DARK JEWELS

Lisa Jackson

 NEW AMERICAN LIBRARY

NEW AMERICAN LIBRARY
Published by New American Library, a division of
Penguin Group (USA) Inc., 375 Hudson Street,
New York, New York 10014, USA
Penguin Group (Canada), 90 Eglinton Avenue East, Suite 700, Toronto,
Ontario M4P 2Y3, Canada (a division of Pearson Penguin Canada Inc.)
Penguin Books Ltd., 80 Strand, London WC2R 0RL, England
Penguin Ireland, 25 St. Stephen's Green, Dublin 2,
Ireland (a division of Penguin Books Ltd.)
Penguin Group (Australia), 250 Camberwell Road, Camberwell, Victoria 3124,
Australia (a division of Pearson Australia Group Pty. Ltd.)
Penguin Books India Pvt. Ltd., 11 Community Centre, Panchsheel Park,
New Delhi - 110 017, India
Penguin Group (NZ), cnr Airborne and Rosedale Roads, Albany,
Auckland 1310, New Zealand (a division of Pearson New Zealand Ltd.)
Penguin Books (South Africa) (Pty.) Ltd., 24 Sturdee Avenue,
Rosebank, Johannesburg 2196, South Africa

Penguin Books Ltd., Registered Offices: 80 Strand, London WC2R 0RL, England

Published by New American Library, a division of Penguin Group (USA) Inc. *Dark Ruby* was previously published in a Topaz edition. *Dark Sapphire* was previously published in a Signet edition.

First New American Library Printing, August 2005
10 9 8 7 6 5 4 3 2 1

Dark Ruby copyright © Susan Crose, 1998
Dark Sapphire copyright © Susan Lisa Jackson, 2000
Excerpt from *Dark Emerald* © Susan Lisa Jackson, 1999

Library of Congress Cataloging-in-Publication Data

Jackson, Lisa.
    Dark jewels / Lisa Jackson
       p. cm.
    Dark ruby—Dark sapphire.
    ISBN 0-451-21690-3
       1. Wales—Fiction. 2. Middle Ages—Fiction. I. Jackson, Lisa. Dark sapphire. II. Title

PS3560.A223D37 2005
813'.54—dc22   2005047952

Printed in the United States of America

Contents

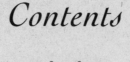

Dear Reader,

What a great surprise! When my publisher suggested we put together a two-in-one package of *Dark Ruby* and *Dark Sapphire,* I was ecstatic. These two books, coupled with *Dark Emerald,* were part of a series I had so much fun writing!

I remember writing *Dark Ruby* and wondered what would happen if a thief was trying to steal an incredible, mysterious stone and was caught by the beautiful but desperate heroine. Hence the story of Trevin and Lady Gwynn began. When they first meet, the sparks fly, seduction sizzles and a secret bargain is struck. Trevin is only allowed his freedom if he agrees to one night of fiery passion. . . . Thirteen years later the lovers meet again. Their secrets and lies begin to unravel, and danger lurks in the shadows.

In *Dark Sapphire,* a beautiful lady, Sheena of Ogof, is forced to stow away on a dangerous vessel only to be discovered and brought before the infamous Captain Keegan. Keegan's a man who has no use for a woman, except for the fact that Sheena has a huge bounty on her head, and the captain plans to collect the reward. However, upon the ship, he discovers he's intrigued by the rebellious beauty and realizes that he's met her before, long ago, in another time and place. Just as he couldn't resist her then, he can't resist her again, and the two of them are bound to each other by forces linked to a dark, fascinating blue stone.

Both these books are rife with desire, destiny, and deception. *Dark Ruby* and *Dark Sapphire* are adventures set in medieval Wales where castles, kings, knights, and sailing ships are surrounded by mystery and dangerous seduction.

I think you'll love these books, and what a deal—two in one in this *Dark Jewels* anthology. Enjoy *Dark Ruby* and *Dark Sapphire* and look for *Dark Emerald* as well.

As always, let me know what you think of *Dark Jewels* by visiting my Web site at www.lisajackson.com or emailing me at lisa@lisajackson.com.

Be prepared to be swept away!

Lisa Jackson

DARK
RUBY

*To all my friends and family
who have supported me through
the toughest time of my life:
I love you and will
remember you forever.*

Prologue

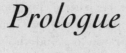

TOWER RHYDD, WALES
1271

Glimmering in the dying firelight, the jewels in the ring winked a deep bloodred. Beckoning. Seducing. Begging to be taken by trained fingers.

From his hiding spot behind the velvet curtains, Trevin wet his dry lips, rubbed the tips of his fingers together, and tried to quiet his thundering pulse. At fifteen he was a thief and a good one, an orphaned waif who stole to survive. Never had he attempted to snatch anything so valuable as the ring left carelessly on the window ledge. But he was desperate and the jewels and gold would fetch a good price, mayhap enough to buy a decent horse since his efforts at stealing one had gone awry. Painful welts on his back, the result of the farmer lashing him with a whip, still cut into his skin and burned like the very fires of hell to remind him that he'd failed.

But not this time.

Now he would have the means to escape Rhydd and his sins forever.

He listened but the lord's chamber was quiet. Aside from the occasional tread of footsteps in the hallway, the rustle of mice in the fragrant rushes tossed over the stone floor of the castle, or the hiss of flames in the grate, there was no sound but the pounding of his heart.

Noiselessly he slipped between the drapes and stole across the rushes to the window where he plucked his prize and stuffed it swiftly into the small pocket sewn into the sleeve of his tunic for just such spoils as this. Holding his breath, he started for the door only to hear a breathless woman's voice coming from the hallway.

"In here, Idelle. Quickly."

Trevin's knees nearly gave way as he realized the lord's wife was on the other side of the oaken door. He had no choice but to duck back behind the curtain and hide himself in the alcove where Baron Roderick's clothes were tucked. *Help me,* he silently prayed to a God who rarely seemed to listen.

The door swung open and a rush of air caused the fire to glow more brightly. Golden shadows danced upon the whitewashed walls.

Trevin dared peek through the heavy velvet and watched as Lady Gwynn yanked her tunic over her head, then tossed it carelessly onto the floor. With a bored sigh, she, now clad only in her underdress, dropped onto the bed.

Trevin's groin tightened at the sight of the lacy chemise against Gwynn's skin. Idelle, the old midwife and a woman many proclaimed to be a witch, shuffled into the room and closed the door behind her. Half blind and a bit crippled, Idelle held some kind of special power and even though her ancient eyes were clouded a milky white, she seemed to see more than most people within these castle walls. 'Twas said that she had the uncanny gift of searching out a man's soul.

" 'Tis the time," she said in a voice not unlike that of a toad. Carefully she set her basket of herbs and candles on a small table. She laid each wick upon a red-hot coal from the fire until all the beeswax tapers were lit. Once the flames were strong and flickering in the breeze, Idelle reached into a pouch in her basket and dropped a handful of pungent herbs over the table. Some sparked in the candles' flames and the scents of rose and myrtle blended over the odor of burning oak.

"Then let's get it done." Squirming upon the coverlet Lady Gwynn lifted her chemise over her legs and hips. Trevin was suddenly much too hot. High and higher the chemise was raised until the sheer fabric was wadded beneath her breasts.

Though he knew it a sin, he could not drag his eyes away from her naked body. White and supple in the quivering firelight she rolled toward the old woman.

Trevin clamped his jaw tight. He couldn't resist eyeing her flat white abdomen, the slight indentations between her ribs, and the nest of red-brown curls that seemed to sparkle in the juncture of her legs.

His throat turned to dust. So this is what a noblewoman looked like beneath her velvet and furs. Oh, what he wouldn't give to run one of his callused fingers over that soft irresistible skin.

"There ye be, lass. Now, let me see what ye've got." Idelle knelt at the side of the bed and her fingers, knotted with age, moved gently over the younger woman's smooth belly. Groping and prodding, she murmured something in the old language, a spell mayhap, as it was common knowledge that she prayed and offered sacrifices to the pagan gods of the elders, just as the man who had raised him, the sorcerer Muir had. "By the gods, 'tis no use." With a sigh, she shook her graying head. Sorrow added years to a face that was barely a skull with skin stretched over old, bleached bones. " 'Tis barren ye be, lass. There is no babe."

"Nay!" Gwynn cried, but lacked conviction.

Sadly, Idelle clucked her tongue. " 'Tis sorry I be and ye know it."

"And wrong you be! Oh, please, Idelle, tell me I am with child," she insisted desperately.

"Nay, I—"

"Hush! There *is* a child. There must be!" Stubborn pride flashed in the lady's eyes as if by sheer will a baby would grow within her womb. "Oh, dear God you must be mistaken!" She whispered, though her chin wobbled indecisively.

Try as he might Trevin couldn't draw his gaze away from her. She pushed her chemise upward to the juncture of her arms and for the first time in his life he saw a noblewoman, a beautiful lady, naked. He'd caught glimpses of serving wenches and whores, of course, but never before had he seen the wife of a baron. His mouth drew no spit as he looked upon the sweet roundness of her breasts. Her nipples were small and pink, reminding him of rosebuds. His damned manhood, always at the ready, became stiff.

"Touch me again. Try harder to feel the babe," Gwynn pleaded, though she seemed resigned, as if she understood her fate.

Regret drew Idelle's old lips into a knot. She laid the flat of her hand beneath Lady Gwynn's navel, closed her sightless eyes, and whispered a chant. Upon the bed, the naked woman lay perfectly still.

With a sigh, Idelle removed her spotted fingers. "There's nothing."

"What will I do?" Gwynn asked, swallowing hard.

"I know not."

"Mary, sweet mother of Jesus, help me," Lady Gwynn whispered from her bed—the lord's bed. If the baron had any idea that a poor stable boy—nay, a thief—had seen his wife naked, there would be hell to pay. Trevin would probably be drawn and quartered, his spilled guts fed to the castle hogs. He shuddered at the thought but still could not draw his wayward gaze away.

Her eyes were wide with fear and she bit into her lower lip. The candles near the bed gave off black smoke and the tiny flames reflected in tears drizzling from her eyes. Saint Peter, she was a beauty. "If I bear not a son, my husband will kill me."

Trevin's heart gave a jolt. He'd heard stories of the lord's cruelty, but to kill this woman—this beautiful wife?

"Nay, he would never—"

"Don't lie to me, Idelle." Gwynn sat bolt upright on the bed, her pointed chin thrust forward, her chemise lowering over those perfect breasts. Frightened, she curved the fingers of one hand over the midwife's scrawny arm. "There *must* be a child."

"I'm sorry, m'lady, 'tis ripe ye are, that I know. Aye, but—"

"I *will* bear my husband a son!" Gwynn's pretty face twisted from desperation to a sly expression that reminded Trevin of a wolf coming upon a wounded lamb. "I . . . I . . . slept with my husband each night before he rode to battle," she said softly, as if to convince herself, "I tried, oh, how I tried. . . ."

" 'Tis a pity, to be sure."

"And I did what you advised," Gwynn added, as if her childless state were the old midwife's fault. With one hand, she gestured to the beeswax candles dripping near the bed. "I added myrtle, oak, and rose to candles. I drew fertility runes in the sand and lied to Father Anthony when he caught me practicing the old ways." Her eyes slitted and a cunning expression overcame her perfect features. "Then, to atone, I prayed on my knees on the cold stone floor of the chapel for hours upon hours, hoping God would answer my prayers. I did everything I could and yet you dare tell me there is no babe."

Idelle frowned and rubbed at the sprinkle of whiskers upon her chin. "I'll not lie to ye, m'lady."

"For the love of Saint Jude!" Gwynn hopped off the bed and walked barefoot through the rushes to the small window cut into the chamber wall. Moonlight streamed through the opening and fell upon her beautiful, angry face while casting a silver sheen to her fiery hair. "You must help me."

Idelle clucked her tongue while worrying her gnarled fingers. "I tried. By the gods, I tried, lass. But sometimes when a man and woman lay together, a child eludes them."

"But why?" Gwynn asked, frowning and tapping her fingers in agitation along the whitewashed wall.

"Who knows?"

"God is punishing me, though 'tis the baron's fault."

Idelle lifted a graying eyebrow. "His fault?"

"Aye, but he will kill me if I give him no sons," she said again, turning and resting her head against the sill. Trevin cringed. If not for the shadows, she would see him. "Was not his first wife, Katherine, found dead in her bed"— she waved a hand at the pile of furs on the curtained mattress—"this very bed after six years of marriage and no children?"

"Aye, but—"

"Strangled, they say, or suffocated."

"The Lord denied it, even unto Father Anthony."

"And his second wife, Rose, drowned when she, too, was unable to give him a babe."

" 'Tis true," Idelle agreed, rubbing her knuckles until Trevin thought she might work the skin off her bones.

Gwynn sighed loudly. "Lord Roderick is a young man no longer. He wants sons and I, Idelle, will give them to him, one way or another."

Trevin bit his lip. He'd heard the talk whispered by the servants in the solar, scullery, stables, and throughout the barony. Even peasants in the village suspected that Baron Roderick had suffocated his first wife, drowned his second, and took another—this one, Gwynn of Llynwen, a woman of fifteen for the singular purpose of bearing him an heir. A son. Trevin swallowed though his throat was dry as sand.

Through the crack in the drapes, he watched as the lady's eyebrows drew together and her gaze moved swiftly over the window ledge. "My ring," she whispered, distracted for a moment as her fingers ran over the stone and mortar. Trevin's heart stilled. Guilt pierced his soul. " 'Twas here but a little while ago . . . the ruby my father gave me . . ." She bit her lip in vexation. "I know I put it here. Oh, for the love of Saint Mary, my mind is gone with all this worry about a babe!"

Trevin didn't dare breathe as she stooped to sweep the rushes with her fingers, as if the jewel had fallen onto the floor. Idelle, too, began searching and the damned ring burned a hole in Trevin's sleeve.

"How very odd . . ."

"Could ye have misplaced it, m'lady?"

"Nay. Nay. It was here. Right in this very spot. I know it!" She slapped the ledge with her palm and then her gaze inched slowly around her chamber.

Sweat dripped down Trevin's spine as she stared at the curtains. Trevin froze. Could she see him? Did his eyes reflect in the dim candlelight? Had he moved and caught her gaze? He closed his eyes to slits, mouthed a silent prayer to a God he didn't trust, and swallowed a lump as large as an egg that had formed in his throat. Sweat rolled down his muscles though the autumn breeze rushing through the window was cold and caused the embers in the fire to glow a scarlet hue that cast bold red shadows upon the walls. Christ Jesus, how had he ended up here—trapped like a cornered fox?

Lady Gwynn sank to the floor. "I cannot worry about the ring right now," she said, her voice soft and forlorn. "Not when I need not a ruby but a babe."

"Would that I could conjure up a child, but . . ." Idelle shook her head and scratched at the hairs sprouting upon her chin. " 'Tis not possible."

Standing, Gwynn turned her thoughtful gaze back to the midwife. "You could be mistaken."

"Oh, m'lady, would that I were."

"My time of the month is not for a fortnight yet. Only then will we know for certain."

"But—"

"Leave me," Gwynn ordered, dashing away her tears and plopping back on the bed. She tossed her long auburn curls in spoiled disdain. "I'll hear no more of your heresy, old woman. I'm with child, I tell you as sure as there is a God, I am carrying the son of Roderick of Rhydd."

"Would that it were so."

"It is, I tell you. Go." Gwynn hitched her chin to the door and there was nothing for the midwife to do but gather her basket of herbs, candles, and knives and start for the hallway.

However, at the door, Idelle hesitated and shivered as if the cold touch of winter had invaded her soul. "Lady," she said, casting a worried glance over her shoulder, "do not contemplate that which is forbidden."

"Forbidden?"

"I see it in your eyes, child," Idelle said, her voice a worried whisper. "If you consider trying to trick him—"

"Hush!" Gwynn said, her cheeks flaming. "You speak nonsense and what can you see, half blind as you are?"

"My sight is from the soul. Be not foolish," the old woman cautioned, as if she could read the dark turn of Lady Gwynn's thoughts. She cleared her throat and added, "If ye be so troubled, I could send for the priest."

Gwynn let out a breath of disdain and waved Idelle's offer away. "Father Anthony and his prayers and penance are not what I need. Why the man asks to be flogged so hard that blood stains his shirt in order that he appear a servant and martyr of God I understand not."

"Mayhap he has reason to repent."

Gwynn sighed. "He is a man of the faith."

"Aye, but even a man who speaks the words of the Father is made of flesh and bone."

"Be that as it may, I'll not speak to him of this. 'Twould but cause him to stutter and gulp so hard his Adam's apple would bob as fast as a hummingbird's wings in flight." Gwynn's smile wasn't kind. "Please, leave me now."

"As ye wish, child, but take care."

Eyes squeezed shut, Trevin counted out his heartbeats as he heard Idelle shuffle from the room. The large door creaked open only to close with a thud and the chamber was silent aside from the hiss and pop of the fire.

Now, if only the lady would lie on the bed and fall asleep, he could make good his leave. The ring would be his and he would leave Rhydd and his past far behind him.

"Come here."

Her voice seemed to echo through the room.

Trevin's muscles turned to stone.

"Come here," Gwynn ordered again and Trevin prayed there was a cat lurking in the shadows somewhere that she was calling. "You there, boy, behind the velvet. I know you're there."

Holy Mother of God.

He dared open his eyes to stare straight into hers as she was standing before him, her face looming in the crack of the curtains.

There was nothing he could do but slowly edge away from his hiding spot and stand before her in his bloody, mud-stained tunic. She was a small thing, inches shorter than he, but she held herself erect and stiff, as if she were looking down on him with all the power of the barony. "You heard me speaking with the midwife."

It wasn't a question.

"You know of my . . . difficulty."

Sweet Mary she was staring up at him with eyes the color of the forest at dawn. "Aye."

"And I know who you are. The thief who was bold enough to steal my ring from my chamber."

His jaw grew tight and hard.

"This blood—" She touched his shirt with a long finger and eyed the scar that ran along his hairline. "Yours?"

"Some, mayhap."

"Another man's as well?"

He didn't answer. Wouldn't incriminate himself.

"Did you kill him?"

He remembered the ire on the nobleman's face, Ian of Rhydd, Roderick's brother, when he'd realized that his bejeweled dagger had been stolen on the streets of the village. He'd spied Trevin pocketing the prize, caught him by the collar, and slapped him hard.

"You'll not best me, you filthy urchin!"

"Won't I?" Trevin had flipped the knife into his fingers and Ian had turned his wrist, the sharp blade slicing down the side of Trevin's face and neck.

Blood had gushed.

With all his strength, he'd kicked Ian of Rhydd in the groin. The older man had let out a bellow like a wounded bull and Trevin, blinded by the blood running down his face had lashed out with his newfound weapon, taking off a piece of the nobleman's ear. Then he'd run as far and as fast as his legs had carried him. He'd dashed through the muddy, dung-strewn alley, dodging carts, peddlers, and such, reeling off corners and wiping his eyes as the blood had dried. He'd ended up here deep within the castle walls where no one would think to search for him. No one but the lord's comely wife.

Now, Gwynn's lashes thinned a bit. Stepping away from him, she said, "My husband would flog you and throw you into the dungeon to rot for your sins. And," she held up a finger, "if he thought that you'd been spying in his chamber and had seen his wife without her clothes, he'd whip you within an inch of your life, then gut you and spill your innards for the dogs while there was still a breath of life in your body."

Again, the truth. Trevin's insides turned to jelly but he didn't flinch, just held her gaze steadily. "Is that what you want, m'lady?" he finally asked, unable to still his sharp tongue.

"What I want is a babe."

She looked at him and he sensed an idea forming in her mind—an idea that, he was certain, would scare the liver from him. "So what are we going to do with you?" she asked.

His heart was a drum. If he made a run for the door, she would scream and call the guards and the window was far above the ground; he would break both his legs if he attempted to jump into the bailey. There was no escape unless he were to grab her swiftly and cover her mouth with his hand. And what then?

She smiled and tapped a fingernail to a front tooth that slightly overlapped its twin. "Thief," she said, nodding in self-approval as her idea took shape. "I have a bargain for you."

"A bargain?" He'd been in enough tight spaces to smell a trap when one was being offered and yet he had no choice but to listen.

" 'Twill not be unpleasant," she said, clearing her throat as if her plan scared her a bit. "I . . . I want you to spend the next three days here in my bed, getting me with child." Her face flushed a deep shade of red and she avoided his eyes as if suddenly ashamed. "No one will know you are here, trust me, and on the third night, I will see that you are able to leave Rhydd with a fine horse, a purse full of gold, and a new name. Nary a soul will know what became of you unless you are foolish." Again she narrowed those dark-lashed eyes thoughtfully as if weighing each part of her plan, testing it carefully, wondering if she, a lady of noble birth, could trust a man who had entered her chamber only to rob her.

His heart was pounding wildly, his erection was full and hard, yet he knew that bedding her was a mistake he didn't dare make, that to touch even one hair of her gorgeous head was as dangerous as stepping through the very portals of hell.

"Come, boy, please," she entreated and for a second she seemed a scared little girl, one he would love to protect. "All I ask is that you lay with me, and . . . and . . . afterward you'll leave here a free man." She reached forward, wound warm, soft fingers around his wrist, and drew his hand to her breast.

He felt the smooth flesh through her chemise and a bud of a nipple against his open palm. *Oh, Mother Mary, what was this tormented ecstasy! This was wrong . . . so wrong.* His chest was as tight as if barrel staves had surrounded it.

" 'Tis a sin," he said, his voice low and rough, not sounding at all as if it belonged to him.

She closed her eyes a second and bit her trembling lower lip. Squaring her shoulders, she nodded solemnly. "Aye, 'tis a sin, and we know that you would never sin, eh, thief?"

"Sweet Jesus."

"This is not the time for prayer."

"But—"

"I'm asking you to help me," she said simply and innocence overshadowed her display of cunning. She was one moment a vixen, the next a frightened girl.

And he, damn it, was only a man. A weak man.

Gaze locked with hers, he let out his breath. Slowly he ran his thumb over the hardening bud of her nipple and heard her sigh, as soft as the wind rustling through the dry leaves still clinging to the trees.

"This is wrong."

"But it will save my life and yours." She smiled slightly, sadly, as tears again filled her hazel eyes. " 'Tis no choice we have, thief. Come to the bed. Save your soul as well as mine."

"God help me."

She lifted her arms and circled his neck in an embrace he couldn't avoid. Oh, God, how he ached. Desire pounded through his head. Need pulsed hot in his veins.

Tilting her head she offered him the seductive white column of her throat. "Please."

He could resist no longer. A groan of surrender escaped from his throat. His mouth crashed down upon hers eagerly, as if he'd expected this moment in time to be his forever, as if destiny had claimed him.

Her lips parted willingly.

His blood was liquid fire. Hot. Dark. Wanting.

She quivered.

Could it be that this beautiful lady actually wanted him?

Trembling, he lifted her from her feet, carried her to the bed, and fell with her onto the fur coverlet. His hands found the hem of her chemise, his cock was thick and ready to burst, and he never stopped kissing her as she unlaced his breeches and peeled off his tunic.

This is madness, Trevin! Stop before you cross a bridge that leads to damnation.

Anxious fingers skimmed the muscles of his shoulders, the few hairs on his chest. So hot he was sweating, he kissed her hard, his tongue probing, his hands upon the laces holding her chemise closed.

His tunic slid to the floor and the ring, gold and deep dusky scarlet, rolled into the rushes.

"I knew it," she whispered. "You're a bold one, thief."

And stupid to be contemplating bedding the baron's wife. But his head was thundering with want, his flesh ready and as he shoved the chemise up her body, he parted her legs with his knees, shed all doubts, and thrust deep into her warmth, only to feel resistance, then a rending.

She let out a soft cry of pain.

He didn't move for a second. Lust thundered through his body and yet something was wrong. Very wrong. "For the love of . . . you . . . you are a virgin," he whispered, his voice raw, his mind screaming at him that he'd been played for a fool.

A tiny pool of blood stained the furs beneath them.

Firelight played in eerie shadows against the walls.

"Aye." Again tears starred her lashes.

His mind was swimming in murky waters as he stared down at her vexed face, her skin glowing gold in the flickering light. "I heard you tell the old woman that you thought you were with child." Oh sweet Jesus 'twas all he could do to concentrate to not move and feel her feminine warmth rubbing against him.

She didn't say a word, just stared up at him through her tears and, swallowing hard, scaled his ribs with warm fingers.

"The baron will—"

"Never know of you. Trust me," she begged. " 'Tis my worry, not yours."

"How could he—?"

"Shh. There are some secrets between a man and a woman that are not to be shared with another. Come, thief, do not stop now." She touched him so gently he wanted to believe in her forever. Slowly, she rubbed her smooth skin against him, lifting her hips, and touching his flat nipples with her thumbs. "Love me."

"Nay, I—"

"Love me, please."

Oh, glorious torment, he couldn't resist. Moaning in surrender, he caught her rhythm and was unable to keep from delving into her sweet heat again and again, faster and faster as the world caught fire behind his eyes. With a primal cry, he spilled his seed into the most secret part of her.

"Yes, thief, yes," she whispered, suppressing a sob. " 'Tis good you be."

And a fool like no other!

Falling against her, crushing her breasts, feeling her arms wrap around his sweaty torso, he found no joy. No satisfaction. For deep in the marrow of his bones he knew with a deadly certainty that this single act would be his undoing. Though Lady Gwynn had seduced him, the truth was that he, an orphaned stable boy who had been raised by a magician with a lust for wine had become a thief and had, in his most bold and stupid act stolen not only the lady's ring, but Baron Roderick of Rhydd's wife's virginity.

'Twas no doubt, there would be hell to pay.

Chapter One

"'Tis bad news I bear." Muir, self-proclaimed sorcerer and often times the village idiot slipped, like an eel through clear water, over the threshold of the countinghouse. Carrying a cane that was more for appearance than use, he cast a furtive glance over his shoulder, as if sensing he was being followed into this private room so near the lord's chamber.

Trevin was not amused by the elder man's theatrics. Muir was known to overplay a part; his dramatics were a bit of his questionable charm. Seated at a small, scarred table near the single window, he looked up from the feeble accounts the treasurer of Black Oak had recorded. "Come on in, Muir," he suggested, leaning back in his chair until the front legs were elevated from the floor. "Do not be shy."

"Ye mock me, boy," the old one grumbled.

"You mock yourself."

"Ah, 'tis a sorry orphaned lad I raised into the lord of this fine castle, one who minces words with me."

Trevin let the chair fall back to the floor, the legs banging and startling Muir.

"But I lose myself. There is news from Rhydd."

Rhydd. The bane of his existence and the beginning of his journey to a barony he'd never wanted and now was forced to rule. Trevin's jaw grew tight and the blackness that forever darkened his heart seemed only to deepen. The quill snapped between fingers that ached to do something, *any*thing other than oversee the daily routine of a castle he'd won by a lucky roll of the dice. He was sick to the back teeth of grumbling peasants, lazy servants, crumbling walls, and a treasury with no coin. "Bad news?" he asked in a slow, angry whisper. "Is there any other kind?"

"I take it the ledgers bode ill." Muir leaned heavily upon his crook and fastened his good eye on the man he had raised from a whimpering blue-lipped babe. He was the only man within the walls of the keep who had no fear of Trevin's black rage.

"Aye, the ledgers bode ill. Very ill. As they always do." Trevin rubbed the ache from his shoulders, then, disgusted, slammed the ledger book closed. A cloud of dust swirled upward. "But tell me of Rhydd."

"I've seen a vision."

"Ah." Trevin folded his arms over his chest and tried not to notice the stale odor of wine that was forever Muir's companion. After all, he'd grown up witnessing the old man's fondness for the cup. "A vision of Rhydd. What this time?"

"There is trouble brewing in the keep."

"At Rhydd?" After thirteen years he could not hear the name of that castle without thinking of the nights he'd spent in Lady Gwynn's bed and the fact that nine months later she'd borne a son. His son. A boy he'd allowed to be named after another, all for the price of a ruby ring, jeweled dagger, and a few gold coins.

"The Lord Roderick returns."

Trevin's head snapped up. His muscles tightened. "He's been locked away at Castle Carter—"

"I know, I know. For as long as there has been peace, but now he's escaped and is returning to Rhydd."

"You *saw* this?"

"Aye." Muir nodded. "In a dream."

"A dream you had after falling asleep from too much ale?"

"Nay, m'lord—"

"Don't call me that." Trevin found it bothersome that the man who had raised him would refer to him as lord, sire, baron, or any such nonsense.

"But ye be the ruler here now."

"Aye, because I was lucky with the dice and won the castle from an addled old man who'd been far too deep in his cups. But we stray from the point. Many of your 'dreams' and 'visions,' Muir, have come to mean naught."

"In the past, aye, I know." He bobbed his bald head eagerly. "But this time 'tis true. If ye do not trust me, then be so good as to speak with Farmer Hal who came from Castle Carter with the news of Roderick's escape as well as a cart of fodder corn and seeds for the planting season."

Trevin couldn't help but raise a disbelieving eyebrow. "The good farmer comes with the news to Black Oak just as you see your 'vision,' Muir? 'Tis lucky timing, is it not?"

"You doubt me? Me who raised you from a sniffling, scrawny babe?"

"Never," Trevin said and would have smiled at his mentor's furrowed pate if he were not disturbed by the news. He snatched the book of ledgers and placed it in an oak and iron chest, then hesitated and, for an unknown reason, picked up a small faded pouch wherein a ring was hidden—the darkly jeweled ring he'd stolen from the Lady of Rhydd. Though in need of coin or food or a steed many times over the years, he'd never sold that little bit of his past that reminded him of her. Fool. He slipped the ring into a pocket, then locked the chest securely once again.

This was not the first time Muir had predicted a shadow over Rhydd, but in this instance, the old man seemed more sure of himself. "Let us see what the farmer has to say." Swiftly, he ushered the magician out the door and turned the key in the lock.

Muir, despite his claims of pain in his knees, nearly flew down the stairs, the skirts of his sorry-looking tunic sailing behind him, the eyes of the ever-vigilant dogs watching him as he hurried past their resting spot on the landing.

One let out a short "woof," then hung his head as he spied Trevin.

Hal, the farmer, was in the bailey arguing over the value of his seeds as he measured them for the steward. " 'Tis the best beans in all of Wales, you can be sure," he was saying, but paused in his boasting as Trevin approached.

"Muir tells me you bring news from Castle Carter," Trevin said and, as the old man had predicted, the farmer told him of Roderick's escape from the dungeon.

". . . yea, the baron is expected back at Rhydd within a few days," Hal said as the first few drops of rain fell from purple-bellied clouds scudding slowly across the sky. " 'Tis a pity, if ye ask me, m'lord, for 'tis no secret that Roderick is a hard ruler." Hal shook his head. "Thank our Lord that the lady was able to bear him a son, elsewise I fear she would have met the same fate as those who had wed the baron before her."

The muscles in the back of Trevin's neck twisted into tight, painful knots.

"Now, no doubt, he'll want more sons."

"No doubt." Trevin left the farmer and the steward to argue over the price of seeds and walked across the mashed grass of the bailey. Fingering the hilt of his dagger he silently cursed the fates that had caused him to steal Lady Gwynn's ring so many years ago. As he had promised her on their parting, he should have forgotten that he had sired a son, that the boy now residing at Rhydd was his own flesh and blood. He could not cast that memory aside. Nor had the years diluted his need to see his boy, to claim him. If anything, his desire to give Gareth of Rhydd his name was stronger than ever.

There had been a time when he'd believed that he would father more children, that this very castle would be filled with so many of his sons and daughters he would rarely think of his firstborn, conceived in sin, raised as another man's heir. But time and fate had played their cruel tricks upon his plans and now, he was certain, Gareth of Rhydd would be his only child; the only son he would ever spawn.

For nearly a year he'd struggled with himself, remembering his bargain with Gwynn, his promise of silence about the boy's begetting. He'd kept the secret for years, secure in the knowledge that Roderick, bound forever a prisoner by Baron Hamilton of Castle Carter, would never guess the truth, never put the boy in danger.

"Lord Hamilton was never one to be trusted," Muir said as if reading Trevin's mind and flipped the hood of his tunic over his head as the rain pelted from the sky. His one good eye stared without blinking at Trevin. The old man had always had the disturbing ability to see into his young charge's soul at the most dire of times. 'Twas a constant battle to keep the sorcerer from looking too closely and spying Trevin's weaknesses. "Ye, m'lord, have a duty to protect yer—"

"Devil be with you, Muir," Trevin grumbled as the wind slapped against his face in icy gusts. "And don't call me lord."

Muir waved off his protest. " 'Tis only ye who has to deal with the darkness in your soul. Only ye who have to face yer Maker and—"

"Oh, for the love of Christ!" Squinting against the rain that ran down his face and neck, Trevin threw an irritated glare up at the menacing heavens. His old bargain with Gwynn be damned. He'd pay her back tenfold, but by the gods of good and evil, he was going to claim his son.

"Holy Father forgive me, for I have sinned . . ." Gwynn whispered her prayers in the nave, hoping that her request wouldn't fall upon deaf ears. Surely God wouldn't forsake her now—or would He? She thought of all the spells she'd tried to weave, the runes she'd drawn, the pagan chants she'd murmured in the vain hope that her husband would never return. She'd lain with another man, deceived everyone in the castle, claiming her son was Roderick's child.

Selfish, selfish woman. Creating a child so that you could live and now you have a son more precious than life itself.

Raindrops pounded upon the ceiling and the wind rushed noisily outside as Gwynn prayed.

For thirteen years she'd been favored. Her husband had been wounded in battle and held prisoner at a castle to the north without ever setting eyes upon the son she'd sworn was his. The ransom that Ian, his brother, had offered had been turned down by the Baron Hamilton of Castle Carter, the ruler who seemed to find some perverse pleasure in holding Roderick as his prisoner.

There had been, at the behest of Ian, a few failed attempts at freeing Roderick. The attacks on Castle Carter had been futile, costly in men and arms and Ian had finally given up. Gwynn had fervently hoped that she would never have to see the man she'd married again, never have to lie about Gareth's conception.

Gareth. Her son. The boy who would someday rule Rhydd. Spawned by the thief so many years before and passed off as the heir to a heartless man who had murdered his first two wives.

Oh, cruel fate that Roderick was now returning.

As it had so many times in the past, guilt seeped into her soul but she steadfastly swept it aside. Had she not lain with the outlaw, had she not spent three days of bittersweet passion in the lord's bed with him, she would never have conceived Gareth, her sole joy in life, her reason for living. "Our Lord, please hear my prayers," she intoned as the stones of the floor pressed hard against her knees. Stiffening her spine and bowing her head, she closed her eyes. She wouldn't feel any more guilt for bearing a child as bright and true as her son.

"You appear troubled, child."

Gwynn nearly jumped out of her skin. Her hand flew to her chest, as if to hold her heart in place. She'd thought she'd been alone in the chapel and hadn't heard the scrape of Father Anthony's leather shoes on the worn floor or the sound of his wheezing breath as he'd approached.

Her prayers forgotten, Gwynn scrambled to her feet.

"What bothers you?" Father Anthony's gentle voice seemed to reverberate from the rafters though, in truth, he barely moved his thin, white-rimmed lips.

"Oh, Father Anthony . . . you . . . you startled me."

" 'Twas not my intention."

"I . . . I was in need of . . . of solace," she said and saw his bloodless lips curve into a knowing smile.

A tall, thin man with stooped shoulders and a ring of blond hair around a bald pate, he nodded, as if he, too, felt a need for the cleansing of his soul. He laid a long-fingered hand upon her shoulder. "Do not let me disturb you."

"Nay, I was finished," she said and hoped that her cheeks were not as red as they felt. 'Twas unsettling the way he could sneak up on a body.

"You were praying for the b-baron's safe return." Father Anthony's eyebrows raised in silent question and his Adam's apple started to wobble, betraying his anxiety.

"Aye." The lie tripped over her tongue and she cringed inside. 'Twas one thing to stretch the truth to suit one's purposes but quite another to lie baldly to the priest in the very chapel itself. "Thank you, Father," she said.

"Rest well."

As if she could.

"And, please, Lady, do not heed old Id-Idelle and her dark ways. She means well, b-but—" He spread his fingers wide, palms upward, as if he were imploring heaven to understand some great mystery. "She is b-but a woman and a weak one at that. The d-d-devil is always looking for those who are not strong." His gaze held hers. "Do not let Satan fool you, even if he dresses in the guise of a midwife."

"Idelle is no devil."

"I said it not. Just be careful, m'lady. Lucifer dons many masks."

"I know my heart, Father," she said, though she couldn't admit what was in the depths of her soul. Clutching the folds of her tunic, she nodded and slipped out the doorway to the corridor where the candles flickered and smoked.

The thought of seeing Roderick again was like a vile poison seeping through her blood and curdling in her innards. She'd never loved him, had been betrothed by her father, and had spent only two weeks with the older baron before he'd ridden off to battle nearly thirteen years before. Since then she'd been the lady of the castle and had only to deal with Roderick's brother, Ian. She shivered at the thought of her brother-in-law. He was a huge man with meaty hands that were covered on the backside with the same sable brown hair that darkened his jaw.

Though educated, he had a crude manner of speaking and there was no light of kindness in his eyes. Often times when he'd sipped from too many cups of wine, his eyes had narrowed and he'd stared at his sister-in-law in silent, evil regard. His own wife had died two years before. A small slip of a woman with pale skin and eyes that were red from disease and painful tears, Margaret had given up her soul in her husband's bed, leaving him, like his only brother, without any issue. Since Margaret's death, Ian's interest in Gwynn had been bolder than ever and his brooding gaze had grown evermore filled with a hideous lust that made her skin crawl.

At the thought, Gwynn's stomach roiled. She hustled through a door and across a short path to the kitchen where the cook, a tiny freckled man named Jack, was scolding two boys turning the spit on which an ox was roasting. Fat that streamed from the carcass sizzled on the coals and smoke rose up a wide chimney where slabs of meat were hung to cure.

"Faster, faster, you lazy swine," Jack growled, boxing one of the lad's ears. The boy yelped in pain but spun the roasting beast at a snappier pace. His partner, on the other side of the spit, avoided the cook's eyes and put all his muscles behind rotating the cross bar. "That's better . . . much better. See that ye keep it so." Jack's hands fisted and rested upon thin, bony hips. "We wouldn't want to disappoint the lord when he returns, now, would we?"

Both boys shook their heads vigorously while a kitchen girl grinding spices with a mortar and pestle at a nearby table smothered a smile. Finally the cook, turning slightly, realized he wasn't alone with his lazy charges. "Oh, m'lady," he said, showing off uneven teeth and gesturing expansively to the bustle of his workers in the kitchen. One girl was paring winter apples, another plucking the feathers from a pheasant just outside the door. While boys carried bundles of firewood or buckets of wriggling eels, girls toted baskets of goose eggs. "As ye can see we're making ready for the baron's return."

"Good, good," Gwynn said, feigning interest, her fingers fumbling with the cross that dangled from the chain of gold encircling her throat.

" 'Tis an intricate sugar castle we be making and the huntsman has brought us fine pheasants, six crane, and a stag." The wiry man beamed at the thought of his feast. "We've eels from the pond and salmon and—"

"—'tis pleased my husband will be. Carry on," Gwynn interrupted, holding up a hand and heading toward the door leading to the bailey. All this talk of Roderick's return was bringing an ache to her head and pain in her stomach. What was she to do? When he took one look at Gareth . . . *Sweet Mother of the Lord, please help me.* Ever since the messenger arrived with the news that her husband had escaped, Gwynn had been questioning herself, certain that she should have sent her boy to her sister, Luella. As the lady of Castle Heath far, far to the south, Luella would have seen to Gareth's upbringing as well as to his safety. He would have become a page and a squire, learning the skills necessary to become a knight. He would have been safe. Gwynn could have sent word to Luella that Roderick was returning to Rhydd.

Oh, what a foolish, foolish woman she'd been! Had she really thought her husband would be imprisoned forever, or that he would die rotting in that dungeon? In thirteen years she'd become complacent, living within the comfort and safety of Rhydd's thick stone walls, acting as if she were the baron, loving her son with all her heart, her only problem keeping her brother-in-law at arm's length.

Since his wife's death, Ian had become more impossible and bold, trying to corner her alone in dark corridors, brushing against her as they passed, staring at her with narrowed, sinister eyes that sent a chill racing through her blood.

But she would gladly face Ian a thousand times over if only Roderick would never return.

Her soft shoes sank into the mud as she dashed along the path winding through the bailey. Geese honked noisily, flapping their wings and losing feathers as they scattered toward the eel pond. Two boys hauling a dead boar veered out of her path as a young girl lugged a basket of wet laundry away from ropes strung near the north tower. Gwynn barely noticed as raindrops splashed against her tunic. She had to find Gareth and explain to a boy of barely twelve years that his life was in danger from the man who was supposed to be his father. When she'd hastily concocted her plan to conceive a child other than Roderick's, she'd thought that the baron wouldn't know the babe was not his. Only later, after years of loving and doting on the lad would he suspect that the child might not have been his issue. By then he would have accepted the boy as his own or, should he suspect otherwise, not voice his fears as he would appear a stupid cuckold fool.

Oh, Lord, she must've been daft to think she could get away with her plan. But had she not lain with the thief, she would not have had her son. Nor would she have had years of memories of lovemaking. Even now, over a dozen years later, she could still remember the warmth of his touch, the sense of his tongue against her skin, the moist heat his kisses had inspired . . .

"Looking for your son?" Ian's voice echoed through the bailey, ringing off the stone walls and thundering in her heart. She blushed, wondering if he could guess the turn of her wayward thoughts. 'Twas silly and a waste of time to think of the youthful thief who had slipped out of the castle and her life just as she'd asked.

Now, Ian stood, fingering the blade of his knife as he watched a group of boys, Gareth among them, playing with wooden swords they'd constructed. Gareth, taller than the rest, was the most agile. A tight-muscled youth with black curls, sharp blue eyes, and quick reflexes, he was able to leap onto barrels or slide swiftly under a hayrick to avoid the advances of the thicker, clumsier boys.

Tom, the butcher's son, lunged forward with his wooden sword, but Gareth ducked low, spun on one foot, and rolled beneath a peddler's cart. "Clever lad." Ian clucked his tongue and shook his head. "Much more clever than his father."

Gwynn's heart nearly stopped. "Is he?" she replied, lifting her chin though she felt the breath of doom against the back of her neck. She'd learned over the years that the best way to deal with Ian was to defy him openly and not allow him to see any hint of fear.

"Aye." Ian's pale gold eyes became slits and he rubbed the blade thoughtfully over the graying stubble of his beard. He was tall and muscular with a thick neck and sharp-edged teeth. "He'll grow, though, given the time. Surely he'll make his father proud." He chuckled deep in his throat. " 'Tis time Roderick met the lad."

Never. Never will it be time. Despite the cool drizzle, Gwynn's palms began to sweat.

" 'Twill not be long now."

God, please no! "Gareth, come!" she said, ignoring her brother-in-law as the boy spun and, withdrawing a rock from the band of his pants, sent the pebble sailing, hitting one boy square in the buttocks. The lad sent up a howl and

Gwynn had to shout over his cries of pain. "Gareth, please. Come along. Let us prepare to meet your father."

Distracted from his game, her son looked up and was tagged by Tom whose wooden sword caught him between the shoulder blades. "Nay!"

"Got ye!" Tom said, laughing in a way that reminded Gwynn of an ass braying. He wound up again, ready to deliver another blow, but Gareth feigned to the left before diving right and catching not only Tom with the tip of his blade but two other boys as well. Sheathing his weapon in his belt, he hurried to his mother and she, feeling Ian's keen eyes upon her back, ushered him into the keep. " 'Tis time I had a real sword," he said. "I be near my twelfth—"

"We'll talk of this later."

"But, Mother—"

"Later, Gareth." He was changing, becoming a man before her eyes. 'Twas only right that he would want his own weapons. And, considering all that was to happen, mayhap she should have given him more than the small dagger she'd bestowed upon him years earlier. "Remember how I told you that 'twould be better if you went to live with my sister and her husband?" she asked when they were in the chamber where her son slept, he distracted by a pair of dice he'd won from Alfred, the foolish servant whose only talent was to train and keep the hunting dogs fit.

"Aye." Gareth watched her as she threw his favorite tunic, hose, and mantle into a leather pack. Quickly she opened the purse at her belt and withdrew a few coins and dropped them, along with a gold cross she wore at her neck and two rings into the bag.

" 'Tis time that you—"

"What?" As if finally understanding, he paled. "Time I left?"

"Long past time for your training—"

"Nay!"

"Do not argue, Gareth."

His eyes thinned suspiciously as they had more often than not lately. Oh, he looked so much like his father. "But why now, Mother?" he asked.

She laughed, hoping to sound amused, but her voice was hollow from the fear that tore at her insides. "I've been selfish, Gareth, keeping you here when all boys your age and younger are sent off to be pages and—"

" 'Tis because father is returning." He stared at her with eyes as blue and clear as a summer sky. So like the thief.

Gwynn swallowed hard. What could she say? The truth? Admit her lie? Tell her son, the very reason for her life, that she'd lain with a common stable boy-turned thief in order to conceive a child and deceive everyone, including the very child she'd borne? " 'Tis not the time for questions, Gareth, now come along and—"

" 'Tis a sin to lie. You say so. Father Anthony and old Idelle who agree on nothing say so. Yet you are lying, Mother. I can see it in your eyes."

From the age of three Gareth had been able to read his mother's expression with an uncanny observation, though he'd never guessed at the lie that was his birthright.

" 'Tis a difficult time, son. Here, wear this." Gwynn tossed him his heaviest mantle lined in squirrel fur.

"You are afraid."

Sighing, she set the pack on a stool in the corner and shoved a wayward strand of hair from her eyes. "Yea, son. Sit down." She pointed to the bed and for one of the first times in his young life, Gareth obeyed. Firelight played in his black hair and cast shadows on the walls and coved ceiling though it was barely noon. " 'Tis difficult for me to say this," she admitted, tempering her words carefully. "Lord Roderick is not a kind man."

Gareth snorted. The absent baron's cruelty was common knowledge within the steep walls of Rhydd and, over the years of his imprisonment, the stories of his wretchedness had become legendary. Nary a child born within the keep did not know the mysteries of the lord's first wives' deaths.

The tales had been embellished with the passing of time and the gossip circulating from one mouth to another seeped like venom from the inner walls of the castle and through the gatehouse to the village. Few in Rhydd looked upon the baron's return as a blessing.

"I fear him not."

" 'Tis foolish, for I—I worry for you." There, it was said.

"Why?"

"Your father—" Oh, how her tongue tripped on that deceitful word. "—he, he might be displeased to know that you were not sent away as planned, that you are behind in learning to become a page and a knight."

"Bah. If only I had a true sword I could—"

"You will have your bloody sword," she assured him, to stave off the argument and with the final reality that he might, indeed, need a strong steel blade.

"Truly?" He was awed. A smile split his chin and he let out a whoop, reminding her that he, though starting to look a man, was still a boy.

"Aye, aye. But you must hurry now, don your mantle."

"I can learn everything I needs know here," Gareth wheedled, anxious to take advantage of her giving mood.

"Not if you want the weapon," she said, bartering with the youth who had become a master at getting what he wanted from her. "Come, we have no time to waste. Idelle told the stable master to prepare a horse. Charles will ride with you to Heath. Hurry, now, don't tarry."

"There is something more."

"What?" she asked sharply, feeling that with each passing second her son's chances for safety were fleeting. "No, never mind, now come along!" With one hand she grabbed his upper arm, hauling him to his oversized feet, and heading toward the door. She scooped up the pouch holding his few belongings and slung his mantle over her arm.

"Do not send me away," Gareth insisted, his forehead furrowing. "I should stay with you and protect you."

"Protect *me?*"

"If Father has killed his other wives—"

"I will deal with him. Now, do not think such things. Maybe at Heath you'll learn to treat your mother with some respect! Hurry!" There was no time for argument. She shepherded the boy down the backstairs, past the solar, and along the path between the kitchens and keep.

The smells of baking bread and crushed garlic filtered through the alley as they half ran to the armorer's hut where Gwynn procured a fine long sword, sheath, and belt that Gareth, grinning ear to ear, slipped around his thin waist.

"Now, let us be off," Gwynn insisted, her worries growing with each second that passed. Clouds stole the sunlight as the mist turned to thick drops that peppered the ground to collect in muddy puddles. "Come," Gwynn whispered as they ducked behind a grain cart and dashed to the stables where Charles, holding the reins of two of the best destriers in the castle, stood with his back huddled against the rain.

Gareth glanced at his mother for he'd never before been allowed to ride any horse other than a bay palfrey with an even temperament and no speed.

At the lift of his young eyebrow, Gwynn said, "Well, you don't expect me to send you to Heath looking as if we're poor, do you? What would my sister think?" She hugged her son fiercely and fought tears that suddenly filled her throat and burned the back of her eyes. Would she ever see him again, this, her only child?

Finally, she released him and, as if he finally recognized her fears, Gareth stared at her. "Fear not, Mother. I will return."

"Of course you will." She sniffed and cleared her throat.

"Soon."

Oh, her heart tore into small pieces. "Aye. Now. Off with you!"

The black charger, a fiery beast named Dragon, snorted and half reared as Gareth quickly threw on his mantle, grabbed his leather bag, and tried to mount. The huge animal tossed his great head and sidestepped, rolling one dark, distrusting eye at the young man who dared tried to climb upon his back.

"Easy, there," Charles murmured to the horse.

Gareth swung into the saddle and a prideful smile cut across a square jaw where a few early whiskers were beginning to sprout. " 'Tis a grand animal you be, Dragon," he said, taking up the reins.

"God help us," Charles said under his breath. He was quickly astride the other charger, a red-brown animal with three white stockings and a barrel chest. "Let us be off."

"Take care of yourself," she said, raising her hand. But as the words were uttered Gwynn heard the ominous blare of trumpets. *Oh, God, no!*

A shout rang through the bailey.

Gwynn's knees grew weak. *No! No! No!*

But deep in her heart she knew all her plans were for naught. Her chest constricted and despair clutched at her heart.

"Mother?" Gareth asked, his fingers clutching the reins.

She bit her lip. "God help us," she whispered as the wind whipped her skirts and rain fell mercilessly from the dark heavens.

The guard shouted down to the keeper of the gate. "Open the portcullis and give praise to the Holy Father! Lord Roderick has returned."

Chapter Two

"No tears of joy for your husband?" Ian asked.

Gwynn ignored his evil grin and watched in despair as a mangy gray horse galloped through the castle gates. Astride the bony nag was Roderick of Rhydd, or what was left of him. Never a particularly handsome man, he had aged horridly in the thirteen years of his imprisonment. Bareheaded in the rain, his once-reddish strands had become gray and scraggly to match a beard more silver than russet. His shirt was in tatters, his mantle a ragged and dingy green.

All work within the castle walls stopped. Carpenters, masons, and alewives abandoned their tasks to stand in the open doorways of shops. The bee-keeper, farrier, and candle maker clustered near the north tower while boys lugging stones and girls washing wool turned to stare through a curtain of rain at their lord, a man many had never before set eyes upon.

Gwynn swallowed hard and crossed herself quickly at the sight of the pathetic creature who could, despite his shabby appearance, instill a gnawing fear in her heart. Roderick was hollow-cheeked and gaunt of frame, his skin sagging on his bones.

As the horse slid to a stop, he winced as he climbed from the saddle. A pasty-faced boy named George whose skin was marred with blemishes raced across the grass to catch the reins of the master's steed. Another page scurried from the kitchen with a cup of wine.

Roderick drank heartily, red rivulets trailing through his beard, then flung the cup back to the boy. He swiped the back of his hand over his lips. "Bring me more," he ordered, seeming to enjoy casting out a command. "I'll have the wine, along with pheasant and a joint of boar in the great hall."

"Aye, m'lord." The page, ducking his head against the rain, ran toward the keep.

"Brother!" Ian stepped forward while Gwynn tried hard to find her tongue. " 'Tis good to see you again."

"Is it?" Roderick's eyes, the color of ale, appeared murky and haunted. "Why did you not pay a ransom and have me returned?"

"Baron Hamilton did not ask for ransom, would not consider payment."

"Bah! Then why not help me with my escape, eh?" Roderick asked, his nostrils beginning to quiver in rage that had festered for longer than a decade.

"We tried. Thrice within the first two years of your capture. But Castle Carter is strong, the walls impossible to scale, and Hamilton seemed to know whenever we planned an attack." Ian's excuses sounded feeble, even to Gwynn.

"Hamilton is a black-hearted bastard, but his fortress is not secure. I escaped without your help."

"Aye and how did you—"

"A traitor to Hamilton, one in his army rode in the opposite direction to mislead the guards, but he will come through our gates and when he arrives, he is to be brought to me and paid handsomely." Roderick smoothed his mustache with one finger. "You may remember him, Ian. He is called Sir Webb these days. He has ridden with you before. Long ago."

Ian lifted a shoulder and shook his head. "Webb? Nay, I recall not."

Roderick crackled, his laugh ending in a rattling cough. "He was Sir Hamilton's trusted knight, but I persuaded him that he would better serve me."

"You bribed him?"

Roderick grinned. "Aye, and he will lead the rest of Rhydd's soldiers for he, as only one knight, managed to do what, so you claim, my entire army was unable to do. He, alone, freed me."

"But, Roderick, do you think that a stranger will be able to—"

"Enough! We will discuss this later. Now—let me savor this moment." Roderick surveyed the high stone battlements and the north tower where a knight was raising the flag, showing off the green and gold standard announcing that the lord of the manor was home. For a second Roderick's throat worked, then his tired eyes took in the rest of the keep—old familiar walls and turrets as well as huts and buildings added while he was away. "Rhydd has prospered in my absence," he said, as if to himself.

"Aye." Ian clasped him on the shoulder as mist rose from the grass and a dampness seeped through Gwynn's clothes to chill her heart. "But 'tis good you return."

One of Roderick's red-gray brows lifted and he scratched at his beard as his gaze moved past several knights to land full force on Gwynn.

Dear Jesus, help me.

"Wife."

"Husband." Her voice was firm though it tripped over the hated word.

Roderick's murky eyes narrowed as icy fingers of the wind plucked at Gwynn's cloak. "I have thought of you often these past years."

"As I of you," she said.

"As so you should." He eyed her as a man would were he purchasing a new horse. "Tell me, where is my son? I have waited many years to meet him."

Her spine stiffened as if it were suddenly starched. "Gareth," she called, but the boy, always inquisitive, had already slid off Dragon's broad back and had walked, squishing in the mud, toward the man he thought had sired him.

A smile teased the corners of Roderick's mouth for Gareth, not quite as tall as he, was a proud boy with an arrogant tilt of his chin and eyes that missed nothing. Rain flattened his hair and ran down his nose. "Father."

Gwynn's heart ached.

Roderick glanced at the horses and leather pouch. "He was leaving?" Silvering red eyebrows slammed together.

"Aye." The lie was already in place. " 'Tis long past time for his training as a page and squire. I had sent a messenger to Luella at—"

"Had you not heard I was returning?"

Gwynn nodded. "Only this morn, m'lord."

"And yet still you would send my boy away?" His nostrils flared slightly and quivered as if suddenly stung by a foul odor.

"Luella was expecting him—"

"Hush!"

At his harsh command, Dragon snorted loudly and pawed the sodden ground. Charles, who had dismounted and again held the reins of both horses, offered soft words to the animal while Gareth stopped directly in front of Roderick. He did not bow, nor change expression, just stared hard at the older man in the ragged clothes as the heavens poured and gusts of wind tossed damp leaves in the air.

"You are called Gareth."

"Aye."

Roderick's sallow skin suffused with sudden color as he glanced at the peasants and servants gathered in small clusters within the bailey walls. The silence was suddenly deafening. Even the cattle and sheep, penned on the other side of the inner gate, quieted.

"So. You are my son." The baron's gaze moved from the boy to Gwynn.

Gareth nodded, but didn't say a word.

"Then 'tis long past time we met." He placed a gnarled hand upon the lad's shoulder and Gwynn let out a long sigh of relief. Mayhap he was vain enough and his memory addled so that he would not recognize that the boy wasn't his.

"You will not be going to Heath."

"Husband, please, 'tis time," Gwynn insisted.

He waved her arguments away with a flick of his almighty wrist. "We will speak of this later." His gaze again centered on Gareth.

Gwynn's heart hammered in her chest and she saw all the differences in her son and the baron. Gareth's skin was darker, like that of the thief, his hair as black as a raven's wing, his eyes clear and blue. As had been Trevin's. Though Gareth was but a boy, his features were already showing signs of becoming sharp and rough-hewn.

"Saints be praised." Father Anthony's voice rocked through the bailey.

"Christ Jesus," Roderick swore as the priest, robes flapping behind him ran through the wet grass and mud of the bailey.

"M'lord," he intoned and Gwynn thought she saw tears gather in the holy man's eyes. Surely she was mistaken. 'Twas only the rain that ran down his cheeks. "I thought . . . er, I f-feared I would never see you again, that you would never . . . oh, we must thank the heavenly F-Father for your return." He bowed his head and crossed himself swiftly.

A flush stole up Roderick's neck. "Good Father Anthony," he said quietly, " 'tis comforting to know that you were here, asking for blessings of Rhydd."

"My prayers and thoughts were with you." The priest, blinking rapidly, composed himself. "Perhaps we should share a prayer now, thanking the Holy Mother and—"

"Later." Roderick shook his head and wiped the rain from his face. " 'Tis freezing, I am. Now I needs clean myself and eat." He touched Gwynn's arm. "I trust that all has been prepared?"

"Aye, m'lord. Water has been heated and scented, a meal of thanks will be served at your command, and fresh clothes await you."

"As did you." His smile was as cold as the sleet in winter.

Gwynn's teeth ground together. "Aye." *Oh, Sweet Mary, how would she ever lie with him again?* Share a bed and have him reach for her only to touch her with icy fingers and an even colder heart?

"Good." He clapped his hands. "Everyone, go back to work." His mirthless smile curdled Gwynn's blood as he stared one long heart-stopping minute at Gareth again. "There is much to learn. Much that has happened."

"Amen," whispered Father Anthony.

"Aye. Amen." Ian didn't bother hiding the amusement that glinted in his eyes. He's enjoying this, Gwynn thought.

"You, Wife," Roderick added as he started toward the great hall. There was a fierceness to his tone, an edge underlying his words that made Gwynn's insides turn to water. "I will have words with you about our son."

"As you wish," she said weakly. Roderick, seeming to gather strength with each moment he was within the walls of the castle, strode ahead while curious servants and peasants parted whispering among themselves and allowing him a path. Sheep bleated in nearby pens, a raven, cawing wickedly, flew overhead and fat pigeons cooed from their roosts.

"The boy—he looks not like me," Roderick said thoughtfully, his gait increasing.

"He—he takes after my older brother Neal."

"Does he?" Roderick began climbing the steps to the great hall. "A pity Neal died young and no one remembers him."

He knows! she thought, her heart thundering. Of course he knows for unless he's become addled and his memory gone, he knows that he did not get you with child. How could he have? She swallowed back her fear and only hoped that he would rather pretend that Gareth was his son than suffer the indignities of admitting to an unfaithful wife who might charge him with being unable to lie with a woman.

The dogs, ever vigilant, sat on the stoop and with rain turning their gray coats to slimy black, growled at Roderick's approach.

"I'll not have my own beasts distrust me," he said, frowning at the hounds. With a hand, he motioned to the guard near the heavy door. "Kill them and get new ones—young ones who will obey me."

"Aye m'lord," the guard agreed and started for the growling beasts.

"Nay!" Gwynn, who was a step behind her husband, hurried to catch up with him as he walked into the vast open chamber. Closing his eyes, Roderick drew in deep breaths of air, as if his lungs, so long imprisoned, needed to be cleansed with the smoky air within the walls of the keep.

"Please, do not harm the dogs. They have been loyal and have lain in front of the door to my chamber, keeping watch."

Roderick's eyes flew open. "What know you of loyalty!"

"Husband, please—"

"Husband," he repeated with a sneer. "And what should I call you? Wife?" He glanced at the guard, then leaned closer to her, so that only she could hear. "Mayhap harlot would better suit."

Her heart turned to stone.

"Send the dogs back to the kennel," he ordered to the castle at large. "I will decide what to do with the curs later. As for you, *wife*, there is much we needs discuss, but 'twill have to wait. I'm tired and hungry." He shoved the wet strands of his hair from his eyes and surveyed the great hall. Tables and benches filled the fore part of the chamber while tapestries splashed color on the whitewashed walls. Candles burned brightly and the fire hissed as it blazed, warming the shadowy interior. " 'Tis as I remember it," Roderick said, his voice softening slightly. "Ah, Rhydd." He rubbed the tips of his gnarled fingers against the wall in a loving gesture. "I feared I might never return."

Gwynn felt a moment's regret for the man who had been imprisoned for nearly thirteen years, but she quickly reminded herself that he was capable of murder, that his previous wives had died, and that she was fearful for her son's life.

As Roderick stepped onto the dais and sat for a minute in his chair rubbing the worn wooden arms with his palms, she wondered how she could convince him that Gareth was his son. "Go now," he ordered Gwynn. "I will speak to Ian now and later we will talk. Privately. Of your son."

"Our son."

His tired, murky eyes accused her of the lie. "I'll hear no more of your blasphemy."

Panic squeezed Gwynn's heart. So his mind was not addled—he realized that they had never lain together as man and wife. "Do not blame the boy—"

"I know where the blame lays." He propped an elbow on the arm of the chair and rested his grizzled chin in his fingers. "With you."

"Nay—"

"And whoever it was who got you with child."

She gulped. "Nay, Roderick, the boy is yours. As I live and breathe—"

"Hush, woman!" Roderick was on his feet in an instant. He rounded on her, his muscles tense, his gold eyes suddenly ablaze. "You and your boy have made a fool of me within my own keep. Think you not that the servants and freeman can see what I myself have witnessed?"

"If you will but listen—"

"Listen? *Listen?* To what? More lies. You and . . . *that boy* will not cause me the disrespect of all whom I rule."

"He is but a lad—"

"Enough!"

" 'Tis not his fault that—"

Roderick leaned close and very slowly curled his fists in her hair. "If you be not quiet, m'lady," he snarled in a hushed whisper meant only for her ears, "you'll have no room to bargain." His fetid breath surrounded her in a thick, sickening cloud and she could but nod. To disobey him now would only enrage him further and though she had no fear for herself—those days were long past—she knew that he could harm Gareth, her one weak spot. She needed time to see that her son was safely away and if she had to put up with his scathing tongue, or brute strength, or even lay in the bed with him, so be it.

His fingers unwound from the tangle that was her hair, and then, as if sensing the servants' eyes upon him, he grabbed the crook of her neck, dragged her face close and kissed her so hard she thought her lips would be forever mashed against her teeth.

Yanking back his head to a chorus of laughter and well wishes from those observing, he flashed a triumphant smile—the martyred ruler returning to his bride and keep. Gwynn's stomach turned over and 'twas all she could do not to spit on him. Instead she forced back the bile rushing up her throat, managed a poor excuse of a curtsy, and turned on her heel.

Heat climbing up her neck, she heard the jeers, men's raucous jokes, and a few nervous twitters at her expense. Her fists balled and her chin inched upward defiantly as she picked up her skirts and took the stairs to her chamber two at a time.

Only when she was inside the room, the door closed and pressed hard against her spine, did she wipe the filth of his kiss from her lips. No longer could she hold back nature and she retched violently, losing the contents of her stomach in the rushes at her feet.

What was she to do? How could she save Gareth?

There was a soft knock upon the door and Idelle, her stiff, steel-colored hair bristling around her wimple, swept into the room. "By the gods, Gwynn, look at this." Through her clouded eyes, she saw more than many. Clucking her tongue she whipped a rag from a pocket in her apron and began cleaning the soiled floor. "I fear for your life," she said as she gathered the fouled rushes and threw them into the fire. Angry flames snapped and sputtered in revolt. "Roderick is not a forgiving man."

"Nor a kind one."

"Aye." Idelle straightened. Her wise milky eyes met the fear in Gwynn's. "He sees as plainly as I do, lass, that the boy is not his."

"I know." 'Twas in this very room where Gareth was conceived, where she'd lain with the thief so many years before. She swallowed hard and chewed on the corner of her lip. She was not a woman to whimper and whine. She believed that for every problem that arose, there was a solution.

Idelle gave the floor a final swipe with her rag. "You should have confided in me, m'lady. Mayhap I could have helped."

"I—I thought it best to—"

"Lie," Idelle accused.

"Aye. 'Tis no use in arguing about it now. What's done is done. We must but find a way to keep Gareth safe."

"Mayhap ye should tell his father. The one who helped create him."

Gwynn shook her head and began pacing, trying to come up with a plan for Gareth's escape. " 'Twould do no good. I know not what became of him. He was but a thief who lingered too long in my chamber." Sighing, she shook her head. "He may be long dead."

"So think ye?" Idelle asked and again clucked her tongue in a manner that Gwynn found irritating. "Well, wrong ye be, m'lady, for I know of him."

Gwynn stopped dead in her tracks and pinned the older woman with a glare meant to freeze blood. "I believe you not."

"Trevin the thief, raised by Muir, a befuddled sorcerer who knows the old ways. With the jewels ye gave that boy and those he stole off other trusting souls he began his fortune and, in a game of dice, was lucky enough to win Black Oak Hall from the old lord who'd had too much drink and too little luck."

"Nay, ye deceive me." Gwynn sagged against the bed. She'd heard the story, of course. Who had not? Black Oak Hall had a history of darkness surrounding it, of trouble within the castle walls.

Baron Dryw, a fool of a man known to enjoy drink and gambling, had drunk too much wine one evening, invited some of his knights to join him in a simple game of chance, and had wagered his keep only to lose it. Some had said the game was crooked, that the soldier who won had cheated but that he was a fierce one whom no one had dared challenge. Worse yet, the baron had died, and it was oft speculated that the dark knight who took the rule of Black Oak so callously had killed the older man. Gwynn had listened to the gossip with only half an ear, for she cared not what happened in other castles, nor did she know Dryw of Black Oak. "Did . . . did not the new baron wed the old man's daughter?" she asked, her interest piqued as she twisted her wedding ring. Was it possible? The stable-boy-turned-thief had become a baron? A neighbor? One who had never violated their pact upon his leaving so many years ago? Her wretched heart twisted knowing that he was nearby.

"Aye." A shadow passed through Idelle's cloudy eyes. "Faith was Dryw's only issue. The poor lass died in childbirth and the babe was born without drawing a breath." Idelle sighed. " 'Tis much trouble they've had at Black Oak. Some say the castle is cursed."

Gwynn had heard as much for gossip ran swift and eagerly through the land. Had she but listened more carefully to the rumors flowing between castles, she, too, might have divined that Trevin the thief was the black knight who had by less than honest means become baron of a nearby castle, that the father of her son was within three days' ride. That thought should have given her solace. Instead she shivered, as if an ill wind had passed through her body and rattled her bones. "I cannot believe that—"

" 'Tis the truth I tell as always."

"But—"

"Have ye ever known me to lie?"

Gwynn shook her head and rubbed her arms.

"M'lady, please," Idelle entreated as she tossed a final handful of soiled rushes into the fire, then wiped her hands on her apron. "I know 'tis said that Trevin killed Dryw, though no one saw him push the baron from the curtain wall. But I believe it not."

"You trust him?"

"More than I trust your husband."

Gwynn could not disagree. "Why tell me this now?"

" 'Tis a feeling I have deep in me bones. Trevin of Black Oak will come and claim his son."

"Why now?" Gwynn asked, her heart beating a little faster at the thought of seeing him again. "I have his word—"

"The word of a thief and outlaw."

"He has not come forward afore."

"Roderick was not on his way home." Idelle frowned deeply. " 'Twill be evident to him that Gareth is not of his flesh. What then? Will he accuse ye of betraying him? Betraying the castle? I mean not to frighten you, but I worry."

"And what would you have me do?" Gwynn demanded, her head reeling.

"Be careful," Idelle warned, then offered an enigmatic smile. "And trust only your heart, for it is true."

Though a fire blazed in the grate, candles flickered and smoked, the scents of cinnamon, apples, and roasted meat still lingered, the great hall was cold as death. Roderick, clean-shaven and washed, fresh tunic and hose upon him, appeared stronger than he had when he'd first arrived at Rhydd. He sat in his chair with the carved-wood arms as if he'd never left, as if he had every right to rule all those who resided within the curtain walls.

The hall had reverberated with laughter and good cheer, though beneath it all had been a silent tension, dark looks, distrustful glances, and thinned lips.

Toasts had been offered, much wine consumed, and Jack the cook had outdone himself. The sugar sculpture in the shape of a castle had caused a collective gasp from those at the tables below the salt and a smile to light Roderick's grim countenance. Musicians, acrobats, and the jester had entertained them with stories, song, and bawdy jokes. Though she'd sat at her husband's side, Gwynn had barely eaten or spoken. While Roderick had feasted on eel, jellied eggs, pheasant, venison, beef, and plum tarts, she'd not been able to swallow, hadn't so much as dirtied her fingers on her trencher or picked at a bite of bread.

Gareth sat on the far side of Roderick. He had eaten hungrily, without many manners, suspiciously eyeing the man who was supposed to have spawned him. They had barely said a word throughout the meal though Ian, near his nephew, had appeared amused, his cold eyes laughing, his lips curved in a smile that had not been inspired by the musicians and jesters who had entertained them.

But now the great hall was nearly empty, the tables cleared and stacked as

Roderick had ordered everyone back to his tasks. Everyone but family members and Sir Webb, the knight who had helped the imprisoned baron to escape. Webb had ridden from Castle Carter and now stood at the fire warming the backs of his legs. Smelly steam rose from his dark, damp tunic. His brown hair was lank and straight, his face flushed from hours riding in the cold weather. He was a man who did not hide his evil in masks of civility, a soul, Gwynn was certain, who had not one redeeming quality. If ever there was a devil, Webb of Castle Carter was sure to be Satan Incarnate.

"Is there something you would say to me, Wife?" Roderick finally asked, picking at his teeth with the nail of one thumb and watching her every move.

Her heart stilled. Her fingers twisted in her woolen skirt. "Just that I am glad you are safe."

"In what? Twelve, nay, nigh onto thirteen winters, you have no other words?" He reached for his mazer of wine and scowled at its contents.

"Nay, my lord," she said pleasantly though each muscle in her body ached with the strain.

"About the boy?"

Dear God, help me, please. " 'Tis not the place."

"Ah, but it is, Wife," he insisted, rolling the cup between his palms. "You betrayed me."

"Nay—"

Gareth's head snapped up. "Mother—?"

"Do not heed your father. He has traveled far and been through a great ordeal." She held Roderick's hateful gaze. "Husband, I implore you to think before you speak. We should discuss Gareth and his training to be a knight later, when you are not so tired or have not had so much wine or—"

"—or when the boy cannot hear the truth, is that it?" Roderick demanded, leaning closer, the pupils of his eyes wide. "I speak not of his training, for he will have none. Does he not know that his mother is a common whore? A woman who would sleep with another man and pass him off as her husband's?"

"Nay!" Gareth's face flushed red, his entire body shaking.

" 'Tis true. Tell him," Roderick ordered, grabbing Gwynn's arm with fingers that were callused, stained, and surprisingly strong. "Tell him that he is the son of—whom? Now that is the question, is it not?" He pinched her harder, his jaw set and hard as he spat out his words. "Who slept in my bed and got my wife with child, eh? Whose little bastard is he?"

" 'Tis enough of your lies I've heard!" Gareth said, jumping onto the table and snatching up the sword Roderick had left by his chair. "Leave Mother alone!"

"Gareth, stop!" Gwynn said, her heart pounding with dread.

"Bastard." Webb's sword was instantly unsheathed.

"Nay, do not spill blood!" she cried attempting to yank her arm from her husband's grasp.

"You dare defy me?" Roderick's nostrils flared and a sickening grin settled onto his lips.

"Leave her be!" Gareth ordered. He was on top of the table, Roderick's sword raised as if he intended to cleave him in two.

Fear clawed at Gwynn's soul. "Gareth, please, do not—"

"The boy has balls," Ian said as he reached forward to grab his nephew. "But not many brains." Gareth nimbly ducked from his uncle's outstretched arms and knocked over a mazer of wine that had not been cleared. Red liquid ran like blood and Ian's face clouded.

"No brains at all," Webb agreed.

"I said, 'leave her be!' " Gareth ordered, the blade of Roderick's upraised sword glinting malevolently in the shifting light from the fire.

"Get down!" Gwynn screamed, scrambling to get away.

"Hush!" Roderick tried vainly to restrain his wife.

"Let me go, Husband," she hissed, fear taking hold of her tongue. "And you, Gareth, do not do anything foolish!" She stumbled backward. Roderick lost his grip.

He raised a hand.

"No!" Gareth cried.

Slap! The sound of Roderick's hand smacking against her cheek ricocheted off the walls and ceiling. "Scheming, whoring, daughter of Satan!"

Gwynn spun backward, tripping over chairs and the table. Roderick pounced on her and shook her as she kicked and clawed. "I'll see that you get the punishment you deserve, Jezebel." He raised his hand and hit her again. Pain exploded behind her eyes.

"Nay!" Gareth screamed.

The room spun but Gwynn managed to draw some moisture and spit upon the dog who was her husband.

"A pubic flogging until you faint, then I'll revive you and use the whip again!"

"Die!" Gareth swung the heavy sword downward and Webb jumped onto the table.

"NO!" Gwynn's shriek exploded through the chamber.

The blade glanced off Roderick's shoulder and rammed into the dark knight's arm. Blood spurted. Roderick howled. Webb swore and fell back, clinging to his wound, blood running through his fingers.

"Bastard! I'll kill you!" Roderick rounded on the small imposter, reaching into his belt for his dagger. Webb shot forward, Ian hoisted his sword aloft, but

Gareth, atop the table, dodged and ducked, swinging wildly with his deadly blade.

"Miserable cur!" Webb spun and sliced.

Gareth lithely jumped above the sword. Webb jabbed, Ian flung himself onto the table. Gareth rolled away from both men.

"Run!" Gwynn yelled as she climbed to her feet. Her face throbbed but she grabbed a table knife and before Webb could deliver another blow toward her son, she flung the blade at him. It caught him on the thigh and he winced, throwing off his mark.

"Aaaggh!"

Roderick grabbed for Gareth's legs, missed, flailed wildly with his knife, cutting Gareth's knee, sending a spray of blood from an ugly gash as the boy spun, slashing downward, his weapon imbedding in Roderick's side.

With a horrifying wail, Roderick fell across the table, his blood spilling into the pool of wine, the sword imbedded deeply in his body.

"Nay!" Father Anthony ran into the great hall, his vestments unfurling behind him. His face was white with terror, his eyes wide at the carnage. "For the love of all that is holy, stop! M'lord, m'lord!" Crossing himself and mumbling prayers, he flung himself upon Roderick who lay, half sprawled over the table. With a strength borne of desperation, he withdrew the bloodied blade and dropped it onto the floor. "Bless this man, keep him safe." The priest's face was twisted in a grief so deep it tore at the man's soul. "Do not let him die, Father, I beseech thee! Now that he has returned to us, do not take him away!"

Gwynn, still stunned, reached for her boy, pulled him off the table, and whispered into his ear. "Run for your life. Find Idelle or Sir Charles—"

"He will go nowhere!" Ian's voice boomed through the castle. He stood next to his brother who lay slumped over the table. "Guards, grab the boy. He is an imposter. His mother betrayed Rhydd and, therefore, as I am Roderick's only brother, I will rule."

"No!" Gwynn was frantic. Knights appeared from the hallways and several looked to Gwynn. "Leave Gareth be."

Gareth was still wound in her arms and she clung to him as if to life itself.

"I said, 'grab him.' And his lying mother as well," Ian ordered.

Webb staggered forward, swiping the air as if to take her child from her. With only thoughts of saving her son, Gwynn pushed Gareth toward the door and tripped the black knight. "Run! Gareth, *RUN!*"

The boy took off, only to be blocked by three guards, all men Gwynn had once trusted, the heaviest of which grabbed her son and plucked him, swinging and kicking, off the floor.

"Let him go!"

" 'Tis too late, m'lady," Ian said, his face spattered with blood, his expression fierce.

With a last rattling breath, Roderick of Rhydd gave up his soul and slumped to the floor.

"Oh, no. No, no, no!" Gwynn said as hands, someone's hands who was behind her, an enemy she could not see, tried to restrain her. Blood smeared over her sleeves and she realized Webb was holding her fast.

"He's dead! The baron is slain!" the priest proclaimed with tears running down his face. "Oh, Father, who art in heaven . . ."

"You did this, woman!" Ian pointed a long, sanctimonious finger in her direction. "With your whoring ways and evil treachery, you brought death upon your husband. You and your son be murderers."

"Nay!"

" 'Twill be." He glanced around the chamber, as if to see if anyone would dare disagree with him. Servants, peasants, and soldiers had gathered, circling the carnage, their faces ashen.

Pleading, fearful eyes gazed at the corpse of a leader most had never seen. Many made quick signs of the cross upon their chests and whispered prayers while others appeared unable to move.

Ian climbed onto the table, his sword at his side. "Make no mistake," he said to everyone within earshot. "As Roderick's brother, I am baron now. The lady has proved herself to be nothing more than a lying harlot who betrayed my brother by pretending that another man's son was his. The boy"—he swung his bloodied sword in Gareth's direction—"was no issue of Roderick's."

Some of the servants dared speak, but only in low tones, and only among themselves. Gwynn saw them all—Jack, the cook, the beekeeper, Alfred who handled the hounds, the candle maker, tailor, and dozens more, standing transfixed in the great hall, as if rooted to their places.

She tried to pull away but Webb's meaty, stained fingers only gripped her tighter, squeezing her flesh, causing pain to scream up her arms.

"The boy will be hanged at nightfall tomorrow," Ian proclaimed and Gwynn's heart was pierced as though by a lance. She let out a wail that trilled through the turrets. Tears blurred her vision and ran down her cheeks in hot rivulets. "Nay, Ian, you must not. Do what you will to me, but leave Gareth go free."

"He is a traitor—"

"Nay, a boy. A lad who knew nothing. 'Twas I who sinned, I who betrayed Roderick and Rhydd, I who should be punished." Despite the heavy hands restraining her, she flung herself at her brother-in-law, groveling on her knees for her boy. "I will do anything," she vowed, "suffer any punishment, but please, please, let Gareth go free."

From his perch on the table, Ian studied the woman trembling at his feet. Lust, ever his enemy, burned bright in his loins. He'd wanted Gwynn for thirteen long years, had lain awake at night thinking of her, letting other whores touch and kiss his member when it was she he wanted, only she who could quell his passion. Now, through the fates, she would willingly give herself to him. But for how long? Only until the boy was safe, then, he was certain, she would rather die than lie with him. She was a beautiful, prideful woman; one unlike any other and he was moved by her passion for her boy.

And then there were the servants and peasants to consider. Most of them seemed to adore her, many of the soldiers were loyal to her. Were he to marry her, they would swear their allegiance to him. 'Twas a gamble, either way, but he thought the odds weighed heavily in allying himself with this woman. Asides, having her warm his bed was oh, so inviting. "So be it, then, if you agree to marry me and bear me my own sons, Gareth will go free." She looked up at him with hope in her lovely, damp eyes. "If, however, you betray me as you did Roderick, or withhold your favors from me, or displease me in any manner, your son will be hunted down like a dog, hanged, and drawn and quartered. Do you understand?"

"Aye." She nodded gravely, terror distorting the fine features of her face at the thought of her only child so treated.

"Then, Gwynn, arise and stand by my side." He hopped to the floor and glared at the guards. "Let the boy go. He is to be banished from Rhydd, but no harm to come to him."

Gareth's face was white as snow. "Mother, nay—"

"Hush!" Her voice was harsh. "You are to do as Lord Ian says."

"But—"

"Do it, Gareth, and do not argue!" she said firmly though tears again rained from her eyes. The boy had no choice. At a nod from Ian, he was hoisted away and she, pale as death, seemed certain she would never see him again, which, of course, was true. Ian turned to the priest who was still mumbling prayers and crying over Roderick's body. "Get up, Father Anthony, and quit your insipid grieving. You have much to do. Not only have you my brother's body to lay to rest, but you must perform the marriage rites for Lady Gwynn and me."

"Now?" she cried, "But the banns have not yet been—"

"Hush! I am baron and as such I say we are to be wed this day. There will be no postponement." He wouldn't give her even a minute to change her mind. "The boy is not yet out of the castle, so what say you, Bride?"

She swallowed hard, but her small backbone seemed to solidify and her chin, once wobbling, became strong as steel. "Aye, m'lord," she agreed without any further trace of emotion. "Let us be wed."

Chapter Three

The vision came quickly on the third day of the ride. One second Muir was riding upon his gray palfrey, the horse cantering easily toward Rhydd, the next he was in a dark forest, with mists rising up from the ferns and bracken and blood running like sap from the trees. "What devilment is this?" he asked, the pain in his bad eye excruciating as he stared at his feet.

In a misting fog, he saw a snake slithering through the undergrowth. The viper crawled up his back and coiled at his neck, then, with a hiss, it changed, biting its own tail and turning into a chain. Cold, lifeless metal cut into the folds of skin at Muir's neck and blood—was it his?—began to flow as the links snapped, one by one, allowing him to breathe, staining his beard and tunic and disappearing.

"Muir! For the love of God, man, wake up!" Trevin reached over from his horse and shook the older man's shoulder. On the palfrey Muir sucked in his breath and leaned forward in the saddle.

"Be gone, Devil, and take this pain with ye!"

Trevin yanked hard on his mount's reins and the horse, lathered and muddied from hours upon the road, sidestepped, nearly bumping into Muir's animal. The five soldiers behind them slowed their mounts to skidding stops. "What is it?" Trevin demanded as the horses snorted and pawed, their ears twitching, their nostrils quivering nervously.

" 'Tis trouble at Rhydd."

"You told me of this before," Trevin muttered, looking at the darkening sky. It was nearly nightfall and soon there would be no daylight. With the clouds as they were there would be little moon glow or starlight to guide them. "We must be off if we are to make the castle gates before 'tis dark."

"Nay, nay." Muir held a hand to his bad eye, the one that saw nothing, yet somehow foretold the future. " 'Tis blood I see, blood flowing in rivers."

"At Rhydd?"

"Aye. Aach, this pain."

" 'Tis bad, eh?"

"Worse than you can imagine. 'Tis like the bite of a viper that never ends, or the burn of flesh, yet there be no fire. Oooh. By the gods, 'tis a curse, I tell ye."

"For all of us," Trevin said dryly.

Muir scoffed and yanked on the hood of his cloak. " 'Tis no time for humor. There is much trouble at Rhydd, more than I saw earlier." He closed his one good eye and flinched as if a bolt of lightning had been flung from the sky to skewer him. "As I live and breathe," he whispered and jolted again. His horse shied and shook his gray head, rattling the bridle and bit. " 'Tis more than trouble at this castle, m'lord."

"Don't call me—"

" 'Tis a chain I spy, one of links that are bound together. Father to son and son to father, cursed to fight and kill each other."

" 'Tis nonsense you speak."

"Nay, Trevin," the old one disagreed. He tore off the hood of his cloak and glared at the heavens with that unblinking, sightless eye. "God or Lucifer, I know not which."

"I have no time for this." Trevin kicked his destrier and the muddied horse took off again while Muir's smaller mount and those of the other soldiers struggled to keep up as they galloped through the mud.

"I fear there is danger lurking about," Muir called after him.

"You always fear danger."

"Aye. And ye embrace it."

Trevin's mouth lifted in a grim smile. How often had he been called reckless or fearless or just plain stubborn? Too many times to count. Near the river, the road curved and the thickets of oak and pine opened to grassy fields that surrounded the bluff on which the castle had been built.

Gray stone walls surrounded the keep and rose sharply from rocky cliffs overlooking the surrounding woods. High turrets and watchtowers spired from wide battlements and appeared to scrape the underbellies of the dark clouds that rolled restlessly through the heavens. An emerald-and-gold standard snapped in the wind and the portcullis was open wide, inviting visitors inside.

Through the sheeting rain, Trevin pulled up on his mount's reins and gazed upon the fortress where he had become a part of Lady Gwynn's plot. He'd been young and foolish at the time—and willing, oh, so willing. Sleeping in the lady's bed had been sweet sacrifice indeed and he'd never forgotten the feel of her skin against his rough fingers, the way she'd trembled when he'd kissed her, the pure, unashamed wanting within her. Deep within him, a dark, unbidden desire flowed again and he forced it back.

Was she naught but a rich, scheming female whose only ambition was to save her own beautiful neck? Had she not conceived a child, lied to her husband, committed willing adultery all for her own gain?

And what about you? Did you not aid her, do all that she did, to save your skin?

Aye, he was as guilty as she. And now a boy—their son—was in jeopardy.

Turning in the saddle he gave orders to his small group of soldiers. He would enter the castle alone and if he did not return with the boy or get word to his men by the time the guard in the watchtower changed, he told Gerald to return to Black Oak for reinforcements. The others were to sneak into the castle as spies.

There were already those within the keep's well-guarded walls who would aid them for Trevin of Black Oak had men loyal to him, men with pasts blackened much as his own was, hidden within the surrounding keeps, including Rhydd. Those men, traitors to their own barons, were paid to keep him informed and warn him of any attack to be waged against Black Oak Hall.

His plan was simple. He would sneak into Rhydd and meet with Richard the carpenter and Mildred the alewife, both of whom were paid to keep their eyes and ears open. Only then would he speak to Gwynn alone before he started bartering with her husband. He owed her that much for breaking his part of their bargain. His conscience twinged a little for he had a code of honor such as it was. His word was usually good and he had promised Gwynn to keep their secret.

"I like this not," Muir muttered as the men dispersed into the woods.

"Trust me."

"Bah."

Trevin placed a hand on the old man's shoulder. "If my plan goes awry, 'tis your duty to take care of the boy, Gareth."

"Take care of him?"

"If something happens to me, take him to the cave. Wait for me there but two days."

"And then what?"

Trevin shook his head and offered Muir an evil grin. "Then conjure up some spells for me, old man, for 'twill mean that something ill has happened."

"Just as I have foreseen."

"From the bottom of an ale cup."

Muir shook the rain from his cowl. " 'Tis not the time for jest."

"Trust me, old man, all will be well." Trevin turned his steed toward the yawning castle gates and leaned forward, nudging the beast's ribs. The horse responded, tearing off and flinging mud and pebbles behind him.

"I pray it so," Muir called after him, his old voice growing fainter. "I pray it so."

                              *   *   *

"In the name of the Father and the Son and . . ."

Gwynn, kneeling in the chapel next to her new husband and the Lord of Rhydd, didn't hear the rest of the priest's prayer. She was married. Again. To another man she didn't love, nay a man who she was sure was as black-hearted as his brother.

But Gareth would be safe. Banished from the castle forever, the boy would be alone in the world and she would never see him again, but he would live and he was almost a man as it was. Tears touched her eyes and her heart was heavy, but she knew she had no choice.

Father Anthony, his face a pasty white, his voice dull and without life, had finally stopped speaking. It was over. Doom settled like lead in her heart. Oh, cruel, cruel fate. She crossed her bosom quickly.

"Come, Wife," Ian said with a wicked grin as he helped her to her feet. His hand upon her arm was hard, his fingers viselike and sickeningly possessive.

Never had she wanted to be any man's bride and now she was married to a man she despised.

"Wait for me in your chamber as I have some business to attend to." His eyes gleamed with an inner satisfaction that caused her insides to curdle like sour milk. " 'Tis a long time I've waited for this night."

Her stomach heaved, but she managed a thin, sickly smile. She could endure anything as long as she knew Gareth would come to no harm. She started to turn, but he didn't release her. "Gwynn," he said in a whisper. "I know of your temper and your schemes. Make no mistake, you are naught but my wife and can act no longer like the baron. While Roderick was alive, you ruled the castle, but he is now dead. I am your husband and as such I will expect your complete obedience, elsewise Gareth will be hunted down, found, and brought back to be hanged." His fingers tightened over her arm. "Do you understand me?"

"Aye," she said through clenched teeth.

"You will never defy me." He stared at her face and she knew he saw the shadow of a bruise on her cheek, a painful reminder of her last husband's hand.

"Never, my lord," she lied, forcing the hated word over her tongue.

"Good." He smiled smugly, then drawing her near, brushed a kiss across her lips, his beard prickly against her skin. Her stomach roiled but pulling up inner strength, she endured his attempt at tenderness. "Go to your chamber and wait for me."

"I will."

She half ran down the shadowy corridor and tried to convince herself that she could live through anything as long as she knew that Gareth was free and safe.

As she opened the door to her chamber, she found Idelle pouring clean water into the basin. Fresh rushes gave off a heady fragrance and new candles had been lit, their small flames giving off pools of light that caused the colors of the tapestry hanging on the wall above her bed, crimson, gold, and purple to seem deep and comforting.

"So it is done?" Idelle asked as she shook the final drops from her bucket.

"Aye," Gwynn said with an angry sigh. "It seems my curse to be forever wed."

"To the wrong man."

"To any man." Pausing at the basin, she splashed cool water onto her face and tried to think. She could leave. As soon as she knew that Gareth was safely away from Rhydd, she could pack a few things and ride as far away as possible—mayhap to stay with Luella or . . . oh, 'twas foolish to think so. Ian would never let her go. Had she not promised him a castle full of sons? Did he not just vow to hunt Gareth down like a beast in the forest and see him hanged if she were to cross him?

The only way to be certain that Gareth remained safe was for her to pretend to be faithful to Ian. Each day she pretended to obey her husband would give her son that much more time to flee as far away from the castle walls as was possible. He would have to take the fastest destrier in the stables and ride to the sea where he could board a ship for some faraway port.

Oh, if she only had more time to make arrangements. "I must see my son," she decided.

"But Ian said you were to stay here."

"I am but his wife. Not his slave."

"There is not much difference." Idelle's lips pursed into a frown.

"I will see Gareth, Idelle, and I will see him now," she said, the fingers of one hand curling into a fist of determination. "But Ian is not to know."

"M'lady, please, do not anger the lord."

"I will not." She shot Idelle a conspiring look. "Do not say a word to anyone but Gareth."

"I like this not," Idelle worried aloud.

Gwynn flung her favorite cloak over the damask dress she'd worn to become Ian's wife. Ignoring the old woman's warnings, she took the backstairs and avoided the sentries who, thankfully, were dozing at their posts, their heads nodding in time with their snores.

Hiking the hood of the cloak over her head, she ducked out the back door, sending a pair of geese scurrying into the wet grass. Darkness had fallen over the land and aside from the firelight shimmering in the doorways and windows, there was no illumination. Not that it mattered much. Gwynn knew the keep well and as her slippers slid in the mud and wet grass, she dashed along a wide path leading past pens of sheep and pigs to the stables.

Once inside, she lit a candle and was careful to place it on a metal shelf far from the straw that covered the floor. A moist wind caused the flame to flicker and dance and mingled with the scents of horse dung, sweat, leather, and straw.

Wrapping her arms about herself, she sighed and waited.

"So, m'lady, you have found yourself another husband and the first one is not yet buried."

Gwynn jumped. Her heart jolted. The deep male voice came from the shadows behind her. She reached for her dagger.

"Who goes—oh!" Strong, callused fingers covered her mouth and a man's head was suddenly next to hers, looking over her shoulder, his breath hot against her ear. The hand that had scrabbled for her little knife was caught by his other hand. "Fear not. 'Tis naught but a thief."

Trevin? Her legs were suddenly weak as the scent of him—an odor she remembered from their lovemaking—enveloped her. Slowly he removed his hand from her mouth and she licked her lips. Could it be? Was he really here?

Still holding onto her wrist he moved soundlessly into the small pool of light cast by the candle. For the first time in thirteen years, she stared into the disturbing eyes of the thief, the father of her only son. A familiar ache squeezed hard upon her heart.

"You—you scared the devil from me!"

He didn't smile, nor did his fingers unclasp her wrist. His mirthless chuckle was positively wicked and as such disturbed her all the more. "I doubt that's possible."

"What are you doing here?"

"Waiting for you."

Her stupid heart missed a beat.

"We needs talk."

"Must we?" She glanced over her shoulder and tried to pull her arm away. His fingers tightened ever so slightly and she realized that she was trapped. He was much stronger than she, much more agile, much larger.

"What want you?"

"My son."

There it was. Dear God, now what? A weight settled heavy on her shoulders. "We had a bargain."

"I will keep him safe."

"You? The thief?" she mocked. "An outlaw, a swindler who won your barony from a befuddled old man in a crooked game of dice? You will keep him safe?"

"Without a doubt, m'lady," he said with confidence.

Dear Lord in heaven, was that her heart knocking so wildly? She hazarded a quick glance through the doorway again, hoping that Gareth would not

come upon them now, but wait until she'd dispensed with this . . . this interloper. What would she tell her son when he ran through the open door? What
could she say? This man hiding in the shadows, the purported baron of Black
Oak Hall and known criminal was the man she'd chosen to betray her husband?

"I came to claim my son," he said, as if she might not have understood his
intentions.

"Now?" She shook her head. "For the love of God, Trevin, do you not know
what would happen to the lad if it were known that his father was . . . was—"

"Not Roderick?" at last he dropped her hand.

With a sigh, she shook her head. "That much he knows."

"But you did not tell him of me?"

"I knew not that you were the baron of Black Oak Hall."

He studied her for a few seconds, as if she was a puzzle he couldn't quite
piece together. "Had you known?"

"I would not have told him. He's but a lad—too young to understand."

"Let me be the judge of that."

"On your honor, you swore that you would never breathe a word."

"I changed my mind."

"We had a bargain," she reminded him, the stables seeming suddenly
close, the night air difficult to breathe. Thirteen years seemed to fade away
and he was once again her lover, the one man who had heard her moan in
pleasure, seen her stretch against him with the dawn, felt the deepest, most intimate parts of her.

"Aye, and for a few baubles I gave up my son." His voice was low, seductive.

"For a few baubles and your freedom," she said, stepping backward, trying
to break the spell of being so close to him. "If—if you had been caught you
would have lost your hand, mayhap your life."

"I had no choice," he said simply and she felt a horrible misgiving. "For
you, m'lady, would have gladly turned me over to the sheriff. Yours was the
perfect seduction."

She blushed at the memory. At the time he was barely a man, but now, so
close that she could smell the scents of leather and musk around him, feel his
heat, see the dark shadow of his beard there was no mistaking he was a male,
hard and virile and strong.

No longer was he the dirty, misbehaved thief she had forced to do her bidding. No trace of that boy lingered. In his stead, standing in the dusky shadows was a man, a severe-appearing man, with harsh features. Black stubble
shaded a rock-solid jaw, ebony brows and spiked lashes guarded eyes a dark,
intense blue that followed her every move, and lips, once supple with youth,
were now thin as the blade of a dagger. Dressed in black from his muddied

cloak to the tips of his boots, he appeared as Stygian as any devil who had found a way to escape from the very depths of hell.

"Roderick is dead, is he not?" he asked suddenly.

"Aye, but—"

"And you've already found yourself a new husband."

" 'Twas part of a bargain," she said, instantly furious. No longer intimidated, she stepped closer to him and tilted her face upward defiantly.

"Ah, and you, mistress, seem to have a way with such arrangements."

"I keep my word," she said haughtily.

"As I have kept mine."

"Until now."

"As I said, I was cornered as well as young and foolish."

She wouldn't give an inch. Couldn't. Too much, even Gareth's very life, was at stake. "You gave me your word."

"You believed a thief?"

"I had no choice—" she said, hearing his own words coming from her lips.

"Bitter irony, is it not?" he mocked. "No, m'lady, 'tis time I claimed my son."

A horse nickered softly in the blackness and there was the rustle of straw as the animals shifted on the other side of their mangers. Gwynn felt desperation claw at her throat. She needed time to think, to lay plans. "Does Lord Ian know that you're here?"

She felt, rather than saw, him tense. "I've not yet approached the lord," he said, leaning one shoulder against a post supporting the roof. "I thought it best to first speak with you."

"And so you've done," she said, unnerved.

"Tell me, how is it you're married to him before your other husband is in the grave? What kind of bargain is this?"

"One that was necessary," she said, unwilling to give him any further information. "Now, if you will leave—"

"Not without my son."

"He is in enough trouble as it is," she said. "If Ian finds you here, it will only cause more."

"What kind of trouble?"

Gwynn hesitated. "You have heard that Roderick was killed by Gareth?"

"I knew only that the baron was slain." Trevin said, his voice sober.

" 'Twas terrible. Roderick returned and met Gareth for the first time. He realized the boy was not his son and accused me of . . . well, many things. None of them good." She cleared her throat and remembered the clang of swords, the screams of pain, spray of blood, and Roderick's last, rattling breath. "There . . . was a fight and Gareth, in an attempt to defend my honor and, I suppose, my life as well took up Roderick's sword and killed him."

"Jesus, son of God."

"Ian saw it all and accused Gareth of murder. Sentenced him to be hanged."

"Not as long as I breathe."

For some reason, Gwynn felt reassured, though, in truth, what could Trevin do? Was he not assumed to be a murderer himself? She placed a hand upon his sleeve. " 'Tis why I am married again. Ian . . . he only agreed to spare Gareth's life if I would agree to marry him."

With one strong finger, he lifted her chin and gazed at her with night-darkened eyes. "Think you I believe that you sacrificed yourself?"

"I did only what I had to." She licked her lips nervously and his gaze lowered to her mouth. Her pulse jumped as she realized how alone they were, felt a tingle where his finger pressed against the sensitive skin at the underside of her jaw, sensed a dusky yearning in his touch. A flame of desire flared in his eyes and she swallowed hard. Oh, God, what was she doing here with him? Why could she not step away?

"Where is Gareth now?"

"He . . . he has not yet left the castle." With all her strength, she stepped away from him and his hand fell away from her chin as she released his arm. "I await him now."

"Good." Trevin folded his arms over his chest and leaned one shoulder against a post supporting the roof. "Then, m'lady," he said. "I will wait as well."

The ferrets scrambled in their kennels, growling softly, their claws clicking nervously on the wooden floor.

"Quickly, over here!" Ian's voice was but a whisper as he led the dark knight through the herb garden. Webb hobbled slightly, his wound, now stitched and bound still bothering him. They stopped at a corner of the keep, in a sheltered spot near the dove cote where the wind, damp and chill, was not so strong. "Roderick trusted you."

"Aye." Webb nodded and blew on his hands. "He promised to pay me well."

"And you shall be."

To ensure the man's trust, Ian untied a small leather pouch from his belt, opened the bag, and poured the coins into his gloved palm. "For your service to Roderick and your allegiance to Rhydd." He dropped the coins into the pouch again and drew the string. The coins clinked softly—such sweet, sweet music. "You will take the boy tonight and ride for three days, then kill him as quickly and as painlessly as possible."

" 'Twill be my pleasure," Webb said. There was a muffled woof from the direction of the dog kennels a few feet away. "What was that?" Webb demanded, turning swiftly on his heel and reaching for his sword.

"Nothing. Just a nervous cur. You're jumpy, my friend."

"Mayhap from being hacked with your brother's sword." He turned around again and sheathed his weapon, his face paling with the effort. " 'Tis an ill wind blowing through your keep tonight, m'lord."

"A poet be you?"

"Nay, just a soldier for hire."

"You have a job." Another dog started howling and the hound master yelled sharply at his charges.

"Shut up ye bloody mutts, er I'll teach ye a lesson ye'll not soon forget!"

Ian waited a few tense seconds as the dogs quieted. When he spoke it was in the barest of whispers. "You must make it look as if you were attacked by outlaws. You'll say that the boy's brash ways got him into trouble as he tried to elude the robbers rather than give them any of his money." Ian snapped his fingers as he thought. "Take Sir Charles and Sir Reynolds with you. They, too, must be killed, of course, and their corpses returned as well."

"Aye."

"Can you take care of all of them?" Ian wasn't certain for though Webb had proven himself to Roderick, he was wounded.

"I have friends, m'lord. They be only too willing to slit a man's throat for a few coins."

"Good. Good." Ian ignored his twinge of conscience. He was baron of Rhydd now. His word was law. He had to do that which was best for himself as well as the rest of the castle. "My faith is with you."

The dark knight snorted and spat into the garden. "As well it should be, m'lord."

Ian licked his chapped lips. He was no stranger to violence, but 'twas not the lad's fault he was born a bastard, and the boy had killed the one man who stood in Ian's way of ruling Rhydd. In truth, Gareth had saved Ian the trouble of murdering his brother. Now, however, the boy, too, had to be done away with. "His mother must believe that you were laid siege upon. 'Twould be good if you were to have suffered a wound."

"Another?"

" 'Tis well paid you are."

"Do not worry, *m'lord*," Webb sneered. "I will be sufficiently cut."

"Your sacrifice will be rewarded." Ian sighed in relief and picked at the skin flaking from his lips. "No one is to know otherwise. 'Tis between us only."

"Aye, Lord Ian. The truth is that the boy, Charles, and Reynolds were all killed by outlaws who showed no mercy. They left me, too, for dead. No torture or inquisition will ever make me say elsewise."

"Ah, you be a good and loyal man, Sir Webb," Ian said, wondering if this man would sell his allegiance to another for a higher price. He'd met him years ago before Webb had become a knight. Then, he was but a mercenary who had, for a while, ridden with Ian while Roderick ruled Rhydd and was married to his first wife. Ian hadn't trusted the man then, but now, through a twist of the fates, he was forced to depend upon the dark knight. "When you return, you will be paid again, thrice what we agreed upon. Also, lest you think your deeds go unappreciated, I will make you my most trusted knight upon full recovery of your wounds."

"See that I do recover," Webb warned, his voice low and without a trace of jest. "Elsewise the outlaws who be my friends will come for you and your wife."

"Do not fear." They clasped hands firmly and Ian felt the strength in Webb's fingers—stronger than steel.

"So be it." Webb tied the purse to his belt and winced at a jab of pain in his thigh, as if his wound was throbbing.

They parted ways and did not notice the two sets of eyes watching them from a hiding space under the dog kennels. Gareth held the half-grown pup his mother had given him this past boon day, during the harvest season. While trying to keep the playful dog quiet, he had heard each bone-chilling word exchanged between the man he'd thought was his uncle and the knight he'd maimed this afternoon. Ian meant to kill him and Webb was only too glad to do the deed. All of Gareth's bravado evaporated in the frigid night and he shivered as he cradled the clawing, wild hound to his chest. He could not waste a second, for with each beat of his heart he came closer to being discovered and murdered.

He had the coins and rings his mother had dropped into his pack earlier as well as the cross, a dagger, and black cloak. He didn't dare make his way to the stables for fear he would be caught. Though he would love to ride Dragon at a breakneck gallop through the main gate and across the moat bridge to the forest, he couldn't take the chance of running into Webb or Ian. Asides, he would be able to buy a good horse with his small cache should he need one, but, for now, he had to run as far from Rhydd as possible.

"Come, Boon," he ordered softly. He pocketed apples from the storage bin and a loaf of day-old bread being saved for the beggars, then whistled softly to the speckled pup who had more energy than brains.

Not for the first time in his twelve years, Gareth opened the sally port near the kennels, cringed as the huge door creaked on its ancient hinges, and let it swing open behind him as he, still holding the scrambling dog, dropped the six feet to the sodden ground.

He landed hard, twisted an ankle, but took off at a dead run through the swampy grasslands and into the black moat. The water was cold as ice, but he swam the brackish span, his skin turning blue, his body chilled to the marrow of his bones.

Boon, with only his head above the water line, splashed and swam enthu-
siastically at his side.

Teeth rattling, Gareth climbed up the opposite shore and ran, hobbling
across the grassland as Boon shook the water from his coat.

"Come!" Gareth ordered in a hoarse whisper. Sometimes the dog had not
a brain in his head! He whistled softly and Boon bounded to his side.

In the forest it was black as the very depths of hell. Gareth could barely dis-
tinguish the gnarled, twisted shapes of the trees or the path that veered
through the thicket. Still he ran with the pup at his heels.

Vines tripped him. Branches slapped his face. Cobwebs clung to his skin.
Thorns tore at his breeches and his boots were so wet they sloshed, but he
sped along the twisting trails, faster and faster, the burn in his ankle cutting
like a knife, his young heart pumping, his lungs burning, tears blinding his
eyes. He knew not where he was going, but fear chased him on.

"Come, Boon, blast you!" he said, gasping as the dog stopped short and
growled. "Hurry! The devil will have us both if Sir Webb catches up to us."

"Who be you?"

The voice rumbled from the darkness.

"Ahh!" Gareth screamed as a hand, seeming to snake out of the very soul
of the forest, clamped around his wrist in a death grip. "Hush!"

The dog lunged, but the voice commanded, "Stay, beast!" Boon stopped
cold.

The fingers around his arm tightened as if drawn by an invisible string and
yet he saw no one in the dark, gloomy night. "Now, boy, who be ye and what
are ye running from?"

'Twas Satan, Gareth thought wildly, his blood pumping through his veins.
Lucifer had come up from hell to capture him. He tried to speak, but his voice
was lost and for a second he thought he might wet himself. "I—I—" Should
he lie? What if this man, nay this demon, was one of Webb's outlaws, the men
who wanted to slit his throat?

"I know who ye be. Y'er Gareth of Rhydd, are ye not?"

Gareth's tongue wouldn't work and he reached for the knife at his belt
with his free hand. He'd kill this bastard from Hades before the creature had
a chance to slay him.

"Do it not, boy," the voice commanded, "or, 'tis certain ye and this mutt ye
call a dog will both meet yer doom."

Chapter Four

"Something's wrong." Gwynn peered through the darkness and wrapped her arms around herself. She couldn't stand another second waiting for Gareth, of feeling the weight of Trevin's enigmatic gaze as it bored into her back. "He should have been here by now."

Somewhere near the kennels the dogs put up a racket and were rewarded with a stern command from Alfred, the simpleton who had a way with animals but could not communicate with another human being if it were to save his soul.

"You're sure the old woman can be trusted?"

"Idelle? Aye. With my life." Gwynn fingered the worn handle of a pitchfork hung near the door. The bailey was dark, few patches of light glowing from the windows of the huts surrounding the great hall. Only the farrier's forge glowed bright in the night. She shook her head. "Something is amiss."

"Then we must go find the boy."

"Not yet." Thoughtfully she chewed on the corner of her lip. Where could the boy be? Not in his chamber or Idelle would have found him and sent him to the stables. Sometimes he hid in closets and crevices within the castle walls, watching for a game of dice. As she had learned the runes and spells of the old ones growing up, Gareth had learned how to wager at games of chance—so like his father.

She glanced again at Trevin and cursed silently that he should arrive this day, at the very time when Gareth was in jeopardy. A spell came to mind, one that would make an enemy disappear, but she held her tongue because, in truth, she didn't know whether the man before her, the only man to have made love to her, was friend or foe. Her mind told her not to trust him, her wayward heart wanted desperately to believe in him.

"I must go." She started to step through the door, but Trevin wrapped determined fingers around her arm.

"Careful, woman," he said into her ear and his breath caused goose bumps to rise on her skin and oh, so, heart-stopping memories to roll through her mind. "Do not cross me."

"I would not—" she said, but knew the words to be a lie.

"Good, because I have many friends within the walls of Rhydd, men with weapons who would come to my aid." He hesitated, then said, "If there be trouble, seek out the carpenter. Richard."

"The carpenter?"

"Aye, he is a friend."

"And a traitor to Rhydd."

"As you were, m'lady, when you slept with a man other than your husband." She stiffened and tried to ignore the warmth of his fingertips through her cloak. "The people of Rhydd are loyal to Roderick and—"

"Roderick's dead."

"—his wife—"

"You, m'lady, are now married to Ian."

"Oh, bother!" How had her life become so complicated? "Everyone knows I only married Ian to save Gareth's life."

One of the horses nipped at another and the second neighed and kicked in defense.

"Shh!" Trevin commanded and he yanked her hard against him. He blew out the candle and the stables were instantly dark. Through the open door she saw movement as a guard, watching from the north tower, held a torch aloft and called down to the gatekeeper.

"Who goes there?"

"Wha'?"

Gwynn froze and silently prayed that she wouldn't be found hiding in the stables in the arms of the outlaw baron of Black Oak Hall. Hard, inflexible muscles surrounded her and the smell of him, all male and leather reminded her of lying naked in his arms so long ago.

"Hush," he whispered, his breath, warm and inviting as it teased the rim of her ear.

Through her clothes her buttocks were pressed hard against his thighs. He shifted slightly and taut muscles pressed against the curve of her spine. Desire unwanted, raced through her blood though she had no time for such nonsense.

Trevin and his lean body be damned, she had to think of Gareth. Barely able to breathe, she tried to concentrate on anything other than the splay of his fingers over her abdomen.

"I say, 'who goes there?' " the guard yelled again.

Sweet Jesus, let me out of here so that I can find Gareth. Her breathing was shallow and soft and her mind spun in images of Trevin and Gareth, father and son, so alike and yet so different. With each of her breaths, his arms tightened, fingertips brushing the underside of her breasts.

Somewhere in a nearby pen, a cow lowed and the dogs began baying again.

"No one's about, ya ninny." The gatehouse guard walked into the bailey and took a cursory look at the darkened grass. Cupping his mouth, he turned his head upward and shouted, "Stand yer watch and mind yer own business."

"Christ A'mighty, y're in a foul mood."

"Yeah, well, ye got the dogs all worked up again, now, didn't ye?" Grumbling under his breath the guard returned to the gatehouse and the sentry on the wall walk made his way to the tower, his torch a moving beacon.

"Now," Trevin said, his lips brushing against her nape, "go you to the castle and find the boy. Bring him here to meet me."

"I cannot."

"If you do not," he promised, agitation evident in his voice, "I will search him out myself and tell him the truth. 'Tis time he knew whose blood is flowing through his veins."

"That of a thief."

"And worse," he admitted and she thought of the rumors surrounding him. A black-heart. A rogue baron. A murderer and, as always, an outlaw.

"I'll go," she finally agreed as she couldn't stand another minute in his arms. Her blood was heating, her traitorous heart pounding out a wild cadence, and her fears for her son were distracted by visions of lying naked in his arms, letting desire run its wayward course as she felt his weight upon her.

Swallowing hard at the memory, she slipped through the doorway and, without making a sound, darted through the blackest shadows of the bailey. Smoke from the fires of the day lay low and sifted through the damp air as she slogged through the bent grass and mud toward the great hall.

Puddles had collected on the path dampening her skirts and shoes. She had to think, to come up with a plan to save her son. Trevin and his wants be damned. 'Twas Gareth who was in danger.

A scheme was forming in her mind as she rimmed the eel pond and a fish jumped near her feet. 'Twas just a thought at this point, but swirling into a more definite notion. She would bribe the soldiers that were to ride Gareth to the outer reaches of Rhydd. Surely one would take the boy to Heath Castle where Luella would see that he was hidden safely away. Then, much later, would she join him. Somehow, someway she would be with her son again.

But you are married to Ian. At that thought she shriveled inside. How could she lie with him? Sleep in his bed? Pretend that she did not despise him? Her stomach turned over at the thought and she slid out of her slippers to climb the stairs of the keep.

The candles were burning down, their light muted, the smoke hanging in the corridors. Surely Ian had missed her by now and he would want to know where she'd been. She would lie, of course, claim that she'd been restless and had to walk to clear her head of all the pain and suffering she'd witnessed this day. Surely, Ian would expect her to mourn Roderick's passing as well as worry about her son's banishment.

She shoved open the door to her chamber.

She shopped short.

All the spit dried in her mouth.

"Wife." There was no hint of a smile on Ian's wicked face. He sat on the edge of her bed, leaning backward on one elbow, as if he owned the very place where she slept.

Webb, the abomination of a knight, stood near the fire. Blood, black, and caked, stained one leg of his breeches and his eyes, above his beard-darkened jaw glinted with an evil light that scared the liver out of her.

"Where is he?" Ian demanded.

Gwynn's breath stopped. "W-who?" she forced out and willed her feet to keep moving into her room. Being in the chamber alone with these two men caused fear to eat at her innards, but she managed an outward calm. "Who are you looking for?"

"Your son, Wife."

Sweet, merciful Lord in heaven. "Gareth? He is not in the castle?"

"Nowhere in the keep."

"But he must be." Silently she prayed that Idelle had snatched him away and that even now he was riding like a demon to castle Heath.

"We've searched everywhere."

"Everywhere," Webb repeated, then spit into the fire. The flames crackled.

"But the castle is large, with many hiding places. You know how Gareth is, still a boy. Always teasing and playing."

"He's gone." Ian's voice was flat.

"Nay. I do not believe that—"

"The sally port was not barred or locked. A guard found it creaking open and he's certain it was secure when last he passed it. Also, the pup that you gave the boy is missing."

Gwynn's knees weakened. Was Gareth with Trevin? Had they escaped together? The sally port, usually guarded, was the back door of the castle, positioned high above the moat, a means of escape if ever Rhydd was under siege. She shrugged. "I know not where he is."

With a snort of contempt, Webb limped to the window and regarded her silently.

"You can do better than this, Lady," Ian said, scratching his beard. "Do not lie to me. Tell me where he is."

"I swear to you on my life, I know not."

"So be it." Never taking his eyes off his wife, Ian pushed himself lazily to his feet. As he approached Gwynn she was aware of how much larger he was than she. Sighing he reached for his belt and began to slowly unbuckle the leather strap. Fear scraped down her insides. "Now, Wife," he said as the buckle gave way and the belt slipped into his fingers, "my patience is gone. 'Tis time to tell me where you have hidden the boy. I want not to harm you, but, if needs be, I am willing to do what I must to rule this castle."

"And that includes flogging me?" she demanded, refusing to show him any of the dread that was strangling her.

"It only means that I am not afraid to make anyone, even my new bride, bend to my will." He fingered the strap. "Pray that I won't have to use force."

"Do what you will," she said meeting his gaze. "I fear you not, Ian. Nor will I ever."

"Who the devil are you?" Gareth demanded as he tried to yank his shoulder away from the claw holding it firmly.

"Know you not?"

"Be you Lucifer?"

"By the gods, boy, would Lord Trevin have sent you to the devil?"

"Lord Trevin?" Gareth tried to view the man—for he appeared to be a man rather than a forest monster—who held him fast, but it was too dark to see much except his white beard and the moving hole that was his mouth. "You talk in circles. Now leave me be."

"Not yet, m'boy. 'Tis my duty to keep ye safe, so I'll have no more of yer sass."

"Your *duty*?"

"Aye, to Trevin of Black Oak."

"Speak you of the outlaw who stole the castle?" Though shivering Gareth spat on the ground. "I've heard of him. Old Bart said he is a cheat."

"Mayhap."

"One who bested an addled, drunken old man who was foolish enough to bet his barony in a game of dice."

"Well—"

"Then, Bart says, when the lord recognized what he'd done, this Trevin, who was but an outlaw knight, ran the lord through and tossed him into the moat!"

"Nay, nay, nay. Who is this Bart?"

"The best huntsman in all of Rhydd . . . well, he was until he lost his fingers to a wolf."

"Bah! He knows only half the truth."

"Nay, Matilda—she scrapes the hides from the huntsman's kill, she, too, says Trevin of Black Oak is a murdering thief."

"Well, she is a liar and the old man—Bart or whatever is his name, he be a fool. Don't ye know better than to listen to women? They be the bane of a man's existence, let me tell you. Now, come along."

"Bart is not a woman."

"Ah, well, some men, too, they are not to be trusted."

"I'll go nowhere." The man not only spoke like he was truly daft but he reeked of sour wine.

"I've food and a warm fire, lad, now come along afore whoever it is y're runnin' from finds ye."

"Leave me be!" Gareth started to struggle and it took all of Muir's strength to hold him down. The dog yapped wildly again and jumped up and down, snapping his ugly jowls. "You—beast—get back!"

"Nay, Boon, attack. Attack!" Gareth kicked and landed a blow to Muir's shin.

"Miserable brat. If ye were not the son of—" He bit down his tongue though his leg smarted. "I'm here to help ye, if ye would but calm down."

"Help me?"

"Aye. To save ye from those that would rather see ye in yer grave before ye reach thirteen years."

The clawing, scratching, and kicking stopped. "You know of them?" he asked.

"Aye. Down, ye little cur!"

"Boon, stay!" Gareth commanded as he eyed this bearded man who held him in his aged hands. He was a short man with an expanding girth, flowing beard, and gravelly voice. His breath stank of sour wine and, even in the blackness, Gareth sensed that his clothes were those of a pauper and there was something not quite right with his face.

"Why be ye here in the forests of Rhydd?"

"Waiting for you, of course."

"Of course," Gareth mocked and the old man sniffed in disdain.

"We must be off. If ye've escaped, then there's trouble brewin' just like I saw in my vision."

"Vision? What be ye? A wizard?" Gareth doubted it. The old man was a drunk, little more. Any vision he saw came from the bottom of a cup of ale unless Gareth missed his guess.

Muir sighed theatrically. "Right now it seems I'm a pitiful man with a boy who asks far too many questions and a dog that would like to bite out my throat. Hurry along this way, would ye, and be quick about it."

Gareth whistled for the pup.

"Oh, do be quiet," Muir grumbled in irritation. He'd never much cared for lads of this age. Too old to be innocent and too young to know anything of any substance, they were trouble through and through. Trevin, at twelve, had been more difficulty than he was worth. Muir had been forever getting that one out of trouble.

"Where are we going?"

"Someplace safe."

Gareth fell into step with the old man who held on to a cane, but never used it, and found his way to a horse that was tethered to a small sapling. Bridle jangling, the palfrey was trying to pluck a few meager blades of grass in the darkness.

At that moment the pup gave out an excited yip and there was a baying of hounds in the distance.

"Saints be damned." The dogs of Rhydd would be released to hunt him down like a wounded stag. "Climb up, then," the drunk insisted and Gareth had no choice but to follow this crippled old man who mounted the horse with surprising ease. He clucked to the beast and though the forest was dark as pitch the palfrey clipped at a fast walk.

Again the dogs let out a chorus of baying that paralyzed Gareth. His teeth chattered and he closed out his mind to memories of slicing through Roderick's flesh with his sword. 'Twas far different from the games he played with Tom, the butcher's simpleton of a son. The feel of metal piercing skin and scraping bone was sinister and cold. He held tight on to the pup, feeling the dog's warmth and wishing that all this trouble had never started.

If only Lord Roderick, the man he'd thought to be his father, had never escaped.

"Hurry along," the magician urged to the horse.

Their path was crooked and doubled back upon itself several times, enough that in the thick rain-washed night, Gareth, who knew the forest as well as the back of his hand, was completely turned around. Finally the old man guided the beast through a glen and around a small lake. On the far side, in a copse of dense bracken and fir trees, he dismounted and showed Gareth the thin slit of an entrance to a cave.

"This is the safe place?" Gareth whispered. He could have done better by himself.

"Trust me."

"I know you not, old man." He was suspicious. Why should he trust this old coot? Was there anyone he could believe in?

He watched the would-be magician pat the horse and tie him to a scrawny tree. "Come you, boy. 'Tis time to eat."

Gareth's stomach grumbled as the ancient man paused to light a single torch from a stash near an outcropping of rock. The ancient one's back was to the boy and Gareth saw nothing but a ragged black cape with a dusty hood and boots that were in sorry need of new heels and soles. Holding the torch aloft, he led Gareth down a dusty trail inside the cavern.

"Be there bears in here, or badgers?" Gareth asked, wishing he'd been clever enough to pack his quiver and bow with him as he strained to see into every nook and cranny of the cavern. His only weapon was a dagger and it seemed small at the thought of snarling wild creatures with sharp fangs.

Boon wasn't much help. The pup whimpered and followed close on Gareth's heels.

"Nay. Naught but a few bats."

"But—" He swallowed back his fear. Droppings and bleached dry bones from several beasts littered the floor. Overhead the rustle of wings was ever-present. Gareth had to remind himself that being here with the old man was surely better than being alone in the forest certain that at any second Sir Webb would leap from the darkness to slit his throat.

" 'Tis empty, I say. Would I bring ye to face some hideous, fanged beast if 'twas my bidding to keep ye safe?"

"Nay, but—"

"Hush. All yer questions rattle around in my brain and cause my head to ache. Here we go now—" He placed his torch to a pile of dry sticks already laid in a circle of well-worn stones. With a crackle and spark the fire caught, flames and smoke rising over upward. Gold shadows played upon the uneven rock walls and the ceiling where roots tangled and weaved.

In one corner were two pallets and upon them furs that were old and dusty. The dog sniffed around the darkened corners, his breath moving the dust and dirt of the cavern's floor.

"Here we be, home sweet home," the cripple muttered and turned to face his young charge.

A scream died in Gareth's throat.

The old man was hideous. He had but one eye and his face was disfigured.

The magician smiled and showed off a few remaining teeth. "This," he said, motioning to his face, "is what happens when a lad gets too cocky and thinks he can best a stronger foe."

"But—but you have only one eye."

"Nay, son, I have two. One that sees as the rest of the world does and one that has visions that no one else views." He settled onto a large rock and placed both gnarly hands around his cane. " 'Tis a curse. Until I was blinded and bleeding, I was no different from the other men in the town. But I was caught robbing a rich man . . . well, there is more to the story but 'tis best if ye hear it later, if at all. The long and short of it is that I was nursed back to health by an old woman who taught me of my magic."

He frowned at the memory. " 'Twas then I learned to use my other faculties. My ears and nose became my eyes. My fingers gave me sight as my vision failed me and when at last the bandages were removed, only one eye saw the light of day. The other, though, came to behold that which others could not see—the dark of the night."

Gareth's skin crawled. "Who are you?"

"I be called Muir."

"Of Black Oak?"

The old man smiled that crooked grin. "For now I belong here, in this cave. Take off your wet clothes, place them near the fire here, and warm yourself in the bed. 'Twould be my hide if I were to deliver ye to Trevin and ye be ill. Go on now—" He waved Gareth toward the pallets, but the boy didn't move.

"What does this Trevin want of me?"

Muir hesitated. "He'll have to tell ye himself, boy, but trust me that he is no friend of Ian of Rhydd's."

"Where is he now?"

"That, I'm afraid, I know not." The old man scowled, then eyed Gareth's pack as the pup turned several circles before settling his head on his paws and watching the boy. "Did ye think to bring anything to drink with ye?"

"Nay."

Muir sighed and rolled his good eye toward the ceiling. "I thought not. 'Tis my lot in life to forever have a dry throat and parched tongue."

Gareth, taking off his shirt, didn't believe the old goat for a minute. However, for now, he had no choice but to trust him and hope beyond hope that Webb or any other of Ian's soldiers didn't find the cave. For as safe as the old man thought it was, the cavern was a trap as it had only one entrance.

If they were discovered, they were doomed.

She had betrayed him. As surely as the moon was hiding behind the clouds, Gwynn had double-crossed him. Silently cursing himself for being a fool, Trevin slunk through the shadows and made his way to the keep. He heard the sounds of the night, the river flowing wildly on the other side of the castle walls, an owl hooting in the forest, and pigs grunting and rooting in their sties.

Why had he trusted her? Had she not used him before? Seduced and bartered with him? Traded him his freedom for a few nights in her bed? The wench had no heart, no morals and certainly no loyalty.

Except to the boy. She seemed genuinely concerned about her son and his safety. *His* son, he reminded himself as he skirted the fish pond and slid noiselessly into the keep. Something was amiss, he was certain of it. The dogs in the kennels were restless, the doves in the dovecote disturbed, and Gwynn had been gone far too long.

He'd seen her enter the great hall and followed her path, his boots muted on the rushes. Several knights dozed at their posts; another two were engrossed in a game of chess, still one more was lifting the skirts of a maid near the doorway to the chapel. The image of the woman's legs wrapped so eagerly around the knight's torso burned deep into Trevin's brain. It had been long since he'd been with a woman and holding Gwynn so tightly a short while earlier had brought his cock to attention.

Not since his wife had died had he bedded a woman, nor had he wanted one.

Until tonight. The smell of Gwynn's hair, the feel of her ribs rising and falling beneath firm breasts, the nip of her waist in his palm and her rump, round and yielding against his legs had been too much too bear. He had not time for the distraction of a woman, any woman, least of all Gwynn and yet here he was, climbing the stairs to her chamber, hiding in the shadows, his heart thudding expectantly.

There had been many women since he'd first made love to Gwynn all those years ago, but never had any touched him with the same primal, aching passion. He'd told himself it was because she'd been his first lover, a forbidden fruit, but now, as he made his way to her room, he felt the same breathless pang of desire squeezing his innards as he had so long ago.

He crouched near her door and heard her voice through the oaken panels.

"I swear to you, Lord Ian, I know not where Gareth is."

"Liar!"

"Nay, do not—"

Slap!

Trevin sprang to his feet. He kicked hard. The door gave way.

Sword drawn, he leapt into the chamber.

"What the devil?" Ian demanded, his gaze moving from his beautiful wife, standing proudly before him with her fists clenched, to the doorway. "If it isn't the thief." He held his belt securely in one hand while the other was raised as if to strike again.

"Leave her be," Trevin ordered and noticed a dark knight in the corner.

"She is my wife."

"And you, Lord, are destined for hell if you do not lower your hand."

Trevin's voice was deadly and he glared at the new baron of Rhydd in seething, barely leashed fury. "Gwynn, leave."

"Nay, Trevin, this is not your battle." Gwynn tossed him an anxious glance, silently begging him to hold his tongue.

"Isn't it?" He sheathed his sword but kept his gaze fixed on the two other men in the room—both now his sworn enemies. "I know you." Ian's lips curled. "You're the pathetic little cur who stole my dagger."

"Aye, and sliced your face."

Ian's right hand flew to his cheek and he touched a scar that ran near his hairline.

"Get out of here now, Gwynn," Trevin ordered, smelling a fight that was soon to erupt. From the sheath strapped to his belt he grabbed the dagger.

"I see you have it still."

Trevin grinned wickedly. "Here." He tossed the bejeweled knife at Ian. Rubies, emeralds, and sapphires glimmered in the firelight as the little knife sailed across the chamber to land in the lord's outstretched palm. "I was but borrowing your weapon."

"Ye be Trevin of Black Oak." Webb's eyes were mere slits, visible only as they reflected the light of the fire. "Ye killed Baron Dryw."

"What business do you have here?" Ian asked, slowly circling Gwynn, his eyes never leaving Trevin. His fingers tightened around the knife's hilt.

"I come for my son."

Gwynn sucked in her breath and shook her head. "He knows not what he says."

"Your son?" Ian asked. "Your son?"

Trevin nodded.

Gwynn was frantic. "He knows not—"

"The boy, Gareth?" Dark eyebrows raised in surprise and he barked out a jaded laugh. "*Your* son? You, a lowly thief, a mere boy yourself at the time, you fathered the lad?" Disbelieving, Ian looked at Gwynn, saw the stain on her cheeks, her eyes snapping fire. "For the love of God!"

"Where is he?" Trevin demanded.

Ian fingered the dagger. "You slept with Roderick's wife while he was away at battle?"

"You suspected Gareth was not my husband's issue," Gwynn interjected, her voice trembling slightly.

"But I knew not that you were whore enough to sleep with a common thief, a man not worthy of polishing Roderick's shoes."

"What does it matter who is Gareth's father?" she said while Webb rubbed his leg and slid his sword from its sheath.

Ian's lips curled into a snarl. "I hoped that you had better taste, Wife. That at the very least you could have done your whoring with a nobleman."

"Where is the boy?" Trevin asked as Webb, sensing Ian's intent, began circling the other side of Gwynn.

"A good question." Ian rubbed the whiskers upon his chin and the scar running along his hairline seemed suddenly more distinct. "I was just asking the same of my wife."

"By beating his whereabouts from her?" Trevin's fingers tightened over the hilt of his weapon. Sweat collected at the roots of his hair.

"The boy killed my brother, the baron. His punishment is to be forever banished from Rhydd."

Trevin lifted a shoulder. "Then, mayhap, he has saved you the trouble by leaving himself."

"Nay! He would not have left without talking first to me," Gwynn insisted, desperation echoing in her voice.

"Make your leave, lady," Trevin warned.

"Stay!" Ian ordered.

"Now!" Trevin yelled and Gwynn fled to the door. Ian hurled his dagger at Trevin, but the younger man ducked and spun. Thunk! The knife buried itself in the oaken planks of the door.

Webb rounded on the interloper. His sword sliced the air. Trevin drew in his stomach but the tip of Webb's weapon slit his cloak and cut his flesh. Gwynn wrenched the dagger free and flung it at Webb. The blade lodged in his shoulder and he shrieked like a gutted pig. Blood oozed down his arm as he yanked the hated dagger from his flesh.

"Run!" Trevin yelled and this time she flew through the door. Trevin, backing up, carving the air with his sword, followed, only to hide in a corner as Gwynn fled down the stairs. Crouching, he waited and as Ian dashed down the stone steps, he readied his sword.

"Guards! There is a traitor. A criminal! Catch him!" Ian rounded the corner. Trevin swung. His sword sliced and held in shinbone. Shrieking in agony, Ian rolled down the stairs.

Trevin raced upward, through the solar and onto the ledge of the window. With a leap, he flung himself through the air, caught hold of another window ledge, then slid down the stone walls, scraping his fingers and body until his feet hit the thatched roof of the carpenter's shop. His bones jarred. He bit his tongue. Pain screamed through his body.

"For the love of God, man," Richard cried as Trevin rolled down the thatches to the ground, "are ye truly daft?"

Trevin's body ached and blood seeped through his tunic and cloak, but, as arranged, Richard handed him the stolen guise of a soldier of Rhydd. "Where's the boy?"

"Already gone, it seems." Trevin stripped and with Richard's help, donned the armor. The smells of sawdust and wood were cut off as the helmet was forced upon his head. Dogs barked, soldiers yelled, horses neighed nervously, and the ring of boots upon stone thundered.

"And the lady?"

"Did she not come here?"

"Nay. I've seen her not."

"Then I must stay."

"You cannot."

Could he leave Gwynn? Trevin remembered her cheek, bright with the pain of Ian's hand, and for what? Not telling him where her son was? Now she had betrayed him, gone against his word. The torture Ian would inflict upon her would be merciless. Damn that woman.

"I cannot leave."

"You will be killed, and I as well. In our effort I have detained one of Ian's soldiers, mayhap have killed him." Richard's voice was harsh. "My family will suffer and my wife is with child again."

"I will not leave her."

"You must, Trevin, or I will turn you in myself." Richard's face, skeletal in the dark, was set with a fierce determination Trevin recognized. "I will see to the lady."

"There is no need," a hushed voice said as Idelle slipped through the doorway. "She is safe."

"Here at Rhydd?"

"Nay."

"She's left the castle?"

The old midwife ducked into a corner, behind a stack of posts. "Do not worry over her, Trevin of Black Oak. You have your own dark heart to mend."

"How am I to know that she is safe?" he asked.

"Trust in the Lord."

"This from you—the woman who is known to cast spells and conjure demons?"

"The lady is well. She bid me tell you. Now, go, or Ian will have your hide and ours as well."

Trevin felt a lie brewing in the air. "You be certain?"

"On the lives of the lady and her son, I swear to you Lady Gwynn is safely away. Now, you, too, must leave."

Trevin didn't bother to argue. He had to trust the old woman. But, he swore under his breath as he joined the other soldiers grabbing their mounts from the stable master, if he ever saw Gwynn of Rhydd alive again, he'd personally shake the living devil from her.

Or, he thought angrily, make love to her until neither of them had an ounce of strength left in their bodies.

"Let us pass, 'tis the lord's bidding," Father Anthony ordered as he led the ass and a cart laden with caskets. Wheels protested under the dead weight of the load and the donkey brayed loudly, protesting his dark task.

Deep within one coffin, Gwynn squeezed her eyes shut and silently cursed Idelle's morbid scheme for her escape.

"Now?" the guard asked. "But there be—"

" 'Tis Lord Ian's request," Anthony insisted as Gwynn, hearing the argument, dared not move. She was pinned beneath the cover of a dead corpse, a thin peasant woman who had worked spinning and dying wool until the cough that had rattled deep in her lungs and become so persistent and painful, it had finally taken her from this world.

"I heard not of this."

"You hear of it now," the priest insisted.

'Twas all Gwynn could do not to scream or retch, but she closed her mind to the brittle woman lying atop her and remembered that she would soon see her son again. She had no more life at Rhydd and, if only she could escape, she would be able to find a way to Heath Castle, which was only a fortnight's journey to the south on foot. 'Twould be treacherous, but she had enough jewels and coin with her to hire a horse and guard, if only she survived this horrid part of her journey. Why must the sentry be so stubborn? Though the night was as cold as death, she began to sweat.

"I was told not to let anyone pass." The guard sounded certain and Gwynn's heart sank.

"Even against the Lord's bidding?"

"Who've ye got?"

"Bartholomew, the miller."

"Aye. He keeled over this morn."

"Then the girl, Kate, who drowned in the mill pond, and Brenna, one of the women who worked with the fleece."

"Well, ye won't mind if I have a look, now, will ye?"

"You t-t-trust me not."

" 'Tis my job, Father." There was the stomp of feet and the cart jostled with the guard's weight. *Dear God in heaven, please save me.* With a wrenching squeak one of the coffin lids was raised. Golden light shined through the knotholes of Gwynn's box.

Sweat soaked Gwynn's skin. Breathing was nearly impossible.

"Yea. 'Tis Bartholomew, poor old sod. A better miller we'll never have."

"Aye, 'tis true," Anthony replied, his voice nervous as the sound of horses and soldiers reached her ears. Shouts, jangles of harnesses and armor, the anxious whinnies of steeds being mounted.

The second coffin was pried open and the guard sighed. " 'Tis hard to see a child so. I saw her just yesterday chasing the piggies."

"Listen, man," the priest said solemnly. "Th-thi-this is enough desecration of the d-dead!"

"As I said, 'tis my job. 'Tis not that I want to look upon the dead, believe you me." The guard's bar squeezed through the lid and box of the coffin and creaking, the top popped open. Gwynn felt a rush of cool, welcome air. She closed her eyes but could see through her lids some flickering orange light as the sentry held his torch aloft.

"Ahh, Brenna. We'll miss ya, lass."

Do not let him see me, please God. Gwynn held her breath and the seconds stretched endlessly.

"Hurry, man."

With a thud the lid was in place again. "Ye may pass."

Thank you, Gwynn said silently. The cart started rolling forward again and Gwynn suffered the stale air and close quarters gratefully as the scrawny woman's cold hand brushed against hers. In the dark, she heard the portcullis clanking open and the echo of the ass's hooves as it pulled the heavy load over the bridge crossing the moat.

Only a little while longer would she have to endure this misery. However it seemed forever until the priest ordered "Whoa," and the wagon stopped its uneven movement.

"God forgive me," he muttered as he pried the lid open and yanked Brenna's breathless body off Gwynn. Without wasting a second, Gwynn scrambled free and bit her lip to keep from retching as she climbed out of the coffin and down the side of the cart.

"Thank you, Father," she said, shuddering as he gently replaced Brenna's body into the casket. "And, Idelle, thank her for me as well."

He frowned. "Idelle. 'Twas her idea."

"But it would not have worked had you not helped."

He sighed and glanced at the castle walls. "Be well, m'lady. And, p-p-please, think fondly of R-Roderick."

"And you, Father Anthony."

"Aye, now be off before we both be caught and end up praying for our souls at the gallows."

"Bless you." Lifting her skirts, she hurried through the cemetery, dodging graves and their tombstones as she made her way through wet grass and weeds to the forest.

No matter what else she encountered, she would find her son.

And what of his father?

She felt a little guilty about leaving Trevin in Rhydd but knew deep in her heart that he would find his way safely free. She fingered the pouch of jewels she'd put in the pocket of her cloak. She couldn't think too much of Trevin. 'Twas dangerous.

After thirteen years she'd thought any emotion she may have felt for him would be long dead. Oh, how very wrong she'd been. As she thought of his body pressed so closely to hers in the stables, her thoughts spun out of control. Her heart began to beat wildly, as if in anticipation of his kiss.

Foolish, foolish woman! What think you? You know better than to give your heart to a thief, for if you do, you can be certain he will surely steal it.

Chapter Five

Curse and rot his foolish hide, where the devil was Trevin? Muir paced through the mist, his good eye trained to the east, his patience wearing as thin as the dew-soaked spiderwebs glistening with the coming of the dawn. Three nights he'd waited, two long days, expecting Trevin to appear, only to be disappointed and stuck with the lad and his incessant questions.

"Why must we wait for him?"

"Is he naught but a murdering thief?"

"What does he want with me?"

"Come, old man, let us be off."

Chatter, chatter, chatter coupled with the half-grown hound's yipping caused Muir's head to pound. The dog was always running off chasing birds and rodents and anything that dared move within his earshot. Oh, 'twas a pitiful lot old Muir had been handed and not a drop of ale or wine to help ease his burden.

"So where is this thief-baron?" Gareth asked, stretching his gangly arms over his head and blinking from recent sleep. The damned cur was beside him, yawning and showing off clean white fangs.

"He'll be here." Or would he? Had he not said wait but two days?

Gareth scowled. "How do you know?"

"Because he keeps his word."

"Oh, I'll just wager he does. The murdering, thieving, cheater who stole his castle from a half-daft old man? *He* keeps his word?" Gareth shook the dust from his hair. "Bah!"

"Ye must have faith, boy."

"Why? I needs be off."

"Do ye now? And what will keep ye from fallin' arse over crown into the hands of Baron Ian's soldiers?"

"I fear them not," Gareth said boldly.

"Then a fool ye be, for they'd just as soon slit your throat as speak with ye."

The boy had the brains to shudder and look over his shoulder as if he expected the soldiers of Rhydd to be hiding in the thicket of oak trees guarding a small pond. Oh, he was like his father, he was, and, a bit like his grandfather though that thought rankled Muir and, as always, he held his tongue. Trevin's ancestry was a secret he would keep with him to the grave.

Muir had raised Trevin from a babe, taught him the ways of the streets, turned his blind eye as all too easily Trevin had learned how to slide a penny out of a rich man's purse. As a lad, he'd asked often enough about his mother, but Muir had kept his promise and had lied to the boy, telling him he knew not who had borne or spawned him, that Trevin, as a swaddled babe, had been left on the doorstep of his hut. Over the years, as Trevin had grown working as a stable boy before he'd decided thievery was an easier lot, he'd quit questioning his birth.

So now, what to do? Muir and the boy could not stay here much longer. The lad and pup were growing restless, the horse needed more feed than the forest offered and the few stores he had with him—smoked meat and bread—were about gone. Eventually, should they stay, they would be discovered. However, they could not return to Black Oak for a while for fear they might encounter Ian of Rhydd's soldiers along the road.

He considered using a spell or two, then discarded the idea. What he really needed was a cup of ale. Mayhap more than one.

The sun peeked over the eastern hills, sending forth a blaze of light that burned through the mist and caused long shadows to fall over the damp ground. Muir took the sunlight as a good omen. They would wait one more day and then, by the gods, they would break camp.

And go where?

For the love of Myrddin, 'twas a vexation.

In the middle of the first night, wearing the colors of Rhydd, Trevin had let his horse lag behind the rest of the mounted soldiers, then turned his steed into the forest. He'd ridden far to the east following the course of the river, crossing the swift-moving current where the waters were shallow. Once on the far bank, he'd avoided the main roads, traveling on deer trails and shepherd's paths that slashed through the hills and cut into the dense forests.

He'd urged his horse onward mostly at night, hidden and rested his steed during the middle of the day and used his own sense of direction as well as the pale light of the moon and stars whenever the heavens were clear.

Finally, convinced that he'd created a cold, endless trail for his enemies, he'd forced his horse to swim across the river again a few miles downstream from the cave.

He'd hoped to miss the search party. However, the new Baron of Rhydd's soldiers were nothing if not dogged. They had not given up their search. Twice Trevin had spied groups of warriors, search parties of trained huntsmen and hounds who had fanned through the forest. The dogs had galloped wildly, sniffed, bayed, and turned in circles of confusion, causing their keepers to order them onward and snap whips at their backsides. Each time Trevin had eluded his pursuers, but his luck would not hold forever and, he feared, Ian of Rhydd would never give up.

Now, 'twas dusk again and, with his stomach growling from lack of food, he'd renewed his journey. He had to make his way to the cave and find his boy. Ian had not had enough time to mount a siege of Black Oak Castle, but 'twas only a matter of days.

What if Muir had not found Gareth? What if the boy was again in Ian's cruel hands? What of Gwynn? Had she escaped the walls of Rhydd or was she again facing the brute who was her husband? Trevin's back teeth ground together at the thought of Ian's hand slapping her, his foul mouth kissing her. Though Gwynn was legally Ian's wife, Trevin couldn't accept the thought of the older man bedding her.

'Twas he who should make love to her as he had in the past. 'Twas he who should feel her lips move sensually upon his skin, he who should taste the sweetness of her and watch her silver-green eyes widen as he entered her. Ah, sweet Christ, how he would love to entwine his body with hers.

Bitterly he thought that lying with her might be a way of savoring a dark revenge against Ian, but he discarded the idea quickly. Though Gwynn was no saint, he would not use her so cruelly. Nor did he dare care for her. He'd made a vow . . .

Did Gwynn not lie with him for her own purposes?

He swore under his breath. Gwynn, damn her, was sinful vexation! Where was she and how had she, in so few hours, become his concern? 'Twas his boy he was after, not the woman who bore him. Yet she filled his thoughts, day and night. Be careful.

For years he'd considered her spoiled and vain. Hadn't she bargained and lain with him to bear a child and pass the boy off as Roderick's to save her own pretty neck? Beautiful, she'd been, and passionate. The days and nights lying with her had been pure heaven though she'd been coldly plotting to achieve that which suited her.

The years, rather than ravage her beauty, had been kind and bestowed upon her a depth, a nobility, that he hadn't expected to find. No longer was she a scheming vixen. She appeared to be willing to do anything, even marry Ian of Rhydd, to save her son—*his son*—from the hangman's noose. As beautiful as ever, she now possessed a spark of pride that he couldn't trust. Nor did he want to.

His dark thoughts chased through his head as he turned onto a little-used road leading through thickets of bare-branched trees to an old, abandoned mill he'd used as a lair when once, long ago, he'd been an outlaw. A smile toyed upon the corners of his lips for he missed those bawdy irreverent days when he along with others much like him had banded together. He was much better suited as a criminal than a nobleman, he thought and wondered at the turn of events that had led him to rule Black Oak Hall. 'Twas a joke.

He drew up the reins and his horse slowed near a stream that splashed over rocks and pooled near the ruins of a toppled stone tower. A rotted water wheel moved listlessly, broken paddles causing the axle to creak and lurch as it turned slowly with the current.

". . . and keep him safe."

Gwynn's voice floated on the breeze as if from a dream.

Trevin slid out of his saddle quietly and, leading his horse, made his way through a patch of undergrowth to a shady glen where Gwynn, her back to him, drew the three-clawed rune that looked like a rooster's foot, then tossed dust into the gathering darkness. A small twig of mistletoe—a herb for protection—was laid at the base of an ash tree.

Christ Jesus, she was beautiful.

In the coming night, the wind caught in her skirts and played with the long, fiery strands of hair that had escaped her hood. She turned her face to the sky and murmured words he didn't understand from lips he'd kissed so long ago, lips he'd never forgotten. He'd heard from his spies at Rhydd that she'd practiced the dark arts she'd learned from old Idelle, but until this moment, he hadn't believed the rumors.

She fell to her knees and bent her head, whispering a prayer to the Christian God over her pagan scratchings in the dirt.

His lungs constricted, as they seemed to each time he looked upon her. As he watched, her lips moved soundlessly yet he knew she was praying for the safety of their child. A boy who was not with her. Pagan rites and Christian prayers, whatever was necessary to keep Gareth safe.

Her mount, a sorry-looking beast favoring his right foreleg, flicked his dark ears then let out a whinny. Gwynn turned quickly, her face set as she reached to her belt where a small dagger was sheathed. "Who goes there?"

"Shh."

Her eyes widened in fear for a second before they found his. "For the love of God, Trevin, you nearly scared the life out of me! You wear the colors of Rhydd." Relief stole over her features. "I thought you were one of Ian's men."

" 'Tis but my disguise for my escape."

"So you are alone?"

"Aye."

"Where's Gareth?" she asked hopefully.

Trevin's stomach tightened into knots. "I had hoped he be with you."

"Nay," she said and again worry caused lines to purse her lips and etch her forehead.

"Have you not seen an old magician in the forest?"

"Magician?"

"Yea, a sorcerer who has little hair, a thick white beard, one good eye, and a lust for wine."

Slowly she shook her head and her eyes narrowed in suspicion. "Tell me not that you are trusting this . . . this drunk of a wizard with my son's life."

"Gareth will be safe with Muir."

"Oh, for the love of all that is holy!" She threw up her hands and stared at the dark heavens as if hoping for divine intervention. Her cheeks were a sweet pink hue, her lips darker still. He felt an unwanted tightening in his groin and silently called himself every kind of fool. " 'Tis a madman you are, Trevin of Black Oak," she chastised with a tired sigh. "An old man with one eye and a need for drink?"

"A good man he is."

"Aye, and probably spends his days trying to turn water into wine."

"I think he leaves that for the Son of God," Trevin replied without hiding any of his sarcasm. "And who be you to judge, lady. Did I not catch you chanting a spell?"

"For Gareth's safety."

"Aye."

"And for my horse who is lame," she said with a scowl. "I bought him from a farmer who assured me he was sound, but—"

"Let me look." Trevin approached the animal and watched the gelding's muscles quiver and ears flatten in distrust. " 'Tis all right," he said softly and ran practiced hands over the beast's muscles, encouraging the bay to lift his leg. The horse snorted, but complied.

In the darkness, Trevin bent the animal's leg and caught it between his thighs. Gently prodding, he found a stone, lodged deep in the center of the gelding's hoof and as he touched the embedded pebble, the horse let out a whinny of pain and tried to pull away. "Don't move, you devil," Trevin commanded, but could not dislodge the sharp little rock.

" 'Twill have to wait till morn," he said as he allowed the palfrey to stand on its own again.

"We cannot. We must find Gareth."

"With a lame horse?"

"If we must walk—"

Voices, muted and distant, reached him. As quickly as lightning striking, he grabbed Gwynn and clamped a hand over her mouth.

"Wha—" She struggled against him until she, too, heard the thud of hooves and jangling bridles that rippled through the forest. Gwynn froze. All protests died on her lips. Through her small body, he felt her heart pounding in fear.

Torches winked with an eerie golden light from the main road, two single rows of eight flames blinking behind the trees, but moving ever steadily toward the old mill.

"Come," he whispered into her ear.

In silent agreement, they took up the reins of both their mounts and dashed swiftly through the creek. The horses splashed but didn't give out a betraying neigh. Water, cold as a January snow seeped through his boots and worry gnawed deep at his soul. He would not let them find her, would die rather than let her be taken by Ian of Rhydd's men.

That thought jolted him. Why did he care? Aye, she was Gareth's mother, but nothing more. Comely, yes. Smart, aye, but worth giving up his life?

Gwynn slipped but didn't cry out.

Trevin caught her arm before she fell and was completely immersed. He didn't let go, but pulled her through the water and helped her up the slick mud of the far bank.

Noiselessly they ducked into a dense copse of pine trees just as the small company of soldiers reached the clearing surrounding the mill.

"We'll camp here," a strong male voice that caused Trevin's innards to congeal ordered. Webb, huge and imposing, swung off the back of a sturdy black destrier with a crooked blaze. Landing with a curse, Webb limped to the gaping door of the mill and rubbed his arm. "Bastard of a boy. I can't wait to get me hands on that one."

Beside Trevin, Gwynn tensed, her face as pale as death.

"He'll learn who to slice with a sword or the devil will take my soul," Webb vowed.

Gwynn gasped and would have jumped forward to defend her son, but once again Trevin held her fast. One hand clamped over her lips, his other arm banded her body as she strained against him. "Later," he mouthed against her ear, for he understood her need to do bodily damage to the man who threatened their child. 'Twas all Trevin could do to restrain himself and the furious woman in his arms. "Leave him to me." His lips curled, his eyes slitted, and every muscle in his body coiled as if for a fight. He would have liked nothing better than to slam his fist into Webb's ugly jaw, but now was not the time.

Patience, as ever, was a virtue.

Carrying a torch aloft, Webb hitched himself into the mill. Trevin tracked his enemy's movements within the building by the shafts of light that spilled through the cracks in the mortar and the few windows.

The small army was going to settle for the night. Soon all but a sentry or two would be asleep. "Come," Trevin whispered into Gwynn's ear and, thank the saints, for once she obeyed.

He led her and the horses along a dark trail away from the clearing and up a steep hill. As night settled around them and the dense forest grew black as pitch, they plodded slowly, inching their way forward through overgrown branches or stumbling over exposed roots and mole holes. Winding ever upward, the path was steep and Gwynn's gelding plodded reluctantly, limping on his foreleg and pulling against the bit.

"We must make our leave," Trevin said as they reached a knoll unfettered by trees. Wind raced across the hill, bending the grass, smelling of rain. "But we go too slowly afoot, your horse is lame and my mount is tired." He rubbed his chin as a plan formed in his mind. 'Twas a risk, but one worth the price. He smiled to himself. "I think it best if we borrow a few horses from Sir Webb."

"What?" Gwynn said and in the moonlight he saw her beautiful eyes round as she understood his meaning. "Nay, Trevin, 'tis too dangerous. Webb would like nothing better than to have the excuse and opportunity to kill you."

"I thought you wanted to slit his throat yourself."

"I would if I could save Gareth, but Ian will only send more men and then, I, too, would be found guilty of murder." She scowled in the darkness, her face puckering in worry. Aye, she was as beautiful as a goddess and just as scheming.

"No harm will come to my son," Trevin pledged. "Trust me." He handed her the reins of his horse and slid the bridle from the lame gelding's head. "Release this one," he ordered, "and ride mine ever south. I will catch up with you."

"No, I don't—"

"Listen, woman, 'tis our only chance."

"And if you do not return?" Her chin jutted proudly forward, her eyes held his. Oh, how he wanted to reach forward and stroke the smooth skin stretched upon her jaw, but he didn't. He had no time to lose himself in her, no time to contemplate his baffling fate of caring for her, no time to think of a promise he'd made long ago, to another woman.

"I will be back."

"Brave words from a foolish man. What happens if you are captured?" Her chin wobbled slightly, as if she were afraid for him, as if she cared a bit. But surely he was imagining things; she thought only of herself and her boy. "How shall I find this Muir and my son?" she asked sharply.

"Muir and Gareth will find you."

"So now I am to trust some half-blind drunken sorcerer and a boy."

"Nay," he said and gave into a foolish impulse. Though he knew it was a mistake, his arms folded around Ian of Rhydd's bride and he lowered his head, his chilled lips claiming hers in a kiss that brought back memories from another time, another place. She jerked back, only to sag against him and sigh, her resistance fleeing upon the wind. A tremor slid through his body and desire, unwanted and wild, stormed through his blood. He pulled her roughly to him and kissed her until his head was spinning. "You are to trust only me, m'lady," he said into her open mouth. "Only me." He released her swiftly and she nearly fell. Dear God, what had he been thinking?

"Trevin—?"

He turned on his heel. "I will find you," he promised and damned himself. Memories crowded into his mind.

Vow to me, Trevin, that you'll never love another woman. Swear it. His dying wife's words haunted him still.

His response rang hollowly through his soul. I swear. On my life, Faith. I will never love another.

By the time Trevin reached the encampment, the torches had burned low. Two soldiers guarded the tethered horses and though he'd hoped to find the sentries asleep, they stood together, talking and joking and seeming as if they would never nod off. One was a burly man whose laughter was but a rasp, the other was gaunt and tall, the kind of man who was little more than a skeleton sprinkled with a few pounds of flesh and skin. He held the other guard's attention, telling bawdy tales that came to Trevin's ears in bits and pieces.

". . . a sweet plump arse she had, that one . . . lifted her skirts for any man who would buy her a pint . . . her friend was a shrew, cackled like a mud hen . . ."

In the shadows of the trees Trevin slid his dagger from its sheath and held it between his teeth as he crept between the horses' legs. His plan was simple: Slide the bridle he'd brought with him over the head of the strongest of the lot, cut the line holding all the animals together, slap as many as possible on their rumps and as the steeds squealed, wheeled, and reared in panic, steal away in the ensuing melee. By the time all the beasts had been rounded up and it was discovered that one was missing, he and the horse would be long gone.

". . . I tell ye, mate, a better little ride ye'd never find this side of . . ."

Smiling grimly to himself, Trevin found the horse he recognized as Webb's charger—a strong black stallion with a crooked white slash running down his nose. Carefully, his gaze fastened on the two guards, Trevin laid a hand upon the destrier's thick neck. Hot flesh quivered beneath a smooth coat. The horse sidestepped and snorted and Trevin ducked as one of the guards' gaze swept toward him.

"Quiet," the big man growled and for a few seconds there was no noise save the breathing and stomping of hooves. The charger shifted and a heavy hoof landed on the toe of Trevin's boot. Pain screamed up his leg and he nearly dropped the knife from between his teeth.

An owl hooted and again the horse shifted. "Oh, bugger," the guard said. " 'Tis only a silly bird. One I'd shoot with me arrow, if 'tweren't so dark." He turned back to the other sentry and slowly Trevin let out his breath. He was sweating, his muscles so tense they ached.

Without so much as the clink of the metal fasteners, he placed his bridle over the black's head. The charger rolled a white-rimmed eye, snorted, and kicked. Another horse shrieked in pain.

"Say, wha—?"

Trevin didn't wait. He grabbed the knife from his mouth. With one swift stroke, he severed the rope binding the herd together.

"Did ye hear somethin'?"

"Oh, Holy Christ!"

Trevin hoisted himself onto the black's back. The horse reared. Other animals screamed, bucking and rearing. Tethers snapped. Leaning low on his mount, his head pounding, Trevin slapped several stallions on their rumps with his reins.

Hooves thundered.

Frightened neighs rang through the woods.

"Halt! Who goes—oh, fer the bloody love of Saint Peter!"

Horses scattered wildly. Hoofbeats rumbled through the forest. Branches snapped. The guards yelled.

Trevin clung to the back of the destrier, ducking low, heading him toward the creek.

"Sir Webb!"

"Wake, ye bloody fools!"

"What in the devil's name?" Webb's voice boomed through the night. "Get them! Damn it all to hell, catch them!"

Trevin spurred his mount toward the creek.

Horses shot through the trees.

Guards chased after them.

"Move, damn you!" Trevin ordered.

The charger took the stream in one leap. With a jarring thud he landed on the other side and tore up the hillside. Branches slapped at Trevin, the horse stumbled several times and shouts and frightened whinnies chased after them. "Come on you miserable scrap of horseflesh," Trevin growled, hugging low, urging the beast forward and smiling to himself. "Run!"

"What the bloody hell happened?" Webb yelled, but his voice was muffled over the sound of the charger's hoofbeats and heavy breathing. Trevin didn't hear the response, but grinned grimly to himself at the thought of besting the man who had sworn to kill his son.

Gwynn glanced over her shoulder. It had been hours since Trevin had left her on his fool's mission and her heart beat with a steady rhythm of doom. His silly plan could have turned against him; mayhap even now he was Webb's prisoner, beaten and bloody, forced to reveal Gareth's whereabouts. At that thought she clucked to the horse, forcing him from a slow walk to a quick trot. The moon was low, the air chilly with a wind that cut through her damp cloak and tunic. She'd met few travelers this night, only a lonely friar upon a donkey and a farmer driving a team of oxen struggling with a heavy wagon. Both meetings had been hours before, when darkness was new.

With icy fingers she touched her lips and remembered Trevin's kiss, so hard and firm and hot. A deep ache settled far below her stomach and she called herself a dozen kinds of a fool for the sinful want only he seemed to be able to inspire within her. Whether she liked it or not, she was a wedded woman once again and though her marriage vows were falsely given in exchange for her son's life, they were nonetheless considered sacred by God and church.

What foul luck she had.

Had she learned nothing in thirteen years? Her traitorous body even now remembered the touch and feel of a young thief's hands. Hands that trembled as he stroked her breast, fingers that were warm and steady and knowing. Now that boy was a full-grown man, mayhap a murderer but surely the father of her only son. He was a man to avoid, an outlaw baron whose castle was stolen in a game of chance. Oh, wayward, wayward heart!

Far in the distance, hoofbeats rang through the night, as if the rider were trying to outrace Satan himself. Trevin. Surely he'd finally caught up with her. Or was it someone else? One of Ian's men? A robber or other criminal escaping justice? Her mount was tired and she couldn't outrun a fresh horse, nor would she want to if the rider proved to be Trevin, yet there was no place to hide, no cover of building, bridge, nor woods in this section of rutted road. Though the moon was but a slit behind thin clouds, the fields on either side stretched into the gloom.

From the sound, only one rider approached, so Gwynn pulled up her hood and slid her dagger from its sheath. Should the lonely horseman be someone other than Trevin, she would be ready.

Glancing over her shoulder she saw a dark form approaching, a rider hunched over the shoulders of a huge destrier. The steed was mud-speckled and lathered and even in the darkness, Gwynn recognized Trevin's tall shape. He rode easily, as if he'd spent his entire life upon such a magnificent animal.

Her stupid heart leapt and Trevin's smile, a slash of white, caused an answering twitch in her own lips. Ah, he was a handsome one, she couldn't deny it. Even in the darkness, his eyes shone bright, his dark jaw was hard and square, and his shoulders wide and muscular. He drew back on the reins and his horse, blowing loudly, fell into step with hers. "Did I not tell you I would return?" he asked.

"Aye."

"You doubted me." His voice held a note of jest, as if he were pleased with himself.

"Always."

" 'Tis a mistake to underestimate me, Gwynn." He let out a laugh that echoed across the barren fields. "Sir Webb discovered that tonight. Now, not only is he half crippled—"

"That be Gareth's doing."

"Was it?" Trevin's laughter again rippled across the night-shrouded countryside. "Good. Now, the dark knight has no horse." Trevin patted his steed on his sweaty neck.

"So Webb will be more determined than ever to find us and Gareth," she said, failing to see any humor in the situation. "I'm afraid all you've done is make him a more treacherous enemy, Trevin. Now, 'tis certain he will not rest until he's captured our son."

"He won't get the chance," Trevin assured her, but the smile fell from his face and his countenance turned fierce as a cornered wolf. Gwynn shivered as a gust of wind swept over the land and chilled her to her very soul.

God help us, she silently prayed, but felt the knell of doom ring deep in her heart.

Chapter Six

"You helped her escape!" Ian pounded a fist upon the table in the great hall while that spineless worm Father Anthony shivered and shook in front of him.

His mazer of wine spilled, red liquid splashing onto the scarred oaken tabletop. The man was a buffoon.

The hounds, miserable animals, had been sleeping near the keep's door. At the outburst they jumped to their feet and began barking wildly.

"Shut up!" Ian ordered and both animals circled and settled back to their positions, letting out disgruntled woofs as the priest, fool that he was, licked his lips anxiously.

Ian turned his attention back to the pathetic excuse of a man before him. Were it not for the fact that Father Anthony was a man of the cloth and respected by everyone in the castle, he would have flogged a confession from his lying tongue.

"I know n-not of wh-wh-what you speak, m'lord," the good priest insisted, sweat sliding down the sides of his face, his Adam's apple bobbing nervously, his beringed fingers playing with a heavy gold cross suspended from a chain upon his neck.

Ian wanted nothing more than to clasp the links of that chain in his fist and choke the fool. Instead he motioned for the page who was quick to wipe up the mess and refill his cup. "Do not lie to me, Anthony. Need I remind you 'tis a sin to lie?" He lifted a skeptical eyebrow and watched the skinny man squirm deep in his vestments. "No one left the castle that night but the soldiers and you. All soldiers except one have been accounted for. Somehow the thief managed to disguise himself as one of my men and soon we will find the missing sentry's body."

That thought rankled as well, for it meant either the men he trusted to guard the castle were bloody fools or there was a traitor in their midst. "As for the lady, she made her escape with you."

"B-but, my lord, the guard, he ch-checked the coffins."

Ian's head throbbed, his legs where Trevin's sword had sliced into his shins ached painfully and the mortification of being played for an idiot by the likes of Trevin McBain confounded him. This stuttering idiot of a liar did nothing to help his disposition. "Now," he said with false patience, "you may tell me the truth in here alone and be saved the public humiliation of a trial." He sipped from his cup. "You will not win."

"But—"

"The sentry who checked the coffins that you carted to the graveyard now says he can't remember if he saw all the bodies."

"But he opened each casket!" Father Anthony argued. "There was the miller, Bartholomew, and Brenna, and the little girl, Kate. You must believe—"

"What I believe is that you were a loyal and trusting servant of my brother, but that your allegiance to me as the new baron lacks sufficient . . ." he looked toward the high ceiling, where years of smoke had darkened the trusses, searching as if he expected to find the correct word in the dusty rafters, ". . . well, let us say portent."

"Please, m'lord, t-t-trust me." Father Anthony knelt on the other side of the table, his Adam's apple bobbing nervously. "I am but your faithful servant."

'Twas sickening, this display of false loyalty. "There are ways to test your devotion, you know."

Anthony gulped.

"Would you drown in the river if held under, or would your faith save you? Could you walk along a bed of coals and your skin not be burned, or, if you were unfaithful, would—"

"Please, you m-m-must believe me, Lord Ian. I am a true servant of Rhydd."

He was near the breaking point and Ian was relieved. He hated to see a man of the cloth grovel.

"We'll see what the guard has to say." Ian snapped his fingers and motioned to a knight standing at attention near the door of the keep. "Call in—"

The door flew open, banging against the wall and sending the dogs into a barking frenzy. Sir Webb, his face flushed, his dark eyes flashing, was fairly shivering with rage.

Now what? Ian wondered, knowing instinctively that Webb was not the bearer of good news.

The dark knight strode into the great hall. "M'lord," he said through clenched teeth, then cast the priest a look that would melt the strongest steel. "I needs to have words with ye."

"And I with you." Ian waved off the priest. "I'll deal with you later."

"Th-th-th-thank you, m'lord." Father Anthony, sweating and scurrying away like an insect, took flight. Muttering to himself, he disappeared up the stairs.

Ian braced himself for what he expected was a round of bad news and a bevy of excuses. "Where is the boy?"

"We found him not."

"I assume you took the trouble to look."

"He's a slippery one, he is."

"Right." His headache pounding, Ian took a swig from his mazer. "What of McBain?"

"Disappeared as well," Webb growled, rubbing the shoulder where he'd been stabbed. "With, I fear, my best horse."

"Wait a minute. Were you not to take a search party out and then, peel off so that you could put an end to the boy's life? I expected you, and your party, to return with a few corpses and another wound for your trouble." Ian struggled to his feet and his legs burned with sudden pain—fresh, hot, and angry— that screamed up his shins and festered in his knees. He sucked in his breath and glowered at the knight in whom his brother had devoted so much trust. "You have failed me."

" 'Tis only a delay."

"You were paid."

"Not yet enough," Webb said, unmoved.

Wincing, Ian fell into his chair and ground his teeth against the pulsating sting that the thief had wrought. "Do not dare to say that you have not at least returned with my wife."

Webb's lips lifted into a sneer. "She, too, has vanished."

Ian's eyes closed for a second. Cretins. He was surrounded by moronic, simpleminded Cretins. He saw a movement in the curtains that separated this room from the hallway and wondered who was listening in the shadows. "Lady Gwynn has not vanished," he said, motioning to the crevice where whoever was hiding lingered. "She is somewhere. Hiding. Searching for her child."

"Mayhap with the thief," Webb admitted. Quietly he walked around the table. "Though they left not together, we found a lame horse near the mill where mine was taken and tracks of two animals as well as boot prints, some belonging to a fair-sized man, the other much smaller, belonging to a woman."

"So you're telling me that my wife is with Trevin of Black Oak." He had expected as much, of course. Gwynn had been aided in her escape by McBain, but he'd been told that they had somehow left the castle by separate means and he'd hoped that they were not together. Jealousy spurted through his blood. For years he'd waited for her—his brother's wife who had so callously slept with another man and borne a child whom she'd portrayed as being

Roderick's spawn. A lying whore, she was, but a beauty he'd wanted for as long as he could remember even when he'd been married to that watery-eyed lass, Margaret. What a cold fish she'd been, lying and not moving as he'd entered her. Her bed had been like a tomb.

But with Gwynn things would be different. She was a fiery one, his brother's wife. Ian's crotch tightened in anticipation. He could not wait to bed her. He would watch her eyes round as he penetrated her fiercely, claiming her as his own, feeling her soft body close around him. He would take her over and over again, in as many ways as he wanted and each time he'd feel a renewed power in her submission.

Mayhap Trevin, the thief, could watch her taming.

Webb opened the curtain and found a woman cowering in the alcove. Frannie the weaver. Brown hair, doe-soft eyes, teeth a little too large, and small lips. "Why are you not at your loom?" he asked.

"Forgive me, Lord Ian, I am but checkin' these curtains. The mistress . . . she, er, she told me we would be needing to clean these or replace them . . and I was wondering how much velvet 'twould take . . ."

Ian didn't believe her for a minute. There were many servants loyal to Gwynn within the castle walls, freemen and peasants who would gladly turn on him if she but gave the word. "You may take the measurements later," he said. "And should you breathe a word of what you overheard here, good woman, your days here would be numbered."

She gulped. "But, m'lord, I—"

"Do not test my patience."

With a quick curtsy, she turned and, heels clicking, scurried away.

"A spy?" Webb asked.

"Mayhap." Ian stroked his beard. He felt the undercurrents of dissatisfaction in the castle, had heard a few servants gossiping that he'd forced Gwynn to marry him, that he'd banished her son. He would have to tread lightly for he didn't relish the thought of an uprising.

"M'lord"—Webb's voice brought him out of his troubled thoughts—" 'tis tricked I was," he admitted. "And it cost me my best charger. But now the outlaw has not only stolen a horse from Rhydd but kidnapped the baron's wife. Surely there should be a price placed upon his head."

Ian glared at his brother's most trusted man. In truth he despised Webb, for the dark knight had ruined his plans in helping Roderick find freedom that Ian had paid for dearly. Keeping Baron Hamilton in gold had been costly, but Ian had been assured that Roderick would never escape. Until Sir Webb had ruined his plans. 'Twas lucky that fate had stepped in and the baron's false son had run him through, killing Roderick and ensuring Ian's rule. "You will be paid well for your trouble, Sir Webb, I've told you as much. But you've failed me. I wish you to kill the boy, capture the thief, and bring my beloved wife back to me." The smile he pasted upon his face was cold as death. "Is that too much to ask?"

"Nay, m'lord," Webb said, but his eyes flashed in anger and Ian realized that the dark knight liked taking orders from no one, including the new master of Rhydd. Webb could, for the right price, turn against Ian.

"Take fresh horses and rested soldiers—ten of each—and find the traitors. Deal with them as we have planned. Leave the rest to me. As soon as I've healed enough to ride, I will lead an army to Black Oak and lay siege upon the keep of the bastard who dared defy me and made my wife a traitor to her own castle." He rubbed the bandages on his legs and winced at the pain.

Trevin of Black Oak had been bold enough to wound him twice. The scar running down the side of his face had never disappeared and now, this new ringing pain in his legs. "Trevin McBain will be captured, tried, and proved to be a murdering kidnapper. The gallows will be too good for him." Ian warmed to his thoughts. "I'll see him drawn and quartered, his entrails spilled and his head cut off to be displayed from the north tower where all in the castle, including my wife, will be reminded of the price of disloyalty."

He motioned to a page with stringy hair and a bad complexion for yet another cup of wine. His legs felt a little better. The pain pounding through his brain had dulled. Time was, as it always had been, on his side. He just had to remember to be patient. 'Twas difficult. Very difficult.

" 'Tis daft you be," Gareth said as he watched the old man draw stick figures in the dry soil near the mouth of the cave. He was strange with his one eye, need for drink, useless cane, and gnarled fingers. He talked of curious images, of bloody links of a chain, of a future of ruin, of visions seen through a sightless eye. Daft. That was what he was. Mindless.

"Nay, child. Hush and keep that infernal dog away from me." The pup was playing, romping through the thickets, startling winter birds and growling at unseen prey scrambling through the underbrush.

"Boon is no trouble," Gareth muttered, his stomach grumbling in protest.

"Hush, child, ye disturb me thoughts."

The pup, ever curious, bounded over to the magician and grabbed at the ragged end of his cloak. Snapping firm jaws around the muddy hem, he pulled backward, nearly toppling Muir in the process. "By Pwyll, ye're a wretched little cur. Get away."

"Pwyll's a demon," Gareth protested.

The pup growled and backed up, shaking his head swiftly from side to side, ripping the old cloth.

"I should turn ye into a toad, or a snake or tortoise, ye dumb mutt." Muir lifted his cane as if to strike the dog or cast a spell.

"Nay!" Gareth leapt forward, but the pup scrambled away, the tired fabric of Muir's cloak tearing. As the cane came down, Boon, tail tucked beneath his legs, dashed into the forest, only to turn and peek backward, his face nearly hidden by the fronds of a fern, the prized piece of cloth dangling from his mouth.

"Ahh, now see what he's done." Muir glanced at the sky and rubbed his forehead as if staving off a great pain. With a quick damning glance at the dog, then a longer look at the cloudy heavens and position of the sun, were it visible, he muttered, " 'Tis time we were off."

"I thought we were supposed to wait for your friend."

"Aye, but we've tarried long enough as it is." Muir's eyebrows collided over his scarred visage. "Unless we want to face Ian of Rhydd's wrath."

Gareth was glad to be away from the cave. Inside, the darkness seemed to close in on him and the dusty air was hard to breathe. Asides, he was tired of sitting and waiting, of trying to trap rabbits and squirrels who seemed far more clever than he suspected. Without his bow and quiver filled with arrows, he was a useless hunter. Even the fish in the stream escaped his hands. He whistled to the pup, who, still keeping a wary eye on Muir, crawled from the bracken, the scrap still hanging from his jaws.

The magician paid no attention to the dog. "Come along, come along," he said, as if, after days of inactivity, he was anxious to be gone. " 'Tis less than two days' ride to Black Oak."

"Why must we go there?"

" 'Tis safe."

"Did you not say there would be a siege on the castle?"

"Aye, but 'tis not yet."

"How do you know?"

"I have seen it."

"Yea, yea, as you have seen so many things that make no sense through that bad eye of yours."

"All will be revealed in time," Muir said pointing toward the cave with his cane. "Now, do not dawdle. We must gather our things and be away. There is fine food and drink at Black Oak."

Gareth's stomach squeezed at the thought of trenchers of gravy, sausages, a joint of venison, and banberry tarts. His mouth watered at the thought of jellied eggs, stuffed eel, and hunks of bread with butter and honey dripping onto his fingers. For a moment his hunger outweighed another more pressing concern, a thought that had nagged at him ever since escaping Rhydd. "What of my mother?" he asked as thoughts of sizzling meat and sweet pies disappeared. "Is she safe?"

"That I cannot say."

"Of course she is not; she married Sir Ian." Gareth frowned at the thought. He'd never trusted his uncle, had always considered him lazy and lustful. All too often Gareth had seen the older man leer at girls decades younger than he and though he'd been married to Margaret, he'd lifted the skirts of many a kitchen maid.

For as long as Gareth could remember he was uncomfortable around Ian and had known that the old knight had lusted after his mother.

"She married Ian so that I would not be killed." The idea galled him and since leaving the castle guilt had been forever his companion. "I needs know she is safe."

"That I have not seen," Muir admitted.

"Some visions you have, old man. Seems they only come when 'tis convenient for you."

"Let us not argue."

"She is married to a pig," Gareth said, wishing he could have the pleasure of running Ian of Rhydd through.

"Boy!" Muir's voice brought him back to the here and now. "Get on with it, would ye?" The old magician had flung a bridle over his horse's head. " 'Tis time."

Gareth helped the old man onto his nag and then with Boon bounding behind them, followed the plodding horse. Deep in his pocket, he rubbed a smooth stone for luck. As much as he wanted a hot meal and a softer bed than the pallet within the cave, he needed to know that his mother was safe.

The cave was empty.

Trevin used still-warm coals to relight the fire. Though there were signs that Muir and his young charge had recently occupied the place, it was now vacant except for a horde of bats that hung upside-down in the cracks and crevices of the roof.

Gwynn sighed in vexation. Her heart had been filled with hope that she would be reunited with her son, that she would see his young face again and know that he was truly safe.

Now, she was certain he'd been here, so at least he was alive. She noticed the pup's paw prints along with two sets of boot prints. They could be from someone else, she supposed, but chose to believe that Gareth had found the magician and they were on their way to safety—wherever that might be. She sent up a prayer of thanks and promised herself to cast another spell for his safety.

Overhead the bats returned, their wings fluttering as they found their roosts and close together, hung upside-down, creating a large undulating mass near the door and moving restlessly as the fire caught and flames crackled.

Gwynn rubbed her arms and told herself not to worry. The bats and insects scurrying into the dark corners were creatures of the earth, nothing to fear. 'Twas men and weapons who were her enemies.

Hanging her cloak on a root that protruded through the ground, she slid a glance in the outlaw-baron's direction. Broad-shouldered, lean-hipped, he was taller than she by a head. His jaw, now dark with stubble, was square, his features harsh, his eyes a bold blue that she'd found intimidating. There was an irreverence to him that beckoned her, a prideful intolerance to pomposity and arrogance.

A quiet man who had kept his dark thoughts to himself during their journey, whose countenance was often grim and brooding, he'd ridden without rest. His eyes had forever scanned the horizon and his mouth had been set in a line so thin and determined he appeared unapproachable, a man who needed no one.

Nonetheless, she had trouble believing him to be a killer. Aye, he had probably slain an enemy or two during battle, but she doubted he had murdered the old baron of Black Oak. Trevin McBain was ambitious, yes, and could have easily duped a drunken old man into losing his castle in a game of dice, but murder? She shivered and refused to consider him capable of tossing an old man off the wall walk to his death.

"Where is Gareth?"

"He and Muir and the dog were here"—he pointed to footprints and paw prints in the dust—"not long ago as the embers still hold some heat. Now, they are on their way to Black Oak."

"Or, after leaving here, they've been captured," Gwynn said, her darkest fears resurfacing.

"Muir would not allow it."

"Oh, and is he magician enough to vanish into a vapor and take Gareth with him?" she asked as dry moss and tinder caught fire, causing flames to crackle noisily and smoke to roll toward the blackened rocks overhead.

"You, too, dabble in magic."

"I claim not to be a sorceress." She watched the shadows play upon his bladed features and felt a restlessness deep within her. "I cast spells, aye, but they are more like prayers for good luck, health, good fortune. I draw runes hoping for blessings, but I cannot cause a person to disappear."

"The boy will be fine."

"How know you this?" she demanded as he settled upon a rock and stirred the coals with a long, charred stick.

"Because Muir raised me." He looked up at her and held her gaze for but an instant. In that heartbeat her mouth turned dry as the dust of the floor. She cleared her throat and shifted her eyes so that he was only in her peripheral vision. "I knew not my mother. My father—" He lifted a disinterested shoulder. "Who knows? 'Twas Muir taught me to slip a coin from a purse and slide a ring from a bony finger. 'Twas he who fed me and gave me a bed on which to rest. He bade me learn of the church as well as the ways of the old ones and never did he place me in danger. With him, I was safe."

" 'Tis different with Gareth," she pointed out as she sat on a flat rock next to the fire and warmed the soles of her boots. "Ian has proclaimed him a traitor and a murderer. Though he promised to only banish the boy if I married him, I have broken my word and, therefore, no matter how much magic your sorcerer may conjure, our son is in danger."

"You broke your word to Ian," Trevin said, his eyes darkening, "because he struck you."

"He is my husband," she said simply, the thought curdling her innards. How could she ever return to him? Allow him to touch her? Lie with him?

"Aye, and he would as soon kill our son as not." Trevin climbed to his feet and dusted his hands. "You are right. Gareth will never be safe until Ian is dead." He stared straight at her. "Nor, m'lady, will you."

That much was true, but she could always throw herself on the new lord's mercy and hope that there was some shred of decency in Ian of Rhydd's vile heart. "I will go back to him, appease him. Mayhap he will leave Gareth be."

"Nay."

"But, if it means my boy's life—"

Trevin crossed the short distance between them and grabbed her by the arm, hauling her to her feet. "Listen, woman," he said through lips that barely moved. "I will not have you place yourself in harm's way."

"I have no choice."

"There are always choices. Only weak minds settle for the first option." His gaze met hers again and she was lost. Her pulse pounded in her ears and she told herself to step away from him, to toss off the hands that clamped over her arms and yet she could do nothing save swallow hard. "You, m'lady," he drawled, "have always done what was necessary to get what you wanted. You slept with me to get you with child, you ruled Tower Rhydd as if you, a woman, were the lord, and when it served your purposes, you married your brother-in-law."

"To—to save my child," she said as he cocked his head and observed her as if seeing her for the first time. He was so close. So near. 'Twas far too dangerous to let him touch her. His scent permeated her nostrils, his fingers were warm through her clothes, and her lungs felt as if they could not draw another breath.

"You, Lady Gwynn," he said in a voice that was barely audible, "are unlike any woman I've met."

She didn't know if he meant his words as a compliment or insult, but didn't care. Her heart was pumping wildly and she couldn't draw her gaze away from the hard set of his mouth. "And . . . and you, thief, you are like no other man."

"Aye." His breath fanned her face and teased her hair, the hands around her arms released only to clasp at her back and drag her even closer to him. "Oh, lady, how you vex me," he whispered, his voice tortured. "Would I had never met you." His head lowered and, for a heartbeat, he hesitated, his mouth hovering a breath above hers.

She licked her lips nervously and he groaned. "Damn you, woman," he ground out just as his mouth claimed hers. She should stop him, push him away, and yet she couldn't. Warm and supple, his lips molded to hers and a tingle whispered over her skin. Her head spun and though she knew she was playing with dangerous fire, that she had to break away from him, pull back from the sweet seduction of his kiss, she couldn't summon up the strength.

Years she'd waited to feel like this, for the magic of this man's touch. How many nights had she envisioned just this embrace? How often had she dreamed of his touch only to awaken alone, yearning and covered in a sweet, dream-induced sweat?

His tongue pressed anxiously against her teeth and willingly she opened to him, her mouth accepting the intimate intrusion as if they had been lovers for years.

Groaning, he dragged her closer still, bowing her back as he kissed her, hands splayed upon her spine, hips thrust forcefully against the juncture of her legs. She felt his heat, the hardness of his member, the pulsating pressure of his body so close to hers.

Let me be strong, she thought, but was ultimately weak. Desire stormed through her blood and deep within that most feminine part of her she began to ache. His tongue stroked hers and she wanted more; to touch him everywhere, to let her mouth and fingers explore his hardened body now that he was a man. Images of lying naked with him glided easily through her wanton mind and she wondered what would it hurt to have him, the only man who had known her, be with her again.

His fingers found the ties of her tunic and as the fabric parted, he kissed her throat with lips that were as gentle as they were firm.

Her breasts ached and her breathing nearly stopped as he kissed the top of one breast, exposed above the neckline of her tunic. Beneath the velvet, her nipple hardened expectantly, as it hadn't in so many years.

"You were wrong," he said, his lips leaving a hot trail against her throat.

"W-wrong?"

"You are a witch."

"Nay." Warmth seeped from her womb to run in a hot current through her blood.

"But you enchant me, little one. Far more than you should." With a sigh he lifted his head and curled his fists in the strings of her tunic. "There is no time for this and . . . and I want it not."

Disappointment welled deep in her heart as sparks drifted toward the ceiling of the cave. She felt the struggle within him, didn't understand why he held her possessively yet tried desperately to push her away. "But—"

"And you are another man's bride. My enemy's wife."

"In body but not in spirit."

One side of his mouth lifted in a cynical smile. "In the eyes of the law and church." His hands dropped and he stepped away from her, as if being so close was perilous.

"It stopped you not before," she reminded him.

"Aye, and since then I've been cursed."

"As have I." Suddenly cold, she reached for her cloak, flung it over her head, and wrapped the voluminous dark blue folds more tightly around her torso. Her lips still tingled from Trevin's kiss, her body was still warmed by his.

Eyeing her, he said, "As long as Lord Ian lives, you will be at his mercy."

Her spine stiffened and fury snapped her head up. "Make no mistake, I will be at no man's mercy, outlaw."

His grin held no mirth and, as if he were making a vow to himself, he proclaimed, "Do not worry. I will see to the new Lord of Rhydd and do what is necessary."

Fear slithered down her spine as she understood. "You mean to slay him?"

Trevin's eyes glittered ominously. "If needs be."

"Nay, outlaw, he is a treacherous man," she said, and grabbed his arm only to release it quickly.

"So am I." He winked at her, but beneath the glimmer in his eye, there was something more, something deeper and darker that he refused to confide. "Stay you here and wait."

"Nay—"

"I'll ride to the next village and listen to the gossip, to discover if Rhydd's soldiers are on their way to Black Oak."

She eyed the interior of the cave with its scattered, bleached bones, bat droppings, and winged inhabitants. She was not one easily frightened, but the thought of staying here by herself was unnerving.

"I will be gone but a few hours and will return before the morning."

"You'll be captured."

"Trust me, Lady Gwynn. I have evaded far more clever enemies than your husband."

"But he has soldiers and—"

"Shh." Again he grabbed her. His lips found hers in a kiss that stole the breath from her lungs and caused her heart to beat in a wild, wanton cadence. Her knees began to crumple. "Wait for me," he commanded, then that same sense that something far deeper was bothering him, that he was holding back, rippled through her.

"What if you don't return?"

"I will."

She raised one eyebrow skeptically and he kissed her lightly on the lips again.

"Have I not gotten you this far?"

"Aye, you've managed to anger my husband, place my son in grave danger, dupe Ian, wound his most trusted knight, steal Webb's horse, and bring me to this . . . this—"

"Hiding place."

"—tomb. We are no closer to finding Gareth than we were on the night we left Rhydd."

"You are impatient, m'lady."

"I worry for our son."

"Fear not."

Oh, if only she could trust him, believe that he would save Gareth. She kicked at a pebble with the toe of her boot. "So be it, outlaw. I will wait one day. But, if you do not return by nightfall tomorrow, I will leave."

"And go where?" he asked, tightening his belt.

"Heath Castle."

" 'Tis a long journey."

She tossed her hair from her face. "At least I'll not be cowering in a cave with only bats as my companions."

"You'll be no closer to finding Gareth."

"Mayhap not. But then again I told him to meet me at my sister's, and he would be there now had he made good his escape and not been captured by your magician friend."

"He is safer with Muir."

She wasn't certain in this gloomy hiding spot. The thought of staying here without Trevin was terrifying, but her pride forbade her from voicing her fears. "As I said, *m'lord,* I will wait until dark on the morrow."

He turned and walked to the entrance of the cave. "Trust me," he called over his shoulder as he disappeared through the boulders that guarded the cave's entrance.

Her heart sank as she heard the sound of hoofbeats fading into the distance.

Trust me.

Oh, sweet Mother Mary, if only she could.

Never had she felt more alone.

Chapter Seven

The old man was an idiot, Gareth thought, standing on his tiptoes on an overturned barrel as he peered through the slats of the tavern's window. Not a magician, not a sorcerer, not a wizard of any kind. Just a plain old fool of a drunk who rambled on and on about "the circle" with its broken links and bloodstains. 'Twas naught but a foolish man's chants and no amount of amulets or eyeing the horizon or pointing his stupid cane toward the heavens would change the fact that Muir was naught but a lowly thief.

As Gareth waited in the shadows, his teeth chattered and goose bumps rose on his flesh. The moon rose ever higher in the sky. The interior of the shabby inn was dark, the only light from a meager grouping of candles and the embers of a dying fire. Men clustered around tables, laughing and joking and Muir, curse his hide, buried his nose in the bottom of a cup.

'Twas certain Muir practiced the dark arts frowned upon by the church, though Gareth had seen no indication that the withered one was truly a magician. The only spirits he seemed to raise were those that passed over his lips from a cup, and the spells he tried to conjure were always a little mixed up and never seemed to work.

As for his prophesies, they were enough to scare Gareth, though he would never admit as such. All that mumbling about a dark circle and links of a chain. Father to son and son to father, or some such blither-blather. The old man was daft, pure and simple, though his mutterings spooked Gareth just the same. All the gibberish of replaying history, of sons killing fathers made his blood run cold.

"Some magician," Gareth mumbled to Boon who paced at his feet, sniffing the ground and whining as if in full agreement. "If he's so clever, why can't he conjure up a cup of ale or wine instead of having to come here?"

Boon sniffed at a stack of crates near the back door. The stench of garbage hung heavy in the air and voices from the inn filtered onto the street where shops and inns lined the heavily traveled road. Horses snorted, cattle lowed, and even an occasional rooster crowed, though 'twas after dusk and the temperature was low enough to cause Gareth's breath to fog. "Come on, come on," he muttered as he witnessed the old man rub his head and hold up his cup for another fill.

" 'Tis doomed we be, dog," Gareth muttered and considered leaving Muir to his own devices. So what if the thief-baron wanted him to stay with the ancient one? With a limp and only one good eye, Muir was more hindrance than help. Asides which, Gareth was worried about his mother. If he had any brains or guts at all, he'd leave the drunk here, ride back to Rhydd on the horse, and run old Ian through. But the thought of actually killing a man—any man— caused ice to settle in his innards. The taking of a life wasn't as courageous and noble as he'd once thought and the memory of shoving his sword into a man's flesh, only to see the lifeblood seep out of him, caused Gareth's stomach to turn sour.

Coward. Would you rather your mother gave her life to old Ian? He shuddered and wished Muir would give up his lust for drink and get on with their journey. "We've cast our lots with a simpleton, I fear, Boon." However, angry as he was with the sorcerer, he felt a bit of fondness for the old man. Hadn't Muir fed him, found him shelter, and although nagging him all the way, assured him that there would be safety soon? Mayhap the old man wasn't so bad after all.

Boon whimpered. The pup was standing on his back two legs, his front paws stretched against the barrel. He yipped for attention, his tail whipping frantically in the air. " 'Tis a good dog you be, Boon." Gareth reached down and patted his dog's head. "But keep quiet. Muir will be along soon." He blew on his thumbs to shake off the chill and hoped he wasn't lying.

The thud of hooves caused him to lift his head and climb off the barrel. He sneaked through the alley to the front of the inn where he saw the band of soldiers approach. Riding double file and wearing the green and gold colors of Rhydd, they entered the town at a fast trot.

Sir Webb, his countenance grim as death, his mouth a seam of undeterred purpose, rode in the lead.

All the spit in Gareth's mouth dried. He hid behind a cistern and prayed that the pup, distracted by a rat scurrying along the fence, wouldn't show himself.

"Here." Sir Webb's voice boomed through the night and ricocheted through Gareth's head. "We'll take sustenance and rest, then make camp on the far end of town."

Christ the Savior! Gareth slunk in the shadows, his feet moving swiftly as he made his way to the back door and slipped into the warm kitchen where a large woman, sweat dripping from her red face, plump fingers curled around the crank of a butter churn, was seated on a stool. The paddles within the churn clicked steadily in time with the movement of her arms. "By the gods, lad, ye scared the devil from me, ye did!" she cried. "Who be ye to be slithering around the shadows like a snake off a cold rock?"

Gareth had no time for pleasantries but he hoped he didn't appear as frightened as he felt. "Please, good woman, would you be so kind as to send the old man with the bad eye back here?" he asked anxiously. Suspended on a hook over the fire, a black kettle of stew was simmering and giving off the heady scent of cooked mutton. Gareth's stomach rumbled.

"What?" She shook her head as she continued to churn. "Go get 'im yerself, boy. Can't ye see, I'm churnin' here? I'll not 'ave me butter go soft or sour."

" 'Twill not. Now, please," Gareth said, then jumped at the sound of snoring. He spun and found a scrawny man sleeping with his head propped against a stack of firewood.

"Ye're not hidin' from someone, are ye?" the woman asked, her bushy eyebrows slamming together as she rubbed the side of her face on her shoulder to wipe away her sweat.

Gareth shook his head. "Nay, but—"

"The sheriff, is he lookin' fer ye?"

There was no arguing with her. "No." Gareth walked to the doorway separating the back room from the rest of the tavern and opened it a crack just as Sir Webb, his mail chinking loudly, entered the room. Conversation stopped as the customers sipping ale looked over their shoulders to view the new patrons.

Gareth's heart dropped to his feet. He couldn't show himself as the dark knight would certainly recognize him. He swallowed hard as Muir lifted his good eye and stared at the soldiers filing into the establishment and calling for ale.

"Oh, wouldn't ye know it?" the fat woman grumbled at the sound of so many new voices. "Nary a soul all night and now an entire army barges in." She turned her head. "Will. Will, wake up, would ye? Get another cask and help Bess out front, we've thirsty men—in armor—from the sounds of it."

With a sharp snort, the snoring stopped for a second before continuing evenly.

"Will!" she said sharply, and with a cough the scrawny man awakened and hopped to his feet.

He took one look at Gareth and ran a hand over his eyes. "Who the devil are ye, lad?" His front teeth were missing and his skin was splotched.

" 'E's not sayin', so don't bother askin', jest git the damned cask and help

Bess out front, would ye? Oh, fer the love of Zeus." She sighed and stopped churning, her paddle slowing. "I'll do it."

Frowning, she mopped her brow with the back of her hand, then wiped the sweat away on her apron.

Gareth's heart was knocking wildly in his chest as she pulled the door open further and stepped into the front of the tavern. "What can I get fer ye, my good men?"

"Ale. Fer all who wear the colors of Rhydd." Webb's voice boomed.

"Good. Good. 'Twill be but a minute while me husband opens another cask."

With shuffling feet and a few words, the soldiers climbed upon the benches near the fire. Elbow to elbow, they sat, leaning on the heavy table and stretching the crooks of their necks or joking among themselves. Gareth watched through the slit in the door and was relieved to see that Muir had the good sense to keep his face averted, as if he'd found the fire suddenly fascinating.

As the fat woman poured ale into cups, Webb rubbed his shoulder and scanned the room. "We be lookin' for Trevin of Black Oak," he said, wincing slightly.

Gareth took little pleasure in the fact that he'd wounded the dark knight. All he'd accomplished was angering Sir Webb and making him determined to hunt him down.

"Ye seek the baron?" She carried a tray of cups to the table and began setting them before the men.

"Aye, he's a murdering thief, that one. Have you not heard that he killed Lord Roderick and stole his wife?"

So, Muir was right. His mother was with the outlaw. Gareth didn't know whether to be pleased or worried.

"What say ye?" The woman slopped ale onto the table and was quick to wipe it up with the discolored hem of her apron.

" 'Tis said he cheated Lord Dryw out of his castle, then killed the old man when he protested. Threw him off the tower."

"That much, I already heard," the woman said as her husband, grumbling under his breath and laboring with the weight of another barrel, brushed past Gareth. For a moment his view was blocked and when Will and the cask moved out of his line of vision, Muir was no longer near the fire, as if he had truly disappeared. Slowly Gareth inched away from the door, ready to sprint into the alley.

A horrifying yowl screamed through the night.

Feet and fur flying, a gray cat dashed into the kitchen and sped through the crack in the door. Boon, yipping wildly, streaked by, fast on the tabby's heels.

"Nay!" Gareth whispered, lunging for the pup, but the dog galloped into the tavern.

"Say, wha—?" Will sputtered as the cat ran between his legs.

Men laughed, a serving girl screamed, and the dog, still barking madly, chased the terrified cat until it climbed up the alewife's voluminous skirts. "Ouch, Sweet Mary! Puss, stop it! Get yer damned claws off me!" Ale sloshed, men laughed, Boon leaped up at the cat, his paws clawing at the ever-moving skirts. "You, mutt! Out with ye," the woman ordered, kicking at the noisy, jumping dog while the cat pounced from the woman's broad hips to a post. Puss scrambled upward to the exposed beams of the ceiling.

Boon, barking his fool head off, circled the post and jumped up and down.

"Cursed mutts. Always comin' in." The woman reached for a broom near the hearth and began swiping at the pup.

"Hey, ain't that the pup—?" Webb asked.

Gareth nearly died.

"Aye, from Rhydd. The lad's—"

Gareth gave out a sharp whistle and the dog stopped, turned, and ears cocked, fixed his puzzled gaze on the back room. "Come!" Gareth ordered from his hiding spot.

"Who goes there?" Webb's voice reverberated through the inn.

He wasn't about to leave his dog. "Boon!" Gareth held the door open but stayed in the shadows.

"It's the lad" another voice said. "He called that mutt of his Boon."

"Fer the bloody love of Christ, get him!" Webb ordered and Gareth scrambled backward, knocking over a sack of flour and spilling white powder on the floor. He nearly fell, stumbled against the hearth where the stew was boiling, and burned the back of his arm against the blackened pot as he unsheathed his dagger. How small the knife seemed when he thought of Webb's men, all of them with swords or maces and armor.

The dog barreled through the door. Gareth wasted no time. He was down the steps and running through the backyard. Behind him, he heard the sound of soldier's boots and rattling swords as Ian's men swarmed through the kitchen.

"Wait!" A voice, soft as the wind and vast as the sea, commanded. " 'Tis not the lad ye want."

No, Muir! No! Don't do this!

Muir! Gareth's footsteps faltered.

"Take me to Ian of Rhydd and we'll barter."

"What? You, old man?" a strong voice hooted.

"I am a magician."

"Bah! And I'm King Edward."

Laughter roared through the inn as the men hesitated.

"Lord Ian will speak with me," Muir insisted. "Or I shall call upon the Morrigu, the Great Mother—"

"Get out of me way, ye one-eyed pagan fool. We'll hear no talk of the warrior goddess 'ere."

Gareth spun and ran through the yard, along a pebbled street to a small opening in a fence. With the dog racing behind him, he slipped through the crack, scraping his leg, sprinting in the darkness, away from the main part of the town. Behind shops, under dark stairways, past closed doors, he ran. Chickens flapped their wings and clucked from their coops, other dogs barked, and Gareth stumbled over stacks of firewood and kettles used for washing.

His lungs burned. His head throbbed. His legs ached.

But he couldn't stop.

He heard the men behind him, boots pounding in the mud, curses ringing out, voices fading as he zigged and zagged through the town and into the surrounding forest. His breath seared his lungs, his legs ached, but still he kept going. He didn't know which direction he ran, but found solace in the woods, for there were trees to climb, bushes for cover, trails that wound in differing directions. He stumbled over roots and low branches, but kept on through the darkness, knowing he was losing his pursuers as their voices and footsteps became more distant.

Cramps tightened the muscles of his calves and he had to stop, his stomach gurgling. Gasping for breath, he suddenly retched and hung his head.

Please God, save me. Save Muir. Save Mother.

His head swam. He couldn't think.

Please, help me. Please.

He fell into a wet pile of leaves and waited. What could he do? Muir was certainly caught, for the old man had no spells to make him vanish, and now Gareth was alone in the gloomy forest with only a hungry dog and a bad sense of direction for companions.

"Great," he muttered, sick at heart. "Just bloody great." He had several choices, none of them worth the time of day. He could try to free Muir by chasing after the soldiers, but then he would put himself at risk, or he could try and find the bastard who, according to the wizard, had kidnapped his mother—the murdering thief.

And where would the man be going? Most likely back to his ill-gotten castle. As would the soldiers. 'Twas a mess to be sure. He closed his eyes and envisioned his mother's face. Never had he thought he would miss her. Never would he admit to caring so deeply for her. He was, after all, nearly a man.

But he had to save her. As she had saved him.

And what about Muir? Do you not owe him your life as well?

He covered his face in his hands and tried to think. He would save the old man, of course he would, but first he would find his mother, and if that meant facing the outlaw, so be it. If, as Muir implied, Trevin was returning to Black Oak, then by a pig and a portal, Gareth would be waiting for him.

" 'Twas like a bad dream, I tell ye," Bess insisted as she spoke to Trevin in the shadows behind the inn. "And the soldiers they be lookin' fer ye and that wife ye stole." Bess, who worked at the inn, was a sweet thing with a small waist, large breasts, and hips soft enough to comfort an ailing and needy man, but Trevin wasn't interested. Nor had he ever been, though he'd known her for years. "I pretended not to recognize yer name," she said, "and most of the louts, when Sir Webb's back was turned, they were only interested in gettin' their 'ands up me skirts."

"Some things never change, Bess," Trevin said.

"Now, fer you, m'lord—" She smiled coyly and Trevin sighed.

"Tell me of the lad."

"I saw no boy—only the one-eyed man who started talking as if 'e was daft, I tell ye. Babbling on and on about the chain, father to son, son to father, blood to blood, or some such nonsense. Now, Lizzie, she's the cook, she seen a youth in the kitchen, but 'e and 'is bloomin' 'ound got away. Tore off down the back alley, like 'e'd seen a ghost, Lizzie says."

"He got away?" Trevin felt a ray of hope.

"As far as I know, but the old man, the magician, he wasn't so lucky. Sir Webb, he 'auled 'im away, tied and bound like a roebuck on a huntsman's staff."

Trevin's back teeth ground together. Muir and his cursed lust for ale. Now he was captured and the boy . . . oh, for the love of St. Peter, the boy was God-only-knew-where and wandering around the forest. At least he was alive. "Thanks, Bessie," he said as the voluptuous miss leaned forward, offering him a moonlit view of plump breasts rising invitingly above a square neckline.

" 'Tis many a favor I'd do fer ye, m'lord," she intoned.

"You've done enough." He handed her a coin and her lower lip stuck out fetchingly.

"I'll 'ave none of yer money, Trevin of Black Oak. I knew ye when ye were a whelp of a lad, a thief and no better than the lot of us."

"Who says I've changed?" He dropped the coin between her breasts and she giggled as he climbed astride Webb's destrier. "This goes no further, Bess."

"Aye, I've never seen ye, ye black-'earted bastard, and 'ere—ye asked fer food, did ya not?" She handed him a cloth sack that smelled of baked bread.

"You're an angel."

"Oh, go on!" She blushed in the moonlight.

With a mirthless laugh Trevin yanked on the reins and his horse wheeled. "Hiya!" The game horse broke into a gallop. Trevin rode east through the town, hoping Bess caught sight of his leaving. Though he trusted her, he wasn't going to let her witness anything that might lead her to guess where he and Gwynn were hiding. Who knew what hidden eyes had observed his tryst with her? Only God could guess how much she'd say if offered the right price or if she were threatened by Ian of Rhydd's blade. No, neither she nor anyone else lurking about this village would guess his destination by his direction.

With the moon as his guide, he rode past several farmers' fields before doubling back and skirting the town.

So Gareth was free, but where? And Muir, curse him, what had he been thinking, pausing for refreshment before making his way to the castle?

Eyes narrowed against the blast of icy wind that tore across the land, he spurred his mount onward. To Gwynn. At the thought of her and their last stolen kiss, his chest tightened. God in heaven, he'd never been able to get that woman out of his blood, not even while he was married to Faith. Guilt pricked deep into his brain like a thorn into flesh. His dead wife deserved a far better husband than he'd ever been. Faith had loved him and he had never returned the fervor of her passion. Because of Gwynn.

A woman who would sell her body to save her son.

God help them all.

The road forked and he headed west toward the cave. The stallion's strides never faltered though lather sprinkled his coat and mixed with the mud splashing onto his chest and legs as he ran.

" 'Tis a fine beast ye be, Dark One," Trevin said, urging the steed ever onward. Harsh thoughts tangled in his mind. He could do nothing for Faith; she was lost to him and to this world, but Muir, the man who had raised him, was another story.

Webb would return Muir to Ian who would probably try to torture the truth from the old man. But Muir was nothing if not clever and when the spirits of the cup did not cloud his mind, he was a match for any man, even the new ruler of Rhydd. The aging sorcerer's magic did exist, but, Trevin had decided, it came with quite a bit of luck and sometimes, in the worst situations, had forsaken him completely.

There was no time to waste. Trevin would have to fetch Gwynn, take her to the safety of Black Oak, then with his company of men, return to Rhydd to free the wizard.

Which was exactly what Ian would be expecting.

Surprise would not be on his side. He would have to be crafty. He smiled as the horse labored on. Somehow he would best his old enemy.

One way or another.

*   *   *

Gwynn stepped into the stream and sucked in her breath. 'Twas near freezing and she felt her skin turn blue, but she only shivered for a second before walking into the deepening pool. She was determined to scrub some of the filth from her body. She'd spent days on the road, time in the cave, and the final hours before nightfall she'd been on her hands and knees, collecting herbs, berries, and roots. Though skilled with dagger, bow, and sword, her true strength came in the casting of spells and healing.

She had once laughed at Idelle and her pagan ways, but over the past thirteen years, she had learned the power of yew, ash, foxglove, thistle, and the like. She was a Christian woman, aye, and prayed to the Holy Father, but she, too, trusted the old ways and believed in Morrigu, the Great Mother and her gifts of the earth. In her struggle to find and save Gareth, Gwynn vowed to use any skill, spell, or weapon that might help.

All that mattered was her son.

Slowly she sank onto her knees. She bit her lower lip and closed her eyes as the icy water splashed the sensitive spot at the juncture of her legs. She sucked in her breath in a hiss and as her body numbed to the cold, she scrubbed, using the brook's current and a handful of moss to wash away the dirt beneath her fingernails, between her toes, and in her hair. The water was fresh, cleansing, and gave her clarity of mind.

What if Trevin didn't return? What if he had no word of Gareth? What, oh dear Lord in heaven, what if her son was already dead! Do not think such, she told herself as she tossed water onto her face and blinked against the drops that lingered on her eyelashes. Surely he was safe and well, ensconced in Black Oak where Trevin's servants would provide for him and his soldiers would protect the boy. Trevin would see that each sword and shield at Black Oak would be raised to safeguard his only son.

Though she did not yet completely trust the thief-turned-baron, she believed that he cared for Gareth. Why else risk Roderick, and now Ian's, wrath? Why ride in the darkness, stealing uniforms and horses and seeming to be concerned for her? She was not foolish enough to think that the thief cared a whit for her, nay, she was Gareth's mother, nothing more. He still considered her the self-centered bride of Roderick who had done anything, even cast aside her virginity, to dupe the old man into thinking he'd spawned a son.

'Twas a long time ago.

Before she'd been a mother.

Before she'd known the fear for a child.

Before she'd fallen in love with a rogue.

Her eyes flew open. Love? In love? Nay, her thinking was addled, her worries over Gareth clouding her mind. She loved Trevin not. He was but a means for her to save her son. Nothing more. She wasn't a silly ninny of a woman who would confuse love with lust.

Still the thought disturbed her.

She lay in the stream and let the water float her body in slow circles where the current played in a lazy whirlpool.

Trevin.

The outlaw.

She'd known him a short time and yet, she feared, she was beginning to trust him. Oh, foolish, foolish heart. He was a thief and mayhap a murderer.

And the father of your son.

Trevin of Black Oak was not a man to whom any sane woman would lose her heart. He was too gruff and grim, too brooding, and too self-important, always giving her orders. But only for a while. As soon as she and Gareth were reunited, they would leave the robber-baron in their dust. His thoughts of her and his son would be but a memory.

There was no other way.

She wasn't in the cave. Trevin held his torch aloft and searched the blackened interior, but aside from coals still glowing in the fire, there was no sign of her. "Damned fool woman," he muttered, disturbing the few bats that still hung from the ceiling and feeling a deepening ache in his heart, an ache he quickly ignored. He had no feelings for the woman. None.

Angry, he walked outside. Why did she leave? Had she not promised to wait? From the corner of his eye, he caught a movement near the trees.

He extinguished his torch in the mud. No reason to have an enemy spy him. Stealthily he unsheathed his dagger and readied himself for a fight. If Webb had found the cave and Gwynn. . . . Rage, as dark and wild as a devil's heart, pounded through his veins. He would kill anyone who—

He came upon her horse still attempting to pluck a few blades of glass that glistened silver in the moonlight.

Could she have been taken? Had Sir Webb and his band of cutthroat soldiers from Rhydd stumbled upon her? The thought hit him hard and for an instant terror seized his heart in an iron-fisted grip. Surely the men wouldn't have stolen her and left her horse.

Silent as death, he stole through the underbrush, searching the area until he heard the splashing of the stream and saw her body, white and pale, as she floated completely nude in the river.

His gut tightened.

A fire started to burn in his loins.

Quietly, he sheathed his knife.

Her white breasts rose above the waterline, their dark nipples pointing toward the starry heavens. Lower, the patch of dark hair was stark against her fair skin and caused a living, breathing lust to flow in his veins.

She was as beautiful as he remembered and he considered lying with her. 'Twould be sweet torture. But she was another man's wife, whether by choice or force, 'twas no matter.

As she was Roderick's wife when you last made love to her.

How easily she had bartered away her virtue, but he did not blame her. Surely she gave up her virginity in an attempt to save her life. Would not he have done the same?

He wanted her. Damn it, he wanted her more than 'twas sane. *Remember Faith and your vow to her.* Guilt took a stranglehold on his soul. He'd never loved his wife and felt a deep remorse. She'd died only days after their daughter and she, with pain-racked eyes and weak fingers, had begged him not to give his heart to another. She knew he would find solace in another woman, she only had asked him never to give his heart.

Now, he cleared his throat and Gwynn jumped, water splashing, her hair falling into her eyes as she attempted and failed to hide her breasts and legs with her hands. "Wh—who goes there?"

"Cover up," he said, catching sight of her tunic, chemise, and cloak dangling from the branch of a nearby tree. Swiftly he retrieved them all. He was about to toss the garments her way so that she could dress, but she held up a hand.

"Wait. Just . . . just hold them and turn your back. I do not wish them to fall into the stream and get wet."

If he hadn't been so worried about Gareth and Muir, he would have refused to do her bidding and enjoyed her vexation as he watched her walk proudly and naked as the day she was born from the stream. But there was no time.

"As you wish, m'lady," he agreed, for he understood the reasoning in her command. Slowly he turned, holding the clothes outstretched as she splashed out of the stream and snagged each piece from his hand. Hazarding a glance over his shoulder, he caught a glimpse of her struggling into her chemise as it clung to her wet body. Her navel was an inviting slit, her ribs, as she reached upward, visible slightly beneath full breasts that would easily fill a man's hand or mouth.

His cock thickened as moonlight washed over her and the dark nest of curls above her thighs shimmered. She caught his glance and frowned as she tugged on her clothes. "Where is Gareth?" she asked.

"He escaped."

"I *know* that much. Where is he?"

"Not with Muir."

"What?"

He turned as she was cinching a belt around her small waist. "Muir was captured."

"Oh, merciful Jesus." She paled even more.

"But Gareth was not caught." He explained all that he knew quickly while she interrupted, peppering him with questions, worrying aloud, and generally becoming more and more anxious as the seconds ticked by.

"We must find him. Do you think he went back to Rhydd? To Black Oak or mayhap to Heath and Luella?"

"Do not worry. Wherever he is, I will find him."

"But where? Oh, poor boy." She wrung out her hair with her hands and paced at the side of the creek. "We must—"

"I said 'I'll find him.' " His voice was firm, his anger rising.

"Aye. As you said I was to 'trust you'? Was that not the last order you gave me?" She threw her hands toward the black sky.

"Calm yourself."

"Tell me not what to do, Outlaw," she shot back.

"Then hear me out."

"Why?" she demanded. "So you can lie to me again? So you can tell me to 'trust you'?"

"So that we can find our son."

"Ha! Is that not what we have been attempting? I have listened to you, followed you, waited for you," she said, her face a mask of rage, his own temper wearing thin. "And to what end? You know not where Gareth is, if they've captured him, hurt him, or what's become of—ooh!"

"Hush, woman!" He grabbed her roughly and intended to shake some sense into her. But as his hands spanned her rib cage, his fury gave way to the sweet seduction in her eyes. "Curse you, woman," he growled, then kissed her. Long and hard and with all the pent-up desire that had been tormenting him for days, he covered her open mouth with his. Her lips were chilled, her flesh beneath her clothes trembled, and for a second he thought she might slap him. Instead she yielded, her body sagging against his, her lips returning the fever of his kiss as if she, too, had waited for just this moment to lose herself in him.

Though there was little time to spare, though the moonlight would soon give way to dawn, though she was the last woman on earth he should desire, he couldn't resist the sweet temptation of her lips, the pliant softness of her body, the urge to take and conquer this woman with her blistering tongue and gorgeous face.

She sighed into his open mouth and his tongue pressed ever forward, touching hers, rimming her lips, exploring the slick moistness of her mouth.

Heat invaded his blood and his cock stiffened in anticipation as he dragged them both to the ground with his weight. A dozen reasons to stop this madness seared through his brain only to be chased away by the hot, dark lust that burned through his body and seared his soul.

Trembling, his fingers fumbled with the laces of her cloak. Anxiously he drew the unwanted garment over her head. His lips brushed a kiss over her neck and his blood thundered in his ears. He wanted her. More than he'd ever wanted a woman. More than was right.

Remember Faith. That you loved her not. Because of Gwynn. Did you not vow on her grave that you would never . . .

She shuddered and whispered his name against his ear. His lips moved downward and discovered the enticing circle of bones at the base of her throat. She tasted of water, smelled of the forest, and felt warm and safe on this cold, dangerous night.

God help me.

One hand untied her belt. The other reached beneath the hem of her tunic.

"Trevin," she whispered. "Do not . . . oh, please—"

She arched against him as he slipped the tunic over her head, the damp chemise clinging to her skin. He saw two dark circles where her nipples pressed against the frail fabric and he lowered his mouth over one inviting breast, kissing and sucking, closing his eyes as desire overcame reason.

He needed Gwynn. He needed her now and the devil could hang any reason for not having her—even his own faithless promise to a dead wife.

Lying above her, he kissed her lips. One hand tangled in the wet strands of her hair, the other surrounded a breast. He felt a need as strong as life itself. To bury himself in her, to dance in the sensual rhythm of lovemaking as she writhed beneath him and called his name to the heavens, to spill his seed within the warm haven of her womb was all he wanted.

"Trevin," she said again and he lifted his head to kiss her once more. Her hands found the ties of his mantle and tunic and helped him toss the unwanted clothes aside. He shivered, but not from the cool night air, nay, from the heat that ran beneath his skin. Her fingers traced the cords of his muscles and the scars that marred his body. She quivered with need. He held back, for he didn't trust himself. When she reached for the laces of his breeches, he grabbed her hand. He could not. He would not.

This was madness.

"Nay, little one," he whispered and with all the strength he could muster fought the urge to take her. He strained against the fire in his loins. Slowly, he pushed up the hem of her chemise and lifted her legs over his shoulders. "Tonight is yours, love. So that you may forget."

"But—"

"Shh," he breathed against her and Gwynn no longer protested. She closed her eyes and sighed as he touched her, his lips creating a special magic, his tongue probing and lapping as she seemed to melt into a sea of sensation.

He smiled to himself for he sensed that for the moment he'd chased away her fears for their son.

And what of you, Trevin? What of the promise you made to Faith? He squeezed his eyes shut and forced aside the memory.

For a few moments in this inky forest all that mattered was the heat between them, the desire that held them fast.

He did not think about the morning.

Tonight would be hers.

Chapter Eight

"What's this?" Ian asked, as Webb, nudging an old man in front of him, crossed the bailey to a corner where targets had been mounted. For the first time in days, the sky was a brilliant shade of blue and a weak winter sun struggled to give off some much-needed heat.

Ian, who had been sighting his weapon, lowered the heavy crossbow as the ancient one approached. He was hobbled, his hands bound behind his back and he stumbled across the uneven grass. He stopped a few feet away from the lord of the manor and raised his head to meet Ian's gaze. Ian recoiled in disgust. Webb's pauper of a prisoner had but one eye. The other was sightless and scarred. Who was this man and why did Ian feel the taunt of a hellish memory tug at his mind?

"We found not the boy, m'lord," Webb admitted. His shoulders were stiff, his mouth a grim line.

"For the love of Christ—"

"But this man, a magician he claims himself to be, was seen traveling with a young lad who looked much like Gareth."

Ian walked toward the two and regretted his quick movement as pain exploded up his legs. Damn Trevin of Black Oak. That bastard would roast in hell for all the trouble and agony he'd wreaked. "The *boy* escaped?"

"He was hidden, m'lord, but we found this one"—Sir Webb shoved the old one forward and he stumbled to one knee before finding his balance again—"with his nose in a cup at an inn. He calls himself Muir and will not speak of his companion."

"Did no amount of . . . persuasion loosen his tongue?" Ian asked while trying to place the ancient one. *Muir.* Had he not heard the name before? The magician—if that's really what he was—again seemed vaguely familiar and teased the corners of Ian's memory, never quite coming into focus. Had they met before? When? Why would he not remember such a vile, ugly visage?

Webb lifted a dark eyebrow. "I thought mayhap ye would like to do the persuading yourself, my lord."

Ian turned the suggestion over in his mind, but couldn't imagine flogging this pathetic pauper. Nearly crippled, he was, and half blind. Ian would find no satisfaction in whipping the already hunched back. "Mayhap, in time," he hedged, "but we will kill him not. If we keep him here, there is a chance the boy or some of his accomplices might return to try and free him."

"Aye." Webb actually grinned as a hawk circled high over the battlements. " 'Tis an opportunity too good to resist."

Thoughtfully, Ian rubbed the stubble on his chin. "Be ye a sorcerer, then, old man?"

"Some say." The wizard had the audacity to stare him coldly in the face, and Ian fought the urge to shudder at the hate he felt emanating from that one seeing eye.

"I care not what 'some' say. What say you?"

" 'Tis only magic if ye believe."

"Tangled words from a fraud," Ian said, then added, "or from bait, for that is what you are, old man, bait for your friends."

"Ye would be wise to fear my friends," he replied, unruffled and prideful though he stood in a dirty, tattered coat that dragged on the ground and was so ragged it hardly covered his age-bent shoulders. "And, m'lord," he added with no hint of a smile, "ye would be wise to fear me as well."

"You? *You?* Do you jest?" Ian laughed at Muir's audacity though he felt a niggle of fear. The sorcerer was too smug. Too arrogant. And ugly. "Look at you, old one, you've got one foot in the grave as it is. 'Tis not I who is tied like a trussed boar. If ye are able to conjure up some magic, 'twould be wise to start now." He motioned to a page standing near the target. "Retrieve the bolts!"

"In time. Trust me, m'lord," Muir mocked. "I will use my magic in time."

"You've run out of time."

Muir's eye held not a bit of warmth. "We shall see."

Though there was no reason to think it, Ian couldn't shake the sensation that the temperature within the bailey had dropped. 'Twas as if a cold wind had raced across the bare brass to swirl around him and yet the air did not move.

The page returned with the bolts and once again Ian picked up his crossbow and pointed it toward the tarp that had been painted to look like a soldier, then spread across a pile of hay. "Take him away," he ordered the guards, tired of the uncanny look in the old man's eye. "Lock the wizard in the dungeon, but see that no harm comes to him. I wish him to stay alive."

"Aye, m'lord," a soldier, a skinny man named Harold, agreed as he shoved Muir's thin shoulders. "Come along now."

Nearly falling, Muir turned to cast one last bone-chilling look over his shoulder. " 'Tis sorry ye'll be, Ian of Rhydd. Very sorry."

Though he knew not why, the lord felt a sudden and nameless fear.

Why she listened to him, she didn't know, but Gwynn, for once in her life, hadn't argued and had ridden with Trevin to Black Oak Hall. She'd hoped that Gareth would be waiting for her and, as their horses galloped through the crumbling portal of the bailey, she knew she'd been foolish. Gareth would not have come here without the magician.

So where was he? On the road to Castle Heath? Returning to Rhydd? Please, God, keep him safe, he is but a boy.

Black Oak Hall was nearly in ruins, though there were efforts, it seemed, to fix the chipped mortar in the walls, and replace rotting beams in the huts propped against the great hall as well as rethatch sparse roofs.

"Lord Trevin returns," a watchman yelled from the highest tower and Gwynn, glancing upward, shivered as she remembered the story, that the castle was cursed, had fallen upon bad times. Was that the turret from which Baron Dryw had fallen—or had been pushed—to his death?

"Lord Trevin!"

" 'Tis good y'er home, m'lord."

"Make way, make way."

Voices, echoing the guard's words, clamored with excitement. The farrier left his forge burning brightly, carpenters laid down their hammers and saws, the armorer who had been cleaning mail in sand brushed off his hands and loped across the bailey. As it was just past midday, the keep, smaller by far than Rhydd, bustled with workers and animals, peddlers, and a band of musicians.

Trevin reined to a stop and Gwynn, slowing her own mount, felt lost, as if she were alone in an unfamiliar land. She searched the faces staring up at her hoping against hope that she would spy her boy, but nowhere in the gathering crowd was there any boy resembling her son. Her heart dropped. Where was he? Captured with that simpleton of a magician? Rotting away in some dungeon at Rhydd? Lost or hurt in the forest? Set upon by outlaws or wolves?

Stop it, Gwynn! Gareth's a clever boy. Have faith. With fierce determination, she hiked up her chin, swallowed back her fears, and stiffened her spine.

Trevin slid off his mount and tossed his reins to a bug-eyed page who eyed Webb's charger warily. The horse tossed his great head and snorted as the nervous boy led him away.

With strong hands, Trevin helped Gwynn from her saddle and gave the reins to another, even younger boy with strawlike hair that stuck out in ungainly tufts and a smile missing more than one tooth.

"Thank the Good Lord for your safe return, Lord Trevin," a scrawny priest welcomed. He was a foot shorter than the lord of the castle and completely bald, the only hair on his head being a reddish beard. Freckles spattered his face, crown, and neck.

" 'Tis good to see you again, Father." Trevin clasped the man's bony outstretched hand.

"And you as well."

"M'lord!" A steward strode forward, his boots squishing in the wet sod of the bailey. He was as tall as Trevin but without an ounce of fat or muscle upon his bones. "Welcome home," he greeted warmly. "You're looking well and that steed"—with appraising eyes he glanced to the stables where Webb's charger was tethered and already being groomed—"he will make a fine addition to the herd."

"Won't he?" Trevin replied with a half smile, his eyes glinting in blue devilment. "I borrowed him from . . . an old friend."

Gwynn let out a puff of disgusted air. Old friend? Webb?

"Borrowed? As in permanently?" the steward asked, reading the baron's thoughts.

"Most likely."

Oh. They are used to the outlaw-baron and his thieving ways, Gwynn surmised. Funny, but she didn't think of Trevin as a thief any longer, but then she was being silly. Just because he'd kissed her to the point of her nearly losing consciousness was no reason not to see him for what he truly was.

"We were worried when you didn't return. Sir Gerald said you would arrive soon, but I admit I had feared the worst."

"No reason, Emerson," he said. To the steward and the others who had crowded around them, he added, "I'd like you all to welcome Lady Gwynn of Rhydd. She is my guest and will be treated as such. Whatever she wishes is hers."

"Welcome, m'lady." The steward bowed grandly. "I'm Emerson and pleased to be at your service."

Gwynn nodded, though she had no time for pleasantries. *Where was Gareth?* Scullery maids, alewives, gong farmers, farriers, and carpenters were filling the bailey. Children followed after their parents, boys and girls with freshly scrubbed faces, or runny noses as the air was cold but, of course, Gareth was not among them.

"The lady has come here looking for her son, a boy by the name of Gareth. Twelve years old with black hair and blue eyes, about so high—" Trevin held his hand at the level of his shoulders. "He was probably traveling alone, mayhap without a mount."

"I've seen no unknown lad," Emerson responded, his brow furrowing in concentration as he shared a glance with another man, a soldier, as if for confirmation.

"Nor I, m'lord," the knight with curling blond hair agreed. "I've stood guard at the gate as well as the west tower. No boy of that description, save Jake, the armorer's son who we've all known for years, has been to Black Oak."

" 'Tis true." A fat woman with hips that seemed to float beneath her tunic and a dingy white scarf wrapped around her head approached. Her hands were chapped raw, her apron splattered with blood. A girl of three hung on her leg, peering at Gwynn with curious, wary eyes.

"You know me, m'lord, I'm the eyes and ears of this 'ere castle and if old Mary ain't seen the lad, he 'asn't been 'ere." She gave a clumsy curtsy and shook her head. "Sorry, m'lady, but I've seen no boy who looks like yer son."

"Nor I," the priest agreed.

Bone tired, Gwynn wanted to break down and cry, or shake the living hell out of Trevin and demand that he find their son, but she stood as she was, dirty but proud, a mother worried sick for her boy. Her heart was heavy, her muscles ached, and she longed for the peace of mind that had eluded her ever since she'd heard that Roderick had escaped and was returning. 'Twas only days ago and yet she felt as if weeks had passed. She was tired, hungry, and irritable.

The whisper running through the crowd of peasants and freemen was that no boy matching Gareth's description was hiding within the crumbling walls of Black Oak. Gwynn's hopes fell onto the cold, sharp stones of reality that Gareth was captured or lost or worse. *Dear God in heaven, was it possible that he had died and she was unaware of the tragedy?* Her heart twisted painfully. Surely she, who had brought him forth into this world, would feel the rending of his life if he'd died.

Even Trevin's broad shoulders seemed to slump a bit, as if he, too, were realizing how futile their search might be. He took Gwynn's hand and led her toward the great hall. "Come. We'll eat and rest, then I'll make plans and find the boy."

"*You'll* make plans? *You'll* find him?" she repeated, her eyes narrowing. "Make no mistake, *m'lord*, I will not be left behind. If there be a plan to save Gareth I will be a part of it."

"It may be dangerous—"

"Think you I care? We are talking about Gareth, Trevin. My son!"

"And mine."

The door to the great hall opened as they climbed the stairs. Inside the interior was lit with hundreds of candles and wall sconces. A huge fire in the grate crackled and popped, giving off warm golden light that reflected on the whitewashed walls and caught in Trevin's eyes. For the first time in days, Gwynn felt warmth against her skin.

Servants scurried about, knights stood at their stations, pages walked swiftly along the corridors. Already a table was being prepared with wine, apples, cheese, and loaves of wastel.

"I knew not when ye'd be back, m'lord," a man with great jowls and silvering hair said. "If ye but give me a few minutes, I will have a feast for ye the likes of which ye haven't seen since the Christmas Revels."

Trevin waved off the man's concerns. "Do not worry, James," he said as he held a chair for Gwynn positioned next to his upon a raised dais. Gratefully she sank onto the seat. "As hungry as we are, we will eat what you've prepared and think it the best in all of Wales."

The cook's chest puffed up in pride. " 'Twill be, I swear. But for now, please, enjoy this bit of nothing, then rest a little, but the time ye've slept and changed, well . . . all will be ready." He clapped his hands and several pages scurried out of the great hall through a back door. "I've already ordered water heated and hauled to your chamber as well as to the lady's room."

"Good, good." Trevin settled into his chair—the lord's chair—a carved oaken piece that she suspected had belonged to the previous baron. He leaned low on his spine, and sliced cheese, apples, and bread, which he offered to her. As they ate and drank wine, Trevin listened attentively to problems that had occurred in the keep. The master builder was concerned about the wattle and daub walls being washed with lime, the carpenter was unhappy with his latest apprentice, the steward was certain that someone in the kitchen was stealing spices, and the armorer was worried that there wasn't enough steel to make the weapons that were sorely needed. There were other squabbles as well, but Gwynn hardly listened as she bit into a slice of tart apple. She was too tired to think of anything but her lost son and his rogue of a father.

Trevin would forever be a mystery to her. An accomplished outlaw, he could steal a man's horse from beneath his nose. A reluctant ruler, he nonetheless listened to the troubles and problems within the castle walls with a just ear and clever mind. A considerate lover, he could make her think of nothing save the touch and feel of him. And now, his new role, that of father, one he seemed to savor.

As men and women from the castle stopped in to welcome him back, meet the lady, or give him news, gossip, and complaints about the travails of Black Oak, Trevin listened, though he, too, appeared anxious, his skin tight over his cheekbones, his lips thin and bracketed with deep grooves.

Gwynn couldn't help but stare at him. How had she come to care for a man she didn't trust, didn't really know? Why did her silly pulse leap each time he looked her way? Did she not have enough problems, worrying about Gareth's safety? She could not, would not be distracted by this outlaw baron. Yet, she couldn't help but appraise from beneath the sweep of her lashes.

Aye, he was a handsome man. His hair, black as the night, fell fetchingly over eyes the shade of a summer sky near dusk. His skin was dark, as was Gareth's, and his smile, when he reluctantly offered it was a crooked slash of white that had, she supposed, melted the hearts of many a maid. Had not she herself been blinded by his black-hearted charm? Had she not let him undress her and touch her and kiss her in places only a husband should know of?

She felt a blush steal up her neck and in that moment, Trevin glanced in her direction, his eyes holding hers for half a heartbeat. Her lungs were suddenly too tight, her breath lost somewhere in the back of her throat. 'Twas as if, in that single instant, he could read her mind and see the wanton path of her thoughts.

She turned her attention to a loaf of white bread and sliced off a slab. What was wrong with her? She couldn't be around him without thinking of their lovemaking. Even riding in the saddle, watching his stiff back as he sat astride Webb's stallion, she was reminded of his touch. Between Gareth's whereabouts and Trevin's kiss, she thought of little else.

Conscious that he was watching her, she slathered her wastel with butter, then drizzled honey over the slice. What was she thinking? She couldn't allow images of Trevin's body to distract her. All she should be considering was the safety of her son. Nothing else mattered. By the time she'd finished the bread, her fingers were sticky and she licked them, only to notice Trevin's eyes regarding her in silent amusement. Embarrassed, she accepted the wet cloth and bowl of warm water from a page and refused to meet the glimmer in his gaze.

After more apologies and promises from the cook of a feast "like no other ye've ever seen" to be prepared for a later meal, Gwynn was shown to a chamber near the priest's quarters. A fire had been lit, the room was warm, and a tub of water with lavender-scented steam rising from it had been placed near the foot of the bed.

The bath looked like pure heaven.

A gap-toothed girl with red ringlets and freckles bridging a pert nose was wringing her hands near the tub. "I'm to bathe ye, m'lady," she said with a curtsy she hadn't yet perfected. "Me name's Hildy and if there's anything ye need, ye're but to ask me."

"Thank you." Gwynn decided to make a friend of this silly lass who seemed as if she'd never attended to a lady before. Though she knew she should insist upon being with Trevin every instant, demand to be a part of any plans he had to save Gareth, she couldn't resist the thought of fragrant, warm water running over her skin. With Hildy's help she stripped off her dirty clothes and sighing in contentment, settled into the hot water.

"Oooh, I've longed for this," she admitted. Her skin tingled and she used the scented soap to clean her hair and fingernails. As the moist heat enveloped her, she was reminded of her last cleansing and Trevin coming upon her while she bathed in the creek. All too vividly she remembered the magic of his lips and how possessively his hands had been on her body when he'd kissed her so intimately.

The silly little maid clucked on, talking about everything and nothing all at once. "—the baron, Lord Trevin, I, um, I thinks he's a good man no matter what some of 'em say."

"And what is that?" Gwynn asked, rotating her neck.

"Well, y'know, that 'e killed Baron Dryw just to keep the castle and he married Lady Faith to make certain that 'e didn't lose it. 'Tis a pity about her, fer she loved 'im, that she did. Never believed that 'e killed her father and always 'oped that 'e'd learn to love 'er back, poor thing."

"He loved not his wife?" Suddenly the twit had all of Gwynn's attention.

"Who knows?" Hildy lathered Gwynn's hair with fingers that were surprisingly strong. "She didn't think so and that was what mattered."

"But still she loved him?"

"With all her poor 'eart." Hildy took a pitcher from the shelf near the fire and filled it with water from the tub. Slowly she poured it over Gwynn's soapy curls. "She thought that bearing 'im a babe would turn his 'eart to her, she did, but then, ah, well, the baby came backwards and the midwife couldn't save it—a girl, Alison, they named 'er. Lady Faith"—Hildy cleared her throat and blinked rapidly—"she . . . she bled to death still 'oldin' the poor dead little lass in 'er arms. 'Twas pitiful." She took the time to make the sign of the cross over her breasts and water from her hands sprayed and dripped with her rapid movements.

"Yes . . . yes, it was," Gwynn agreed, horrified by the story but touched by Hildy's adoration of Trevin's wife.

"The baron, 'e blamed 'imself, if ye ask me."

"Why?"

"Because 'twas the bloody truth." Hildy lowered her voice as she wrung the water from Gwynn's hair. " 'E never loved Lady Faith, you could see it in his eyes. If ye ask me 'e's not capable of love. 'E's a looker, aye, and a decent man most of the time, I s'pose, but 'e's got a heart of stone, that one. I pity any woman who's foolish enough to give 'im 'er 'eart."

"So do I," Gwynn admitted.

"When Faith and the baby died, 'e . . . well, 'e became even more unhappy, or so it seems." She glanced up at Gwynn. "I tell ye, sometimes I think there be a curse cast upon Black Oak." Shaking her head, Hildy stacked towels on a stool near the tub. "I'll be right back, m'lady," she said as she made her way to the door. "The baron's ordered ye clean clothes."

"Kind of him," Gwynn said under her breath. She bathed until the water cooled and closed her eyes as Hildy came and went, laying out dresses upon the bed, then cleaning Gwynn's shoes and boots with a smooth cloth before setting them near the hearth to dry. A dozen scented candles burned, the fire crackled, and Gwynn, for the first time in days, felt a sense of contentment. If only Gareth were here and safe, she could find some peace here at Black Oak.

With Trevin? Peace? Remember, he's an outlaw—some think a killer. All he wants from you is your son. Nothing more. You are only the woman who brought forth his heir. She didn't want to believe her nasty thoughts. Had Trevin not loved her thoroughly the night before, giving rather than taking, offering pleasure rather than demanding it? *Because he wants you to trust him, to fall into his trap of seduction, so that you'll be lulled into the very sense of peace you're experiencing. Don't be fooled, Gwynn, Don't let any man manipulate you again, especially not a rogue like Trevin of Black Oak Hall. Remember what Hildy said—that he was incapable of love, that he didn't even love his wife.*

But then had she loved either of her husbands?

The water finally grew tepid and reluctantly Gwynn toweled off before choosing a lacy chemise and a velvet and brocade gown the color of wine. The dress was heavy but warm as it hugged her breasts and fitted easily over her hips before sweeping the floor.

" 'Tis beautiful ye be, lady," Hildy said in awe as she wound ribbons through Gwynn's still-damp hair.

"Did this dress belong to the lord's wife?"

"Aye." Hildy handed her a braided silver belt that slid easily around Gwynn's waist, then stepped back, clasped her hands together, and sighed. "The lady never wore it as she was with child during the time it was sewn and then, poor dear"—again Hildy deftly made the sign of the cross over her own chest—"she had the babe and died. 'Twas a pity, sure and simple. She was a kind one, was Lady Faith. True of spirit and soul. She was there that day, y'know, the day that her father fell to his death."

"She was?" Gwynn asked, cringing at her own curiosity.

"Aye, walking through the gardens. Lord Dryw and Sir Trevin were up on the wall walk, arguing loudly, and then, suddenly, it looked as if they 'ad come to blows and the baron pitched over the edge, right through the crenels and landed in the bailey just short of the old well." She shook her head and scowled, then crossed herself yet again. " 'Twas a sad day for all of us."

"Sir Trevin was with the baron?" Gwynn clarified.

"Aye." Hildy nodded her head and her springy curls danced around her face. "But 'e did not kill the lord. 'E did not. 'Twas an accident." She was arguing with herself, as if it was she, not Gwynn, who needed convincing. "Even Lady Faith, she believed him, elsewise would she have married the man who killed her father? I think not."

"You saw the accident?" Gwynn asked, swallowing hard.

"With me own two eyes. First the lords were talkin', then arguin', then fightin', y'know, kind of shovin' each other, and then . . . then the baron he cursed Sir Trevin, told 'im 'e'd see 'im in 'ell. Then . . . then . . ." her breathing was uneven, her eyes focused on a distant image only she could see, ". . . then he tumbled through the crenels and let out a horrible scream." Closing her eyes, she shuddered as if she could feel the thud of the body as it landed. " 'Twas awful, m'lady."

"It sounds so."

"Lady Faith, she . . . she never got over it, but married Trevin anyway. Cursed, I tell ye. We all be cursed by a hex that no one can break."

"Hexes are meant to be broken," Gwynn said, as much to appease the superstitious girl as anything.

"Not 'ere at Black Oak. I know. I've been 'ere since me poor ma birthed me and I've seen death and ghosts."

"Ghosts?"

Hildy nodded. "Aye; they walk the curtain wall and I've thought 'twas one of them undead who shoved the baron to 'is death. The devil, 'e never sleeps, ye know."

"I've heard," Gwynn said dryly.

"Yea, and sometimes methinks 'e lives in the very dungeons of Black Oak. Why else would Baron Dryw's life be taken or Lady Faith's? And little Alison, why should she not be born to grow up, eh?" She cleared her throat. "The baron, Lord Trevin, there isn't a day 'e be 'ere at the castle that 'e doesn't visit the grave."

"Of his daughter?" Gwynn shivered.

"And 'is wife. 'E may not have loved 'er while she walked this earth, but now, me thinks, 'e misses 'er sorely. Oh, 'tis a sorry lot we be, 'ere at Black Oak." She sniffed loudly, then asked, "Think ye that ye can lift the hex that's been placed on us all?"

"Me?"

"I've seen yer 'erbs, m'lady, and there is a rumor about that the mistress of Rhydd is a sorceress."

"I claim not to be anything of the kind."

"But ye will 'elp us, won't ye?" She bit her lower lip and kept her gaze fixed on the floor. "Ye see, 'tis not just fer meself I ask, but fer the babe within me." She rubbed her belly with gentle hands. "I be with child." She smiled and blinked. "But I 'ave no 'usband and I pray that the curse of Black Oak is upon me not. I . . . I would not want to lose my babe as Lady Faith did."

"You will not. You are young and strong."

Hildy shuddered inwardly and shook her head, tossing the curls about her face. " 'Tis not enough. There 'ave been three babes born this year past who 'ave not breathed a breath of life. Others 'ave died in their cradles, not yet seeing their first summer." She was pale as a new moon. "I want only the best for my little one. Surely ye, a mother, can understand."

"Aye." Of course she could.

"Then, please, m'lady, use whatever magic you 'ave to put an end to the bad spell cast over this keep."

"I—I'll try. But I cannot promise 'twill work."

" 'Tis enough," Hildy said, brightening.

Shaken, Gwynn smoothed the folds of Lady Faith's dress. Not only was she wearing another woman's gown, but had kissed that woman's man as if he were her husband. She felt suddenly like a traitor to a ghost she'd never known in life. The story Hildy had spoken was bone chilling and yet she had to know more about Black Oak and Trevin, the father of her child. "So tell me," she encouraged as she stepped into a new pair of boots that Hildy had scrounged up, "of Muir."

"Oh, 'im!" Hildy waved a hand in the air. "No one knows if 'e's a sorcerer or nay. True, 'e seems to see things out of that bad eye of 'is and some of 'is spells appear to work, but then there's times when 'e's in a stupor and doesn't make a lot of sense, if ye ask me. 'E and the baron, well, they go way back, came 'ere together, they did, but to me way of thinkin' Muir's just plain odd. 'E didn't bother castin' any spells to scare away the curse, let me tell ye."

"You don't trust him?" Gwynn asked.

"Oh, 'e 'as a good enough 'eart, I s'pose, but 'alf the time methinks 'e's as daft as the town idiot."

This was the man in whom Trevin had entrusted Gareth's life? But then what did Hildy really know?

They talked on and Gwynn rested a little, dozing off on another woman's bed before a knock on the door signified that dinner was ready. "I'll be 'ere to serve ye, m'lady," Hildy said as Gwynn started for the door. "Lord Trevin asked me to be yer personal maid during your visit."

" 'Twill be short, I'm afraid."

The girl's sweet face folded in upon itself. "But the baron, 'e said ye'd be stayin' a fortnight or so—"

"Did he?" Gwynn gathered her skirts in one hand. "Well, he was mistaken. I'll be leaving soon to look for my son." She swept through the door and silently added, *And no one, not God Himself, or the damned baron of Black Oak is going to stop me!*

Hurrying along the corridor, causing the candles to flicker and smoke as she passed, Gwynn startled a cat who let out a yowl and scrambled out of her path. Down the stairs to the great hall where Trevin was already seated, she flew. He lifted his gaze at the sound of her steps and for the span of a short breath she was caught in the seductive blue of his eyes. Her feet faltered a step, her willful heart hammered a quick double-time for a second. A knight, the blond one known as Stephen, helped her to the main table.

Most of the guests were seated upon benches positioned at an angle below the dais supporting the main table. Heads turned toward her and curious sets of eyes watched her as she took a seat next to Trevin's.

"My lady," he said with a cock of one dark, insolent brow. " 'Tis breathtaking, how you look."

She flushed and lifted her chin. "Thank you, my lord." Smothering a smile, she added, "May I say the same to you?"

He snorted a laugh. "You may, Lady Gwynn, do anything you wish." His smile was positively wicked and her stupid heart pounded even more wildly. His hair was freshly washed and attempted to curl, his square jaw freshly shaven, his eyes dancing a mischievous blue in the candlelight. He wore fresh clothes, all black, trimmed in leather and studded with silver. He looked dark, dangerous, and more outlaw than baron.

"The dress suits you."

"Does it?" She cleared her throat and was lucky to find her voice. " 'Tis the first thing here that does," she teased, wondering why she would bother to flirt with him. She eyed their guests but aside from a few curious glances, no one seemed to be unduly interested in them or their conversation.

One side of Trevin's sensual mouth lifted. "Hildy did not please you?"

"Nay, she's a good lass, but—"

"The chamber was not to your liking?"

"The room was fine, but I'll not be a prisoner here, *m'lord*."

"Never."

A page filled their cups with wine.

"Good, then I'll be able to leave at will and search for Gareth."

He didn't reply as the cook, James, chose that moment to enter, leading servers with heavy platters of food. He'd not been lying about a feast of the highest order. Trenchers of brawn, pheasant and gravy, salmon, heron and eggs, tarts and pies, and a stuffed peacock with his quills attached were carried to the head table. Again, Gwynn shared a trencher with Trevin and was treated as if she were, indeed, Mistress of Black Oak Hall. Serving maids and pages attended to her every need, bringing her warm wet cloths to clean her fingers, offering her wine or ale, asking if she would prefer salmon to eel or peacock to pigeon. As quickly as she finished eating one course, another, as savory as the last, was brought in.

Trevin ate heartily, as if he'd not seen food in the span of a full moon, and she, though worried sick about her son, couldn't resist the scents of spices and the taste of hot, fresh food.

Musicians played and acrobats performed as if the meal were a special event and most of the guests seemed genuinely glad for Trevin's safe return. Yet, behind the smiles and good cheer, lurking in the shadowy corners of the castle, buried just below the surface of the jubilation, Gwynn sensed a current, an invisible stream, of ill will. Not all in the castle seemed to trust their lord. Gwynn, as she picked at a joint of venison, wondered at the strain she sensed existed within the ancient walls of Black Oak. 'Twas almost as if the ghost of old Baron Dryw hid in the darkest corners of the keep.

A shiver, soft as the footsteps of a specter, climbed up her spine. She told herself that she was being silly, that Hildy's claims of curses and ghosts had colored her feelings for the castle, but she couldn't shake the sensation that something was wrong, very wrong, at Black Oak Hall.

After the meal, as pages were clearing the tables and the dogs were scrounging for scraps that had fallen into the rushes, Trevin remained in his chair and spoke with those who worked and lived under his rule. There seemed no rules about who could approach him. Everyone from the hound master who had lost his best bitch to illness, to the beekeeper who was concerned about the size of the straw skeps, appeared to need a word with him.

There were those who kept their distance, of course, and Gwynn wondered if they were the men and women who did not trust him, who thought him to be a thief, a cheat, and a murderer. How many knights and soldiers thought him the killer of Lord Dryw? Would they take up their swords against him or steal into his room in the dark of night to slit his throat?

She shuddered at the thought, but glanced at him again. A strong, agile man, he was all sinew and bone, muscle and fierce determination. Surely he could see to his own safety.

He turned, his eyes catching hers for an instant, and she looked quickly away, embarrassed at her wayward thoughts. The disturbing part of her own inner struggle was that she was beginning to care for the thief, not only because he was the father of her child, but because there was a part of him that touched her in a way no other man had. 'Twas foolish, of course. Feeling anything for him other than suspicion was dangerous. As Hildy had warned, Trevin of Black Oak was not the kind of man to whom a woman should be losing her heart.

But, curse it all, she was.

Chapter Nine

"'Ere ye go, ye one-eyed bastard!" The guard, a squat, burly fellow with black hair growing profusely upon his arms, cast Muir's cane into the cell, then locked the door. "Now, I'll 'ave no more whinin' from the likes of ye."

"Thank you," Muir said and hid his smile. He'd been complaining about not having his cane ever since being tossed into the dungeon. 'Twas an ugly place. Water seeped through the walls and pooled on the floor covered with dank, sour straw. Rats, beady eyes reflecting the orange glow of a few torches, scurried through the cages where emaciated men barely survived. Muir had learned most of the inmates were newly incarcerated, those who had dared question the new baron's right to rule, and already they were in sorry shape.

The guard turned back to his chair and table where he was busy sharpening knives on a whetstone. The scraping of metal against rock was rhythmic and most of the inmates sat as if in a trance, neither speaking nor moving about.

Muir waited until the guard was bent over his blade and the candle that served as his only illumination showed his face set in deep concentration. Only when the magician was certain the sentry had forgotten him did he move to the darkest corner of his cell and with steady fingers unscrew the false bottom of his staff. From its hollowed-out center, he pried moss and stones, amulets, berries and herbs, a candle and, most importantly, a knife so small it could be hidden in a man's palm or if the owner was very careful, inside his mouth—a tiny, perfect little blade that was able to pick locks as well as slice through flesh. Muir smiled to himself and hid the knife in a special pocket sewn into the sleeve of his ragged cloak.

He replaced the rest of his possessions quietly and decided to wait until the time was perfect to make good his escape. First, he would gain information, listen to the gossip of the castle and discover what exactly Ian of Rhydd had planned. Then, he would disappear, but not before he relieved the baron of a few jugs of his finest wine.

Satisfied that things would turn out well, he closed his eye for a short nap only to feel a searing pain burn through his brain. "Jesus, Lord have mercy," he muttered between clenched teeth. His sightless eye stung in an eruption of pain that caused him to double over and clutch his face.

"What now?" the guard demanded, scraping back his chair.

" 'Tis nothing," Muir lied, hoping to stem the ache that burned as if he were being branded.

"Then shut up!"

"Aye."

The vision hit him hard. With the gale force of a storm. He saw all too clearly the images of boy and pup stalking through the forest. Gareth and his infernal whelp. The boy wandered easily through the thickets, the dog at his heels, and all the while murky shadows drew nearer, following the lad with a deadly certainty that made Muir's heart stop. Just as the darkness attempted to cover the boy, Muir heard him cry out and chains rattled sharply, showing themselves in a coil like that of a labyrinth, blood dripping between the rusting links. Father to son and son to father.

"No!" Muir cried, realizing that the old secret was about to be revealed, that all he'd worked for his entire life was going to be destroyed. Oh, Morrigu and Cerridwen, let this happen not!

"Shut up, old man, or ye won't live long enough to see the gallows!"

"Aye, aye," he managed to whisper and wished for a long, calming draught of ale. Clutching his cane as if it were the staff of life, Muir rested his back against the cold stone wall as the pain subsided.

There was no hiding, no sliding away from destiny. Fate had seen to it that Gareth's future was placed squarely upon Muir's stooped shoulders.

'Twas certain that if he didn't find a way to conjure up a bit of magic—a miracle no less—he, Trevin, Gareth, and Lady Gwynn were doomed.

'Twas time the tables were turned, Gwynn decided as she sneaked from her room and through the dusky corridor to the lord of Black Oak's chamber. She hazarded one quick look over her shoulder as she climbed the short flight of stairs, for she could not allow anyone in the keep to know her plans.

As she passed a dark, empty alcove, she felt a coldness emanating from the spot, as if an invisible tempest had cut through her to chill her blood. Was the castle truly haunted as Hildy had insisted?

'Tis naught but a silly girl's imaginings, she chastised herself, but shivered just the same.

She reached the door to Trevin's room and hesitated. Earlier, as the meal was cleared away, Gwynn had overheard Trevin speak in hushed tones to two of his most trusted men. Sir Gerald and Sir Stephen were to meet him in his room before the moon had risen over the west tower. She, complaining of a pain in her head, had made her way to her own chamber, insisted that she was a private person and would have no chattering maid sleep in her quarters with her. Only after Hildy had disappeared down the stairs, had Gwynn slipped into the empty corridor.

"God be with me," she whispered.

Once inside the room, she closed the door softly behind her and paused to scan the large chamber. Tapestries hung upon whitewashed walls and a spoked chandelier with unlit tapers was suspended from a high, domed ceiling. A fire crackled cheerily in the grate and sconces held candles that had burned low but offered a soft golden glow that played upon the walls and ceiling.

The bed was low to the ground and offered no hiding place beneath it. A bench, three-legged stool, and a writing table were arranged near the hearth. A wardrobe stood against the wall, but she dare not hide within it as surely Trevin might take off his mantle and hang it within. She eyed the ornately carved cupboard and decided if she were to hold her breath in tightly, she could hide behind the heavy piece. 'Twas a small space to be sure, the wardrobe too massive for her to move, but if she inched her way in, she would be able to hear what happened in the room and once Trevin had fallen asleep, sneak away.

There was no other place to stow herself, so she edged behind the wide wardrobe. A mouse scurried from beneath her feet and cobwebs clung to her face and hair, but she was able to press her back against the wall. Her breasts were crushed by the oaken backing of the cupboard, her lungs constricted, her nostrils filled with dust. She let her breath out slowly, found she could breathe just barely, then waited as the sounds of life in the castle filtered through the windows and crept up the stairs. Soft conversation, rattling dishes, chinking armor, and the ring of hammers kept her from falling asleep on her feet. Once in while a dog barked or an owl hooted. Doves and pigeons fluttered to their roosts as life in the keep slowed.

After what seemed like hours she heard footsteps on the stairs before the door creaked open. Swords and spurs clanked and male voices she barely recognized heralded the lord's return.

The bench scraped against the stones of the floor as a group of men, none of whom she could see, settled near the fire.

"Tomorrow we leave to find Gareth," Trevin said.

"And what of the lady?"

"She stays."

Gwynn bit her tongue, though her blood boiled.

"Knows she this?"

"Nay, but, Stephen, a woman would only slow us down and we need speed and quick wits."

"Aye, m'lord," a third voice interjected. "If there be battle we must not worry over her. She would only be more trouble than we need."

"I think she will not like this." Stephen sounded worried. " 'Tis her son."

"A woman knows not what she wants," the third man said.

Gwynn's fists curled so tightly she felt her fingernails bite into the soft flesh of her palms.

"True enough. A woman is foolish thing." Trevin sounded smug and Gwynn's temper soared to the heavens. To think she'd actually thought she was falling in love with the stupid thug! "She will stay here and wait in case the boy returns."

"We will ride to Rhydd?"

"Aye, but we'll split up; one party will be the decoy to lure Rhydd's soldiers in the wrong direction, the other will actually scale Rhydd's walls and save Muir."

"The magician?" A snort of disdain. "Why save his flea-ridden hide? Did he not lose the boy?"

"Do not forget," Trevin said sternly, "Muir raised me. I entrusted him with the lad and if he's held prisoner, 'tis my doing, as surely as if I'd led him to the dungeon myself. I'll not have his death on my head."

The others grudgingly assented and they made more plans, talking and arguing while Gwynn stewed behind the wardrobe. Oh, how she wanted to leap from her hiding space and tell all the men, especially that arrogant Trevin McBain, thief, liar, and seducer, what fools they were, that a woman would only aid them in their quest. Gwynn was as good a shot with an arrow as most men and though a sword was too heavy for her to swing for hours, she was dangerous with her little knife. Asides, she used her wits more often than her muscle to get what she wanted. Trevin, though he knew it or not, could use her to help him find Gareth.

She couldn't hear all their plans, though, as more often than not their voices were low and muffled, muted by the other sounds of the castle.

The fire popped and sizzled, dogs barked outside, the wind rattled through the slats over the windows, and every once in a while there came a harsh rap upon the door. Each time there was a knocking upon the worn oak planks of the door, Gwynn's heart pounded in trepidation for she feared that someone had looked into her room, found her missing, and was alerting the lord. She strained to listen and bit her lip. None of the disturbances were about her, however, and eventually Trevin's soldiers took their leave.

Thank the Lord.

Their footsteps dulled and the door of the room closed firmly.

Gwynn, hardly daring to breathe, didn't move a muscle.

A lock clicked.

No! Where did he keep the key? Was she to be locked in this room alone with him?

Sweat dotted her scalp and her palms itched. What was she to do? Wait until morn when she would surely be found missing?

Think, Gwynn, think! She had no choice but to wait until he was fast asleep, then she could search for the key, unlock the door, and sneak silently back to her room. In the morning he would discover that someone had been with him and left his door unlocked, but she had no other option. This chamber was far too high for her to dare to leave by way of the window. If she jumped into the bailey, she would surely break her neck.

Dear God, help me. She was not going to be left here at Black Oak, treated like a well-kept prisoner while her son might be in danger.

The minutes ticked by and she heard Trevin unbuckle his belt and remove his boots. The sounds brought images to her mind that she forced back but she felt the cupboard doors open as he hung his tunic and breeches upon a peg therein. Sweat collected on her brow, palms, and spine as his scent reached her. She let out a long breath when the wardrobe doors finally shut and his footsteps over the rushes indicated that he'd crossed the room.

Please let him sleep long and hard, she silently prayed as he tossed a last chunk of wood onto the fire and then, she assumed, dropped onto the bed.

Now, all she had to do was wait.

An insect of some kind walked along the back side of her neck. She couldn't move, didn't dare scream, so endured the passage of the bug as it crawled over her shoulder and along the neckline of her bodice before thankfully taking its leave. Her fingers were curled into fists and she closed her eyes, concentrating on the sounds emanating from the bed. Was that steady, regular breathing she heard or the soft moan of the wind? Did the lord snore slightly as he rustled under the covers or was the noise only the trick of her imagination willing him asleep. Did Trevin drop off easily or did he toss and turn, vexed as the hours of sleep eluded him?

What did it matter? In the morn he would discover that someone had been lurking within his chamber and made good his escape. Certainly he would consider her a suspect. What then? Would he change his mind and instead of keeping her a spoiled, guarded guest, lock her in her room or worse yet, angrily toss her into the dungeon?

Nay. She had only to remember the way he'd touched and caressed her. Surely he wouldn't cast her into a dank, horrid corner of the castle.

She rested her forehead upon the back side of the cupboard as her legs began to ache from standing in one position. Oh, Lord, she couldn't stay here all night. Squeezing her eyes shut, she hoped to hear any noise to indicate that someone was about, but the castle was quiet and aside from an occasional muffled cough or rustle of mice in the rushes or wind sighing through the turrets, she heard nothing.

'Twas now or never.

Slowly she inched sideways, barely making a sound aside from the hammering of her heart. She peered from behind the wardrobe. The room was dark save for the embers glowing in the hearth.

Trevin lay on the bed, unmoving, his clean-shaven face in shadowy repose, golden light gleaming against his shoulders and catching the swirling, dark hair that grew across his wide chest. Her abdomen tightened at the sight of him, for the blankets had shifted and covered only a small section of his body. One strong, muscular leg was exposed all the way to his hip and Gwynn felt a familiar fluttering in her stomach. She dragged her eyes away from the enticing curve of his buttock and turned toward the door.

One step. Two.

"Leaving so soon?"

Oh, Sweet Jesus no! The sound of his voice stopped her cold.

"Why, Lady Gwynn, did you hear every detail of our plan?"

Dear God in heaven, give me strength.

"Did you not think I spied you cowering behind the wardrobe like a thief caught in the act?"

Slowly turning to face the bed, she saw the sparkle of amusement in his eyes, the slash of white as he grinned in bemused satisfaction. Oh, how he enjoyed mocking her.

"Well, now, *m'lord*, it seems we are even."

"Are we?"

"Aye. I caught you hiding in my cupboard years ago and now you've found me out."

He stretched lazily and the mischief brewing in his eyes warned her that there was more trouble heading fast in her direction. " 'Tis true enough except for one small detail."

Whatever it was, it sounded dangerous. "I know not what you mean."

"Well—" He swung both legs out of the covers and stood. She gasped and forced her eyes to stay focused on his face for he was naked as the day he was born, his manhood visible in a thatch of dark curling hair. "—as I recall, I was forced to bargain with you, was I not?"

Oh, merciful God! Her pulse was thundering, her blood racing. Her throat was dry as desert wind in summer, her blood as warm as a vat of water left neglected on the fire. "You . . . you broke your part of the bargain," she reminded him.

"After thirteen years."

He was standing directly in front of her, so close she smelled the maleness of him, felt the heat of his body, noticed a trace of desire in his gaze.

Help me, she thought, knowing she was already lost.

"If I remember correctly, lady," he said in a voice that seemed lower in timbre than she remembered, "to atone for my having eavesdropped on your conversation with the old midwife, I was to spend three days in your bed."

Oh, God. She swallowed hard.

"Now, what say you? Would it not be only fair if we were to strike a similar pact?" He lifted a finger and traced the curve of her jaw.

She shivered, her insides warming, but managed a condescending smile. " 'Twas a different time, different circumstances. Had I not got with child my husband would have had me killed."

"If he'd not been conveniently imprisoned." He lifted her hair from her neck, leaned forward just a bit, and pressed his lips to the sensitive spot behind her ear.

Her knees turned as soft as Cook's pudding and she closed her eyes. "Imprisonment is never convenient."

"Nay?" His lips were warm and oh, so, seductive as they moved against her skin. Desire awakened deep in the deepest part of her.

"Nay."

"How would you have explained the babe? Surely he knew that you were not carrying his child as you were a virgin when you took me to your bed."

The same question she had refused to answer so many years ago. He tugged on the neckline of her dress and kissed her bare shoulder. A deep lust stole through her blood. " 'Tis of no matter now." She cleared her throat, ignoring the passion he, and he alone, stirred within her. "I should take my leave—"

"Not yet, love."

She closed her mind to the endearment as she knew in her heart that he'd said the same words to dozens of women. She shouldn't fall into his seductive trap and yet when his arms surrounded her and he tipped her face up to his, she didn't stop him, couldn't find the strength to deny what she wanted so desperately. As he pressed her clothed body to his naked legs and chest, she felt all her resistance fall away.

Desire, her long-hated enemy, dared sear through her brain as well as the most intimate recesses of her body. *Please, God, if You be listening, help me. Give me the strength to stop this madness.*

But God turned a deaf ear to her pleas.

The laces of her dress gave way easily, the heavy fabric parting to drop in a wine-colored pool on the floor. Strong hands spanned either side of her rib cage, warm fingers searing her skin through the sheer fabric of her chemise.

His lips found hers and she sagged against him. Though she knew that what she was about to do was a sin; that in the eyes of God and the church she was a married woman, she could not find the resistance to stop the course of their twined destinies. Her pulse pounded, her breath was shallow, and all she knew was the touch and feel of this one harsh man.

Oh, Trevin, do not hurt me.

His mouth was hot, hard, and insistent. His tongue pressed against the seam of her lips and she opened to him, felt a thrill of anticipation as his tongue darted and played, plundered and danced with hers.

She welcomed him, tasting and touching as passion ruled her soul. Her arms wound around his neck, and her breasts, deep within her chemise ached for his touch.

"Oh, woman, what am I to do with you?" he said on a sigh.

Anything and everything crossed her mind, but she held back the words and kissed him until she was breathless.

With a moan, he dragged her closer. One callused hand lifted her leg to his waist and already melting inside, she felt his manhood pressed hard against her mound.

Don't do this Gwynn. Think! Consider Gareth! Remember that you are another man's wife! Know that nothing good will come of lying with the thief. And yet she was unable to stop herself. Her hands explored muscles as corded as thick rope, an abdomen as hard as a shield, chest hair coarser and springy to her touch.

He groaned against her ear as his weight dragged them both downward to topple onto his bed. Firelight played upon the angles of his face, accentuated the scars crossing his shoulders and back, and sparkled in his hair and eyes.

Lying atop her he kissed her eyes, her throat, her cheeks. "Ah, Gwynn," he whispered, his breath whispering across her body. " 'Tis beautiful you are." He kissed her breasts, first one, then the other, through the lace of her chemise until the fabric was so wet it was sheer against her skin. Tongue, lips, and teeth caressed her. Hot. Wet. Hard. She moved against him, wanting more as desire pulsed wildly through her. Faster. Hotter.

"You be so sweet, a temptress, to be sure," he said as he rimmed her nipple, so dark against the fine lace, with his tongue. Licks of desire swept through her, tingling her skin and creating a moist yearning deep in the most feminine part of her soul.

"And you . . . you be a smooth-tongued rogue."

"A rogue is what you want, Lady Gwynn." He lifted his head and stared at her with eyes a dusky shade of blue. "Say it."

"Nay, I—"

He kissed her nipple again, drawing hard, suckling as if he were but a babe. "Say it," he whispered across the breast.

"Nay."

"Oh, woman." He lifted the hem of her chemise and as he found her lips with his mouth, he discovered the rest of her with one strong hand. Fingers touched and probed and heat spiraled deep in her moist, intimate cavern. Sweat slid down her spine and she began to move, the wanting deep within her urgent and untamed. "Tell me you want me."

She licked her lips and he groaned before kissing her again. His hand moved. She bucked upward. He caught her and slowly let her down again. Her breath stopped in the back of her throat as he touched her in a spot that sent tingles through her body. As firelight turned his skin a deep shade of gold, she nodded. "Aye, thief, I want you."

"And I want you, love," he admitted with a scowl. "More than I've ever wanted a woman. 'Tis cursed I be with the want of you and I fear I'll be forever damned."

With one strong hand, he yanked the chemise over her head and settled his length to hers. Hard muscles collided with her softer flesh and the torment in his eyes faded. "The devil take tomorrow, may this night last forever," he whispered as he kissed her again and while holding her close, parted her knees with his. Gwynn stared up at him as he touched her with his manhood, gently prodding, not quite delving deep, causing her to lift up her hips.

Perspiration dotted her body. Need burned bright at her core. Still he teased, just gently nudging, but not quite entering as she writhed with the want of him.

"Trevin . . ." Her voice was but a desperate whisper. "Trevin . . . please," she begged, hating the sound.

"For you, love." With a single thrust he drove into her. Her heart pumped. Her lungs burned. The walls of the castle seemed to shift. He withdrew slowly only to plunge into her again. "Trevin!" Her fingernails dug into his shoulders and she moved with him. Slowly at first, then faster and faster, until she couldn't breathe, didn't think, was lost in the wonder of making love to him.

The years spun away and she was giving him her virginity once again, rising to meet him, whispering his name, holding on to him as if he were the only man in this world.

"Gwynn . . . Gwynn . . . Faith . . . forgive me . . ."

With a triumphant cry that shook the battlements and echoed through her heart, their souls collided and they were joined as if forever. His seed spilled into her and though she was married to another man, she knew in her heart that this thief, who had won his castle in a crooked game of chance, was the only man she would ever truly love. Even though as he'd loved her, he'd cried out his dead wife's name.

Chapter Ten

The embers of the fire had burned to naught when Trevin slipped quietly from beneath the covers. Gwynn rolled over and sighed softly. He froze, expecting her eyes to flutter open but she began breathing in a gentle rhythm again. His heart ached at the sight of her, asleep and innocent in his bed, her hair tangled and falling in red-brown ringlets over her smooth, bare shoulders. Thoughts of their recent loving—hot and wild and sinful—seared through his brain and it was all he could do not to take her into his arms again.

He'd only feigned sleep and as she'd snuggled against him, her naked body nestling to his, he'd struggled to stay awake and let her sleep, for he was determined to leave her.

He resisted the urge to bend down and kiss her forehead, or climb back into his bed and love her thoroughly again. But there was no time and before he left the keep, as was his custom, he had one more duty to accomplish.

Without donning his clothes he unlocked the door and slipped out of his chamber into the cold of the hallway. Quickly he ducked into another room where, without any noise, he threw on his tunic, breeches, mantle, and boots. As quietly as a cat stalking prey he hurried down the dark stairs.

Outside there was muted activity in the bailey. Armor, food staples, and tents were already packed into carts. Oxen were being yoked and some horses had been saddled and stood nervously waiting, their breaths fogging in the cold night air. Seven of Trevin's most trusted men were riding with him while Sir Bently, who was still recovering from a nasty wound received on a hunt for a wild boar, would stay at the castle and keep his eyes on Gwynn. It was Bently's distasteful duty to restrain the lady and keep her safely within Black Oak's walls. Trevin didn't envy the man his task.

Several of his men had collected near the stables, choosing their mounts and checking saddles, bridles, and weapons.

"All is nearly ready," Sir Stephen said. He thumbed the edge of his sword to test its sharpness. The blade glistened pure silver in the moonlight.

"I will be but a moment."

"Take yer time," Sir York said, yawning. A big man with a blond beard and round belly, he was tightening the cinch of his mount's saddle and was in no hurry to leave the comforts of the castle.

Trevin ducked behind the stables, through the outer bailey and motioned for the guard to open the gate. Rattling and clanging, the portcullis was raised. Trevin walked briskly up a well-worn path leading to the cemetery where pale white tombstones and wooden crosses marked the graves. His footsteps didn't falter as he wound his way to Faith and baby Alison's grave.

Pain tore at his heart and guilt, as always blackened his soul. He knelt on the damp moss and grass and closed his eyes. How had he come to this? From thief to outlaw to ignoble baron? Half the people under his rule thought him a savior, the rest considered him a demon who had heartlessly stolen an old man's castle, then killed him, and married his only daughter.

Pride kept his backbone stiff, fury clenched his fists, and remorse tightened his jaw.

He envisioned Faith as he'd last seen her, weary and in pain, still holding a babe that had been dead for two days. "Do not love another," she'd begged, agony showing in her eyes. "Trevin, please do me not the dishonor." She'd clutched at his arm, tears drizzling down her hollow cheeks. "I loved you. Dear God, how I loved you. Please . . ." She'd coughed and choked and he'd drawn her into the circle of his arms. "Vow to me, Trevin, that you'll never love another woman. Swear it."

"I swear. On my life, Faith. I will never love another."

He'd believed those words. Had known deep in his heart that he wasn't lying. But now, Gwynn of Rhydd had caused him to doubt all that he'd held true. He swallowed against a throat clogged with emotions he'd tried to bury.

"Forgive me," he said, as if his dead wife and child could hear him. "I . . . I tried, and . . . I failed. Both of you." His throat worked as he thought of his only daughter, born without taking a breath and the woman who had given her life to bear him an heir. "I am but a man, Faith," and the admission tore at his soul, for he'd betrayed her and the vow he'd made. "I did love you, you know," he said, glancing up at the moon and shaking his head at his own folly. "I just didn't know it until you were taken from me."

He thought of those dark days after her death, the loneliness and regret that had shredded his heart, the pain in his soul for the child who he would never swing in his arms or let ride upon his shoulders. He'd never known Alison, but he missed her sorely and it was her death that had led him on his quest to find his son. He would not lose another.

"I did not mean to lie to you," he said to Faith. "I never meant to love another woman, I thought I was incapable, but . . ." He let his words drift away on the breeze. Did he love Gwynn? Was it possible? Or was he confusing love and lust?

Reaching into the pocket of his mantle, he found the small pouch he'd put there days before. He untied the little purse and shook its contents into his palm. The ruby ring winked darkly in the night. "Curse you," he said, examining the jewel that he'd had with him all these years. Why? He'd told himself that he'd kept the ring for luck, that it was a symbol of his freedom for the coin and jewels Gwynn had given him so many years before. It had given him the means to ascend from lowly stable hand and thief to knight and eventually Lord of Black Oak Hall.

A station he regretted.

His fingers wrapped around the cold, heartless stone and wondered at the course of his destiny. "I miss you, Faith," he admitted, for the first time, since her death. "But I cannot live a lie."

So what was the truth? That he loved Lady Gwynn of Rhydd? His jaw hardened and he dropped the stone into its pouch. No. For the rest of his days he would love no one, not even the beautiful mistress of Castle Rhydd. Their lives seemed forever entwined because of Gareth, but he would not be foolish to lose his heart to the woman.

He slipped the pouch into his pocket and glanced at the black sky where the moon and stars shone bright. A breath of cold wind, as ancient as time, touched his cheeks. It was time. Renewed of purpose, he strode back to the castle. His new mount, Dark One, Sir Webb's charger, was waiting impatiently for him, pawing the damp ground, sidestepping whenever anyone came close to him.

Trevin touched the horse's quivering hide. With a grim smile he silently gave the signal for his small band to ride out, away from Black Oak Hall and toward Rhydd to find his son.

Casting one final glance over his shoulder to the keep where Gwynn was sleeping soundly, he felt another needle of guilt pricking deep into his soul. He'd tricked her, but then, hadn't she schemed to do just the same to him? Hadn't she been lurking in his chamber, eavesdropping on his plan to rescue Gareth? She deserved to be held captive for a few days.

After all, 'twas for her own good.

"Shh!" Gareth whispered into Boon's cocked ear. " 'Tis soon we'll both be able to feed our faces." Forlornly the little pup whimpered. Gareth's own stomach rumbled from lack of food and his legs ached from trudging for hours upon the deserted road. His last ride, on the back of a farmer's wagon, had been long ago and not for the first time did Gareth give himself a hearty mental shake that he'd left old Muir's horse back at the tavern. He'd been scared to the point of losing all the spit in his mouth and that explained why he'd run so fast and far.

It couldn't be because he was a coward. Not him. Or was it so? Doubts crowded through his mind that was already filled with guilt and remorse. Oh, what a selfish brat he'd been. If given one more chance to make amends with a mother who had spent all her life caring for him, he would take it. He thought of the times he'd crossed her, lied to her, sneaked out of the castle, and scared her out of her wits.

But he'd make it up to her. He would. If he just got the chance.

He should have flung himself into the fray at the tavern and tried to save the magician. Instead he'd fled like a fearful old woman. Well, he'd surprise them all, he thought as he carried the pup toward Rhydd. He hoped to be within a mile of the castle by dawn, sleep most of the day away in a hiding spot near the creek, then sneak into the castle just as the sun was setting and the guard was changing. He had enough friends within the castle walls to protect him until he found a way to save the old man. Surely Tom would aid him, and Alfred, the hound master and . . . well, there were sure to be others. Aye, his plan would work and he would avenge himself. He had to.

"I'll run old Ian through," he boasted to the pup though he didn't feel quite as sure of himself as he sounded. Even with a silver cast of moonglow, the forest was spooky. Leafless trees raised their spindly, crooked arms to the heavens and bracken and berry vines, lifeless and skeletal, hid all manner of creatures that he felt watching him with nervous eyes. As for killing a man, he'd done that once and felt not a speck of satisfaction for taking another's life. 'Twas not noble.

Again his stomach rumbled. Oh, to have a joint from one of Jack, the cook's, fat pheasants, or a slice of sweet pie, or a sizzling sausage. Even pottage, which the peasants ate, would go far to easing the emptiness in Gareth's belly.

"We'll find something soon," he told the dog and knew he'd have to rob a farmer's henhouse once again for fresh eggs or chickens for poor Boon. Though Gareth had been able to pluck a few winter apples from the barren trees, the dog ate not the fruit and his ribs had begun to show. "When we get back to Rhydd, I promise you, you'll have the finest scraps from the lord's table." The pup, as if understanding, wiggled against him.

The night was clear, the air brisk, the forest silent. Gareth wondered of his mother—what had happened to her? And the old magician, was he already dead or held fast in one of Rhydd's dungeons? Trembling, Gareth pulled his mantle closer over his chest. He hoped there was still time to save Muir and for the first time in his twelve years, he wished he'd paid more attention and listened as his mother and old Idelle had cast spells or drawn runes in the mud. He could use all the help he could get, even if it came from pagan rites.

Soon he heard the rush of water and knew he was approaching the river that ran past the castle. His heartbeat quickened in time with the increased pace of his footsteps. *Rhydd.* 'Twas odd how he felt about the castle in which he'd grown up. He'd enjoyed living there as the son of the baron, but now that he was no longer blood kin to Roderick, knowing that his mother had deceived everyone in the keep as well as Gareth, he felt a desire to return to his home and quieter days. Though he could not.

He reminded himself that he was banished. Being found anywhere near the curtain walls would spell certain death. Ian, whom he'd thought of as an uncle for all his life, was a cruel, heartless man; the thought of the black-hearted bastard being wed to his mother caused a foul taste to crawl up his throat. To rid himself of it, Gareth spat and Boon let out an excited yip.

"Nay! Hush!"

The trees gave way to brush and Gareth paused. Situated on a hill, looming dark and foreboding, stood Rhydd. A fortress. The keep of a cruel interloper. The only place Gareth had ever called home.

Tomorrow he would render his own personal attack against the current baron. He would sneak past the guards and— He jumped as he felt the tip of a cold steel blade press against the back of his neck.

He dropped the dog.

Boon let out a disgruntled "woof" as he hit the ground.

Gareth nearly lost all the water in his bladder.

"Well, well, boy," a nasty male voice intoned. "Who are ye, or should I guess? Don't tell me now . . ."

Gareth reached for his dagger.

"I wouldn't." The point of the sword pricked his skin. He froze. "That's better. Now be a smart lad, will ye? There's still a chance ye might live, Gareth of Rhydd, but, 'tis a slim one, to be sure. I, for one, will not be wagerin' on yer miserable hide."

Bam! Bam! Bam!

Ian's head reverberated with the infernal pounding. Too much wine. That was it, he'd drunk far too much wine.

"Lord Ian!" Again the horrid racket.

"Go away!" he grumbled.

"But, m'lord—"

"Hush, man!" opening one eye slowly, he glared at the door to his chamber and tried to still the dull roar drumming through his brain. He wiped a hand over his face and stretched in his bed when he caught sight of the lovely wench lying, drunk, upon the covers of his bed. Her skin was white and flaw- less, her hair a fine flaxen hue, her eyes—now closed—wide and blue and she could ride a man half the night, but, by the saints, she wasn't as smart as the tired old gong farmer and the ox he used to pull his cart of manure from the bailey. She hadn't stirred throughout the racket.

The sentry wouldn't give up. "Lord Ian, if you please—"

"Bloody hell, what is it?" Ian demanded as he climbed from the bed, threw on a black robe that had once been his brother's, crossed the room in three swift, painful strides, and flung open the door.

"I hate to bother ye, me lord," the rail-thin sentry apologized, his Adam's apple working when he caught a glimpse of the girl on the bed. " 'Tis the boy—Lady Gwynn's son. One of the soldiers found him lurking in the woods and—"

"Where is he?" Ian demanded, his headache suddenly forgotten. He nearly smiled. Could it be that his luck had changed?

"Downstairs in the great hall—"

Ian wasn't listening. He shoved the man out of his way and flew down the curved stairs though his legs still pained him and the robe billowed behind him like a mainsail in a brisk wind.

Finally!

The object of all of his wretched searching and nightmares had, indeed, been captured and now stood shivering in front of the fire. The new captive held on to a pathetic dog as if to life itself and flinched whenever one of the guards touched him or tried to get him to move.

"Leave me alone, ye dirty curs," he growled, though Ian thought his bravado was forced. The boy was so scared he shook.

Nonetheless Gareth still seemed to have some fight left in him. All the bet- ter. Ian cinched the belt of his robe and couldn't help grinning. "Well, well, well, look what the cat dragged in."

" 'Twasn't a cat, but an ass who hauled me in here," Gareth shot back.

"Pretty harsh talk from the boy who killed the baron."

The brat had the audacity to lift his head and hold Ian's furious gaze with his own. Though the boy was dirty and skinny and held on to the damned dog as if he thought he could protect the wriggling little beast, the cocky little son of a bitch still acted as if *he* were lord of the castle.

"You're in trouble, boy."

Gareth didn't reply.

Sir Webb and another soldier, a weasly looking man with bad skin, guarded their young charge with their swords drawn, as if they thought the urchin had a chance at besting them or outrunning them.

"Where did you find him?" Ian crossed his arms over his chest and circled the bane of his existence. Oh, 'twas sweet pleasure to have finally caught another one of the traitors. First the magician, now the boy, next the thief? Or that Jezebel of a wife of his?

"Lurkin' about in the forest, 'e was, m'lord," the scarred-faced soldier replied. "He seemed interested in that sorcerer, prob'ly came back to try and free 'im."

Gareth's jaw tightened defiantly. Apparently the guard had guessed the boy's intent.

"I figured ye'd want to see 'im."

"That I do." Ian let himself have the satisfaction of a smile.

"What shall we do with him?" Sir Webb frowned at the boy as if Gareth had manifested himself as Lucifer.

"I'd say hang him in the morning, but that might not be wise."

"You'd better kill me quick," the whelp had the guts to say. His blue eyes flashed courageously and Ian couldn't help but feel a tad of respect for him. "Elsewise I'll hunt you down and run you through with your own sword!"

"Will you?" Ian laughed at the boy's ridiculous sense of nobility. "I don't think so."

To prove his point, Gareth spit on the rushes at Ian's feet.

"Bastard!" Webb backhanded the boy and sent him reeling against the wall. Gareth's head snapped. His bones crackled. The pup gave out a pained yelp and fell to the floor. Paws scrabbling, he ran to a table and cowered beneath it.

Blood drizzled from one corner of Gareth's mouth but he managed to stay on his feet as he wiped his lips with the back of his hand. Smiling, he spit again. This time the bloody wad landed on Webb's boots.

The dark knight grabbed him by the collar. "Listen, ye thankless little brat," Webb warned in a low whisper. "I'll gladly kill your dog, then, after ye watch him die, I'll tan his spotty hide and pick the meat from his bones."

Gareth turned a sick green color.

"Believe me, I wouldn't think twice about killin' ye as well. 'Twould do me heart good."

Gareth blanched but he met the soldier's harsh gaze with nary a glance away. "Rot in hell."

"Nay, son, that be yer privilege."

"Let him go," Ian ordered.

Webb, after a second's hesitation, released his grip on the boy.

Gareth stumbled backward a step and wiped the blood from the side of his face with the back of his hand. If looks could indeed kill, Sir Webb would have keeled over on the spot.

Turning his harsh gaze upon Ian, he asked, "Where's my mother?"

"Know you not?" Ian scowled. He'd hoped the boy would have information about where Gwynn was hiding.

"Nay, but I think you do." His blue eyes simmered with hate and for an insane second, Ian of Rhydd experienced dread. This boy was the son of the outlaw. "So tell me, 'uncle,' where is she?"

" 'Tis a good question." Ian's eyes met Webb's for a second and he shoved his hands deep into the pockets of the black robe.

"He was alone," Webb explained, his cohort nodding.

"Unfortunate." Ian's mind as already turning toward the future and how he would recover his wayward wife. "However, she'll come looking for him." He hooked a thumb in Gareth's direction. "Just as this one crawled back here for the magician, the lady will come searching for her son."

"Aye." Webb licked his lips and grinned wickedly. "See, boy, 'tis not so bad. You want to see your mother and she'll return for you. You be the bait."

But Ian's thoughts weren't finished. "McBain will no doubt join her," he thought aloud, bile climbing up his throat as he considered the slippery thief who had lain with Gwynn so many years before. "For some reason, he seems to have decided to claim the lad."

"Claim me?" Gareth repeated. "What mean you?" Obviously confused, he dabbed at his bloody lip with the edge of his sleeve.

"Oh, did you not know?" Ian asked with feigned innocence. He was only too glad to give the lad the bad news.

"Know what?" The boy was wary.

"That you, pretender to the throne of Rhydd, were spawned by a common thief?"

The boy shook his head. "Nay—"

"Oh 'tis true."

Horror dawned in the boy's blue eyes as he put the hidden pieces of his life together. "But my mother—she would not have—" He shook his head with surprising calm. "I'll listen to no more of your lies."

"Think on it, lad." Ian enjoyed watching the naive whelp's features twist in disgust as he considered the means of his conception.

"And you thought you were of noble birth, eh?" Webb added with a snort. "As fer yer mother, who knows what happened? Either she's a whoring slut who would spread her legs for the common man or she was compromised by the thief."

"Liar!" Gareth lunged, flinging himself at the knight, but Webb was ready. With a hefty shove, he heaved the kid onto the table and pressed his weight onto the boy. "Come on again, lad. I'll give ye more," he promised.

Gareth rolled to his side, his head hung over the edge of the table. He retched violently, his entire body convulsing. Had he anything in his stomach, Ian was certain he would have vomited the vile mass onto the rushes. As it was he clutched his guts and fought tears of indignation. "Nay," he said, over and over again. "Nay, nay, nay."

Straightening, Webb laughed wickedly and Ian suppressed his own urge to grin from ear to ear. At last his plan was beginning to work.

"You're a murderin' bastard," Gareth flung out recklessly.

"Careful, boy. Remember who was born with no sire," Ian said, then turned to Webb. "Take him down to the dungeon and make sure that everyone in the castle knows that he's being held until I decide when he'll go to the gallows."

Gareth paled.

"My pleasure."

"Oh, and see that a messenger is sent—nay, a traitor who is wounded, would be better—to Black Oak Hall with the news that Gareth of Rhydd is imprisoned here and sentenced to die." He slid the boy a glance. "That should send your mother running to save you, don't you think?"

"Go to hell."

Ian laughed. "You'll be there long before I arrive."

The lad straightened and sucked in his breath, but wouldn't give Ian the satisfaction of begging for his life. Instead he glowered at the lord of the castle as if Ian were but a useless insect he would like to squash beneath his boots. "I be not dead yet."

"Nor will you be until my wife returns."

"She is not—"

"Oh, yes, son. She is married to me. Legally. And she'll return. For you."

Gareth's eyes darkened in the same manner that did Trevin's of Black Oak. "And she will save me."

"Against all my men? I think not," Ian said but felt a premonition of dread crawl up his backside.

One corner of Gareth's mouth lifted into a hard, determined smile, another reminder of the thief. "Think again, for you know, she will punish you a thousand times over if any harm comes to me, Boon, or Muir."

"Oh, and how will she do so?"

" 'Twill be a simple matter," Gareth said, spitting blood onto the floor. "Remember, Lord Ian, she is more than a woman and much more than my mother."

"Is she?" Ian asked, bored with the conversation. His headache was returning and he had many more hours in bed with the wench, though she was as dull as one of Father Anthony's sermons. "We'll see."

"Aye, that you will."

"Take him away. He speaks nonsense." Ian stretched the muscles of his shoulders and considered a time when Gwynn would warm his bed. Oh, by the gods, then his revenge would be sweet.

"Be forewarned," Gareth said boldly as two guards slipped gloved hands beneath his armpits, dragging him forward while a third rounded up his dog. "My mother will not stand for this."

"What can she do about it?" Ian was tired of the boy's veiled threats.

"You don't want to know," Gareth warned, craning his head so that he could meet Ian's tired gaze. "But forget you not that she is a witch."

Ian shook his head and felt a weary sadness for the boy who believed so passionately in his mother. "Nay, child, Lady Gwynn is nothing more than a whore and a cheap one at that."

As soon as Gareth was out of earshot, Ian turned to Webb. "Now, see that one of the knights loyal to the lady, Sir Reynolds, mayhap . . . nay, Charles, Sir Charles would be the one. Make sure that he knows that Gareth is about to be hanged."

"Tonight?"

"Aye," Ian said, walking to his chair and staring into the dying coals of the fire. "Make a racket, talk about it, pretend that you are drunk, if it comes to that, but see that Charles awakes and hears the news. Then keep the castle gates open and follow him. 'Tis my guess he will ride to Black Oak Hall."

"You want me to sneak into the castle," Webb said, his eyes lighting with a gleam of satisfaction.

"Nay. Follow him closely so that you see where he goes, then wound him so that the lady and thief understand that the boy's plight is serious."

"Gladly."

Ian held up a hand. "But kill him not. He must get the message through."

"Aye, my arrow flies true. I will be able to give him a mortal wound that will sap out his life slowly."

"You were supposed to kill the boy before and make it look as if you were wounded yourself, yet you failed me."

" 'Twill not happen again," Webb vowed, sliding his jaw to one side. "I rarely fail."

"See that you don't."

Webb rubbed his beard, creating a scraping sound that irritated Ian. "Are you sure you do not want me to follow Charles and kill not only him but the others as well?"

Ian shook his head. "Death will come to those who deserve it," he said, "but I want to face my wife and the thief first." His muscles tensed as he considered them together. They had been lovers in the past and, he suspected, were again. "My justice will be slow and damning," he said, savoring the words. "Trevin of Black Oak will die knowing who it was that killed him."

* * *

Gwynn stretched languidly on the bed, memories of making love to Trevin still weaving in warm, sensual ribbons through her mind. Ah, 'twas sweet heaven to lie with him. Smiling, she slowly opened her eyes and reached out a hand to touch his warm body, only to have her empty fingers stretch and touch the cold far side of the bed.

Her eyes flew open and she sat bolt upright.

She was alone.

The bed was empty save for her.

Cold certainty settled into her heart, for she knew as surely as the sun would rise again that Trevin had duped her.

The fire had died and the lord of Black Oak's chamber was cold as a cistern.

"Oh, for the love of Mary." She pounded a fist against the covers, for she'd been played for a fool. He'd left Black Oak just as he'd planned. Without her.

"Thieving, black-hearted, son of a dog!" she muttered as if he could hear her. She threw off the blankets. While she'd been caught up in the rapture of making love to him, he'd used her, over and over again, until she, spent, had fallen asleep in his arms.

Oh, what a ninny she was. To forget her fears concerning Gareth, to wash away her worries of Ian, she'd let herself be caught in the sweet seduction of the outlaw. "Stupid, stupid girl!" she chastised as, shivering, she flung on her clothes—well, Faith's clothes—then quickly finger-combed her hair and used water from a basin placed near the now-cold grate to splash over her face. Angrily she shoved open the door to the corridor half expecting a guard to place himself in front of her and order her back into the room, but the hallway was empty.

Good. She'd not be held prisoner; not by any man and least of all by Trevin of Black Oak. The nerve of the man seducing her, luring her into bed, then tempting her with sleep.

Was it any different from how you treated him in years long past?

Stomping her foot in frustration, she startled a cat that scurried out of her way. She was down the stairs in a matter of minutes and stopped in her own chamber where her boots and cloak were waiting. She didn't have time to change into her own clothes, lying clean and dry upon the end of the bed, but she searched for her weapon, the dagger in which she placed so much trust and discovered it, along with her pouch filled with the herbs, berries, and roots she'd gathered for the casting of spells, missing.

"Curse and rot your wretched hide, Trevin McBain," she muttered as she tossed her cloak over her head. Still lacing the mantle, she made her way downstairs and hoped beyond useless hope that she had misjudged him and that Trevin was still in the castle, that she had jumped to the wrong conclusion. Mayhap he was in treasury checking the keep's records, or eating a mid-morning meal in the great hall, or walking through the bailey discussing supplies or repairs or the selling of oxen with the steward.

Aye, and mayhap you be a simpleton!

In the great hall, pages were setting the tables onto their legs and dragging benches into place. The cook was shouting orders, and servants darted through the hallways and up the stairs.

Gwynn ignored them all and nearly ran into the priest near the courtyard door. "Oh, Father Paul," she said, quickly crossing herself. "Could you tell me where Lord Trevin is?"

"The baron? Did he not tell you?" Paul's graying eyebrows became one and his lips stretched over his gums. "I believe—yes, I'm sure that the steward told me—the baron was leaving this morn with a band of soldiers—his best. Was he not searching for your son?"

"Yes . . . yes, I think so," she said, angry all over again, though she attempted to hide her true feelings. "He has already departed?"

"I know not," the man admitted. "I only assumed—"

"Aye," she said, turning to the door. There was a chance that she could catch up with him.

"We should pray for their safe return."

"Of course."

The priest brightened. "Good. I'll see you in the chapel and there will be no more of this talk"—he fluttered his fingers nervously—"of devil worship."

"What?"

He leaned closer to her, as if he expected the very walls to hear his next words. "There is no reason to deny it, m'lady. 'Tis said that you practice the dark arts."

"Nay," she said quickly. "I am but a Christian woman, who prays to our Father as well as enjoys the gifts of the earth He gives us." There was no reason to explain to this man of the cloth that her spells and runes were but another means of trying to save her son, that she would attempt anything, aye, even bargain with the devil himself, if 'twould keep Gareth from harm. "Peace be with you." She reached for the handle of the door.

"Oh, there ye be, m'lady!" Hildy's voice preceded the rustle of her skirts as she hurried down the stairs. "Good mornin' to ye, Father Paul," she added crossing herself with the speed of a lizard scurrying to the safety of tall grass. "Lord Trevin said that I am to be yer maid and I fear I've failed ye as I've been tendin' to the dye vats this morn." She held up her hands and showed that the flesh on one arm had turned a bright shade of blue. "I splashed a bit as I was turnin' the cloth and old Mary, she was passin' by and told me to get back to me task. As if she can order anyone around," Hildy sniffed. "She's but a butcher's wife and has not the skill or patience for the dying of wool."

Gwynn had not time for the little maid's prattle, but she was trapped.

" 'Tis of no matter," Father Paul said, waving away Hildy's wounded pride with a flip of his pious wrist. "You must tend to your own business, which is, as you say, attending to the lady."

"I need not a maid," Gwynn argued as precious seconds ticked by.

"But Lord Trevin said—"

"I don't care what he said," Gwynn cut in.

"No, of course not, m'lady, I didn't mean to say that—"

"Do not worry yourself." Gwynn managed a smile for both priest and maid. "I will let you know when I need your services, until then you can go back to the dye vats or whatever other task is yours."

Leaving Hildy standing with her mouth agape and the priest gently shaking his head as if he saw within the mistress of Rhydd the very vestige of evil, Gwynn gathered her skirts and made her way outside.

Sunlight danced over the bailey. Geese honked loudly, flapping their great wings as they scattered by a pond where boys were busy trying to catch toads. Other, older youths hauled sloshing buckets of water from the well to the kitchen while girls, giggling and laughing, collected eggs in baskets or gutted fish in a trough near the kitchen door.

"Hurry, ye wretched snails!" the cook hollered. "I can't be boilin' pottage without water, now, can I?"

Gwynn ducked down an alley behind the kitchen where the scents of smoke and drying herbs vied with the warm odors of baking bread and the sizzle of venison. Two women were separating milk from cream while another milked a cud-chewing spotted cow.

Around the corner she dashed, her heart in her throat, her eyes searching the bailey, but nowhere did she see Trevin. *Face it, Gwynn, he used you.* Pure and simple.

She passed the garden and spied the stables at the far side of the inner bailey.

"Hey! Not now!" the candlemaker yelled at boys lugging pails of animal fat into his hut. "By the gods I've got no more room fer it this morn . . . oh, put it in the corner and be off with ye."

Clutching her cloak more tightly around her throat, she made her way to the stables where she surveyed the horses and with a sinking sensation realized that not only was Sir Webb's charger missing, but the horse she'd ridden—Trevin's steed—as well. Blast the man! He'd tricked her rather than the other way around as she'd planned. Well, she wouldn't stand for it and as she eyed the horses in the stables and those who were penned in the outer bailey, she mentally chose which one she would steal, a fiery-tempered dappled animal who appeared sound and swift.

Now all she needed was a little help to make good her escape and that 'twould be a simple matter.

But first she planned visits to the apothecary, the kitchen, the armorer, and finally the candle maker to replace the items Trevin had stripped from her. 'Twould take a little time, but she would soon be off to find her son.

She rounded a corner and nearly ran over the hefty knight known as Bently. "Oh."

"M'lady," he said, favoring his right arm that was in a sling from some hunting injury. "I've been looking for you."

"Have you?" The worry lining his brow gave her pause. "What can I do for you?"

" 'Tis my duty and my pleasure to be your personal guard."

"My what?" she asked, smelling a trick.

Two youths—a boy and girl—rolled a hoop as they raced by. Laughing, they yelled and hollered as they ran past and a dog dashed yapping at their heels.

"Your guard, m'lady."

"I need not someone to watch over me." Quiet fury seeped through her veins.

"The baron, he asked me, to—"

"Do not trouble yourself, Sir Bently. As Lord Trevin must have told you I ruled a castle by myself. Now, if you'll excuse me—" She bunched her skirts, but the man was persistent and wouldn't be deterred.

"I cannot. 'Tis my obligation to be with you and protect you."

"While I'm inside the castle?" she asked, wanting to strangle the man who had so recently loved her.

"Aye."

"And if I choose to go out?"

His gaze shifted away for a second before returning to hers. "The baron, he thinks it would be safer for you to stay inside."

"Does he? But that's impossible."

"Nay, m'lady, 'tis the way it must be."

He actually had the decency to look sorry, but Gwynn, anger invading her blood, wasn't fooled so easily this time. She sensed that he was a man who could not be moved. His mission was to see to her safety and she didn't doubt that he intended to do just that. She had no option but to pretend to agree.

"Fine, Sir Bently, though I like it not. I will wait until the baron returns and take up my, what would you call it, not my imprisonment or captivity, surely"—

the guard winced a little—"but mayhap we'll refer to it as Lord Trevin's questionable hospitality."

"Thank you," he said and his eyes told her he didn't believe her entirely.
She would have to be patient and time, she feared, was running short.

" 'Tis nearly time for a meal and Cook's outdone himself again."

"Good." She forced a smile though it pained her. "If I might change into a suitable dress—"

"Surely, Lady Gwynn."

"But you'll stand guard at my door?"

He was solemn as death. "Aye. As the lord ordered."

"Then, Sir Bently, let us not tarry," she said, sidestepping a puddle and eyeing the gate where the portcullis was open, but soldiers watched those who entered and departed with ever-sharp eyes. Damn that black-hearted McBain! When she caught up with him, Gwynn silently pledged, he would rue the day he thought he could outsmart her.

Chapter Eleven

"Why did you not tell me?" a voice in his dreams asked.

Muir snorted and turned over, then felt young fingers gripping his shoulders and digging into his old muscles.

"Wake up, would you?"

Muir stirred, his body aching. Who was bothering him? Slowly he opened his good eye to stare into the face of Gareth of Rhydd. His heart stopped for a second. By the gods, would nothing go as it should? "What the devil are ye doin' here?"

"A better question would be how did a magician let himself get caught and thrown into a dungeon?" the lad asked, eyeing his surroundings and shaking his head at the dark, damp interior of the prison.

"There are some things, boy, ye do not know about my magic," Muir grumbled.

"There seem to be things *you* do not know. It appears to get you into more trouble than it rids you of."

Muir stretched and felt his spine pop. Ach, what he would give for a pint. "Have ye not heard that patience is a virtue?"

"Patience?" the boy repeated, kicking at the filthy straw and sending an old piece of bone scuttling across the floor. "How can anyone be patient while rotting away in a prison?" He turned suspicious eyes on the old man and added, "Asides, *magician,* you lied to me."

"I tell only what is true."

"Then who is my father?"

Muir opened his mouth and shut it again.

"Is he Trevin of Black Oak?"

So the truth was out and the cursed prophesy was starting to reveal itself.

"Hey, quiet down!" the guard grumbled from the chair where he had been dozing. Other prisoners glared at Gareth from their cells, but said not a word as the argument continued.

"Can you not speak, eh?" Gareth whispered. He paced from one end of the small cell to the other. "Why did you not tell me that the thief and . . ."

"Killer? Is that what's troubling ye, boy. Listen to me, Lord Trevin murdered not anyone including Dryw of Black Oak. Hear not idle gossip, Gareth, lest you become the subject of wagging tongues."

"Oh, and you be a good one to talk." Gareth flung his hands upward as if in supplication. "You lied."

"To protect you."

"Little good it did."

"Because you returned," Muir guessed.

"Aye, I was an idiot."

Muir liked the boy despite all his impudence. "So ye came back to save me, did ye?"

"Yeah, as I said, a fool I be."

"And an insolent pup who is feeling sorry for himself."

Gareth sniffed and rubbed his nose with his dirty arm. There was blood on his chin and anger burning bright in his eyes. "They have Boon, too. Sir Webb plans to kill him."

"Oh, for the love of Saint Peter. Sir Webb won't harm the pup," Muir said, seeing that the boy was truly disturbed. "As for us, we'll be free soon enough." He cleared his throat and fastened his good eye on the sentry. "Fear not, for I will get us out of here."

Gareth rolled his eyes. "Oh, so now that I am here, you can suddenly make iron bars bend and stone walls disappear."

"Aye, in a manner of speaking." Muir couldn't help but smile as he thought of the little knife still tucked into his secret pocket. "Truth to tell," he boasted, "I can do even better."

"Can you now?" the boy scoffed, clearly disbelieving.

"Have a little faith, Gareth. We will be out of here afore too long."

"One minute is too long." Clearly the boy had no trust and Muir, despite his bold words, didn't blame him.

" 'Twill be me 'ead if Mary finds out I went against the lord's wishes." Hildy placed a basket of eggs on the edge of the bed in Gwynn's chamber.

"By bringing me these?" Gwynn asked, raising an eyebrow. She had no time for the maid with her silly superstitions. Sir Bently had been her shadow and she had to find a way to detain him as she carried out her plan.

"Not the eggs, m'lady." Hildy quickly scanned the room with her eyes as if she expected to find someone, mayhap one of her ghosts, to be hiding in the corners. Satisfied that she and Gwynn were truly alone, the girl lifted a few speckled eggs from the basket and moved the linen liner. Hidden beneath the cloth were the herbs and dagger that had been taken from Gwynn's chamber. "I thought ye might need these . . . fer the spell."

Gwynn was surprised at the simple lass's ingenuity.

Proudly Hildy lifted her chin. "Lord Trevin, he ordered all yer weapons taken and Mary—ye know which she is, the fat 'un who s'psed to be 'elpin' 'er 'usband with the butcherin' but she's got 'er big nose in everyone's business, that she does, thinks she can tell us all what to do. Well, anyway, she told me to take away anything of yours that might 'ave to do with the devil and the castin' of spells. Was after me like a 'ound on a wounded rabbit, so to get her off me back, I stole yer things, gave them to Mary, then, when she wasn't lookin', swiped 'em back again."

Gwynn couldn't believe her good luck. "Won't she ask you for them?"

Hildy grinned. "Not fer a while. She thinks me a silly girl without a brain in me noggin and I, I lets her think whatever she wants. 'Tis easier that way. Right now she suspects her own boy Elwin of doin' the deed. " 'E's a mean one, Elwin is, always givin' 'er trouble."

"I see," Gwynn said, less interested in the snits of the peasants and servants than she was of her own plight.

" 'Tis important that ye get rid of the curse on this keep and I wasn't about to let old Mary thwart ye."

"Good thinking," Gwynn said, but her own thoughts were running ahead to her escape. If Hildy were more clever than she first guessed, Gwynn would have to tread cautiously. "Now, with these things you've returned to me and a few more I bartered from the apothecary and candle maker, I think I've got all I need. But, we have to have privacy and, 'tis best for the kind of spell you want cast to be done in the forest."

"The woods?"

"Aye. 'Tis more likely Morrigu and Owein Ap Urien will hear us if we be in the solace of the forest, especially if we are close to water." She lowered her eyes and added a small lie to enlist Hildy's help. "Asides, you told me of the ghosts that walk the walls of Black Oak. We needs to be far from the castle walls if we are to keep the ghosts from interfering with our spells."

"Oh." Hildy nodded and bit her lower lip, as if she believed every word. "But if Lord Trevin finds out that I helped ye . . ."

"Do not worry about him. I will see to the baron. You only needs worry about Sir Bently, Mary, and the rest of the servants who might notice my leaving. I have a plan."

"A plan?" Hildy's eyes narrowed suspiciously.

How much could she trust this girl? After all, despite her worries for her unborn child, Hildy was loyal to Black Oak. But time was fleeting by and Gwynn had to hurry if she were to catch up to Trevin.

"If I am to save your babe and the unborn of others in this castle, I must cast my spell while the ghosts and demons of this castle sleep, while the sun is high."

Hildy nodded her head but didn't seem convinced.

"Lifting a curse is not an easy task."

"Nay, I s'pose not."

"So I will need your help while I steal one of the baron's horses."

Hildy's mouth rounded and her eyes widened. Again she glanced nervously over her shoulder. "Oh, no. 'Tis one thing to dupe Mary about a few 'erbs and weapons that weren't 'ers to begin with, but steal from Baron Trevin . . . I cannot."

" 'Twill save his castle from the dark powers you say reside here."

"I know . . ." Hildy rubbed her lips nervously with the tips of her fingers. "But—"

"And 'twill save your child."

Again the girl hesitated and her forehead wrinkled. Absently she touched her flat abdomen. "Could . . . could ye also ask that a man fall in love with me and give me babe a name?"

"Which man?"

"Why the babe's father. Sir 'Enry."

Henry? The young knight with shaggy brown hair and sad, distrustful eyes. He was Hildy's lover? Gwynn had seen him only once and thought him a pitiful excuse for a knight, couldn't understand Trevin's faith in the boy, but now, she had no time to argue. "Consider it done," Gwynn agreed impatiently, "as long as you allow me the time to get away from Sir Bently."

"And steal a horse. Oh, m'lady, 'tis mad ye be."

Gwynn ignored Hildy's worries. "Are you with me?"

The girl hesitated, then nodded. "I'll do what I can."

"Good." Gwynn breathed a sigh of relief. She was anxious to get on with her plan for as the minutes passed, Trevin was getting farther from this castle in the search for their child.

One way or another, she intended to join him.

"We'll camp here for the night." Trevin swung off Dark One at the edge of a river that cut swiftly through the deep hills. A clearing at the edge of the forest would provide room for the tents as well as accommodate the ox cart. His horse waded into the shallows, lowered his head, and drank.

The men who rode with him dismounted while Sir York, driving the lumbering spotted ox, found a place to leave the cart. As he unharnessed the beast, Trevin watched his men work together. Ralph and Henry would take their bows and quivers in the search for fresh meat. Stephen and York would set up camp. Winston would tend to the horses while Nelson stood guard and Gerald scouted the road between the camp and Rhydd.

Everything was in place, so why did he feel so restless, as if something was amiss? His muscles were tense, his teeth on edge, but there was no cause for his worries. The supplies were plenty, the weapons strong, the animals and men healthy and yet . . . he felt anxious and sensed that there was danger. Mayhap that was why he had not shared his plans with his men.

Or mayhap it's the Mistress of Rhydd who vexes you. He plucked a reed from the water's edge and chewed upon it as he watched the men moving quickly about their tasks, but he was distracted with memories of Gwynn lying warm and naked in his arms.

Deciding that he was borrowing trouble, he helped in pitching the tents and watering and feeding the ox and horses and pushed all wayward thoughts of Gwynn aside.

Henry, the least capable of the lot, returned with three rabbits, which they skinned and gutted, then roasted over the fire. Gerald hadn't returned by the time the meat was roasted and again Trevin, as they sat near the fire and picked at the meat, felt a niggle of distress. He sliced a loaf of bread all the while searching the shadows, listening over the roar of the river for the sound of hooves.

"He should be back," Ralph said, as if reading Trevin's thoughts. A thoughtful man, he was prone to worrying. "Gerald. What takes him so long?" He bit into a shank of rabbit.

"Mayhap he ran into Ian's men," York remarked.

"Nay, he'll be here." Stephen skewered a piece of meat with the tip of his knife, then slid it between his teeth. "Have patience."

"On this fool's mission?" Henry scoffed. He shook his shaggy head and watched sparks rise to the heavens. "If ye ask me we all be lucky to be alive."

"Well, nobody's askin'," York said and several men chuckled.

Henry raised a pious eyebrow. "Wait and see," he warned softly. "I go now to pray."

"Good. Take yer time." York shook his head as Henry ducked into the woods. " 'E takes this life far too seriously."

"He's young," Trevin said.

"And green. Why 'e comes with us, ah, well, m'lord, 'tis your battle."

Trevin shook his head and took the jug. "Nay, 'tis all our fight. We all have reason to distrust Rhydd and the baron who rules there."

"Amen," York agreed.

"Aye. To Ian's death!" Winston muttered. "He and that dog of his, Sir Webb."

Ralph snorted, "Death to them all."

Trevin lifted the jug to his lips and swallowed. The hearty ale seared a path down his throat to settle like fire in his belly. He passed the jug to Ralph, then wiped his mouth with the back of his hand.

The men joked and grumbled, laughed and continued to pass the jug. Henry returned and several others took their leave to relieve themselves. There was a bit of discord, but they seemed well suited.

"I'll take first watch," he said when the jug was empty, bellies filled, and the fire burned low.

"Nay, m'lord, 'tis my duty," Nelson insisted.

Trevin agreed and slept uneasily, tossing and turning on his pallet, worrying for Gwynn and Gareth and wondering if he was able to help them. Near dawn he heard the hoofbeats, hard and steady, pounding through the forest.

"Who goes—" Nelson demanded as Trevin stepped out of his tent.

Breathing hard, lathered and covered in mud, Gerald's horse raced into the camp only to skid to a stop. " 'Tis bad news I bear," Gerald said as he swung from his saddle and Nelson grabbed the reins of his charger. "Trouble on the road." He was gasping for breath, his face splattered with dirt.

"What trouble?" Trevin demanded.

"I was on my way to Castle Rhydd when I spied a knight, his tunic stained scarlet with blood, riding the opposite direction, toward Black Oak. An arrow was lodged deep in his shoulder and another in the beast's flank. I called to him, but he heard me not and clung to the saddle for fear of toppling over. I know not who he is but he wore the colors of Rhydd and was kicking the horse like a wild man, so that the animal would continue to run."

Trevin scowled. "And then?"

"I rode back here as fast as the horse could run. I know not what happened, m'lord, but I fear we may be walking into a trap."

The worries that had been with Trevin since the onset of his mission turned darker and more dangerous. They were but one day's ride to Rhydd, and two days to Black Oak. He rubbed the tension from his muscles as the sun began to rise. "Stay here," he told the small band of men. "Wait for me. I'll be back and we'll continue our journey."

"Where are you going?" Stephen asked, rubbing his eyes as he stretched out of one of the tents.

Trevin had walked to the line where the horses were tied and found the reins of Dark One. "I know not, but I'll be back."

"And if you're not?" Henry asked, his dark eyes suspicious.

"Return to Black Oak in three days. Until then, wait." He threw the saddle on his stallion's back, then sent up a prayer for Gwynn and Gareth's safety. Fear threatened his soul, but he pushed it far away.

Neither Gwynn nor her son would come to harm. He would see to it.

And what if you fail? His mind teased as he tightened the cinch, then climbed astride. He wouldn't. He would save his son and the woman who bore him or die trying.

"Y're sure this was your father's best horse?" Orwin, the stable master of Black Oak, was short and squat, an ox of a man with dull little eyes sunk deep into his head and arms as big as hams. The beast in question was running in circles on a tether that Orwin held in one meaty hand. With his other he snapped a whip and the horse clipped from a walk into a trot.

A boy of about six or seven watched the horse being put through his paces and nodded at the question. "Aye, this one, Paddy, he be a good horse. Pulled me dad's wagon, he did."

Hildy and Gwynn approached, staying close to the stables and away from the bite of the whip and the blast of wind that blew across the short grass of the bailey and brought the first clouds of the day. Gwynn was at her wit's end. It had been two days since Trevin had left and there had been not a chance for her to escape, nor the means.

"You know, yer mother, she's supposed to give the baron the best animal ye've got for heriot."

" 'Tis a bad tax, me ma says."

"But the law."

The boy, pigeon-toed and plain, nodded, though Gwynn decided he knew nothing of taxes or laws or heriot. All he understood was that his dad was gone and now the lord, the thieving, murdering lord of Black Oak, was taking his mother's best horse. Gwynn felt more than a second's misgiving. The boy's mother was right. Heriot was a bad tax. "Paddy here"—the lad said, motioning to the sickly looking nag—"was me dad's mount."

"Humph." Orwin, turning and keeping the leash taut, clucked and the animal reluctantly increased his stride into an uneven canter. "I'll have to see the rest of his horses. There, ye be, ye old nag." He slowed the animal to a walk and finally to a full stop. With practiced hands he examined the horse, running fingers along the gelding's back, then carefully prying open his mouth. "Tell yer ma I'll be needin' to speak with her. If this gelding"—he took his fingers from the horse's maw and hooked his thumb toward the sorry-looking nag—'is the best, as ye say, 'tis a pitiful herd ye have."

With a shrug, the lad took the reins of his horse's bridle and climbed astride his bowed back.

"Now, m'lady, sorry fer the wait." Orwin wiped his hands on his soiled breeches. "How can I be of service?" His smile exposed crowded, yellow teeth.

"I need a horse." Gwynn decided to be firm and insistent. Though she intended to steal an animal if necessary, she'd try first to coax one from the stable master.

"Do ye?" Stains from sweat darkened the green of his tunic and though it was a breezy afternoon, perspiration dotted his upper lip and ran along the edge of his jaw. "Beggin' yer pardon, m'lady, but Lord Trevin himself told me you were to stay within the castle walls."

She'd anticipated this, but Trevin's orders boiled her blood just the same. "So I've heard, but 'tis foolish for me to stay. If it's the horse you're worried about, I'm a good horsewoman. I'll take care of the baron's steed."

" 'Tis not the horse that concerns me, m'lady. The lord, he said—"

"I'm not his prisoner," Gwynn cut in swiftly. She was tired of excuses to hold her at Black Oak. She'd been polite and hadn't wanted to offend Sir Bently, James the steward, and priest, or anyone else who tried to make her at home at the keep, but the truth of the matter was, she could stay no longer. "I may come and go as I please."

"Nay, nay, I know that. The baron, he was clear about that, said you were his guest." Both his eyebrows raised, as if they were one. "Said that Sir Bently and Hildy, here, were to see after ye."

"And a good job they're doing," Gwynn agreed. "Now, if I may have a saddle, bridle, and the gray horse . . ."

The man was used to taking orders, but was still unsure. "Baron Trevin, he told me that ye'd try to . . . well, leave the castle."

Gwynn lifted her chin and stared down her nose at the man. "As well I should. If I were a prisoner, would I not be locked away in my room or a dungeon?"

"Aye."

"And did not the baron tell everyone to see to my needs?"

"Yes, but the lord, he was afeared for your safety. Said that there were men at Rhydd who would want to do ye harm."

"How can they harm me if they be at Rhydd?" She smiled beguilingly though she had to grit her teeth. Who was this man—this stable master—to tell her whether or not she could leave the castle? Even while she was married she could do as she pleased. *Because your husband was held hostage.* Nonetheless, she had been her own overseer for the past thirteen years and wasn't about to let some servant determine her fate. Soon enough, when she had to face Ian again, her destiny might change, but not before. She held her head a fraction higher and was about to order the man to prepare her mount when the sound of hoofbeats pounded through the bailey.

A trumpet sounded.

"Open the gates, for Christ's sake," a guard ordered to the gatekeeper.

"But 'e bears the colors of Rhydd—"

Gwynn's head snapped up. Her heart turned to stone.

"For the mercy of the lord, open 'em. 'E's wounded, 'e is!" the guard cried. The portcullis rattled open and a horse and rider flew into the outer bailey.

"Who's that?" Hildy asked as she turned. "Oh, m'God, 'e's bleedin', 'e is."

"Oh, no!" Dread cast its horrid net over her soul. She recognized the rider as Sir Charles, the one man in whom she would have entrusted her son's life. Blood poured from a wound in his shoulder and his horse, lathered and wet with sweat, stumbled. The shaft of an arrow protruded from one flank and a dark purple stain ran in a hideous rivulet down the animal's back leg.

"Sweet Jesus!" Gwynn whispered, then more loudly, "Charles!" She sprinted across the bailey, her skirts flapping behind her, her slippers sinking into the soft, wet loam. "Get the physician," she ordered Hildy. "And . . . and my herbs. Now!"

"But, m'lady, d'ya think—"

"I said, 'Now!' "

Charles's normally robust skin was pale as death and his left arm didn't move. Blood crusted on his tunic. He toppled from the saddle and into Gwynn's arms. "Sir Charles," she whispered as she lay him on the damp ground. "Oh, nay, nay!" He barely breathed and his eyes as he stared at her were like glass. "Charles, listen to me, I know you can hear me. You are here at Black Oak Hall and safe. Do not let go. Hang on, please . . . Charles . . . Charles?"

"L-lady Gwynn?" he asked, his voice a rasp.

" 'Tis I."

Charles had been with her for as long as she'd been mistress of Rhydd. He'd stood at her side and spent long hours with Gareth, teaching him how to use a bow and arrow or hoist a sword or read the sky for the weather. He'd been her champion as well as her friend. She couldn't lose him. Wouldn't.

"Listen, for 'tis news I bear . . ." He coughed, his chest rattling, pain causing his face to blanch, his features to twist in agony. Though he looked at her, she was certain he was sightless.

"Shh. Save your strength."

He coughed again as peasants and servants hurried forward. Mary's harsh voice barked orders. "Give 'im room, would ye? Lousy clods. Make way. And someone—you, Orwin, do *something* with that poor 'orse, would ye?"

"Where is the physician?" Gwynn nearly screamed as clouds covered the sun.

" 'Tis Gareth," the wounded soldier said, clutching at her arm desperately.

"Gareth?" Her blood ran cold.

"Aye . . . at Rhydd . . . in the dungeon . . ."

"No, Charles. You are mistaken, 'tis the pain speaking," she argued, though she had no reason to doubt him. "Gareth . . . Gareth is safe!" *How would you know?*

"M'lady, 'tis true. He . . . he will be hanged."

"Oh, God." Fear gripped her insides and she could barely breathe. She wanted to tell him he was lying, but could not.

"He . . . he is w-with the old one . . . the magician . . . I had to tell . . . to tell you, but I was discovered by Sir Webb. 'Twas . . . his arrow that wounded me . . . another that found the stallion . . ." His voice faded with the rising wind.

"Charles! Charles!" Scared to the very pit of her soul, she held him close, felt his blood flowing onto her dress as thunder rumbled over the land. "You must not let go!" *Dear God, save this man and save my boy. Do not let him die!*

Vestments caught in the wind, Father Paul ran through the crowd and upon spying the dying man, fell to his knees. "Our Father who art in heaven . . ."

"I found 'im not!" Hildy pushed her way through the throng. "The physician be not in his quarters and no one in the castle knows where 'e's hidin'. A bloomin' fool, 'e is, if ye ask me." Breathless, she handed the basket of eggs, now cracked and running, to Gwynn.

Though she wanted to give up, to fall into a puddle of tears and lift her fist to the heavens in frustration, Gwynn gritted her teeth and managed to gather her courage. Someone had to see to the wounded knight and then to free Gareth. "Sir Charles is to be taken to the great hall—the solar," she ordered and two men whom she'd never seen before stepped forward and began to gather the wounded knight into their arms. "Careful. Please." To Hildy, she added, "I will need hot water and clean towels, candles, and red string."

"Aye," the lass said as the two men carefully carried a moaning Sir Charles into the keep. "You," she whirled on Sir Bently. "If you plan to follow me, make yourself useful. See that the horse is attended to and watch for any more wounded." Grimly she added, "Charles may be but the first."

"Yes, m'lady."

The stable master urged the fallen stallion to his feet.

"Ah, 'e's a beaut," Orwin said, more interested in the new addition to Black Oak's stables than the plight of the soldier.

Gwynn, mindless of the crowd that had gathered and the first drops of rain beginning to fall, pushed her way through the curious people to the great hall. She thought of Gareth in Rhydd's dungeon. *Dear God, keep him alive, please. And if that magician is worth anything, may he cast a spell and find a way to escape.*

Where was Trevin? Did he know of Gareth's plight? Her heart ached, but she could not worry, not until she was certain Sir Charles was being tended to.

In the solar Sir Charles was stretched upon a table, the life forces seeping from him with every second. He had lost conscious thought and when Gwynn leaned close to his ear and whispered his name, he didn't move.

" 'Twill be all right," she assured him, though she doubted her own words. "Rest easy, Sir Charles." Father Paul entered and shook his head. "Do not lose faith," she reprimanded him crossly. "We'll not be hearing last rites."

With the help of two women, Gwynn stripped Charles of his tunic and saw the gash, a fresh, gaping wound that sliced through his skin and flesh that was scarred from battles that were waged in the protection of Rhydd and the mistress of the keep. Guilt pricked at Gwynn's soul. How much pain had this proud man endured while protecting Castle Rhydd as well as her honor?

" 'Tis deep," one of the women said, gently touching the wound and shaking her head.

" 'Twill be fine." Gwynn swabbed the cleaved skin clean of blood and dirt.

" 'Tis mortal," the second one argued with a sad cluck of her tongue.

"We know that not. Come, no more of this talk. We must stitch him." Gwynn had seen to wounds before and though Charles's cut was severe, he was a strong man. While the priest crossed himself and, closing his eyes, knelt in a far corner and prayed for Charles's soul, Gwynn washed the wound with the hot water and towels Hildy had carried into the chamber, then began stitching.

" 'Tis too late, I fear," the girl said, but Gwynn would not listen to Hildy's concerns. Carefully, she sewed Charles's muscle, sinew, and skin together, then washed her hands.

"You may want to leave now," she said to the priest as she reached into her basket.

"Why . . . oh, nay," Father Paul said when he saw her withdraw her knife and candles. "You will not call up the spirits in this house, m'lady."

"I will do what I must." She leveled a glare at the man of the cloth and he sighed, imploring her with worried eyes.

When she refused to give in, he let out another long-suffering sigh and fingered his rosary. "I'll pray for your soul."

"As I will pray for yours."

While the ashen-faced priest and the women within the solar looked on, Gwynn lit candles and dusted the air with herbs for healing. Softly she chanted a spell, then tossed bits of apple, rose, and wild cherry onto the flames of the tapers and the fire burning on the hearth. "Save this good-hearted man," she asked, twisting knots in a red cord and tying it carefully around Charles's shoulder.

"Please, Lady Gwynn, do not use the dark powers here!" Father Paul beseeched again.

"I only asked for help."

"But use of the dark arts is forbidden. Please, I beg of you again, do not blacken this Christian keep."

"I seek help wherever I can find it," Gwynn snapped and laid her hands upon Charles's chest. Closing her mind to the priest's request, she concentrated only on healing, on letting her energy flow from her palms into the source of his pain. In her mind's eye she saw the wound from within, felt the heat and cold where Sir Charles ached.

When her energy started to fade, she said, "I bid you well, Sir Charles."

He did not move, but she sensed the lifeblood that had been flowing out of him was staunched. Her legs were weak, her body drained as she pocketed her dagger and herbs. While the priest dropped to his knees near the window and the women tended to the wounded soldier, Gwynn slipped through the open door.

On the stairway she met the physician, taking the steps two at a time and breathing hard. "The patient?" he asked.

"Is alive. In the solar." She pointed the way and leaned against the cool stone walls of the stairway as candles flickered in a dim, honey-colored light. There was nothing more that she could do for Sir Charles, brave knight that he was.

But she could help her son. Before Ian had the boy hanged.

Thank God fate had given her a new opportunity to escape.

While the keep was still abuzz with Sir Charles's arrival and Orwin was trying to save the wounded charger, Gwynn planned to leave Black Oak and ride to Rhydd. Sir Bently was busy elsewhere and Hildy, too, was no longer attached to her.

She thought of Trevin, but decided to stay as far away from the outlaw as she could. Not only could her heart not be trusted whenever he was around, but he had seduced her, then imprisoned her in this very keep.

Her willful heart ached for she feared she would never see him again, but there was no time to be lost. Nay, she must ride to Rhydd alone. Once within the keep she would throw herself onto Ian's mercy. Bile rose in her throat, but she swallowed it back. She could endure anything, even sharing Ian's bed, if he would but let Gareth go free.

"Be with me," she prayed, needing strength.

Her first concern was to find a horse. The gray came quickly to mind, but Gwynn wouldn't be picky as long as the animal was fleet and sure. As she hastened down the remaining steps, she sent up another prayer for Gareth's safety and her own ability to steal one of Trevin's horses. That thought warmed the cockles of her heart.

No one accosted her as she made her way through the great hall and opened the door.

Outside the day had turned to night with the cover of clouds. Rain pelted from the sky and slanted with the harsh fury of the wind. Girls hastily tried to take down laundry that had been strung near the herb garden. Boys hunched their shoulders against the wind and rain as they drove sheep into pens at the far end of the inner bailey while Gwynn, ducking through the shadows, hurried past.

In the stables, Orwin was tending to the wounded horse, talking more gently than Gwynn would have guessed. Several boys who helped him with the herd were caring for the other palfreys, chargers, and jennets in the stables and there was no chance she could take one of them without being caught.

Her heart plummeted as she backed away from the stables and squinted through the storm. At the corner of the mason's hut she stopped short as she spied not one, but two horses tied to iron rings at the farrier's shop. The smith was at the forge, his back to the animals and before Gwynn thought twice she strode boldly forward. Her hands fumbled slightly but she managed to untie the bridle of a dun-colored gelding. His black mane and tail caught in the wind, his ears pricked up as she approached. He let out a soft nicker as Gwynn, without the aid of a saddle, swung across the animal's wet back.

The farrier didn't look up from his work.

Heart pounding, Gwynn pulled her cloak and hood more closely about her face and though one guard shouted at her as she rode through the gate and under the portcullis, she ignored him.

"Halt there, you!" he yelled.

"Hey! Wait! Was that the lady?" Sir Bently's voice rang from the western watchtower.

"Oh, for the bloody love of Christ!"

"If that be her, the baron 'e'll skin us alive!" Bently sounded frantic and Gwynn experienced a pang of guilt that she immediately pushed aside. "Move!" Gwynn ordered, leaning forward. "Run like the wind!"

The horse responded. His strides lengthened. His hooves pounded the road. Through the rain he ran, passing travelers, oxcarts, and wagons. Flinging mud with his hooves, neck stretched forward, he galloped, the wind forcing Gwynn's hood off her face, catching in her hair and causing her cloak to stream behind her like a banner. "Run," she ordered the horse. Would the soldiers follow? Oh, Lord, she hoped not, for not only would she be trying to outrace the knights of Black Oak, but she could be leading them straight into the waiting army of Rhydd. Even now Ian's soldiers could be on this very road. "Run! Run! Run!"

If she were smart, she would take to the little-used paths and trails winding through the fields and hills that separated the two castles. She could use the forest as cover and still, if she rode day and night, be able to reach Rhydd sometime the day after the morrow, albeit not before dusk. Not that it mattered. She had no plot to save her son other than offering herself and her undying loyalty to Ian and though the thought galled her, she swallowed back her foolish pride. 'Twas worth the sacrifice if only Gareth were allowed to live.

And what of Trevin?

"Black-hearted bastard," she growled as the rutted road, empty and scattered with puddles, stretched into the forest. How could she have been so duped by his lovemaking? At the thought she felt a tug on her heart and an answering pull deep in her womb. How could he love her so thoroughly, then heartlessly leave and hold her hostage in his own keep? Oh, when she got her hands on him, she would place them around his thick neck and . . . and what? Strangle him? Shake some sense into him? Or kiss him until both their knees were weak?

She had been foolish to give herself to him, to have lain in his arms, dozing and waking over and over again to the warm inspiration of his kiss and the scorch of his naked skin upon hers.

True, he had been her only lover. Oh, she'd slept with her first husband, shared his bed, and wondered at his cold nuzzlings.

Despite her vocal dismay and arguments, her father had bargained with Roderick of Rhydd, much as he would have negotiated the sale of a prized destrier.

She'd left her home and on the day of the wedding her husband had informed her that he expected her to bear him many sons. That night and for several weeks thereafter she'd shared his bed, attempted to submit to the foul act, and was subjected to Roderick's passionless kiss and cold hands. Aye, he'd mounted her, but never had his member held an erection, never had he been able to penetrate her. He'd blamed her, forced her to do despicable deeds that had failed to make him hard.

On the day he'd left to do battle, he'd tried again, insisting that she shame herself by kneeling like a dog so he could take her from behind. She'd suffered the indignity only to feel him fail yet again. He'd slapped her hard across her bare buttocks, then left, telling her that should she not deliver him the heirs he wanted, she would regret it.

His meaning had been clear. He had two dead wives who had foolishly not borne him children.

'Twas no surprise when Idelle, in Gwynn's chamber thirteen years before, had revealed that she wasn't with child and yet she wouldn't believe it. 'Twas only luck and Trevin's mercenary streak that had brought him to her chamber. 'Twas that first afternoon when she'd lost her virginity to a thief that she'd learned of lovemaking and had yearned, over the years, for more.

Trevin, blast him, hadn't disappointed her. If anything, his touch, now that he was a full-grown man, stoked the fires of her passion more readily than before. Despite her anger, she knew that she would never feel for another man the intensity, the lust, damn it, the love, she felt for him.

'Twas her very private secret. No one, especially not the thief-baron himself, would ever know the feelings buried deep in her wayward heart.

Through the rain she rode never seeing a sentry or knight from either castle.

Sometime during the night, when her fingers were frozen around the reins and her legs numb from the ride, the clouds parted and the showers that had followed her like a hex evaporated into the darkening sky.

Jewel-like stars were flung across the black heavens and a lazy crescent moon hung low in the sky, offering some meager silvery light.

Her horse was tired, lather and mud darkening his gold coat, and she, too, felt a weariness settle deep in her bones. Though the urge to ride onward, to keep going until she was at the very battlements of Rhydd, was strong, she had no choice but to rest.

" 'Tis good you've been," she said, stroking the horse's thick neck as she reined him to a walk.

At the edge of a stream, she dismounted, letting the horse drink as she washed her face and hands. Her back ached, her legs wobbled from hours in the saddle and yet she opened her pouch and tossed dust into the air for Gareth's safety.

"Now for you, Hildy," she said, as if the girl were with her. Carefully she drew runes in the creek bed, then cast a spell that she hoped would dispel the curse Hildy was certain had been leveled against Black Oak Hall. The girl was silly, of course, but worried for her unborn child.

"Be with them all," she prayed to a God who had seldom listened to her as she led her horse to a tiny glade where winter grass offered him some feed. Once he was tethered to a young sapling, she found her own shelter under the spreading branches of a long-needled pine tree.

The ground was dry, old needles offering some cushion against the hard earth. Pulling her cloak about her, she ignored the pangs of hunger in her stomach and the foolish longing she felt for Trevin. She had only to think of their last night together to remember the way her skin tingled at his touch, the warm possession of his mouth molding to her lips, the heady sensation of strong male muscles pressed urgently to hers.

"Stop it," she mumbled. She needed to sleep, to prepare for the next day when she would have to face Ian of Rhydd. Her husband. That thought rankled her sourly, but she was reminded of Gareth and her heart turned to ice. He could not die! She would do anything, *anything* to save him.

She had no time to think of the lying bastard who had loved her so thoroughly, then left her without a word.

Slumber came easily. She was listening to the jangle of her horse's bridle as he plucked at grass, the sigh of wind through the branches overhead and the croak of a solitary frog when consciousness gave way to dreams.

Only much later as an exposed root poked into her back and she shifted did she hear another sound—the crackle of a stick being broken and the soft tread of boots. Fear shot through her blood. Instantly awake, she seized the dagger from its sheath.

"So, the lady awakes," a familiar male voice said.

Her heart jolted.

Trevin of Black Oak, damn his lying hide, strode out of the shadows. Tall and imposing, he crossed his arms over his chest and glowered down at her. "Why is it, woman, that I'm not surprised you disobeyed me?"

Chapter Twelve

"I'll take no orders from you." Gwynn scrambled to her feet. Her pulse throbbed. Her heart thundered and she wanted to shake the very life from the man who dared stand before her. "How did you find me?"

"Luck," he admitted with a smile that was a jagged slash of white that flashed in the darkness. Dressed in black, a new beard shadow roughening his chin, Trevin glared at her with eyes as dark as midnight and she was reminded of looking into those very eyes while he had made sweet, slow, sensuous love to her. For the express purposes of lulling her into trusting him. Oh, what a simpering fool she'd been.

"Luck," she repeated, taunting him. "Like the kind of luck you had when you won the castle from Lord Dryw?" He didn't bother to answer and she stepped closer to him, her fury mounting as she remembered each incident of mortification she'd faced at being held hostage, for that is what it was, at Black Oak Hall. "You . . . You had no right to try and keep me prisoner!"

" 'Twas only to keep you safe." His voice was low, like the sea at the turning of the tide.

" 'Tis not your concern, *my lord*." Gossamer clouds scudded in the heavens, partially hiding the stars, and the forest seemed to close around them as if they were the only two people in this world. "I-I can take care of myself."

"Can you?" A dark eyebrow cocked insolently and he stared at her so long and hard she could suddenly barely breathe. Her abdomen tightened, her diaphragm pressed hard against her lungs.

She heard the sounds of the night, the hum of insects, the soft hoot of an owl and the rush of water as it tumbled over a creek hidden behind the thickets of oak and fragrant pine. Oh, what cruel fate that he could turn her thoughts to such a jumble when they had no time, no time at all to rescue Gareth.

"Have I not for the past thirteen years?" she managed to demand. "Not only did I look after myself, but our son as well all the while ruling a castle."

"Yea, and now you are a bride who has run from her husband, our son is banished and might face death, and your castle is in the hands of a man who is your sworn enemy."

"All because of you!" She would not let him turn this all around. 'Twas his fault as much as hers. She tossed her hair from her eyes and one side of his mouth lifted in amusement as he extracted a long needle from the tangled curls. His fingers grazed her cheek and all the spit in her mouth disappeared. Fierce but tender. Threatening but gentle. So was Trevin the outlaw.

Her stomach did a slow, sensual roll and for a second she thought only of kissing those hard, blade-thin lips and tumbling to the ground with him. But she could not. There was too much at stake. "Do you know that Gareth has been captured?"

"No." His countenance was instantly grim.

" 'Tis true, Trevin. Though he was sorely wounded, Sir Charles rode to Black Oak and told me that our boy is now captive. It seems both he and your magician friend have been cast into the dungeon." Her heart was heavy with the thought of her son lying in the rotting prison beneath the towers of a castle he'd known as his home.

Trevin's jaw tightened and his eyes glittered with a seething, deadly rage. "One of my men saw a wounded man wearing the colors of Rhydd riding to Black Oak. He also spied Webb, who we think attacked him."

"Aye, Charles said as such. No doubt Ian ordered Charles slain to prevent him from reaching me with the news of Gareth's imprisonment." Gwynn shook the pine needles from her hair and fingered her dagger.

"So it seems." He glanced at the night black heavens, then back to Gwynn. "Worry not. I will free both Gareth and Muir."

"Nay," she said, for as angry as she was with him, she knew that if he were to face Ian, Trevin would meet his end and the thought of his death, of never seeing him again was a torment she could not bear. "I will go. Ian will bargain with me."

"Bargain?" He snorted.

"I will offer myself as trade."

"What makes you think he will honor a bargain made with a woman who has already pledged herself to him?" Trevin rubbed the muscles of his neck and his eyebrows were drawn together, his eyes narrowed thoughtfully.

She'd considered this herself and had no answer. "I think . . . at least I hope that he will want to please me."

"And if he does not?" Trevin asked.

Her gaze locked with his. "Then I suppose I will have no choice but to rely upon you, thief."

Trevin leaned down so that his gaze was level with hers, his breath warm as it touched her skin. "Make no mistake, woman. No harm will come to our son," he vowed.

"How can you be certain?"

"Your husband is not foolish enough to risk my wrath." His nostrils flared in the darkness. "Asides, he is using our son as a lure." Trevin's gaze met hers again and in one heart-stopping second she was lost to him. "He dares not harm him as it is you he wants."

"And you."

He took her hand and pulled her away from the tree. "Nay, m'lady, Ian wants me dead—or alive so that he can make a spectacle of killing me."

"Then I will give myself—"

"He will not get the chance," Trevin vowed.

"But—" The vision of Trevin bloodied from Ian's sword was too much to bear. "—you do not know him. He may be much older, but he is quick with a sword and knife."

"Not quick enough, m'lady," Trevin promised. He wrapped a strong hand around the nape of her neck and drew her head closer to his. "As long as I live and breathe, you will never give yourself to that cur."

"But for Gareth—"

"Shh. Know you this," he vowed, his breath whispering across her face. "I will never let you down, Gwynn of Rhydd. Nor will I let you place yourself or our son in danger. If you have faith in nothing else in this world, believe that you can trust me above all else."

She swallowed hard and tried to slow the heat rushing through her blood. But he was too near, too male. The quietly disturbing scents of musk and leather mingled with the rain-washed smell of the forest. She felt his heat, knew a gnawing primal lust that was beginning to burn through her veins. "I—I can't."

"Try," he murmured, his lips brushing hers ever so gently.

Oh, God, was that her heart knocking so loudly?

"Please, Trevin . . . oh, nay . . ."

With pale moonlight caressing his face, he took her into arms as strong as barrel staves and pressed cool, insistent lips to hers. She felt a desperation in his kiss, a wild need that pierced her soul.

There was no time for this madness; she could not place her faith in a man who would sneak away from her bed and hold her hostage. She could not, would not . . .

Resistance fled.

Her chilled, ready lips parted as if of their own accord. His muscles strained as he kissed her, as if though he wanted her, needed her, he, too, was battling his desire.

All too willingly she accepted his tongue, warm and wet, as it entered her, touching, searching, playing with hers.

He trembled violently and she was lost to him yet again. Knowing she was making a mistake, she leaned against him and wound her arms around his neck.

"Sweet Jesus," he whispered. "Forgive me."

His weight dragged them downward and Gwynn closed her mind to the doubts that sped through her mind. Aye, this was wrong. Aye, she might regret the glorious act for the rest of her life, but nay, she would not stop it from happening. Tonight might be the last night they would ever be together, the last time she would feel his kiss, the last moment she would ever feel his welcome weight upon her. Without another doubt, she closed her eyes, drew from his strength, and felt this dark, unforgiving night wrap around her as she gave herself to the only man she had ever loved.

"I hate the bastard." Gareth rocked back on his heels in this hellhole of a prison and glared at Muir. Cold, beaten, and hungry, Gareth wanted the truth.

The old man stirred but didn't waken.

"And I think you be a lying one-eyed fool."

"Say . . . what?" The old magician, lying on his side, stretched and opened his eyes.

"Trevin of Black Oak. The murderin' thief. I hate him. He be *not* my father." Gareth wasn't going to believe any such poppycock. So his father wasn't the baron. Fine. He didn't need a sire. He'd gotten along well enough so far without a father . . . well, except that now he was being held prisoner in a rotting dungeon and scheduled to be hanged.

"Ah, boy, Trevin's a good man." Muir was quick to hold up a hand when he saw the protests forming on Gareth's tongue.

"I don't see how," Gareth growled as the guard, keys clanging, opened up the cell door. Rats scurried through the filthy straw.

"You. Old man. The baron wants to 'ave a word with you." The guard belched and scratched at his protruding stomach while Muir struggled to his feet and, wincing, stretched his back until it made a series of pops. "Come along now."

Gareth saw the ghost of a smile pass over the sorcerer's lips. "Find out about my mother," he begged, "and Boon." He held onto the grimy bars as Muir, led by the guard, was shepherded out of the dungeon. 'Twas a horrid place with rats and mice crawling through the holes in the crumbling walls and a stench that reeked from rotting food and urine.

If his mother could see him now she would keel over. Better that she never know. Oh, Mother, he thought, I've failed you. He'd never expected to miss

her, had often thought her bossing was a bother, but oh, what he would give
to have his blissful, naive life, when he was considered the son of the baron,
returned to him.

"Fresh straw for the prisoners," a voice called down the stairs and Gareth's
eyes rounded when he spied Tom, the butcher's son, hauling a bundle of
straw upon his back. "Where do ye want it?"

The only guard left in the dank chambers was seated upon a bench under
one low-burning torch. "Anywhere," he muttered. "Who cares? Their sorry
lives are worth naught."

Tom, clumsy with his burden, unloaded his bundle near Gareth's cell and
as he untied the twine he whispered, "God's eyes, Gareth, how did ye get
caught?"

"Does not matter."

"I always said you be a fool." Thick fingers fumbling with the twine, Tom
glanced over his shoulder. Assured that the guard wasn't looking, he slid a
small handful of straw between the bars, then straightened.

"What of Boon?" Gareth asked softly.

"I know not."

"Hey! What's going on?" The guard, realizing there was conversation between prisoner and laborer, reeled and glared at Tom with suspicious eyes.

"Nothing. The poor sod's wanting me to get him some of Cook's sausage
for him. Ha!" Tom spit on the floor, then turned and made his ungainly way
up the steps.

"No talkin', y'hear me?" the guard grumbled, his gaze moving suspiciously
from cell to cell.

Gareth didn't answer, nor did he touch the small bundle of straw that lay
so near his fingertips. Only when the sentry's attention was drawn to another
prisoner, did Gareth's fingers search the dried bunch to find a slingshot fash-
ioned from bone and leather. There were no pebbles within the bundle but
'twas not a problem as the stone walls of the dungeon were crumbling and the
mortar chipping away in bits and pieces. Ah, Tom wasn't such a bad lad after
all, Gareth thought, his fingers curling possessively around his newly gained
weapon. He couldn't wait to use it against some of the brutes who had hauled
him in here.

Let anyone dare lay a hand on him. The fool would be lucky if he didn't
lose an eye for his efforts.

"I know you." Ian stroked his chin carefully as he sat, one leg crossed over the
other in his chair. The great hall was nearly empty, but the tantalizing odors
of seared meat and spices lingered in the smoke-scented room. A wooden
mazer dangling from the fingers of Ian's one hand held wine, and the sweet

perfume of fermented grapes teased Muir's nostrils almost to distraction. A few guards were stationed near the doorways but they seemed disinterested in their lord and only snapped to attention when a fetching lass swung by. "We've met somewhere."

"Everyone within the kingdom has heard of Muir," the magician said sarcastically. Oh, for a mere sip from the lord's sweet cup. " 'Tis my powers that set me apart from the rest."

"Do not jest," Ian ordered, rubbing thumb and forefinger together. " 'Tis just at the edge of my memory. I cannot remember where or when, but I will." His lips flattened over his teeth as he concentrated. "In time."

Muir kept his expression bland for 'twould only cause harm if the new lord's memory suddenly returned and he recalled the damning truth. 'Twas years before, aye, when both Muir and Ian were young men. Guilt settled in his bones for 'twas they who had started this horrid bloody chain. "I see not why you keep the boy in the dungeon," he said.

"He's a traitor. He killed the baron."

"Nay, nay." Muir shook his bald head. "He's but a lad who was foolishly protecting his mother's honor."

Ian snorted and to Muir's disappointment, drained his mazer. "Honor?" He shook his head and the veins in his face became visible with a slow-burning rage. "There is no honor or virtue in being a thief's whore." Wincing as he stood, he withdrew his sword and studied the long, shiny blade as it reflected the gold shadows of the fire. "But I will deal with her as well. She will be here soon, for I sent her a gift—a bloody messenger with the news of her son's imprisonment."

Muir felt a dull ache in his bad eye.

"The thief will follow."

Pain, swift and sharp, pierced Muir's brain. He doubled over and clutched his eye. Not now! He could not have a vision now, but sure as he was born, it came, in full view he saw Trevin and Gwynn together, riding toward Rhydd.

Toward Ian's soldiers.

Toward the gallows.

Toward death.

He could summon no spit in his mouth and his heart seared as if it had been burned.

Ian's voice came as if from far away. " 'Tis only a matter of time and then, old man, revenge will be mine."

Nay, 'twill be mine, Muir thought as pain ravaged his body. *And you, Lord Ian, will pay for all your sins.*

Trevin cursed himself up one side and down the other. 'Twas a fool he was and there was no doubt of it. Levered upon one elbow, he stared down at Gwynn, still slumbering, unaware that dawn was casting its first gray light through the forest. A solitary winter bird had begun to warble its lonely song as dew drenched the boughs of the surrounding trees.

She was a beauty. No doubt of it. Her skin was white and pure, her hair in red-brown ringlets framed an oval face with a strong nose and pointed chin. Fine, curling lashes brushed the tops of high cheekbones that were a soft peach color. Her lips were parted, her breath regular, and he knew that beneath the cloaks that had been their blankets her naked body was firm and wanting, a glorious place of pleasure and sanctuary.

A place you vowed never to visit.

He gritted his teeth, his jaw growing hard. Never had he felt this way for a woman, but this one, with her fiery temper and quick tongue, had somehow wormed her way under his skin. He could not seem to get enough of her and though his member was sore from all the times he'd entered her, still he wanted more.

Gently he brushed aside a wayward curl from her cheek and wondered why she was forever on his mind. 'Twas not because she was beautiful, others were so. Nor was it because she was the mother of his son, again, other women could have borne him children if he so desired. Nay, there was more to it. She intrigued him with her forest-green eyes, quick smile, and fertile mind. She was brave to the point of being foolhardy, outspoken for a woman, even of her station, and a person who seemed to believe not only in God but in the Earth Mother and magic as well.

Not that Trevin blamed her. Often times, it seemed, God turned a deaf ear to prayers. Had he not seen it himself when Faith and baby Alison had passed on? Guilt took a stranglehold of his heart and squeezed with iron-clad fingers. He should have loved Faith; but he had not. Though he'd been true to her and never lain with another woman, he had not cared for her with the same intensity that he felt for this sharp-tongued female.

Even though Gwynn was married to another.

Oh, fool that he was, he seemed unable to stop bedding her while she belonged to his enemies. First she'd been Roderick's wife—well, at least in name. Now she belonged to Ian. Christ, Jesus, could he not be with her while she was between husbands? Mentally he kicked himself from one side of Wales to the other.

He knew of false marriages. Had he not married Faith out of guilt for winning her father's castle, then watched in horror as he'd flung himself to his death? His attempts to save the old man had been futile and had turned on him. Many who lived within the walls of Black Oak and had watched him wrestle with Dryw had assumed that Trevin had pushed the old lord through the crenels to the cold stone courtyard rather than believe that he'd tried to save the drunken fool. Either way he'd lost and, as atonement, he'd married Faith. 'Twas his fault she'd lost both father and home and he needed to assuage his guilt.

But loved her, he had not. At the birthing of their daughter, he felt close to her and had wrapped comforting arms around her when the baby had refused to draw a breath. He'd held Faith and the stillborn babe as she'd cried and tried to help her accept the loss of their child. She had refused.

He hadn't been able to save her, either. As Faith had lain upon her deathbed, he'd vowed he loved her but she'd looked at him with sorrowful eyes and shook her head.

"Do not lie to me, Trevin McBain," she'd said, lifting a weary hand and stroking his hair.

"I would not."

"Oh, you be fond of me. Aye, even care for me a bit," she'd said with a weak smile, "but do not shame us both by a lie."

He'd kissed her cold lips and she, still holding the dead child, had begged him to never love another.

Vow to me, Trevin, that you'll never love another woman. Swear it.

He'd sworn upon her grave that he would never marry again, never pretend to love another. He'd managed to keep that vow until this morning as he gazed down upon the one woman who could bring him to break that oath.

Another man's wife.

Even now he wanted to wake her with a kiss. Instead he fought the powerful urge to take her yet again, and angry at fates, shoved his legs through his breeches and threw his tunic over his head. He would not think of their lovemaking again, for it only clouded his mind. He needed a clear head and aside from that he had a new problem—what to do with her. He was not surprised that she'd duped his sentries; many of them were untrained and disloyal. He'd taken his best men from the castle, aside from Henry, the boy he'd knighted out of obligation.

"Lady," he said, his voice rougher and deeper than was usual as he gently shook her shoulder. "Awaken. 'Tis time we meet with the others."

She stretched and smiled up at him, her eyes, when they opened, green shot with silver. "Mmm. Oh, m'lord," she said with a naughty wink, "have you not the time to kiss me again?"

"Nay, we must away—"

" 'Twill not take long," she cooed and he was undone yet again. Cursing his weakness, he hauled her into his arms and kissed her as the sun crested the eastern hills. Her warm, sleepy body molded to his and he knew deep in the darkest part of his soul, he was lost to her. He would have this one last union, for there would be no others and when she realized how he plotted to thwart her, she would be furious with him and never have want of his kiss.

'Twas bittersweet, this loving, and he kept his eyes open as he watched the sunbeams turn her hair to fire. Forever would her image be burned into his brain for 'twould be the last time his gaze caressed her flawless skin and never again would he sense her breath catch in her throat, feel the soft whisper of her fingers searching through his chest hair to discover his nipples, or experience the slick sensation of her tongue slide intimately over his skin.

Almighty God, he would miss her.

But he had no choice.

"We must help them, I tell ye," Idelle insisted. She paced in the small chapel and skewered the priest with a look she hoped would make him squirm. Some man of the cloth he was, always having a page flog him until his back bled—'twas addled.

"I cannot go against the lord's wishes."

"Why not? Oh, a fool ye be, Father Anthony."

" 'Tis not God's will." He wiped a gold chalice with his sleeve, then placed it into a cupboard with silver and gold crosses, goblets, and leather-bound tomes.

"Do ye think 'tis God's will that Lady Gwynn's son be locked away like a criminal?"

"He's a traitor. He killed the lord." A great sadness stole across his face. " 'Tis the law." Father Anthony locked the cupboard and tucked the key in the deep pockets of his vestment.

"And ye, being a priest, are bound by higher laws, are ye not? Are not God's covenants more dear than earthly decrees and possessions?" She stared pointedly at his carved, locked cupboard.

"Who are y-you to lecture me, woman? I know of your dark arts. Have I not turned a blind eye when you mention the names of the pagan gods? 'Tis said you cast spells and chant not the prayers of the church, but rave of devils and demons and the like. 'Tis time you came forward, daughter, and c-cast away your evil ways."

Idelle stood toe to toe with the priest. Her eyes might be weak, but her heart was not. " 'Tis not evil I worship, Father, but all things good and wise. I have faith in the Christian God, aye, but there is magic in the earth, wind, and sea that I will forever use. Asides, we have no time to argue about good and evil, for we both know what they be. We are talking of a youth, Father Anthony, Lady Gwynn's boy and of an old man who is dying."

"The magician."

"Aye."

"He, too, practices that which is forbidden. I prithee, Idelle, s-s-search your heart. L-l-look to God."

"And I prithee, Father Anthony," she said, her milky eyes focusing upon him, "look to your own soul. Who are ye to point a pious finger? I know of ye, Anthony, as I birthed ye to yer poor dead ma. I've watched ye grow from a lad to a man and I, too, have turned a blind eye to all that ye've become."

He swallowed hard. "I-I d-d-do not know wh-what you mean."

"Sure ye do, Father." Idelle, through the clouds in her eyes, noticed his Adam's apple twitch nervously. "Now, think of the good of Rhydd, the people within, and especially Lady Gwynn and her son."

"I—I will pr-pray on it."

"Do so." Idelle deftly crossed herself and genuflected at the altar, then she turned quickly and left the fool of a priest. He was a sorely troubled soul, one who could not look into a mirror without cringing. She only hoped he would search his heart, for she desperately needed his help if she were to free the lady's boy.

The last of the complaints had been heard and Ian's head pounded. The arguments were petty. One peasant argued with his neighbor over the size of his land, a starving farmer begged forgiveness for poaching a stag in the woods, and the cook whined on and on that the steward wasn't keeping stock of the spices and that the multure, fee for milling grain, wasn't enough to keep up with the demand of flour for bread. 'Twas too much for Ian and he wondered how Roderick, then Gwynn, had kept everyone in the castle at peace. Though he'd watched her over the years and offered his advice, even overseeing some of the work, Gwynn, in her husband's absence, had managed to rule Rhydd as well as raise that confounded boy without any outward trouble. Nor had he, while she was in charge, sensed any of the simmering rebellion that he now felt existed within the keep.

He stood and stretched, ignoring the pain in his legs. His wounds were healing and soon he would bear only scars from Trevin of Black Oak's sword.

"Bastard," he spit out as Webb, who had watched the lord dealing with his villeins from his post near the door, approached. "Have you news of my wayward wife?" he asked, knowing the answer.

"Nay. She be a slippery one."

Ian could not disagree.

"As she's with Trevin of Black Oak, she is even more difficult to find."

Ian saw the amusement in the knight's eyes and knew that Webb was not alone in his silent laughter at the new baron being cuckolded.

Most people in the castle, himself included, believed that Gwynn was with Trevin. Was he not the father of her child? Had he not lain with her years before? Her marriage to Roderick hadn't stopped her from bedding the thief, so surely her vows to Ian, given as the result of a bargain for her son's life, would be taken no more seriously.

He wanted to put Sir Webb in his place, but bit back a sharp retort, believing, as always, that he who gets the final laugh enjoys it most, and no one, not the thief or Ian's whore of a wife would get the better of him.

"You are a soldier," he said slowly to Webb, "one who managed to help my brother escape a prison where he'd been held for years. Surely a mere slip of a woman and a common thief are not so clever as to elude you."

The light of cruel merriment in Webb's gaze faded. " 'Tis only a matter of time."

"Good." Ian lifted a lofty eyebrow. "I would hate to think my trust in you was ill placed."

"Nay, m'lord," Webb said stiffly, but hesitated. "However, there is the matter of payment."

"Payment? For what?"

"Recovery of the boy." Webb's lips tightened a bit.

"I did promise that you would be paid, did I not?" Ian stroked his chin. "And, I suppose that even though the lad did practically walk into the keep, that you should have some reward."

The tension in the dark knight's face relaxed a bit.

"I will see to it," Ian said with a nod. "but since the task proved easy, I want you to do more for me."

"More?" Webb's back stiffened and Ian waved away his doubts. "Worry not, I said I will pay you for Gareth, and so I shall. 'Twas our bargain. Now I want you to ferret out the traitors within the castle. Trevin and the lady could not have escaped without help. Listen to the gossip, have our trusted men search through the hiding spots here at Rhydd, watch everyone more closely, and find out who would pledge his fealty not to me if the truth were known."

Webb leaned upon his sword. "Have you anyone you do not trust?"

"I trust no one." Motioning for two mazers of wine, he waited until a scrawny page had done his bidding, then sat with Sir Webb at the table. "Start with the old woman—the midwife—who attended to my wife."

"Idelle?"

"Aye. Though she is nearly blind, she sees all." Ian swirled his cup. "Then, look to the freemen. The butcher has distrust in his gaze, the carpenter is too silent, and the mason is a brooding, gloomy soul."

"Think you they are enemies?"

"Mayhap." Ian took a sip and let the wine slide down his throat as he swirled his cup. "But there are others as well, soldiers within our army who would take up arms against me if there were a choice between my wife and myself."

"What of the priest?" Webb asked.

"Father Anthony?" Ian scowled. There had always been something that bothered him about the man, but he could never put his finger upon what the trouble was. "Nay, he's a coward, to be sure. Spineless and jumpy, but he was loyal to my brother and would dare not defy me." He thought hard for a second, but dismissed Webb's concerns. "Worry not of him."

"Lord Ian!" A guard approached. "We found Sir Keenan naked as the day he was born, dirty and stumbling around the forest."

"Sir Keenan?"

"The knight who was missing on the night when Trevin of Black Oak escaped," Webb said, his hand upon his sword.

"Aye," the guard agreed.

"But he is alive?"

"Barely. He collapsed afore we got him through the gate. He babbles like the village idiot and says nothing but nonsense. We—we carried him as far as the atilliator's shop, for the old man is his father."

Ian's mouth drew into a hard, unforgiving line. "I will see Keenan now. Mayhap he will remember what happened that night and know who the traitors were who helped the outlaw escape." 'Twould be sweet vengeance to discover who was disloyal to him, sweet vengeance indeed.

"When I find out who the traitors are, I will see that they are punished to within an inch of their miserable lives." He drained his mazer and slammed the empty cup onto the table. Looking at Sir Webb, he added, "When I'm through with them, they'll wish they'd never been born."

Chapter Thirteen

"Trust you the atilliator?" Webb asked as they strode across the bailey. Fog was settling over the river and blanketing the castle in its filmy mist. Ian slid a glance at the dark knight. "Did I not say that I trust no one?"

" 'Tis wise."

Though life in the castle seemed to go on as usual, there was an undercurrent of disloyalty, as dark and murky as a whirlpool, that Ian sensed swirled maliciously along the paths and alleys of Rhydd. 'Twas nothing he could see, just a feeling that there were those that would like nothing better than to slit his throat.

But who?

The gong farmer was mucking out the stables and nodded as they passed. "Good day, m'lord," he said, smiling widely as if he didn't know that he reeked of manure, as if he were innocent of anything close to treason.

Sheep bleated from the pens. A pig squealed in protest as the butcher's son managed to get a rope around its thick neck. Hammers rang loudly. The wheelwright mended a cartwheel and the carpenter shored up a truss supporting the roof over the roosts of the game birds that were kept alive until the cook needed them. They nodded, said a quick, "M'lord," in greeting and went about their tasks as if nothing was wrong. Were they loyal, or just good actors? He didn't know. But he'd find out. One way or another.

With Webb beside him, Ian strode past the armorer's hut where the burly man was sharpening swords upon his whetstone. The screech of metal upon whirling stone screamed through the bailey.

As he finished each weapon, the armorer passed it to his son who polished the sharpened blades until they gleamed bright and deadly. Both man and son nodded to Ian, but did not meet his eyes. 'Twas a bad sign. Very bad.

"Look hard at those two," Ian whispered to Webb. Was the sword maker loyal to him or to his Judas of a wife?

Ever since Gwynn's escape Ian had felt distrustful, dangerous eyes upon him and glacial stares from those who questioned his reign. Even among the servants in the kitchen and laundry there was a quiet, though ever-present dissention, a current of disloyalty that seemed to slither along the walls and hide in the shadowy corners of the castle, pooling and turning, waiting insidiously so that it could, when he least expected it, destroy him.

'Twas unsettling and he slept not only with his sword at his side, but a hidden blade beneath his pillow. He heartened himself with the knowledge that all the ill will would dissipate once Gwynn was returned and took her rightful place at his side, the mistress of Rhydd.

If she did.

The door to the atilliator's hut was open and inside, upon pegs were broken crossbows in various need of repair. The room was small and close. Parr, the man responsible for making crossbows, was a tiny man whose small stature belied his strength.

"Ah, m'lord, 'tis glad I be that ye came to see the fallen warrior," he said, nodding and rubbing the knotty fingers of one hand with the other. Paid well for his skills, it seemed unlikely that he would betray the lord, but Ian withheld judgment as his eyes adjusted to the dim light.

Sir Keenan lay on the table. A dirty blanket had been tossed over him, but beneath the old rag, he was pale as death and quivering, his eyes wide, spittle sliding from one corner of his mouth. "Nay . . . nay . . . oh, Christ Jesus . . ."

The physician, aged and stooped over, was peering into Keenan's glazed eyes and shaking his head. "He is near gone, m'lord."

"Well, do something. I needs speak with him."

" 'Tis naught to do but force water over his lips and wait." The shriveled man clucked his tongue and frowned, his forehead wrinkling in deep, worried furrows. "Sir Keenan? The lord, Ian of Rhydd, he is here and needs a word with you."

"Nay . . . no . . . no . . ." he continued to whisper through blue lips.

Ian had seen enough. "Keenan! What the devil happened to you?"

The man didn't glance in the lord's direction, just stared at the dusty beams over his head though, Ian suspected, he saw a vision known only to his eyes.

"Keenan, wake up!"

Still the man shivered and shook and didn't answer.

"He has cuts and bruises and this—" The physician's balding pate wrinkled as he lifted the blanket to show the soldier's chest where three large, even gashes ripped through his skin. The blood was dried, the wounds festering. "Mayhap a bear, or wolverine or other beast."

Webb slid his sword from his hilt. "There are ways to make him speak."

"Nay. He is lost. Put that away!" He motioned to Webb's weapon. Though patience had never been one of Ian's virtues and his temper was near the breaking point, he knew that Keenan would not awaken with a blade at his throat. To the physician, he said, "As soon as he wakes, send for me—no, better yet, move him into the great hall and keep a guard with him. I'm to be called immediately when he stirs."

"Aye," the physician agreed, "but I fear—"

"Where was he found?" Ian was in no mood for excuses or explanations.

"A mile away from the castle, wandering around in circles."

Ian sighed. "We will learn nothing more here. We must wait until Sir Keenan awakens."

"*If* he awakens," Sir Webb clarified and Ian's foul mood only worsened. 'Twas as if the devil himself was his enemy rather than a mortal man—nay, a lowly thief. *Have faith,* he silently told himself as he returned to the great hall. 'Twas only a matter of time. Sooner or later Trevin would return and then, by God, Ian would be ready for him.

"We'll split into two groups." Trevin, fingering his dagger, squatted near the fire where two ducks and a rabbit were roasting on a spit. Fat dripped and sizzled on the coals, flames sparked and flared, and smoke curled upward through the leafless branches of the trees to the winter-blue sky.

His band of soldiers, eight men in all, gathered around him, and gave Gwynn a wide berth. She'd noticed their elevated eyebrows when Trevin had brought her to the camp, caught glimpses of shared glances and expressions ranging from amusement to disapproval as Trevin explained that she'd tricked Sir Bently and escaped the gates of Black Oak.

"The first group will be led by you, Gerald. Take Henry, York, Winston, and Nelson." With his knife, Trevin motioned to each of the men. "You will be the decoy party and will lead Ian's soldiers on a wild-goose chase away from the castle."

"Ye will not be with us?" Henry asked, obviously confused.

"Nay."

"Then why will they follow us?"

"Because they will believe I am with you. You cannot let Ian's soldiers get too close because one of you will be riding my horse—the steed that belonged to Sir Webb—and as you will all be wearing helmets, it should not be difficult to lure them away from the castle. They will think I am the rider upon Dark One.

"What if they do not follow?" Winston asked, pondering the situation and twisting the end of his mustache.

"Believe that, above all Webb will want his horse. 'Twas a bitter humiliation to lose such a steed and Webb is a prideful man. Now, once Ian's army has left Rhydd and given chase to you, the rest of us will enter the castle."

"Including the lady?" Sir Henry wasn't happy at the thought.

"Aye. She will be with me." Trevin's gaze locked with that of the younger man to quell any further arguments. "But we will need further deception," he said to the group at large, "one of you must dress as a woman."

All motion stopped. Sir Winston's fingers held firm to the end of his mustache.

Henry had been scratching his head. His hand stayed atop his crown.

Nelson had been picking his nails with his knife and cut himself at Trevin's words. "I must've heard ye wrong, me lord?" he said, sucking the blood from the pad of his thumb.

York had been whittling and the curls of pine wood dropping from his knife halted.

"I mean it. Ian's men will be looking for Gwynn so one of you will don her cloak."

"Nay." Henry shook his head. "I ain't dressin' up like no lass, you can count on it. Come now, m'lord, ye must be joshin' us."

" 'Tis no joke."

"Oh, me sweet mum!" Henry rolled his eyes to the heavens as if his dead mother could hear him.

All of Trevin's trusted men raised their eyes to stare at Gwynn with a mixture of awe and disgust. She wrapped her arms around herself as eight pairs of eyes appraised her mantle—which was a deep blue—nearly black—and trimmed with white fur. 'Twas distinctive, to be sure, and the new baron of Rhydd had seen it often enough.

"Won't they think you kept her at Black Oak Hall rather than risk her getting wounded or seized?" Nelson asked.

"They could," Trevin agreed, then one side of his mouth lifted in his crooked, devilish smile. "But Ian knows her well. He would expect her to escape from my capture just as she slipped through his fingers and the very gates of Rhydd. A woman who hid herself in a coffin to escape will do anything on her quest."

"A coffin?" Henry was horrified, his face white as a new moon.

" 'Twas empty, eh?" Ralph asked.

Gwynn's voice was strong. "Nay, Sir Ralph, I hid beneath a corpse of another woman."

Henry jumped to his feet as if he'd been bit. "Ach! A dead woman? Mother of Mary." He shuddered, then, as if sensing the others thought him a coward, he cleared his throat and calmed a bit. " 'Tis . . . 'tis clever ye be, m'lady."

"Thank you, Sir Henry." She didn't believe him for an instant.

Trevin swallowed a smile. "So. 'Twould make sense to think that Lord Ian will be looking for his wife."

At the word wife, Gwynn cringed. How could she be married to one man and love another? This past night, beneath the pine tree, she'd made love to Trevin time and time again, quivering in anticipation of his touch, reveling in the ecstacy of his embrace, crying out his name as the night birds cooed and dawn crept over the eastern hills.

Now, she looked away from the censure in his eyes and pretended interest in the charred meat sizzling over the fire. Using one of Trevin's gloves to keep from burning her fingers, she lifted the spit from the flames. Upon a flat stone, she cut the birds and rabbit into quarters, then let the men use their knives and hands to claim pieces of the small feast.

" 'Twill not be that bad," he told his men as they settled back on their haunches or upon rocks or roots from the surrounding trees. "The lady's cloak is large enough that one of you could throw it over your own clothes and use the hood to hide your face."

"But what of our helmets?"

Trevin's jaw tightened at Henry's question. "He who wears the cloak goes without his helmet."

"Ahh."

This was the man who had got Hildy with child? Gwynn wondered. Between the two of them, did they have but one working brain? Gwynn held her tongue but thought the girl was better off without such a mindless self-serving man as a husband. Why Trevin had chosen him to come on this journey was a mystery to her for the soldier—not much more than a boy—was willful, stubborn, prideful, and dim. A bad combination in Gwynn's estimation.

She picked at her joint of rabbit as the men, eating and passing a jug of ale around the fire, discussed at length how they planned to thwart Rhydd's soldiers. As the hours passed and the ale flowed, each soldier in the group retold his own story, why he held a personal grudge against Ian or Roderick or Rhydd.

Nelson's nose flared as if he smelled a foul odor when he told the story of his sister, who, at a tender age, had been raped by Sir Webb. York's tale wasn't any better. His entire village had been pillaged by Ian and a band of Rhydd's soldiers long ago, while Roderick was still alive. A few years back, Henry as a youth had been spying upon one of Ian's men as he'd cheated at a game of chance. When Henry had been foolish enough to speak up, the cheat had lost his wager and his pride. Later he'd taken the time to beat Henry and leave him for dead.

And so it went. Each of Trevin's men was not only on a mission for his lord, but was also seeking his own personal brand of revenge.

At least they were dedicated to their cause, Gwynn thought, though she was anxious to be off. Trevin had explained that they were to wait and arrive near the gates of Rhydd as the sun was setting and twilight made seeing difficult. As the fire dimmed and the ale wore off, Trevin kicked dust onto the coals. He spoke in a whisper to Stephen and Gerald, the leaders of the two groups of soldiers and though Gwynn strained to hear what he was saying, no words reached her. Stephen nodded and picked at a glistening amber flow of pitch that ran down one of the fir trees that ringed the clearing. Squinting hard, Gerald scratched at the stubble of his beard.

When they were finished discussing whatever it was that was so private, Trevin cleared his throat as he spoke to the rest of the men, "There is something you should all know about me and the lady," he confided.

Gwynn's head snapped up. What now? Her eyes met Trevin's and she knew in an instant that he intended to tell them the truth of Gareth's conception. *No. Not now.*

"The boy we are trying to save, Gareth—"

"Nay, Lord Trevin," she cut in, then crossed the short distance between them. Desperate to keep their secret, she touched his arm. " 'Tis not the time."

" 'Tis long overdue." He drew his arm away from her fingers and eyed each man in turn. Gwynn braced herself and pride kept her chin lifted though she felt the slow warmth of humiliation crawl up the back of her neck to color her cheeks.

The forest was strangely silent. Pale sunlight dappled the ground. "The boy who we are trying to save, Gareth of Rhydd, is my son."

No one moved for a second. Henry's Adam's apple worked and he avoided Gwynn's eyes.

Trevin pocketed his knife. "The lady and I knew each other long ago and I allowed Gareth to be claimed by Lord Roderick. 'Twas a lie. One I have oft hated and one I should have renounced long ago, but Lady Gwynn and I struck a bargain and thought it best that Gareth know not who sired him."

Ralph let out a soft whistle.

Winston kicked at the dirt with the toe of his boot.

Stephen grinned as if pleased.

Gwynn wished the earth would open and swallow her, so that she would not have to suffer this embarrassment. Surely all the men would realize that Gareth was conceived while she was married to another and though her vows to the other man were not her choice, though her father had sold her like a prized rooster, she had sworn before church and state that she would be Roderick of Rhydd's bride and as such be forever faithful to him. No one here would understand her reasons.

Trevin's band of soldiers were uncomfortable. York fidgeted. Nelson cleared his throat. Others shifted and looked away. Only Sir Stephen raised his eyes to search Gwynn's face.

"I, for one, pledge my life to find the lord's boy and keep him safe." He stood and flung his sword into the soft ground. The blade stuck. " 'Tis my honor to do so."

"Mine as well," Gerald agreed. He jabbed his sword into the earth. "I will not rest until the baron's boy is returned to him and the lady."

"Aye!" Winston's sword joined the others, as did Ralph's, Nelson's, and York's.

Only Henry appeared to have misgivings. He eyed Gwynn and chewed on the side of his lip. His hand sweated enough that he had to rub it on his tunic. "I—I, too, pledge myself to ye, Lord Trevin," he said, swallowing with difficulty as all eyes were upon him.

"But you are troubled."

"Aye." He nodded and puffed out his chest. " 'Tis the lady. m'lord. I like not riding with a woman to do battle. I trust them not."

Trevin's smile was cold as death. "I assure you, Lady Gwynn can ride as well as any of you. Her aim with a bow and arrow is equal to most soldiers'."

Sir Henry's expression said it all. He didn't believe her capable of anything other than spinning, embroidery, or bearing children.

They had no time for this. Gareth's life was dependent upon this motley group of soldiers, including Sir Henry. "Mayhap the knight would like a demonstration," she said, keeping her anger under control, though, in truth, she would have loved to slap the upstart. "Sir York. May I borrow your quiver and bow?"

"Nay, nay, 'tis not necessary," Henry said. " 'Tis not that I doubt the lady's accuracy with a weapon but . . . but . . ."

"Say it, man, we have not all day!" Trevin said.

" 'Tis said she's a witch, m'lord." His eyes were round with worry.

"What?" Trevin asked.

"Aye, that she practices magic and the dark arts, and calls upon demons and . . . prays not to our Father." Quickly, he crossed himself, as if he expected Gwynn to level a curse upon him and send him to the pearly gates this very instant.

"Did not Muir also call up the spirits?" Trevin asked.

"Only when they came from a cup of ale."

At this some of the men tittered.

" 'Tis true," Gwynn said, stepping closer to Henry and smiling coldly. She was tired of the young knight's whining. "I am a witch." 'Twas time to teach the fool a lesson.

Trevin muttered something about stupid, hardheaded women under his breath. "Please, m'lady, do not—"

"But he's only heard the truth and if he returns to Black Oak he will learn that I worked my magic trying to save poor Sir Charles from a mortal wound. He will also know that I stopped outside of the castle walls and tried to remove a curse that some of the people within Black Oak's walls believe has been leveled against the keep. Aye, Sir Henry, I scribble runes in the sand. I chant spells and pray to the Holy Father in the hope that someone, whether it be Morrigu or Mary, is listening and will help me in my quest to save my son."

"But—" Henry licked his lips. " 'Tis a sin."

"Enough of this!" Trevin hissed.

Gwynn wasn't deterred, she stood close enough to the young knight to smell his sweat. "I have never yet cast a spell to harm anyone, but you surely test and vex me Henry of Black Oak, and if you do not help Lord Trevin and me in our quest for our son, I might be tempted to try out a few spells known to cause warts to form, or an eternal itching to consume a man's body or . . ." She paused as if to think and noticed that all the knights had become deathly quiet as they stared at her with worried, skeptical eyes. ". . . there is one that causes a man's cock to shrivel and become useless for all his days. Let me see, I will need the wishbone of a drake. . . ." She reached toward the burned, picked-over carcass of one of the birds.

Sir Henry gasped and not for the first time Gwynn wondered how this simpleton had become a knight. Stupid, easily goaded, and without courage this boy/man was surely unworthy of his title.

"Here we are," she said, lifting the bone in question and holding it close to the lad. "Now with a little thistle and Saint John's Wort and—"

"Nay!" Henry seemed about to lose control of his bladder.

"Enough of this teasing," Trevin cut in. "We have serious business to attend to." He sent Gwynn a glare that would slice to the core of a lesser woman's heart. "You, lady, will stop your silly incantations and Henry, you will accept that Lady Gwynn will ride with us and ride well. You are to defend her, to protect her, to honor her, and most of all allow her to use her weapons, whatever they be."

"But if she starts callin' the spirits and—"

"*Whatever* they be," Trevin repeated, his voice ringing through the surrounding hills. "Now, do you all understand our task?"

"Aye, m'lord."

"Yea."

"As ye wish."

They were all in agreement, it seemed, and even Henry nodded and pledged himself to the duty at hand. Trevin eyed Gwynn and she, though her back was stiff as a flagpole, acquiesced. " 'Tis nothing I want more than to free my son."

"Good. Let us break camp. Sir Gerald and his men will lead the soldiers off through the woods and to the north. After the commotion has died a bit, we will enter by way of a peddler's cart."

"You have this wagon?"

"Aye." Trevin and Stephen exchanged a quick, mysterious glance that bothered Gwynn. "Bought and paid for. 'Tis waiting for us." He kicked more dust over the coals and, satisfied that the fire was extinguished, motioned for all his men to pick up their weapons. "Let us be off!"

The peddler's cart wasn't much to look upon. Mud caked the spoked wheels and the few wares displayed had seen better years. Tin and silver trinkets, dusty furs, and bolts of cloth that had begun to fade were some of the items for sale.

The donkey harnessed to the wagon had a dull, winter-shaggy coat and listless eyes that surveyed Trevin's band of men without any interest. Ears turned backward, one back hoof cocked, he dozed in the afternoon breeze.

"Whatever you paid for this, 'twas too much," Gwynn whispered to Trevin as she pulled on the reins of her horse and surveyed the rig.

"Ah, m'lord, I had about given up on ye." The owner of the wagon was a rotund man with a girth as wide as the cart's wheel. His tiny mustache and pointed little beard appeared out of place over his thick jowls and he reminded Gwynn of a hog with his tiny sunken eyes and short nose.

She changed her mind when he grinned, showing off perfect teeth and those tiny eyes glimmered with merriment as he gazed upon Gwynn. "M'lady," he said, taking off his hat and bowing so low as to nearly sweep the ground with one hand. "Me name is Fitch and 'tis my pleasure to meet ye."

"As it is mine to meet you, good sir," Gwynn said, noticing for the first time that his thumbs were crooked and barely moved as he gestured.

"I hear ye are on a journey to save yer son. Godspeed to ye."

"Thank you."

He handed Trevin the reins of the cart. "And ye, m'lord, know how I feel about Sir Webb. If I can be of any assistance in cutting out that devil's wretched heart, I'd be glad to ride with ye."

"The cart and ass are good enough," Trevin said. "Thank you, Fitch."

"No thanks I need, m'lord. Just your assurance that this good earth will be rid of the likes of that viper."

"Rest assured."

A trade was made—two of Trevin's horses for the wagon and donkey and the peddler rode off. Only when he'd rounded a bend in the road did Trevin turn to his band. "Now, 'tis time. If our plans go awry and you are captured, remember there are those at Rhydd who are true to Lady Gwynn and myself. You can trust Richard the carpenter, and Mildred who brews ale."

"Aye, and Idelle who is a midwife," Gwynn added.

Trevin looked each knight in his eyes. "If you are caught, I will save you. 'Tis my vow."

"What if ye be the one who is captured?" Henry asked.

Trevin's smile was wicked. "Do not worry."

"But—"

"Do not try and save me, for I will fight my own battle. 'Tis enough that you have come with me for my son's sake and to save Muir's hide." He eyed the lowering sun. " 'Tis time."

"Oh, fer the love of Saint Jude," Henry grumbled as Gwynn removed her cloak and handed it to the smallest of the knights. Grudgingly he donned the mantle, pulled the hood over his head, and peeked sheepishly from its shadowy, fur-lined depths.

"Oh, ain't ye a cute thing?" York teased and winked at Henry.

"A rare beauty, 'e is, er, she is," Winston agreed and hooted.

"Enough!" Trevin's voice brooked no authority, but he could not hide the devilment in his own eyes. "Now, Sir Gerald, be off with ye. Make haste."

"Come along," Gerald said, clucking to his mount and riding away.

"Ye, too, sweetie," York stage-whispered to Henry and was rewarded with a glower.

"Leave me alone, ye big braggart." Henry gathered up his reins and guided his horse after Sir Gerald's.

"Oh, I like a lass with spunk, that I do—" York's voice faded as they rode away and a flock of birds flew overhead.

"They joke when they should be serious," Gwynn said.

"They are good men."

She didn't doubt their intentions nor their dedications, just their judgment. "God be with you," she whispered as the last of the group rounded the bend. Her worried heart sank. How could she possibly trust this band of ruffians, and not even particularly bright ruffians, to accomplish Trevin's plan? Gareth's safety was at stake, if, indeed, he was still alive, and the thought that his future depended upon duping Ian's men with the likes of Sir Henry made her blood turn to ice. Nay, she could not count on those buffoons for anything.

"Do not worry," Trevin said, as if reading her mind. "All they needs do is provide a distraction."

"I pray to God that they can do it," she said fervently, sending up a prayer before climbing off her horse.

"We will leave the horses here with you, Sir Ralph," Trevin ordered. "You are to take them back to Black Oak with news that our mission has failed and we have been captured if we don't return by morn."

The knight seemed about to argue, but held his tongue. "Aye, m'lord," he agreed.

"Stephen, you will take off your armor and wear the clothes Fitch left behind." He reached into a side panel of the cart and found a filthy pair of breeches and stained gray tunic, which he tossed to the blond knight. " 'Tis your job to convince the guards at Rhydd that you are truly a peddler. As no one in the castle has seen your face before, 'twill not be a difficult task."

"What of us?" Gwynn asked.

Trevin's smile was positively evil. "You and I, m'lady, shall ride in here." He reached beneath the rig, unlatched a metal bolt, and displayed the false bottom of the wagon.

"What is this?"

"Fitch is more than a peddler," Trevin replied.

She should have guessed. She eyed the dusty, hidden compartment. "He's a thief like you."

"And a smuggler of cats and men or pieces of gold. Aye."

"Why does he hate Sir Webb?"

"Did you not notice his hands? Sir Webb was the man who broke his thumbs and told him he was lucky that they were not cut off."

"He was caught stealing?"

Trevin nodded. "Aye, a loaf of bread for a starving child."

"Oh." Gwynn had new respect for the rotund man whose features resembled a pig ready for slaughter.

"Don't misunderstand. Fitch would steal from a poor man as well as a rich one. He is truly a criminal."

"But his heart is good."

Trevin lifted a shoulder. "Most times, though some might disagree." He motioned to the dark compartment beneath the floor of the cart. "We have no more time for gossip," he said. "Come, m'lady, your coach awaits."

She hesitated. Something felt wrong about this. Very wrong. Yet, 'twas a clever way to enter the castle unnoticed and she had no choice. She had to trust Trevin, for he wanted only to save their son as much as she did.

"Hurry and slide to one side as there must be room for me as well."

Gingerly she crawled under the wagon and slipped into the tiny, dark confines of the wagon. Dust swirled around her and she sneezed. Trevin followed her beneath the wagon, but instead of climbing inside, he swung the door shut.

Thunk.

It was suddenly dark as night.

"Nay—"

With a clunk, the bolt slid into place.

"Trevin!" She pounded on the sides of the cart as she realized that she was trapped. He was abandoning her! Oh, for the love of Saint Peter. He couldn't be doing this. Wouldn't! No! No! No!

" 'Tis for your own good."

"You demon! You can't do this! For the love of God—" She kicked and pounded, furious with herself for trusting him and burning with rage that he would trick her. Again.

His voice was muffled but she heard him say, "Take her back to Black Oak and stand guard at her door. 'Tis your duty to keep her safe."

"Nay!" Tears of frustration burned behind her eyes. What a fool she'd been. How many times would she let this man dupe her? "Trevin, please, I needs go with you. For Gareth." She thought of her son in that dark horrid dungeon. "Do not do this!" she begged. "Trevin!" She kicked hard and pounded until her fists began to bleed, but to no avail.

Did Trevin not know that Ian would kill Gareth if she did not return to him? Was he willing to gamble with their son's life. "Curse and rot your hide, Trevin of Black Oak, let me out!"

"As you wish, my lord," Sir Stephen said as the wheels creaked and started turning. The cart jostled in the rutted road.

Gwynn gnashed her teeth and fought her stupid tears. Whether she liked it or not, she was on her way back to Black Oak Hall. Away from Trevin. Away from Gareth. Away from any hope of ever seeing her son alive again.

Chapter Fourteen

"What the devil are you doing?" Gareth asked, his voice filled with horror. The old man had truly gone daft, for he'd smoothed away the straw on the floor of the dungeon and somehow—Gareth wasn't exactly certain how he'd accomplished this—Muir had begun to bleed from his finger. Chanting words that made no sense, he let the blood flow onto the floor in a snakelike pattern that coiled evilly.

"Shh." Muir grimaced and squeezed harder as he continued his task while the goosebumps on Gareth's skin began to rise. From the bench near the stairs the sentry snored loudly, his mouth open, his head bent forward as he dozed.

"I like this not," Gareth whispered.

"Nor do I, but 'tis necessary."

"Why?"

"Do you want to escape this dungeon? Aye or nay?"

"Aye, but—"

"Then pretend to be asleep and have no more questions," he ordered and added under his breath, "Silly, miserable youth." The drops of blood continued in their coiled labyrinthine configuration until the old man was satisfied.

"Now what?" Gareth asked as Muir sighed and sat on the floor, his back propped against one wall.

"We wait."

"For what?" Gareth was confused and he didn't like the old man talking in riddles.

"Until 'tis discovered."

"And then?"

Muir smiled. "Then, my boy, ye will see magic unlike any ye've ever seen."

"From you?" Gareth snorted in disdain. "I doubt it."

Muir's good eye was fast upon him. "You will see."

Gareth was sick of the riddles, the talk, and no deeds. He had his own way out of the dungeon and it didn't take chants or spells or scribblings in blood. Nay, with his slingshot he'd be able to wound more than one guard, dash up the stairs, and breathe fresh air again. He wasn't going to listen to Muir's silly ramblings and boastings that were naught. "I'll believe it when it happens."

"So be it," Muir said and closed his eyes. "Before this night is over, son, your mind will change."

Gareth snorted in disbelief and yet he felt a breeze, cold as snow, upon the back of his neck though there was not a breath of fresh air in this dank pit. Shivering, he ignored the old man's advice and rummaged through the filthy rushes for another stone to add to his growing pile. The addled wizard could believe in sorcery or pagan gods or demons for all Gareth cared. He, more practical, would depend upon his quick wits and his weapons.

His callused fingers encountered a chipped bit of daub from the wall and he smiled to himself as he pocketed what would become another pebble in his growing arsenal. Aye, whenever the soldiers came to take him to the gallows, they'd be in for a surprise. He'd give them a damned good fight.

His head plumped by pillows, Ian glanced down at his flagging member and cursed silently. Why couldn't he find hardness with his comely wench? Her skin was dark, nearly swarthy, her hair jet black, her eyes, wide with fear, a deep shade of blue. He'd forced her to straddle him and she'd complied, but still he felt no welcome warmth or tightening of his crotch.

"Damn it all to hell." He shoved her off him and scowled darkly. Though he'd lived nearly five decades he had the body of a younger man and very rarely could he not take a woman. Usually when that unlikely event had occurred 'twas because he'd consumed far too much wine.

Not tonight. This evening he'd swallowed hardly a drop as he'd waited for news from Black Oak Hall. Surely Sir Charles had reached the keep long before now. Aye, he'd been wounded, but he was a strong man and Ian was certain he would have made the trip. As foolishly loyal as the man was to Gwynn, he would have staved off death until he found the lady. Only then would he have dared give up his soul.

So, Gwynn, if she was at the keep as Ian suspected, would have heard that her precious son was imprisoned. She wouldn't think twice but would make haste to return either to beg for Ian's pity and oh, that thought was pleasant— or try to devise a way of helping the lad escape. Either way, Ian's wayward wife would return.

He couldn't wait.

But what of Trevin—the Outlaw Lord. Ian's muscles tensed at the thought and he shifted in the bed. The thief could not be ignored. No doubt he, too, would return. Ian planned a surprise for that one. For the humiliation of stealing his bride, the man would pay with his life, but first, as vengeance for the agony he'd inflicted in Ian's legs, Trevin of Black Oak would suffer, long and hard, in full view of everyone in the castle. Especially Gwynn.

The thief would be an example to anyone who considered going against the new ruler. There were others as well, men and women, servants and peasants who were more loyal to Lady Gwynn than to their new lord. They, too, would be publicly destroyed.

As would the boy. Gareth could not be allowed to live.

Yea, Ian thought, gazing at the tapestry of a great stag that hung near the fire, all he needed now was patience and a little relief.

"Touch me," he ordered roughly to the woman in his bed.

"M'lord?" the wench asked, her voice soft as a doe's breath.

"I said, 'Touch me' and be quick about it."

Biting her lip she reached under the covers of the bed and he felt her fingers, young and nimble, surround him. He closed his eyes willing an erection, but still did not respond. By the gods, what was wrong?

"Stroke!"

She gave off a soft mew of protest.

"Just do it."

She began her ministrations and he sighed. 'Twas as if a weight were pressed onto his chest. All this worry about his traitorous wife, her son, and the damned thief caused his head to pound. Oh, when he got his hands on that woman who had wed him. . . . At the thought of Gwynn he felt the first stirrings of desire course through his veins. Uppity, she was, the little snipe. Oh, when he finally took her, 'twould be pure ecstasy for him. He would not hold back, but mount her like a stallion and make her scream out of need. He knew how to satisfy a woman, but with Gwynn, 'twould not be a mating for pleasure, but a challenge, a show of power. He would make her squirm and beg and then plunder her body.

Mayhap the thief would get to watch their fierce coupling before he was put to death.

His cock began to throb though the girl had the touch of a blacksmith and worked with leaden hands. With Gwynn 'twould be different. And he would make her pay. For lying with the thief she would have to atone with her hands, her lips, her entire body. That thought, of her doing his bidding, whatever he wanted, caused him satisfaction.

He glanced down at the girl in his bed and for a split second he remembered another woman, so long ago it seemed as if 'twas someone else's wife.

That one, too, just past girlhood had raven hair and eyes as bright as sapphires. Comely and tart, she'd been the sister of a man who had interfered when Ian, much younger then, had made his advances known. The woman had declined and he, randy from a recent battle, had refused to take no for an answer.

"Yes, yes," he said as the wench in his bed continued to rub him, but still the old memory wrapped around him like a shroud. His breathing was ragged, his chest ready to explode, but he could not forget that other act so long ago.

'Twas in a forest, where the girl had been gathering mushrooms. Ian had spied her and the brother and wanted her. When she'd refused his lusty advances, he'd had no choice but to take her by force, using his dagger to encourage her into submission.

The brother, a slight man with a fierce countenance, had jumped him from behind and in the ensuing fight Ian had used the knife he'd held at the woman's throat to hobble the man. One cut to the leg, another to the arm, and a final blow to the face. He'd fallen then, screaming, his hands over his wounds, blood streaming through his fingers. The woman had been hysterical, but, as her brother lay bleeding to death, Ian had mounted her. The rest, robbing her of her virginity and spilling his seed into her, had been easy.

He'd left that particular village feeling strong and powerful. A true ruler. It hadn't mattered then that his brother, the eldest, would inherit Rhydd. He'd proved himself not only as a warrior, but as a man.

Now, years later, the ghosts of his past haunted him and though the girl in his bed was scared but willing, he could not hold a damned erection. There were too many distractions and the truth of the matter was, he decided as he rolled away from the girl and motioned her to leave, he would not be satisfied until he could have his wife.

And have her he would.

"We cannot stop now," Sir Gerald insisted. "We be but an hour's ride from Rhydd."

Henry wasn't going to be bullied. "I needs to piss."

"Ye should have thought of it afore."

" 'Tis nervous, I be." Henry pulled up on the reins and with Gwynn's cloak around him, he climbed off his steed. As they had ridden ever closer to Rhydd, the air had seemed to become thicker and damp with a soft shroud of fog. " 'Twill take but a minute."

Sir Gerald glowered from beneath his helmet, but he raised his hand, silently imploring the rest of the small party to halt. "If anyone else feels an urgency," he invited, but the rest of the men waited as Henry hid behind a small copse of fir and oak trees, bundled Gwynn's long mantle, unlaced his breeches, and let loose a long stream.

Finishing, he took a chance, ducked further into the woods where the foliage was dense and dark and there, where needles and dry leaves littered the ground, Henry dropped to his knees. Crossing himself quickly he tried to rally his courage, for his was a quest that was as dangerous as it was difficult.

He had not long been a knight and never would have become one had not his father died in the saving of Lord Trevin's life. At the memory of his slain father, blood pooling around his body, Henry's stomach twisted and the same sour taste that he'd experienced on that horrid day again crawled up his throat.

Lord Trevin, in an act of gratitude, had knighted the slain soldier's only son and, Henry feared, already had begun to realize that he'd made a mistake. Though he fervently wanted to please the new master of Black Oak, Henry could not. The new lord was not worth the dung of his father's destrier.

Did not Lord Trevin consort with a married woman?

Did not he trust her though she practiced dark arts and pagan magic?

Had he not killed Lord Dryw?

Had it not been for Trevin would not his father be alive today?

Had he fathered a child of another man's wife?

Henry spat and felt pain pounding behind his eyes. Trevin of Black Oak, a thief by trade, was not a man to whom Henry, nor his trusting father, should have sworn his allegiance, his fealty, or his life. The new lord of Black Oak was but a fraud, a man who kidnapped another man's bride, a man who cheated at a game of dice to win a castle, a man who had a murdering black heart.

A crow flew overhead cawing loudly.

"Forgive me, Father, for I have sinned," Henry whispered, his heart hammering wildly as he prayed in the wisping fog. He thought of Hildy and the fact that she was with child—his child. He should not have lain with her and yet she was so comely, warm, and soft. She offered sweet haven when his life was so confused. "Help me in my efforts to serve Ye. Be with my unborn child and sweet Hildy. I vow, if I am victorious in my quest, I will marry Hildy and give my son a name and forever be Your devoted servant."

"Hey, Henry!" Gerald yelled from the road. "Are ye not finished?"

"Aye about," he said, angry that his prayer was interrupted.

" 'E even pisses like a woman. Takes all day," Sir York observed with a chuckle and Henry's blood boiled.

He'd show them all. More swiftly than he wanted, he ended his prayer and stood, dusting the stupid woman's cloak he'd been forced to wear. Another humiliation he had to stomach at the hands of Lord Trevin. Well, not for long.

He appeared from behind the trees and York, astride his destrier, let out a long, low whistle. " 'Tis beautiful ye be, lass," he said.

"Yeah and what would ye know of beautiful women," Henry retorted with a swagger as he approached his horse, "when every one ye've ever been with 'as been ugly as a vulture?"

"Fortunately there 'aven't been many," Sir Winston added with a smirk, his mustache twitching.

"Enough of this nonsense!" Gerald eyed them all gravely. "We have not the time. There is much to do and nightfall fast approaches."

Henry swung into the saddle. His hands were sweaty on the reins, his mouth dry as wormwood, his heart racing. He, too, had much to do before the coming night and he was ready. 'Twould be sweet vengeance to prove Trevin of Black Oak the murderin' bastard he be.

Gwynn's legs had lost all feeling and her back ached as she bounced and jostled inside the dark compartment. How many times would she let Trevin play her for a fool? If she ever got out of this cursed box on wheels, she'd find a way to get even with him.

Would you? that pesky voice inside her brain demanded. *Remember his lovemaking, remember the way you felt as he kissed you, remember how easily he bent your will to his.*

Never again, she vowed as one cartwheel hit a rock and swerved slightly.

"Oh, Gareth, I fear I have failed you," she muttered, then gave herself a quick mental kick. She couldn't give up. 'Twas her duty to save her son and no one, not even Trevin of damned Black Oak was going to stop her. Somehow, some way she had to trick Sir Stephen. That would be difficult, for, of all of Trevin's soldiers, he seemed one of the smartest and most loyal.

She pounded upon the flooring of the cart. "Sir Stephen! Please. Stop!"

"Nay, m'lady," he replied, over the creak of wheels and rattle of the peddler's wares.

"But I need to relieve myself."

"Then ye best be doin' it in there."

"Please, do not make me soil myself."

He didn't reply.

"I could cast a spell on you and force you to do my bidding."

He chuckled. "Aye, so ye say."

"I jest not."

"Neither do I."

So he wasn't superstitious. Damn the fates.

"Ye may as well sleep and not waste yer breath on me," he said, "because unless Satan himself stops me, I'll see that ye be safely to Black Oak."

There had to be another way. For the dozenth time she let her fingers skim the interior of the compartment, from corner to corner, over the rough boards, picking up slivers for her efforts. She discovered where the bolt was driven into the false bottom, but it was secure and all she received for her efforts of trying to move it were bloody fingers and broken fingernails.

She closed her eyes and concentrated. She was in a box—a wooden box made of planks fastened together. Atop the box was the floor of the cart and above that foldaway shelves and cupboards holding the peddler's wares. Nay, she could not find a way through the upper flooring.

She couldn't give up! Nor could she rely on silly luck.

Again she searched the base and this time her fingers traced each board. Under one of her shoulders, she felt a knothole large enough for three of her fingers to delve through. If she moved slightly, the hole would allow a little light into her dark coffin, but not much as dusk was shadowing the earth. Craning her neck, she was able to see the axle that ran between the two front wheels. If somehow it could be broken . . . she still had her dagger, but there was no way for her to reach through the boards, and aside, the knife was too small to slice through a solid oak rod.

But there had to be a way.

Think, Gwynn, think! You're a clever woman. You ruled a castle in your husband's absence. You found a way to stay alive when Roderick threatened your life if you didn't give him a child. You tricked Sir Bently and the guards at Black Oak into letting you go free. Certainly a simple wagon can't trap you!

Notion after silly notion entered her head, only to be discarded. Night was falling swiftly and with each turn of the wheels she was being hauled farther from her son. Farther from the man she loved.

Though she was furious with Trevin for deceiving her, she still worried about his safety. If Ian discovered him, he would be tortured and killed. Ian of Rhydd was not a kind man nor a patient man. Even if she returned to the castle and threw herself upon his mercy, she didn't know if he would let Trevin and Gareth go free.

But 'twas the only chance they had.

Again she eyed the knothole. She forced three of her fingers through the small space. The fourth would not fit. She reached into her pouch, withdrew her dagger, and discovered it, too, would fit. But still it was a useless weapon . . . or was it? Perhaps if she . . . Her mind spinning with a new idea, she used her tiny knife to start ripping her tunic. First one strip, then another and another which, with pained fingers, she laboriously tied together in tight knots. "Holy Mother, please let this work," she whispered as once the tunic was completely destroyed and she was shivering with the cold, she tied one end securely to her dagger, which she used as a weight.

If she could drop it through the knothole and it would catch on the ground, there was a chance that the cloth strips would wind along the axle until they reached the wheel whereupon the torn pieces of fabric would wind in the spokes and clog the wheel so badly that Stephen would have to stop the cart.

And then what? Still, he would not open the hatch. Nay, she was doomed to return to Black Oak.

Nonetheless she let her knife drop. It hit the ground, bounced upward, and caught around the axle. Slowly her handmade rope began to slide through the knothole, winding as she'd hoped upon the axle. She rubbed her arms to keep from freezing and felt a change in the pace of the donkey as the wagon slowed.

"Come on, come on," Stephen yelled to the beast. "Hey, what—" The cart began to turn in a circle. "Straighten out, you stubborn beast."

Gwynn crossed her fingers.

"What in the name of Saint Jude?"

The wagon slowed to a stop and bounced as Stephen hopped onto the ground. "What's the matter with you?" he asked the donkey. "Oh, for the love of Christ. What the devil?"

"Sir Stephen, please," she said. "You must let me out."

"After what you did? By the gods, you might've ruined this cart and then where would we be?"

"I . . . I had to get your attention."

"By disabling the wagon? God's eyes, m'lady, what does that help?"

"We need to save Lord Trevin."

There was silence.

"Please, just listen to me, I beseech you." She didn't bother masking the desperation in her voice. "My husband . . . the Baron of Rhydd, he'll kill Lord Trevin if he but gets the chance."

"He won't."

"You don't know Ian," she cried. "Please, we must save him and Gareth. I can do nothing from here or Black Oak Hall." When he didn't respond, she added, "I know the lord thinks he's saving me, that I would only get in the way, but you must believe me, I've lived at Rhydd for over thirteen years and I know the castle like the back of my hand. I can save Trevin and Gareth."

"You're but a woman—"

"I was the mistress of Rhydd. I ruled the castle alone. I have servants, soldiers, and peasants within the walls of the keep who would do my bidding if only I can get to them. Trevin knows not who is ally or enemy. Please, we must hurry. There is little time."

"I cannot go against the baron's wishes."

"Of course you can when 'tis to save his very life! Sir Stephen, I know you to be loyal, aye, but smart as well. Please, I implore you, open this hatch," she ordered. "I would offer you coin, but I know you be a noble man who would be offended. However, whatever it is you desire, I will grant it to you. All you need do is let me escape."

She felt the shift in the air; knew he was weighing his options. Fiercely loyal to Trevin, he nonetheless wanted to help him.

"You and I—together we can aid the baron in his quest. What good is it for you to dress up like a peddler and spend two days' journey upon the road when you could be taking up your sword and fighting Black Oak Hall's sworn enemies?"

"I cannot listen to your prattle—"

" 'Tis not prattle, Sir Stephen. Tell me, how would you feel if the lord and his son died and you were busy driving a donkey and a woman away from the battle?"

Again silence.

"Sir Stephen, have you thought of it?"

"Aye—"

"Is not the lord's life worth his wrath?"

"Oh, by the gods, I should be bathed in hot oil for this," he grumbled, but she heard a wrenching of metal and a loud click as the bolt gave way, the hidden door opened, and fresh air invaded the dark interior of the box.

Gwynn didn't waste a second. She dropped to the ground before he had time to change his mind. Cold air rushed across the earth and brought goose bumps to her skin.

"Oh, for the love of God. You've got no clothes—m'lady, please!" Stephen stood and worked the latches on the top of the cart. Averting his eyes, he dug through the wares and came up with a leather tunic with metal studs that looked as if it were made for a small boy. "Here, until we reach Black Oak—"

"We go not to Black Oak," she corrected, as she drew the tunic over her head and cinched a small corded belt around her waist. He found a hat as well as she tied her hair onto her head before donning the hat. She eyed the peddler's cart with a scowl. "Can the wheel be fixed?"

"Aye." Stephen bent on one knee, sliced the tattered strips of fabric away from the axle, and after cutting her little knife free, handed the dagger to her. "Your weapon, m'lady."

"Thank you."

"Now," he said, straightening and wiping his hands on his too-small breeches. "I will take you back to Castle Rhydd and accept my lord's ire even if he banishes me, but I want your promise that you will do as I say and stay out of danger." His blue eyes were troubled.

"I swear. Except that I must talk to Ian."

"With me," he insisted. "Elsewise I will take you to Black Oak Hall if I have to carry you over my shoulder like a sack of flour."

"But—"

"Do not argue, m'lady. I fear not your sharp tongue, your little dagger, or your spells of nonsense. Nor do I fear Lord Trevin's wrath or Ian of Rhydd's blade, but I will not go against my lord's wishes without your oath that you will obey me and, when we meet up with him again, the Lord of Black Oak."

The words stuck in her throat and Stephen stood as if rooted to the earth of that very spot in the road. He folded his arms over his great chest and waited. "What will it be, Lady Gwynn? Back to your hiding spot in the cart and on to Black Oak, or will you do as I ask on our way to Rhydd?"

"I have no choice."

"Then say it."

"I, Sir Stephen, I will do as you ask." 'Twas a lie, but a small one, just a fib, to assure her that she would have a chance to save Gareth.

"Do not cross me, m'lady."

"I will not. Now, come, let us be off. There is no time to waste!" She climbed onto the driver's bench and Stephen, grumbling under his breath that he was the worst kind of fool, climbed aboard and took up the reins.

Night had fallen, they were hours from Rhydd and Gwynn worried her dagger in its hilt. What if they were already too late?

"Swear to God, Sir Webb, they were out there. Five, maybe six of 'em. all wearin' the colors of Black Oak Hall." From the watchtower where they stood peering through the crenels the guard made a sweeping gesture toward the forest where a thick mist was beginning to rise.

Webb eyed the young sentry as if he'd gone daft. "Why would they show themselves? If I were to try and sneak into another's keep, I would disguise meself so as not to warn me enemies."

"I know not," the young man said, his thick eyebrows butting together. He was a serious lad with dirty-blond hair, dark eyes, and a crooked nose. Webb had never known him to lie or make up stories, but then times were strange and as the lord had pointed out, no one was to be trusted. Not even this snot-nosed soldier. "I know what I saw and there were half a dozen men and a woman—aye, 'twas a woman's cape, like the lady's."

"Lady Gwynn's?" Webb asked, more interested.

"Aye. I've seen her wear it afore—deep blue with fur—white fur lining it."

"She would come this close to the castle? Why take the risk?" Webb fingered the hilt of his sword and stared at the darkening forest with its eerie, shifting blanket of fog. Though the soldier had no reason to lie, Webb smelled a trap. "Prithee, what else did ye see?"

"Your destrier."

"What?" Every muscle in his body tensed.

"The black with the off-center splash of white down his nose or his damned twin," the boy sentry insisted. "Swear on me poor mum's grave that the leader was ridin' 'im."

Anger, hot and dark, shot through Webb's veins. The damned thief had made him look a fool at the mill that night by stealing his favorite mount and now he was parading the beast, flaunting the fact that he'd bested Webb. "And the woman in the cloak was with him and his band of men?"

"Aye." The youth's head bobbed up and down faster than a chicken plucking up bugs. "I don't think they thought they'd be seen as 'twas nearly dark and the fog, it was shiftin' in, but my eyes are keen."

"So they are." Was it possible?

"Could they not be going to make camp in the forest nearby until they are ready to attack?"

" 'Tis a small amount of men," Webb thought aloud as he rubbed his chin.

"And a woman," the sentry reminded him. " 'Tis truly what I saw."

"And they rode toward the river?" Webb sighed. 'Twas a cold night and fog, damp and cloying, had begun to roll over the curtain walls and into the bailey. The thought of chasing through the woods and coming up empty-handed again wasn't appealing, not when there was a cup of ale and a game of dice to be had. This sighting of an enemy army could be naught but a young guard's overexuberance. "Did you see any of the men close up?"

"Nay," he admitted, "but the mantle the woman wore was Lady Gwynn's, I be sure of it."

"Or like hers."

He lifted a shoulder and had the decency to look worried. "I thought the lord would want to know."

"Aye. That he will," Webb thought aloud and considered how much of a reward he would pocket if, indeed, he captured Trevin of Black Oak as well as the lady. 'Twould be well worth giving up a cup of wine, warm fire, and a game of chance.

Asides, his interrogations had gone badly. The mason had known nothing, the carpenter had been close mouthed with a hard glint in his eye. An odd one, that. As for Mildred, the alewife, she had been scared, to be sure, but her mouth hadn't been pried open and Parr, the atilliator, had seemed innocent. Webb hadn't tortured anyone, not yet, and though it bothered him not to inflict pain, he preferred to use the whip or brand or knives only if other means were not effective. He'd planned to speak with old Idelle on the morrow and that wasn't a pleasant thought. The midwife gave him the chills. Those near-blind opaque eyes saw far more than a normal person's. The chants she whispered as she moved about the keep caused his innards to turn to pudding.

She was a daughter of Satan and there was no doubt of it.

"Find a replacement for your watch, I want ye to ride with me and show me where the bloody bastards went. I'll get the others," Webb said, as there was no other option. Mayhap the thief was foolhardy and desperate to save his son. Certainly the lady would risk anything for the boy. Aye, 'twas possible that Ian's plan was working.

Webb hurried into the turret and took the stairs leading ever downward. He'd wake up the houndmaster to ready the dogs, and take a dozen of Ian's best men. If the thief was stupid enough to ride up so close to the portals of Rhydd, Webb would personally drag him before the lord and if the lady . . . Webb's thoughts strayed into perilous territory when he considered Ian's wife. Unlike any woman he'd ever seen before, she was beautiful, smart, and sharp-tongued. Webb usually liked women who were pretty and stupid, willing to do whatever he wanted without too much of an argument, but Gwynn of Rhydd was the exception—a fiery challenge. He wondered, not for the first time, what she would be like warming a man's bed, then, as he shoved open the door to the outer bailey and stepped into the damp mist, he pushed those wayward thoughts aside.

She was Ian of Rhydd's wife, lady of the castle, and Webb would think of her as such. Nothing else. To do otherwise would spell instant death.

Instead of the thief, it could be he who would end up dangling by the neck from the hangman's noose. Webb had worked too hard and too long to let his eager cock determine his fate.

But he had to remain cautious. There was a chance that the sentry was mistaken, that there was no small army from Black Oak, or, that he'd mistakenly identified a group of travelers as enemies, or . . . was it possible? Could the sighting be part of Trevin of Black Oak's plan to lure some men away from the castle and ambush the lot of them?

Webb glanced over his shoulder as he made his way to the kennels and some of the hounds began to bark. Was it his imagination or were there enemy eyes already watching his every move?

Curse it all. He'd never felt a moment's fear in his life, until he'd come across that slippery thief with the cold blue eyes. Christ, the thief caused a blade of dread to twist in Webb's guts.

The sooner the bastard was caught and brought to Ian of Rhydd's swift justice, the better.

Webb's mind worked feverishly as he awakened his men—his best soldiers.

Some would ride with him, the others would stay, awake and alert, to defend the castle.

Trevin of Black Oak wasn't going to outsmart him and make Webb appear the fool again. 'Twas time to even the score.

Chapter Fifteen

The fog was a blessing he hadn't expected. It rose from the river, enveloped the castle, and provided Trevin with a cover he might not have otherwise found in the shadows of Rhydd's watchtower. He grinned to himself as, with a clang the portcullis rattled open and two files of Rhydd's best soldiers mounted on steeds worthy of battle galloped through. They carried torches that burned bright in the night but gave off small illumination in the gloom.

"Ride, you bastards," he muttered softly and spied Webb's stiff back as the dark knight rode upon a pale charger. The company seemed to be made up of Rhydd's best soldiers, but nowhere in the small army did he spy the lord of the manor. So Ian of Rhydd was still within the curtain walls.

Good. Trevin wanted to deal with the baron personally.

Before the guards had a chance to lower the gate, he slipped into the bailey. Like a wolf slinking through a dark glen, he made his way unnoticed to the carpenter's hut and silently sneaked inside.

"Richard?" he whispered as his eyes adjusted to the dark interior. " 'Tis I—"

"Yea, I know who ye be," Richard said from his bed jammed into a back corner of the shop. "Be quiet, will ye, or we'll all be killed." Tools lined the walls and the scent of sawdust and raw wood was heavy in the air.

"Richard?" The carpenter's wife, Maggie, rolled over as he climbed out of bed.

"Shh, wife. 'Tis only Trevin."

"Ach. The baron, y'mean. I *know* who he is and what trouble he brings to this house," Maggie grumbled over a yawn. "Whether ye be a thief as I knew ye years before or all high-and-mighty Lord of Black Oak, 'tis a dark cloud ye carry with ye, Trevin McBain."

"Hush!" Richard ordered.

"Hush, yerself. Here I am, with child now, and Trevin, oh, excuse me, his lordship, comes in and ye're ready to lay down yer life. Haven't ye suffered enough?" She sat up in the bed, held the covers around her ample breasts, and pouted. "I needs ye, Richard. I love ye."

"Aye, and ye hate Lord Ian as much as I do."

Maggie, sighing theatrically, fell back to the pallet. "Oh, all right," she groused. "What do ye want me to do?"

"Pretend that nothing is amiss," Trevin said, his voice low.

" 'Tis a miracle ye want from me then."

Richard turned and reached for a tunic hanging on a peg. As he did Trevin saw his back, white skin marred by dark, ragged welts.

"You've been flogged," Trevin whispered, fury burning through his veins.

"Within an inch of his life. Because of you, McBain," Maggie was anxious to tell him. "Sir Webb that devil was on a tear. Lookin' fer spies, he was."

"Worry not," Richard said. "Sir Webb first came sniffin' around, just askin' questions, of not only me, but others as well. When he found out nothin' he resorted to . . . stronger measures." Richard found his sword and strapped it onto his belt. "I kept me tongue quiet, as did everyone, even old Matilda when they threatened to burn her fingers one by one. She's a tough old hen, I'll give her that. Now, my friend." He looked up and grinned in anticipation. "What have ye got in mind?"

" 'Tis time to take the castle away from the lord."

"Oh, is that all?" Richard mocked.

"Nay, we need to free Muir and Gareth as well."

"And did ye bring an army to help ye?"

Trevin shook his head. " 'Tis only I, but Lord Ian's best soldiers have ridden out of the castle to be led on a merry chase."

"So, then, have ye got a plan in mind?"

"A simple one," Trevin said.

"From you, would I expect more?"

"Be sure this plan, 'tis one that works," Maggie mumbled from beneath the covers.

"To be sure," Trevin agreed. "Now we need to quickly round up the men to take over the great hall and the dungeon."

"Gladly," Richard said and Maggie, from the bed, sighed dramatically.

"Be on your guard," she advised, her eyes shining in the dark.

"Always," Trevin vowed as he opened the door a slit and stared through the crack. When he was certain the sentries weren't looking, he and Richard would launch his personal attack to save his son.

"Good work." Gerald held tightly to the reins of Dark One as the charger sidestepped and snorted, nervously shifting in a tight circle.

"Here they come." From their vantage point on a hill, Trevin's men could barely discern the looming darkness of Rhydd. Shrouded in the fog, the fortress was black except for two columns of torchlights shining weakly in the gloom.

"Like a dog to a bitch in heat," York said and Henry watched, his heart beating rapidly, his body bathed in a cold, worrisome sweat.

The five of them sat astride their mounts waiting to lead the warriors from Rhydd through the forests and hills. But Henry had his own plan, a scheme that didn't include racing along the edge of the river to disperse on differing trails through the woods while Ian of Rhydd's soldiers stupidly split up and followed their lead.

"Now!" Gerald said as the lights shone brighter. He kneed the black stallion and snorting, the beast took off. Tail aloft, hooves clanging on stones, the charger raced through the dark trees. Winston, York, and Nelson took up their reins and their mounts, too, raced through the underbrush and damp mist.

"Guide me, Father," Henry prayed, trailing behind, his steed's gait an easy canter along the wide path. The sound of the river, water rushing through the canyon, met his ears and he told himself to have faith. He was doing that which was right. *Remember your father, how he died needlessly, taking an arrow meant for the outlaw-turned-baron. Remember Lord Dryw. A good man. An able leader. Murdered by Trevin.* His breathing was labored, sweat running in his eyes, Lady Gwynn's mantle billowing over his bay's rump as he slowed his horse, fighting as the animal tossed his great head, anxious to be part of the ever-fleeing herd.

"Hold back," he said to the horse as the trees gave way to a strip of rocky shore that bordered the black, racing water. The others had already urged their animals onto the sandy beach, hoping that their pursuers would catch glimpses of the small army before each rider turned into the dense foliage once again. Nelson's mount splashed along the river's edge, York's hugged close to the trees, Gerald and Winston rode together in the middle of the sandy strand. Henry hung back, his trepidation mounting as wisping trails of fog separated him from the others. Certainly this was the right thing to do— the most noble of acts. Or was it?

His throat ached in fear and for the first time he doubted the wisdom of this one, rash act. Hoofbeats sounded behind him. Men's voices, unfamiliar voices, caught up to him. He swallowed hard and sent up another prayer. "Please, Father, keep me safe. Let me follow the courageous noble path worthy of—"

"Hey! There's one!" he heard as he wheeled his mount.

"Do not harm me," he yelled. "I am with you."

" 'Tis the lady—" one of the riders, dark and ghostlike as he appeared in the haze, yelled.

"It don't sound like 'er."

"Use caution. She is not to be harmed." Webb's voice boomed through the fog. Bobbing lights burned ever more brightly. "Stay your weapons!"

Soldiers on huge horses emerged from the mist to surround him and his nervous stallion.

Henry began to tremble. "Do not harm me for I wish to join you," he said as he tossed off the hood of Lady Gwynn's mantle. "The lady is not with us as we—the other four riders and I—are part of a decoy mission."

"Decoy?" Webb thundered, his mount mincing as it approached.

"Aye. Trevin and the others, the lady included, stayed back and planned to take the castle."

"Four of them?" Webb asked.

"There are others inside; those not loyal to Ian of Rhydd." Oh, he hoped he'd not made a horrid mistake in throwing in his lot with Lord Ian and this surly knight.

"Why, pray tell," Webb said, guiding his horse so close to Henry that the beast's hot breath shot down his leg, "should I believe that you've turned traitor?" His face was wet from the mist and glowered darkly in the dim, flickering light of the torches. "Could you, too, not be part of a trap?"

"Because I tell the truth. I—I am Henry. Sir Henry." Why wouldn't they believe him?

"You be a knight?" One of the soldiers laughed and another joined in. Henry squared his thin shoulders and tried to hold up his wobbling chin.

"Hush!" Webb glowered at this company and his face took on the visage of Satan incarnate. "Tell me, Sir Henry, why ye have turned against the man for whom you ride?"

Sweat trickled down Henry's cheek and settled in the sparse hairs of his beard. "I trust him not. He killed Lord Dryw and . . . and my father lost his life saving that of the outlaw." His reasons, nay his convictions, sounded feeble and unfounded.

"Ye expect me to believe you?"

"Aye." Henry nodded quickly, his eyes darting as the soldiers seemed to draw nearer, evil messengers from hell getting ever closer. His horse tossed his head nervously and Henry had to fight every instinct he had to kick the steed and try to race away from the sinister forces he suddenly realized were at work here. " 'Tis . . . 'tis the truth I say, Sir Webb. This be not part of a trick. If . . . if ye do not believe me, ye can take me hostage, but please, please trust me, Trevin is at this moment inside the gates of Rhydd. He will not rest until his son is free and Lord Ian is dead."

"What of my horse?" Webb asked, his countenance menacing.

" 'Tis ridden by one of Trevin's men, part of the deception, as is this mantle of Lady Gwynn's."

"Where is she?"

"We left her with a peddler, but . . . but I think Gerald, one of the knights, said that she was to be returned to Black Oak by Sir Stephen, another one of Trevin's knights."

Slowly Webb unsheathed his dagger. Leaning forward in his saddle so that his face, a mask of dangerous fury, was within inches of Henry's, he whispered, "Listen to me, *Sir* Henry, I will trust ye for a while. We'll return to the keep and if I find that ye have deceived me, I will personally cut out yer lying tongue and throw it to the dogs, do ye understand?"

Henry nearly fainted. He swayed in the saddle. "Aye. Aye. But 'tis the truth I speak," he managed to say as Webb leaned back, pulled upon his white steed's reins and the animal, rearing, wheeled and nearly fell against Henry's mount.

"To Rhydd," he said and Henry felt a moment's relief. "And you"—he pointed a gloved hand at a burly giant of a knight—"Sir Patrick, make certain our prisoner does not escape."

"Prisoner?" Henry said as someone slapped his mount's rump and the edgy horse leaped forward. "Nay, Sir Webb, I am not a traitor to Rhydd."

"Nay? A man who turns his back on his lord is not to be trusted. This, I know."

"But—" *Prisoner? No, this was all wrong!*

"Ye didn't think ye'd be a guest, now, did ye?"

"I thought I would ride with yer men."

"Did ye?" Webb's laughter was dull and wicked. "You be a simpleton, then. 'Tis a miracle you be called a knight. Come! Once we secure the fortress, then we shall retrieve my horse and find the lady." He spurred his mount and the white stallion took off like a shot, galloping fearlessly into the thick darkness.

Henry, astride his steed, was swallowed in a sea of horses, soldiers, and torches. Though he felt betrayed, as if he'd cast his lot with the wrong madman, he had no choice but to follow.

"Help! Guard! Please, help me with the old one. He's . . . he's dead!" Gareth cried, banging on the iron bars of his cage with his fists.

"Dead?" the sentry, a behemoth of a man whose only speed was slow, asked. "Nay, he's just sleepin'."

"He breathes not! He . . . he has no heartbeat! Please call for the physician."

"If he be dead, then 'tis already too late." With a snort of disdain, the man climbed from his bench and lumbered through the murky darkness to the cell. "He looks fine to—what the devil's that?" Frowning, his heavy face distrustful, he opened the cell door and walked inside.

"I know not," Gareth said, eyeing the rune that Muir had bled from his own body onto the cell floor. "Did you not hear the old man rambling on and on and drawing on the floor?"

"Nay . . ." The sentry slowly shook his massive head. "I listen not to the prisoners." He scratched his crown and his face pulled into a confused frown.

"Well, he did and then . . . then he lay down as if to sleep and died . . . I swear it!"

The guard didn't move, nor did he approach the old man who lay motionless on the filthy rushes.

" 'Tis the mark of the devil," the thickheaded sentry whispered, fear flaring his nostrils.

"No . . ."

The guard, rather than enter further into the cell as Gareth had hoped, backed out and closed the door with a clang. "I'll not be in any place where Lucifer sleeps," he insisted and a few of the other prisoners grumbled their agreement. "Hey—John, you at the top of the stairs. Go and get the priest."

"Why?" a voice yelled down.

"Do it and do it now unless ye want to find yerself in the maw of hell!"

"Go and get 'im yerself!"

"Gladly." Backing up the stairs he disappeared and Gareth kicked at the straw in disgust.

"He believed you not," he whispered, thinking Muir's plan to trick the guard had been feeble at best. "We needs to do something else."

The old man didn't stir.

"Did ye hear me?" Gareth asked, moving closer to the corner where the sorcerer slept. "We needs—oh, God." Muir was not sleeping as was the plan. Nay, he lay, not breathing, his one eye open and staring sightlessly. "Oh, no, no, no!" With footsteps as cold as an ogre's breath, fear crawled up the back of Gareth's spine and wrinkled his scalp. "Help!" he cried again, more loudly this time.

"Oh, shut up, would ye?" a ruffian grumbled from his cell.

"You shut up, Reginald," his cellmate shot back.

"Help!"

Gareth's heart thundered, his palms sweated. He'd never liked the old man, not really, and yet he felt a horrid loss in this dank, close prison with its dripping walls, rotting straw, and hidden rats. To be in this dungeon, alone, without anyone with whom to speak was unthinkable and the sorcerer for all his faults was a good old sod. The world seemed to collapse upon him and

Gareth realized the futility of his plight. He thought of his mother and tears burned the back of his eyes, tears he would never shed for 'twas weak to show how much he missed the woman who'd borne him.

All of his bravado failed him and though he tried to summon a drop of courage, he had but to look at the old man, his mouth agape, his chest not rising, his scarred eyes open and Gareth wanted nothing more than to climb through the damned bars and escape. His slingshot was tucked into his breeches and he had more than a handful of pebbles in his pocket, but he was so scared he could think of nothing more than getting away from the dead body.

"Hey, is the old sod really dead?" one of the other prisoners asked.

"I'll be buggered. Are ye sure?" another joined in. "Ain't 'e some kind of magician or somethin'? Maybe 'e's just in a damned trance."

"Aye and I be the King of England."

The men chortled and told more jokes, but Gareth didn't listen. He stared at the stairway and silently prayed for the priest, the guard, *anyone* who would remove the body.

It seemed like hours before he heard voices and saw the dance of golden shadows from a torch playing against the bottom of the steps.

" 'Tis too late for last rites," Father Anthony was saying as he, grim faced, along with the guard and old Idelle entered the dungeon.

"This place be a disgrace," Idelle said, shaking her aged head as if she could see through eyes that had turned a milky white. "If the mistress was still in charge—"

"Well, she ain't and this is the way Lord Ian likes things," the guard said as he reached for his keys.

"Gareth, lad!" Idelle's wrinkled countenance lightened with a grin. " 'Tis troubled I've been, knowing ye were here." She hugged him fiercely and again those dreaded tears came to his eyes. Idelle, so close to his mother, had always been good to him. "I've tried to come and see ye, but Lord Ian had forbidden it."

"Where is my mother?"

"Oh, would I to know," she whispered, kissing the top of his head before turning to Muir's still form.

"Look, there, on the floor!" The guard pointed at the rune Muir had created with his own blood. " 'Tis the mark of the devil, I tell ye."

"Nay," Idelle dismissed the man's fears. " 'Tis only a drawing about life."

The priest, trembling, made a quick sign of the cross, then leaned over Muir. "This poor soul—"

At that one of the magician's hands moved.

"Achh!" The guard yelled.

"Holy Father." The priest backed toward the cell's door and Gareth, heart beating faster than a rabbit's, yanked his slingshot from his breeches, loaded, and fired a piece of mortar. Ssst! Crack! The rock hit the sentry squarely on the back of his head.

"Ouch! Say what?" He turned just as another piece of flying mortar shot into his forehead. "Ach! Stop!" Another shot. This one to an eye. "Stop it, ye've blinded me, ye filthy little bastard." With one hand over his wound, the other to his sword, the guard didn't expect another sharp stone to launch into his gut.

"Jesus, Mary, and Joseph, stop him!" He yanked out his sword but not before Muir jumped to his feet and imbedded his tiny knife into the guard's neck.

"Run!" he ordered.

Blood spurted and sprayed. The sentry swung wildly with his sword and Gareth took off like a startled colt. He didn't wait to see what happened to Father Anthony or Muir or Idelle. He ran up the stairs two at a time and threw open the door to the bailey where fog shrouded the keep. He slunk through the shadows, hanging close to the curtain wall and thankful for the mist that was his cover. Two sentries guarded the main gate and the portcullis was down. No escape there. He inched around the edge of the keep until he came to the kennels where the dogs, already restless, woofed softly at his approach. Alfred was nowhere in sight, so Gareth let himself into the pens and was nearly knocked over by Boon.

Tail whipping, the pup yipped and danced at Gareth's feet. "Hush," he ordered, picking up the wriggling mass. Most of the grown dogs, those trained for the hunt, lifted their heads, then lowered them again as they were used to the boy visiting at odd hours. He held his puppy close and felt the wild, erratic beating of Boon's heart. "Shh," he warned, trying to stay in the shadows.

Muir, the old goat, had duped him. Why hadn't he told him that he could put himself into a trance or whatever it was and appear dead? Gareth shivered as he carried Boon out of the kennels and sat behind the huge kettles used for washing clothes. He had no plan for escape, but knew it would have to be done quickly, before everyone in the castle was looking for him.

On his feet again, he made his way past the ferret kennels where the nervous beasts were pacing restlessly in their cages. Boon stiffened, but didn't bark as they passed only to stop at the end of the kennels and view the sally port where a sentry, a young lad from the looks of him, was positioned. He wore no helmet so there was a chance that Gareth could use his slingshot against him, but he had only one more pebble. 'Twasn't enough. He needed a pocketful of rocks and then he'd attack the guard and set himself free.

Once he was outside of the walls of Rhydd, he'd do as his mother had ordered him and head south. In a few days' time if he walked partway and caught rides on carts, he'd arrive at Heath Castle where his mother's sister Luella was mistress.

Except he had no money or jewels. Those his mother had given him before were with Muir. Gareth had nothing, not a single coin. Unless . . . He smiled to himself in the darkness. So his father was a thief, was he? Well, Gareth could be one as well. He'd steal a dagger from the armory, bread and apples from the kitchens, and a few jewels from the castle treasury, for unless Ian had changed things in the short time he'd become lord, Gareth knew where the spare key to the treasury was hidden.

Something was wrong. Terribly wrong. The sounds of the castle were different. In his sleep he'd heard men shouting, horses neighing, and the excited barks of the hounds. Ian had incorporated all these noises into his dreams, but now, though the fire had burned down and the torches were dark, he sensed another presence in his chamber.

He reached to the side of the bed where his sword was lying, but his fingers found only cold stone and thick rushes, no metal blade.

His heart hammered and he turned, expecting to find his dagger and its sheath near him on the pallet, but it, too, was missing.

"So you finally awaken."

The voice was that of his enemy. The thief.

"I thought I might have to slit your throat while you slept."

As Ian's eyes adjusted to the darkness he saw his nemesis, dark and foreboding, looking larger than ever as he stood near the window. In one hand was Ian's sword, in the other his knife.

"How did you get in here?"

"Through the front door."

"Guard!" Ian yelled, but Trevin crossed the room and was upon him, his own knife pressed against his throat.

"I've dispensed with those loyal to you," he said in a harsh whisper that turned Ian's blood to ice. "Now, I think you should get dressed and come with me."

Gwynn eyed the sky and wished for moonlight and a swifter means of getting to Rhydd. They'd traveled for hours, she and Sir Stephen, and finally they were near, though the tired ass lagged and 'twas only the reins slapping him on his buttocks that kept him plodding along.

The air here was dense with fog and cold enough to freeze flesh. Gwynn blew on her hands and hoped beyond hope that she was not too late, that Trevin was safe and Gareth . . . oh, if only he were alive and somewhere safe.

"Cannot we move faster?" she asked, not for the first time.

"Would that we could, but 'tis not possible."

Time was ticking by so quickly and Gwynn shivered to the marrow of her bones. She should never have let Trevin trick her so, never have trusted him and yet, furious as she was, her heart was with him and the few men he'd taken.

'Twas a fool's mission but she couldn't quell that little bit of hope that burned bright in her heart. Surely he was safe. He had to be. With Gareth. Oh, what she would give to see her son again, to embrace him. If only she could see them both one last time, she would be able to give herself to Ian and be his dutiful wife.

The idea was pure poison and it turned sour deep in her belly, but she would find a way to survive being Ian of Rhydd's wife, suffer any indignity he suggested as long as Trevin and Gareth were safe.

She sent up yet another silent prayer and somewhere in the forest nearby a wolf gave up a lonely cry. The donkey, so listless moments before, bolted and the cart rolled forward at a faster clip.

Rhydd was close now. She could feel it in her bones, but along with that welcome sensation was a dark fear that those she loved most in the world were in danger . . . or worse yet, neither had survived.

Gareth couldn't believe his good luck. His pockets bulging with jewels and coins he'd taken from the countinghouse, the puppy tucked under one arm, he dashed along the curtain wall, pausing behind a wagon to scan the bailey.

All the sentries were missing, away from their posts, and he had the vague feeling that something was amiss, something more than his escape from the dungeon. Was it possible old Muir had finally cast a spell that worked and all the guards had fallen asleep at their posts, or mayhap, after the fight and confusion in the prison could it be that the sentries were scouring the castle looking for him?

Gareth didn't stop to think too hard. All he knew was that the gatehouse appeared empty and though the portcullis was lowered, it was a simple matter of raising it and slipping through. It would take time and agility, for the minute the huge metal gate began clanging upward, the castle would be alerted. Then he would have only seconds to race down the stairs and dash through the gatehouse to freedom outside the castle walls.

Cautiously he slunk along the edge of the walk, squinting so hard through the fog that his head ached. His slingshot was tucked into the band of his breeches and in the hand not holding the dog, he carried a dagger.

He reached the gatehouse and holding his breath, slipped through the open door and up a winding staircase. He expected to run into a guard hastening down at any second, but heard no sounds and the torches and candles in the sconces on the walls had burned low, some mere embers that cast little light.

Heart thumping, he reached the winch room, then realized he couldn't open the portcullis without another man's help. "Damn," he muttered under his breath as Boon gave out a yip and scrambled out of his arms. "Shh!"

"I wondered when ye were goin' to arrive."

Gareth froze, then watched in wonder as Muir, cackling, appeared from a dark alcove. So the old man did have a little magic in him after all.

"Hurry now, boy. We have not much time. Grab that handle!"

Gareth did as he was told though he wondered at the old man's strength. The gate was heavy, meant for two stout men to reel it upward and yet there was no other way. If he and Muir and Boon were to escape, they had to open the gates.

"The prisoners have escaped!" A guard was yelling, his voice rolling through the bailey as Trevin, his sword still at Ian's throat, pushed his captive through the doorway of the great hall. No other men came running, and the few sleepy-eyed servants who appeared in the windows did not seem inclined to help the anxious sentry.

Trevin smiled to himself. Richard and the other men they'd gathered must have been victorious in their efforts of subduing the few guards and soldiers left in the castle. He leaned forward and said into the older man's ear, "Now 'tis time for you to smell the stench of the dungeon." Trevin prodded Ian with the tip of his blade.

The sentry, running toward the great hall, was tackled by a clumsy lad no more than thirteen. They rolled on the grass until Richard, hiding behind a broken wagon, leapt forward and helped the awkward boy restrain the guard. "Sorry," the carpenter said, looking up and appearing sheepish. "We missed this one. Good work, Tom."

"The rest?" Trevin asked.

"Most have either sworn allegiance to you or are in the dungeon."

Ian's shoulders slumped as if a weight had been placed squarely upon them. In the poor light, he appeared old and tired.

" 'Tis as it should be," Trevin said.

"Nay, 'tis not all good news. A few men loyal to this one"—he spat on the ground at Ian's bare feet—"escaped and the boy and sorcerer are missing."

"What?" Trevin's fingers tightened over his sword. "Missing?"

Richard nodded gravely. "I led the group into the dungeon, but the guard was already dead, the boy and Muir gone, and all that was left was a strange, bloody drawing on the cell floor."

"All for naught, thief?" Ian asked, one eyebrow lifting.

"Where are they?"

Ian shrugged. "I have no idea."

Trevin believed him, but felt a moment's fear. "Search every inch of the castle," he ordered his men but as the words escaped his mouth, he heard the creak and groan of ancient gears. Rattling like the chains of dying prisoners, the metal portcullis slowly raised. "No!" he yelled for just as the gate opened, the hollow, damning sound of hoofbeats rang through the bailey. "Close the gates!" he ordered, "For the love of Christ, lower the gate!" But it was too late. Through the fog he saw two figures, an old man and a youth, slip out the door of the gatehouse while, riding through the unguarded portal was a company of soldiers, torches held high.

In the lead, his sword drawn, the blade gleaming a malevolent gold in the light, was Trevin's old enemy.

Sir Webb, hatred distorting his features, had returned.

The only object between him and the outlaw baron was Trevin's son.

"Gareth, run!" Trevin screamed. "Here, take this one!" He shoved Ian toward Richard and ran across the bailey, his sword raised, fury and fear pumping through his blood. "Run, damn it, boy, run!"

But it was too late.

"Get him!" Webb ordered. Two men jumped from their steeds. Another took quick aim. The dog, which Gareth had been holding, dropped to the grass and yipping, scuttled away.

"Nay!" Trevin vaulted a pile of firewood in his path, landed quickly, and didn't miss a stride as he ran. He was only fifty yards from the boy.

Thwack!

The first arrow hit Gareth in his leg. He screamed and the sound echoed in Trevin's heart. Writhing in agony, the boy fell. His slingshot slipped to the ground. With a whimper, the puppy ran further into the shadows.

Another deadly hiss.

Thud. The second arrow lodged in Gareth's shoulder. Again that horrid, shrill scream.

"Nay!" Fury, as black as a demon's heart tore through Trevin. He raced forward, his sword raised, the keening scream of denial he heard, torn from his own throat. He swung and one of the archers fell with a sickening thunk. Horses whinnied and reared. Men shouted. Swords flashed in the ghastly orange lights. Metal clashed. Grown men yowled in pain.

"Stop him!" Webb's voice thundered above the horrid cacophony.

An arrow hissed through the air, whizzing by his head.

Another sizzled as it passed.

"Trevin! Watch out!" Richard's voice. Somewhere nearby. Or far away. Men scrambled off their horses and in the midst of the soldiers, captured, his face white as death, was Sir Henry.

Thwang!

Pain exploded in his thigh. Trevin stumbled. His sword nearly fell from his hand. He forced himself onward. "Gareth!"

An archer sighted on his boy.

Trevin threw his sword. It hit the archer and sliced deep.

Screaming, blood spraying from his chest, the soldier dropped to his knees, clutching the weapon that was ending his life.

"Stop this bloodshed! In the name of the Almighty, I implore ye!" Father Anthony, robes flying behind him, descended through the dark bailey like a furious, avenging angel from heaven. "D-d-do not—Oh, merciful God!"

Trevin was at Gareth's side. His dagger was in his hand. "Stay back!" There were other men about. Some rushing from their huts, others taking up weapons. Whether for him or his enemies, he knew not. The torches reflected on the thick mist and in the wild eyes of the restless steeds and the flash of weapons.

Dogs barked, horses snorted, and in the distance he heard a baby crying. Men were shouting or screaming, the sounds jumbling in his mind.

An arrow hissed by his ear. Another pierced his shoulder. "Gareth, get up. Run."

" 'Tis too late," Muir, appearing through the fog, was suddenly at his side. Gareth lay unmoving, blood staining his tunic.

"Nay. He will live and survive and—"

" 'Tis too late for all of us," Muir said.

"Never!"

Trevin reached under the boy, intending to carry him to the keep. "Gareth, lad, rest easy. I will see to you," he promised, staggering as he lifted the boy and the pain of his own wounds burned through his muscles.

"Stop!" Ian's voice was cold as the bottom of a well. "Traitor. Murderer. Thief!"

Trevin pushed onward. The words were far and distant, their meaning unclear. A roar, like the sound of a mighty, tumbling waterfall, filled his head. If he could get Gareth to the keep, lie him on a bed, all would be well.

And what of Gwynn?

By the gods she was beautiful. If he could see her again. Just once. He fought the pain and the darkness that threatened his vision. The dull roar in his head grew louder, like the sound of the sea pounding the shore. *Gwynn, love, I will see that our son is safe. Remember that I love you as I have loved no other. . . .* With a shake of his head, he cleared his mind. He could not lose his senses, not yet.

"Did you not hear me?" Ian roared.

Trevin trudged onward, his legs heavy, his feet stumbling in the blood-stained grass. He would save his son. If he'd done nothing of purpose in his vile life, he would save his boy.

Sweat poured from his skin. Blood flowed from his wounds. Pain gnawed at his body and soul. Still he trudged forward. 'Twas not much farther.

"Run!" Richard yelled. "Trevin, please . . . all is lost! Save yourself!"

Ian, who had managed, with the help of the miller to wrest Richard's weapon from him, watched the fool carry his boy toward the keep. With each step Trevin of Black Oak faltered yet he kept onward, intent upon his mission, caring for a child he'd never really known.

The battle was nearly over. Webb's soldiers and weapons were strong; the insurgents—peasants and servants—were no match for trained warriors.

Ian turned to a marksman who had slain several men in the uprising. "Take care of the traitor," he said and watched as the archer drew back on his bow, aiming at Trevin's back.

"NAY! TREVIN!" A woman's voice, his *wife's* voice, shrilled. Ian turned and saw Gwynn, her face a mask of horror running through the bailey. Her feet were swift as she passed the soldiers who had managed to round up most of the traitors. She had just arrived in some sort of cart and was dressed in men's clothing, leather tunic and breeches. Her hair streamed behind her, tears ran from her large eyes and never had she looked more beautiful. "Stop this! Ian, I beg you, please—"

Trevin, hearing her voice, turned.

The archer released his missile.

True to it its mark, the arrow whistled through the air and lodged deep into Trevin's shoulder, only inches above Gareth's head.

"Nay, nay, nay!" she yelled, racing over the wet grass and through the thick mist, speeding closer.

The outlaw baron staggered. His son rolled to the ground and with one final look at the woman racing through the gloom, he fell.

"Trevin! Oh, no, no, no!"

She tried to race past him, but Ian would have none of it. This woman had humiliated him before. She'd run off with the thief on their wedding night, slipped away from him and caused him to be a buffoon to his own men. She was not to be trusted, never to be let out of his sight again. For all he knew she could already be carrying another of the outlaw's children in her womb.

That nasty thought curdled his blood.

Though he was nearly fifty, he was quick and he caught her. He reached for her arm and she, flying around empty carts and splashing through the edge of the eel pond, jerked her elbow away from him. As if his very touch repelled her.

Wicked little slut.

"Stop, wife!" he commanded and when she attempted to keep running, he tackled her, knocking her onto the muddy grass. Tears still pooling in her eyes, she tried to push him away and when his grip around her only tightened she pounded his chest with her fists.

He pinned her with his weight and grabbed her hands so that she could no longer strike him. So close he could smell the scent of heather in her hair, he heard his men surround them, knew that Webb and his soldiers were witnessing the taming of his woman. "Listen, you little wench," he breathed hard into her ear. "If you value the lives of your lover and your son you will get up and stand with me as my wife. You will find a way to repair your dignity as well as mine."

"I cannot."

" 'Tis your choice, m'lady," he said, seeing the righteous fury flashing in her eyes and feeling her breasts, beneath him, rising and falling with each of her shallow, indignant breaths.

"I would rather die."

" 'Tis not your life with which I barter."

Every muscle in her body stopped moving. Finally, he had her full, though unwilling, attention.

"If you do not do as I ask, I'm afraid, they'll both die."

"No!" She twisted, trying to catch a glimpse of her beloved and their child.

Her faith in the thief was enough to make a man sick, though he was awed by her courage and the fervency of her emotions. " 'Tis your choice, sweet," he said, trying to keep the snarl from his voice. "If you do not stand by me they will die, either by the wounds they have received this night or by having their necks snapped in the gallows as soon as they are strong enough. So make up your mind. Now. Just remember, their fates rest with you."

Chapter Sixteen

"Why not just kill 'em?" Webb asked as he picked at his thumbnail with the tip of his dagger. He leaned against the stones of the grate as servants scurried, eyes averted, in and out of the curtains and up the stairs. Guards were posted at all the entrances of the keep, ready for an attack, should one come from Lord Trevin's loyal soldiers at Black Oak. Though many of the peasants and servants were in prison, there were enough to run the castle, though all of those couldn't be trusted. Not yet. There were dozens of pairs of eyes and ears that were watching and listening.

Ian sighed. He would have to be careful if he wanted to earn the trust of those whom he ruled.

A spark shot from the fire in the great hall and he kicked the dying ember back to the flames. It had been two days since the attack by the outlaw and he would like nothing better than to put an end to Trevin McBain's miserable life, just as he'd promised Gwynn. Nothing better. But he had to think in larger terms, about the future, about his wife, and his power. As for the boy, well, once again, it had to appear to Gwynn as if Ian were a forgiving man even though he'd shown his true colors on the night of the attack. He'd kicked himself several times over for her to see the hatred that blackened his heart.

Gwynn was the key. The sorry fact was that he was afraid he loved her. The image of her face, twisted in pain and fear as she'd raced across the bailey intent on reaching her child and lover had seared through his brain. He doubted it was possible that she would ever care so much for him. He'd once only wanted her submission, her taming, and cared not if she loathed him. Now he needed more. Not just her expressionless compliance, but her heart as well.

" 'Twould be easy enough to kill 'em," Webb said, frowning as he cleaned each of his filthy fingernails.

"Aye, and then what? They will die anyway, but I needs not hasten it along. Let the midwife chant her spells and burn her candles." He fluttered his fingers in the air as if waving off a bothersome fly. "Allow the priest to pray and flog himself in atonement." That one, Father Anthony, was an odd man. Never had Ian seen a man so intent on doing himself physical harm. "Do not stop the physician from testing urine, or letting blood." He leaned forward in his chair and rested his elbows on the trestle table as he eyed the candles burning brightly within the ring of interwoven antlers suspended from the ceiling. Webb was an imbecile who thought only of the moment at hand and Ian, though it was against his nature and who would like nothing better than to slit the outlaw's throat, tried to be patient. "I want to rule with her at my side. For that she must trust me."

"Why?" Webb spat into the fire and sheathed his blade. He wiped his nose with his sleeve and eyed the lord of the manor as if he were weak. " 'Tis too late for trust, m'lord," the dark one snorted with a cruel laugh. He reached for the mazer of wine he'd left on a corner of the table.

"Do you not know it's never too late?"

"Oh, aye, and now ye'll be quotin' scripture or some such rot to me. Ah, Lord Ian, a fine and righteous and pious man ye be." He laughed again and Ian seethed, his neck growing warm. As soon as things at Rhydd quieted and he and Gwynn were ruling the castle amicably, he'd find a way to dispose of Webb. He was a good warrior, true, but he felt no bond with the man who had helped his brother go free after Ian had paid dearly to keep Roderick imprisoned. Webb would have to die for that mistake.

Ian leaned back in his chair and propped a boot onto a nearby bench. Today he was feeling his years. Five decades and no heir. 'Twas time to change that, if he could. Margaret had given him no sons, nor had any of the wenches he'd bedded claimed he'd fathered their children. Then there was the sorry fact that his wife might be pregnant with the thief's issue yet again. Had they not been together, spent nights alone or only in the company of Trevin's men?

Anger surged through him, that same bloody anger that was fed by his hatred. He touched the side of his face, his fingers tracing the wound the thief had given him. Oh, how he longed to kill the bastard. 'Twould be so simple. Webb was right.

But Ian would have to be patient. If Gwynn was with McBain's child, then the babe would never survive the birth. Ian would see to it. He would not be played for the fool his brother had been. But until the child, if there was one, was disposed of, he could not chance bedding Gwynn. If she did get with child, how would he know whether it was his or the spawn of the thief's?

He had to wait.

Either she was pregnant or would, soon, have her time and the laundress would know. But there was no reason he couldn't hurry McBain's death along, was there? Who would know? Mayhap, for once, the dark knight was right. "I will think on it," he said. "Now, tell me, what of the magician?" Another burr under his saddle.

Webb scowled into his cup. "Disappeared."

"Impossible."

"He must've ducked out the gate before we closed the portcullis. In all the fighting and with that bloody fog, 'twas hard to see."

"He's here. I can feel it." Ian sipped from his cup and tried to dispel his thoughts about the old sorcerer. There was something about the old cripple and his bad eye, something he should remember . . .

He heard footsteps on the stairs and looked up to see Gwynn accompanied by two guards descending into the hall. Dressed in deep, red velvet, her hair braided away from her face, her chin lifted, she was as beautiful a woman as he'd ever seen. And she was his wife. A fleeting sensation of pride swept over him until he remembered she might be with child. A babe without any of his blood running through its veins.

"Wife," he greeted, standing and pulling out her chair. "Come, come, there is much we needs discuss."

"I want to see my son," she said, her cheeks two bright spots of color.

"And you shall, as soon as he improves—"

"Now!" she insisted. "I needs see him, touch him."

There was pain in her green-gray eyes and he knew he had no choice. If ever she was to trust him, to love him, he would have to accord her this one small wish.

He inclined his head. "I will see to it."

She stiffened for a second and distrust marred her beauty.

Ian glanced up at one of her guards. "When we are through here, the lady will visit her boy."

The ghost of a smile touched the edge of her lips. "And Lord Trevin?"

His patience snapped. Murdering the thief in his sleep sounded better all the time. "Nay. He, though being attended to, is a prisoner. The same as the others. As soon as he is well enough, he will be sent to the dungeon to await my judgment." Ian had to be careful. He wanted her trust and confidence; he hoped someday she would care for him just a little, but he refused to look weak. He reached into his pocket. "By the way, I found something of yours."

"Wha—? Oh, merciful God." Tears filled her eyes as she watched him twist the ruby ring in his thick fingers. She'd not seen it in thirteen years, yet she recognized the ring Trevin had stolen from her, the one she'd eventually given him in order to keep his silence about Gareth's conception. Now it winked in the firelight, dark facets sparkling as Ian placed the stone in her palm and she curled her fingers over it.

" 'Twas with the thief," Ian admitted and her heart tightened in pain.

In all the years they'd been separated, Trevin had never given away the ring, never sold it. Tears filled her throat. "Thank you," she said.

"Anything for you."

She saw a glimmer of love in his hateful amber eyes. "Then please, m'lord," she asked, her words tumbling out, "forgive those who rose against you. Do not seek vengeance against the carpenter, the alewife, and all the others who were caught in the fight. Have the gallows dismantled. Show some pity, some caring for those you rule and let the soldiers of Black Oak go free—"

"I cannot," he said simply. "Though it grieves me, Lady, those who rose against me must be punished."

"But they did it for me."

"Then they will have to learn who the lord is. You are but my wife and though 'tis my every wish to make you happy, I cannot appear weak. Now, go, see the boy and"—he glanced up at the guards—"my wife may see the midwife who will attend to her from this moment on. She will no longer be locked in her room, but"—he added when she lifted her head expectantly—"for the time as it is, she must remain within the great hall."

Gwynn didn't know whether to thank him or demand more freedom. She opened her mouth, saw the set of his jaw beneath his silvering beard, and she nodded. "Thank you, m'lord," she said, still clutching the ring. If he were willing to concede her this much freedom, she would take it and plan accordingly.

" 'Tis nothing, Gwynn. I only ask that you believe I want to please you as I hope you want to please me." His benign smile was not to be trusted, for the gleam in his eyes reminded her that he'd lusted for her long and she knew him not to be a kind or forgiving man.

"Aye, m'lord."

"Take her to her son."

Heart pounding, she allowed herself to be led away by the guards. Finally she would be able to see Gareth, to touch his face and hair. If only she could do the same for Trevin. She ached to touch him again, to kiss him, to tell him how much she loved him. . . . She walked along a corridor to the western edge of the great hall and up the stairs. All the while she squeezed the dark ruby so tightly it nearly drew blood, then at the locked door in the towers, she slipped the ring upon her finger.

Gareth was in a small, windowless room resting upon a tiny bed. One candle burned in a sconce and the air was thick with the smell of death. For the first time she believed that she might truly lose her only child. Grief, ugly and creeping, gnawed at her. "Oh, Gareth," she said on a sigh as she fell to her knees and touched his forehead. His skin was hot, his eyes closed, and he moaned softly. Tears burned behind her eyes as she saw the blood-crusted bandages wrapped over his wounds, one in his chest, another in his thigh.

"I'm here," she said, holding his hand, now larger than hers, in her fingers. *Please God, save him. Please hear my prayer.* "Gareth, I will stay with you. But please, awaken." Her heart was heavy, for he did not stir and the thought that he might never awaken tore at her. Guilt took a stranglehold of her throat and she wept, her tears staining his blankets and dropping onto his skin. "You have been my life, son," she admitted, "and you will always be."

Pain seared through his body. Every inch of his skin felt as if it were charred with red-hot coals and he couldn't open his eyes. He heard people, the priest, the old midwife, voices he didn't recognize, but Trevin knew he had one foot on the path to hell.

Gwynn. Where was she? Had she escaped? No. He'd failed. Somehow she'd returned to Rhydd and tried to save him and the boy. His head pounded. He'd failed Gareth as well. His only son; now, without a doubt, if not dead already, on his way to the gallows.

"He awakens." The priest again.

"Nay, he only stirs." Idelle's voice, as if from the far end of a corridor.

"Will he live?"

"He is strong of heart but who knows? His wounds were deep, and if he survives 'tis only to face the hangman's noose." Cold, brittle hands smoothed his hair from his face.

"Let us pray."

Idelle agreed and as he drifted in and out of consciousness, Trevin heard their whispered prayers for his wayward soul. He felt himself slipping away, but fought hard. He could not give up. Not while there was a breath of life in his body. Not while Gareth was alive and needed him. Not until he was certain Gwynn was safe.

"Ye must eat, m'lady," Idelle said as she eyed Gwynn's untouched trencher of brawn that lay, where she had placed it, upon a small table in Gwynn's chamber.

"I'm not hungry." Gwynn paced from one side of the room to the other, pausing to look out the window and cringe each time she viewed the gallows, hastily constructed and nearly ready should they be needed. Ian had savored the irony of having Richard, the wounded carpenter, oversee the building of the very structure that would eventually take his life. No amount of pleading from the carpenter's wife, or from Gwynn, could convince him to spare

Trevin's accomplice. All the men who had taken up swords against Rhydd that night had been shackled in the dungeon, including Henry, who, it seemed, had been a traitor to Trevin's cause, though he was loudly complaining of his treatment according to some of the women who had taken food to the prison.

With the exception of Muir, they'd all been caught. The old man had vanished from within the fog-encased bailey. No one had seen or heard from him since and it had been days . . . long, sad lonely days that had bled into one another. She found her only solace in the fact that both Gareth and Trevin were alive, if only clinging to life.

She spent a large part of her days with her son, the rest here, in her chamber, for though allowed the freedom of the keep, she had not the heart to take up her duties as mistress to Lord Ian. She cared not about the herbs, gardens, nor the books or records nor the damned cloth that needed to be purchased. Nor could she stand the fighting between the cook and steward.

All that mattered were Trevin and Gareth. Somehow she had to free them both. There had to be a way. There had to! She clenched her fist and felt the ring upon her finger—the ruby. The depth and darkness of the stone gave her strength.

"But ye must think of the babe, if not yourself," Idelle said.

Gwynn knew the old woman was right, of course, there was the chance that she was starving a child, should there be one growing within her. Ian suspected that she had made love with Trevin and as such, was waiting to see if she was pregnant before taking her to his wedding bed. He wanted his own heirs and wasn't about to be duped into raising another man's child as his own the way his brother had been. So she had some time; not much, but a little.

"Tell me again of Trevin."

"He grows stronger, aye, but does not wake. He is guarded at every hour and when 'tis time and he has healed, he will be taken to the dungeon where, along with the rest of his men, he will await his trial."

"You mean his death," Gwynn said, worrying the ring in her fingers.

"Aye."

"You are allowed to see him?"

Idelle nodded.

"Then you must take him a weapon, a—"

"He does not waken. 'Twill do no good."

"But we must save him."

"And risk Gareth's life?" Idelle asked, shaking her head, her half-blind eyes sad. "Do you not think that Lord Ian's retribution would be swift and sure if Trevin were allowed to go free?" She picked up the tray of uneaten food. "Let him go," she advised. "M'lady, Lord Trevin's destiny is now in his own hands."

"Nay—"

"Think of your son. His son. What would he have wanted?"

"Then you must help me. I have to see Trevin one last time." She was desperate. "Is there nothing you could put in the guard's food to make him drowsy? So that I could visit Trevin for but a few minutes."

Idelle hesitated. " 'Twould be difficult."

"But not impossible."

Slowly the old woman nodded. "Nay, not impossible."

"Then, please, Idelle, do it."

"Ye will not be able to leave this room unnoticed. Ye may rove free, but you are watched."

"I will go at night."

"A guard is posted at your door."

"I know the guard and his ways." Gwynn sensed the old woman weakening.

" 'Tis too dangerous. Ye will be caught."

"No. Bring me animal fat and I will grease the hinges and do not worry about the guard."

Idelle hesitated.

"Please, Idelle," she said firmly. "Do this for me."

With a shake of her graying head, the midwife rolled her opaque eyes. "As you wish, m'lady."

For the first time in a week, Gwynn felt a ray of hope pierce her dark soul. She wouldn't give up. She couldn't. Twisting her ring, she walked to the window and eyed the gallows—built squarely in the middle of the bailey for all to see. Richard was at his post, chained and guarded, as he instructed younger men to pound nails and shore up the posts that would eventually end his life.

Unless she did something.

But what? The question haunted her and kept her awake at night. Now the wheels were set into motion. She had a chance to see the only man she'd truly loved. Somehow she had to find a way to save him.

Think, Gwynn, think. You're a smart woman. You've ruled this keep. Your son and the man you love are dying. You have no time. Hurry!

"In the name of the Father and the Son and the—" The priest's voice stilled and he froze as Trevin skewered the man with a deadly gaze. "Oh—for the love of God, you live!"

"Shh!" He'd been waiting for days and now, as night was falling, he knew it was time to return to the living. He'd awakened to broth being spooned down his throat but had kept the presence of mind to feign the same deep sleep that had kept conscious thoughts at bay. He swallowed, but was unable to speak for a second.

"I am p-p-pleased that—"

"Hush!" Trevin ordered in a harsh whisper. "Give me your cross."

"What?"

"The cross!"

"Oh. Nay, I cannot—" Trevin's hand shot out and wound in the folds of the priest's vestment.

"If not for me or Gwynn, then for Roderick," Trevin forced through cracked lips. "I have heard your prayers, Father, when you thought you were alone and I know that you broke your vow of celibacy, but not with a woman." The priest nearly fainted, then slowly, his glance sliding toward the closed door, he lifted the chain supporting the heavy gold and silver cross that hung from his neck. With shaking fingers he handed the chain to Trevin, who snatched the cold metal and stuffed it under the thin blanket covering his body. "Speak of this to no one and I will keep your secret."

"I—I—"

"Shh. Get out." Trevin closed his eyes and held on to the metal. At first he hadn't believed Father Anthony who, in his rambling prayers, had continually begged forgiveness for his own sins of the flesh with the lord of the castle. 'Twas no wonder Roderick had been unable to get Gwynn with child. He'd been in love with a man. The thought knifed through Trevin's innards and disgust brought bile up his throat, but he would not think of the two men together, nay, but concentrate on the fact that now he had a weapon. Cold metal filled his palm and he brushed his fingers over the pointed tip of the cross. Now, he had to wait.

But not for long.

Muir's old bones ached from hiding in a small space below the loom, a place Idelle had hidden him on the night of the escape. He'd been brought food and water and even a pint now and again while he'd waited, hoping that the soldiers would believe that he truly had vanished, or, if not that, at least think that he scuttled away through the open gate.

But he would not leave Trevin. Not when there was a breath of life in his old body or any in his young charge's. For he still considered himself Trevin's guardian and whenever that thought faded, he had only to think of his sister, Cleva, and the cruel, ruthless soldier who had raped her. Muir, who had robbed the man earlier, had tried to stop the travesty, of course, had attacked the man as he'd unlaced his breeches, but the soldier had been swift with his blade and had swung fast, nearly killing Muir and leaving him blind in one eye.

Muir shivered in his hiding spot, little more than a grave it was, with straw for a bed and rats for companions as, overhead, the weaver kept at her task, the shuttle clicking loudly as the threads were woven.

He remembered the blow, strong enough to cleave a man, but it had glanced off his hard skull, slicing through his eye as he'd fallen and in that moment a great light had seemed to glow in the forest. From that moment on, he'd had visions, cursed as they were, and he'd heard his sister's screams as the young soldier—brother to the lord, Roderick of Rhydd—had mounted her, raping her over and over again while Muir could do nothing to save poor Cleva.

Nine months later she'd birthed Trevin and, after forcing her brother to promise to take care of the baby who only reminded her of that one, violent, dark act, had drunk enough hemlock to kill herself. There had been nothing Muir could do to save her and he had raised her son—Ian of Rhydd's son— as if the boy had been his own. He'd sworn to his sister that he would never reveal the name of the boy's father or tell him how he'd been conceived. Only then had Cleva been satisfied. For all these years he'd kept his promise, but now, with the circle of fate ever tightening, he saw all his best intentions sliding away.

He banged on the false door with the hook of his cane and the clicking halted. The weaver, a stout woman with fair skin and merry blue eyes, kicked off the rushes and opened the trap door. Fresh air flooded the small niche and filled Muir's old lungs.

" 'Tis time," he said and she, worrying her lower lip, only nodded. She was one of the few in the castle who were loyal to Lady Gwynn and detested Ian of Rhydd, yet had managed to escape prison.

"God be with you, Muir," she whispered as he ducked behind spindles of colored thread mounted on pegs near a back wall.

"He always is." His legs were cramped, his blood felt as if it were congealed and a tingling sensation in his feet and fingers made walking and holding his staff difficult, but as evening was soon approaching, he had little time to spare. His vision had come earlier and, if it could be trusted, an army was nearing.

None of the soldiers who guarded the roads leading to Rhydd had discovered the men as they sneaked through the forest on foot, but Muir could sense them approaching, had seen through his pained blind eye, that they slunk at night through the forest. They were the men loyal to Trevin—Sir Gerald, York, and the rest. Now, he had to do his part, which was simple. He would steal the keys from a guard, unlock the dungeon, freeing the men inside, then have them overcome the guards of the sally port and throw long ropes down the outside of the curtain so that more armed warriors could scale the walls and save them all.

The scents of warm bread and roasting meat hit him as he slunk behind the kitchens but he ignored the rumbling in his stomach. Barrels of wine were being rolled into the wine cellar and he licked his lips as he thought of the nectar within the oaken casks, but he kept to his mission. Now was not the time to give in to his lust for wine. There would be time for sampling the barrels soon. If all went well. If it didn't . . . then his thirst for the spirits would be forever quenched.

Gwynn watched the moon rise and waited until the sounds of the castle had muted and the farrier's hammer had stilled. The geese, ducks, and chickens had roosted for the night and the torches had burned down and were but smoldering. The gallows, skeletal and foreboding, were visible in the moonlight, so she looked not through her window.

Asides, she had a mission.

She cracked the door slowly and the old creak of hinges no longer squeaked as she'd greased them with sheep fat Idelle had stolen from the kitchen. Her boots, too, were soft and silent as she watched the guard at his post. He never dozed and took his job quite seriously, but she knew he could be distracted, and as she waited, her heart pounding, sweat dripping from her forehead, she saw the comely kitchen girl who met him regularly at night.

He spoke—a quick joke. The girl giggled and tossed her head as he approached. They embraced and for a heart-stopping moment Gwynn remembered making love to Trevin deep in the forest—his touch and the feel of his mouth upon hers. She licked her lips and once the two lovers were caught in each other, she slipped from the room, closed the door softly behind her, and took the corridor to the steps that ran to the back of the castle.

Heart thudding, she made her way through the hallways to the far tower of the keep, the one where not only Gareth but Trevin was housed. She'd asked about him, but the gossip that had returned to her had been in snippets and contrary. Some said he was hovering near death, others thought him stronger by the day, but never had he awakened. Idelle seemed to think that he might forever be in this state of near-death and that thought was the worst of all.

Let him live, she silently prayed as she climbed the stairs to the room where Gareth lay. No guard was posted at his door, so she stopped, walked noiselessly into the small room, and brushed a kiss across her son's forehead. "I miss you. The pup is waiting for you as I am, Gareth." Her throat swelled shut and she fought tears, as she did each time she visited him.

It pained her to leave him, but she had another mission tonight. Quietly she walked to the top floor of the tower, her back pressed against the wall as she climbed the stairs, for she feared that she would be spotted.

She hoped that Idelle's herbs had worked and the sentry was sleeping. She paused, straining to hear the sound of snoring, but the hall was silent. No sound greeted her and she hurried up the final steps only to send up a quick, silent prayer and round the final corner.

The guard was missing. No one stood at his post and the door to Trevin's room was ajar. For a moment her stupid heart leapt and she thought that he'd escaped, but as she inched forward and peered into the tiny chamber, her blood turned to ice. Trevin lay on the bed. Unguarded. Unmoving.

Her heart shattered. He was dead. Oh, no. "Trevin," she whispered, falling to her knees and taking his still-warm hand in hers. "Oh, love, no, no, no." Inside she was dying. How could she have loved him so long and never told him? How could she have regained him only to lose him all over again? Tears burned behind her eyes and fell onto his body, bare aside from the bandages that were wrapped over him. "I love you," she whispered, sniffing and holding him. "Forgive me, but I loved you with all my heart and love you still." Desperation tore at her soul. Grief raked through her body and her years ahead— alone, without him, seemed long and purposeless. She reminded herself that she had Gareth, that part of him would live on through their child and also that she might have another babe growing deep within her. "Trevin, please . . . please do not die. I need you, I—"

"Touching."

The voice curled with acrimony and Gwynn started. She turned and saw Ian looming in the doorway. But he was not alone. With him was the magician, hobbled it seemed, his hands bound behind him and the woozy guard as well, trying and failing to keep his eyes open. A small cry escaped her lips.

Hot amber eyes burned in anger. Ian shoved Muir into the chamber and ground his teeth together. "I tried to be patient with you," he growled. "I gave you freedom. I didn't kill your bastard of a boy, I—"

"You only stayed away from me because you thought I might be carrying Trevin's babe," she accused, standing up to him, glaring back at eyes as deadly as a wolf's. Tears ran down her cheeks and pain burned deep in her heart, but she wouldn't back down, not ever. "And I am with child." Her voice shook with pride and she hoisted her chin even higher. "My time has come and gone and I know that I carry Trevin of Black Oak's child in my womb."

The minute she said the words she regretted them.

"Whore!" Quick as lightning he grabbed her. "You vile, worthless slut, there's no reason to hold back any longer, is there? I've waited long for this—"

"Leave her be!" Trevin's voice rasped through the darkness.

Gwynn jumped back. Her heart soared.

Ian whirled and glared at the bed. "Dare you speak, thief?"

"Trevin?" The dead weight within her dissipated as he opened his eyes. She tried to reach him but Ian shoved her roughly aside.

"I should have done this long ago." A dagger glinted in Ian's hand.

"No!" Gwynn cried. The blade slashed downward. "Nay!"

Trevin's arm erupted from the covers. Metal met metal in a sickening clash.

"Oh, God, no—"

The sharp tip of Trevin's cross plunged deep into Ian's belly.

"Aaagh—" Blood poured from the wound. Ian staggered backward.

Gwynn screamed.

" 'Tis true, 'tis true, father to son and son to father—" Muir mumbled seemingly horror-struck as Ian reeled against the wall, his dagger falling from his hand.

"What?" Trevin asked, blood staining his hands as he pushed himself upright.

" 'Twas your destiny. Ian of Rhydd is your father."

"Nay!" Trevin bellowed, his face still white as death.

"Holy Christ . . . the girl in the forest . . ." Ian's eyes glazed over and he mumbled incoherently. "I . . . knew . . . oh, Christ in heaven . . . what have I done?"

"She was my sister." Muir's voice was flat and hard.

"Who?" Trevin asked, his eyes dark with a quiet, nagging certainty. "Who was?"

"Your mother."

"Nay—"

" 'Tis true," Muir insisted.

"You are my . . . son." Ian's face was slack, his breathing labored as he slipped to the floor. "My only . . ." His voice faded and he breathed his last rattling breath.

"Oh, God." Gwynn was shaking. Ian was Trevin's father. She was in love with the son of the man . . . but it didn't matter, she told herself firmly. Nothing did other than Trevin and Gareth's safety.

"I . . . can't believe." Trevin's face was twisted in pain. He moaned from the deepest reaches of his soul. "Nay. Nay. Nay! NAY!"

"Believe," Muir insisted.

"Never!"

"You must, Trevin, for it is the truth."

"It . . . it is hell," he whispered, painful white lines bracketing the corners of his mouth.

Gwynn, shaking off all the anguish that tore at her, flung herself onto Trevin, the only man she'd ever loved. "You live. Think not of anything else!"

"But, my father—"

" 'Tis of no matter." She held his face in her hands and rained kisses over his cheeks and lips. Tears ran in crooked paths from her eyes. "You live. Oh, Trevin, you live—"

"But—"

"Shh. Think not of the pain. Look at me." When he failed, she pressed harder on his cheeks. "Look at me!"

Slowly he raised his eyes and the torture in his eyes found hers. "You live! I—I thought you were dead. Now 'tis not the time to think of anything but living."

He swallowed hard, cast one last look at the dead man, and shuddered. "Aye," he finally agreed with a half smile as if he, too, could shake off the torment at least for the moment, "I live, and I shall, I fear, for a very long time." She kissed his face and shoulders and refused to think of the slain man so close at hand. When Trevin glanced once more at the corpse of his father, she kissed his eyelids, forcing him to think only of her.

"I love you," he said when she finally lifted her face from his.

"What?" She froze, hardly daring to believe what she'd heard.

"I love you, Gwynn of Rhydd, and I have for all of my life. From the moment I spied you in your chamber years ago, I lost my heart to you."

She felt as if her heart would break with love for this man.

With one finger he lifted her chin and stared deep into her eyes. "Why did you think I kept your ring for all those years?"

She shook her head. "I know not."

"Because every time I looked at that dark ruby that sparkled in the light, I thought of you, Lady. Every time. Even when I was married to another." His eyes held hers. " 'Tis my curse to love you, Gwynn, a curse I will bear for the rest of my life."

"Oh, for the love of all that's holy," Muir said, "would ye give up this silly talk and cut me loose? There's wine to be drunk."

Footsteps sounded on the stairs and Trevin jumped to his feet, grabbing Ian's knife and ready to slay whoever entered. He shielded Gwynn's body with his own. "Halt!" he commanded as Stephen's face came into view.

"Nay, m'lord, do not harm me," he said. "Gerald and the others have come and freed the prisoners. We have taken the castle. Sir Webb is behind bars, but Ian . . ." His gaze moved over the small room to rest on the still form of the dead baron. "Ah. All is well."

"Aye." Trevin's arm circled Gwynn's waist.

Stephen cut off Muir's bonds and the old man rubbed his ankles and wrists. " 'Tis time to celebrate, methinks."

Relief caused Gwynn's legs to buckle, but Trevin held her steady. He looked into her eyes and kissed her. "Now, take me to my son and"—he threw Muir a dark look that brooked no compromise—"I'll hear no more of this nonsense about Ian being my father."

"But—" Muir said.

"I said, 'tis never to be spoken again. But . . . I will want to know of my mother."

One side of Muir's mouth lifted. "As you wish, sire."

"Don't call me that."

Together Gwynn and Trevin made their way down the stairs to the chamber where their son lay as she'd left him, unmoving, white as death. "He does not hear me," she said, tears stinging her eyes. Oh, if only Gareth would rise up.

"I know what the lad needs. I'll be back soon." Stephen, none the worse for his days in the dungeon, left them alone for a few minutes.

Trevin looked upon his son and love crossed his features. "He will live," he predicted. "He has not stayed alive all these days only to die."

"I . . . I . . . I pray it so." Gwynn could not think of life without Gareth. Would God be so cruel to give her Trevin again only to steal her son's life? Her insides shriveled at the thought and she clung to the man she loved, the father of her boy.

Trevin's arm tightened over her shoulders. "Have faith." He kissed her slowly upon her lips and images of making love to him filled her head.

"I love you, thief," she whispered, her lips trembling into a bit of a hopeful smile.

He traced those lips with the pad of one callused thumb. "As I love you, Gwynn. As I love you."

Surely God would not punish them, give them this precious love only to wound them by taking their boy. And yet . . . *Have faith.* Trevin's words echoed in her heart and she vowed to trust in him, in God, and in the powers of all things good on this earth.

But Gareth didn't move.

Tears burned behind her eyes as Stephen returned with the puppy who wriggled in his arms.

The big knight bent down, allowing the pup to nuzzle Gareth and anxiously wash the boy's face with his slick tongue.

"Come, lad, your Boon needs you," Stephen encouraged.

Nothing.

Trevin's face was a mask of tension.

Gwynn bit her tongue and swallowed the tears that were thick in her throat.

"I love you, son," Trevin vowed.

"Oh, Gareth, please wake up," she whispered.

No movement.

The dog gave out a lonesome, pitiful howl and Muir sighed as loudly as the wind upon the sea. " 'Tis too late."

"Nay!" Gwynn wouldn't give up.

Boon yipped.

Gareth moved slightly. Or was it the torches casting hopeful shadows over his face?

"I need you," Gwynn said, hardly believing her eyes.

"Aye, and so do I." Trevin brushed the hair from Gareth's forehead.

The boy's eyes fluttered open for a second.

"Gareth?" Gwynn dropped to her knees and took one of his hands in hers. "Can you hear me? Gareth?"

"He will be fine," Stephen predicted, winking at Trevin as Gareth stirred and moaned from his bed. "But he'd fare much better if his mother and father were married, I think."

"Married?" Gwynn repeated.

" 'Tis only a thought . . ."

"But a good one." Trevin, his eyes glistening, lifted Gwynn to her feet and cupped her face between his big hands. "What say you, m'lady?" he asked, his eyes holding hers. In that blue seductive gaze, she saw her future, her love. "Will you marry me?"

She glanced at Gareth, breathing easier it seemed. Her boy. His boy. Their first. There would be more. Many more. If she could but trust her heart to him.

Had she any choice?

She tossed her hair over one shoulder. "Marry you, eh?"

" 'Twould be my honor if you became my wife."

"And mine, if you were to be my husband."

"Good, good, now. Let us celebrate." Muir was down the stairs, moving more quickly than anyone would guess a man who professed himself to be a one-eyed cripple should be able to travel. Stephen carried Gareth, the puppy loped behind, and Trevin, holding Gwynn's hand, walked her to the great hall where Muir was already ordering pages to bring mazers of wine.

Once the cups were filled he lifted one in a toast. "To the baron and his wife, may they live long and prosper."

"Here, here," the voices of those who served them faithfully rejoined.

Trevin tipped the edge of his cup to hers. "To you, fair lady," he said and she laughed merrily. Life was as it should be.

"And to you, thief." Her smile was wickedly seductive. "You know, you stole my heart a long, long time ago."

"Aye, lady, as you stole mine." His arms surrounded her, his mazer fell to the floor, and he kissed her until she couldn't draw another breath. "May you never give it back."

Epilogue

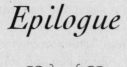

TOWER RHYDD
SUMMER 1287

Trevin stretched and felt his wife's body curling sensually against his. A cock crowed in the yard and already he heard sounds of the castle awakening. He'd learned to love his life here at Rhydd and a smile grew across his jaw, for he would spend the day hunting with Gareth.

His boy had survived his wounds and accepted Gareth as his father. With Muir and Boon as his constant companions, Gareth had gotten into his share of trouble, but no more than his father had years before.

He heard a giggle, then another, and lifted an eyelid. "Who goes there?" he demanded to a chorus of childish laughter. An impish blue-eyed face with a mop of dark curls poked from behind one side of the wardrobe, while a red head—the spitting image of her mother—eyed him from the other side.

Twins! His twins.

"What are you two doing?" he demanded, his voice fierce. The girls weren't afraid but ran forward, each throwing themselves upon him as he wrestled with them in the bed. With a yawn, Gwynn slowly opened her eyes.

"Get up! Up! Up!" they insisted.

"Demanding as your mother, you two are," he teased.

"And stubborn as their father." Gwynn hugged her girls and kissed their crowns.

Things had worked out well, he thought. The traitors had been dismissed, Hildy had married Henry and had come to Rhydd to be Gwynn's maid, and Trevin had finally forgiven himself for loving her. He'd made his peace with Faith, but he was still troubled by the fact that he was Ian of Rhydd's son.

He would never think of it again and concentrated, instead, on his own growing family.

"There ye be, ye little scamps!" Hildy scolded as she walked into the room. With her hands on her hips, she sighed and rolled her eyes. "Come along, now, and I'll show ye how we gather eggs."

"They'll break them all," Gareth said, sticking his head into the room and skewering his father with an impatient look. "Are ye not coming? 'Tis nearly light. Muir is waiting . . . or he was when I saw him last, although he said something about tasting from a new barrel." Gareth shook his head and waved at his father to come hither. "We must hurry or he will not want to join us."

"I'll be along," Trevin promised.

The girls, laughing, hurried away with Hildy fussing and muttering under her breath as she shepherded them down the hallway.

"I will wait for you at the stables. Come, Boon." Gareth whistled for the hound, then left them alone. The door banged shut and they were alone for a few fleeting moments of peace.

Trevin reached for his wife. He kissed her neck and she snuggled against him.

"Have we time?" he asked, one hand cupping her breast.

She laughed deep in her throat. "I know not." Her eyes danced mischievously as she reached for him. "But I think if you are a true man, you can be quick to satisfy a lady, can you not?"

"I can only try," he said, teasing her nipple with his thumb.

"Then try, thief," she suggested as she kissed his lips and melted against him. "Try very, very hard."

DARK
SAPPHIRE

Author's Note

For the purposes of this story I used a little artistic license and embellished Captain Keegan's ship, the *Dark Sapphire,* and made it slightly more grand than the vessels of the time.

Prologue

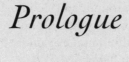

At last he would become a man.

Gritting his teeth, Keegan pulled back on his oar with all the strength of his fifteen-year-old muscles. The wind shrieked and howled with the coming of the dawn, and the sea was choppy, white caps boiling around the small craft. Keegan's heart thudded wildly. His blood lust ran hot, the thrill of a battle at hand. Finally. His fingers curled around the oars in a death grip as he saw himself, sword drawn, ready to slay any of his father's enemies who attempted as much as the hint of a fight.

Others in the small craft were not as inflamed as he.

Hollis, the old goat, was the worst of the lot. Even now he was complaining.

"Ye be on a fool's mission, I tell ye, Captain Rourke," the old man warned Keegan's father as the tiny rowboat pitched and rolled on the angry, dark waters of the bay. "There be no good come from this."

Rourke was having none of it. With a grunt he, too, rowed inland, helping drag the small craft toward the ever approaching shore. "'Tis time to face Jestin again." His eyes narrowed. "Past time."

"Ach, by the saints, ye be mad."

"I swore I'd return, and so I have. The term of the bet is up. Twenty years have passed. Now, row!" Captain Rourke ordered, and Keegan swallowed a prideful smile. His father would not be intimidated by the old man's ranting.

"For the love of all that be holy, listen to me. Ye may be the captain, but ye keep me on to be yer adviser, do ye not?"

"Not today."

"Oh, bloody Christ, why do I bother?"

Rourke's head snapped around, and he impaled the older man with his glare. "Quit worrying like an old woman. I say we meet Jestin, and we meet him. I vowed to see him in this lifetime again, and today be the day!"

"'Tis better to forget what happened."

"And next ye'll be tellin' me to forgive as well," Rourke sneered as the wind licked at his hair.

"And ye'll not be listening to that, now, will ya?" Hollis threw up his hands as if in supplication to the stormy heavens, abandoning his oar. "I may as well be talkin' to the wind, but the fact of the matter, Rourke, is that what happened between ye and Jestin was long ago. It matters not now. Ye've got yer ship and yer son and—"

"Damn it, old man. Row!" Rourke barked as a wave splashed over the side. Salt water as cold as ice rained down on Keegan.

As one the crew threw their backs into maneuvering the craft over the rough waves. The smell of brine was thick in the dark morning air, the taste of salt settling on Keegan's lips, but his blood was on fire, his eager pulse pounding at the thought of meeting his father's old enemy. Oh, to finally be part of a battle, to embrace the fight, should there be one. 'Twas what he'd dreamed of, what he yearned for.

Hollis, true to his nature, would not stop forewarning doom. "If ye don't care about yerself, for the love of God, Rourke, think of the boy. Vengeance has no part in Keegan's life."

Keegan bristled and drew hard on his oar, nearly standing as the little boat pitched and bucked. He spat into the sea. He was no boy. Nearly fifteen, he was almost a man. His body was testament to it. His voice now cracked and lowered, the hint of whiskers speckled his chin, the muscles of his arms and legs had become strong, and more often than not he awoke with his manhood stiff and hard as the main spar of the *Warrior*, his father's ship. Nay, he would not think of himself as a lad. As usual, old Hollis with his hook of a nose and dark eyes sunk deep in his skull, was seeing the devil in every corner.

"My son stays with me," Rourke insisted.

"Even if ye go to yer grave? Will ye be takin' him with ye at his young age?"

"I'll not be dyin' today Hollis."

"I might remind ye that Jestin is the lord of Ogof, and he might not agree. He has no love of ye, Captain."

"Nor do I of him." Rourke snorted, and Keegan's heart swelled with pride. His father was captain of his own ship, a brave man who, though sometimes a swindler, smuggler, and thief, never fell victim to cowardice. Unlike jittery old Hollis. Oh, why hadn't Rourke left the anxious, aging man back on the ship where he belonged?

"Ye be temptin' fate, Rourke, ye know ye are," Hollis worried aloud, and the aging man's concern only served to irritate Keegan further. The old goat was forever worrying about storms, and sea serpents, and witches and the like. More often than not Hollis paced the deck, praying and crossing himself and glancing with anxious eyes at the heavens.

As if God was listening to him prattle on and on. Humph!

Even now the old worrywart was muttering a quick prayer. As if in response, his hood was snatched by the fingers of the wind, exposing his balding, spotted pate. Long silvery strands of his hair whipped over his face.

Keegan swallowed back a grin and, along with the other men, a few of his father's best archers and swordsmen, rowed as one, guiding the bobbing craft over the waves and ever closer to the rugged shoreline near Ogof just as dawn was breaking.

Sweating despite the bitter cold, Keegan hazarded a look at the mouth of the bay, where the *Warrior*, the only home he'd ever known, lay anchored. The sails had been lowered, and the masts, like long, skeletal fingers, stretched upward toward the dark clouds.

"What do ye hope to do, arriving here at the home of yer enemy unannounced?" Hollis demanded, taking up his litany of doom again.

Rourke's eyes narrowed. "Settle an old score."

In all of his fifteen years, through rough seas and stormy weather, Keegan had never witnessed the glint of raw vengeance that now possessed his father's eyes.

Hollis opened his mouth to speak, then snapped it shut as he took up his oar again. The small craft crested a final wave, and the men climbed out of the boat to pull it ashore.

Keegan caught his first glimpse of Castle Ogof. Spread upon the surrounding hills, the heavy gray curtain wall rose and dipped with the terrain and reminded Keegan of the spiny back of a slumbering dragon, napping in the foggy October air, ready to be awakened at the first scent of trouble.

He pulled hard on the rowboat's line as his boots splashed through the tide pools. Sea foam and icy water swirled around his ankles, but he took no notice. His eyes were focused on the behemoth of a castle stretching above the bare-limbed trees. So this was where the enemy abided. Fine. Good. Keegan couldn't wait.

"You," Rourke said, pointing a gloved hand at one of the *Warrior* deckhands, "stay with the boat."

"Aye, sir," the sailor replied sharply, as if anxious not to face Rourke's old nemesis. Probably a coward.

Keegan himself was unafraid. He lusted for the thrill of sword play, the exhilaration of besting another warrior. He wore his bone-handled knife proudly strapped to his waist, and inside one boot, another smaller knife with a wicked little blade, was hidden. If there was to be trouble, he was ready. More than ready.

Rourke walked swiftly across the rocky beach, and the older man hobbled over the jagged stones to keep up with him. "Let us turn 'round quick as a flea jumpin' upon a cur." Hollis sent one last, longing glance back to the ship that rolled on the current far in the distance. "I've a bad feeling about this."

"You always have a bad feeling," Rourke countered, tall and strapping in a long surcoat. Deep brown and trimmed in black fur, the coat billowed as he walked without giving any evidence of the hidden pockets deep inside—pockets that held all manner of treasures, tricks, and weapons.

"'Tis better not to wake the demons of the past," Hollis grumbled, nearly slipping as his legs, used to the slippery, oft angled decks of the *Warrior*, had difficulty reacquainting themselves with land.

"And I say 'tis better to claim revenge."

Hollis, pausing to catch his breath, stopped at the edge of the beach. Craggy cliffs rose overhead, stretching upward to the swollen gray clouds roiling overhead.

"Come along," Rourke said, eager to get to the castle.

Hollis struggled to keep up. "Ye lost Bertrice fair and square to Lord Jestin. I was there," he huffed, his voice strained. "Now, that be twenty years ago, 'tis over and done with. There is naught that can be accomplished by trying to best the lord now."

Rourke glowered at the shorter man, and his expression was as thunderous as the swirling waters of the sea.

"Some women ye never forget, Hollis. Ye know this yerself. Some women get into yer blood and burrow deep into yer heart. Ye have no say in it, no means to get rid of it." He glanced at Keegan and laid a big hand upon his son's shoulder. "That's the way of it, boy," he admitted, sadness tempering the rage that had been burning in his eyes. "Stay away from women. All of 'em. They be the curse of each and every man, I tell ye true. When first Eve gave Adam that apple in the garden, 'twas just the beginning of it, to be sure. Just the beginning. Now, 'twas twenty years to this day that I left; 'tis time to fulfill my promise."

Jaw set, Rourke hurried to a path that cut through a small barrier of leafless trees. There the trail widened and joined a muddy, rutted road that wound ever upward to the foreboding castle.

Though the day had barely begun, Rourke's small band was not alone. Carts dragged by straining horses and filled with fine wares inched through the mud. Peddlers swung their whips and cursed their beasts.

Snap! "Hurry along there, Black."

Crack! "Ye can do it, ye miserable, useless piece of horseflesh. Put yer shoulders into it or I'll be sellin' ya to the tanner!"

Women lugging baskets, children clinging to their skirts, soldiers atop fine steeds, huntsmen dragging their early morning kills, all entered the behemoth of a castle through its great maw, where the portcullis, like sharp iron teeth, had been drawn up. Rourke stated his business to a sentry, and though few would recognize what he'd done, he quietly slipped the man a coin or two from one of the many pockets within his robe.

"Ye may pass," the man said, his eyes gleaming, thick fingers surrounding the silver pieces.

Some of Keegan's bravado slipped a bit as he followed his father into the outer bailey of Ogof and noticed the wary sentinels standing guard on the wide curtain wall. Archers and swordsmen, soldiers, knights, and all manner of men who had sworn to defend this monstrous fortress regarded the procession through suspicious eyes.

Keegan doubted if his father had enough coins to bribe them all.

He swallowed back any bit of apprehension.

Nay, he was not afraid.

Squaring his shoulders, he hurried to keep up with Rourke's long strides and took comfort in the knife strapped to his waist.

There was a rumble behind him, and a woman shrieked and jumped.

Hoofbeats, fast and furious, thundered through the gate.

"Halt!" a guard shouted.

Whirling, Keegan leaped. A sweating horse and rider flew past.

"God's teeth!" Hollis cried, scrambling out of harm's way.

Laughter trilled from the rider as the bay jennet, dark legs flashing, nostrils distended, ears flattened, bolted into the inner bailey. Astride the galloping beast was a girl, skirts bunched to her knees, her head tucked low, her dark red hair streaming behind her like a banner.

Awestruck, Keegan could only stare.

The horse was wet, breathing hard, its chest splattered with the same mud that flecked the girl's oval face. Her skin was white, her small jaw set, her eyes flashing pure devilment. She pulled back on the reins. The bay slid to a stop, and the she-devil hopped lithely to the ground.

Leaning forward, she patted the jennet's wet shoulder affectionately, and Keegan felt a tightness in his chest, a swelling in his breeches. "'Tis a fine horse you are, Shamrock," the girl said as the mare tossed her head. Flecks of lather speckled the horse's dark coat.

Breathless, her cheeks rosy, her eyes as blue as a summer sea, the rider swiped her sleeve over her face.

"What were ye doin' takin' the mare out so early?" a man admonished. He was crippled up and barely as tall as the girl, but he took the reins with curled fingers and clucked his tongue. "The lady, she'll not be happy."

Laughing, the redhead winked. "When is she ever? 'Tis not Fawn's nature." Wiping her hands on her skirt, she ignored the fact that she was being watched. "See that Shamrock is cooled, Del, and given extra oats as well."

The old man wavered. Frowned. Slid a worried look at the mare. "Farrell will report your takin' of the mare to yer father, I'm afraid."

"Let him."

"But he be the stable master, and—"

"And he cannot tell me what to do." She shook her mane of tangled red curls, and a precocious smile curved her small pink lips. "Asides, this will give him something to stew over."

Del snorted. "And stew he will, mark my words." He wrapped the reins around his gnarled fingers and, clucking to the horse, ambled off. The woman-child cast a look in Keegan's direction, paused but a second, arched one arrogant eyebrow, and then, as if he was of no interest whatsoever, turned on the heel of her muddy boots and half ran through a gate toward the center of the keep.

Keegan could barely move. She was, without a doubt, the most beautiful girl he'd ever seen. A vision of innocence and mischief.

"Come along," Rourke prodded, his expression darkening as he caught his son's fascination.

Hollis sniffed as he surveyed the interior of the castle. "'Tis bigger than I thought." The grooves furrowing his brow deepened. "Lord Jestin has done well."

Rourke shot him a look that silenced the older man as they strode through the very gate where the girl had disappeared. Keegan, his father's mission temporarily forgotten, trained his eyes ahead to catch another glimpse of the fiery-haired girl.

"Holy Mother," Hollis whispered once inside.

Men shouted orders, women chattered, and the smells of smoke, dung, and the sea blended together. Hammers rang, the skeps in the windmill whooshed, a potter's wheel creaked, and dogs barked over the hum and bustle of people working. Boys stacked firewood. Girls hung laundry. Young children scattered chicken feed or gathered eggs. The tanner was scraping a bear's hide clean, the blacksmith's bellows hissed and puffed, while a mason's chisels cut stone and women toted buckets of water toward the kitchen.

From the corner of his eye, through the knots of workers, Keegan spied the girl trying to shove her tangled hair into a circlet and veil as she hurried toward the chapel. At the door she smoothed her skirts, took a deep breath and, frantically making the sign of the cross over her small breasts, cast a glance over her shoulder. Her gaze collided with Keegan's again and his heart stopped.

She didn't move for a second. Blue eyes narrowed appraisingly. Keegan couldn't breathe.

Without a word, she dashed inside.

Absurdly, Keegan wanted to follow her, took a step in that direction, then felt a hand on his shoulder.

"Careful, lad," his father warned.

The door of the great hall opened fast, banged against the wall.

"Rourke!" a man's deep, resonant voice boomed from inside the great hall.

"Christ Jesus," Hollis whispered under his breath. "'Tis the devil Jestin himself."

Dressed in polished boots, thick breeches, and a tunic lined in silver fur, the lord of Ogof strode onto the top step of the keep. Barrel-chested, with fiery hair stuffed under a hat, he oozed authority. His expression was harsh, his jaw as hard as the very stones that had built this castle. "So ye've finally returned, have ye?"

At the sound of his voice all work in the castle ceased. Hammers stilled, the blacksmith's forge was forgotten, chisels and files were set aside.

Suddenly silent, the air in the bailey seemed to thicken.

A prickle of apprehension caused the hairs on the back of Keegan's neck to rise.

Rourke squinted up at the baron. "Aye, Jestin. I've returned. As I vowed."

"'Tis too late."

"Never. We agreed. Twenty years."

The lord's face folded in upon itself. "'Tis too late if it was wanting to see Bertrice again, you were. She's dead. Been gone five years."

Rourke paled, his knees seemed suddenly about to give way, and his mighty shoulders slumped. Not a sound was issued from the crowd that had circled around. "'Tis a lie ye speak." Rourke's voice was a whisper.

"Nay. 'Tis true."

The wind blew as cold as Keegan had ever felt.

"For the love of God," the captain said in a low voice filled with despair. For the first time in his life Keegan saw his father sketch a quick sign of the cross over his chest and close his eyes. Seconds passed, then slowly, as if somehow finding a new sense of purpose, Rourke managed to straighten his spine. "My . . . my condolences."

"Accepted." Jestin cleared his throat. "I've a new wife now." Gesturing toward the open doorway, he motioned with his fingers, and a proud, pale woman, her abdomen huge with child, appeared. She stood next to her husband. Fair-skinned and radiant, she linked one arm through his. "This be Fawn," Jestin said as Rourke frowned, and somewhere far off a sheep bleated. "She's the lady of Ogof now."

In his peripheral vision Keegan saw the red-haired girl slip out the door of the chapel. Yanking at the circlet, she moved silently and swiftly across the dead grass to stand near a doorway at the side of the keep. At the sight of the pale-haired woman standing next to the lord, the corners of the girl's mouth turned down.

"Lady Fawn, this be Captain Rourke." Jestin introduced them.

"M'lady." Rourke, ashen-faced, managed a stiff bow.

She nodded slightly, a smooth, smug smile stitched tightly to her lips. "Welcome, Captain," she said, though her eyes belied her civility. Cold and calculating, they regarded Rourke and his small band of men with an icy consideration that chilled Keegan's blood.

Rourke studied the ground for a moment, then slowly raised his gaze to meet that of the lord of Ogof. He cleared his throat. A vein throbbed over one eye. His hands clenched. "'Tis sorry I am about Bertrice, Jestin. I loved her true."

The lord's lips flattened as the first drops of rain began to fall from the heavens. Lady Fawn's eyebrows elevated just a fraction, as if she'd heard new gossip that she could use to her advantage at a later date.

"Since I be here already, I see no reason why ye and me, we can't have another toss of the dice," Rourke suggested as a pig squealed from a pen somewhere.

Raindrops began to fall more steadily, splashing against Keegan's head and running down his neck, sliding from the roofs and puddling on the ground.

Jestin shook his head as the peasants and servants gathered around. "There is no point to it now."

"Are ye no longer a gambling man?" the captain asked.

A pause. Jestin chewed the corner of his lip.

"Mayhap your new wife disapproves," Rourke suggested.

The baron's spine stiffened. Red eyebrows slammed together. "I do as I wish, but 'tis busy I be."

"Too busy for a quick game?"

Jestin cleared his throat, caught a disapproving glance from Lady Fawn, then disregarding her, said, "And what would be the stakes?"

"Oh, we will start small." From one of the many hidden pockets within his surcoat, Rourke withdrew a thick pouch that jingled and chinked invitingly. "Just a few coins, but . . . if it pleases ye, we could raise the stakes a bit after a game or two, just as we did before."

"And what would you have to offer?"

Rourke hitched his head backward in the direction of the bay. "If ye come up with somethin' interestin', I've got me ship I'd be willin' to wager."

Nay! The *Warrior* was their home.

Hollis lost all his color. "Do na be teasin'," he warned the captain in a harsh whisper. "Jestin, he hates ya sure, fer Bertrice loved ye once. He'd take yer ship without thinkin' twice, he would, and then where would ye be? Where would the boy be?"

"I'll not lose," Rourke insisted, then more loudly, "Have we a bet, then, Baron? What would ye put up?"

"Not my castle, you know that." The lord's eyes narrowed as he looked west and, as if he could see through the curtain wall and watch the *Warrior* rolling on the gray waters of the bay, a greedy, lustful expression took hold of his features. "Ye'll wager yer ship?"

"Aye. What have ye to put up?"

The baron's gaze landed full force on the captain. "I'll make it worth yer while, Rourke, if we get that far."

"I would not trust the captain," Lady Fawn admonished, touching her husband's arm again.

"Nor would I, but 'twould be good to best him." Again Jestin's gaze narrowed on his old foe. "Then, in with you and we'll see if luck is on yer side this time." He snapped his fingers, servants scurried, and within minutes the captain, Hollis, Keegan, and the few other men who had rowed ashore were inside the great hall, the two old adversaries seated at a scarred trestle table, a wooden cup rattling with dice, mazers of wine at their fingertips.

Rushlights and candles glowed from sconces, a huge fire crackled and popped in the grate, hungry flames licking logs that glowed red, while men and servants shuffled around, searching for a better view.

"Saints be with us," Hollis whispered as a crowd gathered around the game.

"Tell me of Bertrice," Keegan demanded.

The old man scowled so deeply that ridges appeared in his brow. "She was beautiful and sinful. Your father was in love with her. So was Jestin. She . . . ach, she flirted with both men, used one against the other, fanned the fires of this rivalry, let me tell you." Hollis sighed and shook his head as the dice rattled like bones in the hull of a ghost ship. "So finally, when she could not make up her mind, twenty years ago this very night, the two men threw the cups. With each toss of the dice the winner banished the loser to a year away from the woman who would be his bride. The game went long into the night, but as dawn approached, your father had lost not only his money but his woman, and twenty years of life that could have been here. 'Tis then he took to the sea forever."

"Why have I not heard this before?" Keegan demanded.

"Because the captain wished it so." The old man laid a hand on Keegan's shoulder. "Women, they be the bane of a man's existence."

"And how would you know?"

The old man snorted. "All men who have lived beyond their youth know."

Keegan asked no more but watched with the others. Pages poured wine. Lady Fawn, her once serene face drawn into a mask of silent condemnation, sat at her husband's side as the stakes were raised quickly. Merchants, peasants, even the priest, a potbellied man who rubbed his rosary beads nervously, huddled near the gaming table.

Keegan stood close enough to see the sweat on his father's brow, the determined gleam in his eye. This was not mere sport. Nay. The tossing of the dice ran much deeper than simple gamesmanship. A tic above the lord's eye was proof enough that each man felt the same prideful need to win. Both men drank and gambled, and for a while they both won, but as the hours passed and the stakes increased, slowly Jestin's winnings mounted. He beamed and ordered more wine; Rourke frowned, counted his money, and tossed back mazer after mazer as more men—soldiers, merchants, visiting lords, and servants trying to look busy with their tasks—surrounded the table.

Keegan was jostled and pushed.

The stench of sour ale mingled with the odor of smoke and roasting meat wafting in from the kitchen.

"Out of me way, lad," a bear of a soldier with foul breath and a sheathed sword ordered, elbowing Keegan away from the table.

"Aye, let me have a look," another insisted, one hand on the hilt of his weapon. He was as large as the first, had no teeth, and wore the scars of battle upon his brutish face. Keegan was elbowed and shoved farther from his father. It was not a good sign, and the fear in Hollis's eyes for once seemed well founded. Rourke had drunk far too much, was reckless with his bets, and Jestin's well-armed men were edgy and alert.

The coins on the table were piled high, and Jestin, with a flip of his wrist, threw the dice. As the cubes rolled out, he let out a whoop, and Fawn's placid face split with a wide, relieved grin. "Beat that if ya can," the lord crowed, pounding a triumphant fist on the table. His eyes gleamed, his face ruddy. A buzz swept through the crowd, and Rourke took up the cup, rattled the dice, and threw them across the table. A poor toss. He rolled again. No good. Keegan's heart nearly stopped, for in this game the third toss was the last.

Swearing under his breath, Rourke threw again.

The cubed and marked pieces of bone rolled to a stop. The roll was better but not enough. The captain had lost.

Rourke's massive shoulders slumped. He swallowed without a sip of wine.

Keegan bit his lip.

"Christ Jesus," Hollis whispered as Jestin, his cheeks puffed by a self-satisfied grin of victory, leaned across the table and scraped all his winnings across the table toward him.

"So ye've come to me door just to be beaten again," Jestin gloated, and several of the servants started back to their duties. Keegan's heart was hammering. Why had his father lost? It was unlike him. And unnecessary. "You're like a stupid cur, you are, Rourke, never knowing how to stop the beating." He laughed, and most of the men joined him.

Rourke mopped the sweat from his brow, settled back in his chair, and scowled. His color was high, his eyes dark with shame and rage. "We not be done yet."

"Nay?" Jestin said, and downed his mazer, then clapped his hands while a page hastily refilled the empty cup. "Face it, man, your luck's run out if you ever had any. Which I doubt." More laughter rolled through the cavernous room.

"I've still got me ship."

The crowd stilled.

Keegan's heart leapt to his throat. *Not the* Warrior. Surely his father had brought up the ship only as a joke.

Hollis stepped forward and, placing a hand on the captain's sleeve, whispered loud enough for Keegan to hear, "Nay, Rourke, this bet, 'twould be no good. Let us be off, now. Ye came, ye had yer chance, but 'tis over."

"Shut up, old man." The captain fished inside his tunic and retrieved the title to his ship, a faded yellowed scrap that he slowly unrolled. "I'll wager the *Warrior,* but ye've got to come up with more than a pile of coins."

Jestin eyed the ownership papers. "Ye be sure of this, Rourke?"

"Nay, he's not certain," Hollis said, "Ye can see he's in his cups and—"

"What have ye got?" Rourke demanded.

Their eyes locked, and Jestin's mind was made up. "Give me but a minute," he said, and took his leave. In the time he was gone, Hollis pleaded with Rourke while Keegan, eyeing the restless crowd, worried about his father. The castle dogs, two gray, speckled beasts, watched his every move through suspicious gold eyes.

"Think, man," Hollis pleaded. "The *Warrior,* she be all ye have in the world aside from yer lad. What happens to Keegan if ye lose her?"

"I won't."

"Ye've said that before, but—"

"Enough!" *Slap!* Rourke cuffed the old man across his face. Hollis stumbled backward. Didn't so much as whimper. Just held his jaw.

"Don't—" Keegan jumped forward. Never had he seen his father strike the older man.

"Nay, lad, do na interfere," Hollis warned, holding his chin with one hand and stretching his arm outward as if to stop Keegan from tangling with the man who had sired him. Rubbing his jaw, he said to Rourke, "'Tis mad ye be, Captain."

"Go to hell," Rourke growled.

"Oh, I be already there," the old man said, "all because I've followed ye."

"'Twas nothing I asked of ye!" Rourke tore his eyes away from the wounded man and watched as Jestin and a solitary soldier, a swarthy, muscular man, returned.

"Will this do?" Jestin asked as he sat in his chair and opened his fist. Resting in his palm was the finest gold ring Keegan had ever seen. It glittered in the firelight, and the huge stone that was set into the heavy prongs winked a vibrant, seductive blue.

"Sweet Jesus."

"Not the stone."

Several men gasped. The room went silent. Was it reverence that reverberated through the whitewashed walls, or foreboding?

Two stumbled backward quickly.

Hollis swore under his breath. "By the gods, 'tis the cursed Dark Sapphire."

The man near him swallowed—whether in lust or fear, Keegan knew not which. "Holy Mother protect us."

"'Tis said the owner will have good luck always," Jestin said, but Hollis shook his head violently.

"'Tis cursed," he whispered loudly in the captain's ear. "Ye know as well as I do, 'tis the Dark Sapphire of Ogof." Hollis's thin skin was drawn tightly over his skull. "The jewel brings its owner not luck but damnation. 'Tis the downfall of men, and kingdoms and armies."

Rourke's eyes thinned. His lips flattened. "'Twas Bertrice's ring."

"Once," Jestin admitted. "I gave it to her. 'Tis the Dark Sapphire of Ogof."

"But it was to be mine," Fawn said swiftly. "Do you not remember, husband? You promised me the gem."

"If you bore me a son, which you have not."

Tears sprang to her eyes. "I am with child now! 'Tis but a few weeks until the babe be born, and he will be a strong, fine son to you, the boy you have always wished for. No longer will Sheena be your only issue." She reached for her husband's arm, her fingers curling in the fabric of his sleeve. "Do not risk the ring."

He yanked his hand away. "If I win, I'll name the damned ship for you, and we will still have the ring."

"But—"

"Hush, woman!" He held the ring beneath the captain's nose, and the room was silent as a tomb. "What say you, Rourke?"

Keegan's father regarded the gem as if he couldn't draw his eyes from its seductive blue brilliance. He was not alone. Many within the thick walls of the keep were in awe of the sparkling stone. Rourke swallowed hard. "Aye, 'tis a bet," he said, and placed the *Warrior*'s title on the table, securing the curling edges with a candle. "But not just the ring. The money as well."

"So be it." Jestin slapped the ring atop the ragged, faded papers, shoved the pile of coins to the center of the table, and settled back in his chair. In the hushed room the blue gem glimmered.

Eerie.

Dark.

Tempting.

Rourke picked up his cup.

"The ring is not yours to give!" a strong feminine voice—one that Keegan recognized—accused. "'Twas my mother's!"

Keegan's eyes were drawn to the girl with the wild red hair as she pushed her way to the table. Insolence held her chin high. Anger sparked in her blue eyes.

"Did she not ask that it be given to me when I marry? Is that not what you've told me again and again as I grew up?"

This girl was the lord's child? With her impertinent grin, wild hair, and smudged dress? "It was never to be given away. Not to her," she insisted, eyeing Fawn, "nor him." She pointed a condemning finger at Rourke.

"'Tis mine to do with as I please," Jestin said. "I need not answer to you."

"But—"

"Oh, for the love of Mary!" Fawn said in great irritation as she motioned wildly to an aging serving woman. "Zelda, please take her to her chamber and see that she causes no more trouble!"

"Do not even try it," the girl spat.

Fawn looked at her husband, silently blaming him for his daughter's impudence, then wiggled bejeweled fingers impatiently at the maid. "Just get her out of here. Now."

Zelda nodded, attempted to do as she was bidden. Lanky and gaunt, she was as tall as most men but ungainly as well. Though she gave chase to the nearly grown girl, she was no match for the lord's daughter. The girl was as clever and agile as she was speedy. She darted through the throng as quickly as a mouse scurrying through sacks of grain. Sidestepping a page, she slipped around a column and ducked behind a curtain.

The older woman lost her, but Keegan followed the redhead's every move with his eyes. Aye, she was a sassy, impudent one, bound to give her father and whatever man dared try to tame her trouble. But she was as fascinating as the blue stone in the ring.

"Roll!" Baron Jestin ordered. Uninterested in his saucy daughter's antics, he turned his back to the stir and eyed the ownership papers of the *Warrior* with more than a trace of avarice.

Rourke shook his head, sat back in his chair as the room grew still as the middle of the night. "'Tis your turn."

"So be it."

Keegan drew his eyes back to the table. Again a hush swept through the room. All his father owned in the world was at risk along with a pile of coins and a ring the likes of which few men had seen, a stone whose facets reflected blue crystal brilliance in the hundreds of candles that illuminated the great hall.

"'Tis a fool Lord Jestin be," one man, a merchant from the looks of him, whispered to another. He leaned heavily on a cane of polished wood.

"Aye, but this be not about the gem," the other said. Dressed in deep forest green with a thin beard, he rubbed the back of his neck. "Nor the ship."

Keegan, standing near the two, his heart drumming in his eardrums, strained to listen. His nerves were frayed, his stomach clenched.

"Bertrice of Llwydrew," the first man said, as if just now remembering the events of twenty years ago.

"Yes, Bertrice. A beauty like no other. Blessed with eyes the color of the sky and the reddest hair ye've ever seen." The man in green lifted one hand and fanned his fingers at the memory of the winsome Bertrice's tresses. "It seemed to catch fire in the morning light."

Just like her daughter's, Keegan thought, realizing that this girl was the daughter of his father's love.

"Who knows what she thought of Jestin and Rourke's wager over her? Or the fact that Jestin won."

Keegan listened for all he was worth.

"And Rourke took to the sea, he did. Swore he'd never marry. Had himself a bastard or two, methinks."

The top of Keegan's ears burned, for he knew little of his own mother—a tavern wench who hadn't wanted to be bothered with a child. He had no memory of her, and whenever he'd asked, his father had grown silent and stern. Even old Hollis, whose tongue was never still, could not be cajoled into speaking of her.

The two men moved on, and Keegan wove through the crowd to stand behind his father. It wasn't like Rourke to lose; not only was he clever but crooked as well. A blackheart who shamelessly drank and smuggled, Rourke was also a cheat who, if the situation called for it, would do anything to win.

Today was no exception. 'Twas hard to spot, but Keegan's trained eye had caught Rourke's sleight of hand more than once. In a game where a man was given three tries to best his score, Rourke had slowly lost. A few times Keegan was certain his father had switched the dice, but with each bit of trickery, the captain had not won. Now Keegan understood why. Only when the stakes were high enough would his father take advantage of his opponent.

Feet shuffled in the rushes. Servants peered through the curtains. From the corner one of the castle dogs growled, as if the shaggy cur could feel the tension in the room. Faces were strained, muscles taut, eyes focused on the battered planks of the table.

Side bets were being waged among the soldiers and peasants who had gathered.

"A sack of grain on the lord," one man with crooked teeth whispered to another.

"Amen to that. I'll put up me best mule on the captain there."

"'Tis a fool ye be, Luke, but I'll not be arguin' with ye. I could use me a new ass."

Keegan swallowed hard, and as he found a spot behind his father's shoulder, he noticed the lord's red-haired daughter on the far side of the table, partially hidden in the shadows of a curtain. For a second she caught his gaze, and a hint of a smile brushed her lips. Though she didn't speak, he felt that they shared a secret together amid the crowd and the thickness in the air.

His head pounded and he bit his lip.

The dice rattled. "'Tis now the time ye will rue your wager," the lord said.

Keegan dragged his eyes back to the game.

Jestin tossed the cubes onto the table.

The bits of bone rolled to a stop.

A wide, self-satisfied smile stole across the baron's ruddy face. He snagged up two of the cubes, threw them again, then nearly leaped in the air when they landed beside the others. "Beat that if ye can! I need not another roll."

Keegan gulped. The baron's score was high, nearly impossible to break.

"I'll give it me best shot." The captain was solemn, but in his eyes there was a glitter of hatred that rivaled the gleam from the blue stone he sought to win.

He shook the dice in the cup.

Conversation stopped.

All eyes followed the snap of his wrist.

Thwap! He dropped the cup onto the table, then poured out the tumbling bits of bone.

The first toss was no good.

Rourke grabbed the dice again. Rattled them hard. Slapped down the cup.

Smack. Again the pieces of marked bone spilled onto the planks.

Once more the score wasn't enough.

Jestin let out a breath of air, and to hide his smile, he took up his cup, threw back his head, and drained his mazer. The soldiers of Ogof hooted and clapped each other on the back. Fawn sighed. Laughter rippled through the great hall.

Rourke snapped up the cup in a deft motion that defied most gazes, but

Keegan saw the trickery as the new dice fell from his father's sleeve and the old ones were stashed within a hidden pocket. Easily. Perfectly. Seamlessly. Rourke gave the cup another shake. "May luck be with me," he whispered fervently.

Whap! The cup hit hard on the table. The dice tumbled rapidly. They rolled the length of the table to land directly in front of the lord of Ogof. And they spelled his doom. Fawn gasped, looked about to faint.

"Christ Jesus," one man whispered.

"The captain won!" another, a man who had bet on Rourke, cried. "Can ye believe the luck?"

Jestin's jaw slackened.

"There ye be!" Rourke's smile belied his deceit. Half standing, he reached forward to scoop up his winnings.

Keegan's fingers sought the handle of his knife. Surely it wouldn't be this easy.

"Nay, Captain," Fawn said. She'd turned the color of milk without any cream. "This . . . this . . ."—she pointed at the table where the game was so recently played—"is not right!" She turned accusing eyes upon her husband. Her voice was an octave higher than it had been. "Surely, you couldn't have lost the ring."

"'Tis done," Jestin said with a scowl.

"Nay. It cannot be so." Slowly, she turned her head and her eyes fastened on Rourke. "He cheated," she said without much conviction. "No one could be so lucky. No one."

"It seems I was."

She wasn't about to be dissuaded. "Didn't—didn't you see him cheat, Sir Manning?"

"That I did, m'lady," the brute of a knight beside Jestin agreed without a moment's hesitation. The smell of a fight charged the air. Swiftly, Manning unsheathed his dagger.

"Nay!" Keegan cried, but the warrior was lightning quick. The blade glinted in his hand. He slammed his wicked little knife down into the back of Rourke's hand. Pinned it flat to the table.

Blood spurted. Rourke roared in pain. Coins clattered to the floor. "Bastard," the captain hissed.

"Ye should never have tried to cheat!"

Stripping his knife from its scabbard, Keegan sprang forward.

A soldier with foul breath pushed Keegan. "Get back, boy!" Holding Keegan on the floor, he managed to scoop up a fistful of the scattering gold. Swords rattled. Women screamed. Men grabbed their weapons. Others scrambled for the coins. The captain reached for his own blade with his free hand.

"Kill the bastard," someone commanded.

"He tried to trick the lord."

"Nay, 'twas a fair game."

"The dice were weighted," Jestin snarled, throwing the bit of bones onto the floor. He reached for his sword. "You always were a filthy, lying cur, Rourke. 'Tis a blessing Bertrice never had to lay with the likes of you!"

Reeling free of the big man, Keegan sprang at the baron. His fingers coiled around the hilt of his knife.

Crack! Pain exploded behind his eyes. His knees wobbled.

A huge arm threw him to the floor, where he sprawled upon the rushes. A soldier stripped him of his weapon, slashing his arm as he tried to roll away.

"Father," he cried, but his voice was drowned by the crowd. With horrified, blurry eyes he watched as Rourke struggled against the blade impaling his hand on the table.

"This'll teach ye for not playin' fair," Sir Manning snarled, holding fast to his knife so that the captain was nailed by his own flesh. Rourke writhed. His weight pulled over the table. Blood and coin and candles fell to the floor.

Hot beeswax from the candles sprayed Keegan's arm. Flames from the fallen tapers found the dry rushes and raced, crackling in deadly brilliance along the floor. Keegan's heart raced. Fear throbbed through his bloodstream.

"Fire!"

"Bloody Christ, get the pails. We needs water here!"

"Fire!"

"For the love of God, get water!" Smoke billowed through the keep.

Women shrieked, men grunted, swords clanged, bodies crashed into each other.

"Call the guards," Fawn screamed above the din, but the soldiers were already filling every inch of the smoky hall. Fire snapped, racing up the curtains. Sparks ignited the tapestries. Keegan struggled to climb to his feet.

"Let there be no blood spilled," the fat priest ordered, choking, but it was too late. Soldiers swarmed through the castle, and Rourke's few men, though struggling hard, were bested.

The papers declaring Rourke captain of the *Warrior* crackled as they caught fire. People ran in all directions. Babies cried. Water was thrown from buckets, and Keegan, struggling to his feet, fell against the table and saw the ring. Glowing with an eerie brilliance, it had slipped to the floor.

"The sapphire! Get it," Fawn screamed through the thickening acrid haze.

A woman's dress caught fire. She screamed and fell to the ground, rolling out the flames. Smoke clogged Keegan's lungs and filled the chamber.

Keegan grabbed the gem.

"Take yer soul to hell, Captain," Jestin roared, and from the corner of his eye, Keegan saw the lord lunge at his father.

"Nay!" Keegan cried. Horror pounded through his head. He was too late. With a primal yell of triumph, Jestin rammed his sword through Rourke's chest. Blood gushed from the wound. Rourke screamed in pain. The blade protruded through his back.

"Noooo," Keegan screamed, horrified. He tried to reach his father, was pushed down again by the crowd. No! Nò! No!

With a groan Rourke slumped to the floor. His eyes threatened to close, but his gaze fastened on his son. "Run, Keegan," he ordered weakly, blood oozing from his lips. "Save yerself. Oh, Christ . . ."

"No!" Keegan cried again, barely able to breathe. Flames raged in the curtains, blackened timbers creaked ominously, and Keegan was sure he'd entered a portal of hell. Nearby a man howled in pain, and not far away someone was sobbing through strangled prayers. "Nay, Father—" Tears streamed down his cheeks, and his throat was raw, hot with smoke and utter defeat. "I cannot leave you." His father, his brave father, couldn't be dead.

"Get out!" Hollis cried as he was dragged away through a wall of smoke and flame. "Run! The devil be after ye!"

"Shut up, old man!" Manning kicked past a dying soldier, his eyes narrowing on Keegan.

"No, oh, nay!" Again Keegan struggled to his feet, was knocked down, and as Manning swung his sword, Keegan caught hold of one meaty arm, raked the ring down already wounded flesh, and was flung across the room, the gem still clenched in his bloody fingers. "Meet yer doom," Manning yelled, raising his sword high as Keegan slithered along the floor, past burning tables and slain warriors, toward a corner. But the big man, swinging his deadly blade, stalked him. "Come here, boy," Sir Manning ordered, blood trickling from one eye. "There be no escape."

The tiny knife in Keegan's boot pressed hard against his flesh. He reached down, pulled out the weapon, was ready to lunge at the black knight but waited, his chest on fire, his head throbbing. When the murdering bastard was close enough, Keegan would leap to his feet and slice Manning's thick, ugly throat.

Through the smoke the big man trudged. Timbers groaned. People screamed. Keegan's fingers tightened over the hilt. *I'll kill you, come on, just come on.*

"Watch out!" a woman shrieked as a horrid rending sound nipped through the hall. The walls quaked.

Crash! Thud! A huge beam collapsed. In a cloud of dust it bounced and landed between Manning and Keegan.

"Get the boy!" Manning yelled, blocked by the burning timber.

Another beam groaned, threatening to give way.

Smoke and dust obscured Keegan's eyes, but he scrambled through the rushes, crawling backward as more timbers gave way and stones began to tumble from the walls.

Water from buckets splashed. Flames sizzled.

"Come with me." A voice—the woman-girl's voice—commanded.

His eyes burned and he couldn't see, but he felt her warm fingers nearly circle his wrist.

"Hurry!"

Scrambling to his feet, he ran blindly, stumbling forward, led by her hand as they dashed around corners and through a maze of smoke, crumbling stone, and flames.

"Duck."

"What?" He ran smack into a wall.

"Through here! Now!"

"But—"

"I said, bend down!" she yelled, and he obeyed, coughing, still clinging to the damned blue ring in his free hand while the fingers of his other were twined with hers. Through a hallway and another door that led to the chapel. "This way. Hurry! By the gods, do you want to be burned alive or kilt by Manning's blade?"

Running swiftly, she led him through another door. Faster and faster, down steep stairs that led to a dark chamber that smelled of death, where the sounds of the screams and fire were faraway, muted, and the scrape of rats' claws more defined. Slipping a key from her pocket, she unlocked a thick barred door and dragged him through. Once they were on the far side, she kicked the door closed. The lock clicked into place.

"Now, follow me." She, feeling along the narrow hallway, ran easily onward. The floor was moist, as if it were earthen, and slanted downward. He stumbled. She held him up. They ran as if Satan were breathing down their backs.

Unable to see her, he clung to her hand, trusted her. Around a sharp corner, through another door where the smell of must and decay entered his nostrils, he kept up with her, though he felt as if he were treading where no man had dared walk for centuries.

"Come along! Hurry!" she insisted, and still the floor sloped downward, steeper and steeper, as they were forced to slow to a walk. Another doorway and he smelled salt air. The temperature dropped and the sounds of voices, of fear, the smell of smoke, had disappeared.

"What is this?" he asked. His voice echoed. Was it his imagination or could he hear the distant roar of the sea?

He felt one wall with the knuckles of the hand that held the cursed gem. It felt moist, cool, hard as granite.

"For the love of Morrigu, run! I lead you to safety."

"There be none."

"Come *on!*" she urged, and he smelled the ocean. "There be steps here. Be careful."

Not steps, but crumbling stairs that were slick and cold, yet Keegan hurried. The roar of the tide swelled louder in his ears, and the smell of salt air cleared his head. Slowly he saw a bit of light that became brighter as the stairway opened onto a vast underground cove. A rotting dock jutted into the deep chasm, and a tiny rowboat undulated with the movement of the tide.

"What is this?"

"There be no other way back to your ship. Sir Manning has killed the man who was guarding your rowboat and claimed it for Ogof. 'Tis only a matter of time, once the fire is put out, before the army will take over your father's ship."

He hesitated, bit his lip, and eyed the small boat and the cave's entrance to the open sea.

"Why did you do this?" he asked, looking at her for the first time since they'd reached daylight. Her face was smudged, her fine dress torn, her hair more tangled than ever. "Why did ye save me?"

"Because I want you to take me with you," she said earnestly.

"But you be the daughter of the lord."

"Aye, but not of Fawn. She—she is a witch." As if she expected him to disagree, she grabbed his mantle in desperation. "You must help me leave this place."

Keegan hesitated. What would he do with the girl aboard the *Warrior*? If he made it to the ship. Here she was a rich man's daughter. On the sea she would be at the mercy of the men. No longer would his father steer the helm. Nay, he could offer her nothing.

"I cannot."

"You must." Her face fell, and for a second she seemed crushed. It was all he could do not to wrap his arms around her.

Something in Keegan's heart tore. "'Twould not be safe."

"But I would be free."

"I think not."

A look of hard determination crossed her features. She dropped her hands and glared at him. "Listen, boy, take me with you, or I myself will take you back to the soldiers and my father." To prove her point, she pulled a small knife from her pocket and waggled it under his nose.

Keegan nearly laughed, but she was serious, her chin thrust forward, her small pink lips compressed. So full of life. So demanding. So spirited. So much trouble.

"Well?" she said. "We have not much time."

"No, girl, we do not," and for the life of him, Keegan didn't know what possessed him, but he swept her and her silly little knife into his arms and kissed her hard on the lips. She gasped, tried to draw away, but instead dropped her weapon and sighed. Deep inside, he felt a new fire burn through his blood. In his breeches his manhood swelled and throbbed, and for a second he thought of nothing else but kissing her and touching her and . . . and . . .

He stopped then. Stepped away, stared into her suddenly glazed eyes, and took a deep breath. "By the saints," he whispered, then ran down the slippery, rotting dock, to the small craft that looked as if it might sink at any minute.

She let out a yelp and followed him, but he was fast, untied the boat, and shoved off. The current did the rest, pulled him out to sea so quickly that she couldn't jump on board.

"Curse you, boy!" she cried, stomping an angry foot in frustration. "Curse your soul to hell!"

"It's already there," he said, unable to call up a smile.

"Morrigu and Pwyll, hear my prayer against this son of the devil who would abandon me . . ." She raised her fists, and though he could no longer hear her voice, he was certain she was calling up all manner of spirits to arrest him. He took to the oars and refused to look at her standing at the dock, for there was something dangerous there, something that was far more frightening than any of Lord Jestin's soldiers. It had nothing to do with demons and curses but with emotions he'd heretofore not known.

The brave, impetuous girl had touched his soul somehow, and that would never do. Her kiss lingered on his lips, her curse ringing in his ears. He finally glanced over his shoulder as the tide swept him out to sea, and he saw the *Warrior* riding high above the waves. No, he had no time for a woman.

"There he be!" a hard voice yelled, and as he glanced toward the beach where his father's rowboat had been dragged, he saw three soldiers. An archer took aim and shot.

Thwang!

Keegan threw himself to the bottom of the boat.

Ssst!

The arrow hissed over his head. He flattened to the tiny craft's ribs. Prayed. Didn't move for heart-stopping minutes, but the little boat was drifting down the shoreline, out to sea, far from the *Warrior*. He had to get to the ship. Holding his breath, he sat upright, lifted the oars, and fought the sea.

He threw his back into the effort, saw, from the corner of his eye, another deadly missile sizzling. He flinched. Not quickly enough.

Thud!

Sharp and hot, the arrow's steel tip pierced his clothes and skin, buried deep in his shoulder, burning like a flaming coal. Blood trickled from the wound. *Thwack!* Another shot aimed over the waves.

Hot pain exploded in his chest. His body jolted.

The world seemed to topple and spin.

Sky and sea became one.

The boat rocked wildly.

Keegan fought the pain, battled the blackness that threatened him. He tried not to give in to the seductive sleep that would dull the ache in his body and soul.

But he failed.

As he slipped beneath the gentle cover of darkness, his mind swam with vibrant thoughts of the plucky red-haired girl and her kiss—still warm upon his lips. 'Twas his first and, it seemed, 'twas destined to be his last.

Chapter One

*B*am! Bam! Bam!

"What the bloody hell?" Keegan growled from his bunk.

"Captain. I hates to disturb ye, and ye know it, but there's trouble afoot. May I have a word with ye?"

Keegan opened a bleary eye. His cabin, lit only by a single candle mounted in a lantern hung near his bed, flickered and swayed with the roll of the sea.

"Captain! Can ye hear me? 'Tis Hollis and I hate to wake ye, but I needs speak with ye."

"Trouble?" Keegan repeated, his head feeling as if it might split wide open.

"Aye!"

"Pirates?" God's eyes, Hollis was always conjuring up the devil, certain there was a horrid looming disaster afoot. The old man seemed certain the *Dark Sapphire* was cursed to her very keel.

'Twas enough to try a man's patience. But then, he'd saved Keegan's life. Hollis was, and always had been, loyal and true. But a pain in the backside.

"Nay, Captain, there be no pirates," Hollis yelled.

"Are we taking on water? Is the ship sinking?"

"No, but—"

"Are the men planning a mutiny?"

"Nay, nay, not that I'm aware of, Captain, but—"

"Then go away." Keegan rolled over in his small bunk and jammed his eyes shut.

"Nay—"

"Leave me be!" He was cross and had no time for the old man's pointless worries.

There was a pause, then Hollis's nasal whine yet again. He wasn't a man to give up. "If ye'd please jest let me have a word with ye, Captain Keegan . . ."

"Bloody Christ." Snarling at the intrusion, his head thundering from too much ale and too little sleep, Keegan tossed back the fur covers and, without bothering with his dressing gown, threw open the door.

There was a gasp—for a second Keegan thought it sounded like a woman's voice—from the dark stairwell. But that was impossible. There were no women aboard, and they'd set sail three days earlier. A gust of bracing wind cut through his skin. "What is it, Hollis?" he demanded as his eyes adjusted to the darkness. "And whatever it is, it had better be good."

"Oh, sweet Jesus, Captain, if ye'd be so kind as to cover up—" Hollis's round face was illuminated by a lantern he'd hung on a hook near the door. Above his scraggly beard one cheek bore four red welts that had been scratched deep into his skin, his sparse hair stuck out at all angles, and one of his eyes was nearly swollen shut.

"What the devil happened to you?" Keegan asked as he noticed the rope, a thick coil that wrapped around Hollis's hands and trailed behind him and ended with a knot over the bound wrists of a captive.

A woman.

A dirty, bedraggled mess of a woman, but a woman nonetheless. *Jesus Holy Christ, where did she come from?*

"Tell your man to untie me," she ordered, tossing off the hood that had covered her head. Wild red hair caught in the candle glow as it framed a smudged face with high, prideful cheekbones and fierce blue eyes that cut him to the quick. Perfect teeth flashed white against her filthy skin. For a heartbeat he thought he knew her. There was something about her that instantly triggered a dark, forgotten memory that refused to spark. Nay, 'twas impossible. "I am not a slave! Nor will I be treated as one!"

"Who the hell are you?" He ignored the unlikely thought that he'd met her before.

"She's a stowaway, that's what she is."

"I asked her." Irritated, Keegan leaned a scarred shoulder against the door frame and folded his arms over his chest. "What's your name?"

Aside from the howl of the wind and the roar of the sea, there was only silence. The bit of a woman had the audacity to hold his stare, and there was something in her eyes that gave him pause—something that tugged at the cor-

DARK SAPPHIRE 259

ners of his memory yet again. Had he seen her somewhere? Defiantly she raised the pointed little chin of hers.

"She ain't sayin,' Captain," Hollis finally offered. "I found her in the hold, hiding behind the ale casks." He cleared his throat and shifted so that his shadow fell across Keegan's bare loins.

Keegan didn't give a damn what the woman did or didn't see. "What were you doing in the hold?" he demanded of the scruffy, prideful wench. "For that matter, what in God's name are you doing on my ship in the middle of the night?"

"Hidin', that's what she was. And up to no good, let me tell you," Hollis answered in his raspy voice. "Nearly tore me apart, she did. Clawed and hissed and spat like a damned she-cat. This one's the spawn of Lucifer, I tell ye. She's cursed this ship, to be sure."

"Have you, now?" Keegan asked.

She didn't bat an eye, just met his gaze with the angry fire of her own. The barest trace of a smile slid across her lips. "Oh, yes, Captain," she confided in a husky voice. "As surely as the moon rises behind the clouds and the wind screams over the sea." She took a step toward him without a trace of fear. "I be a witch sure and true. I've sent many a fine ship to the depths of a watery hell, and if you do not set me free at the next port, all of the wrath of Morrigu will be upon you."

"Morrigu?" Hollis whispered, horrified, his eyes rounding above his beak of a nose, his skin ghostly pale. His throat worked. "The goddess of death," he whispered.

"Oh, she is much more than that," the woman taunted, turning to stare down the man who had the audacity to leash her. "Fate and war ride on her wings. Destiny is her companion." Despite her bonds, the she-devil advanced upon her captor, and though much smaller than Hollis, she seemed to tower above him as he cowered in fear. "Morrigu's vengeance will be swift and harsh. Trust me. She will have no mercy on you, you pathetic insect of a man, or you, Captain Keegan." Whirling suddenly, she faced him. Fierce eyes, dark with the night, bored into him. Red, wild hair caught in the wind. "This ship and all those aboard will be doomed to the most painful and vile of fates if I but say so. Death will be a blessing."

Keegan laughed despite his headache. She seemed so certain of her gifts of death and pain. "Will it, now?"

"Do not mock me!"

"Oh, wench, I would not," he lied, but couldn't stop the smile he felt slide across his chin. "Curse away," he said, unable to hide the amusement in his voice. He motioned toward the decks with one hand. "'Twill not be the first time the *Dark Sapphire* has been damned."

She flinched a bit at the name of the ship.

"Nay. Do not!" Hollis's voice squeaked as he spun on a heel, his terrified gaze landing full on Keegan. "Be ye losin' yer mind, Captain? We . . . we wish not the wrath of the fates upon us. Morrigu, do you not know of her power, of her wrath, of her—"

". . . hold upon you?" Keegan demanded, tired of the game. "Even though you somehow managed to bind the witch's hands? Why has Morrigu not saved you, wench? If she be so powerful, why are you tied like a dog?"

The woman's expression was pure cunning. "For she is patient, Captain. Unlike mortal men."

Laughter erupted at the top of the stairs. Several deck hands coughed and snorted.

So the woman had already caused a stir among the men. 'Twas no surprise and yet a problem that irritated Keegan. His crew was a randy lot without much conscience or many scruples. A woman cast among them was certain to cause jealousy and trouble. Mayhap old Hollis wasn't so far off from the truth—that this wench would bring nothing but disaster to the ship and the men aboard her.

Keegan's amusement disappeared. He glowered up the stairwell to the darkness where the faces of his men were hidden. "Everyone back to his watch or work, and you"—he fixed his eyes on Hollis and hitched his chin toward the cabin—"bring her inside."

"Nay!" She threw herself backward, and the rope slipped through Hollis's fingers. He toppled to his knees as Keegan snagged the leash and wrapped it skillfully around his palm.

"Do not bother fighting," he warned the arrogant bit of womanhood. "There is no place to run."

In the weak light her expression changed. Fear, though fleeting, darted through her eyes, and an expression of defeat crossed her features, only to be quickly replaced by steadfast determination. Holding her head high, she followed him as he tugged on her tether and led her into the small confines of his cabin.

Dusting off his breeches, his pride completely undone, Hollis followed, barely sliding through the door as Keegan slammed it shut. From the corner of his eye Keegan noticed that the woman was assessing every square, naked inch of him. Worse yet, it was having an effect. His damned manhood, so long dormant, was responding.

His teeth ground in frustration. Just what they needed—a damned woman with her talk of spells on the ship.

Turning his back to his new prisoner, he dropped the rope and plucked his mantle from a hook near his bed. Deftly he threw the cloak over his head and didn't bother with the laces.

"Leave us," he ordered Hollis, who was planted firmly in front of the door. "Wait. Get some water—enough for the lady to drink and wash with." Beneath her grime he noticed a spark, a flicker of intelligence. "And have a tankard of ale as well as bread and meat sent up."

Hollis's bushy eyebrows shot upward. "You want food?"

"For the lady."

Hollis made a disparaging sound deep in his throat. "Water be precious. There be little aboard."

Keegan sent him a hard stare. "Water and soap. Aye, bring soap as well."

The woman stood stiff as a broomstick.

"But—" Hollis attempted to protest.

"Do it! Now." Keegan threw the man a look that could cut through steel.

"As you wish." Hollis, with his rapidly bruising cheeks nodded, though he glanced at the woman as if she truly were a curse come to life.

"Be quick about it, then. My guest waits."

"Guest?" Hollis repeated.

"She'll be staying here. With me."

"Nay!" She turned on him so swiftly her black cloak whipped about her legs, parting enough to allow him a glimpse of her dress. The fabric had once been a silvery gray but now was splattered with dark stains.

"You have no choice." Keegan rubbed the back of his neck and looked down upon her, for she was a mite of a thing, all bravado and little flesh. He glanced at the door through which Hollis was quickly disappearing. A salty breath of sea air seeped inside. "Well, that's not quite true," Keegan amended, rubbing his jaw thoughtfully. "If you would rather, you could take your chances with the rats and the crew, but let me warn you, lest you decide too quickly. The men who serve me have only one virtue—they are loyal to me. I ask no more of them. I know naught of who they really be or of what they have done to make them want to work here. They could be honest seamen or they could be cutthroats or thieves, traitors or debtors, murderers or worse. I know not. I care not. As long as they give me an honest day's work and remain true to me and this ship, I ask no questions."

"Ah, Captain, 'tis a fine assemblage of men you've gathered," she mocked, but beneath her show of courage she was not so brave. He noticed that her throat worked, and she sneaked a worried glance at the doorway.

"There's nowhere to go, you know. Now that we know you be on board, you cannot hide. You either stay here in the cabin with me, take your chances on deck or in the hold with the men, or dive into waters that are cold as ice and filled with all manner of creatures." He sat on the edge of his bed.

Her lips pinched in a display of defiance, and he could imagine the wheels turning in her mind as she conjured up some ridiculous means of escape.

"So now, woman, 'tis time you told me who you are and why you are hiding in my ship." He reached forward and she, who had been bracing herself against the sway of the carrack's floorboards, nearly jumped out of her skin. "I'll not harm you. Well, at least not yet." He took her hands in his, and when she tried to resist, to pull away from him, his thin patience snapped. "Do you wish these bonds removed?"

She froze.

"I thought so. Be still." He started untying the knots, keeping his eyes on his work though her breasts were heaving in front of him and through a gap in the laces of her cloak he caught a glimpse of white skin and the dusk of cleavage. Again his manhood responded, growing thick, hard, and needing relief.

Setting his jaw, he ignored the sensation; 'twas foolish to even think of it.

"Now," he said, his head bent over his task. The light was poor and Hollis's damned knots had swollen tight. "Who are you?"

A moment's hesitation. "Victoria."

"Victoria?" he repeated, knowing it to be a lie. "From where?"

"Rhydd."

"So far inland?" He glanced up at her, noticed the blanching of pale skin beneath a layer of mud and grime. She nodded, red hair seeming to catch fire in the candle's glow.

"Where did you board my ship?"

She bit her lip.

"Not from Rhydd."

"Nay. I—I got on at Gwagle—"

"Why?" The knot was loosened and the loops of rope fell away. Swiftly, she drew her hands from his, rubbing her wrists and sneaking a longing glance at the door.

Hollis, grumbling under his breath, returned with a large platter upon which was balanced a small pitcher of water, tankard of ale, crust of bread, and several strips of dried venison. A cat slithered between his boots, nearly tripping him.

"Damned beast," he growled, "Go after the rats, would ya, now?"

The creature let out a pitiful cry before slinking from the cabin.

"Just set everything there," Keegan ordered, motioning to the bedside desk. Hollis was quick to do his bidding, adding a bit of soap and a cloth from his pocket to the tray he set on the small table. With a disapproving look at the captive, he made a quick sign of the cross over his chest and, mumbling about sea witches and hexes, slipped through the door.

It closed tightly behind him. The woman—Victoria—started. No, now she was not so bold.

Rubbing his whiskered chin thoughtfully, Keegan leaned over the table. "If you got on the *Dark Sapphire* in Gwagle, you've been with us for three days." Again she flinched at the mention of the ship's name. Now, why was that? "If you boarded earlier, then it's been longer still. You must be hungry, thirsty, and would probably like to clean yourself." He paused, picked up a piece of venison jerky, and took a bite. She followed him with her eyes. Aye, she was starving, just too damned proud to admit it. Her small shoulders were squared beneath the muddied finery of her cloak. At first he'd thought her an alley wench, a poor woman, presumably a whore, but that was before he noticed the fur lining her mantle and the embroidery that was visible on her dress when she moved. This woman was no pauper. She carried herself with a regal bearing and looked haughtily down her small, straight nose, though she was in no position to argue with him.

Keegan chewed thoughtfully and tapped the remainder of his portion of smoked meat against his cheek. "So what have you to say for yourself . . . Victoria?" Waiting, he took a long drink from the tankard. Again she watched his movements. "Why did you steal onto my ship?"

Victoria gritted her teeth. Her stomach rumbled, and her mouth was dry as parchment. Lord, what she would do for a swallow of water or ale. But she couldn't tell this devil of a captain the truth. She couldn't confide in anyone and expect to live. Her skin itched, her muscles ached. Shuddering inwardly, she remembered the past three nights of hiding aboard this ship, listening to the sound of tiny, scurrying claws, feeling the rats climb over her feet, across her shoulders, or through her hair as she nodded off. Even now, just at the thought of the vermin, her skin crawled.

"You're running from something," he decided, his eyes narrowing in the frail light. Another bite of jerky. He chewed deliberately. "What is it?"

"'Tis not your business."

"You're aboard my ship. Without my permission." Another precious swallow of ale. "Seems like that makes it my business."

"I'll—I'll pay you for passage." The ship rocked slightly, the candle flickered.

"With what?"

"When we dock, I'll make arrangements to see that you're compensated," she insisted.

"How?"

"'Tis not your worry."

"'Tis precisely my worry." Frowning, he offered her the tankard. "How do I know that I can trust you?"

She held the cup in both hands, took a long swallow, felt the cool ale slide down her throat, and forced herself not to gulp it all down so fast she would vomit. Slowly, she lifted the metal tankard from her lips. "You know not that you can put your faith in me, of course, but I give you my word."

"Your word?"

"Aye." She took another swallow, and he shook his head at the folly of it all. She pinned him with her gaze. "I promise," she said slowly. "I will pay you and well, Captain. Of that you can be sure." Her mind was reeling, her thoughts pricked with fear. She had not known the name of this ship when she'd boarded or that of the captain. Could it be? Could this strong, strapping man be the boy . . . ?

His gaze raked down her body, and she was well aware of her sorry state, the rips and tears her mantle had endured as she'd raced through underbrush, the tiny scratches on her face and hands, the blood staining her skirts . . .

The moments dragged by.

She forced her mind to the present. This man Keegan held her fate in his callused hands.

Her pulse raced anxiously.

Outside, the wind moaned as the ship rocked.

"We dock in a week's time, Victoria," he finally said, his gaze assessing her reaction. "You have until then to convince me that you have a way to pay me for my inconvenience, that you are not on board to steal from me and that at the time we lay anchor there will not be authorities ready to storm the boat and search for you." He leaned closer to her, and she saw that his eyes were the same steely color as the sea in winter.

"There will be no trouble," she lied.

"We'll see." He stood, towering over her, and she noticed his bare legs, all sinewy, tough muscle and dark hair. She kept her eyes averted though she'd witnessed his sheer nakedness only a few minutes earlier, had surveyed strong back muscles covered with tight skin that bore the marks of floggings, old scars that had never faded. And then there was his manhood; she'd glimpsed that as well, though she'd studiously avoided staring at the juncture of his legs.

Once she'd been curious about men.

But no longer.

Never again.

"Eat." He nudged the platter toward her. His teeth flashed white in the depths of his beard.

Her stomach grumbled, and it was all she could do not to eat greedily. The bread was dry and hard. Delicious. The jerky was tough and salty. It tasted like heaven. Never had she been so hungry.

"Why were you hiding in my ship?"

She nearly choked on a bite of bread.

"As I said, 'tis my guess that you were running from someone." The *Dark Sapphire* pitched and rolled. "Probably the soldiers." Her back stiffened and he nodded, "Oh, yes, they were there at Gwagle. I met their leader, Sir Manning of Tardiff . . ." His eyebrows drew together as he considered the name—as if it had some significance but was lost on him. Sheena's heart turned to ice. "He was searching for a woman, a murderess. But this woman's name was Sheena, not Victoria."

Suddenly her appetite disappeared. Her stomach threatened to give up everything she'd just swallowed.

"It seems this Sheena was recently married and killed her husband, the Baron of Tardiff. She then stole some of the jewels from Tardiff's treasury." Sheena began to shake inside. *Be calm, this is but a test, one you must pass.*

"This murdering wife, she led the soldiers on a merry chase. They tracked her to Gwagle only to lose her again." His lips pursed and he pointed at her skirts. "Now *Victoria*, your dress, beneath your cloak, appears stained with blood." He leaned closer to her. "A bit of a coincidence, wouldn't you say?"

She set aside the tankard, gathered her strength, and though the tip of her nose was mere inches from his, met his gaze steadily. "All I ask of you, Captain Keegan, is safe passage. I said I would pay you and I will, so, please, give me the same respect you bestow upon the men you hire. Inquire not of my past. Ask only that I be loyal to you, and hold me to the bargain we have struck."

"You are in no position to bargain," he pointed out.

"But you agreed." She saw hesitation in his eyes and something more, something indefinable. Again she was set upon by the unsettling feeling that she'd met him before, long ago. The name of the ship should have been warning enough. But was it possible, was this surly Keegan, the upstart of a boy she'd saved—the handsome, cocky bastard who had allowed her to save his life, only to kiss her and leave her stranded in the cove? But that was impossible. That boy had been killed. She'd seen his death with her own eyes.

"'Twould be a mistake to cross me," he was telling her.

"As it would be to cross me."

The hint of a smile touched thin lips surrounded by his dark beard. "Is that a challenge, lady?"

"'Tis a fact."

His gaze traveled to her mouth. "Is it now?" So close she could see the streaks of blue in his gray eyes, she was, for a second, lost in his gaze. He suddenly straightened and she swallowed hard. If he wasn't the boy—then who? A man so like him as to be his brother? His twin? Dear Lord, maybe she was imagining the likeness. The boy was dead. *Dead.*

"Well, Victoria, we shall see." Again he took in her sorry state, and involuntarily she squared her shoulders.

His black eyebrows drew together. "Your clothes be dirty and damp. Mayhap you would like to change."

She nearly laughed, knowing she was lucky to have escaped Tardiff with her life, much less any possessions other than the three stolen stones. "I be sorry to disappoint you, Captain," she said, her gaze lowering to his bare legs, "but I am wearing all that I have, which is more than I can say for you."

"You're a bold one for being my captive."

"Ah, so there it is," she retorted hotly, meeting the dare in his eyes with that of her own as the timbers of the ship creaked. "A captive. Did you not tell your man that I was a 'guest'?"

His lips compressed. He looked as if he wanted to step forward and strangle her.

"Or was that just a lie, a reason to keep me here alone with you?"

Shaking his head at her impudence, he bit out, "Be you careful, lady, for that tongue of yours has a way of getting you into trouble." He turned his back to her, kneeling at the side of his bunk. "And it be my guess that you've found enough of that already."

She opened her mouth, then snapped it shut as he pulled out a deep drawer from beneath his bed. Inching nearer to the door, she watched as he rummaged through the garments, obviously searching for something she could wear, though nothing he could own would fit her, as he was nearly twice her size.

Yet he uncovered a bag that was tucked beneath a pair of breeches. "'Twas a good thing I thought better of throwing this into the sea," he muttered under his breath. Withdrawing a large, coarse sack that smelled faintly of lavender, he straightened and untied a fraying drawstring.

He reached inside, and to Sheena's amazement, he retrieved a wine-colored gown embroidered with gold thread. Without a second's thought he tossed the dress to her, then pulled out another gown, this one deep blue, the sleeves quilted in silver and lined with black fur. "Wash yourself and wear whichever of these you wish," he said, dropping the second gown over the first.

Dumbfounded, she shook her head. "I cannot."

"Why?"

"Because they—they must belong to someone," she said, running her fingers over the plush pile. The dresses were as fine as any she'd ever seen, meant for a lady.

"Aye," he said, his voice without emotion, his expression harsh and dark. "They once belonged to my wife. Now, Victoria, they be yours."

Chapter Two

What to do with the woman? Keegan asked himself over and over again. In the darkness, beneath the rigging and masts he paced as he eyed the slice of moon with a jaundiced eye.

Victoria she claimed to be. Victoria of Rhydd. Yet she was lying, he sensed it. And he'd met her before. The more he'd spoken with her, the more certain he'd been, but where? When? For the life of him he couldn't remember. But wasn't that as it had always been, ever since the dark time?

The soldier he'd spoken with in Gwagle, a knight with hard eyes and severe features, had sworn he was looking for Sheena of Tardiff, a murderess.

Sheena. 'Twas an unusual name. Keegan paused, placed both hands on the railings, and looked ahead, past the prow to the night-shadowed horizon. He had heard the name once before, he was sure of it, but that memory, along with far too many others, had been lost to him. *Sheena.* He rolled the name through his mind, and it evoked a response in him—a mixture of emotions from anger to something akin to love. 'Twas folly.

But not only the name. The woman was familiar as well. Or was she? Sweet Jesus, was he imagining it all? Had she, as she had threatened, cursed him? Had she done so in another time and place?

"Oh, for the love of the saints," he growled. How could he even know if they'd met before? With all the mud and grime upon her, she was nearly disguised, mayhap a tavern wench in finery, or a daft woman of means who had wandered off and boarded the ship by mistake.

Clasping his hands behind his back, Keegan began pacing the deck in agitation, hunching his shoulders against the bracing wind, feeling the salt spray upon his face, spying the great sails billow as the *Dark Sapphire* cut through the inky waters. Silently Keegan swore at the fates that had delivered him a stowaway—a bit of a woman who had the nerve to climb aboard his ship and the impudence to talk back to him. Though he was uncertain that he'd met her before, he was convinced she would bring him nothing but trouble.

Aye, she had to be the runaway bride. The blood stains on her dress were testament enough against her. And her bearing, the way she angled her chin, the fire of contempt in her eyes, led him to believe that she'd been born privileged. He leaned over the railing, his fingers curling over the strong wood. He watched a bank of filmy clouds scud across the thin slice of moon as he considered his captive. He couldn't find it in his heart to think that she had actually slain an unarmed man.

"God's eyes, what does it matter?" She was running from something and, like everything else aboard this ship, would fetch a fair price whether she paid him herself or he was forced to ransom her back to Tardiff—if that's where she belonged. Let her face justice or her husband, if the bastard be still alive and not dead as the soldiers claimed, or whoever bloody well else claimed her.

Keegan had learned long ago to never trust a woman; they were simply irrational creatures whose only purposes were to give pleasure and provide heirs. His own mother was proof enough of that. At the thought of the woman who had borne him, his lips flattened against his teeth. He'd never known her, never laid eyes upon her sorry face . . .

"What have ye done with the stowaway?" Hollis's voice was thin over the rush of wind and the soft moan of the sea. Smelling of ale and cradling a lantern so that the candle within the glass shelter would remain lit despite the breeze that howled off the sea, he sidled toward Keegan and leaned his rump against the rail.

"She is in my cabin."

"Ye trust her there alone?"

"Where can she go?" Keegan asked, but, in truth, he didn't trust her at all; the very fact that she was on board bothered him. "I doubt she'll make her way back to the hold with the rats, and she seems far too cunning to throw herself overboard."

"A pity, that." Hollis was nervous. He gnawed his lower lip and sniffed loudly. "I would not take me eyes off her if I were ye."

"And why is that?" Keegan asked. "What possible damage can she do?"

"She be a woman. Is that not trouble enough? And from her own lips she admitted to being a witch, that she could call up the Morrigu and—"

"Bah! I'll hear no more of this nonsense." Keegan pointed a long finger at Hollis's nose. "That kind of talk is for gossiping old women who have nothing better to do than spin tales of treachery."

The candle's flame flickered, casting tiny golden shadows over Hollis's fea-

tures. "There be rumors, Keegan. Some of the crew were in the tavern at
Gwagle, and while they were drinking ale and flirting with the whores, a band
of soldiers from Tardiff arrived. Their description of the husband killer they
were chasing is the same as that of the woman. Did ye not talk with their
leader yerself?"

"Aye. Sir Manning of Tardiff."

"But dinna let him board."

"Nay. I trusted him not." Keegan frowned.

"Nor would I."

"You know him?"

"Nay, nay," Hollis said hastily, mayhap too hastily. His eyes didn't meet
Keegan's. "So what of the woman?"

"She claims her name is Victoria."

"Do you believe her?" There was a shadow of something more than this
simple question in the older man's eyes—a shadow that quickly slipped away.

"Nay, do you?"

"No." Hollis shook his head with authority. His sunken eyes narrowed.
"And she did stow aboard. She be runnin' from something. Mayhap she sliced
the man's throat while he slept, as the soldiers claim. 'Tis more than possible,
me thinks. She's not to be trusted, Captain."

"No woman is," Keegan said, "but I doubt she will kill anyone on board."

"Why not? She may well be daft."

Keegan laughed bitterly as overhead the sails flapped with a change in the
wind's direction. "Daft?" The ship shifted and pitched, turning into the
breeze as the helmsman steered ever northward. "Aye, she probably is, old
man. What sane person would take refuge in this ship of cutthroats, thieves,
and fools only to hide in the hold with the stench of bilge water and the feel
of rats?"

"Oh, listen to ye! Jokin' about it all when I'm worried about the ship and
the men aboard her."

"You're only worried about your own sorry hide," Keegan said as Hollis's
candle died and the older man cursed.

"Hells bells, Captain, if all I cared about was me own fortune, ye'd not be
here yerself, now, would ye?"

"Nay, I suppose not." Keegan slapped Hollis affectionately on his stooped
shoulder. If not for the ancient one's true heart years ago, Keegan would have
died alone in a tiny boat. But the old man had saved him from a warrior's
arrow, stayed with Keegan during the weeks it had taken to heal, been at his
side as he'd lain on a pallet, unaware of the world around him. 'Twas true:
Keegan owed the old man his life.

"And the men, they be a restless lot. She may be no beauty, that one, but it matters not. A skirt is a skirt to many of 'em." He sniffed loudly. "I'm just askin' ye to be careful with the stowaway. She's touched by the devil, that one is."

"I'll see to her. Rest easy, old man. I thought she needed some privacy to wash up a bit and change."

"Change?" The old one lifted a bushy eyebrow and coughed. "Into what? Breeches?" Hollis threw up an age-spotted hand. "So now she's going to look like one of the deck hands, is she?"

Keegan snorted as he thought of the wench and the cleavage he'd seen as she'd leaned toward him. "If she be mistaken for one of the men, Hollis, then we've all been at sea far too long."

Mentally kicking herself, Sheena considered escape. Of course there was none. She'd trapped herself aboard this ship in the middle of the sea, with a brooding, dark captain whom she didn't trust for a second—a man whom she'd met before. She was certain of it. But how was it possible? It had been years but . . . was it reasonable . . . had her eyes betrayed her that day? Had that horrid, Judas of a boy somehow survived? This hard-edged captain with the black beard, wide shoulders, and gruff voice, could he be the wounded son of a captain she'd helped escape from Ogof so many years earlier? If so, why hadn't he remembered her? Oh, if he be the same rogue who had left her in the cove that day when she'd risked her life for his, he would not think anything of betraying her yet again and turning her over to Sir Manning. At that thought her stomach soured.

She worked feverishly, stripping off her mantle and gown, then ripped out the hem of one sleeve and removed the jewels she'd hidden there. For a few seconds they winked in the frail candlelight—blood red, brilliant green, and shimmering gold. They had been part of her dowry, the only valuables she now owned, and she wasn't about to lose them. She had no string to sew them into the new gown, and didn't dare cram the gems into some knothole within the miserable captain's quarters for fear of never being able to retrieve them again.

For the moment, lest she be caught with the valuable stones, she wrapped the gems in a piece of cloth from her dress and stuffed them into the toe of her boot. Then she began scrubbing, hard and fast, working up a lather on her face and hands. There was little water, but using it sparingly, she even managed to rinse some of it through her hair before it trickled down her neck, shoulders, and breasts.

Goose bumps appeared on her skin, but she rubbed hard, washing away the dirt, the grime, the blood and the painful, dark memories . . . oh, sweet Mary, the horrifying images that stalked her as relentlessly as did Ogof's soldiers.

"Stop it," she told herself as she rinsed the lather away. "'Tis no good to think of it." As she bathed she again considered escape and found no answer. Until the ship docked, she was a prisoner of a captain she dare not trust. "So be it, then," she murmured and spied the mazer left upon the small desk. Grabbing the cup, she hauled it to her lips and in one quick gulp finished the ale. Then, with an eye on the door, she grabbed the blue gown, tossed it over her head, and felt the smooth brush of velvet over her skin.

It smelled of lavender and was soft as down. Fur lined the collar and cuffs. She laced the bodice, and though the dress was a little too large, it was heaven to have fresh clothes brush against clean skin. Without benefit of a mirror, she finger-combed her hair, then spied her pool of clothes cast onto the floor.

Her dress and mantle were ruined, her chemise and stockings black with dirt. Quickly she searched the pocket of her filthy gown and retrieved her small knife.

The old fool who had stumbled into the hold to tap a cask of ale and caught her dozing had been so startled he hadn't had the brains to search her pockets, thank Morrigu. She thought for a moment and considered the old one who had caught her—was he the same man who had been with the boy? Oh, by the saints, 'twas true. The man had been hauled to the dungeon but had somehow escaped in the confusion of the fire eleven years ago. Had he somehow caught up with the boy, the one she thought was dead, and found a way to heal him? Holy Mother, what was this? Her knees wobbled. What trap had she inadvertently thrown herself into? Had she only known the name of the ship as she'd run up the gangplank, mayhap she would have chosen an alternate means of escape.

But there was none. *Even had you known this was the* Dark Sapphire *you would have rushed aboard.* "Think not of it now," she warned, and deftly tucked her sharp little dagger deep into a pocket of the dress—the captain's wife's gown, she reminded herself, and one that, from the look and feel of it, had never been worn.

Fleetingly she wondered about the woman who had married such a formidable man, then cast those thoughts aside. "It matters not," she reminded herself.

With the remaining drops of water in the pitcher, she soaked her undergarments as best she could. Using the last bit of soap, she scrubbed until her fingers were raw and she heard the sound of footsteps on the stairs outside.

Sheena froze for a second. "Sweet Mother, help me."

The captain was returning.

Or was it another of his men?

She lifted her hands from the wash. Her stomach tightened as she slipped a hand into her pocket and her wet fingers surrounded the hilt of her knife.

The door swung open.

With a rush of cold wind that caused the lantern to flicker, Captain Keegan with his damnable broad shoulders, beard-darkened jaw, and suspicious gaze ducked inside.

Sheena felt more than a moment's fear. In her lifetime she had been frightened of little, but this man, with his harsh expression, mirthless laughter, and haunted eyes scared her. She had met him before; now she was certain of it. But either he had forgotten that horrid tragic day, or he was keeping his knowledge to himself.

His hair was black as midnight, his skin nearly bronze, his eyes the color of steel. He was angles and planes, tight skin stretched over bone and sinew and muscle. She doubted many men were bold enough to cross him.

"Well, well, well," he said, smoldering eyes assessing her slowly from the top of her damp hair to the toes of her boots where her jewels were lodged. One of his eyebrows cocked. "Lady Victoria."

"I did not say I be a lady."

"You did not have to."

"And how would you know?" Did he remember?

He grinned, a wicked slash of white. "'Tis evident."

Her spine stiffened and she hiked her chin upward before she realized that in so doing she'd proved his point.

Sheena's heart raced, and she felt as naked as if he'd actually seen her without any clothing whatsoever. He closed the door slowly behind him. The latch fell into place. She nearly jumped out of her skin.

The cabin seemed suddenly close and far too small for the two of them. The floor rolled with the tide, and Sheena, balancing herself against the gentle rock, couldn't take her eyes off this man, could barely breathe.

"For the rest of the journey," he said slowly as he appraised her, "you will remain at my side."

"Your side? Why?"

"For your own safety."

"What care you about that?"

"Not much," he admitted, his lips pursing. "Just protecting my investment."

Her blood ran cold. "Your investment?"

"Aye, you have agreed to pay me when we dock. How you will accomplish this, I know not and I care not. If you do not pay as you have promised, I will be forced to call upon the soldiers of Tardiff; it seems there are men who are searching for you, men who might pay well to have you returned to them."

"You would ransom me?" Disappointment tore at her soul. The candle in the lantern flickered. Why had she considered him the least bit different from any other man she'd ever met? Had he not left her once before, shown his true side then, when he was little more than a lad?

"Aye, m'lady." He nodded and glanced at her one last time. His eyes darkened a bit. "Now climb into the bunk."

"What? Think you that I will gladly warm your bed, then you be sadly mistaken." Dear Lord, her heart was pounding so crazily, she was certain he could hear it. He, if he be the same man, was the first she'd ever kissed, the only one who had made her blood race wildly, her mind fill with wanton, unthinkable images. "I'll not—"

A strong hand reached out and circled her wrist. "Hush. I mean you no harm," he vowed, his face so close to hers his breath raced over the skin of her cheek. She noticed the shading in his gray eyes—the hard glint of determination. He was not a man who was used to being challenged. "I'll sleep on the floor."

"But I cannot—"

"Do not argue." His fingers tightened. "And do not be foolish enough to think that you might trick me. If you try to escape, remember, there is no place for you to run. Your virtue is safe with me, but I can not promise the same of the men. If you leave this cabin, no place on board will be secure." His fingers tightened, the warm pads pressing against the inside of her forearm, feeling her pulse, which was throbbing in dread. "Not on the deck, or in the hold, or even the crow's nest. They will find you. And you will be sorry."

She swallowed hard.

"Do you understand me, lady?" he demanded, and she couldn't summon enough spit in her mouth to answer. She couldn't imagine sleeping in his bunk, or having him so close. "Do you?" This time he yanked her arm.

Dear God, what did she get herself into by boarding this ship? "Aye," she whispered.

"Good. For I am weary and tired of dealing with half-drunk mates and lying women, so take to the bed, go to sleep, and pray that you find the sense to speak the truth to me in the morning."

Sheena opened her mouth to argue, then shut it quickly. And though it galled her to no end, she moved around the man, who seemed to fill the room with his presence, then sank onto the hard mattress. She expected the captain, despite his promise, to follow her. She was sweating with fear, the fingers surrounding her dagger wet, her grip so tight her joints ached.

She saw him move toward her.

She would not let him touch her, not let him do the unthinkable . . . oh, dear God in heaven, not yet, not here, not with this man, or any man.

All her muscles tensed. Her eyes burned but were dry.

Touch me and meet your doom, she thought silently, though even with her knife, she knew she was no match for him.

He sighed loudly and blew out the candle.

Sheena strained to see, but there wasn't the tiniest bit of light in the cabin. *Dear Lord, please, help me . . .*

True to his word, he didn't slide into the tiny space with her. Instead she sensed that he had settled on the floor. At least for the moment, it seemed, the captain had decided to leave her be.

She didn't release her death grip on her dagger, but some of the tension in her body eased. For the first time in three days she was able to stretch out, and her muscles, cramped and aching from too little sleep, relaxed. The ship rocked gently on the sea, and though she tried to stay awake, to be ready should the fierce one change his mind and try to climb into bed with her, she closed her eyes. Exhaustion took its toll. Despite her need to be wary, within a heartbeat Sheena drifted off.

"I'll hear no excuses!" Lady Fawn hoisted her considerable bulk from her chair in the great hall of Ogof. The baby, soon to be born, kicked deep in her womb, reminding her of her mission, the urgency of the task at hand as she advanced on Sir Manning, her one true ally, as he warmed his back-side near the fire in the great hall. "How could you have let Sheena elude you? For God's sake, she's little more than a child and a pampered one at that." Fawn threw an angry look toward her husband, Lord Jestin, who was no help at all in this matter. He sat in his chair, sipping wine from a wooden mazer while staring at his wife as if she'd gone completely and utterly daft.

It seemed to Fawn that Jestin grew older and fatter by the day, and the man she'd thought she'd married, the strong warrior, was slowly withering beneath his bulk. Fat as he was, he was only a shell of the man he'd once been. Sheena was his firstborn daughter, the only child from his union with Bertrice, his pathetic, sickly whore of a first wife whom he'd loved so fervently that he'd given her a ring the likes of none other. The gem had been worth a king's ransom, and he'd promised it to his second wife. Fawn felt the sword of injustice pierce her heart again, as it had over and over in the years she'd been married to the oaf. Bertrice had died when Sheena was but a girl, and from that point on Jestin had doted on the precocious, snotty child. Jestin had treated Sheena as if she were his son, for the love of St. Peter, as if Sheena were his only heir. He had favored Sheena over his other daughters, the three girls Fawn had borne him in rapid succession, as she was as anxious as he to bring forth a son.

A foolish old man, Jestin had let his firstborn run wild and even allowed her to play with the peasants' children. He'd taught her how to ride and use a bow and arrow. 'Twas hideous, and now he was paying for his mistakes.

All because the fat bastard had never stopped loving his first wife. In the years since Bertrice's death her memory had evolved into that of a saint. A shrine had been placed in the chapel, fresh flowers and candles lit every day. *St. Bertrice*—the wife who had raised her skirts and spread her legs for another man, but Jestin had seemed to conveniently forget all that. Oh, he was getting more disgusting by the day, Fawn thought bitterly, then realized that Manning hadn't answered her.

Were all men imbeciles?

She turned her attention back to her most trusted knight. "How is it possible that this—this snip of a girl has been able to vanish and leave the best huntsmen and soldiers in all of Ogof and Tardiff combined looking like fools?"

"She is either exceedingly cunning or very lucky or both," Manning said, his color high, his eyes, so very dark and wickedly seductive, clouded.

"A clever girl she is," Jestin added, with more than a touch of that galling pride that Fawn found sickening.

"Forget not that she be a murderess!" Fawn whirled on the balding old man to whom she'd given the best years of her life. "If you do not remember, husband, 'twas Sheena who killed my brother, your best friend, the man to whom she pledged her love forever." Tears filled Fawn's eyes, tears of grief, regret, and guilt. Angrily she dashed them away as dozens of candles flickered cheerily. Tapestries draped the tall whitewashed walls, and the scent of dried flowers in the rushes strewn over the cold stone floors met her nostrils, reminding her of all that was hers, all that would belong to her unborn son. This keep, once nearly in ruin from the fire when Captain Rourke had died, was strong again, built to her specifications, the envy of other baronies. And it would be her son's.

Sheena couldn't get in the way.

Sighing loudly, Jestin set down his cup, climbed to his feet, and rounded the table. He placed a calming hand upon his wife's shoulder. "Now, now, do not upset yourself, Fawn," he suggested, and slid his hand down the smooth wool of her dress to caress the roundness of her swollen belly. "Think of the baby."

"I am!" she snapped back, then caught herself and placed a hand over his. "Please, husband, do not doubt that everything I do, every breath I take, all of my plans are for the child. Our son." She felt the heat of Manning's gaze upon the back of her neck, but refused to glance in his direction.

"'Twill be all right," Baron Jestin whispered, linking his fingers through hers, and she knew again he was a fool, a poor, pathetic man who gambled and drank too much. Were it not for her, he would surely have lost his barony years before. 'Twas she who kept everything running smoothly. Jestin did little more than hunt these days and preside over the peasants' measly squabbles.

"Lady Sheena will be caught," Manning said, and when she looked over her shoulder, Fawn saw jealousy in the set of his jaw. The fire crackled and popped behind him, throwing his magnificent body in stark relief. His tunic and breeches were dirty, still wet from his long ride through the rain, and yet Fawn's heartbeat raced at the sight of him. "This I promise you," he vowed, his gaze holding hers.

"So your allegiance is to me?" she teased.

"The lord, of course," he sneered, but Jestin didn't notice the disdain in his voice. "As I am loyal to Tardiff, so I be loyal here. Have I not been your servant for all these long years?"

"Aye," she said, smiling, for Manning had proved himself time and time again. She felt a ray of hope, but before she could answer, the steward rounded a corner at the base of the stairs leading to the second floor. Wearing his forever dour expression and a brown cloak that had seen far better days, he walked with silent footsteps. "M'lord," he said, and lowered his head a bit. "If I may have a word."

"'Tis late, Allen." Jestin was tired; it was evident in the heavy bags beneath his eyes. How long had it been since he'd seemed a youthful man? There had been a time when he was dashing and proud and filled with a powerful passion . . . but that had been years ago.

"Yes, yes, I know," the steward apologized, hesitating as he glanced at Manning and Lady Fawn. Clearing his throat, he said, "'Tis a matter of much importance."

"Is not everything?" Jestin sighed and rubbed a hand around the back of his neck. "What is it?"

"'Tis the cook. He knows not how to use the spices sparingly, nor does he discipline the boys who work for him. There is so much waste and—"

"You deem this important enough to interrupt us?" Fawn asked, stepping toward the rail of a man.

Allen lowered his gaze. "'Twas the first time I could speak with the baron."

Jestin lifted a once red eyebrow that now bristled with long gray hairs. "I will have a word with him."

"Thank you, m'lord." Allen drew himself to his full height.

"If it is not one thing, 'tis another," Jestin said irritably. As the steward hurried silently out, Jestin offered his wife a smile begging her patience. "This will take only a few moments."

"Aye," she said frostily. "Why you keep him on, I cannot imagine."

"Because, Fawn, he is loyal. He cares. Elsewise why would he bother me?"

"Because he longs for power." Couldn't the old fool see what was so blatantly evident? "As do all men."

"And women. Forget not the ambitions of women." He pushed his weight from the chair. "I will be back."

"Nay," she said hastily. "I am so weary 'tis hard to keep my eyes open. I am nearly finished here, and when I am I will meet you in our chamber." She forced a smile on lips that felt as if they would crack from the strain.

"So be it, and you, Sir Manning, find my daughter and bring her back to me." He hesitated. "Alive and unharmed. Your men are to find her and escort her to Ogof, but should anyone lay a hand upon her, I will have his head."

"Aye, m'lord," Manning agreed.

With a nod, Jestin followed after the damnable steward. Fawn stilled her tongue until she could no longer hear her husband's heavy tread on the curved stairway and she was certain he was out of earshot. Eyes scanning the dark corners and curtains where servants were known to eavesdrop, she slowly turned to Manning.

"Remember," she said, touching the tall knight on his arm as she lowered her voice. "Sheena may be the lord's daughter, but she is a criminal as well. Not only is she a thief, but a murderess—"

"M'lady—"

"Shh." She placed a finger upon his lips, forcing his silence, as the castle walls could not be trusted. There was forever a twit of a laundress, the silent priest, or a manservant lurking in the corners, hoping to hear a bit of gossip to spread throughout the streets of Ogof. "Remember that above all else." Fawn angled her chin upward to gaze upon Manning, silently daring him to argue with her as she withdrew her finger.

"What I remember, m'lady, is that you and I have a bargain."

"Aye, we do, Manning. We do."

Chapter Three

"Damn that woman," Keegan growled to himself. He cracked open an eye. Every muscle in his back ached from his cramped position on the floor by the door. His head thundered from too much ale and too little sleep. Christ Jesus, how had he been cursed with such a bad turn of luck? What fate had he crossed that he now had to endure the next week with the lying chit?

And who the bloody hell was she? He dreamed he'd known her long ago, and in his dreams he saw smoke and fire and a beautiful, headstrong red-haired girl upon a blood-bay horse that reared and pranced to a backdrop of flames. The girl had tossed back her head and reached her small hands to the heavens as if to invoke the spirits, but he'd still had the urge to kiss her as she'd never been kissed before. . . .

He'd awoken in a sweat, the images receding quickly, the mixture of emotions—desperation, fear, and love—ebbing away.

He must've known her. Hearing his spine pop, he rolled to his feet. As the first shafts of morning light pierced through the small window, he stared down at his newfound burden. Fast asleep, breathing deeply, she sighed. Untamed hair fanned around her small, heart-shaped face, where a crescent of fine lashes caressed the tops of her cheeks and her tiny lips parted with each breath. Aye, she was a beauty, despite what Hollis might say, but she was trouble of the worst kind. He knew it in the deepest part of his soul.

He turned away quickly but caught sight of the tops of her breasts rising and falling in a smooth rhythm above the square neckline of Brynna's dress— a velvet thing that she'd never had the chance to wear. Remembering Brynna, he scowled. The woman he'd made his wife had been fair-skinned and even-featured, with almond-shaped eyes that could round in innocence or slit in cunning. With sable-colored hair and an air of mystique, Brynna had been seductive and treacherous.

Not unlike this woman with her strong chin and sharp tongue. One more glance in her direction convinced him he'd seen her before. He just couldn't place where. Or when. His mind clicked back to images of his travels, the towns where he'd docked running the length of Wales. Had he seen her in a market? In a tavern? An inn? On the street?

Was she the Lady of Tardiff? A woman who had slain her husband and robbed him? Never in his life had Keegan been close to Tardiff Hall, though he'd heard of it.

Or did you meet her in the black time—that part of your life you remember not?

Vexed, for he had no answers, Keegan dressed quickly, pulling on breeches and boots, a tunic and mantle. As the mystery woman lay sleeping in his bunk, he walked noiselessly from the cabin. Dawn was just breaking over the eastern horizon, the soft gray of morning parting the mist that rose from the sea. To the east, through the thin veil of fog Keegan spied the coastline of Wales, where the bare mountains of Snowdonia spired upward.

On deck the men were stirring and mumbled greetings as he strode past. Big Tom was already swabbing the deck, his mop moving evenly over the floorboards, Cedric was checking for tears in the mainsail, and a third man, Reginald of Hawarth with his straight back and thin mustache, was on his way to relieve the night helmsman.

None of them was the man he sought, but as he glanced up at the top castle on the foremast, he spied Wart and waved him down. Within seconds the agile little man had shimmied down the spar, swung onto the rigging, and dropped to the deck at Keegan's feet.

"Ye be lookin' fer me, Captain?" Wart asked, his ruddy skin creased, his body tough as old leather. He was a loyal one, Wart was, though his past was as murky as the sea before a storm.

"Aye, I've got a mission for you."

Bushy eyebrows raised expectantly. "A mission, is it?" He glanced to the shoreline barely visible in the distance and scratched his beard with the fingers of his left hand—there were only four. A thick stump was all that was left of his thumb. He'd never explained the loss, and Keegan had never asked.

"'Tis that why ye've had old Seamus take us so close inland?"

"Yes." Keegan clapped him on the shoulder and together they walked toward the bow.

"It has somethin' to do with the stowaway, I bet. The lady. Ah, but she's a looker, that one. Even in the dark, wearin' rags, a man with any eyes in his head could see she's a beaut."

"Is she, now?" Keegan mocked.

"Don't tell me ye ha'na noticed or I'll call ye either a blind man or a fool." Wart chuckled, and the laughter deepened into a cough that rattled in his thin chest.

"'Tis said you were once a spy," Keegan said.

Wart stiffened. The smile that had begun at one side of his sharp jaw disintegrated. "I was told when I signed on the *Dark Sapphire* that a man's past was his own." Pale lips flattened over his crooked teeth. "That no questions would be asked about his reasons for joinin' the crew."

"I asked nothing," Keegan said, eyeing the horizon. "'Twas merely an observation. I need someone I can trust to take a small boat ashore, sell it, gather some information, and meet up with me when we dock at the next port."

"Do ye, now?" Always ready for adventure, Wart notched his chin toward the land. "What kind of information, eh?"

"You're to see if the woman be who she says. Victoria of Rhydd."

"You think she is lying?" Wart's eyes blinked rapidly.

"She is a woman, is she not?"

"Humph. There be no denyin' that, I'm afraid." Wart sighed. "'Tis been a long while since a lady walked these decks." As if he'd realized he'd said too much, he quickly cleared his throat. "Is there anything else?"

"Nay, only the truth." A twinge of conscience assaulted Keegan, but he ignored it. If the woman had lied, then 'twas best that he found out now. "You've heard of soldiers from Tardiff searching for a woman who murdered her husband. Lady Sheena, wife of the baron."

Wart whistled long and low. "The murderess?" he said, new respect in his voice.

"Mayhap. These soldiers, they are willing to pay for her return."

"And you think the stowaway might be that woman?" Wart rubbed his hands, either from the cold sea breeze or the thought of ransom.

"You know me, Wart," Keegan said simply as they reached the forecastle and he glared at the rugged shoreline of the coast, green hills emerging more clearly as the fog dissipated. "I trust no one."

"Especially someone who hides in the hold with rats."

Especially a woman.

Wart winked. "Consider it done, Captain. Consider it done."

Sheena stretched and pulled the coverlet to her chin. She nearly smiled in the warmth of the bed until she felt a gentle rocking and her eyes flew open. Oh, Lord! Where was she?

Not in a bed. Nay, she was lying in a small bunk.

Oh, God.

She remembered. All too vividly.

She was a prisoner on this ship, the very one she'd snuck onto. How had she been so stupid as to stow away on the *Dark Sapphire* with the beast of a captain who was holding her prisoner? Aye, this morning she was certain he was the boy, and had somehow survived an archer's wound and the stormy sea. Too many facts assured her of the truth. Was not the old man the same who had escaped? Was not the name of this ship the same as that winking blue stone he'd stolen—the sapphire that had belonged to her mother? So he was older, taller, with wide shoulders, muscles, and raven black hair covering his jaw and chin—aye, he was the same betraying beast who had left her to deal with her father's wrath all those years before.

She cringed as she thought of the punishment she'd endured, how she'd nearly been banished, how ever after she'd been at Fawn's beck and call. She'd been imprisoned within the walls of the keep, forced to become a lady, never allowed to ride Shamrock through the surrounding fields, disallowed from the hunt, kept away from playing with the servants' children and, at every turn, Lord Jestin had threatened to marry her off to anyone of his choosing. In the end, he'd waited long and eventually given her to the worst possible choice. She shuddered when she remembered the mockery of a marriage ceremony at Tardiff Hall and the man who thought he owned her and could therefore treat her worse than a slave.

"God help me," she whispered as she thought of her escape and how she'd hidden from Sir Manning's men until they cornered her in Gwagle.

And she'd willingly boarded his cursed ship! She flung an angry fist on the bed as she remembered the horror of the chase through the town's crooked streets, the jangle of bridles, thunder of steelshod hooves, rattle of swords and the mind-numbing fear of being caught by Tardiff's merciless soldiers. All other avenues of escape had been blocked. She'd been forced to board the *Dark Sapphire* and had hidden in the hold until Hollis had discovered her.

Now Sheena was sleeping in the captain's bed. Had she traded one horrid fate for a worse one?

"You had no choice," she reminded herself, and banged her head as she sat up. "Damn." Rubbing the bruise, she climbed out of the tiny compartment and glanced around the room—the harsh captain's private quarters. The candle in the lantern had burned out, but a shaft of light streaming through a small window illuminated the wood-paneled room. A small desk had been bolted to the floor, the narrow bunk surrounded by a few drawers and a cupboard. A cloak and mantle hung from the hooks near the door, and there was barely enough space to turn around.

"'Tis time to face him," she told herself as she adjusted her wrinkled dress—Keegan's wife's gown. What poor woman had been foolish enough to marry him? Keegan's bride probably had had no choice in the matter. Or else she'd been taken with the beast's maleness.

'Twas not worth worrying over. She prayed the door wasn't locked. She didn't trust the blackheart of a captain for a second and suspected that he would try to jail her. Aye, they had a bargain, but it meant naught. The man was the spawn of Satan, she was sure of it. She yanked the door open.

Mayhap dealing with Tardiff's soldiers would have been safer.

At that thought her blood ran cold, and she climbed the short flight of stairs to the main deck, where the breeze was stiff and smelled of the sea. By some means, either fair or foul, she had to escape. As soon as the ship approached land, she would steal a rowboat and make her way to shore. From there she would take seldom used roads ever eastward. She was adept with a bow as well as a sword, and with the proper weapons she could fend for herself until she came to some obscure village where, using the jewels for money, she would establish herself.

As what?

A seamstress? Nay, her stitches had always been poor and weak.

A midwife? While growing up at Ogof, she had witnessed the birthing of cattle, sheep, pigs, and horses in the stables and fields of the castle, but she'd never seen a baby brought into the world.

A cook ? Or tavern maid? At the thought of serving raucous men, soldiers, tradesmen, peddlers, and merchants anxious to get away from their duties or nagging wives for a few hours, gathered together laughing, telling bawdy stories and trying to get a glimpse under her skirts, Sheena could not hold back a grimace of distaste.

For the moment she would not worry about what she would do once she had escaped this ship. No reason to put the cart before the donkey. First and foremost she had to find a way off the *Dark Sapphire*.

On deck, the wind slapped her face. Overhead, the sails billowed full and the ship cut through the clear blue waters while onboard men of all shapes and sizes scrambled from one end of the decking to the other. Chains rattled, flags snapped, and sailors barked orders at each other. Some of the crew washed the deck, others dumped buckets of bilge water overboard; still others scrambled up the rigging and adjusted the huge white sails, booms and yardarms.

On legs that were far from steady, she picked her way across a grating to the rail. Though the sea was calm, the ship still rocked along with the contents of her stomach.

"Well, look at that, would ya?" a deep male voice said behind her. She didn't bother to turn around, but shaded her eyes with a hand and looked eastward to catch a view of land in the distance.

"That be the stowaway," another man answered in a nasal tone. "Mayhap we should be spendin' more time in the hold with the rats, eh, Big Tom?"

"No tellin' what might happen if we did." Deep laughter rolled Sheena's way. 'Twas all she could do to tighten her jaw and keep from giving the scally-wags the tongue-lashing they deserved. Seamen were, in large, a superstitious lot; if they bothered her further, she would cast a spell in their direction and let them discover if there was any power to it or not. The taller of the two was a muscular man with thinning blond hair. His nose was crooked, as if it had been broken more than once, a scar ran from one ear to his chin, and one cold blue eye was slightly larger than the other. He sniffed loudly.

"Outta me way!" a huge voice boomed behind her. She jumped back as a heavyset man lumbered forward with a bucket filled with dead rats. Her nose wrinkled as, with only a second's curious look her way, he tossed the furry carcases overboard. "Who are ye?" His eyes were small and close together, his lips thick around few remaining teeth, his belly protruding farther than his chest.

"She's my guest." Keegan appeared from the other side of the mainsail. Dressed in black, his chiseled jaw set, his eyes narrowing on the crew members, he strode across the deck easily.

Sheena froze.

"And as my guest," he continued, "she will be treated with respect. Is that understood, Maynard?" The wind ruffled his raven-black hair, his jaw was set in stone, his eyes fierce and burning as they pinned the three idle seamen.

"Aye, Captain, aye." Maynard, his head lowering, his tiny eyes downcast, hauled his pail with him and hurried away.

All hint of amusement fell from the faces of the other two men.

"You, Tom, have you nothing better to do than joke here with the lady?" Before the man with pale hair could answer, Keegan added, "I thought you were to help James fix the bilge pump."

Tom's cracked lips pursed, and he seemed about to argue but clamped his jaw shut. Keegan's gaze was already upon the smaller of the two. "Jasper, if I'm not mistaken, you were to take inventory of the casks of wine and ale this morning."

"'Tis right ye be, captain," the shorter man agreed, nodding frantically. One of his eyes drooped. His face was ruddy as if he stood on the decks of this ship in all weather and rarely had use for a razor. Under the captain's fierce glare, Jasper scurried off like a crab seeking a rock for shelter. Tom wanted to argue. His nostrils flared and his fists clenched, but he, too, ducked beneath a shroud, two thick ropes leading from a masthead, and van-ished from view.

Keegan's gaze followed Tom as he leaned a hip against the railing. Then, as if satisfied that the sailor had indeed gone about his duties, he turned angry eyes upon Sheena. "As for you, woman, did I not ask you to stay in the cabin?"

"Aye, but I'll not—"

"What you'll not do is argue with me." Irritation laced his voice, and she bristled. Aye, he was an intimidating man, but she'd grown up with bullies, soldiers, and the like. Though Keegan was taller than most men, his shoulders wide as an ax handle, and he carried himself with the air of someone who had given commands all his life, she wouldn't let him order her about.

The ship rose upon a swell, and Sheena fought nausea. She was certain her skin had turned the color of pea soup.

"I needed fresh air." She inched her chin up a tad. "And worry not about my safety. I take care of myself."

"Not on my ship."

"Anywhere."

"Nay, woman, not anywhere. Not here. Not on the *Sapphire.*" Irritation tugged at the corners of his mouth. He raked stiff fingers through his hair as he spied a boy of about eleven high on the rigging, hanging onto the main yard. Impish eyes peered through an unruly curtain of brown hair, and a crooked smile twisted the lad's mouth. "Back to work, Bo," Keegan ordered.

"But I be workin'."

"Is that what you call it?" One of Keegan's eyebrows rose in doubt, but for just a second Sheena saw a hint of a kinder, softer man, one with a soul and a sense of humor, behind the captain's gruff exterior. Had she misjudged him? Nay, she had but to remember how he had abandoned her when she had risked her own life for his.

"Aye," the boy answered, his small chest puffed out.

"Well, if you think you will be paid for hanging onto the mainsail as if you were a monkey, then you'll have to think again."

The boy laughed out loud, a bubbling sound that caught on the wind. Beneath the beast of a captain's beard his lips twitched a bit.

"Is that yer lady, Captain?" the impudent lad, leaning off one of the yardarms, asked.

"She is my guest."

"Why?"

"'Tis none of your concern."

"Methinks she be your woman."

"Nay, Bo," Sheena said, twisting her neck to better view the boy. She shaded her eyes against the sunlight dazzling off the sails. "I be no man's woman."

"No?" Obviously he didn't believe her.

"Mayhap you would like her to be yours," Keegan suggested, and from behind the Bonaventure mast there was a rumble of laughter, wheezing chuckles. Unseen eyes had watched the display.

Keegan's expression turned cold. He grabbed the crook of her arm and steered her toward the prow of the ship as it cut through the swells. Steely fingers held her fast. Boots rang on the decking. Overhead the huge sails filled and flapped as sunlight spangled the water. "I'll accept no back talk from you," he said slowly. "Not in front of my men. Not on my ship." He leaned down so that his face was near enough to hers that their noses nearly touched, and she couldn't help but notice the hint of blue running through his gray eyes. "Listen, Victoria of Rhydd," he whispered as her queasy stomach quivered. "On the *Dark Sapphire* I am the rule. No one questions me, no one argues with me, no one dares speak against me. My men are loyal to me, the ship, and each other. You are but a guest, an uninvited guest at that, and certainly one who will follow my rules."

"Or?"

"Or what?"

"It seems you were about to threaten me," she said, biting back hotter, angrier words while fighting the sourness in her belly and bracing her legs against the rise and fall of the deck.

"I do not threaten, lady." His gaze drilled deep into hers. "But I expect to be obeyed. Is that understood?"

Oh, how she would love to defy him, and she would. But not now. For the moment he had the upper hand. "Clearly."

"Then I will have no trouble from you?"

"Oh, aye, aye, Captain," she spat out sarcastically, her temper flaring despite her attempts to hold her tongue. Her head ached where she'd bumped it, her stomach threatened to disgrace her, the jewels crammed into the toe of her boot cut into her flesh, and she was angry with herself for ever climbing aboard this cursed chip. "Or," she said, as if a sudden thought had struck her, she added with mock sweetness, "mayhap I should call you lord. Or master. Or both?" He grimaced, but she couldn't still her sharp tongue. "Is it possible that God Himself takes orders from you?"

"Only when He's aboard this ship, Victoria," Keegan said, his teeth flashing against his bronzed skin. "But, aye, then He surely does. And when I suggest He stay in the cabin, He doesn't argue. I expect no less from you."

She was about to challenge him again, but the fingers around her elbow dug into her flesh. "Remember, not only do we have a bargain, but I saved your neck the other night. If not for your taking safe harbor aboard this vessel, those soldiers would have found you and don't—" He pressed a finger to her lips as she started to protest. "Don't even think of arguing with me. 'Tis of no use. Until we dock, you are to stay by my side. Once ashore, we'll conclude our business, you'll pay me for my trouble, and then you can be on your way."

For a second she only stared at him. 'Twas all she could do not to rip her arm from his, kick him in the shin, and curse his sorry soul to the darkest depths of hell, but she restrained herself. Instead she yanked her arm from his. Like it or not, for the next few days she would have to obey him; she'd given up all freedom when she'd run up the gangway of his bloody ship. Short of throwing herself overboard, she had no escape.

As if he could read the capitulation in her eyes, he slowly grinned, and for a second the bastard was nearly appealing. Nearly. She smoothed the folds of her skirt, felt the brush of velvet of another woman's dress on her palms, and asked, "Is this how you speak to your wife?"

His smile fell away. A tiny muscle worked in his jaw. "No longer."

"I would hope not."

He looked at the sea for a second. One fist balled up and he let it fall against the railing before his eyes found hers again. She felt a chill as cold as the sea pass through her bones. Pain, quickly disguised, slid through his gaze. "My wife is dead, Victoria," he said through lips that barely moved. "Brynna died three years ago."

"Is there no word?" Fawn asked, tucking a braid behind her ear as she walked through the garden. Marigolds and roses were showing their colors, and she should have found some joy in their beauty, but she didn't. Not today. She felt like an old plow horse as she plodded toward the bailey. Her ankles were swollen, her entire body misshapen, and she was tired of the ungainly weight. Allen, that skeleton of a steward, was with her. He was an odd man, one who made the hairs on her arms stand on end.

"The lord has not yet returned from his hunt," he observed tonelessly.

"Nay, I care not about the hunt," she snapped, her temper quick to fire these days. She watched a thatcher repairing a roof. "I was speaking of Sheena. Has she not yet been found?"

"Sir Manning has not returned, but it has been only four days since he departed."

It seemed like an eternity.

Though Fawn hated to admit it, she missed Manning. She had told herself that she would only use him. He was strong, cunning, and brave, and above all ambitious far above his station in life—the perfect choice to help her with her plans. And yet she was nervous. Anxious. So impatient.

Oh, bother, mayhap it was only her condition. Pregnancy always seemed to cause her brains to curdle a bit. She paused to rest on a bench near the chapel. Bees buzzed through the showy blooms, and the air was heavy with the scents of flowers and spices, as the cook had demanded rosemary and sage be planted in clumps near the kitchen.

From her position Fawn observed a woman retrieving honeycombs from the bee skeps mounted high on one turret. On the flagstaff over the woman's head the standard of Ogof, emblazoned with a blue and gold dragon, snapped in the brisk morning breeze.

Fawn folded her hands over her protruding belly and felt very much like the oldest and ugliest sow in the castle pigsty. The baby moved within her, and she told herself to be patient, that this child was worth every morning of illness, every day that her ankles swelled, every hour of discomfort. This babe, her son, would be Lord of Ogof.

And Tardiff.

Finally.

"The minute there is word, you are to tell me," she said to the steward, who was standing near her, nervously shifting his weight from one foot to the other. Idly she wondered if she was to puncture his veins, would she find blood—or ice water.

"As you wish," he agreed, nodding as he took his leave. Oh, he was harmless enough, she decided, though she was suspicious of anyone and everyone within the keep's thick walls. No one, it seemed, could be trusted.

Even Sir Manning, a voice inside her head warned, though she ignored it. She motioned to the ninny of a girl who was attending her. "You, Sarah, fix this!" With one chubby finger Fawn pointed at her wayward coil of hair, and the scrawny little maid came over and began fussing with her tresses. "Where is Zelda?"

"She be in the keep, m'lady. She wasn't feelin' well, and she asked me to attend to ye for a bit," the twit replied. Fawn was instantly irritated at the old lady in waiting—she'd never liked her. Never. She'd inherited the dour woman from Bertrice.

"Zelda should have spoken to me herself."

"Aye." Fawn felt a tug on her head as Sarah reattached the braid. "There ye go, m'lady. Good as new," she said.

Fawn opened one eye slowly and the girl's face loomed into view. She could have been pretty, Fawn supposed, if not for large, crooked teeth and a weak chin. Not that it mattered. She was, after all, merely a servant. Beauty would have only caused her pain, for all the men in the castle from the lord to the gong farmer would have lusted after her and taken what they wanted. 'Twas a blessing that the poor girl was homely. "That's all, Sarah. Tell the midwife I need to see her in my chamber."

"Aye, m'lady." With a quick bow the relieved girl slipped quietly through a gate to the outer bailey, and Fawn struggled to her feet. She swatted a pesky fly and lumbered to the chapel, where she planned to kneel and pray just long enough so that the priest wouldn't reprimand her. It was important that everyone within Ogof's thick walls believe she was a loving wife, devoted to Lord Jestin, and devout in her faith.

'Twas a bother, to be sure, but necessary. If all was to go as planned.

Chapter Four

"Have I not seen you before?" Keegan asked as they sat in his cabin, she in the solitary chair at his desk, he standing near his bunk.

Sheena swallowed her crust of bread and told herself to remain calm. So he didn't remember. "I think not."

"Nay?" Frowning, he rounded the desk to look down at her. "'Tis familiar you be."

Oh, Lord, should she tell him the truth? Did she dare? She drank a sip of ale and set the platter aside. Upon it were the remains of bread, cheese, and dried meat that they'd shared. "How do you mean?"

Gray eyes regarded her with such intensity that she wanted to squirm beneath his stare. She remembered the kiss they'd shared so long ago, the betraying touch of lips that had turned her bones to jelly and caused her heart to pound as quickly as a hummingbird's wings. But that was long ago—before she'd found what brutal savages men could be. "It's—it's as if I've seen you in my dreams," he said, his gaze narrowing and moving from her eyes to her lips.

A rush of heat burned up the back of her neck as the ship rolled lazily and the timbers creaked. Did he remember? Was he but toying with her? "That I do not know. Your dreams be your own."

"Mayhap, but they be bothersome."

She lifted a brow.

"Yea, as you be, woman. Why did you stow away on my ship in Gwagle?"

"'Tis . . ." She bit her lip and felt the stones in the toe of her boot. She wanted to trust him, to confide in someone, but she didn't dare. Oh, he seemed concerned now, his fierce demeanor slipping to reveal the face of a man who cared, but she knew it to be trickery. Were she to admit—oh, by the saints she would be a fool. "'Tis difficult to explain a private matter. We had a bargain, you and I," she said, and wondered why the small room seemed suddenly closer still, more intimate. "You promised to ask no questions."

"And you promised to pay me." The mask of suspicion fell quickly back into place.

"Aye." She forced the lie over her tongue. "And I will. When we dock."

He wasn't convinced. She saw the doubt etch lines near his eyes and pull at the corners of his mouth. "I will remember, you know," he said, and her mouth lost all spit. "If I have met you before. I will remember."

And what then? she wondered.

"But for now your secret, whatever it be, is safe." With that, he strode out of the room. Sheena let out her breath. Being so close to him, in constant contact, was difficult. There was no place on this ship to run to, no spot in which to hide. Keegan seemed to be everywhere at once, and though she reminded herself that he was a blackheart, a horrid beast who would sell her as surely as not, she caught glimpses of a kinder man beneath his fierce surface.

She'd watched him with his men, and he was forceful, to be sure. 'Twas his way aboard the *Dark Sapphire* and there was no mistake to be made of it, but he was never savage or cruel as he'd dealt with each man's complaints, or arguments, or laziness. In one instance when she'd been on deck, she'd heard him reprimand a spry man who'd been lounging against a barrel of tar used by the caulker, who had also abandoned his task.

"Back to work, James," Keegan had ordered. "And what the hell happened to old George—he's not yet finished caulkin' here."

James had scurried to his feet. "I'll find 'im fer ye, Captain," he'd said, and rushed off as quick as his limp would allow.

Another time she'd seen him approach one of the men adjusting a sail. "Cedric, ye need to be tending that line more closely. Like so." Keegan had taken over the man's task agilely, his muscles bunching. Sheena had tried to look in any other direction, but the stretch of his shirt across his shoulders had held her gaze and she'd imagined his muscles beneath the cloth, hard and rippling, covered with smooth dark skin that bore the scars of ancient floggings. A warm flush had crawled up her skin, and desire, an emotion she was certain had died within her, had suddenly come to life.

She'd turned away quickly, stumbling over a rope, and she'd clumsily made her way back to this cabin only to see her reflection in his mirror. Her cheeks had been rosier than usual, her eyes wide, and she was sick with the thought that she'd actually found him attractive. "You be daft," she'd berated herself. "A fool of a woman. Remember, Sheena. Remember who he is."

But the feeling had persisted, and she'd found herself following him with her eyes, watching him deal with each of his men.

"Jasper, mind that ye don't leave the pulleys to rust. Ye know better," he'd said, clapping the crooked man on a shoulder one afternoon.

The very next day, as the *Dark Sapphire* had cut through the waters of a calm sea, he'd approached the big oaf of a man whose job, it seemed, was to rid the ship of pests. "Maynard, check the inside hull for ship worms—we may need to repair when we get to port," Keegan had ordered, his black hair gleaming in the midday sunlight. Sheena had been standing on the upper deck at the time, searching for the coastline of Wales. Her stupid heart had skipped a beat at the sight of Keegan. Wearing a black tunic and breeches decorated in tooled leather, he walked with authority toward Maynard, who was again tossing his kill over the deck rail.

"But, Captain, the rats—"

"You've been doin' a fine job killin' the beasts," Keegan had acknowledged. "A fine job. But them that's still aboard, they be goin' nowhere, and that bloody cat of yours will tend to them while you check the inside of the hull. Take Bo with you. He can scramble around in the small spaces more easily than you. Report to me about the worms, and then, Maynard, you can get back to the rats."

The big, lumbering man had obeyed without any further argument, and Keegan had flashed him a smile that, though not rained upon her, had touched Sheena's foolish, feminine heart.

And the nights, Lord, the nights were the worst. Knowing that he was sleeping close enough that she could reach down from the bunk and touch him, wondering if he was awake, listening to the sound of his breathing . . . 'twas enough to drive her mad.

"Do not think like this," she warned. "Too much is at stake. He is a man. You cannot trust him." She had only to think of her wedding day to remind herself of the horror of men. She had been certain less than a month ago that she would never want a man again. Whenever she remembered her dead husband she swore all over again to never be with a man. And no man could be trusted. Had not even her father betrayed her?

Sheena hadn't wanted to marry Ellwynn; had fought her father's decision from the moment he'd suggested a marriage to the Lord of Tardiff. . . .

"Nay, Father," Sheena responded when Jestin approached her with talk of a husband yet again. She was in the outer bailey with Bart, Ogof's falconer, at her side, working with a new bird. The falcon, wearing its leather hood, was perched nervously upon Sheena's gloved arm, and she was speaking softly to it, but her voice changed at her father's suggestion.

"I'll not marry Tardiff!" she said, startling the falcon, whose talons gripped harder, wings flapping noisily.

"Ah, Sheena, 'tis time you married. Long past time. Ye be three years past twenty. Ye should have been married long ago and have babes of yer own."

"I be hardly a spinster."

"Nay?" he snorted in disbelief. "Besides, it would be a good match."

"I like him not." The bird cried and attempted flight, but was bound by its tether.

Irritated, Sheena handed the hunting bird to Bart and stripped off her heavy glove. A spring dew collected on the sweet-smelling grass. The sun, shining pale through a thin mist, cast weak rays that warmed Sheena's crown and reflected on the spider webs stretching across the lush blades. Stalking toward the keep, Sheena slid her father a glance as they passed the orchard. Fragrant blossoms hung heavily in the leafy trees. Sheena barely noticed.

"This marriage, it be Lady Fawn's idea," she charged.

"Aye, she thinks 'twould be best for both baronies."

"She wants to get rid of me." Sheena kicked a dirt clod in her path, sending mud and pebbles flying.

"'Tis time her brother married as well."

"He was married before."

"Ah, but poor Lady Alyce passed on."

Sheena shuddered. Alyce had died when she'd been thrown off a horse and her head had struck a rock.

"And now Tardiff is lonely and needs a wife. He be a handsome man, Sheena, with good, profitable keep."

"I trust him not."

"You know him not."

"He be Fawn's brother." In Sheena's mind that alone was enough to condemn the man.

Her father sighed, rested a big hand on her shoulder, and guided her through the gate to the inner bailey. "I'm thinking only of you, Sheena," Jestin persisted. Stubbornly she threw off his hand. "Your mother, God rest her soul, would want you married and bearing babes of your own." He sighed, and there was more than a hint of sadness in his aging eyes. "Bertrice was a fine woman, Sheena."

"My mother loved you," Sheena cried, whirling as they reached the steps of the great hall. "She believed in love and would not want me to marry for the sake of convenience."

"Oh, but 'twas not always so. She grew to love me, but the first years of our marriage I think her heart was with another."

She knew this. "Captain Rourke," she muttered under her breath, refusing to think of the seaman's dead son who had left her standing on the dock years before.

"Aye. Bertrice was very young. Foolish."

Jestin placed one foot on the second step as the door to the keep flew open and the castle dogs ran out. Barking madly, the two swarmed around her father's boots as the kennel master slammed the door behind him, hurried down the stairs, and apologized.

"Do not worry, they are fine with me," Jestin said. He scratched one behind its lopping black ears while the keeper of the dogs hurried off to the kennels. Jestin glanced at Sheena as he continued, "Bertrice, she never said his name around me, held her head high, and eventually forgot him. In time his image faded and she came to know how much I loved her."

"But Rourke loved Mother. That was why he returned here." Again she thought of his blasted son, the one who had disarmed her with a kiss she had never forgotten.

"Rourke was a fool," Jestin said, his face flushing even more scarlet at the thought of his old rival.

"But Mother loved him as well."

"'Tis something we need to discuss. Rourke was . . . a distraction. Nothing more." Jestin patted both dogs on their heads. One leaped up expectantly. "Down," he ordered. To Sheena he said, "I was not a wealthy man. Ogof was not nearly as grand as it is now when I courted your mother. I had spent much of my time in battle, but I knew Bertrice would make me a good wife.

"I swore that I would love her and care for her and that in time she would learn to love me as well." He rubbed the stubble upon his chin thoughtfully. "It took time, Sheena, I'll not deny it. There were moments when I thought she would never come to love me, but I was patient and eventually she realized my love was true."

"And what of Rourke?" Sheena asked.

"Bertrice forgot him." He said it with authority, but Sheena noticed the doubt in his eyes.

"I remember not much of her," Sheena admitted.

"Mayhap I should have told you sooner," Jestin said, wiping some mud from his boot on a tuft of grass, "but you were young and it never seemed the right time. Now that you are about to marry, I thought you should know."

"I'm not about to marry anyone," Sheena corrected. "Least of all Lord Tardiff."

"Have you someone else in mind?"

"I have not yet found the man I love."

"Oh, girl." Jestin ruffled her hair as if she were a tiny child. "This is what I am trying to tell you. Love comes slowly."

"Has it come for you and Lady Fawn?" Sheena demanded.

Her father's expression turned guarded. "That is different."

"How so?"

"I—I needed a wife and a mother for you."

Sheena let out a disgusted puff of air. "She is no mother of mine."

The door to the great hall swung open again. Fawn stepped out of the keep, radiant in golden silk. The Lady of Ogof was followed by her three daughters, towheaded stepping-stones. Mary, the eldest with buck teeth and pale eyes, was twelve years younger than Sheena and a prissy thing who was forever sniveling and spying upon her older half sister. Ann, the middle daughter, was quiet and aloof, while the baby, Lynna, was a playful cherub who brightened upon spying her half sister.

"See-Na! See-Na!" she cried, scrambling down the stairs and running on short, chubby legs toward her. Grinning, Sheena bent down, picked up the imp, and twirled her in the air. Lynna giggled and screamed in delight. Her cheeks were flushed, her blue eyes bright and happy. "More!" she cried when the spinning stopped.

"Careful," Fawn reprimanded. "Don't get her dirty—oh, Sheena, look at you." Frowning in disapproval, Fawn pried the reluctant two-year-old from Sheena's arms. "Your clothes are a disgrace, and your hair, for the love of St. Peter, look at it." Her lips tightened as if pulled together by a purse string. "And you, Jestin, should not be condoning this behavior. Sheena is a woman now, soon to marry my broth—"

"Nay, I will not marry Lord Ellwynn!" Sheena glared at the older woman.

"Of course you will," Fawn snapped, then turned accusing eyes upon her husband. "This is your fault for letting her run wild and treating her as a son. She thinks she has a choice in the matter."

"I do—"

"Hush! I'll have none of your back talk!" Fawn glanced around the inner bailey, where within the stone walls the peasants and servants had stopped their tasks. The dyers tending their vats in a nearby hut were looking up from their work, and the candle maker had come to the door of his hut to see what was happening. Even soldiers on the wide curtain wall were peering down at the inner bailey.

"There is to be no more discussion," Fawn ordered. "Come, girls, and you, Zelda," she added, snapping her fingers at the maid, "See to Sheena. My brother visits tonight."

"Nay!" Sheena's heart dropped.

"Go, daughter," her father said, and she noticed a tinge of regret in his words. "We'll talk later."

"There is nothing more to discuss," Fawn insisted as she gathered her brood, including a fussing Lynna, and returned to the keep. Mary cast a superior look over her shoulder and smiled as if she enjoyed seeing Sheena put in her place.

Sheena wanted to protest wildly, but the harsh slant of her father's jaw convinced her any further argument would be futile. He had set his mind, and at Ogof his word was law—as long as his wife agreed.

Not for the first time in her life, Sheena was embarrassed to be his daughter.

Who was she? Keegan scowled in the darkness. Bits of memory, snatches that didn't quite fit together, pierced his brain. Had he not seen her astride a dark, sweating horse as it raced across a meadow? Had he been in a town where she, mischief dancing in her eyes, had pulled on a circlet and dashed into a cathedral? Was there not a time when she had taken his hand in a dark place that smelled of the sea, drew him to her, and brushed her lips against his? Had she not teased him with a blue stone, holding it before his face only to snatch it away? Were these pictures in his mind, so vivid and real, naught but dreams? Christ Almighty, was this the first vestiges of madness?

He gazed up at the coming stars. Nay, he was not daft, but something was amiss. If only he could remember. Could he have met her in the dark time— the span of months where he was little more than a lad, the time that he had no memory of but had been regaled with time and time again? 'Twas the time when his father had been killed by his old enemy. Keegan had been there, at Ogof, but remembered nothing from the time the ship had laid anchor in the bay until long after, when his wounds had healed and he'd awoken to learn that his father, the only parent he had ever known, was dead.

Even now when he remembered awakening to the sight of Hollis's gaze, he felt a coldness deep in his soul. "Father?" he'd choked out through lips that were cracked and dry. His voice had not been his own, had sounded even to his own ears as if it were echoing through a long, dark tunnel. His head had thundered in pain, and Hollis's words had echoed through the anguish.

"I'm sorry, lad, but do ye not remember? The captain, he was killed."

"Nay : . ."

"Oh, son, 'tis only ye and me and whatever we can scrape together."

He'd fallen into the darkness yet again and then had awoken days after without much memory but with a new, heavy pain that weighed on his heart and burdened his soul.

So how then would he have met this woman? *How?*

His back teeth ground together, and he told himself it didn't matter. Within a few days' time he would be rid of her and be a richer man. And yet he couldn't help listening for her tread upon the decking, glanced far too often over his shoulder to see if she was nearby, looked forward to the nights when he could gaze upon her in slumber even though his shaft was hard and thick and painful.

Aye, 'twould be good to get rid of her, whether she be Victoria as she claimed or Sheena as he suspected.

"Be ye a witch?" Bo asked as Sheena walked up the steps from the captain's cabin. The boy was lugging two pails, one filled with dead fish, the other empty. Sheena was grateful for someone to talk to, even if the subject was a little difficult. The ship was confining, and there were always men about, eyes following her every move.

Then there was that blasted captain, calling her Victoria, acting as if he'd never laid eyes upon her before the night she'd been dragged to his cabin by Hollis, and questioning her as if he truly had no memory. The sooner she was able to escape the *Dark Sapphire*, the better.

"If I were a witch, do you think I'd tell you?" she teased the scruffy-looking boy.

He eyed her suspiciously. "Nay, I'd be bettin' that ye'd cast a spell on me."

"Better be careful or maybe I will," she said, and laughed at the thought.

He didn't share her amusement. "Old Hollis, he be sayin' that ye have some kind of"—he thought for a minute, pulled out his dagger, and waggled it in the air—"some kind of power to call up the gods of the ancient ones."

"And what do you think?" For some reason she wasn't angry, just amused. Dragging in a breath of salt-sea air, she rested her arms on the top of the railing and eyed the horizon, searching for any glimpse of land.

"Mayhap." Bo plopped himself down, one leg stretched in front of him, his back braced against the railing, and pulled a fish out of his pail. As he looked up at Sheena through a shag of brown locks, he slit the fish agilely, slipping a sharp dagger through its skin near the tail and cleaving the flesh to the gills. "I heard ye sayin' ye could cast spells meself that first night ye were found." With a smug smile he added, "I sees more than they all know. Most of the men, they think me slow . . . but I be smart as any of 'em," he said proudly, and she wondered that anyone would mistake his youth for dim-wittedness. "I seen ye cursin' the captain on the first night when old Hollis found ye in the hold. Ye were callin' up the Great Mother—Morrigu—and ye asked her to doom this ship and all of us aboard."

She arched an eyebrow as she glanced down at him. "I only said it was possible."

With quick fingers and his well-honed blade, he scraped out the innards of the fish and ripped out the gills, dropping the guts into his second bucket. The herring's carcass was tossed back into the first pail. "Hollis, he's convinced ye be the daughter of the devil, and he's been bendin' the captain's ear."

"Has he? Hmm. And what did the captain say?"

"He laughed."

So the man did have a sense of humor, even if it was at Sheena's expense.

"Hollis has been sayin' it to the men, too. He's certain ye are here to damn us all. And half the crew—Seamus, Jasper, Cedric, and the lot—they believe him."

Sheena didn't argue against the old man's warnings about her, for if the men feared her, or her wrath, they would leave her be. Or so she hoped.

"So, are ye gonna chant a spell, call up the ghosts of the sea to capsize the ship so that we can all be eaten alive by sea serpents?"

Sheena smothered a smile. "I've been giving it some thought, aye."

The boy's eyes narrowed suspiciously on her. A gust of brisk wind caught her hair and brought a soft salty spray to her face. Overhead clouds gathered, their dark underbellies warning of a coming storm.

"So, Bo, what do you think?"

"Oh, I be sure you're a devil-woman," he said with a quick nod, "but I'm not afeared of ye."

"Nay?"

His smile was bold. Cocky. "Because I be able to take care of meself. I kin wield a blade as well as Big Tom and I'm quicker." He snorted. "The others—they know not what I see, what I hear, what I know." He held his dagger aloft, and a few rays of sunlight piercing the clouds gleamed against the sharp blade. "Ye want to know why I be so certain you be a witch?"

"Oh, please," she mocked, "tell me."

"Because ye've cast a spell upon the captain."

"A spell?" She glanced down at him, certain she would see mockery in his boyish face, but Bo nodded curtly again, as if agreeing with himself.

"Why else would he allow a woman on board?" Bo grabbed another unfortunate, but already dead, fish and sliced its belly evenly with his sharp little knife.

"Captain Keegan knew not I boarded."

"But he did na toss ye overboard when he found ye, did he? He didn't make ye walk a plank, as he said he would if ever a woman stepped on the ship."

"Has he done it before?"

"I donna know."

"If he tossed me overboard, Bo, I would surely drown or . . . or be swallowed whole by those horrid beasts of the sea—the serpents. Is that what you want?"

He thought for a second, the point of his knife nearly touching his chin. "I was but makin' an observation, lady. The captain, if he be true to his word, he

should have wanted ye dead fer trespassin' and stowin' yerself away. So that
the men know he means what he says." He yanked the gills of the herring, and
again slippery organs spilled into the bucket. With a smack the second fish
joined the first, and within a split second a third herring was in one of his
hands, belly exposed, glassy eyes seeing nothing as Bo's wicked little dagger
cut into it. He scowled to himself. "I dinna say I wanted ye dead."

"I should hope not," she said, then cocking her head to one side asked a
question that had been with her ever since the first night of her entrapment
in Keegan's cabin. "What of the captain's wife?" she asked, and Bo became
silent as he quickly dispensed with three more fish.

"I'll not cast a spell on you if you tell me," she said, prodding the boy. He
was chewing one side of his lip as if deliberating how much he should confide
in her.

"I knew her not," he finally said. Again he tossed a cleaned-out fish into the
rapidly filling bucket and snagged up another in his deft hands. "And ye did
not answer me question."

"What question was that?"

"What have ye done to the captain to keep him from throwin' ye overboard?"

"Nothing," she hedged, for she didn't want to think of the bargain she'd
agreed to the night she'd been captured.

Bo snorted in disbelief as he grabbed the final herring and cleaned it swiftly. With one eye peeking upward through the shaggy strands of hair, he
appraised Sheena with a look that called her the liar she was. He tossed the
last fish back into the bucket. Its scales glimmered silver in the faint beams of
sunlight that filtered through the clouds. "For you, the captain, he goes
against his own rules, ye know."

"How so?" she asked, leaning over the rail and searching the depths of the
ocean with her eyes. A salty breeze lifted her hair as she tried not to show too
much interest in the blackheart of a captain, the man who had betrayed her
years before yet acted as if he remembered her not. Was he blind? Or baiting
her? She was not sure of his intentions, and every time she was around him,
she was on edge. Nervous. Off balance.

"He always said there was to be no women on board. None." Bo's lips
pulled into a thoughtful scowl. "And there never was one."

"Never?"

"Nay."

"Not even his wife?"

"I said I dinna know her. Asides, she be dead," the boy said without a bit of
sympathy. He hopped to his feet, grabbed the pail of entrails, and tossed the
contents overboard.

"I know, but when she was alive?"

"She never stepped foot on this ship." Big Tom rounded the foremast. "And well she shouldn't!" He was carrying a coil of rope over one of his massive shoulders, and his expression, as ever, was harsh, his eyes as cold as a winter sea. How long had he been within earshot? Sheena's cheeks reddened as she thought of her questions about the captain.

Tom snorted and spat over the railing. "Women have no place on the sea, and that one, she was a lyin' whore. There be no mistake about it. Killed herself when the captain found her with another man, she did."

Sheena didn't believe the huge man for a minute.

"Carryin' a babe at the time." His nostrils flared, and he hitched the rope higher over his shoulder. "Spoilt she was, but sly as a fox. As beautiful as ye be with a heart as black as the devil's own. Any man who saw her wanted her. Including the captain."

Footsteps rang on the deck behind her, and she knew in an instant that Keegan was near. Her heart sank. Embarrassment stained her cheeks.

"Bloody hell," Bo whispered as he stared over her shoulder.

"Bo!" Keegan's voice heralded his approach. The boy straightened and picked up his catch. "The cook's lookin' fer you."

"Aye, Captain," the boy said, then cast Sheena a glance that warned her to keep what they'd spoken of between them. Then, his hair flopping in the wind, he scurried down the stairs to the lower deck.

"And ye, Tom, have ye naught to do but gossip like an old woman?" Keegan demanded. His expression was unreadable, his eyes dark.

"Ye have no gripe with me, Captain."

"Then why are ye not mindin' the jibs?"

"Because I see no reason for it," Tom said, standing his ground. "Where are we goin' Captain? Why is it ye've taken us so far off course?" Tom's eyes narrowed on the horizon, and he spat on the deck. He pointed toward the east. "Where is the coast land, eh, Captain?" A few sailors inched closer.

Keegan's lips tightened. "We be this far asea because of the shoals, Tom," he said with little patience.

Wiping his nose with the back of his hand, Tom shook his head. Two men who had been adjusting the sails stopped their work.

Keegan's patience was stretched thin. A muscle leaped in his jaw. The muscles at the base of his neck bunched, and he looked as if he wanted to pummel the bigger man with his bare hands.

The ship rocked, timbers creaked, and chains rattled as crew members looked on. The smell of a fight was heavy in the salty air, and Sheena knew, that at the root of it, she was the cause of all the dissension between the men.

"'Tis the woman," Tom charged, voicing her own dread. *Thud!* He dropped his coil of rope.

Sheena wanted no part of being any reason for Keegan's men to challenge him. Right now she needed him and . . . and, truth to tell, she hoped no harm would befall him regardless of their pact.

From the stairway Hollis appeared, his hood blowing off in the wind, his old eyes taking in the scene unfolding beneath the huge billowing sails.

"She's been distractin' ye, Captain, as she has many of the men." Tom hooked a disparaging thumb toward Sheena. "The sea be no place for a woman, a ship no home for a witch."

"The lady has nothing to do with the course we take."

"Nay? Well, I say she's cursed this ship by castin' a spell of doom over it and addling yer mind."

Hollis frowned and shook his head. "Enough of this—" he ordered, but Keegan paid him no heed.

"Tend to the jibs, Tom. Worry not about the stowaway."

Tom's face reddened and he motioned to the older man. "Hollis, there, he agrees with me, no matter what he be sayin' now. And so do Maynard and Seamus. Ye've not been the same since the old man found the witch in the hold and dragged her to yer cabin. She's cast a spell over ye, Captain, I swear it."

"And I say you're wrong. She is my guest. Nothing more."

"Or yer whore," Tom said under his breath.

Sheena's back stiffened. "I be no man's whore," she vowed, her fists clenched as she took a step forward on the slippery deck. Outrage and indignity burned through her blood. "Not the captain's. Not any man's. As for spells, mayhap you should be careful lest I cast one on you."

"Enough," Keegan said, but Sheena wasn't finished. She'd endured much already, and she wouldn't let any of these thugs and cutthroats intimidate her.

"Now, what is it you'd like, Tom, eh? There be spells that make a man blind, or kill him dead, or shrivel his manhood to the size of a babe's finger or—"

"I said enough!" Keegan growled, glaring at her with a gaze that was sure to cut through stone.

"But—"

"Cast whatever bloody spells you wish, Victoria, but do it quietly, alone, in my cabin."

"Careful, Captain, lest I turn my magic on you." A gust of wind slapped her in the face, tore at her hair, but she didn't move as the ship turned into the wind.

"Try it," he suggested without a drip of humor in his voice.

"Nay!" Hollis cried as other men looked up from their work. Keegan rounded on Tom.

"Back to work. All of you." Keegan's jaw was granite. The skin over his face had stretched tight, and deep grooves surrounded his mouth. "As for you, Tom, I warn you, never speak of the lady again lest you do it with respect."

"Bah!" Again Big Tom spat, this time on the deck. "Things are not as they should be, Captain Keegan, and ye know it. We be off course and Wart be missing. What of him?"

The wind shifted. Keegan pinned the big man with his eyes. "I sent Wart ashore a few days past. He took a rowboat and will meet us at the next port."

What was this all about? Who was Wart?

"Why?" Tom demanded, and Sheena realized the answer even before the next words were spoken. "Because of the whore?" Tom asked, cocking his head toward Sheena in disgust.

Keegan lunged forward, his fists curled, his shoulder muscles tight as if he was ready for battle. He stopped short of grabbing the taller man. "You treat the woman as a lady, Tom. Or ye will have to answer to me. Now, go about your duties, and be quick about it or you and I, we'll settle it another way."

"Ye would fight me?"

"'Tis your choice."

Jasper, Reginald, and Seamus gathered on the deck, witnessing this hint of mutiny. They looked at each other, then Tom.

Time froze.

Keegan didn't move.

The sails snapped.

Tom's thick lips curled into a sneer, and Sheena was reminded of the castle dogs, how they crouched and glowered when they'd been cornered and expected a beating from the kennel master. Tom's gaze never moved from Keegan. "Ye be the captain only because ye cheated a man out of this ship in a game of chance," he snarled, rounding a bit, looking for a place to land a blow.

Just like his father before him, Sheena thought, swallowing hard. Had not Keegan's father, Rourke, nearly lost his ship, the *Warrior,* in another game of luck? Instead of winning, he'd given up his life.

"Every man on board knows it."

"'Tis of no matter, Tom," Keegan said, moving with the other man. "Whether I bought this ship, stole it, or built it myself, I still be the captain." Every muscle in Keegan's body was tense, the cords in the back of his neck standing at attention. "And you, Tom, along with the rest of the men, are to obey me. There be no questioning my authority. Ever."

"Then ye be a fool."

"Mayhap."

Tom's gaze darted around the deck, and for a second Sheena expected him to throw a meaty fist in Keegan's direction.

He hesitated, then growled, "It be not worth the trouble." Backing off, he sent a glare of pure hatred in Sheena's direction before spitting again. Finally, he reached down to pick up his coil of rope, tossed it over his shoulder, and strode off, lowering his head as he ducked beneath the mainsail.

"Now, Victoria," Keegan said slowly as he turned to face the bane of his journey, "never are ye to—"

"Captain!" Hollis picked his way across the deck and cast a worried glance at Tom's backside as the big man disappeared behind the rigging of the foremast. "By the saints, Tom, he's always sayin' things he should na. But he means it not. 'Tis his temper only."

Keegan didn't comment.

"Ye know this, Keegan. He's always spoutin' off, now, but he's proved himself true."

Keegan glowered irritably at the older man. Tom's words had cut deep, for what he wanted to do right now was grab the sharp-tongued woman, haul her down the stairs to his cabin, and lock her away where she was out of sight of the men and could not cause any more trouble. But he had to deal with the old man. "What be on yer mind, Hollis?"

"'Tis Seamus. He's ailing and needs be relieved of his duty. It seems he drank too much ale yesterday."

"Come along, then." Keegan strode toward the short stairway leading to the lower deck, where Seamus now guided the ship with a whipstaff.

Seamus barely glanced in Keegan's direction as he approached, nor did he look at Victoria, as the fool woman had come to the helm with him. Keegan's lips tightened over his teeth. He'd known she would cause more than her share of trouble, and he'd been right. Blast her and her damned beauty.

From the corner of his eye Keegan noticed James, who sat with his back against the wall as he repaired a large net. Smothering a grin, James nudged Jasper with his elbow. James's mouth curved into a crooked grin as he whispered into the other man's ear. Jasper barked out a laugh, and Victoria visibly stiffened. Her shoulders squared, her chin lifted proudly, and for just a second an image tugged at the corners of Keegan's memory—a picture of a younger woman, nay, a girl. But before he could quite grasp it, the recollection slipped away. Yet again. But he would remember. Soon. He sensed it.

Her cheeks were flushed in embarrassment, her lips compressed, for she knew that, as Big Tom had voiced, some of the men believed her to be warming Keegan's bed. Well, so be it. Whether she realized it or not, she was safer with him than locked away in the hold.

However, he thought with more than a trace of irony, mayhap Hollis had been right this one time. Perhaps he should have taken the woman ashore the minute she'd been dragged to his cabin.

"Captain," the helmsman greeted Keegan as he approached. A tall, gaunt man with a scraggly brown beard and tired, lifeless eyes, Seamus was holding onto the whipstaff as if it alone were holding him up. His cheekbones were visible beneath skin that was tinged a sickly green.

Keegan minced no words. "Hollis here says you want to be relieved of your duty."

"It might be best, aye." Dead eyes flicked toward the captain. "For now. 'Tis sorry I be, but—" He cleared his throat and looked guiltily at the floorboards.

"Off with you," Keegan said brusquely. He took command of the whipstaff, the long pole attached to the tiller that guided the ship. To Hollis he said, "Find Cedric."

"Aye, Captain, that I will."

"And take the lady with you," Keegan ordered.

Sheena opened her mouth to argue with him, but changed her mind. "I need not an escort," she said instead. She made her way to the upper deck and felt the jewels pinching her toe. She needed to get off this cursed ship and soon. Keegan was not all he seemed. Did he really not remember her? Should she tell him that they'd met before?

She arrived at the cozy little room she shared with the brooding captain, and she collapsed onto the bunk, nearly banging her head, and threw one arm over her eyes. Oh, he was a shameless one, Keegan was and yet . . . a part of her found him fascinating. "Then 'tis a fool you be," she told herself. "He's no more charming than a wolf about to slaughter a lamb!"

Why had he sent the man—what was his name— Wart—ashore? Wart? What kind of name was that? Where had he been sent—to Tardiff? Ogof? Her heart froze. Would Keegan double-cross her, knowingly keeping her captive to sell her back to the men who were chasing her down?

He had no scruples . . . or had he?

Had he not stood up for her on the deck less than an hour before? Had he not taken that horrid Big Tom to task? Not that she couldn't have dealt with the man herself, but the captain had stepped in.

'Tis only because of your bargain, she told herself, but frowned, for there was something about the rogue of a captain she found intriguing.

What was wrong with her? She knew him to be a traitor. Had he not proved that years ago? She couldn't trust him, wouldn't. Nor, even if he held up his end of their pact, could she honor her bargain with him.

At that thought she felt a pang of true regret. She removed her boot slowly and pulled out the stones. They winked in the frail light from the lantern—brilliant, sparkling gems in the dark room. She wondered about the dark blue stone he'd taken—the most valuable of her mother's jewels—the cursed Dark Sapphire of Ogof. Had he sold it and bought this ship, naming it after the stolen gem? Did he still own it? Was it hidden somewhere in this prison of a ship? Or had it been lost in the sea years before when she'd thought he'd been killed in that tiny boat—the one she'd given him?

"It matters not," she reminded herself. As soon as the ship was near land, she would escape and leave Keegan with his mysterious past and seductive eyes behind her.

And then what will you do? Once you flee the Dark Sapphire *and are on land again, what then?*

Mayhap you should go home, Sheena of Ogof. Somehow you must elude Sir Manning's men, sneak into the castle, and find your father alone. Explain to him what happened on your wedding night and then accept whatever punishment he metes out.

She swallowed hard, sat up, and looked into the mirror at her reflection. She was suddenly pale, for the thought of facing the hangman wasn't pleasant. She'd never been one to run from a battle, was usually bold to the point of impudence, and wanted to return to Ogof to explain herself.

Don't do it. 'Twill be certain death, one part of her mind admonished. *But the truth needs be told; leave your fate in the hands of your father. Trust in him. He's a fair man,* the other part of her brain disagreed.

She stuffed the stones into the toe of her boot once again and considered her future. Only two things were certain: She had to escape the *Dark Sapphire* and elude the soldiers of Tardiff. Then she would decide if she would run and hide for the rest of her life, be forever wary, continually look over her shoulder, or return home to her father's brand of justice. "God help me," she whispered, not for the first time, though she expected no answer to her prayer.

Chapter Five

"Say it not," Fawn warned as she lay on the bed in her chamber. She wore only her chemise while the midwife Maven, an aging crone with little sense of humor and a reputation Fawn wasn't certain she believed, poked and prodded with spotted fingers, then shook her head sadly as if there was not the slightest chance of an easy delivery.

"'Tis sorry I be," the midwife admitted sadly as scented tapers, smelling of a mixture of pine cones and acorns, burned beside the bed.

Zelda, her maidservant, stood near the grate, waiting with infinite patience, holding Fawn's clothes while the midwife took her sweet time with the examination.

"Tell me not that the boy is not in position." Fawn was in no mood for bad news. Anxious and edgy, she awaited word from Manning about Sheena. How had that twit of a girl eluded the best men in Ogof for so long?

Maven pursed her already wrinkled lips as a small fire hissed from the grate. Tapestries adorned the walls, and fresh rushes, scented with rose petals and lavender, had been strewn over the stone floor. But today, with the feel of a storm in the air, Ogof held no warmth, no joy for Fawn. Coupled with everything else, the midwife's dour expression was all the more irritating.

"What? What?" Fawn demanded, eyeing the woman who was supposed to give her good news—only good news.

"You told me not to say, m'lady, but the babe, be it boy or girl, has not yet turned. If it does not—"

"*He.* If *he* does not," Fawn corrected, sitting up in bed and yanking down her chemise over the protrusion that had once been a waist so small a man's hand could span it easily. "'Tis a boy I carry. Forget that not."

"Aye," the woman said, though from the shadows in her eyes it was obvious she still had doubts. Fawn didn't. Secretly she'd ridden to the edge of the forest where the fortune-teller Serena dwelled in a crude hut.

Serena had placed warm, knowing hands upon Fawn's naked belly and, closing her eyes, had told Fawn the truth—that the child inside her womb was male, was destined to rule and would be as strapping, cunning, and fierce as his father. Serena had said that the child had all the qualities of his ancestor, Llywelyn the Great, and Fawn believed every word. Serena's prediction was a good sign, to be sure.

"If *he* does not turn, the birthing will be difficult," Maven said softly. A breath of wind rushed through the open window, and the embers of the fire flared and cast shimmering golden shadows on the whitewashed walls.

"I have born three babes." Fawn snapped her fingers at Zelda as she stood. The older woman was quick to help her don a green tunic and darker surcoat. "And aye, their births were not pleasant, but not so difficult, either." With Zelda's help, Fawn adjusted the tunic, frowning as she had to stretch the fabric over her distended belly.

"This child is larger."

"'Tis not a simpleton I be," Fawn shot back, angry at the tight fit of her gown and the fact that the midwife should bring up her ever increasing size. "Boys often are." Fawn managed a smile despite the old woman's concern. Discomfort aside, this birth would be a blessed event, the likes of which Wales had not seen since the Llywelyn himself had been brought into the world. Jestin would be proud.

But then, he was a fool.

"But, m'lady, sometimes, if the babe does not turn and is born back end first, even if it—he—survives he may . . ."

"May what?" Fawn snarled. "Tell me not that he would be crippled or . . . or . . ." Dread froze her heart. "Or that he might be born an idiot, for that is blasphemy, Maven. Do you hear me? Blasphemy!"

"I said it not."

"Good." Fawn would not worry about the midwife's concerns. "'Tis up to you to see that the babe is born healthy. I trust you are able to do it."

Maven chewed her lower lip. "I have lost only three in all the years that I've birthed babes, m'lady."

"And this one will not be your fourth," Fawn insisted. She grabbed the midwife's gown, her fingers curling in the worn fabric. "Remember that this child is destined to rule not only Ogof but Tardiff as well. Now, be off with you!" She released the wretch and heard the sound of thunder cracking over the distant hills.

A storm was brewing.

As the midwife, hunch-shouldered and grim, scurried out of the room, Fawn glanced at the window. Why had Manning not returned with news of Sheena? Absently she touched her belly and felt the child growing within her kick. Hard. Ah, he was a warrior, this one. Very soon she would have a son. And then, by all that was holy, that old man of a husband of hers owed her a jewel, and not just any bauble, oh, no. She expected a ring with a stone as awe-inspiring and dazzling as the Dark Sapphire of Ogof had been—the treasure he'd bestowed upon his first, pathetic wife. Nay, whatever prize he gave her, it would have to be *more* valuable than that damned ring.

Sheena tossed and turned on the bed as the wind howled across the ocean and the ship pitched wildly. She couldn't sleep, though it wasn't because of the roll of the sea; she'd become used to the rise and fall of the ship as it cut across the waves. Nor was it from worry about being captured by Sir Manning and his army of thugs. She felt safer aboard the ship than she had on land. But the captain, she found him disturbing, and though she reminded herself that he'd betrayed her once before, that he was only keeping her on board because it spelled a profit for him, she felt herself melting where he was concerned. Not only was he strapping and handsome, but she'd seen beneath his gruff exterior another man, one who might just have a soul.

"Do not even think it," she worried aloud, tossing off the covers and wondering when he would return to the cabin. *If* he would return. She was becoming charmed by him and had even pretended sleep to watch him remove his tunic and breeches, though in the dark she'd seen very little of him aside from corded muscles and a swirling mat of black curls upon his chest. All else was lost to her.

"And a good thing," she muttered, feeling guilty for taking the space where he was to sleep. He deserved better—or did he? Just then she heard his boots ring on the steps outside. Her silly heart jumped, and she bit her lip as he threw open the door and strode inside. His clothes were wet, his hair in damp ringlets, the smell of salt upon his skin. The lantern had burned low, and Sheena, careful not to bump her head, climbed out of the bunk.

"What's this? Can you not sleep? 'Tis the storm. Do not worry, it will be over before morn."

"Nay 'tis not the weather," she admitted, realizing she was wringing her hands and willing them to stop. "I can take your bed no longer." She stood and the ship pitched again. She nearly fell against him, but caught herself and stood toe to toe with him in one of his wife's dresses.

"Why not?"

"'Tis not right." She shook her head proudly. "Though you call me your guest, I was uninvited and I—I . . ."

Her words faded as she realized he was staring at her with his damnably gray gaze that had somehow scraped against her soul. Rainwater ran down his chiseled face and down his neck. Her pulse throbbed in her throat, and she was suddenly tongue-tied. He was far too close, and she remembered all too vividly how it felt to have him kiss her so many years ago. The tiny room seemed to shrink even farther, the flickering light from the lantern casting golden shadows on the dark wood walls and defining the hollows and planes of his face.

"I—I will sleep on the floor."

"I have not asked it."

"I know, but 'tis your bed and, as you so often remind me, your ship." Unexpectedly she'd felt her cheeks warm.

He hitched his chin toward the bunk and sighed. "Now, Victoria, I be weary." His voice was low. Intimate. "Take the bed."

"Nay, I—"

"Do not argue with me."

"But—"

"Oh, for the love of the saints." Quick as a cat springing, he grabbed her by the arms. His fingers tightened. His eyes glowed with the reflection of the candle. "Must you always defy me?" Sheena's blood spurted hot through her veins. She swallowed hard as he slowly pushed her backward the few feet to his bunk. Her calves brushed up against the hardwood frame.

All time stood still. The ship rocked. Somewhere overhead footsteps could be heard and the masts creaked. "Christ Jesus, what is it about you?" he demanded, shaking her a bit. "Why is it that I feel I know you?"

She swallowed hard. Should she tell him? Or would opening the gates to his memory bring with it all manner of demons from the past?

"Get into the bed, Victoria. Now." His mouth drew downward, brooking not a solitary argument. "Alone."

"I do not want—"

"Then I will be forced to sleep with you. Would you prefer that I share the bed with you?"

"*What?*" she cried, her voice low and raspy at the thought of him lying next to her, his body pressed intimately to hers in the small bed. "Nay, I'll not . . ." She gulped, and his gaze was drawn to her neck, watching the movement at the hollow of her throat. She felt dizzy and the roll of the sea only intensified the sensation.

He said nothing, just stared. So near. So distant. And yet she detected a yearning deep within his soul. Felt his desire as well as her own.

"Test me not, Victoria of Rhydd or Lady of Tardiff or whoever it is you be," he whispered in a voice as raw as a winter wind.

She didn't budge, just stared at him in the dim glow of the lantern and licked her lips nervously. The fingers over her arms dug in, and he drew in a swift, whistling breath.

"Either you are an innocent who knows not what she does, or an accomplished temptress who is testing me. Now, woman, get into the damned bunk before I throw you into it." She inched up her chin but didn't have the chance to rebuff him, for he said, "If you defy me, I swear, I may do something I will forever regret."

She didn't ask what he meant. The air was thick with lust and longing, nearly crackling with a need she never thought she would feel. For once she held her tongue, and clearing her throat, she lowered herself onto the bunk. Quivering inside, she closed her eyes and listened as he strode out of the cabin and the door shut with a thud behind him.

"Oh, God, no," she whispered, feeling a deep, dusky ache in the most intimate part of her. Denying the sensations of wanton lust even as they assailed her, she curled her fingers in the coverlet, tried to close her mind to the thought of him without his shirt and breeches, and ended up lying awake half the night, calling herself a thousand kinds of fool because a wayward part of her had found his threat appealing.

God forgive her, after all she'd been through, she wanted Captain Keegan both in body and spirit. Tears sprang to her eyes, but she refused to cry. Not for him. Not for any man.

She forced herself to sleep, reminded herself that she would want no man, and she dozed all the while the ship fought the waves. Time passed. The captain didn't return. She must have fallen asleep, for suddenly she was startled awake. There was a cry—or was it only the moan of the wind?

She slipped out of the warmth of the bed and felt an instant chill. Again the cry. Not bothering with her mantle, she opened the cabin door, where rain lashed from the night-dark heavens. The ship listed to one side, then shuddering, righted itself and, barefoot, Sheena fell against the cabin wall only to hear the cry again.

"Hello!" she yelled, climbing the steps.

"Help me . . . oh, please . . ."

She sprinted onto the deck. "Where are you?" she screamed, her voice snatched by the wind as it shrieked through the masts and the *Dark Sapphire* bobbed wildly. 'Twas as if Satan himself were at the helm.

"Here! Help."

Was it Bo's voice? Heart pounding, feet sliding, she dashed through the rain and the darkness, bending under the boom. "Bo! Where are you?" she cried. Oh, for the love of God, answer!

"Here!" he screamed as the boat rocked and pitched. Sheena's body slammed against the mast. Pain shot through her. Icy rain pummeled her from above. The wind roared and shrieked as she peered into the darkness, straining for a glimpse of the boy.

"Where?"

"Here! Up here!" And then she saw him, a small boy caught in ropes that had tangled in the wind. His dark contorted shape was barely visible against the huge white sails rippling in the wind.

"Hang on," she screamed, and, fearing he might lose his grip at any second, began climbing in the darkness, her toes curling over the wet, swollen ropes, her fingers clawing ever upward. The drenched dress was a dead weight, dragging her ever downward, her hair blew in front of her eyes, and her fingers scraped against the rough cords until they were raw. She forced herself upward. "Hang on."

Bo was caught, dangling half upside down. Somewhere below she heard voices, men shouting as the crew tried to keep the unsteady boat afloat.

Keening wind filled the sails. The ship rocked. Sheena's hands bled. The boy was a dozen yards above her. "Can you see me . . . Bo!"

He didn't respond. His face was white as death. *Oh, God, was she too late? Had he somehow hung himself on the rigging? Had he tangled himself in the complex network of wires, pulleys, and ropes?* "Bo! For the love of God, can you hear me?"

He was closer, only half a dozen yards. Just a little farther. The *Dark Sapphire* shuddered suddenly. Waves crashed over the deck. The wind shrieked and the huge ship listed so far that one of Sheena's legs swung free. Closing her eyes, she clung to the rough ropes, sending up prayer after prayer as men below worked to right the ship. Fear constricted her heart, and she was shaking with the cold. She stretched. "I'm—I'm almost there!" she yelled through teeth that chattered and bargained with God for Bo's young life.

"Lady . . . Lady Victoria," he cried and she was grateful for the sound of his voice.

"'Twill be all right."

"I got meself tangled up. The wind . . ." He tried to sound brave. "I slipped and a pulley hit me . . . and somethin' must've torn and—"

"And we're going to get you down. Right now." Oh, Lord, she sounded more confident than she felt. Slipping one leg through the netting so that she would not fall, she worked with the twisted ropes that bound him, her frigid fingers forcing the frayed cords apart. "Come on," she said. "Easy, now."

As he was freed, he began to move much more agilely than she. "Come on, hurry," he said as the wind tore at her and the rain blurred her vision.

She followed more slowly, careful as she descended, her stomach jolting each time the ship rocked. Her dress was matted against her body, her hair sodden, her flesh chilled to the bone. Her hands were scraped raw on the slippery, coarse ropes. Her shoulders ached, and she bit her lip to keep her teeth from chattering like a ninny.

"Hurry," Bo yelled, seemingly well.

She was halfway down, lightheaded and frozen, when she felt a strong arm surround her.

"'Tis no witch you be," Keegan said, grabbing her and holding her close, his breath warm against her frigid skin. "But a foolish, foolish woman." She was too exhausted to argue, too grateful for his strength to disagree. She wanted to collapse against him, but clung to the ropes high above the deck. "Now, let's get down from here."

"Who's . . . who's at the helm?"

"Seamus. Worry not." With one arm on the main cable and the other around her, he half carried her ever downward, his feet sure, his muscles tight. She wrapped an arm around his neck, felt his warm, wet body pressed tightly to hers. His face was tense against the rage of the wind, but he never faltered, never said a word. Within minutes he'd stepped onto the deck, still carrying her as if she weighed nothing.

Maynard stood near the main mast. "Ye saved Bo's life," he muttered, his voice barely audible over the wind.

"Nay." She shook her head as Keegan carried her toward the stairs. "I helped him."

"No. Ye saved his life." Big Tom agreed, and the surliness that had been his constant companion was no longer with him. The boat listed again, and Keegan barked orders at his men.

"There be work to do!" A cable snapped. The ship pitched wildly. "Get Jasper and James. Someone has to fix the rigging. Now!" he yelled as he carried her across the uneven deck. The two men scurried away, and Sheena struggled to stand on her own feet.

"Do not struggle, little one. I'll carry you." With surprising tenderness, he carried her into the cabin and set her carefully onto the bed.

"Where's Bo?"

"With Hollis. Worry not for him," Keegan said, pointing a finger at her soiled dress. "Take that off before you come down with chills."

"I—I'm fine." She tossed her hair from her eyes and wiped her face with her hands, only to wince in pain.

"Are you?" He bent down and held up one of her hands, exposing the cuts and scrapes in the candlelight. Her fingers were raw, bleeding. "I'll send someone with warm water, soap and a cup of wine."

"Do not bother—"

"'Tis none." He strode to the door, then paused, his great shoulders sagging a bit. With a glance over his shoulder, he said, "'Tis true. For once

Maynard was right. You saved Bo's life. And now I must see to the helm." With that, he was gone, and Sheena had no thoughts of disobeying him for the first time since she had been dragged on a leash into this very cabin on the night she'd been discovered. Tonight, as the *Dark Sapphire* battled the storm that still raged, she sank backward onto the bunk. There was no fight left in her.

The maid was a comely wench if ever there was one, Wart thought as he sipped dark ale from his bench at the tavern. Her hair was braided into a long plait that fell over one shoulder and was the color of wheat at harvest time. Sky blue eyes, a pert little nose and, above the neckline of her dress, white breasts like pillows, soft and beckoning. A man could smother between those inviting mounds, and ah, what sweet death 'twould be. She moved between the tables, avoiding the patrons' hands, for many a man too far in his cups was willing to risk a slap for a chance to pinch her fine arse swinging invitingly beneath her skirts.

"Lizzie, girl, another drink," one man yelled over the noise. Wart guessed him to be a merchant of some sort by the finery of his garb.

The girl picked up a tray of cups filled by a birdlike woman with wrinkled skin who opened casks, brought out steaming platters of food, and anxiously counted the coins that the lass collected. As dried up and drawn as Lizzie was ripe and young, the old hag watched the tightly packed room with eyes that missed nothing. Conversation buzzed, bawdy jokes were passed, raucous laughter vied with the clink of cups, and the struggling strains of a musician who plucked at his lute and sang in a thin, wobbly voice could hardly be heard over the din.

Wart sat and listened. From what he understood, a small army of men had stopped at the inn, soldiers from the south, just the night before.

Lizzie delivered to the merchant a cup of ale, then worked her way down two plank tables to the corner that Wart had occupied for most of the evening.

"Will ye be havin' another cup?" she asked in a voice that was like a songbird. It brought back memories of Wart's first love, a girl who had sworn her heart to him, only to marry the son of a farmer her parents had chosen—his cousin Peter.

"Aye, if ye be pourin', Liz."

She giggled, though he suspected that her flirting wasn't because she was interested in him. Nay, he knew he wasn't a handsome man, but he paid well for his drink, and she sparkled and laughed and brought a bit of joy into his tired, jaded heart.

"And how did ye lose yer thumb, eh?" she asked.

"Defending a pretty lass's honor," he lied. The incident that had cost him partial use of his hand was not worth telling. He motioned her closer. "Ye say there were soldiers in here just last eve?"

"Aye. Half a dozen of 'em, I'd guess. All asking questions, they were." She filled his mazer and, leaning over, offered him a long look at her breasts. Wart's old, lonely member rose in his breeches, and he resisted the urge to shift on the bench.

"What were the soldiers doin' here?"

"Oh, they be searchin' for a woman. A lady, methinks." She lingered, anxious to pass on a little gossip.

"A lady?" Wart feigned surprise.

"Mmm. Lady Sheena of Tardiff." Lizzie leaned ever closer, and the faint scent of honeysuckle tickled his nose. "The knight who be in charge—Manning, they called him—said she killed her husband!"

"Nay."

"On her wedding night." Lizzie moved her head up and down slowly.

"'Tis hard to believe."

"I heard it from the knight himself." Clucking her tongue and shaking her head so that her braid brushed the tops of those supple breasts, she added, "Can ye imagine? She bein' a lady and he bein' a lord. Stabbed him, she did, nearly gutted the poor man."

"Mayhap he did not please her," Wart said, then took a long draught. "It takes skill, ye know, and patience as well. Not all men be able or willin'."

She didn't so much as blink; nor did she blush.

"Lizzie! Make haste, will ye?" the old shrew behind the counter yelled. Oh, she was a nasty one, that. With a shrill voice, beaklike nose, and tiny eyes that sparkled suspiciously, she slammed a tray upon the counter. "There be thirsty men here!"

"Aye." Lizzie started off, but Wart was quick and grabbed her wrist. "These soldiers, were they headin' north?"

"I did not hear." She glanced nervously to the counter, where the nag was watching with her tiny, hawklike eyes.

"Lizzie!"

Wart released her; there was no more she could tell him. He would locate the encampment, listen to the men himself, and then have a word with Sir Manning, find out exactly who the knight was searching for. Victoria of Rhydd or Sheena of Tardiff, it mattered not to him.

He left some coins and a piece of his heart with Lizzie, then walked outside to a night as dark as death and prayed that he'd find the army from Tardiff soon. He'd been too long on the land and was itching to return to the *Dark Sapphire*. He missed the smell of brine and the feel of the ship as it cut through the night-black waters. 'Twas a feeling like no other, a freedom he missed sorely. Despite all the fetching maids in Wales, Wart had learned long ago not to trust them. Now and forever his only true love was the sea.

*   *   *

The ship was too damned small, Keegan decided as he walked to the prow and took in a great lungful of bracing night air. Grand as she was, the *Dark Sapphire* was far too confining. All because of the woman. No matter where he turned, Keegan saw Victoria, and when he didn't, he couldn't help but look for her. Christ Jesus, he wished she'd never boarded the ship, never stowed away. And yet if she hadn't, would Bo be alive this day?

Last night, as he'd held her tight while helping her down the rigging, his memory had flared, and he thought he'd been near to her before, holding her close, running through the darkness . . . and yet just as he was certain the image would come into sharp focus, it had slipped away from him again. Much later, after his watch, when the storm had abated and he had returned to the cabin just before dawn, it had taken all of his willpower not to join her in the bed. He'd ached to touch her, to feel her warm skin against his cold flesh. She'd been in peaceful repose, her red hair fanned around her face, the sweep of her lashes and parted lips as seductive as a siren's call.

Oh, she was a distraction. Not only to him, but to the men as well. All of them. Jasper was completely smitten, and even Big Tom, ever since she'd risked her life for Bo, had started following her with his eyes. Bo, of course, had been won over. Only old Hollis was still wary, and even his harsh attitude against her appeared to be softening. "She be a witch, I tell ye," he still proclaimed, but Keegan had caught the old man speaking with her, even cracking a smile and showing off his snaggled teeth when she spoke with him.

Nay, it wouldn't be long before every man on the ship was besotted with her.

He leaned against the bowsprit that held the jibs in place. It jutted over the night-dark water above the figurehead he'd had specially carved after Brynna died—that of a solitary wolf with painted eyes that were gold as a summer sunrise.

Keegan had always felt at home on the sea, but now he was restless. This night was no different from every evening when he thought of the woman sleeping in his bed. 'Twas all he could do to withstand the temptation of returning to his cabin, locking the door behind him, and sliding under the covers to lie with her. He'd caught glimpses of her in the night when she'd moved on the bed and the candle in the lantern had burned low.

He hadn't been immune to her allure, though he'd gritted his teeth and dragged his gaze away from the curve of her spine, the slope of her shoulders, even a firm, small breast with its button of a nipple that had been exposed for a brief second as she'd rolled over on the bed—*his* damned bed.

The fires within him burned, for it had been long since he'd been with a woman. Too long. And the other night, when she'd defied him by not taking the bed, it had been all he'd been able to do to stride out of the cabin. He had spent the next three hours looking out at the sea, his hands clenched, his mind burning with the want of her.

Last night, with her hands bleeding, her sodden dress molded to her body, her tiny lips chilled, he had forced himself back to his duties.

Now at just the thought of her, his manhood swelled uncomfortably. He stared up at the inky sky, millions of stars winking overhead. The moon was full, casting a ribbon of light on the rippling waters, but his thoughts were far from the beauty of the heavens. No, his mind would not waver from the seductive image of the woman lying in his bed.

Who was she?

What was she running from?

Was she a pampered lady who had actually plotted to kill her husband?

And why did he have the feeling that he had known her once, long ago, that she remembered him? Worse yet, he suspected Hollis was keeping something from him as well. The old man had trouble hiding his true feelings and was holding tight to a secret. What the devil was it?

Questions, like a flock of hungry gulls after a single dying crab, kept circling and wheeling through his mind. Why was he certain he'd seen her before? That red hair, those blue-green eyes, so bright and deep. Bloody hell, why couldn't he remember? "Blast it all," he growled, drumming his fingers on the smooth wood of the bowsprit as he glowered into the starry night and listened to the wash of water against the *Dark Sapphire*'s hull.

He wondered how much ransom he could demand for Victoria and felt a jab of guilt, for she had shown true bravery when she'd saved Bo.

The air stirred, and he sensed a presence before he heard the light tap of boot heels against the decking. Glancing over his shoulder, he saw her, a small thing with wild hair and skin that seemed as white as alabaster in the moonlight.

"Did I not tell you to stay in the cabin at night?" he growled as she approached.

"I could not sleep." She tossed her hair over one shoulder rebelliously. God's teeth, what would he do with her? "Remember, Captain, I be not your prisoner."

He snorted. She was an impertinent thing. And beautiful. Damnably beautiful.

Her eyes slitted in the darkness, and she reached up to twine her fingers in a shroud stretched to the rigging. "Are you afraid that if I walk around the ship I might uncover your secrets?" she baited.

He didn't respond.

"'Tis too late. Some of your men have loose tongues."

"Especially if they be threatened by witchcraft."

Her lips pulled into a little smile. "Mayhap."

"And what have they told you?" He crossed his arms over his chest and leaned back, telling himself that whatever she'd learned, it was of no consequence.

"I know that you be a thief."

He frowned. Didn't say a word.

"And a smuggler. I was in your hold."

He lifted a shoulder and tried not to stare at the hollow of her throat, a seductive, dusky indentation above the tops of her breasts. He clenched his teeth so hard they ached.

"So what is it you carry on board?"

"Other than sharp-tongued stowaways?" he asked.

"Aye." She chuckled. "Tell me, Captain Keegan, what is it you hide?"

"If you found my hiding spots, then you found what was in them. You tell me."

She frowned. Tapped her fingers on a pulley. "They be empty." Lifting her eyes, she stared straight into his, and his gut tightened. He wanted her—God, forgive him, but he wanted her as he'd never wanted another woman. "But they not be empty for long, me thinks," she guessed, hitting too close to the truth. Stepping closer to him, so close he felt the heat of her body, she looked up at him with her incredible eyes, and it was all he could do not to wrap his arms around her, drag her up against his body, and kiss her until they were both breathless. "What is it you do on this ship? What are your secrets, Captain? What is it you're hiding that is so important that you refused to let the soldiers on at the last port?" she asked, unwittingly tempting him.

Without thinking he grabbed hold of her arm. "Whatever be my secrets, they be mine," he said, his fingers circling her wrist and feeling the leap of her pulse. "Mayhap I should remind you that I be not the one running from the law, little one." Her muscles tensed beneath her sleeve, and yet he didn't release her. "As for the soldiers, I allow no one on my ship I do not wish aboard." Roughly he yanked her closer to him. "Except stowaways, and then I throw them off at the next port. In your case I made an exception."

"Because I promised to pay you."

"A promise you cannot keep." He tried not to notice the way her bosom rose and fell with her breaths, or the curve of her lips or the fire in her eyes. She was a stowaway, nothing more. Nothing!

"You have to have faith, Captain."

"Blind faith."

"Aye. You will be rewarded for taking me safely to shore."

"Empty words, Victoria. False promises." His fingers dug into her flesh as the wind snapped in the sails. "Let this be a warning. If you lie to me, if you treat me like a fool, I will not rest until I have chased you down."

"And what?" she threw at him. "What would you do to me then?" Her head inched up mutinously, and her lips quivered in rage. "Threaten me not, Captain," she advised as his blood, suddenly hot, began to pound in his ears. "Just trust me."

He gazed into her eyes a second too long, and rashly, without thinking, he dragged her against him. "'Tis not your position to make demands of me, lady."

"'Tis not yours to order me about."

"I be the captain."

"And I be your guest. Is that not what you told your men?" she challenged, her eyes bright.

He could not resist her. She was as hot as the sun and cold as the sea all at once, her gaze promising him heaven while her lips condemned him to hell.

"And yet you treat me as if I was a prisoner!"

"Are you shackled?" he demanded.

"Nay, but—"

"Chained?"

"Not by iron links."

"Held under lock and key?" He lowered his face, stared deep into those night-dark blue eyes.

She swallowed hard, looked down at his mouth. "Nay," she whispered so softly he barely heard the words over the rush of the wind filling the huge sails and driving the ship through the inky waters.

"Are you not given food and water, precious as it is?" She was quivering now, and she bit her lower lip. "Have I not clothed you, given you my bed, and kept you safe?" He felt her stiffen, her spine become rigid. "And yet you not only disobey me but accuse me of holding you hostage when you, *you*, lady, stowed away on *my* ship, hid in the hold and took refuge here. 'Tis only by the grace of God and my patience that you are safely aboard. We dock in two days' time. Until then I order—nay, I ask—you to obey the laws of this ship and my commands."

She wanted to argue; he saw it in the defiant twist of her neck and the set of her shoulders, but when she opened her mouth to speak, no words flew out. Instead she clamped her jaw shut for a second, as if choking back the words she so dearly wanted to say. Glowering up at him, she finally said, "No man has the right to tell me what I will do. But as we have a bargain, I will try to hold up my end. I will do as you command, and in the end, believe me, Captain, you will be paid for your trouble. 'Tis all that you want."

"Oh, no, lady, 'tis wrong you be," he said, desire pounding through his bloodstream. "There is much more I want from you. Too much." Damning the consequences, he cupped her head and stared deep into her eyes.

As his brain screamed that he was making a mistake which would waken the dogs of hell, he fell victim to temptation and kissed her. Hard, hungry, demanding, he slanted his mouth over hers. The feel of her skin was pure magic. It awakened in him the long dormant feeling of youth. He groaned, expecting her to pull away or to slap him soundly across his chin. Instead she didn't move for a second. Then her lips slowly parted.

Deep inside he throbbed. A memory sizzled through his brain.

His tongue slid easily between her teeth, and the taste of her, the feel of her body as he dragged her still closer, brought his damned manhood to further attention. By the Gods, he wanted her. His body ached to claim her. His brain was in flames, his mind spinning with erotic images and more—in rapid fire succession the hidden doors to his mind were unlocked. Click. Click. Click. Her tongue flicked against his, sending shivers of want through his flesh. His arms wrapped around her tightly, and he kissed her hungrily, anxiously, as the night wind swirled around them and the sea splashed upon the ship.

Drawing back his head, he saw the slumberous passion in her eyes, felt her quiver, knew in an instant who she was.

"Ogof," he whispered. "You're the girl. You, Victoria of Rhydd, are Sheena of Ogof." He remembered their last bittersweet kiss and how he'd left her alone to face her father after she'd helped him escape. "So why are you here aboard my ship?" he asked, holding her at arm's length and staring into her eyes. "For sanctuary or for vengeance?"

Chapter Six

Sheena's mind spun as the *Dark Sapphire* cut through the dark waters and the moon climbed higher in the sky. How could she tell him the truth? Confide in him? Trust him? She struggled for an answer and found none.

"Tell me, Sheena," he said, her name rolling off his tongue as the sea breeze ruffled his hair. Strong arms held her so close to him she was certain the breath was being pressed slowly and ever so seductively from her lungs. "You are that imp, are you not? The daughter of Lord Jestin."

"A-aye," she whispered, barely able to think. So he knew who she was and the fire in his eyes was a cold, hard flame of accusation. Yet he didn't release her. Her heart was racing, her skin flushed and heated, yet the night wind felt cool against her cheeks. *God help me.*

"And you were married to Tardiff."

She gulped.

"Slayed him?"

She closed her eyes as the horrid images assailed her in rapid-fire succession, memories from which she wanted nothing more than to escape. But they chased her down, were relentlessly shadowing her with the pain and torment of her wedding day and night. She shivered, shook her head and tried to pull away from the captain's embrace.

"What?" he asked and his muscular arms seemed suddenly sheltering rather than imprisoning. One hand brushed the hair from her eyes. "What happened, Sheena?"

Something inside her broke when he said her name again. Trembling, she bit back a sob and tried to speak, but her throat was swollen. Tears, those horrid, relentless drops that she'd sworn she'd never again shed, burned in her eyes and, as if he somehow understood her pain, he folded her tight against him.

"Ah, 'tis a beautiful liar you are, Sheena of Ogof," he said and kissed her forehead. She closed her eyes, refusing to cry. She wouldn't allow herself to be duped by this small, uncharacteristic display of tenderness from a man she knew to be a Judas. *Nay!*

She tried to wriggle away. "'Tis . . . 'tis something of which I cannot speak," she said, her voice lower than it should have been.

"You brought danger to the ship and my men," he said.

"You bring it yourself."

"Aye." The tenderness in his voice disappeared. "But never have I crossed Sir Manning again. Mayhap, 'tis time."

"Nay, we . . . we must . . . escape him."

Keegan snorted. "Think you he will stop?" Slowly he pushed her away, his big hands covering each of her shoulders. "He will chase you to the ground, Sheena. Mark my words. Either he will capture you and drag you back to Tardiff, or die trying."

Her knees weakened for she knew Keegan spoke the truth. "Then I must evade him. I must be more clever than he." The thought was daunting, but not impossible. Refusing to be beaten, she tossed back her hair and lifted her chin. "I will not give in."

One corner of Keegan's mouth lifted, as if he found her bravado amusing. "I'm afraid you have more spirit than brains."

"You should know," she tossed back. "'Tis a trait you seem to have honed to perfection."

He laughed then, the deep timbre of his voice rumbling over the flapping of the sails and the rush of wind. "Nay, m'lady," he said, releasing her. "Not a trait, I fear, but a curse."

"Then we both be damned."

"There be no doubt." His smile fell away and again she was staring into those intense eyes. "Now, be off with you before I do something we both will not want to face in the morning."

For once she didn't argue. She had but to think of his kiss and realize should she stay much longer she would find herself in deep, deep trouble. Her blood pounded through her veins, her heart clamored as if a thousand steeds were galloping through it, but she somehow managed to turn on her heel and run across the ever-undulating deck. Her boot heels rang against the steps as she hurried down the short flight of stairs and hurled herself against the door of the cabin.

Once inside, she drew in several calming breaths, touched her so-recently kissed lips and wondered why this man, this vagabond captain could evoke such passion in her. Why was his kiss forever impressed upon her mind? Just as that cursed touching of lips while on the slippery dock all those years ago had left her weak, senseless, her silly mind swirling with wild thoughts, so had this kiss stolen all rational thought from her mind.

She flung herself on the bunk—his bed—and closed her eyes. But the smell of him was in the small cabin and the taste of his skin was still on her lips.

Oh, what a fool she was. She curled a fist and pounded it impotently against the coverlet. God in heaven, why had she challenged the brute of a captain? Had she not learned her lesson about men? And now Keegan knew who she was. Once his mind had cleared, he would certainly now deliver her to Manning, for he knew that she'd lied to him and would surely realize that there would be a ransom paid for her.

Oh, 'twas a trap she'd thrown herself into. She wound herself in the covers and squeezed her eyes shut.

But she wanted him. As a woman wants a man. Idiot that she was, lying under the covers fully clothed, knowing he was somewhere on this ship, she yearned for him.

Are you certain, Sheena? her mind taunted. *Think hard. Do you really want to share this bunk,* his *bed?*

"I don't know," she said aloud, jumping at the sound of her own voice. Only a few weeks ago she'd been certain that she wanted no man to ever touch her again, that her marriage had destroyed any desire she had.

It was an ominous fateful day when Ellwynn of Tardiff arrived to claim Sheena as his bride. The sky was dark as night, thick, swollen clouds threatening rain as Tardiff, dressed in a blue tunic and dark breeches, sailed through the gates of Ogof upon a galloping black stallion. Servants scattered, chickens squawked and flapped out of the way, a peddler yanked hard on the reins of his stubborn mule as the steed barreled into the inner bailey. Girls who had been carrying pails of water let go of their buckets and jumped from the horse's path. Boys hauling firewood to the kitchens nearly let go of their kindling. Aye, the bastard acted as if he were the lord of this very keep.

"You there, page, tend to the horses and be quick about it," Tardiff yelled to Paul, a young, shy boy. As the boy approached, Tardiff hopped off the wild-eyed steed's back. The horse reared and snorted, and as Ellwynn slapped the reins into the frightened boy's palm, the destrier bowed back its great head. The reins nearly slid from Paul's hand, and it was all he could do to handle the beast.

Sheena observed the wild entrance all from her window. Looking down at the bailey, she cringed at the sight of the man to whom she was unwillingly betrothed.

A dozen soldiers, all on prancing, high-strung beasts, escorted Ellwynn.

Dressed in the bold red and yellow of Tardiff, they surveyed the keep and walls of the castle as if they were spies—enemies rather than allies.

Sheena's skin crawled.

Though Tardiff was a handsome man, he was perhaps too much so. His brown hair gleamed with red streaks; his face was chiseled, his jaw square as if it had been hewn by a master mason. On the steps of the great hall he stood proudly, hands on his hips, cape tossed over a shoulder as he surveyed the bailey with a practiced eye.

"Brother!" Fawn cried, streaming out of the great hall as if she could not wait for him to be announced. "'Tis grand you look."

"And you, too, Fawn," he said with considerably less enthusiasm. Though she flung herself into his arms, Ellwynn appeared embarrassed at her display. She wrapped one arm through his, and they walked together to the garden that was located just below Sheena's open window. Their voices, lowered so that the rest of the castle could not overhear, rose on the slight breeze, allowing Sheena to catch each word clearly.

"My men have traveled far. Some are hungry, some need women, and all are thirsty."

"They will be seen to," Fawn assured him, nodding her head rapidly as if in full agreement.

"I knew I could count on you." The Lord of Tardiff laughed, and it wasn't a merry sound. Sheena resisted the urge to spit on him. "So, now, sister, where is the girl who is to be my wife?"

Sheena's stomach turned sour. *Wife.* Oh, sweet Mother Mary, no!

"Come in, come in," Fawn insisted brightly. "She's waiting for you." Suddenly realizing that some of the kitchen maids who had been gathering eggs had stopped to stare at the visitors, Fawn snapped her fingers and commanded abruptly, "Back to work. All of you!" The silly girls nearly dropped their baskets as they dashed off to the kitchen.

"Some of the servants and peasants here appear lazy, sister," Ellwynn observed, peeling away from Fawn's arms and eyeing the blacksmith's and candle maker's huts where children kneeled and played in the dirt. "It surprises me that you would allow this here in your keep."

Fawn's expression turned to ice. "'Tis the baron. He is too soft with them."

"'Twill come to no good. Servants are like dogs and should be treated as such. Rewarded when they please, beaten when they do not. I see no scaffolding for a hanging should there be need of one, no peasant in your pillory, no example set."

"As I said, my husband is aging. He lacks . . . discipline."

Sheena's blood congealed. Though she did not like her stepmother, she had believed that Fawn loved her father.

Fawn sighed loudly and linked her arms with her brother again. "Come in and see the girls. You will be surprised at them. They have grown much since the last time I brought them to see you. And you've never met the baby, little Lynna—"

"'Tis only Sheena I wish to see," he cut in with irritation. "Your daughters are fine, Fawn, to be sure, but I want to see my bride." He laughed wickedly. "She's a beauty and a fiery-tempered lass, is she not?"

"Sometimes too much so."

"Then I shall just have to tame her, won't I? After all, I be baron."

There was a moment's hesitation, and Sheena felt a short burst of hope that her stepmother would caution the bastard to treat her well. But, of course, Fawn only laughed and said, "Oh, would I were a mouse in the corner to witness that. The girl has been a thorn in my side since I came here. Even after that nasty business with Rourke, when she helped the bastard's son escape. Jestin punished her, but in the end, it was just as before. Jestin spoils her and treats her as if she were his son."

"That will change," Ellwynn decreed, and Sheena, her cheeks hot, again thought she might lose everything she'd eaten that day. "I promise that. After the wedding, when you next see your stepdaughter, she will be meek and obedient. I look upon her as a challenge, Fawn, and I will break her spirit."

"We'll see."

"Oh, sister, I rarely lose. This you know."

"Oh, yes, brother," Fawn said with a slight edge to her voice. "For you are the Baron of Tardiff." There was a bitterness in her words that Sheena had never heard before. "Come in, come in. There be food and drink aplenty for you and your men. Sheena will be pleased to see you."

"Nay, I think not. If what you say be true, she will not be anxious to meet a man who intends to bend her will to his own."

"She will get used to it," Fawn predicted.

"Or regret it." He laughed, and Sheena thought it the most wicked, disgusting sound she'd ever heard.

In the forest off the main road, Wart lay on his stomach. The ground was cold, his blood warm from a few too many cups of ale, his skin scratched from crawling through briars and brush to stare at the encampment of Tardiff's soldiers.

Lanterns glowed within the few tents crowded in a small clearing, and a campfire, flames crackling, sparks rising to the sky, burned bright. Soldiers squatted near the ring of stones surrounding the fire as they tended the quail and rabbits that sizzled on a spit. Wart eyed the charred meat hungrily. He'd spent more time drinking than eating in the past few days. His stomach rumbled in empty anticipation and his mouth watered. Yet he didn't move, forced his muscles to freeze as surely as if he were a stag who recognized a hunter's spoor.

The soldiers of Tardiff were a sorry lot in Wart's estimation, a scraggly bunch of men who grumbled, and told bawdy jokes that barely brought a chuckle. Warming themselves by the fire, they rubbed their hands and passed a jug of ale or wine between them. For the most part they groused like a gaggle of unhappy fishermen's wives.

Still he waited, his ears straining, hoping he could hear what he came for without having to approach anyone. From what he'd gleaned, more than a few of the men considered themselves on little more than a fool's mission. They were anxious to return to their families at Tardiff Hall. The names they said were unfamiliar to him: Ellwynn, Fawn, and Jestin—somehow linked. There was talk of murder as well, for the lord—Ellwynn of Tardiff—had been slain by his wife. Few seemed to mourn his passing; most considered him a cruel, useless ruler.

"A bastard if ever there was one," one man with patchy red hair and a pointed nose sniffed as he tore off a piece of charred rabbit, then sucked the bones.

"Aye, mean as a wounded bear, he was," another agreed. He was a portly man with thick arms that bulged as he cleaned his few teeth with the tip of his dagger. "Always kickin' the dogs or whippin' the horses when they be spent."

"Worse than that. He enjoyed wieldin' his power over everyone," a third man, a quiet man who sat cross-legged and stared straight at the spot where Wart lay hidden, admitted. "Baron Tardiff, he had his eye on me daughter, he did, and Kate and I we were afeared he would call for her one night. I thought I might have to send her to live with me sister up ta Twyll, but afore we found means to get her there, he was kilt." The quiet one took a swig from the jug that was being passed, then wiped his mouth with his sleeve. "Good riddance to him, I say."

The wind rustled through the leaves overhead. "So Lady Sheena, she did ye a favor," the round one said.

"Aye, that's what I be thinkin'."

The flap of the largest tent was flung open, and the leader, an ox of a man with a hateful expression and eyes as dark as pitch, strode into the campfire's light. He glanced up at the heavens and frowned. "A storm be brewin'. Christ A'mighty, will nothin' go right?"

"Mayhap this mission be doomed, Sir Manning." The hawk-nosed one spoke up and, as if his muscles were sore, rubbed his forearm with his opposite hand.

"Doomed?" Manning asked, his voice as loud as thunder.

"Aye. The old ones at Tardiff, they claim the Lady Sheena, she be a witch. Is it not possible she cursed us all?"

"You feel cursed, Leonard?"

Somewhere in the distance an owl hooted softly and the wind rushed through the branches of the trees overhead.

Several men shifted uncomfortably as Manning strode toward the fire and loomed above Leonard.

"I repeat only what I heard. Many think Sheena be a witch."

"Gossip. From old women. Nothing more." Manning's suspicious gaze swept the area around the campfire where the men squatted and crouched. "Do any of you others feel as Leonard? Cursed? Doomed?" Before anyone answered, Sir Manning dragged the naysayer to his feet, twisted his arm hard. The man squealed as his shoulder popped from its joint.

"For the love of God, leave him be!" the round one cried, on his feet in an instant.

"Now, I'll hear no more talk of doom or witches," Manning snarled. "There be no dissension in my camp."

Wart was thankful for his nasty little knife hidden deep in a pocket. Sir Manning was a bully, a man who forced obedience by fear, a man who would have no compassion for the woman, if indeed she was Sheena. Two men went to rescue the writhing soldier, forcing his arm back in its socket, and Wart crawled back to the spot where his horse was tied. He didn't want to turn the woman over to the beast who led this band of soldiers, but 'twas not his decision. He would ride to meet up with the ship and warn the captain.

Silently he untied the nag. Some unseen rodent stole through the underbrush in a hurry. Wart didn't move. His ears strained to hear. A twig snapped. Scrabbling for his knife, Wart spun. But it was too late. The tip of a soldier's sharp sword found his midsection.

Wart froze.

"Who be ye?" the soldier asked, his voice echoing over the wind. It was a voice that stirred unwanted memories. Wart gulped.

"Warren . . . Warren of Halliwell?" the soldier demanded, giving his weapon a little nudge. "And what be ye doin' spyin' on Sir Manning?"

"Oh, nay, I weren't spyin'," Wart lied, wishing he could wrap his fingers around the hilt of his knife, but the point of the sword held him at bay. "I did go up and look, fer I'm hungry and weary and—"

"And ye be a liar, sure as I can tell. I've seen ye before, years ago, Wart. I was there the night ye lost yer thumb. The night ye tried to rob me of me finest horse."

"I—I know not of what ye speak," Wart lied, feigning innocence.

"Do ye not recognize me, Warren? Yer own flesh and blood? I be Peter. The man who married your woman? Remember?" Wart's knees turned to water.

"Now, be ye called Warren or do ye still go by Wart, eh? Even if ye seem to have lost yer memory, I haven't."

Wart's heart plummeted. He'd hoped he'd been mistaken. God's teeth, what bad luck!

"Do ya not see that I'm yer cousin?" The pressure on the sword increased, slicing menacingly through Wart's tunic just as the first fat drops of rain fell from the night-darkened heavens.

"Come with me, Wart. I think ye have something to say to Sir Manning." Peter's voice was smooth as warm pudding. "And if he don't kill ye fer spyin', believe me, I will."

Chapter Seven

*S*o the stowaway was Sheena of Ogof.

And, no doubt, Sheena of Tardiff, the woman accused of slaying her husband.

Hiking his mantle more firmly around him, his back pressed against the cabin door, one leg bent at the knee, the other stretched in front of him, Keegan tried and failed to sleep.

The memories were too vibrant. 'Twas as if, in that one kiss, the floodgates of his brain had opened and all the pieces of his life that he'd forgotten rushed forward in a swift, mind-spinning current.

The images were disjointed, but he remembered his father and the crushing grief at the vision of his death. Clearly Keegan recalled the journey to Ogof, his father's mission, the despair at the loss of Bertrice, the rattling dice cups and the fire. But more distinctly, more defined, were his images of Sheena, her red hair streaming behind her as she rode a dark horse as if racing the very wind, the mischievous grin as she, forcing a circlet over her head, ducked into the chapel, and her insistence on saving him from certain death as she'd tugged him through the dank corridors to the cove. But the most brilliant memory, the one that was wedged deep into his brain, was that kiss on the rotting dock, the chill of the air, the warmth of her lips against his, the magical touch and feel of her. He scowled as he thought of abandoning her, of catching a glimpse of her disappointment, the anger as she invoked the furies against him. Only moments later he'd felt the sharp sting of an arrow. He'd given up consciousness with the warmth of her lips still lingering on his.

"Bloody, bloody damn," he growled. And now the girl was a full-grown woman. Sleeping in his bed. And a murderess? A woman capable of slaying her husband? Had it been an accident? How had she come to kill him, if indeed she did? At the thought of the lord he felt a burning jealousy. Who was this man who had won her hand only to have it turned against him? Why had she agreed to be his wife, to obey and honor and love him, then end his life?

It made no sense. Would a woman who was a cold-blooded killer risk her own life not once but twice that he knew of? Not only had she saved him at Ogof all those years before, but she'd climbed the shrouds just the other night to rescue Bo, a boy she barely knew.

No, he wouldn't believe her to be a calculating killer. There had to be more to the tale, more than he'd pieced together from his dealing with . . . His guts knotted. *Manning!* The brute who had pinned his father's hand to the table with his dagger and had tried to kill Keegan. *Manning* was leading the search party. *From Tardiff?* Had the dark knight somehow changed his allegiance?

A thousand questions seared his brain. Some Sheena could answer; others the old liar Hollis might be able to explain. Anger tore through Keegan's veins when he thought of the aged man: Hollis, who had nursed him back to health; Hollis, who had sold the *Warrior* to buy this ship; Hollis, who had dragged Sheena to his cabin on a tether and insisted she was a witch. What was it that the old man feared from her?

Keegan rested his head against the door and stared upward to a pitch black sky where no stars were able to shine through the heavy clouds. Kissing her again had unlocked his memory, aye, but brought with it grief for a father who had died young, new unanswered questions that haunted him as surely as ghosts, and the vibrant images of a sprite of a girl that he'd left to her own fate.

Mayhap he should never have kissed her again. For now the wanting was only worse. Even as the night sky threatened to pour, he was thinking of the sweet, sensual pressure of her lips again.

The mere thought of kissing her caused his manhood to rise and his breeches to become too tight. He imagined the feel of her skin against his, and the hard swelling between his legs began to ache. "Stop it," he muttered to himself, pulling his mantle tighter and attempting to force his thoughts from the woman as the sky opened.

The wind was up, the sails full as the helmsman tacked over the swells. Angry whitecaps rose on the sea, and the *Dark Sapphire* pitched and rolled as she headed ever northward. Soon they would dock, Wart would return, and Keegan would determine what to do with the stowaway.

'Twould be a blessing.

Or mayhap a curse, his traitorous mind taunted. *Could you give her to the soldiers of Tardiff if her life was threatened? What if she did kill her husband, what then? Many of the crew had no doubt done the same, and yet you do not hand them over to the authorities, not even if they have a price upon their sorry heads. And what of Hollis?*

He's the one member of the crew who is certain of her guilt, the one who refuses to trust her at any juncture. Aye, Hollis knows more than he's said all these years, allowing you to live in the "dark time" when your memory was lost to you.

Well, the old man had much to explain, Keegan thought, huddling against the rage of the storm, watching the sails bulge and flap as the wind rose. As rain lashed his face, chilling his skin, he considered the warmth of his cabin, just on the other side of the door. Sheena was within—warm, inviting, seductive. And deadly, he was sure of it. She was like a sweet-tasting poison, a slow but oh-so-tempting death. Gritting his teeth, he silently vowed to himself he would not touch her again. Never.

He had but one more day until they docked, when they would meet up with Wart, and then what? Hand her over to Sir Manning?

How in the name of heaven could he release her to Manning? How would she ever find justice?

And, blast it, he was attracted to her. More so now that he had remembered who she was. Beyond reason.

Aye, she had a sharp, wicked tongue, and he'd experienced more than once the bite of it. Nonetheless, for a reason he refused to contemplate, he looked forward to the sight of her each morn, when her fiery hair was tousled, her eyes still slumberous, her lips spreading into a yawn and her arms stretched over her head as she awakened. He enjoyed her banter and wit, saw that she wasn't afraid of the men, all of whom were now half in love with the witch—well, except for Hollis, of course—but even he was thawing to her appeal while Keegan himself, the man who had told himself all women were the ruin of man, dreamed of making love to her. With each night his thoughts of her turned dangerously erotic.

God's eyes, he would love to strip her bare, cup those firm breasts in his hands, and enter the sweet, wet warmth of her. He would make love to her for hours, until they were both spent and sweating, gasping in each other's arms.

"No!" he growled under his breath as the wind shrieked and the ship bobbed. The rain was unleashed in a torrent, pouring, sheeting, blurring his eyes, stinging his face, and running down his neck. His mantle was soaked, his skin raw and chilled. Not that he cared. He'd been long on the sea, had spent many stormy nights wondering if his vessel would survive a tempest's fury. To this night the *Dark Sapphire* had not let him down.

Lightning split the sky and thunder pealed loudly across the water. Stretching, Keegan climbed to his feet and made his way to the helm, where Henry, the strongest helmsman on the ship, was holding fast to the whipstaff. "I'll finish your shift," Keegan offered, for the man was tired of facing into the storm. There were walls around the helm and a roof that overhung the window, allowing the helmsman a view, but in a tempest such as this, with the shutters open, the wind and rain pelted in.

"Nay, Captain, I can handle her—that is, if the tiller holds true," Henry said. He hazarded a quick glance in Keegan's direction. "Ye're wet as if ye've been swimmin' in the sea. By thunder, Captain, ye best be dryin' yerself out."

"That I will, Henry, after you get a bit o' rest," Keegan insisted, and took over the helm. Few of the men were sleeping this night. Old Hollis found his way to the small room and prayed that they'd be safe, Bo huddled in a corner and tried to act as if he wasn't afraid of the storm, and even Big Tom passed through, eyeing the whipstaff as if he expected it to break in Keegan's hands.

"'Tis a rough one, this," Hollis said as thunder cracked and the helm shifted. Keegan set his shoulders into holding the ship steady. His muscles strained and ached. The ship stayed true.

"We've been through worse."

"But the lady, she hasn't," Bo said. "Is she all right?"

"She'll be fine," Keegan muttered, though he wondered himself.

"Do not worry about her," was Hollis's advice, and he pulled nervously on his beard. The old liar. What other secrets was he keeping? The need to demand answers was strong, but Keegan would not do so with so many crew members about.

"If ye be asking me, I say she's the reason for this storm," Hollis continued.

"Because ye think she be a witch?" Bo asked, then snorted in disgust. "If anything I think she be an angel."

"Be ye in love there, boy?" Jasper said, then went about his business as Bo shot him a look guaranteed to kill. He'd been right, Keegan thought bitterly. Most of the crew were besotted with the woman.

Including you, fool that you be. He shoved that wayward concept aside and with boots planted on the slippery decking strained to keep the *Dark Sapphire* on course.

Henry relieved him just before dawn, but still the storm raged. Cold, furious waves sprayed over the sides of the ship while the wind roared with a voice as deep as if Satan himself were cursing the heavens. Bracing himself against the gusts, Keegan made his way back to the cabin and considered the woman. Was she sleeping through this storm, or was she huddled beneath the blankets cringing in fear? He thought most likely the former, for she didn't scare easily, not even when she'd been little more than a child. Nor did he imagine her holding herself for fear of losing the contents of her stomach, for Sheena had grown to be a worthy sea woman, if there be such a beast, in the past week. Aside from her gender, she was like the men aboard this ship, running, hiding out. The crew of the *Dark Sapphire* were men without pasts, men who had bargained for their lives and agreed to stay aboard or pay to be shipped to a far-off port, far from their mistakes. Keegan had enough cargo—fleece, wool, and twine—to satisfy any officials who demanded to board, but there was a false bottom in the floor of the hold and a space beneath where three or four desperate men could hide. 'Twas a bit of irony that Sheena, had she approached him and paid him for his trouble, could have hidden safely aboard.

As it was, he was caught between trusting her for the fee she offered him and turning her over to those who were looking for her to collect the reward he was certain would be offered by the soldiers of Tardiff. *And Manning!*

For the first time since he'd become captain of this ship he doubted himself, wondered if there was money enough to send Sheena to her fate. Surely he'd saved many a murderer from the gallows before, why not trust the woman? Her money was just as good as any man's.

Lightning forked in the dark heavens. 'Twas a night not fit for man or beast. Rain poured from the sky to run down his cheek. Cold wind sliced through his clothes. His blood was ice.

He shouldered open the cabin door, intent upon having words with the woman, but the sight he beheld stopped him in his tracks. She was sitting on the floor, her eyes closed, her lips moving, the folds of the burgundy-colored dress spread around her like a blood red pool. Murmuring words he didn't understand—was it a spell? Quickly, nearly losing her balance, she scrambled to her bare feet.

"Captain," she said, obviously embarrassed that he'd caught her chanting to whatever pagan gods she believed in. "I—I thought you were steering the ship."

"I was."

She seemed nervous, mayhap because of the storm. Anxiously she glanced at her boots.

The boat shuddered and pitched. She started to fall, caught herself.

"Why are you not in bed?" he asked.

"I couldna sleep—oh!"

Again the ship rocked. Hard. Her feet slipped. Thunder cracked. The ship lurched again. Arms flailing, she toppled forward. Instinctively his hands shot out. He grabbed her around her small waist, held her fast against him.

For a heartbeat she didn't move. Nor did he. She smelled faintly of lavender, her wild hair brushed his chin. Even through the folds of velvet he felt her flesh, heard her catch her breath quickly. She was light in his arms . . . warm. Oh, so enticing. She looked up at him with blue eyes that seemed to see beyond the man to the boy who had kissed her with ardor only to betray her. Her teeth sank into her lip, and Keegan groaned inwardly, for all sense was surely fleeing him. The thought of kissing her lips, touching her white skin, of watching as her pink nipples buttoned beneath his fingers was more than he could stand. Images of making love to her, of kissing her navel and searching out the nest of red-brown curls that surely guarded her womanhood and hid the most delicate parts of her scorched his mind. His frigid blood heated. His pulse throbbed.

"Sweet Mary," she whispered, swallowing hard as those erotic eyes held his.

God help me, he thought as his arms tightened around her. She didn't push him away, yet didn't cling to him as the *Dark Sapphire* steadied. Slowly he released her, but not before the touch of her, the warmth of her body, the scent of her, had burned deep in his soul.

Christ Jesus, how he wanted her. The bed would be warm, her body hot, their passion as wild as this very night. In the light from the lantern he saw that her cheeks were flushed. In the hollow of her throat her pulse pounded.

"The storm will pass." Forcing himself not to reach for her again and tumble onto the bunk with her, he shoved his wet hair from his eyes, strode to the small window, and searched for signs of the coming dawn. The ache in his loins was nearly unbearable.

"If we do not capsize first."

"The *Sapphire*, she's as seaworthy as the best." He glanced back at her and was surprised to find no fear in her gaze. The girl he'd kissed on that rotting dock was a fearless one, possessed of a restless, adventurous spirit. "Worry not." As he peeled off his wet mantle, he noticed she averted her gaze. At first he thought she was embarrassed that he was stripping himself of his sodden clothes, but there was more to her discomfort, it seemed. Suddenly, as if snapped out of a trance, she hurriedly reached for her boots.

"You need not leave." He hung his cloak on a peg, and drips of water puddled upon the floor. "Go back to bed."

She blanched. Her spine stiffened as if a rod had been jammed up it. She began stuffing one foot into a boot. "I will."

"In those?" he asked, eyeing her as she forced the leather up the smooth curve of her calf. He couldn't drag his eyes from her.

"In—in case I needs get up and it be dark and I cannot find them. The deck be too wet to go bare of feet."

"The deck be too wet to walk about it at all." As if she hadn't heard him, she plopped down on the edge of the bunk and bit her lip as she tried to yank her boot higher, though it seemed stuck.

"What were you doing in here?" He motioned toward the center of the wood-paneled room where she'd been kneeling.

"Praying, of course." She looked up at him with luminous eyes, and his gut tightened. Again the ship rocked. The lantern flickered. Sheena nearly lost a boot.

He braced himself. "To Morrigu?"

"To whoever will listen," she tossed back defiantly. The room seemed to grow smaller still, and his mind was filled with thoughts of kissing her and the temptation of her perfect lips.

"Go to bed, Sheena."

"I said—"

"Leave off your boots, throw the covers over you, and go to sleep."

"Why care you what I do?"

"Because, lady," he said, crossing the short distance quickly and grabbing her by the forearms and hauling her to her feet once again. "I be a man without much patience, a man who has been to sea far too long, a man who, like the rest of the men on this ship, would like to bed a woman."

"And—and that be me?"

"Is there another woman aboard?" Her arms were supple and firm beneath his fingers.

"Nay, but if there were . . . ?"

He steeled himself, for he knew that other women had not affected him as this one had. In all his life no other woman had somehow reached beneath his skin and delved as deep as this stowaway of a female had. "Aye," he lied. "No woman would be safe."

Her chin inched up a bit. "I'm not afraid," she asserted, though her eyes betrayed her.

"Then you're foolish."

She stood with such defiance, it was all he could do not to toss her onto the bed and make love to her for the rest of the passage. She managed a humorless grin. "I have prayed to the Great Mother for my safety."

"'Tis of no matter who you pray to. I care not, be it God Himself, the Holy Virgin, or the pagan idols of the old ones. But be warned, Sheena," he cautioned, pointing a long finger at her nose. "I'll not have you chanting and casting spells where the crew might see you."

"Nay?"

"My men, they're superstitious, and . . ." Sweet Jesus, he couldn't look into those night-darkened eyes and not ache for her. His throat was suddenly dry, his groin tight as saddle leather. "They needs have their wits while manning this ship and . . . and I'll not have them distracted . . ."

"You think they be distracted by me?" she asked with feigned innocence. Oh, she was a wicked one, and as the single candle in the lantern cast her face in pale, golden shadows, he remembered the scamp of a girl, his enemy's rebellious daughter who had pleaded with him to take her away from Ogof.

Desire throbbed in his skull. "The crew would be diverted from their tasks by you or any woman."

"As you be?"

"Do not test me."

"I try not." And yet her lips twitched in mocking amusement.

Despite the storm, aside from the fact that she, for all he knew, was running from the gallows, laughter sparked in her night blue eyes. And it was as if they were the only man and woman alive on this storm-tossed ocean, the only two souls in all the known world.

"You be a liar." His hands clenched tightly on her forearms.

"As are you, Captain." Her face was turned up to his, and for the second at least she appeared to have forgotten her blasted boots. Was her smile an invitation or accusation? A temptation to heaven or certain passage straight to hell?

He wanted to shake some sense into her, to make her realize just how dangerous teasing him could be. Instead, without regard to reason, he lowered his head swiftly and placed his eager mouth over hers. Again he felt the sweet torment of her soft lips pressed to his. He thought she might draw back and slap him, might fight and pull away. But she yielded easily. Her mouth opened in silent invitation.

His mind screamed that he was making a mistake he would take with him to the grave, but he gave no heed. He was chilled to the bone, his flesh wet with the clothes on his back, desire pounding a hot tattoo through his brain.

His blood thundered, his skin ached with want, and as he felt the seductive pressure of her lips against his, he forgot every last reason why he couldn't make love to her. His arms surrounded her, and he felt any remaining trace of her resistance melt, her knees weaken, and a sigh, soft as a sea breeze, escape from her throat. From that second on, he was lost to her.

Desire drummed through his blood.

As his body pressed urgently against hers, he imagined stripping her bare, kissing her in every dimple upon her skin, making her tremble with the want of him. Hunger raged, his manhood throbbed, and he twined his fingers through those fiery strands and kissed her as if he would never stop.

Sheena gasped, his tongue slipped past her teeth, and she closed her eyes, wanting more. She told herself that she had no choice, for she had to distract him, to take his mind off her boot where the jewels were hidden. Kissing him was only a ploy, or was it?

As her blood heated, she trembled deep inside. Passion as hot as a smith's forge, and an emotion she'd been certain she'd never feel again, trapped her. Through her dress she felt his hands, strong, rough, anxious. Her resistance crumbled to dust.

She tasted the raindrops on his skin, smelled the salt air mixed with the pure male scent of him, felt hard, strident muscles straining through his wet clothes, and wanted him. Oh, dear Lord in heaven, how she wanted him.

His tongue circled and stroked, flicking against the roof of her mouth, causing her blood to sing through her veins. Never had she felt such elation, never had she tingled so with desire, never had she flirted with such certain disaster, for lying with this man, giving herself to him, could only cause heartache, only bring pain.

Think, Sheena, think. Do not cast off your virtue so easily. Do not fall victim to his sweet, hot seduction. Kissing him is madness! 'Twill only bring you agony most vile. Remember that bastard Ellwynn and how he used you! For the love of all that is holy, Sheena, stop this now!

Before 'tis far too late.

And yet she couldn't. Wouldn't. Captain Keegan was not the spoiled Lord of Tardiff; nor did he try to hurt her. There was no pain, only pleasure, oh, such sweet, delicious pleasure. Sheena's eyes closed. Keegan's hands moved anxiously against her back, bunching the fabric of her dress only to smooth it again, causing goose bumps of desire to rise on her skin, awakening a hot yearning deep within the most feminine part of her.

She lifted her arms, linking them around his neck, pushing her body ever closer to his, until the dampness from his tunic soaked her dress. The heat between them, white-hot and pulsing, caused steam to rise. Her breasts ached to be touched, her heart thudded wildly, and deep inside she hungered with a newfound want.

"Sheena," he whispered. "Sweet, treacherous woman." He pulled her hair and kissed the crook of her neck.

"Ooh." She tingled and lolled her head back, wanting more, so much more. Though she knew she was wading into a dangerous, seductive whirlpool from which she might never swim away, she gave herself completely.

His weight was welcome as it forced her onto the bed. Clinging to him, she felt the bittersweet ache of passion pulse through her blood, sighed desperately as his fingers loosened the lacing at her neck.

"Sweet, sweet lady," he whispered, his lips kissing the corner of her mouth, her eyelids and cheeks before dropping lower. "This be a mistake." His breath brushed warm across her neck and the tops of her breasts.

"Aye." Was that her own voice that sounded so breathless?

"One you may regret."

"No . . . yes . . ." she rasped, unable to heed anything but the hot tide of passion roaring through her blood. Her fingers curled in the bedding as he lowered himself and kissed her neck and shoulder as the laces loosened and the bodice of her dress inched downward, over her shoulders, past her breasts. Cool air caressed her skin, only to be followed by the warm, gentle persuasion of his lips.

Think, Sheena, think. Do not lose your head. But it was too late. The velvet slipped over her flesh. He kissed the tops of her breasts. She squirmed, feeling a hot, desperate ache forming deep within her. The ship rocked, the storm pounded the old timbers, but inside, Sheena was melting, wanting, writhing.

The dress lowered farther and he traced a path with his tongue, sliding along the slope of her breast to a nipple, hard and waiting. Sheena gasped as he took the little bud in his mouth, kissing, touching, laving the nipple while her back arched.

More, she thought impatiently, *I want more,* and as if he understood, he took her other breast in his hand and caressed it, gently at first and then more roughly as he suckled. Her blood was on fire, her mind no longer questioning. Her fingers felt the cords of his neck and drove through his hair. With a growl he ripped off his tunic and was upon her, hard, sinewy muscles running across his shoulders and down the flat plane of his abdomen. She ran her fingers down his arms, felt his strength, heard him sigh into her skin. "'Tis a witch ye be, Sheena," he whispered, his breath rolling across her fevered flesh. "For you have beguiled and vexed me and enraptured all my men." His tongue traveled lower and her lips murmured in pure pleasure as he pulled the dress over her hips and down her legs.

Sweet Mary, she was hot. Even as the boat swayed and the rain lashed the cabin, her blood was near boiling, desire pulsing through her veins. He kissed her navel and she bucked upward, surprised as his big hands caught her, held her in the curve of her spine, and he buried his face in the curls at the juncture of her legs. Fiery as a dragon's breath, the air from his lungs raced through her thatch to the sensitive skin guarding her womanhood. She wriggled, and he kissed her hard, his tongue teasing and playing with the most secret part of her.

As if of their own accord, her hips lifted, and she opened to him, twisting, giving him more intimate access, her mind spinning with the wonder of his touch, the storm within her as violent as that blowing across the sea.

Pressure. Hot and sweet. She was moving, closing her eyes, rocking, harder, faster, feeling his warm, wet touch until at last a dam gave way and with a cry she convulsed, breathing hard, not understanding what had happened.

Her skin was wet with sweat, her heart a drum, her breathing as ragged as if she'd run a hundred miles and yet . . . she glanced up, saw him unlacing his breeches, and the back of her throat was suddenly without moisture. The breeches fell to the floor and she saw his manhood, stiff, hard, thick as he reached for her again.

With strong arms he drew her to him, kissed her urgently, and she tasted herself for but a second as his tongue found and mated with hers and her fingers touched the sinewy strength of his shoulders and arms. Again she felt the warmth, again her blood fired, and as he touched her, she responded, her body still tingling from before, her mind spinning with wanton images of lying with him. The ship creaked and rolled, the bedcovers fell away, and Keegan, dark, mysterious Keegan, kissed her neck and shoulders. Rough, callused hands cupped her breasts, anxious lips kissed her face, hard knees spread her legs as her mind spun. "Please," she whispered, wanting more of him, arching upward.

"Ah, woman, ye vex me," he said, as if admitting weakness, then his lips found hers. She felt him nudge against her, caught her breath as he thrust hard.

She felt a moment's hot pain, gasped, and cried out as his shoulders flexed, and he began to move, slowly at first. She caught his rhythm, rising to meet each of his long, deliberate thrusts, closing her eyes and mind to everything as he began to sweat and breathe as if he couldn't drag in enough air. Faster and faster, as if the ship were spinning in a moon-spangled sea, whirling feverishly.

Hotter and hotter. Time stopped. Sheena closed her eyes, dug her fingers into his flesh as he moved ever more quickly. Sweating, catching his tempo, her mind whirling with flashes of light until she couldn't think, couldn't breathe. The universe was centered in the joining of their bodies, of their spirits. "Keegan," she cried, her voice ripped from her throat.

Her body jolted.

A hot wash of liquid fire exploded behind her eyes. She screamed as she touched ecstasy, her mind no longer with her body.

Keegan threw back his head. Through bared teeth he let out a primal roar somewhere between pleasure and pain.

He collapsed upon her, his skin wet with perspiration, his weight flattening her breasts, his breathing fast and shallow. "By . . . by the gods, woman," he gasped, holding her close, his breath ruffling her hair, "what am I going to do with you?"

"'Twas just what I was thinking," she teased, though as she realized what she'd done, she felt a tinge of sorrow, for now, certainly, she would have to escape. And soon.

"You were a virgin," he said, and she froze in his arms. "So now the question is, who are you? The woman the soldiers are looking for, a murdering bride who did not lie with her husband? Sheena of Tardiff?"

"It . . . it matters not," she said, but as the warmth of lovemaking faded, she heard her own lie.

"Then tell me . . . oh, for the love of Mary." His entire body tensed. His arms tightened to iron bands, as if he suddenly realized the calamity of lying with her. As if, despite what they had just shared, he intended to turn her over to Sir Manning and the soldiers of Tardiff. "Do not lie to me any longer," he ordered, and his voice was suddenly cold as the sea. He glared down at her, and even in the shadowy, flickering light from the lantern, she saw realization and condemnation dawn in his steely eyes.

"'Tis time you told me the truth, Sheena," he said, and all the warmth that had been in his voice had disappeared. "Did you marry the Lord of Tardiff only to kill him on your wedding night?"

Chapter Eight

Sheena swallowed hard. Suddenly she felt foolish. She tried to roll off the tiny cot, but Keegan held her firmly beside him, the length of his naked body brushed up against hers, the springy curls of his chest hair tickling her breasts. "Did you kill Tardiff?" he repeated.

Oh, God. She managed to look up at him, this man who had so recently become her lover. "'Tis said you ask no questions of a man's past when they board."

"Aye."

"And yet you make demands of me."

"Because you did not come aboard honestly, now, did you? And you answered not my question." Steely fingers manacled her wrists. "Are you Sheena of Tardiff?"

"Aye." She nodded, unable to lie a second longer.

"So you married the Baron of Tardiff, then sent him to his grave before he bedded you."

She bit her lip, fought against the terrifying, ugly images that crossed her mind. "There was more to it than that," she admitted, and felt him tense beside her.

"How?"

"He . . ." Oh, God, she would not shed a tear for that bastard who had been her husband, *would not!* "'Twas the wedding night. He, uh, he drank much and . . ." Shivering, she willed hot tears backward, forced her mind to view what had happened as if to someone else, not her. ". . . he tried to bend my will to his."

"You would not take to his bed."

"Nay, I—I was there. I was . . . willing to do what I had promised, but . . . I loved him not. He was my father's choice, the brother of my father's wife. And when we were alone . . . he wanted me to do more than . . ." Her voice faded and she avoided Keegan's eyes. "Tardiff was drunk. He had a knife and brought another woman in, a serving girl. . . . She was Tardiff's lover, and he wanted the three of us to . . ." Shuddering, she sighed, her voice aquiver, Keegan's eyes intense and dark. Unreadable. "I objected and he pulled out his dagger, laid it upon my throat and . . . and I disobeyed him."

Keegan's eyes swept to her neck, and he touched the scratch now nearly healed with one finger. "He did this?" His voice was low. Ominous.

"Aye."

"Anything else?"

"He dinna get the chance," she said, biting her lip and looking away.

"But he threatened you?"

"Promised to cut me if I did not do everything he ordered. We struggled. Fought. I—I was able to wrest the blade from him."

"So you stabbed him." His voice was without condemnation.

"If I had not, he would have done the same to me," she said, not expecting Keegan to believe her. "If not for Fannie, the serving girl, I do not think I would have been able to escape. She helped me and . . . I fled Tardiff Hall."

His hand cupped her naked shoulder, and he forced her to meet his night-darkened gaze. "You did not go back to Ogof?"

"Nay." Sheena shook her head, heard the rush of the wind and the roar of waves battling the *Dark Sapphire*'s hull. "As I said, my father's wife, she is the Baron of Tardiff's sister."

"Lady Fawn," he said as if drawing up an image of the cold, calculating woman.

Scowling darkly, not releasing her, Keegan let out his breath. "So you ran away because you killed your husband and were worried for your life?"

"Yes. There are those who would see me hanged."

"Including your father?" he asked, his jaw tightening as he remembered the man who had slain Rourke so callously. It was all clear to him now, that dark time when he'd been half-besotted with a fiery-haired girl who had helped him escape.

"Mayhap," she said as his grip relaxed, and she, desperate to get away from him, from his bed, from their so recent lovemaking, tried to roll away. He would have none of it and suddenly was upon her, pinning her to the bed with his body. "But—until a few moments ago, you were a virgin. Do not try to lie to me," he said. "What of your husband?"

"We fought before . . . before 'twas done," she said, shuddering at the memory and feeling ashamed as she lay naked with this man, one who was not her husband, one she did not love . . . or could she? Oh, 'twas foolish to think of it.

Bam! Bam! Bam! "Captain? Be ye awake?" Hollis yelled, pounding his fist upon the door.

"Go away."

"But Henry. He needs yer help at the helm."

The ship shuddered, old timbers moaned, and Keegan, swearing under his breath, released her. He rolled off the bed and yanked on his breeches quickly.

Sheena reached for her dress as Keegan crossed the small space and threw open the door.

"What of Henry?"

"He's tired, methinks, or mayhap has been in his cups too much," Hollis said as Sheena swiftly squirmed into the wine red velvet. Keegan was large enough to block most of the door with his body, hiding her from view. If the old man caught a glimpse of her, he was wise enough to hold his tongue.

"Bloody Christ!" Keegan snapped up his tunic and mantle.

"I tell ye true, Keegan, the ship will capsize."

"Not this night. Tell Henry I'm on my way."

"Aye," the old man said, and was out the door.

Keegan whirled on Sheena. "You," he said as she slipped one leg from beneath the bed and reached for her boots. "Stay put."

"But I—"

"Do not argue with me." His eyes flashed and he grabbed his wet mantle. Quickly donning the cloak, he found his boots and pulled them on. "This cabin. 'Tis the safest place for you."

"But I might help."

"You'd be in the way. I need concentration, as do the crew. There be not time for"—he motioned with his hand by his head as if he could not find the right word—"for any interruption." Then he straightened, reached for the door, and paused again. His broad shoulders slumped a bit, and he sighed. "Please, Sheena. Do not leave. 'Tis only that I fear for your safety."

"How noble you be," she mocked, unable to keep her tongue still as the great masts creaked and the wind shrieked.

"Do not test me, woman, I have no time for it." Then he was out the door. It slammed shut, leaving Sheena alone in the bed, listening as his boots rang up the stairs. She counted to ten, then, convinced he would not return, she swung out of bed, tightened the laces of her dress and yanked on her boots. The stones were still tucked inside one, cramping her toes, reminding her that she had little time. If they were to dock the following night, she had much to do.

Once the storm abated, *if* it let up, she would leave the vessel and take her chances alone. The ship would be close to shore and she could lower a rowboat and make her way to land. She felt more than a little tug of regret at the thought of leaving the *Dark Sapphire*, for she had felt an awkward peace aboard the ship, a sense of safety as she'd realized that the soldiers of Tardiff could not discover her as long as the ship was at sea. Asides, she would miss Bo and Jasper and Seamus . . .

And Keegan?

Oh, God, yes! He was gruff, harsh, seemingly unforgiving, a man she'd sworn she hated, couldn't trust. She tossed a glance at the rumpled bed, still smelling of sex. Fool that she was, she knew she'd long for him with all her body and heart.

Angry at the turn of her mind, she gave herself a swift mental kick. This was no time to be maudlin or sad. Just because he'd bedded her was no reason to trust him. Had he whispered that he loved her? Or even cared for her? Nay. He'd mentioned some fear for her safety, but she doubted it was for any other reason than he intended to sell her back to Manning or demand payment from her.

Love?

Never. Captain Keegan knew not the word.

She paused, touched the fine velvet of his wife's dress, and her heart twisted. Mayhap he had once loved, but 'twas another woman, a woman who had betrayed him.

Oh, fool that she was, her heart ached for him, though there was no time for it. She had to plot her escape and make it good.

And it had to be soon.

The ship pitched, masts groaned in the wind, and rain flailed the decks and hull. Sheena sent up a quick prayer for safety of ship and crew. Once the storm receded, she would leave the *Dark Sapphire* and the demanding captain behind.

Her throat tightened at the prospect and she called herself every kind of fool, for she was beginning to care for the brute who steered this ship, the man who had left her standing alone once before.

She gathered up her few belongings and hurriedly finished dressing. Knowing that once she escaped the *Dark Sapphire* she would never see Keegan again, she felt a moment's chill.

Stupidly, her heart tore a bit. She glanced at the bed where they'd so recently made love. Keegan was a bastard, true, a blackheart whom she couldn't trust, and yet a part of her wanted to feel his strong arms surround her, wanted to kiss him and taste the salt water on his warm lips, to lie with him again and experience the thrill of his skin rubbing against hers.

But it could never be.

Theirs was a few short hours of desperate passion, nothing more. She

found her mantle, threw it over her shoulders, and fought this newfound and
unlikely sadness.

She had thought after her horrid, agonizing wedding night that she
would never want a man to touch her again. The memory of that horrible
night lingered with her still. . . .

Sheena whispered her vows in front of Father Percival at Tardiff Hall—
removed from those that she loved. There was an underlying malaise within
the recesses of the dark, unhappy keep, a chill that danced upon Sheena's
neck as she knelt and forced out the horrid words of obedience and commit-
ment. Sheena felt the discontent as she suffered through the knowing glances
cast her way, witnessed the nudges of elbows of the soldiers of Tardiff Hall,
and realized that they were sharing a joke at her expense. Though Tardiff had
raised his cup to her at the meal after the ceremony and had demanded all of
the servants obey her and treat her as a lady, she had caught him winking at a
large-bosomed serving girl. The lass had swallowed a smile and blushed to the
roots of her hair.

Sheena had been mortified, but the worst was yet to come.

That night, after her father and Fawn left Tardiff, she and her new husband were alone in his chamber. Sir Manning, a gift from Lady Fawn, was
posted as a sentry on the other side of the door to the lord's chamber, but
Sheena held no illusions that the dark knight had been left to protect her
as much to see that she did not escape. The surly knight had been her shadow in the days before the wedding. Otherwise she would have fled Tardiff
and its lord.

Ellwynn closed the door with a thud. Turned the lock.

Sheena, shivering inwardly, swallowed back her fear and told herself there
were worse fates than submitting to her husband. 'Twas a man's right and,
she'd heard from the gossiping old women as they'd shelled beans or pared
apples, it could be very pleasant. Sheena had seen dogs and horses mate.
She'd known some of the laundry maids at Ogof who had giggled and told stories of the thrill they'd experienced kissing and loving a man. But to her, with
the Baron of Tardiff, the thought was vile.

Tardiff crossed the room, where a fire was dying in the grate. "Come here,"
he demanded as he stood by a large bed covered with the skins of animals.
Throughout the room small indentations held candles that burned weakly,
tallow dripping down the wall. Two windows were open, but no breath of wind
stirred the single tapestry draped over the bed.

She hesitated.

"I said, come here," he repeated, and his words seemed to echo against the
coved ceiling while the red embers of the fire glowed brightly. His voice was

calm, and he spoke as if to a slow-learning child. "And when I say those words, you reply, 'Yes, my lord,' and do my bidding. 'Tis the same when I command you to do anything. Your response is 'Yes, my lord.'"

"Nay," she said, shaking her head. "I'll not—"

"Come here, *wife*."

She froze.

"Remember, 'Yes, my lord.' And then you do my bidding," he repeated with slow patience.

Anger spurted through her veins. "And when I ask you to do something, will you say, 'Yes, my lady?'"

His eyes flared with silent fury. "Do not make me angry," he warned.

"Then do not order me about as if I were a slave."

He glared at her. One of his nostrils drew up a bit. "Do not make me come after you or you'll regret it. Come, Sheena. Now."

She glanced at the door.

"'Twould be foolish," he cautioned, "and to no avail. This is my castle. My men stand guard and do as I tell them. As you will. Now. Come *here*." With one long, arrogant finger he pointed at a spot on the floor just in front of him.

Clenching her teeth, knowing that to say anything further would infuriate him and only cause her pain, she approached.

"That's better." His eyes slitted and he appraised her. "Now, take off your clothes."

She froze. "But—"

"Do it, Sheena, and do it quickly. I want to see you naked." His lips barely moved when he spoke, and drops of sweat beaded his forehead, slipped through the strands of his hair.

Throat dry, again she glanced at the door, locked and bolted, with Sir Manning posted on the other side. With fumbling fingers she removed her belt and gown, tossing them onto the rush-strewn stones of the floor. She wanted to die, to save herself this humiliation, but death was far from her, it seemed. Shivering, she stood in her chemise and felt as if the entire castle could see her. Tardiff smiled coldly, then motioned with his finger to her chemise. "That as well. Get rid of it."

Gritting her teeth, Sheena obeyed, letting the lacy undergarment slide down her body to pool on the rushes and leave her naked as the day she was born. Though mortified, she managed to stare straight at her tormentor.

His smile was pure evil, made all the more sinister by the dying light. "I see I have bargained well." He twirled a long finger in the air, motioning for her to turn before him. "Aye, ye be a nice piece of flesh, Wife. You will suit me well. Stay." He walked to the fire, where on a small table three mazers of wine were waiting. Sipping from one, he paced the room slowly, his eyes turned in her direction, watching her intently as if searching for flaws and imperfections. "Your father assured me you were a virgin."

She elevated her chin and glared at him, refusing to answer.

"Are you?" He took a long swallow from his cup.

"Are you?" she tossed back before she could think twice.

"Mind your waspy tongue, woman, or you'll pay for your impertinence." He swirled his wine. "But nay, wife," he said, and she cringed at her new title. "I assure you that I am quite skilled in the art of lovemaking. You will be well satisfied."

She didn't respond, just held her ground, squared her bare shoulders, and tried vainly not to tremble. Though patience was not in her nature, she had learned to watch and wait, her father stressing that biding one's time was considered a virtue whenever she accompanied him on a hunt. This night she felt as if she were the prey. But she would wait. Smoke curled up from the nearly melted candles, and the fire gave off a soft hiss.

Sheena's nerves were strung tight, and she prayed she'd find a way to get through the long night ahead. Mayhap the baron, who seemed so fond of wine, would be well into his cups tonight and fall asleep.

She could only hope.

Plucking a small bag from the table, Ellwynn winked at her, then poured out its contents. Vibrant gems gleaming red, gold, and green sparkled in the firelight as they tumbled to a stop.

Her heart was wrenched as she recognized her mother's jewels. "Nay," she whispered.

"Part of your dowry." Ellwynn sighed as he fingered the stones. "A pity the blue one's missing. 'Twas the most valuable of the lot, worth much more than these three together. But your fool of a father lost it in a game of chance, my sister claims." He dribbled the jewels through his fingers. "But this be payment enough, I suppose." He held the gold stone aloft and stared at its many facets. "Asides, it was rumored to be cursed, not that I believe in such things."

Sickened at the thought that her father had given her mother's precious stones to this beast, she dragged her eyes away. As if satisfied with her reaction, he finished his wine, set down his cup, and clapped his hands. "Page! More wine."

With a creak, part of the wall opened up, and through a hidden doorway a page appeared carrying a vessel. He was a gawky boy who averted his eyes as he hurried through his chore. Sheena, burning with embarrassment, turned her back to him and silently wished the horrid man who was now her husband would drop dead in the rushes.

She felt rather than saw the boy leave the jug, then retreat through the hidden doorway.

"Be you embarrassed of your body?" her new husband asked.

"Nay, but neither do I display it!"

"That will change. You have no reason to feel any shame. You are, I assure you, genuinely perfect. As beautiful as any of the stones that were given me for taking you off your father's hands."

She wasn't warmed by his compliment, only sickened. "I will not allow—"

"Lie down on the bed!" Tardiff ordered, cutting off her protests. She heard him loosening his belt. Her stomach clenched, and she slowly sank onto the bed. *It will be over soon, this act of lovemaking, though no one would think of love at this coupling.*

"You can watch me undress, wife," he invited, and she heard him removing his clothes. She didn't move, but he walked in front of her proudly, like a strutting peacock. Though he sickened her, she raised her eyes to his and refused to show him any sign of weakness. He had already discarded his tunic and was unfastening his breeches. All too soon they fell to the floor and he was naked, too. Inside, Sheena shuddered in revulsion. He was a tall, muscular man, strong, but with the hint of soft flesh about his belly—the suggestion that he would someday soon run to fat.

He was carrying his cup and tossed back his wine in one swift motion. "Now, wife, we have business, you and I."

She steeled herself. "Be ye ready for me?" he asked, and when she didn't reply, he laughed as if at a private joke. "Well, ye will be." Calling over his shoulder, he yelled, "Fannie, girl? 'Tis time."

From the hidden doorway a woman appeared. Sheena remembered her—Zelda's daughter. Zelda, who had served Sheena's mother, then Fawn when she had married Jestin. Fannie had been sent to Tardiff to punish some minor wrong Fawn had claimed Zelda had committed. For a second Sheena felt relief—mayhap Fannie would take her place—but knew it was a false hope.

With nary a glance at Sheena, Fannie swallowed hard, crossed the rushes to the naked lord, kissed him soundly on the mouth, and squealed when he grabbed one of her buttocks through her skirt and pinched hard. "Like that, do you, wench?" he asked, his eyes gleaming with a malevolent light as he looked past her shoulder to Sheena on the bed.

"Aye, m'lord," Fannie said, though her eyes seemed to have no luster.

"What is this?" Sheena demanded as the lord guided the girl to the bed.

"Fannie will be joining us."

Sheena's stomach roiled. No matter how distasteful she found Ellwynn, she had never expected this depravity.

"Nay." Sheena spat the word. "'Twas bad enough that I was to lie with you as your wife, but I'll not share the bed with her and you and—"

Smack!

The flat of his hand slammed against her cheek.

Her head snapped back from the blow. Pain exploded behind her eyes. She stumbled backward. Tasted blood. Before she could defend herself, Tardiff lunged. The weight of his body forced her onto the bed. "I've had enough of your arguing with me at every turn," he growled, his eyes dark with hate and more—lust and arousal.

"Get off me."

"Not until I've had my way, wife!"

She struggled. *Slap!* He hit her again. Pain ripped through her.

"Nay." Fannie was shaking her head, holding her arms tightly around her. "Do not hurt her, m'lord, please."

"Stay out of this."

"But—"

"Or you'll get some of the same," he yelled, his face red, a vein pulsing in his forehead as he pinned Sheena to the bed.

"But she's just a girl."

"She's my wife," he snarled, holding Sheena down as she struggled to free herself. She fought from instinct, kicking, clawing, writhing. The more she fought, though, the stronger and more determined he became. His member was swollen and stiff and rubbed anxiously against her abdomen as she tried to push him away from her.

"Oh, I knew you'd have fight in you," he said, panting and sweating and reeking. His eyes gleamed. His mouth pulled back in an evil, ugly grin. "I'll show you what it is to serve a husband." He forced her knees apart with his, and she closed her eyes, told herself to let it happen but couldn't. She twisted, trying to throw him off, but he was too heavy, too intent.

"Fannie," he ordered. "Come here."

"Oh, no, m'lord, please. The lady, she is not yet accustomed to this." Then to Sheena she pleaded, "Please, lady, do not fight him."

"I'll have no back talk from you," Ellwynn snarled, turning his head a fraction and glowering at the serving maid with his hateful eyes. He was panting, tiring. "'Twill be your turn to please me as well, and you'd bloody well do my bidding or I'll turn you over to my men and they be not as kind as I."

Tears filled Fannie's eyes. "A-aye, m'lord," she said meekly. The fire popped and somewhere far away, on the other side of the door, a dog barked.

"That be better." Ellwynn's horrid gaze returned to Sheena. "Now, wife, beg me to take you."

Sheena stared up at him. Clenched her jaw. Felt blood dripping from the corner of her mouth.

"Now."

"I'll beg nothing of you," she vowed.

He grinned. "Nay? Oh, woman, be careful." He was enjoying humiliating her, and at that second she hated him more than any man on earth. Positioned above her, his stiff cock brushing her naked belly, he reached under the bed with his free hand and retrieved a knife, a bone-handled dagger with a hideously curved blade.

"Now, wife, you will do my bidding," he warned. "Or I will be forced to use this." The blade winked in the candlelight. "And I would hate to."

"May your soul go straight to hell," she replied, refusing to stare at the horrid knife.

His muscles flexed and his nostrils flared in rage. "Oh, I intend to, wench. And I'll take you with me."

"I be already there," she swore. She saw the blade move and she reacted, drawing up her knee. Fast. Hard. To connect with his groin.

Ellwynn roared in rage and pain.

"Oh, merciful God, no," Fannie whispered. She gasped in horror, and Sheena tried to slide away as the Baron of Tardiff howled in pain and his body coiled around his groin. Rolling back and forth, swearing loudly, he clenched himself together in agony.

"Now, ye've done it," Fannie whispered, her eyes round in horror as she backed away from the bed. "He'll kill us both."

"Not me, he won't." Sheena sprang from the bed, ran to the door, and pounded with her bare fist on the thick oaken planks. "Sir Manning! Open this door at once. The baron is ailing!" she cried, intending to run past the sentry when he opened the door.

With a roar Tardiff exploded from the bed. "You foolish piece of flesh," he said, flying across the room and throwing himself at her.

She ducked, but he was quick, grabbed her by her hair, and flung her against the wall.

"Ooof." She slammed against the lime-washed stone. Every bone in her body was jarred. A table toppled, candles fell to the floor.

She tried to scramble away, but he threw her against the door.

Bang!

Her head cracked hard against oaken planks, and he pinned the length of her body with his.

"I will have you, wench, and you'll never forget this night. Never forget that I own you." Behind him flames crackled in the rushes.

"You'll have to kill me first."

"So be it." He lifted his hand, and she saw the ugly knife, curved and raised. Her heart pounded. There was no escape.

"Oh, sweet Mary," Fannie whispered. "Look what's happened here!"

Quickly she poured water from a pitcher on the rapidly spreading fire, sending steam and smoke toward the ceiling. "Do not hurt her, m'lord."

"She deserves it."

"But not the knife." From the corner of her eye Sheena saw the woman make a quick sign of the cross over her naked bosom as smoke hung low in the air. "Not the knife, please."

"Lord Tardiff! Be ye all right?" Manning yelled from the other side of the door.

"Leave us!"

"But there be smoke and sounds of a fight and—"

"Leave us!" Ellwynn thundered, the cords in his neck rigid. Quickly he placed the knife near Sheena's throat, and she felt the sting of its blade as it broke her skin ever so slightly.

"Oh, sweet Jesus," Fannie whispered. "Nay . . . oh, nay . . ."

Sheena, Tardiff in tow, inched toward the hidden door. Nervous sweat gleamed on her body, blood dripped from the shallow cut, fear consumed her while the smell of smoke and burnt tallow was heavy in the air.

"By all that is holy and all that is not, I curse you, Ellwynn," she said, holding his ugly glare with her own, but her hands were working, fingers creeping along the wall to an indentation where a candle was burning. "Not only God but the Earth Mother as well shall condemn you."

"So you'll use your witchcraft, will you? We shall see." He shifted. The blade flashed. Sheena spat hard. "Wha—" In the split second that he jerked back, she reached for the candle, grabbed it, and jabbed it in his bare, sweaty abdomen.

Hisssss.

"Aaaaagggghhh."

The smell of burning flesh and hair filled the air. He dropped the knife. The candle fell away.

"I'll kill you," Tardiff screamed, writhing in pain. Sheena wasted no time as he jumped at her. She fell to the floor, hot rushes burning her skin, her fingers curling over the bone hilt of the weapon.

"I'll teach you to—"

She whipped around and without thinking plunged his own knife into his side. Blood spurted from the wound. Tardiff's face blanched. He bellowed in pain.

She ran, stumbled, ran faster. As he fell to the chamber floor, collapsing in a pathetic heap, blood pooling around him, she snatched up her clothes and fought the nausea that burned up her throat. *You've killed him! Merciful God in heaven, Sheena, you've murdered your husband, the lord.* Staggering on legs that threatened 'to give way, she made her way to the hidden doorway, where Fannie, quivering, her eyes wide and disbelieving, waited.

"Oh, my God, oh, my, God . . . oh . . . Run," the serving girl cried. "Run as far as you can, for this one, if he lives, he'll hunt you down like a stag in the forest and kill you sure. And—and take these . . .." She stuffed the stones into Sheena's outstretched palm, closed the door behind them and, using a hand against the wall for guidance, took off at a dead run, leading Sheena down a curved stairway. Tears ran down Sheena's cheeks though she felt no sorrow, her bare feet scraping against the flôor. She and Fannie careened down the corridor, stumbling, falling, scratching themselves as they heard the squeal of terrified mice racing away. At the main floor there was a fork in the tunnel. "Wait." Fannie slipped through a door and returned quickly with a burning taper. "Go that way," she said, "it leads beneath the portcullis and into the moat. Oh, by the gods, ye're bleeding."

"I care not." Teeth chattering, Sheena threw her dress over her body. She had to get out. To find freedom. To put as many miles between her, the dead baron, and Tardiff Hall as she could.

"Then be off with ye. Take care and God speed, m'lady," Fannie whispered, biting her lip and choking back tears. "I—I must go back and sound an alarm, for if I don't, if—if I do not, the lord will kill me as well."

"Thank you," Sheena said. "You didn't have to help me—"

"There be no time for this. Run! Go! Now."

Sheena didn't argue. Shivering with fear, she drew on her boots.

Through the tunnels, cupping the candle's weak flame, praying she would be able to escape, she ran until she reached a door, unlatched it, and smelled the moat in the darkness. She could not see it was so dark, but she sent a prayer toward the heavens and jumped, not knowing if she would live or die.

"You knew who she was," Keegan finally accused, manning the whipstaff. His fingers curled over the long rod attached to the tiller, and he strained against the bucking of the sea. "You knew she was Sheena of Ogof."

Hollis was the only other person in the room besides Bo, who was huddled in the corner and sleeping despite the turbulent, raging waters.

"Why did you not tell me?"

"I thought it best," the older man admitted. "And when I first came upon her in the hold, I dinna know."

"But you did soon after."

"Aye." He rubbed his balding head and bit his lip.

"You claimed she was a witch."

"I wanted ye to stay away from her." He steadied his legs as the *Dark Sapphire* shuddered. "She be the daughter of the man who kilt yer father. She be the one ye left when ye escaped Ogof. She has reason enough to hate ye, Keegan. I trust her not."

Keegan's teeth clamped together, and he steered the ship against the thrashing power of the black water. His muscles ached and strained, and yet he sensed the storm calming, felt the tiller respond. "I never knew you to lie to me, Hollis. I did not expect it."

The old man had the decency to cast down his eyes. "'Twas a mistake. But since you remembered not, I thought it best." He lifted a shoulder and sighed.

"You were wrong."

"Mayhap. But she's cast a spell on ye, lad. She cursed ye, she did. When ye were near death and not awake, healing from yer wounds, ye flailed and cried out, talking of her and the curse. I was sure ye were about to die, I was. Because of her. I tried to tend to ye, to comfort ye, but 'twas as if ye had no mind. I believed she'd damned yer soul to the devil and that was why ye were not wakin' as ye should."

"I believe not in curses."

"Then ye be a fool," Hollis insisted. "And ye did then, when ye were lyin' on the bunk, sweatin' and swearin' and callin' out fer help." His old hands lifted upward. "Rantin' and ravin' ye were, as if Satan himself had taken over yer soul." Sighing, Hollis worried his cracked lips with his teeth. "And then, after all this time, she appears here on the ship, hidin' in the damn hold, the daughter of the man who kilt yer father, the woman who swore vengeance against ye. If not the spell of a witch, then that of a beautiful woman. They have ways of turning a man's head, of telling him what he wants to hear, of getting what they want. She has no reason to love ye, Keegan. Nay, she has all the more reason to despise ye."

That much was true, though Keegan still didn't believe that Sheena had cursed him. "What other secrets are you hiding?"

"None," the old man said so swiftly, Keegan knew it to be a lie.

"Nay?"

"I'm tellin' ye true—"

"What of my mother?" Keegan demanded, thinking back to other times he'd been certain the old man was altering the truth. "Each time I ever spoke of her, you held your tongue, but there was something in your eyes, I know it."

Hollis scowled, picked at his beard.

"What?" Keegan insisted, fury burning through his blood. "What is it you are keeping from me?"

Studying the floor, the old man shook his head slowly, as if arguing with himself. "Lorinda . . . she was my sister."

For a second Keegan didn't move. The whipstaff shuddered. "You lie."

"Nay. 'Tis true. She—she was always a wild one. She met yer father, got with child, and me own father threw her out." Guilt filled his ancient eyes. "'Twas because of me that she came to meet Rourke; 'twas after Bertrice."

Stunned, Keegan sucked in his breath, held onto the long pole attached to the tiller, as if he intended to break the damned thing. "You're tellin' me that you be my uncle," he accused, suspicion evident in his words.

"Aye. 'Tis true."

"And yet you never told me."

"Nay."

"By the gods, Hollis, I should throw your miserable carcass overboard." He seethed as other questions blazed in his brain. "Lorinda." He would not think to call her Mother any longer. "Be she alive?"

Hollis shook his head. "Nay. She died long ago, before Rourke was killed."

A dozen emotions he'd never felt before assailed him as he steered the ship. "How?"

"Ye do not want to know—"

"I do! Tell me." He threw the older man a hard, unforgiving stare and would've shaken some sense into him if he'd dared to release the whipstaff for a second.

"She married a farmer, worked herself to the bone, and took ill the first winter. Died within a fortnight." Hollis frowned. "I was at sea with Rourke and you at the time. Didn't find out that she'd passed on until the next spring."

"So you stayed with my father because of me?" Keegan asked, his mind searching for answers.

"'Twas one of the reasons."

"And the others?"

"'Twas fond I was of your father. And you. And the sea."

"You're scared to death of the sea."

A strange smile played over his lips as Keegan strained against the bucking of the waves. "And yet I love it, I do."

Keegan wiped one hand on his breeches. "Lorinda. Did she ever ask about me?"

Hollis hesitated. The wind shrieked. Keegan felt a bitter disappointment even before the answer.

"Nay."

So that was it. Keegan felt a loss that he would not consider for a mother's love he'd never known. But he'd survived and he would not grieve for a woman who bore him in shame and gave him away. Hollis headed for the door, but Keegan, arms straining, had more questions. "Be there other secrets ye keep, old man?" he asked caustically, his eyes narrowing into the rush of air that swept through the open window.

"Nay."

"No?" Keegan didn't believe him. His mind was spinning with questions that had been unanswered since the dark time. "What of the ring?"

"Ring? There be no ring," Hollis replied, but something flickered in his gaze.

"The ring with the Dark Sapphire of Ogof, the stone you were certain was cursed. What happened to it?" A wave splashed over the deck, the ship shivered. Keegan gritted his teeth.

Hollis bit his lip, glanced up, and Keegan braced himself for yet another lie. "I sold it."

"You sold it? A ring with a stone that valuable?"

"Aye." He nodded, scratched his balding pate, and said, "I barely escaped with me own life, there at Ogof. Had it not been for the fire and the confusion and the lucky fact that the guard who was hauling me off to the dungeon was scared for his child's life, I would have died. Heard her cryin', the guard did, and released me for a minute. I made it to the shore, and while the other soldiers were hurrying to the castle to put out flames, I stole the rowboat we came in on, and found you. Bleedin' to death from arrow wounds ye were and clutching that damned stone as if it were blessed from God. When I finally got ye back to the ship—"

"The *Warrior*," Keegan said, remembering his father's craft and the man who had so bravely manned her, the captain who had been both father and mother to him. For this parent he still grieved.

"As I said, for the first few weeks it was nip and tuck, didn't know if ye were gonna pull through, in a deep sleep ye were—rantin' and screamin' about the curse. I spoon-ladled ye soup and cleaned yer wounds, but I feared that Jestin's army would be after us, so after a week or so, I sold the boat to an Irish sea captain and bought another—this one." He patted the walls with a loving hand. "Used the money from the *Warrior* and the Dark Sapphire as well."

"Who bought the ring? What was his name?" Keegan asked suspiciously as he realized how easily the old man had lied to him over the years. For love? Or for his own gain?

"The owner of this boat bought the cursed gem, I'm tellin' ya. A man who said his name was Kroft, but I be doubtin' that, though I never called him on it. We both had something to hide, he and I. Fer all I knew he was a pirate and had stole this ship. As for the Dark Sapphire, it belonged to Ogof. So we asked no questions and the trade was made. I renamed the ship, just to remember, and set to sea. Ye awoke a week later, but ye didna remember anything. Not the battle, the fire, the stone, yer father's death, not even the girl who helped ye escape."

"Sheena," Keegan said softly, scowling as the lanterns bounced shifting yellow shadows on the walls. The smell of the sea was everywhere. His thoughts turned toward the clouded time that had been hidden from his memory, so long forgotten. He held firm to the whipstaff, fighting the pull of the sea and the strength of the wind, using all his muscles as he guided the ship through the rough water. His shoulders and arms ached from the task. Despite the icy breath of the wind, sweat sprinkled his brow, slickened his palms, and ran down his spine. Gritting his teeth and throwing his back into his work, he wondered what would happen when they docked. He only hoped that Wart was waiting for them and had news of Tardiff's soldiers.

"I dinna want to deceive ye, Keegan."

"But you did."

"Aye." Hollis nodded sadly, though Keegan doubted the old man's show of remorse. He'd had plenty of time to undo his untruth and confide in Keegan. But he hadn't. Hollis's secrets regarding his mother, Sheena, and the Dark Sapphire of Ogof had been locked away for too many years.

Keegan's eyebrows drew together and he turned his concentration to steering the ship. Little by little, as Keegan refused to think of the woman who had borne and abandoned him, or the girl he'd later betrayed and was now his lover, the storm slowly abated.

Old Hollis, curse his sorry, lying hide, was right about one thing, though: Sheena was far more trouble than she was worth.

Or was she?

It occurred to him that he was beginning to fall in love with her, and he quickly banished the thought. Love was only for fools. He'd learned that lesson all too well years before at his wife's hands.

Never again would he fall victim. *Never.*

Baron Jestin of Ogof rolled over and reached for his wife. Though Fawn was heavy with child and refused him these days, he had need of a woman. He was anxious, his cock stiff with want, his mind worried. There were many troubles within the castle walls. The steward was forever prattling that the cook was skimming spices from the larder or that the candle maker was behind, forever in his cups, or some other bothersome concern. Lately there had been trouble collecting wood-penny, agistment, and chimiage. The peasants were cutting firewood, grazing their animals, and carrying goods through the forest without paying the proper taxes.

There had been a restlessness within the castle walls since Sheena left, a cloak of discontent that covered the keep, and Jestin felt as if he could trust no one.

Worst of all, there was another worry he'd been carrying around with him for the better part of a week. 'Twas his piss. Ah, there had been a time when his stream had been strong as a stallion's, and clear; then it had grown weaker and murkier, though he'd ignored it. Now, however, 'twas often black with blood, and he wondered if he was dying. Rotting from the inside out. He'd not yet called the physician, for he did not want to face the truth, should it be so. Asides, the scrawny, balding man would do nothing more than apply leeches to his body to draw out the bad blood.

Jestin decided he was losing enough as it was.

Whatever was wrong with him was his own secret, one he would share with no one.

Fawn's side of the bed was empty. Cold. As was the woman herself. He knew she was fidgety and uncomfortable; the baby was due shortly. Another girl, no doubt. No matter how loudly his wife proclaimed that she was carrying a son, Jestin had sired only daughters. Sheena, the three he fathered with Fawn, and four others that had been conceived when he was away from the castle. All girls. No boys.

None of them were anywhere close to Sheena. Oh, he'd tried to love his other children, at least the ones that were legitimate, but Fawn's issue were petulant and wily creatures, all with big, haunted eyes, milky white skin, pouty little lips, and weak chins. They were a sorry lot; all three of them tied together could not hold a candle to Sheena. Or Bertrice—now, there was a woman. One worth fighting for. Even killing for. Not so Fawn.

Bertrice.

He closed his eyes and remembered the only woman he'd loved. She had been big-bosomed and big-hearted, a beautiful girl with a lilting voice, lustrous red hair, and fetching eyes that had promised him so much.

As they had promised Rourke.

Bertrice's father had been eager to marry her to a lord, and then she'd met the sea captain and lost her heart. Aye, she'd slept with him and had not come to Jestin's bed a virgin, but he'd loved her with all his heart. And even though he'd had to win her hand in a game of dice, he'd never regretted it; even now, when Fawn's sharped-tongue barbs were cast at Bertrice's memory, he had but to walk to the shrine in the chapel and feel the peace of her spirit.

She'd never brought up Rourke again. Once she and Jestin were married, she had not mentioned the fact that Rourke had promised to return in accordance with the terms of their first bet.

Jestin was thankful that she hadn't lived to meet the captain again. He'd lived every waking moment in fear that she would desert him.

Ach, the troubles he had. To think so many envied him being baron. His head pounded with his worries, and his member was so hard it ached. Fawn would not accommodate him. He thought of a serving wench who could handle his needs, a girl who worked in the kitchen with high, firm breasts, teeth that overlapped a bit, and a sparkle in her green eyes whenever she offered him more wine. When he'd teased her, she'd flirted outrageously, and once when she was serving jellied pigeon's eggs, she'd fed him right from her smooth hands. Then as he'd chewed, she'd licked her fingers provocatively. One by one. He'd never bedded her, had tried to remain true to his wife, though he wondered why.

Fawn was not the kind of woman to trust. He'd known as much when he married her, and yet he'd needed a mother for Sheena and a wife who would bear him an heir.

Ah, Sheena. His heart was heavy whenever he thought of his firstborn, and as he slid to the side of the bed and shoved himself to his feet, he felt a jab of remorse. He should not have insisted she marry. Aye, she was well past the age and had refused all suitors, but he missed her terribly and now there was all that trouble at Tardiff.

So where was his wife? He listened to the sounds of the castle starting to stir for the morning, but the door to his chamber did not creak open. Nor did he hear Fawn's tread in the hallway. She'd changed and become different with this pregnancy. She was far more distant and much moodier, forever running to that odd fortune-teller, Serena. Mayhap Fawn was right; mayhap she was carrying a boy child—that would explain the difference in her temperament. Or, mayhap something else was bothering her, something he sensed but didn't really understand—trouble on a larger scale.

His damned shaft throbbed, and he thought if he couldn't mount his wife because of the babe, at least Fawn could offer her hands and mouth as comfort.

But it was evident she was not returning, and despite the chill in the air, his manhood was hard as ever. 'Twas a joke. He was still always ready to bed his wife, and yet when he relieved himself, that same organ of which he was so proud, the one that ensured he'd sire heirs, would offer up colored piss to remind him of his own mortality.

With a grunt he threw on a fresh tunic and breeches and wished his throbbing member would wilt. Grabbing his quiver and arrows, he found the green mantle he used for hunting, as it always assured him of good luck, then walked into the hallway where the guard was dozing. As the door to Jestin's chamber thudded shut behind him, the soldier awakened with a start.

"M'lord," the flustered man said. "Good morning and—"

"Tend to your post," Jestin barked as he strode to the steps usually trod upon only by servants. Every so often the baron took the back staircase just to keep the lazy ones who idled near the windows on their toes.

Outside, it was still dark, the moon high in the sky, no streaks of dawn yet visible. Stars blinked through a haze of clouds, and the bailey was coming alive and filled with the scents of cut hay, salty air, and a lingering fragrance of roses from the garden. Boys were drawing water and carrying firewood; the armorer was sharpening spears and lances by the light of an early morning fire.

'Twas a peaceful time of day, though 'twould soon pass as the cook would be rising, the guards changing, the portcullis raised. The windows of the baker's hut already glowed from the fire where he baked the castle's bread. Overhead, the sweeps of the windmill whooshed. Jestin looked up as a bat flew by.

He ducked, crossed himself, and hoped that seeing the black creature was not a sign of bad luck. As he passed the well a rooster crowed and the dogs, ever ready to put up a ruckus, howled.

"Shut up, ye miserable curs," the hound master snapped, then, upon spying the baron, managed a gap-toothed smile. "Are ye goin' out huntin' this morn, m'lord, and will ye be needin' the dogs?"

"I'll not need the dogs today," Jestin said, shaking his head. "Another time." As the first shafts of morning light pierced the thin haze he strode to the chapel and peered inside. Father Godfrey was at the altar, praying, not even lifting his head as the door opened. The candles flickered at the shrine for his first wife, and he sent up a silent prayer. But Fawn was not in attendance, and Jestin was beginning to doubt her. Forever claiming to be praying for the unborn babe's health, or stopping off at the stables to check on the horses, or walking through the garden, Fawn avoided his questions as to her whereabouts. The feeling that she was lying to him bothered him again, like a slowly festering wound.

Closing the door, he turned and walked quickly to the stables, where the stable master was ordering boys about. A gruff man with an odd-shaped head—the result, gossip said, of his mother being kicked in the belly when she was about to deliver. Whatever the reason, Farrell was an ugly man with one side of his face mashed in. Angry at the world in general, he had a unique touch with the steeds.

"You there, Will, haul the water and be quick about it! The pails be in the corner." As the first boy grabbed two buckets and hurried toward the well, Farrell grabbed the other one and boxed his ears. "And you, Nate, where 'ave ye been these past two days?" He tweaked the boy's ear, and the lad let out a howl that rang through the bailey.

"'Twas me mum. She was feelin' poorly and needed me help with the twins."

"Bah." Farrell spat on the ground. "The next time ye pay yer mom no mind."

"But me dad is dead and—"

"And the lord's horses still need tendin' to." He twisted the upper part of Nate's ear, and the boy let out a pain-filled shriek. Several horses whinnied and snorted nervously.

"Ah, ye cry like a woman. Now grab a shovel and clean the stalls up right quick. Then, once yer finished with that, pick up that pitchfork and start givin' 'em hay."

"But the gong farmer, 'tis his job to clean the dung," Nate complained, fighting tears and rubbing his ear.

"Not today, it ain't," Farrell turned from the lad and dusted his hands. "Ah, m'lord, I was expectin' ye. Got yer steed all saddled, I did." He snapped his fingers. "Nate, get the baron's horse and be quick about it."

The boy hurried the length of the stalls, unlatched one, and led Banner out. A spirited gray, the stallion's ears were pricked forward, his nostrils flared.

"Ye'll not be takin' anyone with ye?" Farrell asked, rubbing one of the horse's shoulders with his big hand.

"Not this time." Jestin swung onto the saddle.

"Same as the lady," Farrell said, his crumpled face frowning a bit. "I told her I did not like her riding out alone. Even though it be near dawn, there be pickpockets and thieves about. A fine lady like her, full with child, aye, she be an easy target," he said, lifting the eyebrow of his good eye.

Jestin's jaw turned to steel. "When did she leave?" he asked.

"Not even an hour ago, maybe less."

"Did she say where she was going?" Jestin hated to ask, realizing the deformed stable master was enjoying the fact that he had a bit of knowledge over on the Baron of Ogof.

Farrell shook his misshapen head.

"But she was alone?"

"Aye. Since Sir Manning was given to Tardiff, she rides alone."

"He was her personal guard," Jestin said, rankled by the undertone in the man's voice but ignoring the suspicions that had begun to germinate in his mind—suspicions he'd told himself were unfounded.

"Aye, and she be missin' him." Hearing the implication in his words, Farrell added quickly, "Manning, he watched over her."

"And was paid to do it." Irritated at the horseman's suggestions, Jestin picked up his reins and clucked to his mount. Banner took off at a trot, anxious to run to stretch his legs.

Jestin needed some time alone with his thoughts. He leaned forward. The horse's strides lengthened. As he neared the main gate, the baron shouted to the guards barely visible in the pre-dawn light.

"You there, let me pass."

"Aye, m'lord," a man's deep voice yelled back. He bellowed orders to someone in the gatehouse. Within seconds, groaning and clanking, the portcullis was raised. Jestin, still simmering at the insinuation of the damned deformed stable master that he might have been cuckolded, kicked Banner in the flanks.

As they passed through the gates, the stallion stretched out, easing into a gallop, his hooves flinging mud, his ears pricked forward.

Jestin guided his mount along the road running parallel to the coastline. Faster and faster until tears stung his eyes and the rutted lane curved upward through the forested hills. Rather than ride to his favorite hunting spot on the ridge, he veered south along a beaten path beneath a canopy of leafy branches. A stag leaped out of the underbrush and sprang over a fallen log, disappearing deep into the forest. Jestin didn't give chase. Barely noticed. His bow, arrows, and quiver were forgotten. He had a new purpose as he rode.

He intended to find his wife, and he wouldn't rest until he did.

Chapter Nine

"Tell us where the woman is," Manning demanded as he pulled off a glove. In the dirt by his feet, coiled like a snake ready to strike, was a whip. "Or, my friend, I assure you, you'll regret it."

"I know not." Wart was sweating, stretched between two men in the clearing, where the fire burned low and the first hint of morning light was visible above the lacy branches. They had been at this for hours—accusations from the dark knight, denials from Wart.

"Ach, you be a fool." Manning picked up the whip and shook the sinister loops free. "Peter here says he knows you as Warren of Halliwell, that you be his cousin, isn't that right?"

"Aye," Peter said, his eyes narrowing on Wart. "And a thief he be, though I be ashamed to admit it. Robbed everyone in town including the baron, stole horses from him and then poached in the forest. Some say he was even a spy. Warren, he be the rotten apple in the family, fer sure. Caused his parents nothing but shame, he did. His old father, he disowned him."

Manning smoothed the whip with his fingers. "Then he's a wanted man with a price upon his head."

"Aye, the Lord of Halliwell would pay well for his return."

"What have ye to say to these charges?" Manning asked.

"Peter's me cousin, aye, and he be a liar. From the time he was a lad he couldna tell the truth." Wart spat out the words though fingers of fear were clutching his heart, making it difficult to breathe. He'd been flogged before, knew the bite of a whip against his back and hated it.

Manning fingered the whip thoughtfully. "It matters not what ye be running from, but 'tis important that you tell me about the lady, Sheena of Tardiff. I know she boarded the *Dark Sapphire*, ye see. I have men posted at all the ports, and one saw her climb the gangplank, so all I want from you is the name of the ship's next port."

"I know not. I told ye I was not aboard any ship."

Manning sighed impatiently, deep grooves visible around his mouth. "Several of my men disagree. They saw you in the tavern the night we chased the lady into the town, and later one man witnessed that you boarded the ship."

"'Twas not me."

"Liar," Peter accused. High overhead, hidden in the branches a crow let out a throaty caw. "I saw ye with mine own eyes, though I could not believe it."

"So, tell me," Manning said, obviously straining to keep his patience under rein, "where is the *Dark Sapphire* going to dock? We know her route was northward, we've checked along the seacoast in the towns where she stopped. I've spies at each village so I will find out the truth, but 'twould be easier and less painful for you if you were to give up that information now."

Wart snorted. "And then ye would let me go free?"

"You would stay on, as my guest, of course . . . until we locate the lady."

"I tell ye, I know nothing about the ship or a woman who boarded."

Manning's eyes gleamed malevolently. All his civility disappeared in an instant. "'Tis your memory that's the problem, man, and I intend to improve it."

Wart braced himself, felt a tingling in his arm.

The dark knight smiled without a hint of mirth. As his men circled around, grinning and wagering on how many lashes Wart could take before he could no longer stand, Sir Manning drew back a huge shoulder slowly. "Turn him 'round," he ordered in a voice that echoed through the trees. Those holding Wart did as they were bid.

Wart closed his eyes. Waited. Sweated. Felt a shift in the air. With a horrifying hiss the whip sizzled through the air. Snapped beside Wart's head.

Crack! It sounded like thunder. A flock of startled quail flew upward in a whir of wings.

Wart steeled himself and turned his head to call over his shoulder, "Ye may flog me within an inch of me life, but I cannot tell ye what I do na know." He had trouble breathing, and his arm, held by one of Manning's oafs, began to feel numb.

"We'll see." Manning's voice was smooth as oiled leather. "Take off his shirt," he commanded, and in an instant, too quickly for Wart to break free, his tunic was ripped over his head.

Wart stared into the forest, and deep in his chest he felt pain, sharp as a pick cutting through his breastbone. He sagged. His captors forced him to his feet.

"I see this is not the first time ye've been punished," Manning observed as he noticed the old welts scarring Wart's back. "I would have thought you had learned a lesson."

"A stupid one he is," Peter said. "Thick-skulled as any mule."

Some of the men laughed. Wart gasped.

"He's afeared, he is. Look at him," one man chortled. But Wart could not respond, couldn't think. His chest was exploding, his lungs gasping.

"He's about to piss 'is breeches."

"This be your last chance, Wart. If you do not want to add to those scars and then, once ye're flogged, taken back to Halliwell to face the charges against you, I suggest you tell me about Sheena and the *Dark Sapphire.*"

Wart held his silence, felt the other man's anger rising.

"So be it." Manning's voice was a death knell.

Snap!

The whip bit into his back like a viper. He flinched. The men held him upright. He couldn't breathe. Blood thundered through his ears.

Crack! Again. Pain ripped through his flesh.

"What say you, Wart?"

He closed his eyes. Tried not to think of the sting. Of the pain. *Help me. By the gods, I'm dying.*

"Fine, then." Some of the laughter from the men died, and the whip sliced open more of his skin. His back was on fire, as if he'd been stung by a thousand wasps. Squeezing his eyes shut, bracing himself against the next blow, Wart sent up a prayer to a God he'd long before forsaken, and before the whip sliced through him again, his entire body shuddered and he felt his soul slipping away from him as blackness, more friend than foe, overtook him.

Lying upon a small table in the hut, Fawn waited as the cherub-faced seer touched her stomach with gently probing fingers. A fire burned brightly in a small grate, and a few candles gave off a golden glow. Several chickens walked along the dirt floor. Fawn, though trying to remain calm, felt impatience grab her.

"Well?" she demanded when the woman with one blue eye and one green didn't say a word. A mottled cat slithering along the wall hopped imperiously to the windowsill and began washing itself. "What of the babe? Is he all right?"

"What does the midwife say?"

"Oh, her," Fawn snorted with disdain. "Maven's an old crone who has not a good word to say to anyone."

"She told you the babe was breech, did she not?" Serena removed her hands from Fawn's naked belly and, before Fawn could protest, deftly picked up a kitchen knife and sliced off a small lock of Fawn's blond hair.

"Nay!" Fawn's hand shot to the tresses of which she was so proud.

"I need this." Serena held the bit of hair up to the candlelight. "You wanted my vision, did you not?"

"Aye, but . . ." Fawn was in no position to argue. "Just don't take much."

"I have all I need." She rubbed the pinch of pale tresses between her slim fingers and eyed each separate blond strand.

"What does that midwife know, anyway?" Fawn complained, her back nearly breaking on the planks of the table. "Maven's a fool. I don't know why my husband keeps her. The same with that old, useless Zelda. What a pathetic excuse for a lady in waiting she is." Fawn shuddered inwardly at the thought of the serving maid with her haunted, deep-set eyes. The woman never smiled. Never. 'Twas as if she had an inner poison running through her blood. Especially since Fawn had sent Zelda's daughter, Fannie, to be a kitchen maid at Tardiff. But Fawn had no interest in having the pretty young maid at Ogof.

Mayhap Zelda would die soon. Fawn could only hope. She felt the same for the ancient midwife. Maven would surely leave this earth before too many seasons passed. Now, if Fawn were baroness, both of the dried-up old hens would be cast out. . . . Ah, well, that would not happen for 'twas her curse to be a woman and put up with and pretend to be subservient to the men who ruled. 'Twas enough to curdle the contents of her stomach if she thought too long and hard on it. Instead she pretended obedience.

'Twas hypocrisy, to be sure, but she'd learned long ago she had to be coy and cunning. Smart and beautiful were not enough. She'd once been outspoken and had only earned herself a slap from her mother and worse from her ogre of a father. Gryffyn of Tardiff had liked nothing better than to lift her skirts and punish her with his huge hand. He had often times hit her hard enough that her bottom had been sore for days. But it was a lesson well worth learning, for now she was about to earn the spoils of her pretended obedience.

Rolling ponderously to her side, she sat up with effort and felt dizzy for a minute. The hut was small and dark, filled with creatures and drying herbs that hung from the rafters. Chicken dung stained the floor and windowsill. Above the door, nailed to the dark wall, were the talons of a hawk, the bleached skull of a stag, and a rusting horseshoe.

"Do not tell me there will be trouble with this birth," Fawn cautioned Serena, for though she desperately sought the truth, she was tired of Maven's gloomy predictions. "I have borne three babes easily."

"But they were different," the woman said thoughtfully as she crossed the small space to the fire and tossed in Fawn's lock of hair. The embers sizzled angrily and foul-smelling smoke curled upward. Serena slowly shook her head.

"You mean because this time I am carrying a boy child," Fawn guessed, though she felt a drip of ice water in her blood as the sorceress's expression turned dark as midnight.

"Nay."

"But 'tis true, this one is different," Fawn insisted, an inner fear nearly strangling the words in her throat. If this child be a girl, oh, nay, she would not even think such heresy.

"'Tis not the babe's sex that concerns me," Serena said, turning from the fire to stare at Fawn with silently accusing eyes.

"Then what?" Fawn slid into the mantle she'd borrowed from an unknowing maid. 'Twas nearly dawn, and she needed to return to the castle. Already she was forming a lie for her husband, that she had visited an ailing woman who needed comfort.

"The babe be not Lord Jestin's."

"What?" Fawn gasped in horror. Her hand flew to her chest with feigned indignance, and warmth swept up her pallid cheeks. How had this woman divined the truth? "'Tis a vile lie you speak, sorceress. Of course my husband is the sire."

Serena studied the wisps of smoke as they disappeared up the charred stone chimney. "Nay, m'lady. This child be sired by a warrior—a fierce one at that."

"The lord is—was . . . a warrior of great renown."

"But he be different. The father of this babe is a warrior who has not yet gotten what he strives for, a man who lusts for more power, a soldier who has recently spilled blood or killed in battle. The lord has not seen war in many years. This warrior wants more and will stop at nothing, even bedding the wife of the baron, to get what he wants. This be the man who is the father of your babe."

"You know this not," Fawn insisted, though she was turning to jelly inside as she edged off the table.

"You come to me for the truth." Serena's expression was without judgment as she leveled her steady odd-colored eyes on Fawn, her voice low but unbending. "You pay me to tell you what will be and I do. Now you would lie to me?"

Fawn felt a knife of desperation slice into her soul. Her throat was suddenly dry as if she'd swallowed sand. "Nay . . ." Abruptly she was anxious to leave, and she delved into a small leather purse, found a silver coin, and left it on the table where she'd so recently been examined.

Outside, hoof beats thundered.

Serena's head snapped up. Fear pulled at the corners of her mouth. Hissing, the cat leaped to the floor and scurried off to hide beneath a stack of wood. A horse snorted. A bridle jangled.

Damn! Fawn's eyes scoured the little cabin for a means of escape. No one could find her here. No one. She started for the door, but it was too late.

"'Tis your husband," the seer declared, still studying the flames.

Fawn's heart dropped. "No, he would not—" Oh, God, was it possible? Serena was not just telling the future, she was warning Fawn. The fortune-teller stepped to the window and peered through the slats of the shutters.

With the telltale sound of a man dismounting a steed, boots landed on the earth outside the door. Heavy footsteps approached.

Frantic, Fawn searched the small hut for a hiding space or a back door or any way to escape facing her husband. There was none. Asides, 'twas too late. Her mare was tethered outside, and there was little doubt the lord had not recognized her horse.

Bam! Bam! Bam! A huge fist pounded on the old timbers. Fawn's bones jarred with each horrifying knock.

"Open up," Jestin roared. "I know you be in there, Fawn. And you, witch woman, if you want not to be dragged back to the keep and tried for heresy, you'll not hide my wife!"

Fawn wanted to melt into the floor.

"I tell you true," Serena said, unshaken by the fact that she was being threatened. "You be carrying a boy child and his birth will be difficult, for he has not turned."

Fawn reached for the door handle.

"And, lady." Serena laid a hand upon the rough wool of Fawn's sleeve. "Your babe was conceived in lust by a dark, angry soldier who would slit your throat as easily as lie with you. Be careful."

"Nay, nay, you lie," Fawn insisted, jerking her arm away, her heart as cold as death with fear. "Shh. No more of this."

"Oh, for the love of St. Andrew!" A boot crashed into the door. The oak bolt shivered. Wood splintered. "Open up! Fawn, I know you're in there."

"Wait!" Steeling herself, Fawn lifted the bar with trembling hands and opened the door to find her husband, his face flushed and livid, his lips tight over his teeth, fury emanating from every pore of his body, glaring down at her in a pyre of self-righteous fury.

"And what be you doing here, wife? Tell me true," he demanded. A vein bulged in his forehead, and his gloved fists opened and closed as if he would like nothing more than to wring her neck.

Fawn drew in a deep breath and formed a lie, but no words escaped her lips. Pain ripped through her body. As excruciating as a stallion's kick to her abdomen, the agony robbed her of her breath. Her knees buckled. She nearly fell to the dirt floor. "Oh, God," she cried, closing her eyes and counting her heartbeats as the sharp agony slowly waned. Sagging against the doorway, she closed her eyes. "It matters not now, Jestin," she said as she gasped for breath and felt a rush of water flow from between her legs. "The babe—your son—is on his way."

Sheena slipped through the door of the ship's cabin and slowly climbed the stairs. The storm was behind them, the water still uneasy, the sky beginning to lighten through a thin mist. She'd rested, never slept and knew that she had to make good her escape before Keegan returned.

Though the wind no longer shrieked across the water, the air was cool and heavy with the smell of brine. The deck was slick and dark, the great masts spiring upward as the *Dark Sapphire* held a steady course.

Somehow she had to get off the ship. Now. While no one was watching over her. Before Keegan returned and she willingly fell into bed with him all over again. Oh, how had she been so foolish as to have made love to him, the boy who had abandoned her, a captain of a smuggler's ship, the man who was secretive and dark one minute, kind and engaging the next? Why did her inner soul scream that she was falling in love with him when she knew him to be a rogue and a blackheart, a man whose life was the sea?

"Because you be an idiot," she growled at herself, and refused to think of the painful emotions burning deep in her heart or the pleasant soreness between her legs. 'Twas daft to have such feelings, and she had no time to worry over them.

Stealing across the deck, she heard voices. Through the shadows of dawn she made out two figures, men who stood near the bow. Though she could not see their faces, she heard their words.

". . . you think the storm was not some kind of spell?" Tom asked, his meaty hands curled over the rail as he stared into the coming morn. The *Dark Sapphire* rocked as if in protest.

"Nay." Jasper shook his head, his hands moving frantically as he spoke. "'Twas but a storm, a bad one, but only a storm. I do not think ye can blame the lady or any kind of witchcraft for the rise of the wind or the anger of the waters. Only God Almighty controls that, and ye'd be smart to pay it heed."

"A woman aboard a ship is a curse," Tom insisted, though he seemed confused, his thick eyebrows drawn together as he battled inwardly against all he had held true. "'Tis known by all good men of the sea." Tom spat into the water as a gust of wind pressed his mantle to his body. "I know she saved Bo but . . . did she not sneak on board and try to hide? Did she not threaten to curse us all? Did not the captain send Wart to find out the truth about her? And by the gods, did he not become smitten with her, same as the rest of the crew?" Tom's voice was filled with worry. "Even Maynard is besotted. And the captain. He not be thinking straight. He's in love with her, plain as I'm tellin' ye. I can see it in his face, the way he looks for her, watches her when she be not lookin'. And that's what I'm tellin' ye, Jasper, no one but a witch could burrow into Keegan's heart."

Sheena didn't move. Her ears strained to hear over the wind, and she bit her lip. Was it possible? Could Keegan love her? Oh, nay, 'twas only Big Tom worrying aloud. He was a man who didn't trust any woman.

"'Tis full of it ye are," Jasper argued. "The captain, well, aye, I've seen him look at the woman with longing, but he'll not put any of us in jeopardy. Wart's gone, true, though I do not know why. But I do na think it has anythin' to do with the lady."

"Bah. Then 'tis a fool ye be, Jasper. I overheard the captain and Wart talkin', I did. And Keegan, he sent Wart to find out if she's that woman Tardiff's army is lookin' for. The one who kilt her husband. Captain Keegan, he wants to know if there's a price upon her head and how much it be so that he can ransom her."

Sheena's heart dropped.

"Would he do that if he was in love with her?"

"He wasn't at the time. Now 'twould be different."

Or would it? Sheena wondered, refusing to think of their lovemaking. Would Keegan give her up to Manning, though he knew the dark knight was brutal? Had he believed her when she'd confided to him about her wedding night, or had he thought her a liar? Did she mean nothing but a few coins to him? Sadness pierced her soul, though she told herself to put it aside, forget Keegan, and make her way off this cursed ship. She couldn't take the chance of trusting him. 'Twas a mistake she'd made once before.

"Keegan knows not what love is." Tom reached for a length of chain. "He dinna know his mother, and that wife of his betrayed him at every turn. He would not trust another woman, nay. That be why I say he be under a spell."

"A spell not strong enough to keep him from ransoming her back to those who be lookin' for her?" Jasper snorted again.

"Ach, I know not. But 'tis plain enough to me and every other man on this ship, Captain Keegan's not the same as he was before he met the woman. And even if she did save Bo's life, she's still treacherous, I tell ye. Mayhap more so as we all want to trust her. She did not come aboard and hide in the hold if she wasn't."

"A pity that," Jasper agreed. "If she be runnin' from somethin', I say she has a good reason. 'Tis not as if the rest of us don't have our own shadows chasin' us."

Big Tom shook his head. "But none of us jeopardize the safety of the *Sapphire*. We've all pledged to protect her. With the lady, 'tis different."

"Let's not be condemnin' her just yet."

"I'm just tellin' ye what I think."

"Well, we'll see, now, won't we? We dock in a few hours."

A few hours? She had only a few hours? And then what? Face Sir Manning? She glanced across the choppy water to the dark coastline, nearer than it had ever been on this journey.

The wind kicked up, and whatever further conversation the two men engaged in was lost to her ears. Not that it mattered. She knew only that she had to leave. She couldn't risk being dragged back to Ogof by Sir Manning and his army of cutthroats. Nor did she want to give Keegan a chance to betray her again.

Determination filled her soul. She could not run forever. Nay, she needed to face her father again, but she had to do it alone. Not as Sir Manning's prisoner. At the thought of the dark knight shackling her, humiliating her, leading her back to Ogof with her hands bound, she felt sick. 'Twas time to return. On her own. She would ride into the castle not a prisoner but a free woman determined to see her father. No longer would she run and look over her shoulder and hide like some night creature afraid of the light.

As damp strands of her hair blew across her face in the salty breeze and the prow of the ship knifed through the gray waters, Sheena realized she could not stay here with Keegan a moment longer. Whether he intended to turn her over to Manning or not, the truth of the matter was that she could not risk falling in love with him.

"Fool," she said under her breath and edged around the mainmast to look to the east and spy the shoreline not far off. Stealing the boat would be difficult, but she had to try. She waited until Jasper and Big Tom disappeared into the hold, then sneaked to the side of the ship where two rowboats were fastened down. Murmuring a quick prayer that she wouldn't be discovered, she untied the heavy ropes with nervous fingers.

"Give me strength," she prayed under her breath, hoping to lift the small craft, but it was heavy, barely moved as she pulled on its prow. *You can do it,* she told herself, trying again, muscles straining, but the damned rowboat didn't budge. Biting her lip, she stepped back and looked for a tool, a board, anything she could use to pry the boat away from the deck and into the sea, but there was nothing except for the pulleys and chains, which would cause too much noise and take too long. She reached into the boat, grabbed hold of one of the seats, and felt the old wood give.

The sky was getting lighter. She was running out of time. She heard men's voices and the shuffling of boots upon the deck. "Come on, come on," she said, trying yet again, her fingers wrapping around the nearly broken seat, her jaw set, her muscles straining. The boat didn't move, not one bloody inch. *Damn!* Clenching her teeth, her hands bleeding, she pulled once more. The seat creaked. She yanked. Wood splintered and the seat broke off in her hands.

Sweating, her muscles aching, she knew she had no chance with the fool boat. Nay, she would have to find another way. She looked up at the rigging, but found no salvation in the tall masts stretching up to the still, dark heavens. The sails were of no help. She quickly eyed the deck, found nothing to help her. "Bloody hell," she muttered. Determined to find a way off the ship, she leaned back against the railing.

"Ye need to rest." Hollis's voice rang over the decking.

"Aye, and I will." *Keegan. Lover. Traitor. Judas.* She scooted behind the stair-well as he approached. "But only for a few hours. Wake me before we dock."

"That I will," Hollis promised. "Do ye think Wart will be waitin'?"

"I hope so."

"If anyone can find out the truth, he will," Hollis said. "And he'll find out where the soldiers are, how big the army is, and what price is upon the woman's head—what ransom will be paid."

Keegan didn't argue.

So he would give her up. Sheena's heart sank as if it were tied to an anchor. Why would she think differently? she wondered as she hid and the two men passed. Had he not as a boy kissed her and then left her on the dock? Was this not the same? Only this time he'd done more than kiss her, he'd made love to her before offering her up to her enemies. A pang of disappointment knifed through her.

Well, he could curse and rot in hell for all she cared, she told herself.

But she could not stay on deck any longer. She had but a few minutes, then surely Keegan would find she was missing. All hell would break out. She had no doubt that Keegan would lock her in the cabin until they docked, and then, oh, dear God, would he really turn her over to Manning?

She couldn't risk it. She heard the door to the cabin open. She looked toward the shore, barely visible through the thin mist, but close enough to give her a chance. Without another thought she tossed off her mantle, hauled the broken piece of bench with her, and climbed to the deck.

"Bloody hell. Where is she?" she heard Keegan say, then, more loudly, "Search the ship!"

Swallowing back her fear, she climbed onto the railing and, before she thought twice, clutched the board to her chest and jumped.

Heart in her throat, she sailed through the air. Feet first she plunged into the swirling, icy water. *Bam!* Her chin hit the hard wood. Pain shot through her jaw. Her mind spun. Down she went, deep into the frigid darkness. Cold as ice, the salty water filled her mouth and nose, clutched at her dress and boots, dragged her downward into the darkness. Her lungs burned. She kicked, hard, upward, where there was so little light.

Her chin ached, the black waters swirled around her. Thoughts of all manner of horrid sea creatures, the very beasts Hollis claimed existed, tumbled through her mind, but she struggled hard, kicking, clinging to the damned piece of wood. *Don't worry about sea serpents,* her mind taunted, *you'll drown or freeze first.*

Her lungs were on fire. She kicked harder. Against the sea. Through the clinging folds of her dress. Ever upward. Her mind spun. Just as she thought she would lose consciousness, her head broke free and she gasped, choking, coughing, kicking madly away from the ship, which loomed much too near. The coast seemed miles away, a dark shadow stretching impossibly in the distance, but she hung onto the board for dear life, forcing her legs to move while the drag of the sea insisted on pulling against her.

Her boots were waterlogged, the stones still jammed tightly against her toes, the long skirt of her dress an anchor, but Sheena was determined to break free and return to Ogof to face her father and whatever brand of justice he would mete out.

Unless the cold sea claimed her first.

Never!

She kicked hard, clung to the board, and headed toward the rugged shoreline. The waves crashed over her, salt water drenched her and clogged her throat. Her mind spun and her body felt as if cold, sharp needles were piercing her skin.

Still she kicked.

Her legs were numb when she first heard her name, lost in the moan of the wind and the crash of the surf.

"Sheena!"

Oh, no. Her throat clogged as she recognized Keegan's voice screaming above the wind.

Go to hell, she thought, squeezing her jittery jaw shut and forcing her heavy legs to move. Tears sprang to her eyes. She saw something—another shadow on the water's surface.

Another wave crashed over her. The board slipped from her fingers. *Nay, sweet Mary, No!* She scrambled, tried to hold the slab of slippery wood, but the angry tide stripped the board from her frozen fingers.

Another wave pounded her. She screamed, swallowed water. Her body flopped forward, closer to the land. Choking, salt water burning her throat, she surfaced. Her arms flailed. Treacherous, foaming water was everywhere. Above. Below. She bobbed up again, spat salt and seaweed. Shivered. Again she was dragged under. Her foot scraped something. A rock. She tried to stand, only to be hurled forward.

Bang!

Her head crashed hard into the jagged rock hidden beneath the water's swirling surface.

Pain exploded behind her eyes.

Her body was tossed as if she were a rag doll. Her arms and legs were useless, the pain in her head blinding. One leg scraped against rough hidden shoals. She gulped water, spewed it up and then swallowed more.

Somewhere there was sky—the pale light of dawn visible in short flashes. Her arms wouldn't move. Her legs were dead. She caught a quick image of the shore, so far away, much, much too far. She would never be able to reach it.

Her body failed her. She couldn't move.

As the water dragged her under she thought of Keegan—tormentor, lover, blackheart. She would never see him again.

All was lost.

Chapter Ten

"Man overboard!" a deep voice boomed across the deck of the *Dark Sapphire*. "Get the boats! Hie! For the love of Christ! Man overboard!"

Keegan's heart plummeted to his knees. *Sheena!* He knew in an instant she'd either fallen or jumped overboard into the swirling, icy depths. Why? God in heaven, why? He raced to the edge of the ship and stared through the rising mist, searching for any sign of her. His gaze roved the sea, hoping to spy her struggling in the gray waves.

"Who?" Bo asked, sliding down the foremast and scrambling over the rigging to land at Keegan's feet. His face was ashen with fear, his mop of hair flat and wet from the mist.

"I don't know," Keegan lied.

"Would ya look at that? Someone ripped apart the rowboat! For the love of Mary, who would do such a thing?" Jasper muttered as all the deck hands scurried, like rats seeking higher ground on a sinking ship. Seamus unlashed one of the rowboats. Tom was working on the other. But Keegan was immobile, his heart dark with dread, every muscle in his body tense, as he squinted into the half-light of dawn.

"Where's the lady?" Maynard demanded.

"In the captain's cabin," Bo insisted.

"Nay." Keegan admitted what he most feared. "She's missing."

The boy blanched even whiter. Chains rattled as a rowboat was lowered.

"What the devil do ye think ye're doin'?" Hollis was beside him in an instant. "Ye can't go jumpin' in after her, Keegan. Think. If she wants to kill herself, well, so be it, but nothin' will be helped if you drown as well."

Ignoring the older man, Keegan kicked off his boots.

"Think, man," Hollis insisted, grabbing hold of the sleeve of Keegan's tunic. "There be no reason to—"

Keegan stripped off the damned tunic, climbed onto the rail, searched the deadly whitecaps, then dove.

"Nay!" Hollis cried.

The sea came at him like an angry, frigid mistress, full of fury and wrath, devouring him. Ice water hit his skin. Salt spray filled his nostrils. He dived deep into the darkness, then kicked upward to the surface, where the roiling water had not an ounce of mercy.

"Sheena!" he screamed. Gray light stretched over the waves. "Sheena, by God—" But his voice was lost over the roar and rush of the sea tumbling ever toward the shore.

He treaded water, turning in a wide arc, squinting toward the shore. His teeth began to rattle with the cold, but inside he was on fire with anger and fear. God's eyes, how could she have been so foolish? The ocean was a sure tomb, a watery grave.

His heart wrenched in a newfound pain. He'd lost a wife already, and though he'd loved her once, that love had been tarnished and betrayed, but this—this feeling of sheer panic and desperation was new to him. It tore at his soul, played havoc with his mind, screamed through his body.

She couldn't be lost. *Couldn't!*

He would find her if it took his last dying breath!

"Sheena!" he screamed again. "Sheena, oh, for the love of God, answer!"

He strained to hear, over the wild thudding of his heart and the crescendo of the sea endlessly pounding the shore, but the only other sound he heard was the clank of chains, the call of voices from the ship urging him to swim back to the safety of the *Dark Sapphire*, screaming for him to wait for the rowboat that was being launched.

Still he swam, keeping his head above the waves, choking on gulps of cold, salty water, feeling his hope ebb as the minutes passed. Why did she fling herself into the sea? Not to kill herself, nay, she was too strong of mind for that, but to escape him and the uncertainty of the docking.

Bloody Christ, it was his fault.

Her death would be because of him.

"Noooo!"

His throat closed as he thought of their lovemaking, so recent, so warm, so filled with passion.

"Sheena! For the love of God, answer me!"

He prayed, his body growing numb, his jaw quivering. For the first time since the dark years, he prayed as he tried to stay afloat, his eyes ever searching.

Please, Father, if you're listening, save her. Take me, but, please, see her safely to the shore and far from the horrors of Tardiff.

Shaking, teeth chattering, breath short and fast, he felt his muscles rebel. He'd had little sleep, had manned the helm and fought the sea most of the night. In the hours he was to rest, he'd been with Sheena—hotblooded virgin. Murderess. Thief. Liar. Stowaway. Lover. His mind spun and he called her name until he was hoarse, and when he opened his mouth, no words came.

He was cold to his bones, yet he felt nothing in his arms and legs. 'Twas as if they were not attached. Water sprayed in his nose, and he coughed as he rotated slowly, scanning every inch of the horizon as he fought the urge to close his eyes.

"There he is!" Hollis's voice came as if from a distance over the dull roar that invaded his mind, penetrated his soul. "Row. Faster. Holy Father, he's about done in. Bloody fool." Keegan tried to swim closer to the shore, but the rowboat was upon him and strong arms surrounded him.

"Nay . . ." he croaked out, his world upside down, his only intent to save the woman he loved.

"Pull him in." Hollis's disgusted voice again. "I'm tellin' ye, I'm sick to death of savin' his sorry skin, I am. But do it and be quick about it."

Someone—no, not one but two big men—dragged him into the small craft and dropped him into the bottom as if he were fish caught in a net.

"Now, row back to the ship. Quickly," Hollis commanded, his voice brooking no argument. The tiny boat moved, tossed about, but Keegan didn't care, couldn't lift his head.

"Captain, stay with us!" Who was that? Seamus?

"We're losin' him, sure." Another voice far away, as if Jasper were at the far end of a long tunnel and calling to him. "Captain, ye'll be all right."

Cold. It was so damned cold. Shivering, clutching himself, thinking of making love to her . . . over and over again . . .

"Where's the lady?" Was it Bo's voice raised in fear? "We cannot go back without her!"

"Row!" Hollis ordered again. "Bloody Christ, men, throw yer damned backs into it!"

"But we cannot leave her!"

"Enough! Shut up, Bo, and row, for the love of God. She's dead already most likely."

"Nay, we must find her, we must—"

There was a scuffle of sorts, and the boy was yelling, screaming, kicking, the boat pitching. Keegan's mind faded in and out, taking him to another time, long ago, on the dock in the cove when first he'd kissed her. *Sheena, oh, love, you were the first . . . and the last . . . And I failed you yet again. Again he was fifteen, full of piss and eager for adventure. Again he was in a bobbing craft fighting for his life, certain that he would never see her again. He felt the sting of the arrow, the curse of her words . . . the pressure of her sweet, sweet lips to his.*

"We'll all drown, you little bugger," Jasper was saying. Or was it Jasper? Keegan could no longer tell. "Now, forget the lady. What's done is done. It's the captain we've got to save."

Keegan tried to argue but only coughed. Didn't know where he was, didn't care, but the weight on his heart, heavy as an anchor, wouldn't leave, trapped the air in his lungs, reminded him that he'd let her go, lost her, the one woman he'd loved. . . .

Someone, Keegan couldn't tell who, threw a heavy wool mantle over him and he lay, shivering, coughing, certain Sheena had died. Because of him. Guilt burrowed in hot, painful holes through his brain. 'Twas his fault she'd jumped, his fault she was now at the bottom of the sea. 'Twas his destiny to forever fail her.

The boy was crying, soft, muffled sobs, and the small boat rocked over the water. Keegan tried to fight the urge to give in to sleep, to the welcome, mind-numbing blackness that threatened him. He was the captain. He had to man the ship. He had to find Sheena, be she dead or alive. But the fight was out of him, and the blackness was soft and seductive, a spell of tranquility that was cast upon him, rolling like the tide and drawing ever closer, blocking out all hint of light until he fought no longer and willingly gave himself up to the peace of unconsciousness.

"Do not push!" Serena ordered as Fawn lay on her small bed amid the chickens and drying herbs in the fortune-teller's hut. Jestin paced through the small shack, his hands clasped behind his back, his eyes averted as if seeing the birth of his own child were unclean. Instead of being a part of the birthing, he glowered into the fire, watching as the embers burned low, the flames reflected in his eyes.

Pain cleaved through Fawn's body. She was being ripped in two, torn apart. Sweating, silently cursing, feeling the horrid pressure with each cramp, she clenched her fists and tried not to cry out. This pain, 'twas worth it. For her son. The next baron, not only of Ogof but Tardiff as well. Aye, she would endure anything for the boy.

"Breathe slowly, do not push."

"I'm not!" she snapped, angry at the fortune-teller, though the woman was but trying to help her bring the babe into the world. "I—I have had three children. Never had I had such horrible . . . oh, sweet Mother." She began to breathe in shallow little bursts of air, braced herself. Sheer agony screamed through her again, blinding, shrieking pain. "Ooohhhh, bloody hell!" she cried out. "By the gods, what's happening?"

Serena, that fool, was at the foot of the bed, attempting to help with the baby, but her quiet words and steady hands were not enough. Something was wrong. Horribly, painfully wrong.

Sweat poured down from Fawn's forehead, drenching her hair, soaking the bedclothes. Blood and water soiled the bed, and yet the babe did not come. "Call for the midwife!" she demanded.

"'Tis too late." Serena's face pulled into a tight pucker of concentration, as if it had been drawn by an invisible and worried string.

"But something's amiss, I feel it, oh, oh, ooooooo!" God in heaven, she couldn't endure much more of this. Each second felt like an eternity in hell.

"'Tis not right," Serena said nervously.

"Make it right!" The Baron of Ogof turned on his heel. "No son of mine is going to die before he's born. You bring him into this world healthy and robust!"

"Aye, m'lord, I am trying."

"'Tis not good enough to try," Jestin growled. "Do it. Do it now and I will forget that you practice the dark arts, that you cast spells and see into the future and are a heathen. Elsewise, if this babe is not born healthy and strong, I will blame you. And trust me, my justice will be swift and harsh."

Fawn moaned in excruciating agony. Morning light streamed through the solitary window, and yet the Lady of Ogof was certain she had fallen into the darkest bowels of hell.

Something tore.

"It's near," the seer proclaimed, her face sheened in sweat, worry drawing lines upon her forehead.

"He," Fawn corrected, desperately. *"He!"* The baby was crowning, she was sure of it. Pressure pounded through her body, squeezed her brain. At last. She began to push, her body convulsing, trying to expel the infant.

"Not yet, 'tis not the head . . . nay, do not push!" Serena ordered, but it was too late. Fawn could no longer control herself. Her body worked feverishly to rid itself of the babe.

"'Tis time, Serena," she gasped, and then screamed so loudly several of the chickens flapped wildly in the rafters overhead. The cat leaped through the open window. Feathers drifted downward.

Flesh tore, blood flowed, pain the like of which Fawn had never felt wrenched all of her organs. Certain she would die right there on the table, she moaned pathetically. The seer pressed her hand over Fawn's abdomen, pushing gently, whispering "God help us all" in a voice so low Fawn barely heard the words. Ever so slowly the baby came into the world, buttocks first.

"'Tis a boy," Serena said as the babe let out a lusty cry and Jestin turned to look at his wife for the first time since striding into the small, dirty hut.

"A son," he whispered proudly, his throat catching. A smile grew from one side of his stern face to the other. 'Twas as if heaven itself had touched him, for the adoration on his face was pure, nearly holy. "Thank God." He blinked rapidly against a bath of tears.

"Aye." Fawn managed a weak smile when she saw the dark-haired infant. Red-faced and screaming he was. Oh, the babe was fine and strong and would be as handsome and brave as his sire—a true warrior. "A son." Relief washed over her as surely as if she'd been bathed by a dozen handmaids.

Her husband, who had been ready to strangle her but a few hours before, was moved to tears. His throat worked and he took his wife's hand in his. His thumb rubbed the top of her palm, and his voice was rough with emotion. "I . . . Oh, wife . . . I have waited long for this moment."

"I as well, Jestin," Fawn vowed. "This one, he be your issue, your heir."

She noticed the cursed fortune-teller stiffen as she cut the cord cleanly, tied it off, and swaddled the babe in an old towel. Serena's lips had tightened, but she kept her eyes averted. She would hold her tongue or lose her life.

"At last." Jestin stared at the red-faced baby as if he were the only child on earth, and when Fawn took her son to her breast, the Baron of Ogof looked on proudly. "We shall name him Daffyd," he said. "'Twas my father's name."

Cuddling the baby close, Fawn shook her head. Wet ringlets fell into her eyes. The babe nuzzled and found her nipple. Latching on, her son sucked so hard Fawn drew in a whistling breath, then said, "Nay, husband, I have thought long on what we should call him. Let his name be as courageous as he will be." She smiled up at her husband. "I say we name him Llywelyn after the great one."

Serena gasped, but quickly disguised it with a cough.

"Llywelyn," Jestin repeated, not spying the sorceress's surprise. Thinking hard and rolling the name around on his tongue, he winked at his wife. "Llywelyn of Ogof." He nodded, as if liking the sound of it. "Aye, wife. So be it. Llywelyn he be." Jestin gently touched the babe's head of fine black hair. "He is not fair like our daughters," he thought aloud, and Fawn's heart stopped for a second. "But my father, his hair was dark as well. A strapping man he was, a true warrior as little Llywelyn will someday be."

"Aye," Fawn agreed hastily. She held her boy child close, for he was her promise, her future, her entire reason for living. This one, he was destined to rule. But not only Ogof and Tardiff, nay, those baronies were not nearly enough. This boy would someday drive fear into the hearts of the English and rule all of Wales.

* * *

Keegan's head throbbed, his body ached, and as he opened a weary eye, he knew something was terribly wrong. The ship was still. There was no movement of the sea, but that wasn't what caused him concern. Nay, there was a deeper trouble, a weight pressing hard on his chest.

And then he remembered. With razor-sharp clarity memories of Sheena sliced into his brain, and the painful thought that she'd died in the sea caused him to suck in his breath.

"So ye are alive." Hollis was in the room, braced against the wall, his old, wrinkled face illuminated by a single candle in the lantern. "I thought ye might be stirrin' soon."

"Where are we?"

"We've docked, Keegan. The ship is sound. We've cargo to unload and some to take on, but we've done nothin' yet. We were waitin' fer you to wake up."

"You might have waited a long time," Keegan observed, realizing he'd been close to death as he sat up and the headache thundering behind his eyes worsened. He looked past the old man to a hook by the door where a dress hung— the blue velvet that was to have been Brynna's but Sheena had worn. He remembered seeing her for the first time in that gown, her red hair tumbling in soft curls to the shoulders, her eyes as blue as the plush fabric, her shoulders stiff with indignity. There had been other times as well, when she'd stood on the deck and the wind had billowed the skirts, or when she'd been undressing, unlacing the bodice with her back turned to him and he'd seen the slope of her shoulders, the curve of her spine, once, the dimples just above the cleft of her buttocks. . . .

"What of Sheena?" he asked, ignoring the pain pounding at his temples and blazing in his muscles.

"She was lost."

"Her body?" he asked, his heart heavy with denial.

Hollis shook his head, his old speckled pate reflecting the lamplight. "Nay. We found no trace of her."

Keegan hadn't expected any better and rubbed a weary hand over his face. He felt a hundred years old. The heaviness in his chest pressed hard against his heart. Never in his life had he known such sadness, such grief. Not even when his father had been killed. This loss was deeper and, he knew, more dangerous, for it played with his mind. Though he'd grieved Rourke's passing, he'd been a child mourning a parent. 'Twas a different agony from this; he now felt that he'd been clawed and gutted from the inside out, that the wounds from which he bled were invisible but carved deep into his soul, far deeper than the pain inflicted by the sea.

He forced himself to his feet and was light-headed but for a second. "Let us start unloading," he said without any enthusiasm, with no speck of life, but another thought struck him. "What of Wart? Has he boarded?"

"Not yet."

"How long have we been docked?"

"Six hours."

"And he has not come aboard?" Keegan asked. 'Twas odd. Wart was loyal and true, had never once been delayed. Though he loved a good pint and a coy smile, Wart had put duty before pleasure many a time. He frowned, glanced at the older man. "'Tis unlike him."

"Aye." Hollis hesitated. He looked at his fingers for a second as if he was troubled but could not easily voice his concerns.

"What is it?" Keegan demanded, rubbing a temple.

"There be another . . . situation."

"What?" Keegan wasn't interested. He found his mantle, hung near Sheena's dress, and as he reached for it, his fingers brushed against the soft fabric. An image flashed behind his eyes, and he saw her as he had the last night they were together, when he'd given in to his desire for her, kissed her and ended up making love to her in this very cabin. He remembered her lips, rounding with surprise as he'd entered her, the hunger of her kisses, the firmness of her breasts, snowy white and tipped with perfect pink nipples. . . . Sweet Jesus, how could he miss her so badly?

Throwing on his mantle, he forced himself to dispel her image, for 'twould do no good to dwell upon it. She was gone. Lost at sea. Driven to her own death because of him.

His jaw clenched so hard it ached. "What else is wrong?" he demanded, reaching for his boots.

"'Tis the soldiers from Tardiff. They want to board and search for Sheena."

"Bloody Christ. Already?" Keegan, ready for a fight, grabbed his dagger and tucked it into his belt.

"They were waiting."

"How did they know we were to dock here?"

"I know not."

Angrily Keegan pulled on his boots. "They be relentless."

"Their lord was killed."

And Sheena died as well. His throat grew thick.

"Sir Manning, he awaits ye."

"Does he?" Keegan's smile was without any humor; his head pounded and his blood knew a new vengeful lust. Aye, he would love a fight. His fingers curled over the hilt of his blade, and his muscles bunched in anticipation of battle with the man who had chased Sheena to the ground. He'd love to strangle Manning's thick neck.

"He wants to search the ship. He's brought a sheriff from the nearest keep with him."

"All well and good," Keegan agreed with more than a trace of sarcasm. He flung open the door of the cabin and stormed up the short flight of stairs to the deck. The brutish knight had already boarded, and along with a small band of his men was a fat, surly-looking man who glared at Keegan.

But Keegan's gaze was centered on Sir Manning. He'd aged over the years but was still as dark and swarthy as he had been on the day that he'd pinned Rourke's hand to the table, nailing him to his fate. Aye, a beast of a knight. Tall and thick-chested, strong as an ox with black hair and a cruel mouth, he seemed as anxious for a fight as did Keegan. "We needs search your ship, Captain Keegan," Manning stated flatly. "We have reason to believe that Lady Sheena of Tardiff is on your ship, and she is to be returned to stand trial for the murder of her husband, the baron." His chin hitched toward his companion. "I've the authority of—"

"Then do so," Keegan invited without a smile, his aching muscles tense, ready to lunge if the chance arose. "There is no woman aboard. I harbor no criminals. But search quickly. We have much to unload and cargo to take on. Two of my men"—he glanced around to the crew, most of whom had gathered on the deck beneath the masts—"you, Seamus, and Hollis as well as myself will accompany you."

"Ye need not bother," Manning said.

Keegan knew his grin was pure evil as he watched Manning's expression turn cunning. The promise of a fight crackled through the air and Keegan embraced it. "'Twill be no bother," he assured the man who was now and forever his enemy. "No bother at all."

Sheena's head throbbed, her body ached, and the world swam before her eyes. Where was she? What had happened? Why did she feel as if she'd been trampled by every last steed in the stables of Ogof?

"She be comin' 'round, Freddy," a woman said, and Sheena tried to open her eyes but couldn't.

"Is that right?" A man's voice. Nasal, disapproving. "About time. I was sure she was dead."

"Near enough. 'Ere ye go, missy. Open up." Sheena felt a spoon pressed to her lips, and then a bit of salty fish broth slid over her tongue to her throat. "Come on, eat a bit, won't ya, girl? 'Tis good fer ye, a bit o' soup."

The man snorted. Feet shuffled and somewhere not far away pigs grunted.

Sheena opened one eyelid with effort. The dim light in the room pierced right to her brain. "Oohh," she whispered, and slammed the eye shut again.

"Now, come on, will ye? Try again, missy. 'Ere ye go." Another drop of soup slid down her throat, and her memory unlocked. She'd escaped the *Dark Sapphire*, jumped into the sea and thought she was drowning. Somehow she must've survived, for if this was God's idea of heaven, he had a very large sense of humor.

Again she opened an eye, and this time her blurry vision focused on the kindly, fleshy face of a woman dressed in drab brown. Tiny eyes at odds with an oversized nose peered back at her. A wide grin, showing off spaces where several teeth were missing, stretched from one plump, vein-riddled cheek to the other. "There ye are . . . see, that wasn't so bad, now was it?"

Sheena stretched, tried to sit up, felt another rip of pain sear through her head, and froze.

"Take it easy, now, lass. Ye've been through a lot, ye 'ave. Me husband Freddy hauled ye out of the sea jest as ye went under. He was out fishin', he was, and pulled ye into his boat."

"That I did. Took ye to the beach," the man agreed. "Laid ye on the sand, but ye didn't move, just lay there like a one-legged crab all curled in on yerself and bruised from 'ead to toe."

"Aye," the woman agreed. "Half dead ye were, but he carried ye here and I've been tendin' to ye ever since."

For the first time Sheena realized that she was in some kind of rough dressing gown, lying on ticking that covered a pallet spread upon the floor. Her dress and chemise were hung on a cord near the fire, pools of water shimmering on the dirt floor beneath the sodden clothing. Her precious boots with their hidden treasure were nowhere to be seen. Panic shot through her cold blood.

"Nay," she cried, pushing up to a sitting position despite her throbbing head and scanning the small wooden building with a fireplace on one end, no windows, but a door that led to what Sheena assumed was a pigsty from the grunts, oinks, and snorts that could be heard through the cracks and knotholes. "My boots—"

"All of yer things are bein' cared for," the woman assured her. She was holding a mazer of fish broth in one hand and a spoon in the other as she squatted over Sheena. "I washed yer dress and under dress, but methinks they may be ruined by the salt water and rocks. As fer yer boots, we—the husband and I—we polished them. Found yer jewels we did. Rest assured that they be safe."

Sheena wasn't certain, but she reminded herself it mattered little. She had nearly drowned in the sea, was lucky to be alive, and had Freddy the pig farmer to thank for it, though it appeared he wasn't too happy about having a guest.

"Who are ye, lass?" he asked, his bushy eyebrows drawing together into a thick line over eyes that were more oval than round. His beard was thin, his cheeks pockmarked, his skin boasting a rash. "What were ye doin' in the tide, eh?"

"Hush, she just awoke. She need not answer yet," the woman said kindly.

"That's the trouble with ye, Esme, you be trustin' everyone, takin' in strays we don't need. What if she stole them jewels, what then?"

"They're mine," Sheena said, her throat raw, her words raspy. "They . . . they belonged to my mother."

"And yer name?"

She couldn't trust this man. Though he'd saved her life and dragged her back to his hut, she dared not admit her true identity. Even now the soldiers from Tardiff could be lurking nearby, searching the villages, fields, and forests for her. "I'm Victoria of Rhydd," she said as if the name had rolled off her tongue all her life. "I was traveling by ship and was washed overboard in last night's storm."

"Bless the saints that ye lived," the woman said, crossing herself quickly and slopping some of the broth onto her apron. "'Tis a miracle."

"Why were ye on the deck in the likes of that tempest?" Freddy asked, eyeing her suspiciously. "'Ave ye no brains?"

Sheena bristled but held her tongue. Let him consider her a twit; 'twould help her. "'Twas a mistake," she said through clenched teeth.

"And nearly cost ye yer life."

"But it didn't. 'Twas lucky that ye were out fishin' so early and ye found her, Freddy, but find her ye did. 'Tis God's will that she arrived 'ere." Esme set the mazer of soup on a small table and rocked back on her heels.

"Oh, woman, don't be goin' on about the will o' God to me. I do na believe in such nonsense." He threw up a big red hand and shook his head. "'Tis not the will o' God that I be raisin' a mean sow and litter of runty piglets. Na, I do na think so and don't be startin' in about God makin' ye barren to punish ye, I'll not hear it." He reached for a ragged hat that hung on a peg near the back door, then glanced over his shoulder. "Unless the good Lord has brought ye to us, lassie, and meant fer me to save ye so that ye could give me one of yer gems. Now, that I'd believe. Maybe he's makin' it up to me that me prize boar, Old Jack, died last winter before he could get the sow with piglets." Freddy's eyes narrowed on Sheena. "Aye, if there be God's work here today, it's to pay me back for years of breakin' me back working the fields, listenin' to the woman here go on and on, and givin' me such poor luck with me pigs." He jammed his hat on his head and walked through the heavy door. "I'll take care of the sow, then I'm off to the alehouse."

Grunts, squeals, and snorts greeted him, and a stench like no other stole into the room. Freddy shut the door firmly behind him, as if to cut off any reprimands from his wife.

Sighing with strained patience, Esme deftly made a swift sign of the cross over her bosom. "He is an angry man, Freddy is," she said simply. "No sons to help him with the farm. Nor daughters." She wrung her hands, then wiped them on her dirty apron and stood. "Sleep now, Victoria. When ye awake again, I'll help ye wash and then ye'll eat some more to get yer strength back."

Too exhausted to argue, Sheena slept fitfully, dozing in and out. She woke to the sound of pigs squealing or the off-key humming of the big woman as she went about her work, stoking the fire, turning the clothes on the line, baking bread over the flames, or stirring her stew pot—a black iron caldron that hung by a hook over the flames.

Hours and minutes blended together. Dreams mixed with what was real, and Keegan the bastard, Keegan the rogue, Keegan her love was ever on her mind.

When Sheena finally awoke fully, she blinked and banished all thoughts of the *Dark Sapphire*'s captain from her mind. Cautiously she raised herself on one elbow and winced at the pain throbbing through her jaw. At least her headache and blurred vision had fled.

"Awake now, are ye?" Esme asked, stirring the simmering pot. "Hungry?"

As if in answer Sheena's stomach rumbled.

The older woman chuckled. "I thought so. 'Tis a good sign, y'see." She found a wooden bowl and ladled some of the stew into it. As Sheena started to get to her feet, Esme shook her head. "No need to get up, lassie, I'll be bringin' this to ya." She rose to her own feet and carried over the steaming bowl. "Can ye take it in yer hands?"

"Aye," Sheena said, and was rewarded with the wooden dish. The smells of fish and spices tingled her nostrils as she began to sip, slowly at first and then, as the warm broth slid easily down her throat, more hungrily. "I'll be gettin' ye some bread to go with that." And within minutes the woman had sliced off a thick slab of wastel and slathered it in butter. Sheena bit into the hard bread and thought it the best she'd ever eaten. Esme's graying eyebrows lifted a bit as if she was anticipating praise.

"'Tis good," Sheena said, nodding and taking another bite. Around the mouthful she added, "Very good."

"Ah, it's nice to have me cookin' appreciated. Freddy . . . well, he's used to it, 'e is." She glanced at the window and noticed the sky had become dark. "'E's been gone long." One big shoulder elevated a mite. "But 'tis 'is way. Now, I bet you'd like to take a look at yer gems, wouldn't ye?"

"Aye." Sheena nodded and finished her soup. Esme padded slowly to the fire, retrieved the boots, and dropped them by the pallet. "Inside they are both of 'em."

"Both?" Sheena's heart sank.

"Aye. A ruby and an emerald. Fit for a queen, ain't they?"

"Well, yes, but—" Sheena reached into the boot, felt around and pulled out the two stones, one dark green, the other blood red. Her fingers searched the entire toe area but found no other gem. "There were three."

"Three?" Esme frowned, her lips folding out thoughtfully.

"Yes, an emerald, a ruby, and a topaz," Sheena said, her heart pounding. Had the stone dropped from her boot as she'd been tossed in the sea? Had it fallen when she'd been carried here to this hut, far from the beach where she'd washed up, or had it been stolen?

"Freddy, he told me there were two in the boot, and sure enough, when I got ye undressed, I found 'em."

"There was another one. A gold stone."

"Are ye sure, lassie? Ye took a knock on the 'ead fer sure, and there be no other gem lodged in either boot." Sheena reached into the second boot, and, as Esme had predicted, her fingers found only damp leather. The gem was missing.

"Ye could 'ave dreamed up the third jewel," Esme said, and took her soup bowl, unconcerned at Sheena's loss.

"Nay, 'twas in my boot."

"Not when ye got here. Took 'em both off ye, I did. There was only two stones. The red and the green." She squatted down close to the pallet. "Ye be a lucky person, Victoria. Very lucky. Not only did ye survive the storm and the sea, but ye've got two precious gems, more wealth than me or my Freddy will see in a lifetime." She glanced at the window, and worry drew thin lines around her mouth and eyes. "He should have come home by this time. There be much to do on the morrow—grain that needs be cut and more fishin', as he cut his trip short this morn when he found ye in the waves." With a heavy sigh of the truly persecuted, she turned to Sheena. Esme pointed a thick, square-tipped finger at the end of Sheena's nose. "Ye can be thankin' the Lord above that we be honest good people." There was the hint of hardness in her gaze as she stared at Sheena. "Mayhap we should pray together; thank the Father that you're alive, in óne piece, and that ye've got your treasure." She made the sign of the cross and bowed her head. From the other side of the plank door a pig grunted and another one squealed.

Sheena didn't argue any further. She didn't know what had happened to the gem, if it had been lost in the sea or stolen by a poor pig farmer, but it was lost to her forever. Esme was right; 'twas fortunate that she was alive.

And then the man she'd pushed out of her thoughts returned with a vengeance, galloping through her mind.

Keegan.

Oh, love. Traitor.

Her heart squeezed painfully, for she knew she would never see him again.

Mayhap it was for the best.

Or the worst.

Chapter Eleven

The farmer was drunk.

And loud.

The most boisterous man in a tavern that teemed with merchants, peasants, soldiers, and the like. A troupe of musicians was trying to entertain. One
was plucking dutifully at a lute, another blew into a pipe, while another, a slim
woman with a sad face, was attempting to sing a ballad of sorts. But the din of
the patrons drowned out whatever sounds they made. The farmer, dressed in
tatters, was by far the noisiest of the lot. Laughing and joking, drinking cup
after cup of ale, he was working very hard at making an ass of himself.

And Manning was not in the mood for it.

The night had been fruitless. He'd boarded the damned ship with its smug
captain and was certain he'd find the woman. Though there were spaces
aplenty in the hold to store men or women, he'd found nothing. But the captain's cabin had been a different matter, and there had been evidence of a
woman; dresses hung by the door. He claimed they belonged to his wife, but
rumor had it she was long dead.

There was something about the man that bothered Manning, something
vaguely familiar. The dark-haired captain tugged at Manning's memory, as if
the knight had met him before. The ship, too, was a puzzlement. With a name
not unlike the damned ring that Fawn had been mewling about for years, the
Dark Sapphire bothered him. Could it be? He narrowed his eyes into his cup
and didn't like the link that was forming in his mind. He didn't like it at all.

He tossed back his ale, then snapped his fingers at a buxom barmaid to
refill his mazer. The music irritated him. He drummed his fingers on the long
plank tables as the serving girl filled his cup and offered him more than a
casual glance at the cleft between those big breasts. Aye, they were inviting,
spilling over the neckline of her dress as they were. But he wasn't in the mood

for a flirtation or even an attempt to lift her skirts, though he assumed 'twould be easy enough. The girl kept her eye on him and smiled fetchingly, the very tip of her tongue rimming her lips when she caught his glance. Aye, she would serve a man and serve him well.

But Manning had not the time or the inclination.

Where was Sheena? Still aboard the *Dark Sapphire*, stowed in some hiding spot he and the paunchy sheriff had overlooked?

He took a long draught of ale, ignored the serving wench, and half listened to the drunken farmer rave on and on about a turn in his fortune. Probably a man who planted by the phases of the moon.

Blast it all!

"Can I get ye ennythin' else, sir?" the barmaid asked as she rested a plump hip on the edge of the table and spoke directly to Manning. "Somethin' to eat?"

"I be fine."

"Ah, and there be no denyin' that," she said with a smile and a lift of one sultry dark eyebrow.

"You're a bold chit."

"When I have to be." She poured more ale into Manning's near-empty cup.

"Hey! Wench. Over here. We be dyin' of thirst!" the farmer yelled, flagging her and waving her over. The men around him, dressed in filthy rags such as his, laughed raucously. "Another pitcher and one fer me friends."

Manning's eyes narrowed on the man. The farmer was far too generous for his station in life. But Manning could not think on it. Not now. He had his own problems. He was certain Sheena was or had been on the *Dark Sapphire*. There were many secrets hidden in that cursed ship's hold, none of which Manning had uncovered. He'd left the brooding captain and the damned ship, then once out of earshot, had posted a guard. The soldier would hide on the dock and watch, keeping track of anyone who attempted to board or leave the anchored vessel. Manning had also instructed the spy to make note of any large crates or bundles that were roomy enough to hide a small woman. If somehow in his search he'd missed Sheena, she wouldn't get off the ship without his knowledge.

Caught in the turn of his thoughts, he slowly sipped from his cup as the music, laughter, and gaiety danced in the air surrounding him. He couldn't dismiss what was becoming more evident.

Manning was convinced that Keegan was indeed the son of Rourke, the captain who had tried to cheat Baron Jestin years earlier. Though Rourke had died, the boy and an old man had escaped.

With the Dark Sapphire of Ogof.

'Twas blasphemy to name the ship after the stolen stone. Idly, Manning wondered if Keegan still owned the jewel that was rumored to be cursed, the blue stone of such myth and legend. Oh, 'twould be sweet revenge if Manning were to lay his hands on the gem. He would pocket it and never mention the stone to Jestin or Fawn.

But first he had to find it.

Along with Sheena. Scowling, he swirled his mazer and stared at the beer sloshing in the cup. That woman had proven him and his troops to be fools. She'd eluded them, evaded them, and seemed to disappear each time they came close to her. God's eyes, all of Tardiff and Ogof were probably laughing that one small woman could outsmart his army.

If only the ship's spy had lived. Mayhap Warren of Halliwell could have given him some more insight, but the poor sod had decided to give up the ghost before Manning's whip had even started to pry open the weak man's tongue.

Another bad turn of fortune.

"Aye! Fill the cups, that's a girl," the farmer crowed and pinched the wench's butt through her skirts as she walked past balancing a tray holding six cups. She started, squealed a bit, and foam sloshed down the sides of the mazers.

"Are ye sure about this, Freddy?" she asked. "'Tis quite a few."

"Get on with it." He showed off a toothy grin. "Old Freddy's luck has changed."

"How so?"

Manning shifted, kept the farmer in his sights. The man was well into his cups and swayed a bit, his speech slurred. "Ah, 'tis me secret," he said, then laughed loudly as the musicians started another song.

Manning wanted to cut out the braggart's tongue, then stuff it down his throat. The smelly, filthy farmer was obnoxious.

Laughing loudly, clapping his friends on the back, grinning widely, his pockmarked face beaming as if he'd just struck gold, he settled onto a stool. There were others in the tavern, a sorry lot of peasants who had spent their entire lives scraping out a living from the soil, paying the lord his due, living from one year to the next, and praying the weather held, his pigs, cattle, and sheep had healthy offspring, and that there was someone who was willing to buy his crops and animals just so he could do it all again the next year.

'Twas a pathetic life, in Manning's opinion. But then, he was an ambitious man. Mayhap too ambitious. His arm ached from flogging the unlucky bastard who'd been spying upon his encampment. The one-thumbed man had just up and collapsed with only a few blows. He'd cried out and stiffened, clutching his chest, his knees buckling. His face had twisted in horrid agony, and he'd been unable to draw in a breath. 'Twas as if his heart had just given out. Before Manning had gotten the information he wanted from him. All he had learned was where the *Dark Sapphire* was docked. Nothing more.

"Come on, Freddy, what is it?" the wench asked, trailing her finger around the pockmarked farmer's neck. "What kind of good luck befell ye, eh?"

"Ah, 'twas a gift from heaven. Brought by an angel." The farmer's tongue had been loosened by too much ale and the thought that he might be able to bed the comely serving wench.

"Bah!" one of his friends said. "An angel, ye say?"

"'Tis true." Freddy nodded emphatically as more ale was poured and sloshed. A fire crackled, giving off heat from one end of the room.

"Let him finish!" The bar wench left her hand resting on Freddy's ragged collar. "What angel?"

"Found 'er 'alf dead in the ocean. Goin' down to her death she was when I plucked her up and—"

Manning's ears picked up. He set down his cup. Focused on the filthy man.

"—and so thankful she was fer me takin' her home and savin' 'er life, she gave me somethin'."

"What?" The wench leaned closer, breathed something into Freddy's ear, and the man actually blushed. With stained, dirty fingers he dug deep in one of his pockets and pulled out a stone—a bright yellow stone that Manning recognized. 'Twas part of Sheena's dowry, given to Tardiff from Jestin.

Manning's pulse jumped.

"Oooh, 'tis a beaut," the girl said enviously.

Several of the farmer's friends whispered among themselves. Other eyes watched as well, and Manning thought there was a good chance Freddy's throat would be slit and his treasure stolen from him before he staggered back to his hut that night. But Manning would see that it wouldn't happen. Nay, he and his small army would be the farmer's guardian angels, for they would ensure that he got safely home.

Once at the farm, they'd remove this stone from Freddy's grimy fingers, take the others as well, and put that damned elusive wench in chains before hauling her back to Ogof.

A smile of triumph twisted across Manning's jaw. His palms sweated in anticipation. Silently advising himself to be patient, he slowly finished his drink and observed the farmer through guarded eyes. Finally, it seemed, Manning's luck was beginning to turn.

"I'll not stay here another second," Fawn insisted. She was lying in the fortune-teller's bed, and the darkness made the hut seem gloomier than ever. In the feeble light from a candle and the dying fire, the bleached bones and talons of dead animals seemed more sinister than they had during the day. The hut was filled with the presence of evil and was no place for a baby, any baby, and certainly not hers—not this boy child who would, she was certain, someday rule all of Wales.

"'Tis best for you to rest," Serena said.

"Not here."

"Just until you and the babe are stronger." Her soothing voice irritated Fawn. How did this woman who had no children of her own know what was best for a newborn and his mother?

"I needs be at Ogof," Fawn argued, eyeing her husband, who had spent the day with her, proud as any new father who had so long wanted a male heir. He could, if he so deigned, see that she and the child were taken safely back to Ogof.

Oh, Fawn longed for the comfort and privilege of the castle, for the servants that she usually found dull and lazy, for fresh water brought to her, a cook's meals and a nursemaid who would take the baby away when his cries became too much for her. She licked her cracked lips and lusted after wine for her throat, soap and water for her skin, and ointment to be rubbed into her sore muscles. Most of all, she wanted the sense of victory and self-satisfaction that would come when she reentered the gates with this boy child, an heir for Ogof and Tardiff. Her heart pounded with expectation. "I must go home."

"In the morning," her husband promised. "When dawn breaks I will ride to the castle and return with a wagon for you."

There seemed to be no changing his mind. Oh, Jestin was a stubborn one, he was. Fawn frowned, but then remembered her secret. The baby let up a wail. Again. His cry was lusty, it was. Jestin paced and Serena, thank God, held her tongue about the child's sire. What did it matter? Since Fawn was certain that she was descended from the true prince of Wales, it was insignificant that this boy child was not of Jestin's blood.

"All in time," she whispered to the downy head as the baby fussed and coughed, nuzzled at her breast, only to turn fitfully away. The cat slunk into the shadow. The Baron of Ogof leaned heavily against the warm stones near the fire while Fawn tried fruitlessly to soothe the little one. 'Twas as if he were angry for being forced into the world. Or at being in this horrid little hovel. "'Twill be fine soon, Llywelyn," she consoled, though his continuous howls were beginning to stretch her nerves thin.

Oh, 'twas torture to endure here at the edge of the forest with only the fortune-teller as a servant. As she tried to hold her newborn close, she wished he was not so loud. She was weary from the birthing, yet the lusty-voiced babe would not let her sleep. Fawn tried to console herself with the thought that his cries were an indication of his fierce, strong spirit, but deep inside she prayed that he would quit squalling and sleep.

Only minutes after he was born, Llywelyn had started crying and had barely stopped for a moment. He'd suckled at her breast, then stopped, screwed up his little red face, and now was fussing at the top of his little lungs.

The blankets over Fawn itched, and she was certain bugs riddled the straw bed upon which she was lying. Her breasts were beginning to fill and she was hemorrhaging more than she had with the girls.

She was hot, threw off the awful blanket, and felt a flea jump against her leg. It was all Fawn could do not to scream in frustration. But somehow she would endure the night. Then she would return to Ogof triumphantly. With her son. The heir to Jestin's barony.

Sheena no longer reigned.

A weary smile stole over Fawn's lips. 'Twas always the same—to get what she wanted in this life, a woman had to sacrifice for a man. Even one who was but a few hours old.

And sacrifice she would.

For this little one would someday prove to be the true prince of Wales— nay, 'twas not enough. Llywelyn would someday throw off the shackles of the English and become the king of Wales.

But why stop there? A tiny smile played upon her lips. This little warrior might just be destined to rule England as well.

"Where is he?" Keegan demanded, his mood foul as he stood on the deck of his ship and his finger curled tightly over the rail. The noises from the town, the turn of cart wheels, whispered conversation, laughter from a pub, all filtered over the steady lapping of the water where the *Dark Sapphire* was anchored. "Where's Wart?" Smoke rolled to the heavens, and patches of light cast from the open windows of some of the buildings gave an eerie illumination to the docks. Gentle fingers of fog were beginning to stretch throughout the town.

"Who knows?" Hollis glanced up at the heavens, with winking stars flung across the dark sky and reflecting in the night-dark waters of the bay. Only the patchy mist rising from the sea dimmed their sparkle. "Mayhap he found a woman or a pint of ale that he could not resist."

"Nay, he would be here." Keegan's body still ached from his ordeal in the water the night Sheena had thrown herself overboard, and his heart was heavy—a weight in his chest. Guilt pounded through his head. If he had stayed with her, or locked her in his cabin, or never been so bold as to have made love to her, she would be alive this night, her blue eyes laughing, her red hair coppery in the dark night, her tongue wicked and sharp as ever. His back teeth ground together as he damned himself to his own private hell and paced the length of the ship, his eyes trained on the docks, where crates and barrels were stacked around great coils of rope and chain. Men walked near the waterfront, some drunk and stumbling, others huddled deep in their cloaks, their voices carrying in the night, their laughter and bawdy jokes ripping over the waves. "Something's happened to Wart," he decided.

"What?"

"I know not, but I intend to find out." With a rush of determination Keegan took the steps down to his cabin, grabbed his mantle, and then made his way down the gangway while Hollis, like an old woman, chased after him, nagging and arguing about his decision to visit the local tavern.

"'Tis not a good idea," the older man advised.

"Never is."

"I mean it, Keegan. Ye escaped with yer life the other night, and now ye be spoilin' fer a fight. I see it in yer eyes, so don't be lyin' to me."

"Then I won't."

He left the old man swearing under his breath and walked swiftly along the piers, where the acrid odor of rotting wood battled the smells of bilge and brine.

Keegan's head throbbed, his stomach rumbled, and the heaviness in his heart refused to leave him. Cramming his fists into the pockets of his mantle, he thought of Sheena. Had he sent not only her but one of his men as well to an early grave, all because of his fascination with the woman?

"Do not think of it," he reminded himself, his boots ringing on the wooden pier. He felt a vein throb over his eye, and as he passed a stack of crates he thought he saw movement, the figure of a man lurking near a piling.

So now you be jumping at shadows, eh? his mind taunted, but his muscles flexed and he felt for the knife tucked inside his belt as he reached the street. Was it his imagination, or did he hear the soft tread of boots scraping along the cobblestones in his wake? He glanced behind him, saw no one creeping through the thin fog, and frowned to himself.

There it was again.

The sound of footsteps.

But who?

Wart?

Or some other presence? An enemy? 'Twas time to find out. Ducking along a narrow alley, he hurried his steps, now certain he was being followed. A smile of satisfaction curved over his lips for the old man, Hollis, had been right. Keegan was spoiling for a fight. And he intended to make it a good one.

Silent as a cat, he moved in the shadows. He passed a tailor's shop, then ducked around a corner. He crossed the narrow alley past a barrel maker's establishment to a stable, where, pausing only to pick up a few pieces of gravel, he lithely swung himself over the gate to land softly on a straw-strewn floor. With a snort, one of the horses sidled away, blowing and mincing nervously as Keegan squatted and peered through the slats.

He didn't have to wait long.

Within seconds a man appeared. Walking so rapidly as to be nearly running, his head swiveling side to side as he searched the darkness, he neared the stables. Though there was little light, Keegan recognized his shadow as one of the soldiers of Tardiff Hall who had been with Manning.

His lips curled and he placed his knife between his teeth.

The soldier's footsteps slowed. He paused at the stable, as if sensing his enemy within the black interior. Keegan felt that tingle of anticipation signaling a fight, the surge in his blood readying him for battle.

Without a bit of noise he flung the pebbles down the street, where they rattled against the cobblestones.

The soldier jumped. He stepped forward again, his attention drawn down the alley. Now! Keegan sprang, vaulting the gate, throwing his body onto the back of the soldier.

"Bloody hell!" The soldier, nearly toppling to his knees, scrabbled for his sword. Muscles bunched.

Keegan's arm surrounded the man, held him fast against his own long frame, caught one of his enemy's hands, and roughly twisted it behind his back.

"Ach! *Awww!*"

In a heartbeat Keegan's blade was at the soldier's throat; the dirty smell of his adversary filled his nostrils. "Drop your weapon."

The sword clattered to the cobblestones.

"Now, soldier, die or speak the truth," he commanded through lips drawn back far enough to bare his teeth.

"Who—what? If it's me money ye want—"

"I have no need of your paltry coins."

"Aagh! Me shoulder. If—if not money, then what?"

"Ye be a soldier from Tardiff Hall."

It wasn't a question, but the man nodded frantically, his skin white in the night.

"What's yer name?"

"P-Peter."

"So, Peter, your leader is Manning, is it not?"

Hesitation. Keegan twisted the man's arm up a notch and pressed the knife closer to his throat. Tendons popped.

Peter yelped. "Aye—aye, Sir Manning."

"Did Manning come across a sailor? A man by the name of Wart?"

Every muscle in Peter's body tightened. His spine was pressed hard against Keegan's chest. "Nay," he said as Keegan twisted his arm ever tighter. The man's voice raised an octave, and from the sudden rush of stench Keegan thought he might have pissed himself as well. "Not that I know of."

"You'd remember Wart," Keegan insisted, sensing a lie. "He be a small man. Moves quickly. Thin brown hair and he's missing a thumb."

"I—I haven't seen 'im."

"Nay?"

"Nay. I—I would've remembered."

"You'd best remember or I'll kill you sure. Stick you like a pig and leave you bleeding here in the street." To add emphasis to his words, he wrenched the soldier's arms and pushed the tip of his knife into his filthy throat. "Tell me!" He felt the man melt in his arms.

"Ah, ah, Wart, he was spyin' on us, 'e was, watchin' our camp and I . . . one of the soldiers found 'im and drug 'im back to Sir Manning," he finally admitted. "Ach, me arm, ye're rippin' it out of me!"

"So where is Wart now? With Manning?"

Hesitation.

Another touch of the knife. The soldier gulped.

"Nay, nay, Manning he be off to the farmer's hut in search of the woman."

Keegan froze. His heart nearly stopped. He felt a thrill of anticipation, then told himself to slow down. Sheena was dead. Killed in the sea. He took a deep breath, then asked, "What woman?"

The horse behind him neighed, and the sounds of the waterfront, laughter, music, and conversation drifted through the narrow alley.

"The lady we be lookin' for. Lady Sheena of Tardiff."

"How do you know this if you've been watching my ship?"

"I . . . was in the tavern and sent to relieve the first man who stood guard."

Keegan didn't trust this liar, and yet a part of him was desperate to believe that Sheena might be alive. Hope sang through his veins but was quickly tempered by reality. 'Twas a ruse, a carefully laid trap. "Why would Manning think the lady be at a farmer's house?"

"Because the man was drunk and braggin' about a half-dead woman he pulled out of the sea. The farmer, he showed off a jewel he'd found on her. 'Twas a golden sapphire, a topaz, one of the stolen gems missin' from Tardiff Hall."

Was it possible? Had Sheena lived—only to fall victim to Sir Manning? Did she have jewels upon her?

"When did this happen?" Keegan demanded harshly, his pulse racing.

"Tonight. Earlier."

"Where is the farmer's hut?"

"I know not—ah!"

Keegan kneed the man in the kidneys. "Lie no more, or meet your doom."

Peter nearly collapsed. "'Tis the truth, I tell ye. Sir Manning rounded up some men and followed the farmer home. As I said, he sent me to relieve Donald. They took off to the east and left me on the docks to watch the ship."

"They will be back for you?"

"Nay. I was to meet up with them at dawn, at the camp."

"Then you shall, soldier," Keegan said through tightly clenched teeth, "but you'll go as my prisoner. Pray that you've not lied to me or I'll send you to your grave."

"'Tis the truth, I swear."

Keegan wanted to believe him. With all his heart he yearned to cling to a shred of hope that Sheena had somehow survived. "Now you'd best be on your knees, asking God that your leader will trade your life for the woman."

Peter grunted. "Then I be dead. Manning has searched too long and hard for this one to give her up now."

Keegan's blood rushed through his body. His injuries no longer throbbed. Did he dare believe that Sheena was alive? Hope chased the demons of despair from his soul, and yet he could not believe she had survived. "If the woman is Sheena of Ogof, I'll barter for her."

"And you'll lose. This is not a matter of money but of pride. She has eluded him much too long, made him look a fool."

Keegan's grip tightened. He felt the desperate man was telling the truth, or as much of it as he knew. But it seemed that a miracle had been performed by the farmer and that Sheena of Ogof and Tardiff, the woman he loved, was alive. Silently Keegan vowed that one way or another, this soldier was going to take him to Sheena and Keegan would help her escape. If he had to slit this one's throat, or slay Manning in the bargain, so be it. If he had to sacrifice his own life, he would. He would not let her be dragged to the gallows.

"Where does this farmer live?"

"I—I know not. Please, trust me . . . I only know that the army was heading north of town." Peter swallowed hard. "In the tavern they would know where the man is from."

"Then we shall go there," Keegan said, his mind clicking into gear as he glanced back at the stable and the horses within. He had no compunction about "borrowing" a couple, or of stealing a nag or two if need be. Not when Sheena's life was in danger.

He prodded Peter toward the tavern. Devising a plan to help her escape the deadly clutches of Sir Manning, he whispered to the sweating soldier, "You best pray that your leader has a change of heart. And now that your memory has returned, Peter, tell me, where is Wart—at the camp?"

There was a pause, and a chill as cold as death slid down Keegan's spine.

"Nay. Not there."

"Where then?"

"In hell." Peter spat on the ground, and there was a hint of satisfaction in his voice. "Sir Manning did the honors of sending the bastard's soul to the devil."

*   *   *

"God in heaven, forgive me," Hollis whispered as he stood on the bow of the *Dark Sapphire*. The lights of town were fading, Keegan had not returned, and all the sins of the old man's past rested heavily on his aging shoulders. He thought of his foolishness, of his pride, of his reasons for betraying all those whom he'd loved. He'd done it for Keegan's sake, or so he'd told himself, but he could not deny a bit of avarice in his black soul.

"Forgive ye for what?" Bo asked, darting across the deck quick as a frightened mouse.

"Many things, lad, many things." Hollis sighed and rubbed the pain from his hands. These days his joints were swollen and knotted, and he knew he had not many years left on this earth. It was time to make his peace.

"Like what?"

"Ye be too young to understand."

Bo snorted, flipped his hair from his eyes, and squared his thin shoulders. "I be almost a man and tired of everyone talking to me as if I were but a boy."

Hollis chuckled to himself, for the boy's bravado reminded him of Keegan when he'd been but a lad and Captain Rourke had still been counted among the living. Keegan, too, had been full of himself, anxious for battle and thinking no harm would ever touch him. 'Twas foolish, of course. Ach, it seemed so long ago now. "You'll be a man soon enough, boy. Do not hope to hasten it along."

Bo climbed upon the rail and glared at the older man. "Where's the captain?"

"'Tis a good question ye ask."

"Ashore?"

"Aye, that much be certain."

"Why?"

"He's off to find Wart, though why they be not back by now, I know not." He glanced anxiously at the star-flung heavens, more obscured as the night fog grew thicker, the lights glowing from the town now blurry. "'Tis a worry."

"All things be a worry to you."

Hollis sighed and he pulled the neck of his tunic closer, as the night was seeping into his bones. "There be much to be concerned about," he admitted, and the boy, tired of talking in circles, hopped down from the rail and quickly scrambled up the shrouds and rigging to the crow's nest. Again Hollis glanced up at the sliver of moon barely visible through the mist, and he felt a premonition of doom. Something was wrong. Very wrong. Elsewise Keegan would have returned.

Hollis felt ancient, and the old fear that he'd doomed Keegan and his ship scraped at his soul. Snagging a lantern from its hook, he used the feeble light from its single candle to guide him as he descended to the hold, where casks of wine and barrels of ale were stacked. Rats scurried out of his path, and he vaguely wondered why Maynard was not after the bothersome pests. In the war against the beasts, Maynard and his cat seemed to be losing.

Easing his body behind a post, Hollis reached upward to an overhead beam where long before he'd whittled out a hiding spot. Standing on tiptoe, stretching as far as he could, he felt the top of the dusty beam with his fingertips, found a tiny nail, and pulled. A small lid lifted and he frowned, for it was becoming harder and harder for him to reach so high. He was shrinking, his spine shortening, and soon he would have to find a new hiding spot for his treasure. Straining, his fingers delving into the small space, he felt the ring, cold metal and icy stone. With effort he pulled it from its age-old niche and held it up to the candlelight.

He'd kept the ring for eleven years, lied to everyone who asked about it, including Keegan. But he'd never had the heart to throw the beautiful gem into the sea, though he'd promised himself he would do it a thousand times over.

But he, like all the men and women who'd owned the jewel before him, had been seduced by its dark brilliance, had ignored the fact that he knew it to be cursed, and kept it hidden from the day he'd sold the *Warrior* and bought the *Dark Sapphire*. He'd even named the ship as a reminder to himself that the ring was hidden in the hold. And in so doing he'd probably cursed the crew.

He'd vowed to get rid of it, but each time he'd tried, he had not been able to cast the stone into the sea. Worth a king's ransom, the ring had been insurance against grave financial loss; Hollis had comforted himself with the thought that should Keegan ever feel the pinch to sell the craft, he would be able to spare him the pain, by offering up the stone to save his nephew's ship.

Or had he simply been bewitched and cursed by the gem?

"'Tis a fool ye be, old man," he grumbled, staring into the deadly blue facets of the sapphire. Oh, 'twas seductive as the most comely wench.

Rather than return the ring to its hiding place, Hollis dropped it into one of his voluminous pockets.

Mayhap this night he would have the courage to throw the damned ring off the bow and into the dark waters of the bay.

Chapter Twelve

Boots clomped outside the door. A deep male voice sang, though very much off-key. In the hut, Sheena raised her head.

Bang! The door flew open. Bounced against the wall.

Reeking of ale and dirt, his hat falling over one eye, Freddy staggered in. A gust of wind chased after him, causing the fire to glow brighter.

"Where 'ave ye been?" Esme demanded. She'd been sleeping on a pallet in a corner near the fire, but she was on her feet, her eyes puffy, her hair standing up at odd angles. "As if I didn't know."

"Just 'avin' a pint or two with some friends."

"It's nearly dawn. And ye've got work to do."

"Ah, Esme, ye worry too much." He shut the door behind him and yawned, showing off crooked yellow teeth.

"One of us must."

"'Tis the trouble with ye, woman," he said, and winked familiarly at his wife. "Always frettin' ye be." Stretching an arm over his head, he started undoing the laces of his tunic with his other hand.

Esme wasn't interested in his sudden turn of affection. "The girl here"—she hitched her chin in the direction of Sheena's pallet—"she claims there was another jewel with her, a golden one."

Freddy's eyebrows lifted high over his eyes, and he turned his palms toward the bare rafters as his bleary gaze turned on Sheena. "I found none, lass. Only the two that were in yer boot. If there was another stone, ye must've lost it in yer swim."

"It was with the others." Sheena rolled to the side of her pallet and sat up. "In my boot. Wedged there. I doubt if it would have fallen out if the others were still there."

Frowning drunkenly, his head wobbling, he said, "Well, now, girlie, Esme was with me when we took yer boots off, and there be only the two stones—red and green."

"But—"

"Ye could search the sea yerself," he said, and chuckled as if he found the thought humorous before turning to look at his wife again. Sheena glared at the man who had saved her, knew he lied, though his wife seemed convinced of his integrity. "Did ye tend to the pigs, Es?" he asked, avoiding Sheena's eyes.

"Don't I always?"

"'Tis a good lass ye be, wife," he said, swatting her familiarly on her rear end. "Hardworking and true."

"And 'tis drunk, ye be, husband."

"Aye. That I canna argue." Swaying, leaning heavily upon the big woman, he waggled one index finger in front of her nose. "But I do na beat ya, now, do I? Newton, the carter, he takes a cane to his wife."

"Yeah, and if I were Newton's wife, I'd take worse to him. Come along, now, Freddy. Let's get ye into the bed. Come on, now."

She managed to turn her husband toward the door.

Hoof beats—hundreds of them, it seemed—thundered outside the door. Horses whinnied and snorted. Bridles jangled. Sheena's heart flew to her throat. Boots pounding the earth outside. *Oh, God!* A deep voice echoed through the night. Sheena's blood turned to ice.

Sir Manning!

Nay!

Bam! Bam! Bam!

A huge fist thudded on the door.

Sheena shot to her feet.

"Now, who the devil is that?" Esme looked at her husband, then the door, and back to Freddy again. "Did ye bring home—?"

"Open up, Fred Farmer! 'Tis the sheriff."

"Oh, bloody Christ," Freddy grumbled.

"What is it ye've done now?" Esme clucked her tongue.

Sheena nearly tripped on the folds of the big dress.

"I said, 'Open up.' I know ye be in there. Saw ye enter meself, Freddy, and there's someone here who needs to talk to ye."

Sheena's heart was a drum. "Do not open the door," she ordered, searching for another way out of the hut. She crossed the room in a second, the hem of the rough dress dragging, the dirt floor cool against the soles of her feet.

"Wait a minute—where're ye going?" Esme asked.

Sheena didn't answer.

"Open up! Fred!" the sheriff commanded tersely. "Now!"

"Break it down." Manning's voice again.

Sheena shuddered. Frantic, she had to find a means of escape.

Chickens fluttered, feathers scattered. The cat hissed. Sheena didn't wait. Couldn't. Throwing open the door to the pigsty, she flung herself into the darkness. The stench was overpowering. Her feet sank into the ooze. Her heart knocked, ricocheting through her brain. *Run!*

More pounding on the front door. Men's voices. Angry. Gruff. Demanding. *Dear Lord, help me!* She slammed the door to the sty behind her but still heard the muffled orders and jangle of swords.

Run, Sheena, as fast as you can! RUN!

Freddy called, "I'm coming, I'm coming—"

Sheena stumbled through the muck. Pigs snorted and galloped out of her way.

Ears straining, she heard the front door burst open, bang hard against the wall again.

Her stomach clenched. Fear drove her onward. A sow grunted.

"Where is she?" Sir Manning's voice demanded as she frantically waded through the dung, mud, and straw. "Where, man, tell me now, or I'll slit your belly—Oh, hell. After her!"

Dear God, no, not like this! Piglets squealed around her feet, the sow snorted and oinked, and in the darkness she bumped her head against a beam on the low-hanging roof. Fumbling, she stumbled away from the house. The door opened.

A lantern illuminated the sty, condemning light catching her in its flickering beam.

"There she is! With the pigs," Manning yelled. "Get her. Now!"

"No!" Esme's voice.

Gasping, dragging herself forward, Sheena ducked beneath the overhang of the roof. Her blood was pulsing through her brain, her legs slogging through the ooze.

"Oh, for the love of God," Freddy growled as she dashed toward a short fence.

Soldiers poured into the enclosure. Pigs shrieked, oinked, grunted, and slopped through the slippery mud.

Sheena rolled over the top rail of the fence that separated the enclosure from a field, landed on the far side, and twisted her ankle. Pain shot up her calf. Still she ran, hobbling through the slimy mud and into the darkness. The smell of the sea was heavy in the air. Fog circled her feet as it rose from the cliffs. Gloomy and gratefully dark, the night was illuminated with only a hint of light from a sliver of the moon.

"There! Shit—get out of me way, you blasted beast!" a man yelled from the shed.

A piglet screamed.

"After her!" Manning ordered, his voice deep, resonant and terrifying.

"She's got away—go out the front!"

Sheena's feet slapped the ground.

The forest wasn't far away, she knew, just on the other side of one of Freddy's fields. She ran by instinct, her legs burning, her ankle on fire. The roar of the sea faded, the smell of salt in the air receding as she headed away from the cliffs on which Freddy's hut was perched. If she could find her way into the trees that spread up the hillside, then hide until dawn, she would be able to steal a horse and—and . . . Oh, God, they were still chasing her. She heard the thud of boots, the shouts of men as they spied her. There was a crackle of excitement, a cry of expectant triumph from a soldier. 'Twas as if he felt the blood lust of a wolf after prey.

Help me, Sheena silently prayed, for the thought of being alone with Sir Manning for even a few minutes was horrifying. The man had no heart, no soul. She would not allow him to drag her back to Ogof a prisoner. Nay, if and when she returned to face her father, she would do it on her own. She'd thought of returning to Ogof when she was aboard the *Dark Sapphire,* and now, as she tried to escape, she knew that she would have to someday walk through the yawning gates of the castle.

Someday.

She couldn't think past the moment and the agony in her ankle. Clenching her jaw, she spurred herself onward, ignoring the pain raging up her leg.

The soldiers were closing the gap, breathing hard, cursing her, commanding her to stop, but the forest was nearer as well. Through the mist tall, dark shapes of trees loomed along the field's edge, protective foliage only a few feet away. Her lungs burned, her ankle ached, and the skirt of the huge dress was caked with mud. It tangled against her legs. *Run. Run for your life, Sheena. Do not give up!* Propelled by sheer will, she found a path in the forest and forced her feet forward as branches slapped her in the face, underbrush snagged her clothes, and her feet tripped over roots exposed on the trail. Her eyes attempted to adjust to the stygian blackness, but with only a sliver of moonlight and a few pale stars as her guide, she was running half blind.

Pain burned in her ankle, but she plunged on, upward through the forested hills. Her only chance was to lose her pursuers in the tangle of oaks and pine. She heard no dogs baying anxiously behind her, so there was hope that somehow, with God's help and her own wits, she could elude them. *Hurry, hurry, hurry!* she silently prodded herself. Deeper and deeper into the thicket. The men were farther behind her now, and yet she felt as if someone was watching her, trailing close at her heels, stalking her.

'Twas only her fear that made her think she heard the snap of a twig so close at hand. The voices of the soldiers were at the base of the hill. The trail forked and she bore right, then dived into a thicket, desperately willing her wild breathing to slow. Her lungs were on fire, her ankle throbbed, her mind reeled as she tried to find some escape.

"In the forest! Sir Manning, she's in there!"

"Oh, for the love of St. Michael, how'll we ever find her?"

"It matters not how, just bloody hell flush her out!" Manning commanded.

Sheena cringed at the sound of his voice, fell back against the rough bark of an oak tree. She was sweating, gasping for breath. Her feet were bruised. Her pulse racing.

"Surround the forest," Manning ordered, his voice far too close. "'Tis but a few trees. We'll work from the outside in."

Her heart plummeted. Somewhere in the uppermost branches of a tree an owl hooted. There was no escape if what he said was true, and she had no way of knowing, for this part of Wales was foreign to her. *Think, Sheena, think. Do not give up!*

She backed up a few steps, her thoughts whirling. She had to get away, to find a place to rest, to—

A heavy hand clamped her shoulder. She jumped. Nearly screamed as another huge hand reached around and covered her mouth.

All was lost.

Her knees sagged.

Mother Mary, help me.

"Shh," her captor whispered against her ear, and for the barest of seconds her hopeful heart leapt as the deep timbre reminded her of Keegan's.

Keegan.

Judas. Blackheart. Lover.

Her soul twisted painfully at the thought of the bastard who had stolen her silly heart. She swallowed hard and turned to look at the beast who held her in a grip of steel. 'Twas too dark to see, and her mind was surely playing tricks upon her. She considered biting his hand, but knew he'd let up a yowl and then all of the cursed soldiers would be upon her.

Somewhere nearby a horse neighed.

Bridles jangled, steeds snorted, and the beams of torches were visible, golden points of light that shined through the branches and vines.

"Be quiet and do as I say." Dear God, he sounded so much like Keegan. Could it be? Nay, nay, 'twas but her willful mind playing tricks upon her.

Slowly he released her. She turned and felt his face with her hands, knew in an instant it was the brooding captain of the *Dark Sapphire.*

Tears of joy filled her eyes.

"Do as I tell you," he whispered in her ear as the soldiers and horsemen

surrounded the forest. "We have not much time." He took her hand and together they ran, stumbling, through the low brush toward the sound of a
stream that rushed and gurgled through a chasm that sliced between the
stands of pine and oak. "Hurry."

She needed no further inspiration. Fear drove her, and she clung to Keegan's hand as the sound of water tumbling and falling, splashing over stones,
became louder.

They reached the bank of the creek, and he guided her around a copse of
saplings, then stopped short. Even in the darkness she saw the man, lying on
the ground and naked as the day he was born. He was wriggling and trying to
speak, but his voice was muffled. His wrists tied, his ankles bound, he was a
big, dark squirming shadow who writhed angrily and could not speak because
of the gag across his mouth.

"Who—?"

"Shh!"

Sheena heard them drawing even closer, men and horses tromping up
the hill. The torches flickered and burned bright, evil lights shining in the
darkness.

Her heart was thudding, fear racing through her blood, but Keegan's hand
on hers was somehow reassuring. He drew her close, and for a split second she
thought he would kiss her. Instead he placed his mouth to her ear. "Now,
Sheena," he said so softly she barely heard him, "take off your clothes."

"What?"

"Just do as I say. And be quick about it."

Through the brush she heard the soldiers approaching. They were getting
far too near. The thought of facing them without any clothing was daunting,
yet she threw off the big, dirty dress and shivered in the barest hint of moonlight. Keegan grabbed the soiled garment and tossed her some garb—men's
clothes, a soldier's uniform of red and gold—the colors of Tardiff's army. It
smelled of urine and sweat. Her stomach turned over, but she closed her mind
to thoughts about the allegiance symbolized by the uniform. Fingers fumbling, feet aching, she donned each piece of the hated, wretched colors of
Tardiff while Keegan cut the man's hands free and forced the dress over his
head.

Seams ripped loudly as the prisoner squirmed, but Keegan prevailed and
soon he'd forced the man to stand up in the foul-smelling gown. Rapidly, as
Sheena yanked on the soldier's boots, Keegan retied the man's hands behind
him, then sliced the rope that held his legs together.

"Come," he said, taking Sheena's hand.

Silently they waded across the stream, where two horses, standing nervously together, their coats wet with sweat, were tied. She touched one sleek

neck. "We will use them later, for escape," Keegan whispered in her ear, "but not yet. Now, scream as loudly as you can."

"What?"

"Do it."

Was he daft? "Nay." The anxious horses tugged at their bits, pulled at the reins.

"Draw the men to the prisoner," he ordered.

"But—"

"If you value your life, Sheena, do it!"

The soldiers were closing the gap anyway.

She swallowed back her fear and let out a cry that echoed through the canyon, reverberating against the hills. The horses pulled hard on their tethers. Limbs cracked and splintered.

"Damn," Keegan swore as the beasts broke free.

"Over here!" one man cried.

Clenching her hand in his, Keegan started down the hill on the far side of the creek. *This is madness,* she thought, for the men were approaching, crashing through the woods.

"Hey! I found her!" a soldier yelled not fifty feet away. Sheena's heart was in her throat, pounding in her ears, her body sweating. "Over here! Sir Manning!"

Hooves thundered up the hill, resounding through the gorge. Keegan's fingers circled her wrist, pulling her behind a tree as a laboring horse, running crazily, splashed up the creek. Leaving Sheena at the base of the oak, Keegan swung onto a low branch that spread over the chasm.

The horse drew nearer. Louder. Sheena cowered behind the bole of the oak.

A massive white destrier plunged into view. Hooves clattered, water splashed. The rider upon the steed's back was a huge, hulking man. One hand held the bridle; in the other was a raised sword that glinted in the feeble light. Sheena's heart froze.

"Where?" Manning bellowed from atop the destrier, and Sheena shrank inside.

As the horse galloped beneath the branch, Keegan sprang upon the rider.

"What the bloody—?" Manning cried, startled.

Together, grappling, both men plunged into the creek. With a terrified squeal the silvery white war horse reared, then bolted forward, his hooves slipping as he tore up the bank. Quick as a cat Sheena lunged. She grabbed the animal's reins as the men, splashing and rolling in the water, grappled and gulped for air.

She forced the wild-eyed steed up the bank, trying to calm him as he tried to rear and pull away. Her leg ached, and in the distance she heard men's voices. Through the trees torches glimmered faintly, burning red and gold in the blackness. "Hey! Look at that!" one man with a nasal voice cawed. "The woman, she's tied, she is."

No! Soon the men would discover they'd been duped. She and Keegan were running out of time, yet the two men battled, kicking and throwing punches, rolling through the rapids, gasping and gurgling, trying to drown each other. Sheena longed for a weapon, any kind of weapon, so that she could help.

"Oof."

"Curse you, you bastard!" *Manning's voice!* So close. He was gasping for breath as he and Keegan swung at each other.

A sword flashed in the darkness.

"Nay!" she cried, springing onto the destrier's saddle. He reared, front hooves flaying the air, back legs slipping on the bank. "Come on, you miserable beast." Slapping the horse with the reins, she forced him back into the creek. He took the bit in his teeth, shook his great head. "Come on, come on," she urged.

"Hey! It ain't the woman!" a man yelled from the direction of the cluster of torch lights.

"Who the devil—?"

"Christ Almighty, it's Peter!"

One man laughed.

Another one cursed. "Bloody hell!"

"Hey! Shut up, would ya! What's that I hear? Sounds like a fight . . . Where the devil is Sir Manning?"

Sheena kicked the horse deeper into the creek. In the splash and rush of the stream she saw fists fly as the men grappled. "Here! Over here!" Manning called, yelling to his troops. He stood and raised his sword as Keegan slipped backward, his feet failing him.

"No!" she cried.

"Where are ye?" The soldiers again.

Manning snarled, "Over here—"

The torch lights started moving in their direction. Men shouted. Feet thundered.

The knight swung downward. Sheena aimed her booted foot, kicked hard. *Bam!* She connected with Manning's jaw. His head snapped back. He fell into the water. Pain exploded up her leg. "Come on!" she yelled at Keegan, offering her hand. He swung up behind her, his clothes sodden, a bloody stain darkening his shoulder.

Pulling hard on the reins, she forced the big horse down the hillside, through the shallow water as fast as the beast dared run. Keegan's arms tightened around her as she guided the steed through the canyon, once again leaving Sir Manning and his sorry group of soldiers behind. The barest trace of a smile came to her lips.

But it was a false sense of victory, for as the creek tumbled out of the forest to slice across the fields, she knew that it was not over. As long as Sir Manning lived, for all the time Fawn was Lady of Ogof, they would chase her to the ground, drag her back to justice, and lie to her father.

She had no option but to return home and plead with Jestin, tell him the truth about Tardiff. She could only hope that he would believe her.

And what will you do with the captain? her mind nagged as the horse tore across the grassland and the sea roared in the distance.

Keegan's arms tightened around her possessively, and it felt so good to be close to him, to feel the front of his thighs pressed into the backs of hers, to sense his manhood pushing against the cleft of her buttocks through the scratchy breeches. She reminded herself that he'd come for her—risked his life for her. Somehow he'd found her and helped her escape.

She wouldn't believe that he had imperiled his life just for the bargain they'd agreed upon—because of the money. Nay, there had to be more to it than that.

Or was there?

Tonight, as a few stars winked through the cloaking mist and the aches in her body eased, Sheena would not think of it.

For the moment she and Keegan were together.

Chapter Thirteen

Manning, his jaw throbbing, his head pounding, his pride beaten to a bloody pulp, watched as the woman he'd chased for weeks and the captain of the *Dark Sapphire* were swallowed by the mist-shrouded night.

Once again he'd failed.

Once again he'd been made to look like a fool.

In front of his men.

He stood on unsteady feet. The rocks in the creek bed were slick, he felt a sense of dizziness, but worst of all he knew he'd been bested. By a mere woman. And Captain Rourke's rogue of a son.

"Bastard," he spat, feeling no sense of satisfaction. "Miserable cur of a bastard."

As the cold water of the creek swirled over the tops of his boots, a new emotion coursed through Manning. Blood lust. He wanted vengeance and he yearned for it so desperately he would gladly have sold his soul to the devil if only Lucifer had appeared in the fog. With or without the dark prince's help, Manning needed to restore his pride.

Long ago he'd agreed to help Fawn because of his hungry ambition. He'd allowed himself to be seduced by her, had come eagerly to her bed, never anticipating that she planned to get herself with child, that he was merely the sire she'd chosen for her babe.

He'd been unable to resist lying with her. Not only was she beautiful and powerful, but the thought that he was bedding the lord's wife, sometimes with Jestin just one chamber away, had fired his blood. The sense of power he gained was as potent and intoxicating as fine wine and brought with it a need for more. Manning was anxious to drop the trappings of a common man, the son of a blacksmith and a woman he'd never bothered to marry. Aye, he craved more for himself, for his issue. Fawn had been his stepping-stone that bridged the deep abyss between poverty and privilege.

Willingly Manning had done her bidding and held his tongue, smug in the knowledge that he was getting a little back at a lord who didn't appreciate him, a man who had, through no effort on his part, been given a better station in life. But his sense of power had been lessened when Fawn had admitted to being pregnant and that she was going to pass the babe off as her husband's. This son was going to rule Ogof and Tardiff, and if Manning dared breathe a word that he'd lain with her, she vowed she would cry rape and have him hanged, then drawn and quartered.

"Do not let the fact that the child be yours give you any illusions, Manning," she'd cooed into his ear as they'd lain naked, drenched in each other's sweat, upon her bed. "I will keep you well, yes, but this boy must, for the time of my husband's life, be considered his issue."

"And what if Jestin is soon called to meet his maker?" Manning had asked.

"All the better . . . after the babe is born. But hear me well, do not cross me or I will see to your death personally."

He'd stared into her cold eyes and believed every word she uttered as he'd placed strong arms around her neck, thrown her onto that smooth back of hers, and mounted her again, pouring his rage and his seed into her as she cried out and begged for more of him. Later, still gasping, she had promised him a share of her wealth, though she would not say how they were going to get rid of the baron.

Now, as he stared through the gloom, he cursed his fate. He was forced yet again to return to the woman who controlled his destiny and admit that he'd been thwarted by Sheena. His jaw clenched so hard his back teeth ached, and his fists curled in impotent fury.

No longer was this mission merely Fawn's will. Now 'twas a matter of pride.

He heard his troops approaching and climbed out of the creek, making his way along the bank to the cluster of torches and the sweating faces reflected in their red-gold light. Smoke singed the air, horses snorted and pawed, and the soldiers were gathered around a woman, a big woman— nay, a man dressed in female garb. "Who have you . . . ?" He let his words fall away as he recognized Peter in the ugly frock. "God's eyes, man, what is this?"

"I was tricked," he said, eyes downcast.

"By the captain?"

"Aye." He gulped.

"And you brought him here."

"He nearly ripped me arm from its socket," Peter cried, mortified, then held his tongue, for the excuse was paltry—the cry of an old woman.

Manning's hands itched to strangle the pathetic excuse of a soldier, but he resisted. Hadn't he, too, been deceived easily, his horse taken from him? By the very girl he was supposed to capture? His blood thundered in his ears. Asides, he needed every man; he could spare none.

"Where's yer horse?" one of his men had the audacity to ask. The soldier was astride a black gelding, his face illuminated by the golden glow of the torch. Theatrically, with eyebrows raised and mouth pulled into an exaggerated frown, as if he were truly perplexed, he glanced around, searching for the steed.

"He was stolen," Manning admitted through clenched teeth and a jaw that still throbbed from the thrust of Sheena's boot. None of the soldiers dared say a word. "And since I am now without a mount, I'll have yours."

The man seemed about to argue, opened his mouth, but looking down at the raw, dangerous wrath in the dark knight's gaze, he snapped his jaw shut and dutifully climbed off his steed.

Manning hauled himself into the saddle, threw a leg over the beast's back, and glanced at the ragtag band of soldiers who were with him. They were all weary of the chase; he saw the defeat in their hopeless, lackluster eyes. "We will not go back empty-handed," he vowed, silently daring any man to argue with him. "Nay. You"—he pointed at a long pole of a man—"will stay near the farmer's house, watch who comes and goes. Sheena might return there." He doubted it, but he could ill afford to let her slip through his fingers again. "And you, Seth, you shall be posted at the ship. The rest of us will try to track down the lady"—he said the word with a sneer—"and we will report to each other. I doubt the captain will go far without his boat." He looked from one tired, distrustful face to the other. "We will catch Sheena and return her to her father. And when we do, each of you will be rewarded. I swear it."

Keegan's shoulder was on fire, pain blazing down his arm as he and Sheena rode swiftly across the night-darkened fields. He gritted his teeth against the pain as the horse labored, long legs stretching over the grass toward the town. Manning's sword had sliced deep, and Keegan wished he'd killed the bastard who had sent Wart to his grave. Guilt burned in his brain, for Wart had been a true and faithful crew member.

But Sheena was alive, and for that he was thankful. He'd been certain he'd never see her again, and to find her alive had been a miracle, had nearly convinced him that God did exist. His good arm tightened around her slim waist possessively, and he wondered what it was about this woman that had made him risk his ship, the members of his crew, his very life for her. Never had he felt this way, not even with Brynna when he was besotted. Brynna had been a beautiful but cold woman who had never been satisfied, who complained of his months away at sea and yet refused to sail with him.

No doubt she'd been lonely, and for that he supposed he didn't blame her for seeking another man's company. But when he'd found her lying in Sir Robert's arms, naked and sleeping in the very bed where they'd first made love, Keegan had turned on his heel and walked out the door. He'd found his solace in the sea and forced her from his thoughts.

Any shame or grief he'd felt, he'd buried deep. No one had seen his pain, and it had lessened.

But when he'd returned and found that she was dead, he'd visited her grave, stood on that hill and looked down at the mound of earth covering the one woman he'd given his name.

"Oh, Brynna, a goose you were," he'd said, his hair catching in the winter wind as it had blown in icy blasts over the cliffs. That she'd been with child had saddened him. Though the babe had not been his, 'twas a shame that it had never been born. Brynna with her sable brown hair, white skin, and eyes as round and brown as a doe's, had been a sad woman who had deserved better than a man who embraced the sea, a girl who hungered for flattery and a man's touch.

They'd both been fools.

Since Brynna there had been no other woman. Until Sheena.

Silently, as her hair brushed against his chest and she leaned over the tiring stallion's neck, urging the destrier ever onward, he cursed the fates that had brought her to him. He'd sworn he'd never let another woman reach into his heart, would hide his soul for the rest of his days.

His mistress had been the sea, and he'd found comfort in her passionate blue depths. Raging tempest or calm, glasslike water, the ocean was his love.

Or had been.

Now, on this dark mist-laden night, with the fullness of Sheena's breasts weighing on his arm, the feel of her buttocks pressed against his manhood, the warmth of her body so near, he wasn't sure of himself.

For the first time in years the captain of the *Dark Sapphire* second-guessed himself. Though he knew he was being foolish, he couldn't stop the emotions that blazed through his soul and tore through his brain. He argued with himself, but he knew he was lost to her. He buried his face in her hair and flexed the muscles of his good arm more tightly around her as he silently condemned himself to the hell of loving her.

Nay, Keegan, the rational part of his mind argued. *'Tis only because you've been long without a woman.*

You'll not feel this way once you set sail again.

She's a passing fancy, nothing to worry about.

You'll soon forget her.

But all his reasons were but poor excuses. He loved her. That was all there was to it, Keegan realized as the horse broke out of the woods and the destrier's strides lengthened over the silvery fields. Like it or not, Keegan, cold-hearted captain of the *Dark Sapphire*, a man who rued the day he'd ever met a woman, was in love with the daughter of his father's murderer.

"Are we being followed?" she asked, daring a glance over her shoulder, and he caught a glimpse of her straight nose, fine lips, and big eyes.

"Nay." Keegan, too, hazarded a look back at the woods, expecting to see the dark shapes of men and horses pouring out of the forest. But so far they were alone.

The horse was laboring, his breathing loud, and Sheena guided him away from the pig farmer's hut and along a rocky outcropping that led past the sea.

"Manning will expect us to go to the ship," she said aloud.

"Worry not. The *Dark Sapphire* was not to wait for me. Hollis is to see that she gets to Drudwy." He felt Sheena relax a bit as she pulled on the reins, urging the tired horse away from the town and into the hills again.

She tried to ignore the feel of Keegan's body against her but failed. Images of their night of lovemaking whirled through her mind in seductive circles that took her breath away. With his arm around her, his well-muscled legs snug against the back of her thighs, her spine pressed into his chest, the movement of the horse as he galloped brought back wickedly erotic memories she'd tried so hard to forget. In the higher slopes she drew hard on the reins, and the horse, his grayish white coat flecked with lather, slowed.

"Manning will not be pleased that you stole his horse," Keegan observed.

"Oh, but he'll like the fact that you lunged at him from the tree, knocking him into the creek." She smiled at the thought that the cursed knight had been bested.

"Aye, we've given him more reason to chase you down."

"He would have done it anyway." She shrugged, felt his breath against the back of her neck.

"Before, he was doing his duty. Now he will have reasons of his own."

"I care not." Sheena refused to be intimidated by the soldier who, at Fawn's urging, had pledged his fealty to Ellwynn of Tardiff. Aye, Manning was a beast, but she would not live in terror. One way or another, she would return to Ogof. There she would face her father and whatever brand of justice he meted out.

"You canna leave without the captain!" Bo's face turned white as a full moon as he clutched the sleeve of Hollis's old mantle.

"I'm just doin' as he told me." Hollis made his way to the helm. He'd already ordered the men to raise the anchors, but the boy was beside himself.

"We must wait."

"Fer what? Sir Manning and his troops?"

"Fer the captain and the lady." Bo limped after Hollis to the helm.

So that was it. He, along with the rest of the crew, had been edgy and glum ever since Sheena had jumped overboard. Even Big Tom, the cruelest man on the ship, had been affected. More surly than ever, he'd asked about Sheena more than once. Ach, though Hollis hated to admit it, even he missed her quick wit, sharp tongue, and dimpled smile. Aye, she'd gotten past his crusty exterior, though he'd never admit it. That was the problem with women; they had a way of burrowing past into a man's thick hide and somehow finding a way into his heart. Had he not seen it with Bertrice and Rourke and now, again, with Keegan and Sheena. Women caused men pain. Even his sister, Lorinda, God rest her soul, had used Rourke and abandoned her son. And Brynna, Keegan's wife, had betrayed him. Oh, they were a sorry lot, women were, and yet men could not live without them.

Hollis had managed to stay out of a woman's path. There had been one woman when he'd been a young man, but he'd held tight to his heart and, as he'd expected, she'd found another. And now this one, this Sheena of Ogof—no, Lady Sheena of Tardiff—she'd captured the hearts of all the men. And like it or not, Hollis, though he knew better, had not been immune. Witch or nay, she'd charmed him as well.

"'Tis a fool ye be," he muttered under his breath. Worse yet, he was an old fool, one who knew better, who had, during the course of his years, seen the ravages only a woman could cause. Wars were waged for women; friends became bitter enemies over a woman's attention. Lives and careers were ruined because of a woman's allure, and if that wasn't a curse, Hollis didn't know what was.

"We must wait longer," Bo insisted, and Hollis jerked his sleeve free of the boy's clutching fingers.

"I said we'll meet up with the captain in Drudwy; 'tis the way he wanted it, and the way 'twill be. Now, off with ye. Go help Cedric mend the sails or George with the caulkin'. There be work to do."

Bo sniffed and tossed his head to rid his eyes of his uneven fringe of hair. "Aye, aye, sir," he mocked, and scurried off with his uneven gait. Hollis was relieved to get rid of him, didn't even run after him and box his ears for his impertinence. The boy was young. Naive. Needed to be seasoned. But at least he was now gone.

Seamus was at the helm. "I don't mind tellin' ya, Hollis, that I don't like this," he said, frowning. "'Tis too dark to try and leave this bay safely, and without the captain . . ." He scowled.

"Ye know that Keegan always leaves the ship in my charge when he's gone," Hollis said. "And have I ever gone against his wishes?"

"Nay, but—"

"Do ye think I'm stealin' the *Dark Sapphire*, then? Is that it? After I was the one who saved Keegan's life more than once, sold the *Warrior* when he was but a lad, and bought this ship for him? After I kept him from the hangman when the sheriff found out we were smugglin' men in our hold? Would ya think I would be doin' somethin' against the captain's wishes?"

"Ye've had words," Seamus said.

"Ach, 'twas nothing. Now, I've told the hands to lift anchor and raise the sails. Either you steer this damned ship or we'll run aground sure."

"Aye," Seamus agreed halfheartedly, and Hollis, despite his assurances to the crew, hoped he wasn't leaving Keegan without any means of escape if he needed it. The old man feared that taking the ship out to sea in the middle of the night was sending everyone on board to a certain death.

Worse yet, Hollis was worried. Again.

About Keegan and . . . yes, about that cursed woman as well. He'd even replaced the ring in its hiding place, once again unable to toss it into the dark waters of the sea.

Aye, he was a fool of the highest order.

And, for the moment, he was the captain of the damned ship.

Bo dragged his sleeve under his nose and thought of a dozen curses that he'd like to shout at Hollis, the old mule. Bo wasn't going to take orders from an ancient man who saw sea serpents at every turn of the prow. Hollis was daft and scared, like a feeble old woman. And Hollis wasn't loyal to the captain, that much was sure.

Bo had proof.

Scowling to himself, trying to walk without a hint of a limp, Bo hurried along the decking. He'd followed the old man into the hold on several occasions, and he'd discovered Hollis doing more than tapping into the barrels of ale and casks of wine hidden deep in the ship's bowels. No, there was another secret the old man kept. Hidden between the stacks one day, Bo had peeked around and saw Hollis enter the hold, slip around a post, stretch tall, then finger open a little tiny opening. He'd reached inside and, as the rats scurried and squeaked and the ship creaked in the wind, Hollis had held up a ring with a brilliant blue stone. Sucking in his breath Bo had stared in awe at the gem winking blue fire from the candlelight. 'Twas like none he'd ever seen.

"Old goat," Bo now growled under his breath as he tiptoed down the stairs and entered the dark room where Hollis's secret treasure was hidden. Once it became known that Victoria of Rhydd was really the daughter of Baron Jestin, Bo had heard the story of the captain's father's bad luck at a dice game where the stakes were Rourke's ship wagered against an incredible blue stone, the Dark Sapphire of Ogof.

'Twas Hollis's ring, to be sure. And it didn't belong to him.

Climbing onto the casks, Bo balanced carefully so that he didn't slip and have his good leg crushed between the heavy oaken barrels. His fingers scraped along the beam, and he found the tiny peg, lifted it, and with the tip of his finger felt inside the small hole. The sharp stone nearly cut his finger as he scooped out the glittery piece of jewelry, looked at it while the boat started to move, then, nearly dropping his prize between the stacks, pocketed the gem.

It wasn't as if he was stealing it, not really. The ring did not belong to Hollis. It should have been Rourke's, if the story of his death was true. If not—well, he'd think about what he'd do with the ring. Until then it was his.

"There has been no word?" Fawn asked as the damned maid picked up the baby and gently swayed back and forth. Zelda was an odd one, dark and mysterious, but she had a way with children. She had treated each of Fawn's daughters as if they were her own; the same would be true of this son. Though Zelda had protested when Fawn had sent the maidservant's only daughter to Tardiff, she'd finally accepted her fate. And now, because of Fawn's own maternal instincts, and since Ellwynn was gone—oh, she felt a sharp pain at that—she had decided to order Fannie returned to Ogof. The truth of the matter was that Zelda would not last forever and Sarah was a ninny. Fannie would make a good serving girl.

"Sir Manning has not returned. Nor have any of his soldiers." Zelda smiled down at the baby, yet no light of happiness brightened her haunted eyes. But then, it rarely did.

"Has Fannie returned?"

"Nay, not yet. But soon," Zelda said, and there was actually a spark of life in the old maidservant. "Today."

"Good."

"Thank you, m'lady."

Fawn waved a hand in the air. "'Tis nothing," she said, somewhat pleased to have the old woman's allegiance if only for a second.

With a sigh Fawn set down her mazer of wine and hoped that the warmth she expected to flow through her blood would come quickly. She was still sore, still bleeding, and anxious to be on her feet again.

Lying in her bed, with the fire in the grate burning bright, the rushes clean and smelling of dried rose petals, the tapestries splashing color against the whitewashed walls, her son finally born and secure as the rightful heir of Ogof and Tardiff, she should have been content. Yet she was restless. She sensed undercurrents of trouble within the dark hallways and wide wall walks of Ogof. Even Jestin, despite his elation with his newborn son, was tense. Distant again.

Because of Sheena.

Damn that girl to the depths of hell.

There was a knock on the door, and Mary, pale hair flying behind her, burst into the room. "Papa said you were here!" the girl said, then spying the swaddled infant in Zelda's arms, walked over to inspect her new brother.

"This is Llywelyn?" she asked. And as she looked at the boy, her top lip curled and her little nose wrinkled, as if she smelled something bad.

"Aye, your brother."

Mary didn't bother hiding her disapproval. "He looks . . . different." Mary was the first to voice what others who had come to view the infant had said silently. Upon entering the room, the servants and peasants had been all laughter, well wishes, and smiles. They'd burst into the chamber bubbling over with excitement, but upon observing little Llywelyn they had, to a one, lost their exuberance, their laughter fading, their smiles becoming hard and chiseled upon their faces.

"Because he's a boy."

"Nay, because he has dark hair and his skin is not so white and . . . and his face . . . it be—"

"Fine. He's fine," Fawn snapped, refusing to believe even for a moment that the boy she'd worked so hard to conceive could be less than perfect. 'Twas true that in the few hours since her son's birth, Fawn had noticed the difference in him. He was not as alert as Mary had been after she'd come screaming into this world, nor were his eyes as bright as Ann's had been and, compared to Lynna . . . well, Fawn wouldn't think such thoughts. Each child was different.

"Give him time," Fawn suggested, irritation lacing her words. "He's only been here a short while, and he was born in a tiny, smelly hut, unlike you and your sisters."

"Why were you there? At Serena's?" Mary asked, losing interest in the babe that Zelda so patiently rocked and held. She flopped onto a corner of the bed. "She's a fortune-teller, right? So why did you want to see her?"

"I don't know," Fawn lied.

"Were you worried about the baby?"

"A little."

"Then you should have gone to the chapel and prayed." Mary nodded and tossed a ringlet of white hair over her shoulder. "That's what you always tell me to do."

"This was different."

Mary didn't argue, but one eyebrow lifted imperiously. 'Twas a pose that reminded Fawn of herself. "He's just another baby," Mary pointed out, and for the first time Fawn considered that her daughter was a little jealous. Not that

Fawn didn't understand. Mary would never be the heir. Never favored. Never become the source of hopes and dreams. Never named after a legendary king. The best she could hope for was to marry a rich baron who was kind to her.

'Twas not fair.

Just as it had not been equal when Ellwynn had been born and Fawn had learned the bitter truth that a person's gender was far more important than a person's intelligence.

Men were destined to become leaders. Women were fated to follow.

Unless they were clever enough to manipulate their men without being found out. Oh, one could never let her husband know that she was plotting her own course and using him as a vessel. No. She had to be silent and appear obedient, even witless at times so that the man was assured that he was the ruler, the one making all decisions. Then and only then would a wife's will be done.

Never would she get kind words for her efforts. Nor would she be allowed a shred of glory.

Glory, fame, and wealth were only for men.

Unless a woman moved in the shadows, whispered lies, hid her true feelings, and was ruthless enough to do what had to be done, no matter how distasteful or bloody it was.

The baby started crying again. "He is hungry," Zelda said, walking to the bed.

Reluctantly Fawn opened her arms and, lowering one side of her tunic, held her son close. Her breasts, large and overflowing with milk, ached; the nipples burned from her attempts at feeding the boy. Again he fought her, suckling for a few seconds only to arch his tiny back and wail to the heavens.

"'Tis fine you be, Llywelyn," she said, though she nearly choked on the lie. Mary hopped off the bed and, with her weak chin leading the way, flounced out of Fawn's chamber.

The horse was spent. Lather foamed against his once white coat, and he was blowing hard as they crested a small hill and came upon a large lake that reflected the stars and a bit of moon. Dawn was approaching, and it was far past time to rest. Every muscle in Sheena's body ached, her spine was stiff, her ankle throbbed.

Keegan, leaning heavily against her, reached over her shoulder and pointed at a copse of trees and outcropping of rock. "There. 'Tis a good place to rest for a while."

With tired arms Sheena tugged on the reins, and the destrier slowed to a walk. Once at the edge of the lake, Keegan swung to the ground and helped her alight as well.

Blood, a dark smear, stained his tunic, but he seemed strong and helped remove the saddle. "I'll walk him a bit," he said. "You find a place for us to rest."

Too tired to argue, she drank from the lake, splashed cold water over her face and hands, then did as she was told, searching beneath trees to find a grassy spot. Keegan led the horse to the water, let the beast drink a few gulps, then walked him around the edge of the lake until the destrier was breathing normally again.

Sheena dug through the compartments in the saddle, hoping to find some food, but there was none. No provisions whatsoever. Ignoring the emptiness in her stomach, she used the saddle as a backrest laid upon the cool ground and closed her eyes but for a minute. She knew that sleep would be impossible, but as she listened to the lap of the water at the lake's edge, she began to breathe slowly. She barely stirred when Keegan, after gritting his teeth against pain as he cleaned the edges of his wound, settled in beside her. She snuggled up to him, whispered something and, sighing, fell into a deep, untroubled slumber.

She seemed younger than her years as she slept, and he smiled as he brushed a lock of her flame-red hair away from her cheek. She was only a few years younger than he and hardly an innocent. He was troubled by the brutality of her husband and what she'd endured, but she seemed to have put it behind her, not unscathed but strong. Aye, she was a unique woman, one not only accused of killing her cur of a husband, but a woman who had outsmarted the soldiers of Ogof and Tardiff combined, a horsewoman whose sharp kick had felled Sir Manning. She'd probably saved Keegan's life, not just tonight but a long time ago when she'd braved her father's wrath and taken his hand to lead him down a secret tunnel to a rotting, hidden dock.

Aye, she was a woman like no other, and as he held her close, he placed a kiss upon her forehead. His heart was tugged. Resting his cheek upon her crown, he listened to the sounds of the dawn. The wound in his shoulder ached but had stopped bleeding. Though he was near exhaustion, his manhood swelled with desire. Fighting the urge to kiss and wake her, to make love to her until they were both lying gasping and breathless, he stared into the sky, where dawn was chasing away the few remaining stars.

The horse, after again drinking from the lake, lay down and rolled, grunting in pleasure, his powerful legs pawing the air until, with a snort, he stood, shook his great head, and began to graze. Mist began to rise off the water, and Keegan, captain of the *Dark Sapphire*, a man who had sworn to trust his heart to no female, knew he would lay down his life for this mite of a woman with the fiery hair and sharp tongue. Never had he felt such a need to protect and possess. Never had he thought of giving up the sea for a woman, but Sheena of Ogof had turned his thoughts around.

His breath feathering her hair, he fell into a dreamless sleep just as the first shafts of morning light began to crawl across the eastern hills.

Hours later Sheena opened an eye to spy a hawk circling high in a cloudless sky. The horse was grazing, and Keegan, his jaw dark with his beard, was snoring softly, his neck at an odd angle, his shirt stained with blood.

He didn't move when she lifted his tunic and scowled at the sight of his wound. It wasn't as deep as she had feared and had already scabbed over, but the flesh around the cut was an angry purple and his chest hairs were matted with dry blood.

She longed to clean the cut, to apply ointment if she had it, but knew he would wake if she so much as touched him. Besides, she needed a few minutes alone in the lake. She was still wearing the soldier's scratchy uniform, and her feet were filthy from running through the pigsty and the forest. Her hair was tangled and clumped, and the lake beckoned.

She slipped away from Keegan and stripped out of the hated, stinking clothes. Kicking off the soldier's boots, she waded into the water. She sucked in her breath as the icy liquid splashed up her legs. Yet it was clean. Bracing. When she was hip deep, she pushed off and swam, dipping her head beneath the surface and feeling the cold water slide over her skin and through her hair. Using her fingers, she combed the tangles from her tresses, wiped the smudges of mud from her legs, arms, and body, then floated on her back and watched the clouds move across the sky just as she had when she was a child. The water chilled her flesh, but her spirit soared, for she was safe and with Keegan, if only for a while.

Lifting her head, she glanced across the water to the grass in the direction where she'd left Keegan. He was missing. No longer lying with his head propped against the saddle.

Her heart stopped.

Fear knifed through her.

Then she saw him emerge from the forest.

Naked as the day he was born. Bronzed skin stretched over hard, sinewy muscles. He stared directly at her, his eyes as gray as the morning dawn.

The back of her throat became dry as a desert wind, for she'd never seen him naked in the light. The blood-crusted gash on his shoulder was only the freshest of scars that were visible on his broad shoulders and wide chest, where a mat of curling dark hair arrowed down a flat abdomen.

Lower still, stiff as a ship's spar, Keegan's manhood rose between hard, well-muscled thighs. Anticipation caused her chilled skin to tingle as he approached and waded into the water. His gaze never left hers and she was suddenly unable to breathe. They had no time to linger, no reason to spend another second here, where they could be discovered at any instant. And yet when he reached her and his arms swept her against him, she didn't protest.

Cold skin suddenly heated. Her nipples were already hard from the frigid water. Her chilled lips met the warmth of his hungrily, anxiously.

With a groan he dragged her closer still. His tongue plunged into her mouth, his lips pressed hard against hers, and he kissed her until her breath was lost deep in her lungs and the liquid fire in her blood spread through her limbs and to that most intimate part of her.

Deep inside she wanted him, yearned for him. Her arms circled his neck as she kissed him feverishly.

You have no time for this, Sheena, no need. This rogue will do naught but cause you heartache and pain. Asides, Manning's soldiers are riding ever closer. Do not dally! Do not tarry. 'Tis suicide.

And yet she couldn't stop. His hands splayed upon her back, the tips of his fingers grazing the valley of her spine. He lifted her to him, kissed one wet breast, and Sheena threw back her head, felt the early morning sunlight caress her skin as his teeth nipped and his tongue licked and his lips sucked.

Her pulse leapt. Thoughts of love pierced the armor surrounding her heart.

"Ah, witch," he said, looking long into her eyes, "'Tis true that you've cast a spell upon me."

She couldn't help but smile as she stood in the water that reached her breasts. Her nipples puckered in the cool morning air. "Aye, Captain, that I have. And so you will please me, over and over again."

"So I have no will of my own? I am here but to serve you?" he mocked.

"Aye. 'Tis so." She nodded curtly, then laughed aloud, the sound trilling over the ripples of the lake.

He chuckled deep in his throat. "Is that my punishment?"

"Oh, nay, Keegan. 'Tis your reward."

A glimmer of light caught in his eyes. "Then I accept it now." Reaching down swiftly, he placed his big hands around her thighs, lifted her up, and lowered her over the thick rod of his manhood. She gasped, her tender skin hot and cold all in one instant. His mouth claimed hers in a kiss of pure possession, and her legs wrapped around his torso. Slowly he lifted her, only to kiss her hard and lower her again.

Dear Lord.

She cried out.

Again, kissing her, his hands hard, he raised her to the tip of his shaft, only to bring her back to him.

Desire shot through her. She kissed him fiercely, hungrily, and moved against him. Pressing hard, increasing the tempo. She wanted him. All of him. God forgive her, she needed him.

Water swirled around them, churning wildly as her breath came faster and faster. He lifted her up and down in a feverish tempo, moving with her. She couldn't breathe, could barely think. Moaning, clinging to his neck, she moved with him as sunlight spangled the water and a breeze laced with the scents of summer swept across the lake. Hotter and hotter, faster and faster, he moved, his head bent backward as he kissed her, her fingers digging deep into the muscles of his neck.

"Keegan . . . oh . . ." She couldn't speak, could not force any words past her throat.

"Ah, love . . . sweet, sweet Sheena . . ."

The first spasm hit and she jolted. Her body convulsed, the sky and water fused behind her eyes, and her spirit soared to the heavens. She clung to him, held his face against her chest, listened to the pounding of his heart and the slowing of his breath.

Only when she was able to take in air again did he let her slide down, her feet sinking into the soft silt at the lake's bottom, the smooth dirt filling the cracks between her toes. "So, witch, did I please you?" he teased, gasping and smiling with the knowledge that she'd been well sated.

"Oh, nay, Captain," she lied with a wink. "I think you need to try a little harder."

"Do you?" A wicked smile slid across his jaw. "Then so be it." He dragged her to him and kissed her hard. His arms surrounded her, his body enveloped her, and she wanted nothing more than to hold him to her for the rest of her life.

It was insane. Daft. She was laying her heart bare, and yet she had no choice. Foolish or not, she loved him. There was naught she could do about it.

He kissed her so hard that her knees began to buckle, and the roaring in her ears was thunderous, wild, like hundreds of horses' hooves thudding wildly over the hard ground. Pounding, pounding . . .

Every muscle in his body tensed. He lifted his head. Sheena nearly fell into the water. "Keegan—?"

"Shh!"

Then she heard it. The earth was shaking. 'Twas not her heart that was galloping but the sound of dozens of horses approaching as fast as lightning.

"Damn! Come! Now!" Grabbing her hand, he dragged her out of the water, did not pause to scoop up their clothes, or the saddle, just the bridle as he ran to the steed, which had lifted his great head. Keegan forced the bit into the horse's mouth, buckled the chin strap and, grabbing the reins in one hand, he lifted Sheena onto the stallion's back. Then he mounted behind her and kicked hard.

"Run, you bastard!" Keegan growled.

The stallion bolted, streaking toward the woods. Across the grassland and into the shadows the horse galloped, long legs eating up the ground, strides lengthening. Tears came to Sheena's eyes, blurring her vision. The thickets of oak and pine loomed closer. *Faster! Run faster, you demon!*

Sheena's wet hair unfurled behind her, slapping Keegan's face as he reached around her and kicked hard. Leaning forward over the destrier's massive shoulders, Sheena could barely breathe.

At the edge of the woods, as the great war horse raced into the dark cover, Sheena dared to look over her shoulder.

Manning of Tardiff's army was just cresting the hill.

Chapter Fourteen

"What mean you that he's not here?" Hollis demanded, wringing his hands as he stared into the worried faces of several members of the ship's crew. For the love of St. Peter, where was Bo? A dozen worries assailed him as he paced the deck of the *Dark Sapphire*. The sun was high, a few clouds moving in, but the ship was steady on her course to Drudwy, the sails billowing full.

"I mean, I checked from the crow's nest to the lowest hold. Even the secret compartments, but Bo, he ain't on board," Jasper said, his good eye squinting in the sunlight.

"Saints preserve us." Hollis studied the shoreline far in the distance and clasped his hands before him, rubbing his aching joints and silently cursing the headstrong lad, who was beginning to remind him more and more of Keegan. At Bo's age, Keegan had been full of piss and nonsense, always looking for and finding trouble. Though they were not blood-related, Bo had learned much from the man who had plucked him off the streets where he'd grown up as a pickpocket and beggar.

"Methinks he got off afore we sailed," Jasper concluded, wiping a ragged sleeve under his nose and sniffing loudly as the ship rolled gently with the tide. "Maynard, he swears he saw the boy scrambling around below decks just before we raised anchor."

Hollis shook his head and felt mist against his bare scalp. There was no turning back, not if he was to meet with Keegan. He made a quick sign of the cross and whispered a brief prayer for the headstrong lad. Truth to tell, there was a hollowness deep inside him, for Hollis had no family but Keegan and considered these men—ruffians, blackhearts, thieves, and thugs though they be—his clan. Brought together by dark deeds of their pasts, drawn by the lure of the sea, a fleet ship, and a captain who asked no questions, the men were like wolves in a pack, each needing the other.

And there were so many terrors in the world. Sea serpents and witches, the devil around every corner . . . Bloody hell, he hoped the boy had enough wits to survive, but didn't believe it for a second.

So where was the bloody pup? he silently asked himself. *Where?* And why had Bo jumped ship?

Because of the woman, his mind taunted. Nary a man on board had been the same since she'd been found and had become a part of their last voyage. Hollis glowered at the lowering sun and rubbed his arms, for he felt a chill as cold as the bottom of the sea. If not for the comely witch who had stowed away, not only Bo but Keegan as well would not now be missing.

"So what're ye gonna do?" Jasper asked, and Hollis sensed the eyes of other men boring into him, expecting him to come up with an answer. George glanced up from his work as he caulked the seams in the deck floor, and Big Tom, checking the rigging, stayed within earshot. Even Maynard, distracted from catching the day's worth of rats, idled near the fore staysail and pretended interest in coiling rope.

"Stay the course," Hollis said, scowling into the wind. The prow of the great ship cut through the clear waters, bearing ever southward. Just as Keegan had ordered. But the weight of the decision burrowed into his conscience, and he feared for the lad's life.

By the saints, if he ever set eyes upon Bo again, he'd grab hold and hug the boy fiercely. Right before he gave the lad the tongue lashing of his life or strangled him for being a damned, mule-headed fool.

The saddle was his. Manning squatted on the beaten-down grass, ran his fingers over the tooled leather, and narrowed his eyes in thought. Sheena had been here. She and the captain. Clothes were scattered on the bent grass— the seaman's garb and Peter's soiled uniform—and there was evidence that someone had slept under the branches of a tree near the clearing. Yet there was no sign of Sheena, the captain of the *Dark Sapphire,* or Manning's precious destrier, the best war horse in all of Wales. Anger coursed through his blood, and a muscle worked in his jaw. He rubbed his thumb against his finger and thought of all kinds of punishments for the pair if he ever caught up with them.

And he would. By all that was holy and all that was not, he would run the snot-nosed daughter of Jestin to the ground if it took the rest of his life.

Manning had prided himself on his cunning, on his sheer brute strength, on his ability to make men quiver in fear. But dealing with Sheena had been different and far more difficult. The wench had proved to be sly as a fox and twice as elusive.

And damned lucky. Oh, God's eyes, she'd been lucky.

Standing, he rubbed the muscles of his back and kicked a stone into the clear waters of the lake. The wheels in his mind turning, he watched the pebble sink to the bottom, sending ripples ever outward as the sun reflected upon the cool surface.

"There be no sign of 'em," Leonard reported as his eyes scanned the edge of the woods, but Manning didn't trust the whiny man to have done a thorough job. Leonard had been ready to give up this mission before it had gotten started.

"Keep looking."

"But—"

"I said, keep looking!" Manning thundered.

Leonard and several others returned to the forest, presumably to hunt for clues, though Manning suspected there were none to be found. The damned woman sometimes left no more tracks than did a ghost.

He spat, studied the countryside and the lake, where a dozen ducks were swimming, quacking and turning their tails skyward as they searched for food. Where the devil was Jestin's wayward daughter? *Where?* She could not have gotten far on one horse with a wounded companion. Manning spat, wiped his mouth, and didn't say a word. He would check the town again, and the farmer's hut, the ship at the dock, and turn over every sorry pebble in this godforsaken outpost before returning to Ogof empty-handed. At the thought he scowled darkly, and had any of his men said a word, he would have cuffed the soldier from here to eternity.

He paced the grass and conjured up excuses to Fawn. None were good enough. As the sun rose ever higher, Leonard and the rest of his sorry band returned. Empty-handed. "We—we searched the clearing here and the undergrowth, but they be gone now. Emberly spied fresh horse tracks, but that be all."

So why did they ride off and not take the clothes or saddle?

Manning tossed the dirty uniform to Peter, then scowled at the captain's bloody shirt and breeches. At least he had the satisfaction of knowing that he'd wounded the bastard. Hopefully it was mortal. Obviously they'd found new disguises, Manning decided, but why not take the saddle . . . unless they'd been found out and left suddenly.

By the Gods, it was his curse to always chase that woman! Even his men were starting to doubt him, and their spirits had sunk. They'd become a quarrelsome lot, and if Sheena wasn't found soon, he feared they'd take up arms against him.

"What now?" one man, a particularly surly knight with rotting teeth and bad breath, asked. He was lean and anxious, always ready for battle.

"We keep looking."

Peter spat on the ground in disgust. "Where?"

Manning thought for a moment, and an idea that he didn't like much formed in his mind. Mayhap Sheena kept escaping because he wasn't relying upon his brains to capture her. A strong man who had always used his size and intimidation to get what he wanted, Manning expected those who argued with him to become scared, to give up rather than fight him or try to best him, for most men knew he would allow no one to win, he would be relentless in hunting them down. But with Sheena it was different. His size and reputation hadn't been enough to intimidate her into submission. If anything, she seemed more determined than ever to thwart him.

Perhaps it was time to change his tactics, to use his mind to catch her. To that end, he might have to give up some time, but rather than keep running in circles, looking like a fool while hoping to chase her down, it would be better to lay a trap. He reached down, felt the soil, and let it sift through his fingers as he considered his options.

Though he hated the thought of it, he would have to backtrack a bit. Consider her next move. He glanced across the lake to the shadowy forest and scowled. She was always slipping through his fingers like the earth he'd just scooped up. "No more," he said aloud. His fist clenched as if he could grab her.

"No more what?" one of his men asked.

No more will I lose. He didn't answer aloud. "Come," he ordered, throwing himself upon Delwyn's horse and jerking hard on the reins. "You, Seth, grab that saddle and the clothes. We may need them." Kicking his mount, he led his tired army away from the lake and toward the farmer's hut where Sheena had once taken refuge. Mayhap Freddy or the woman had learned of her plans in the time she'd spent there. For a few coins, or to avoid a flogging, many tongues had been loosened in the past. Manning doubted it would be any different with the pig farmer. Asides, he had unfinished business with the man. There were the stones to consider, the ruby, topaz, and emerald Sheena had stolen from Tardiff and Freddy had bragged about at the tavern. Manning could return to Ogof with the gems if not the woman. He clucked to the horse and started off at a gallop.

Within hours, they were upon the farm, a small piece of land wedged between the forest and the cliffs overlooking the sea. Manning spied Freddy in the middle of a field, shaking dried acorns out of a large sack while his pigs snorted and rutted near his feet. He tossed the bag over his shoulder and was dusting his hands when he looked up and saw Manning's army. Immediately his ugly face twisted into a grimace of suspicion.

"What is it you want?" he demanded, walking through the muck to the fence. A pathetic creature in tattered clothes, he used one hand to shade his eyes as he glowered up at the dark knight. "Did you not find the woman you sought?"

"I need the stones," Manning said flatly.

"Wha—?" The farmer's expression changed. His eyes slitted like a cornered dog. He was about to lie.

"I know the gems be here, Fred Farmer, so don't bother attempting to lie to me."

"But there be no jewels."

Manning picked up his short whip. "Think hard, farmer, and lie to me not. That night in the tavern, you said that the girl you found was carrying stones with her. More than the gold one you were crowin' about. I heard ye with me own ears."

The farmer didn't move. Swallowed hard. High color swept up his pockmarked face. "I do na know what ye're talkin' about."

Manning edged his horse closer, held fast to his short whip. "Of course you do."

"I was drunk."

"I saw the yellow sapphire."

"'Twas the only one and I had to sell it and—"

Manning leaped from his horse, vaulted the fence, and grabbed the poor idiot by his throat. He brandished his crop as if he intended to slice off the lying bastard's tongue. "Lie not to me, Fred Farmer, or I will kill all yer pigs, burn yer farm, and take both ye and yer wife back to the Baron of Ogof. When he hears that ye've lied to me about his daughter and the jewels she left here, he'll send ye straight to the gallows, make no mistake." He twisted the man's arm behind him and heard sinews and tendons pop.

"Ooooh," Freddy cried, falling to his knees. Manning dragged him to his feet again and snapped the crop near his eyes. Still the fool did not say a word.

"Kill the sow," Manning ordered Seth, and the soldier drew an arrow from his quiver, took aim, and pulled back on the bowstring.

"Nay!" The door to the hut opened, and the man's wife, a big woman with a fleshy face and huge nose, hurried out. "I've got the stones, Sir Manning. They be here, in the lady's boot."

"Esme, no!" Freddy's face fell. All his dreams of riches were about to vanish as quickly as they'd come.

The wife was running, ungainly and heavy, holding a small boot outward and shaking it until it rattled. As if she were eager to give up the treasure. Why? Dozens of sows could be bought with but one of the jewels . . . it made little sense unless she was afraid for her life, or that of her husband. Was she so frightened?

Manning released the farmer, vaulted the fence, and snatched the boot from her fingers. He upended the clean leather, and two stones rolled out onto his waiting fingers. Blood red and forest green, they winked brilliantly in the sunlight.

"Well there, see, Fred, ye fergot that ye had these gems, now, didn't ye?" Manning taunted, tucking his riding crop inside his belt. "Mayhap ye should not drink so much."

Red-faced, looking as if he'd been struck by an act of God, the farmer was clutching his arm with his free hand and trying to hold back the curses that were so obviously close to tripping off his tongue.

The woman was afraid. Her big face was white as death, and a nasty tic was tremoring beneath one eye. Her hands shook as she wiped them on her dirty apron. Manning climbed onto his steed and was about to ride off, but there was something in the air that he felt, something more that he was missing. Aye, he had the stones and they were worth a lot, but the woman . . . she was acting so strangely.

A thought struck him. Hard. 'Twas obvious Freddy's wife wanted Manning gone and fast. As if she was hiding something. But not the stones; she'd given them up easily. Too easily. And not for love of the man or she would have climbed over the fence to his aid, as he looked about to swoon from the injuries inflicted upon him by Manning. Instead she stood on the dirt path leading to the door of her hut—almost as if she were blocking his entrance to her home.

Why?

Was it because she was hiding something more valuable than the gems in her crumbling shack? The air was cool, the sound of the sea beneath the cliffs a steady rush, and yet Esme was sweating, beads running down from her temples. Squinting against the sun, Manning drew his attention to the doorway and thought he saw a movement within the hut.

His heart jolted.

Someone indeed was hiding inside.

A smile twisted his lips, and anticipation fired his blood. Was Lady Sheena so foolish as to return here? Had she no choice? Was it possible she and the captain had been naked—mayhap even coupling—and been startled by someone, only to seek cover in the only place they knew of to find shelter and safety? Or had she returned for her precious stones—the very gems that were now so easily being offered to him?

"Check the house," he ordered Peter and Otto.

"Nay, there is no one," the woman said, frantic, her eyes wide. She swallowed hard. "Ye wanted the stones and ye have them and—"

Otto, the strongest of his men, pushed her to the ground and, sword aloft, lumbered up the path and through the open door.

Esme would not be detained. She scrambled to heavy feet and ran after him. "Nay, nay, there is no one here. Be off with ye now—"

A yowl erupted from the hut, then swearing and the sound of running footsteps.

"God help us," Esme cried as Peter knocked her to the ground and held her there with his blade pointed at the cleft between her breasts.

Manning's jaw clenched. Had Sheena escaped yet again? How? "Let no one pass!" he ordered curtly. "Surround the house!"

But it mattered not. Within a heartbeat Otto appeared hauling a boy with shaggy hair under his arm. The lad was struggling, kicking, swinging wildly with his fists, biting and writhing.

Blood dripped from Otto's ear.

"Bit me he did," Otto grumbled, his face twisted in pain. "Little bastard!"

"Who's this?" Manning demanded.

"No one." Esme rung her hands nervously. "He be but a boy who is staying with us and helping me husband with the chores."

"But not your boy?" Manning said, frowning thoughtfully, for he thought he'd seen the shaggy-haired lad before.

"Nay, but—"

"Put him down." Manning ordered, and wondered where he'd seen the urchin before. "Who be ye, son?"

The kid started to bolt, but Otto was quicker than he looked and grabbed the kid by his stringy hair. "No, ye don't . . ." he warned, holding the boy at arm's length. "He's a bad un, he is. Nearly bit off me ear and kicked me in the shin, he did. Aimed higher, too. Wanted to catch me in me balls."

"Why?" Manning said.

"I've seen him before," Peter offered with a bit of pride. "He be a lad who sailed on Wart's ship. Ain't that right, boy?"

Still restrained, the urchin spat on the ground. "Leave me be."

"Aye." Manning, too, had spied him crawling up the spars of the ship as well.

"'Tis not his fault. I found him in town and he was asking questions about a captain and a woman who'd fallen overboard from his ship. I asked him here to talk to him, to find out about the lady . . ." Esme's voice failed her and her chin wobbled. "He's but a boy."

"You've not seen the woman again?"

"Nay," she said, shaking her head as her husband collapsed against the fence. "But do not take the boy, please. He be but a child." She ignored Peter's blade and walked to the fence. "We—we, me husband and meself, we could use a child. Love him."

"I be not a child!" the ruffian insisted.

"This one could be worth something." Manning was warming to the idea of a hostage. Someone to barter with. Manning felt the hint of a smile tug at his mouth, though he knew the battle was not over yet. But now he had the stones and the boy. Things were turning around. He smiled into the salt-laden wind. "Let us go to the ship."

The insolent pup had the nerve to laugh. "'Tis too late," he taunted. "She's already sailed."

"With the captain?" Manning's blood burned. The kid didn't respond, just taunted him with his eyes.

"Well, it matters not, because I have spies strung up and down the coast-line," he snarled. "Wherever the *Dark Sapphire* docks, I will soon hear of it. The sheriff in town, he will know." The brat spat again. "Bring him!" Manning ordered, and the woman ran after the urchin, shaking her head, a hand to her mouth. Manning ignored her. "If he puts up a struggle, tie him and gag him."

"Nay, please, he is but a boy." The woman was pleading, tears in her big eyes. All this for a child who was not hers. Manning didn't understand. "You cannot take him—" she cried, reaching upward, supplicating.

"I can," Manning said with a knowing grin. "And I will."

"What of the sow?" the archer asked, and Manning realized the man was still sighting on the pig.

Manning looked at the miserable farmer slumped against a fence post and his fat, ugly wife chasing after a child she'd never borne. He glanced at the archer, kicked his steed, and said, "Kill it."

If nothing else, the captain was inventive, Sheena thought, shivering as she stepped into a monk's robe that Keegan had stolen from the laundry of an abbey. As easily as a cat, he'd scaled the walls and slipped naked through the stone corridors.

No one had seen him, he'd vowed once he'd returned, and Sheena didn't really care. She'd hidden in the brush, wondering what she would do if he was caught and detained, which fortunately hadn't happened. At least now she had something to wear again, and she threw on the scratchy vestment and pulled up the hood, hiding her hair and partially obscuring her face.

They'd managed to elude Manning's troops by doubling back on their route, passing the abbey, then heading south again, staying along the coast. At a stable in a small town they had traded Manning's distinctive white steed for two skinny mares which the owner of the stables was more than glad to give up.

"Ye've made yerself a fine bargain, Father," the man had claimed, clapping Keegan on his back and all the while having trouble smothering a self-satisfied smile at the deal he'd struck.

"Aye, I think so, and God will reward you in accordance with your actions," Keegan had replied, sending the stable master's Adam's apple to bobbing rapidly. "He knows your true heart. Bless you, my son."

With that he and Sheena, who had lingered in the shadows and kept her face averted while Keegan spoke with the horse trader, had climbed astride the two sorry-looking jennets and had ridden away.

Sheena had been nervous, forever glancing over her shoulder, but they'd traveled for miles with no hint of Manning's army behind them. They had met other travelers: men and women on foot or horseback, young children often in tow. A band of musicians had passed, as had a peddler with a noisy cart pulled by a team of mules. Not one soldier had crossed their path. Yet Sheena had been wary, her eyes scanning the horizon, her ears straining for the sound of an army. Her hands sweated over the reins as she checked behind them or searched each fork in the road, certain that at any moment the hated knight and his band of cutthroats would appear over the next rise or be waiting to ambush them around the next corner.

Keegan, however, was calm.

She avoided glancing at him, for each time she did, the image of him, naked and strong as he'd ridden with her on the destrier, filled her mind. The few times they'd made love had been glorious, and yet she knew there was no chance of it again; she was about to return to Ogof, mayhap to face the hangman, and Keegan would return to the sea. 'Twas the way it would be, even though she and the handsome, bullheaded captain had argued about it.

Her heart was heavy with the thought of leaving him, but she had no choice. Elsewise she would spend the rest of her life running from the enemy, nervously glancing over her shoulder and watching her back as she was doing now.

And he would forever be the target of Manning's wrath. Only if she gave herself up to her father would Keegan be free. Her throat closed when she thought of the danger she'd brought to him and his men.

Her heart twisted and she sent a quick glance in his direction, catching a glimpse of his angular features and intense gaze. What was it about the man that he was forever in her thoughts? Even now, as she worried about the threat of Tardiff's soldiers, she remembered their lovemaking in the lake and the feel of his slick, wet skin sliding erotically against hers.

Tingling inside, she forced her eyes back to the muddy road, rutted by heavy carts and hoofprints. Each time they had come upon another horseman she had been certain the man was a scout, one of Tardiff's soldiers. But as the hours passed and they neared the town of Drudwy, she felt a sliver of hope that they had evaded the enemy. All the hours spent backtracking and taking side roads and deer paths might have procured their freedom. "Do not count on it," she told herself as more travelers joined them.

She couldn't let her guard down, not for a minute, and there was another problem to consider. Keegan was certain she would sail with him on the *Dark Sapphire,* though she knew she would never board the ship again, never again imperil his crew.

Another thought that had been bothering her surfaced. "Where is Wart?"

Keegan didn't reply.

"You sent him to find out the truth, I heard it myself," she insisted, twisting in her saddle to pin him with her eyes. "Where is he?"

"Dead."

The single word was delivered without any expression.

"How?" she asked, but knew the answer. "Sir Manning."

Keegan's scowl deepened. "He will stop at nothing. No life is sacred." His eyes scanned the faces in the crowd before returning to hers. "You will be safe on the sea," he said again, as if he were reading her wayward thoughts.

"Nay, Captain." She shook her head, for she knew she had to return to Ogof, her home. Alone. "I cannot spend the rest of my life running. Nor can I hide in your ship. Nor . . . Nor can I put any more of your men in jeopardy." Wart had died because of her, and that was the end of it. Bitter cold swept through her bones, for she'd come to care for every man aboard the *Dark Sapphire,* cutthroats or thieves though they might be. She had not known Wart, but mourned his death and felt the stab of guilt that he had died because of her.

"So you would risk your own life?" Keegan asked.

"'Tis my battle and time to no longer be a coward."

"Even if it means facing your death?"

"My father would not sentence me to die."

"You know this?" he asked as they rode through the town gate. "He is not a patient man."

"He is my father."

"Aye and he killed mine."

Sheena lapsed into silence as the horses plodded through the narrow streets. Music and laughter spilled from the open doors of an inn, while a tin smith was offering up his wares and a blacksmith was working at his forge, the bellows hissing, a fire burning bright and hot. Children ran and played, some rolling hoops, others chasing after dogs. Smoke, salt spray, and the smell of fish mingled with dung, urine, and garbage.

On the far side of town was the wharf, and there, among a small fleet of fishing vessels, the *Dark Sapphire* was anchored. A proud smile cut across Keegan's face as he stared at the tall masts knifing upward to the blue, cloudless sky. Her sails bunched upon the yards, the ship was at rest, the smell of the sea heavy in the air. A man was selling fish near the dock, speaking to everyone who passed, offering up herring and cod and crab. His wife sat near him on a stool, gutting the fish and not even looking up to smile as burly men loaded casks and crates onto the other vessels at port.

Keegan pulled on the reins of his mount and reached across to do the same with Sheena's, but as his fingers twined in the leather straps, he froze. Again he looked at his ship, and his smile faded quickly. "Something's wrong," he whispered, his eyes suddenly dark with suspicion.

"What?"

"Where are the men?" His gaze narrowed on the deck of the *Dark Sapphire*, and Sheena, too, searched from bow to stern, seeing not a single member of Keegan's crew.

"Mayhap they are all below deck or in town or . . ." Her voice faded as she felt a presence behind her. The hairs on the back of her neck lifted one by one, and she turned her head, her heart plummeted.

Sir Manning of Tardiff, astride a black horse and proudly wearing the red and gold of the hated keep, was directly behind them. But he wasn't alone. With him the crew of the *Dark Sapphire* filled the narrow cobblestone street. Hands tied, faces drawn, welts visible on some of them, they stood and stared at the ground—Seamus, Jasper, Hollis, Maynard, even Big Tom and the rest. All shackled. All chained. All held prisoner by the rough soldiers of Tardiff.

Sheena's insides congealed.

Manning, dark knight of Tardiff, had won.

"Lady Sheena," he said, his voice rough, his face warm with pride. "'Tis time for you to come with me and face your father, and mayhap your death."

Chapter Fifteen

Keegan's face grew hard as granite as he faced Manning. "I'll take no orders from you. Nor will the lady." He positioned his sorry horse between Sheena's little jennet and the dark knight's steed, but it was of no use. The battle was over. They had lost and Sheena had brought the crew of the *Dark Sapphire* to their certain doom.

Manning's hate-filled eyes were trained on Keegan and satisfaction laced his words. "You, Captain, have no choice."

Sheena's heart ached. She had put these men in jeopardy, had ruined their lives. The battle scars and bruises upon the faces of Seamus, Jasper, even Big Tom convinced her that she had to offer herself up, to save them if she could.

Worse yet, Bo, who had always been so full of life, an imp with bright eyes, floppy hair and a cocky attitude was now beaten, his wrists cruelly bound by thick rope, a gag stuffed in his mouth. His face was streaked with mud, his eyes round with fear, and for some reason, he was being held apart from the others. Oh, God, please don't let Manning hurt the boy. Her throat turned to dust. Somehow, some way, she had to save him. Bo lifted his eyes to meet hers and despite the fear and the tearstains that tracked through the mud, he squared his slim shoulders, silently insisting that he was a man.

"Now, lady," Manning said as his horse stomped impatiently and his weary, angry-looking army surrounded their prisoners. "Finally, you have nowhere to run."

Keegan leaned forward in his saddle. "You have no jurisdiction here, so take your pathetic army and leave the lady, my crew and be off or—"

"Or what?" Manning sneered as the fisherman stopped trying to sell his catch and a crowd began to gather. "You're in no position to bargain, Captain. I've spoken with the authorities here. I will take these men prisoner as they have aided a criminal, a woman who killed the Lord of Tardiff." Manning's

voice was cold as the sea, his demeanor smugly proud. "'Tis finished, Keegan."
He snapped his fingers and motioned and his army circled tighter. Sheena's
horse minced, as the soldiers crushed closer.

"I'm warning you, leave her be, Manning." Keegan kicked his mount, drew
up near the dark knight. His jaw was rock hard, his eyes bright and despite the
horrid odds, he seemed ready to lunge at Manning. "Set these men free; you
have no argument with them."

"'Tis too late. The sheriff has agreed."

"I will go with you," Sheena began, thinking quickly, knowing she had nothing to barter with other than herself. The smell of a fight was heavy in the sea
air and the crew of the *Dark Sapphire*, though a tough bunch of cutthroats, was
no match for the weapons and soldiers of Tardiff. "Just let the others go free
and I will—"

"Nay." Keegan's jaw was set, his muscles bunched, his eyes blazing. His eyes
were trained on Manning, but Sheena saw him size up the crowd, the enemy, the
chances of escape. . . . "The sheriff has no such authority. You will stay with me."

Manning laughed. "I need no one's authority," he argued. "I've had my
men positioned in the towns along the coast, and I've dealt with the law in
each." His eyes narrowed a fraction. "I've been chasing the lady for a long time,
but now, at last, 'tis done."

Keegan's hands gripped hard on his reins. "Let her and my men go free,
Manning, and the *Dark Sapphire* will be yours." He hitched his chin toward the
ship rolling on the swells and Manning flicked an avaricious glance toward the
great carrack with its tall masts and gleaming hull.

"Nay!" Sheena would not have him lose the *Dark Sapphire*. Nor his crew.
"This be my battle. I will come with you, Sir Manning," she said again, tossing
off her hood, "and I will not try to escape, but the crew and ship stay here. With
the captain."

"Oh, lady, you have naught to bargain with." He tossed a smirk at Keegan.
"Nor do you. If I want the ship, I will take her. As for the prisoners, I will de-
cide their fate. Now, we be off! Oswald, round up the prisoners," he ordered.
"Take the captain and—"

"Nay, Manning, listen to me. If you let these men go free, I will come willingly with you, no longer try to escape or thwart you. But please, I beg you, do
not punish them for my sins," she said again, more boldly as the crowd became
larger, gathering around the soldiers and their prisoners. Women peered from
windows, men stopped their work, the fisherman's wife let her knife drop from
her bony fingers as she watched the display. Ignoring warning glances from
Keegan, Sheena lifted her chin and met Manning's cold glare. "You have my
word that I will do as you bid," she vowed.

"And if I do not grant these criminals their freedom?"

"Then I promise you, I will get away from you and free these men, and warn my father that you have no honor, that you killed an innocent man in Wart."

"The spy? Warren of Halliwell be hardly innocent."

Her insides curdled at his arrogance. Keegan seemed about to leap from his mount and strangle Manning with his bare hands.

"'Tis not up to you to decide who lives or dies," she said.

"Nay?" Manning snorted. "I think ye should consider again, *m'lady*. I be here at your father's request."

"I'll deal with Jestin," Keegan vowed.

"Nay!" There had already been enough blood spilled. "This be my battle." Inching her chin up proudly, she slowly eased her gaze over the faces of each of his soldiers. "If you let the captain and crew of the ship go free, I will also promise not to do harm to any of your men."

Manning laughed and the cold sound sent a shiver straight to Sheena's soul. "My men be strong; they fear not a woman."

"Nay?" she asked, lifting a skeptical eyebrow, though her heart was pounding and beneath her rough garb she was beginning to sweat despite the cold. "Not even if I call up the wrath of Morrigu or—"

"Ach, she be a witch," a woman with a hooked nose whispered, gathering her children close and scurrying away.

"I believe not in your witchcraft," Manning said.

"Nor did Tardiff."

Some of the soldiers seemed to pale a bit. A massive bay sidestepped, his iron-shod hooves ringing on the cobblestones, his nostrils wide. Somewhere a man coughed. The wind kicked up. The crowd stepped back a pace or two and a few of the more pious made a swift sign of the cross over their chests.

"Do not test me," she warned in a low voice.

Keegan tossed off the cowl of his robe as he leaned forward in his saddle, his lips flat over his teeth. "My men remain with me, Manning, and the woman stays as well. As I said, for our freedom, you will be given the *Dark Sapphire*," Keegan insisted and again Manning laughed. This time the sound was pure evil.

"But I already have it, you see." Manning reached into his pocket and withdrew a ring with a brilliant dark stone that gleamed in the afternoon light.

Sheena gasped.

Keegan stared at the ring as if it had been ripped from the fleshless fist of a dead man.

"So you recognize it."

Sheena stared at the gem that had once belonged to her mother, had been the object of the horrid wager, had been stolen by Keegan years before. "But how—?"

Keegan's gaze, drawn to the stone for a moment, slowly moved with silent condemnation to Hollis. The old man seemed to shrink into his cloak. "You lied?"

Hollis studied the cobblestones of the street. His shoulders slumped and despair edged his words. "I should have thrown the damned thing into the sea years ago."

"'Twas with the boy," Manning said. "But it matters not. I have everything now, and you, Captain, have nothing but false pride to bargain with. Now, there be no time for argument. Half of my men are going to board the ship and you're going to see that they and the *Dark Sapphire* make it safely to Ogof. The boy here"—he motioned to Bo—"will be kept apart, under constant guard and if there is any whisper of mutiny against me, the guard will slit his throat and throw his scrawny body to the beasts of the sea." Bo gulped and Sheena felt desperation the like of which had never before darkened her soul. If only she could save the boy, or Keegan . . . or the rest of the crew of the *Dark Sapphire*, a sorry lot of criminals that she'd come to trust with her life. She glanced at Keegan one last time and her heart twisted with the knowledge that she would never set eyes upon him again.

The boy she had kissed on the dock.

The man she now had taken as a lover.

Manning snapped his fingers, and seven or eight scraggly soldiers, their boots ringing, stormed up the gangway and onto the ship.

"The rest of my men and I will take the lady back overland. Once there, we will meet, and if you've done your part, I will let your men go free." He motioned to the rest of his small army, most of whom were on horseback. "At Ogof, Lady Sheena of Tardiff will be returned to her father, and the ship will become mine. Baron Jestin of Ogof will decide your fate—whether you live or die. It matters not to me." His smile had faded and pure hatred seemed to ooze from his every pore. "Now, that is how it is to be. I grow weary of this chase and will abide no dissent. If you do not agree, I will be forced to kill your men, one by one, and we'll start with the boy here."

"Nay," Sheena cried.

Manning nodded sharply to the soldier guarding Bo. Swiftly the man pulled out a long knife with a curved blade that glinted in the afternoon light. Bo arched his back and tried to fight, but the soldier put the blade to his throat.

"Dear God," Sheena whispered, tears filling her eyes. "Do not harm him." Surely Manning would not slay an innocent boy and yet . . . she knew how cruel a beast he was. She swallowed the lump in her throat. "Take me back, Manning. Leave these men. Please, I beg of you."

"What, woman? No more threats of witchcraft?" Manning asked with a crooked, self-satisfied smile. His gaze moved away from her to Keegan. "So, Captain, what say you?"

Keegan's face was grim. The veins in his neck throbbed, but his gaze was fastened on the blade at Bo's young throat. The boy shivered with fear, and a drop of blood began to ooze slowly from a tiny cut. "Enough!" Keegan agreed, his nostrils flaring, every muscle in his body bunched. "Let the boy go! Now!" His gaze was hard as he turned to Manning. "As long as you assure me of my men's safety and that the woman will not be harmed, so be it. You and I, we'll meet again in hell."

Manning nodded to the thug and the blade was lifted from Bo's neck. "That we will, Captain. That we will."

Anger roared through Keegan's veins. Fury tore at his soul and guilt, a new and ugly companion, sat heavy on his shoulders. His thoughts were dark and vengeful and the fear in his soul, a fear that Sheena would be forced up the steps to the gallows, besieged him, ripping at his mind with sharp, painful claws.

Somehow he had to save her.

No matter what.

Watching her ride away, her wrists bound, her spine stiff as she sat astride the old mare, had been more than he could bear. He'd pretended acquiescence, taken the helm without argument and steered the ship ever southward while the man who was guarding him began to nod.

The skin was tight and drawn over Keegan's face, his mind turning with plans of besting Manning and saving Sheena, his hands gripping the whipstaff so hard his knuckles showed white as he pretended to comply with Manning's orders. He'd commanded his men to do the same and now, grudgingly, they went about their tasks upon the ship, working under the suspicious eyes of the guards.

They had grumbled and sent scathing glances at the soldiers, but to all it had appeared outwardly that Keegan had complied, that he'd crumpled beneath Sir Manning's will. Some of his own men had looked upon him with disgust, but it had been necessary for the crew to view him with contempt. He had had to appear weak, in order to lure the enemy into believing him to be compliant, his spirit broken, and that he'd lost all fight in him. Bo had been tied and gagged in the hold, one soldier watching him around the clock.

"But why not try to best them," Jasper had complained one twilit evening. "They be a sad lot if ever I've seen one."

"We cannot risk the lady's life," Keegan had replied within earshot of a strapping soldier with a thick, red beard and hands that appeared strong enough to strangle a man and snap his neck.

"We could take 'em," Tom had insisted, his brows drawing together as he viewed Keegan with new eyes, as if his captain had suddenly turned coward.

"I will not put Sheena in jeopardy," he'd said and Tom had spat on the deck, confusion evident on his face.

"This be a ruse," Hollis had whispered to him on the deck near the bowsprit. "I know ye well enough. The rest of the crew they might believe ye to have bowed to Manning, but me, I've known ye since ye were a babe."

"And yet you lied to me about the stone."

"Ach." Hollis had shaken his balding head. "Worry not about the gem now." His hand had reached out to touch Keegan's shoulder. "I'm on yer side. If ye be plottin' a mutiny against the soldiers, I'm with ye, as are the men."

Keegan's gaze had bored into the older man's. He had sensed a presence hiding behind the mainsail. "I would never put Sheena's life in danger, Hollis. This you know. I will do whatever I must to see that she's safe."

Hollis had hesitated, then his old eyes had sparked as if he understood. "Then, ye be a fool for a woman," he had said, though there was little conviction in his voice.

"Mayhap."

"The men be disappointed in ye."

Keegan had slid his gaze to the sail and Hollis had nodded, as if he had understood all too well that they were being overheard. "Tell the men that they are to follow my example. Everyone's life is at stake. No one is to question my authority."

"So be it. I'll make sure they understand," Hollis had said, ambling off and the shadow, still hidden behind the sails, had snuck after him.

Now, as Keegan guided the ship through the night-black waters, positioning the *Dark Sapphire* at odds with the current, he planted his feet, rolled with the decking and, from the corner of his eye, caught sight of one of Tardiff's soldiers lose his battle with nausea and lean over the railing.

Keegan grinned inwardly as a huge swell raised the *Dark Sapphire* high, then dropped quickly.

"God have mercy," the man guarding him muttered. He was a heavyset man who sweated and smelled sour and like all of the tired foot soldiers aboard had never before been asea. It wasn't only the rock of the ship that caused them to be ill, but the heavy drinking, more than the soldiers could handle on the rough sea, and the food, deliberately tainted as it was, adding to their sickness. By now Hollis had caught onto Keegan's plans and had spread the word to the rest of the crew.

"Can ye na steady her?" the guard asked, his skin a pasty shade tinged with green in the lantern light.

"I'm trying my best," Keegan lied and caught a glance from Seamus. A smile played upon the seaman's lips. "Mayhap you would like to take over."

"Nay, nay," the soldier said as Maynard stopped by with his bucket of rats.

"Ye called fer me."

"Do not throw the beasts overboard," Keegan said and nodded at the furry, bloody carcasses in Maynard's pail. "In case we run out of provisions."

"We'll not be eatin' rats!" the guard said.

"Unless we run out of food." Keegan's gaze cut any argument from Maynard's lips. "Sometimes we have no choice."

"God's eyes, who would want a life like this?" the guard muttered and Seamus swallowed another smile as he turned away. "The food and this bloody journey give a man the runs, they do."

"I'll give these ones to the cook," Maynard said, lifting a pail.

"Aye."

"Bloody Christ," the soldier muttered, swiping a palm over his brow. "I'll starve before I eat a rat."

"'Tis your choice."

"I-I needs a drink."

"I've already ordered all the casks opened. There be wine and ale enough to last the voyage."

Keegan tacked again and the ship lurched, the pail of rodents nearly slopping its bloody contents as Maynard hurried below decks.

The guard ordered ale and it was brought, but as the wind picked up, keening across the ocean, Manning's men were restless. Some had drunk far too much, others were listless and tired. All the soldiers were anxious to return to land and Tardiff Hall. They knew naught of the sea, nor of sailing ships, and had to rely upon Keegan and the members of his crew to take them back to Ogof.

It was just as Keegan had hoped.

The tired soldiers, weary from weeks of chasing after Sheena, counted upon the fact that Keegan would do nothing to endanger his men, or Sheena. To be on the safe side, as Manning had ordered, they held Bo in the hold, bound and gagged, as insurance. Should Keegan veer off course, or should any of the men not do as they were told, Bo would be killed.

Or so they thought.

But as they fell asleep at their posts or hung over the deck rail and retched, Keegan gave up the helm to Cedric. He feigned sleep on the floor as his guard had taken the bunk. Snoring softly, his eyes closed, Keegan waited, listening, the sounds of his cabin familiar. Of course he was chained. He had been each night, but what the guard didn't know is that the master key to all locks aboard the *Dark Sapphire* was hidden in a space beneath the drawer in his bunk. Tonight, as the wind raged and keened and the boat creaked, the masts groaning, the rigging rattling, Keegan ever so slowly tugged on the squeaky drawer. It seemed to take hours to inch the drawer open far enough that he could stretch his arm over the space that hid his clothes to the little niche in the back. His muscles ached and he bit hard on his lip as the shackle dug into his calf, but his fingers brushed the metal.

The soldier snorted. Keegan froze. Sighing heavily, his jailer rolled over and Keegan snagged the key, hiding it in the palm of his hand. He waited a few more seconds and as the ship listed slightly, found the lock. With a soft click, the shackles opened and he was free.

Taking the sleeping man's sword from his scabbard, Keegan slipped out the door and locked it firmly behind him. Outside the sky was dark, the wind fierce, the air brisk. He moved stealthily through the shadows, past slumbering guards, into the hold where he found Hollis, wrapped in his cloak, snoring loudly, his head bent at an odd angle. Placing a hand over the old man's mouth, Keegan shook his shoulder gently.

Hollis's eyes flew open. He started to struggle, then spying Keegan in the stygian gloom, he climbed to his feet. "I wondered when ye'd come fer me," he whispered as they slipped silently to a spot on the main deck. "Ye've a plan."

"Aye. Pray that it works. You free the men with this." He dropped the key into Hollis's palm.

"And what will ye be up to?"

"'Tis time to turn the tables on Manning's men. We'll set Big Tom free, and he and I will handle the soldiers. Bring them to the hold where you and the others will be ready to lock them in the chains they've used on us." Keegan's smile was pure evil. Hollis cackled. "Come."

Creeping stealthily, they came upon the guard on deck and Keegan lunged forward, wrapped his arm around the brute's neck, and threatened death with his newfound blade. "Fight me and you'll die," Keegan promised. The soldier, weak as he was, put up no struggle. Within seconds Big Tom was free, rubbing his wrists and anxious for battle.

"I knew ye'd find a way to free us," he said. "I never doubted ye for a second, Captain."

'Twas stretching the truth a bit, Keegan thought, but cared not. "First we free Bo, then the others."

In the darkness, Big Tom smiled. "And then the lady? We'll save her as well?"

"Or die trying," Keegan vowed.

"Then, Captain," Tom said heartily and grabbed the soldier's dagger and sword, "there be no time to waste."

"Amen," Hollis agreed as they slunk through the shadows and into the bowels of the ship. *Hold on, Sheena,* Keegan thought, his eyes straining in the dark, his muscles poised for battle. *I'm coming.*

The night was bitter cold with the promise of autumn. No stars dared shine through the fog that crept stealthily over the ground, yet Sheena recognized the road as it turned toward the great gates of Ogof. They had ridden for days, she was tired to her bones, and she felt no sense of homecoming even as dawn threatened to pierce the mantle of fog surrounding the fortress. Nay, all she felt was dread—deep, dark and terrifying. She had barely slept as she'd always been wary, not trusting any of Tardiff's soldiers who had stared at her with a silent hatred. She'd heard them talking around the fire, picking their teeth with the bones of quail and rabbit, grumbling about the chase she'd given them, arguing among themselves if she were a witch, daft, or just a cold-blooded killer.

Manning had barely let her out of his sight and even when she had to relieve herself, a guard stood nearby. 'Twas humiliating and worrisome, though she'd managed to scratch a few runes in the sand and had even offered up more than her share of prayers to God. She had let the men hear her chanting as if calling up the spirits. More than one Adam's apple had bobbed in worry and the men, aside from the guard assigned to her, had given her a wide berth.

All the better. Now, of course, she had to face her father.

Lord help me, she thought, gathering up her courage and forcing her back to be ramrod stiff as she sat astride her weary mount. *And be with Keegan.* For all of this horrid journey, her thoughts had been with that blackheart of a captain, the man she'd sworn to hate, the man she now realized she loved. With every breath in her body she ached for him, for she was certain she would never see him again. *Oh, love, if I had only told you how I felt.* But she had not known, would not admit it to herself. By the gods, she was a fool like no other. And now she would never see him again, might not know if he lived or died.

Torment, dark and desperate, scraped at her soul.

"Halt! Who goes there?" a deep male voice demanded from the top of the tower. Her heart pounded in fear, and though she had pretended subservience, anger burned bright in her mind.

"'Tis I, Geoff," Manning said, his voice filled with a sickening pride that made Sheena's skin crawl. "And I have with me Lady Sheena. Let us pass."

"Aye, Sir Manning! Open the gates!" Geoff replied, his voice filled with relief and jubilation. So this was how it would be. Even those who had known her since childhood would celebrate her imprisonment, mayhap her death.

With a grinding of gears the clanking portcullis rose. Sheena set her jaw and, her hands still bound, rode into the home that she'd known for most of her life. Through the outer bailey where the quintain was at rest, sheep grazed. The gong farmer rolled out a wheelbarrow of muck; peasants carrying sickles and scythes were walking toward the main gate on the way to her father's fields.

As the army rode to the inner bailey, she felt eyes upon her and heard her name whispered.

"So they finally caught up with her," a man murmured as he hoisted a heavy bag to his shoulders. In the darkness Sheena could not see his face.

"Poor lass, she'll be hanged sure," a woman, mayhap his wife, replied. She carried a basket of candles and was walking to the keep. "And Jestin, her father, he be the one who will have to send her to the gallows. By the saints."

Husband and wife hurried on their way, but the word of Manning's triumphant arrival spread, and peasants and servants alike appeared through the mist. She recognized Allen, the rail-thin steward, and Farrell, the stable master, leading a docile horse. John, one of the pages, smiled shyly, blushing as he saw her. His hair stuck up at odd angles and his teeth were crooked and much too large for his mouth. Harold was walking several dogs which began to bark madly and strain at their leashes, sending up a ruckus loud enough to alert the entire castle. The cook, miller, atilliator, potter, all ran from their huts. At the sight of Sheena, eyes rounded, fingers pointed and a few brave souls even smiled, though most stared at her as if she were a heathen. Children cringed and whispered her name. Mothers held their babes close to their breasts.

"By the saints, 'tis the lady," the potter whispered, his eyebrows shooting skyward.

"I thought she'd never come back to Ogof. 'Tis a miracle, it is," Gillian, the spinster, whispered loudly.

"Or a curse," Owen, a mason, muttered under his breath. Sheena looked away, refused to break down. "Look at her. Her hands are tied."

"'Tis a pity she returns now, with her father as he is."

Sheena's head snapped around. The baron? Something was wrong with Lord Jestin? No.

"Aye. First the sadness of little Llywelyn and now this—his firstborn daughter brought to justice for slaying her husband. 'Twill kill him sure."

A man snorted. "He already be nearly in the grave."

Despite her bonds, Sheena twisted in her saddle and pinned the spinster with her eyes. "What say you, Gillian? What of my father? Be he ill?" Fear gripped her heart.

"Enough of this!" Manning said.

Sheena's wasn't to be put off. Her head swiveled slowly as she eyed the servants and peasants who had gathered. The sun was lighting the eastern sky. "What of my father?" she demanded and there was much whispering between them. Some cringed, others looked away, several looked upon her with pity in their eyes.

"Come. Now!" Manning was impatient.

"Wait! What's wrong with the baron?" she demanded, her eyes sweeping the upturned faces. "Someone tell me."

Jason, the armorer, and a man she knew to be honest as any stepped forward. He sniffed loudly, nodded to her and, swiping his hat from his head, curled it in his fingers. "'Tis a sad day, m'lady. Lord Jestin, he be dyin', lady. The physician, he's been with him since morn yesterday."

"What? Nay!" She couldn't believe the horrid words.

"I lie not."

"Aye, 'tis true." Father Godfrey hurried along the walk from the chapel, his tonsure visible, his fingers twined nervously within the beads of his rosary. "I was on my way to be with him when I heard the dogs—" His eyebrows lifted as he took in her monk's robe. Frowning at the disrespect and blasphemy, he opened his mouth as if to reproach her, but seemed to think better of it. Cleaning his throat, he said, "Ye'd best hurry, m'lady, for he's not much longer in this world." As if to add emphasis a cock crowed loudly.

"Nay, oh, nay. I'll not believe that my father—" Her voice cracked and she fumbled with the ropes cutting into her wrists and swung one leg over her horse's back.

"Stop! We have no time for this nonsense." Manning wheeled his horse, but it was too late.

Sheena threw her weight to one side and tumbled from her bow-backed mount, stumbling as she landed in the soft grass of the inner bailey. Manning yelled and sputtered, but Sheena ran through the throng, past men and women she'd known all her life. Working at the ropes she dashed up the crumbling steps and threw herself against the door to nearly fall into the great hall.

A fire burned low in the grate and rush lights glowed through the corridors. "Father!" she yelled, her voice echoing as servants and sentinels hurried forward. "Father!"

"For the love of Christ! Stop!" Manning yelled, bursting through the door.

"Please. Do not mock the name of the Son," the priest said, his heavy tread following that of the dark knight. Sheena didn't so much as look over her shoulder.

With Manning and the priest hard upon her heels, she raced up the steps to her father's chamber, pounded on the door with hands that were tied together, then shoved against the door and tumbled into the room.

At the sight of her father, she gasped, her heart squeezing painfully for he lay on his bed, his face pale, his eyes without luster.

"Sheena?" he whispered, his voice rough as a light of recognition flared in his eyes. "Sheena? Girl, is that you?"

"Aye, Father!" Her voice cracked. Stumbling through the rushes, she flung herself toward the bed. Tears filled her eyes. "What is this?"

He snorted through his nose. "'Tis said I be dyin', daughter." He smiled feebly and lifted a hand. "But 'tis glad I be to see ye, make no mistake." His lips twitched and he blinked against tears but for a second as she threw herself upon his once-strong body and felt his arms surround her.

"Nay, you be not dying. You are but sick and will improve. . . ." She choked back further words and clung to this man who had raised her alone for so many years, until he had married Fawn. There had been times she'd hated him and thwarted him. Had she not betrayed him by setting Keegan free all those years ago? Had she not wanted to leave then when he'd allowed his new wife to order her about? And had he not given her to Tardiff, insisting she marry? She loved and hated this man all at once, yet could not face his death.

Footsteps thundered through the door.

"'Tis all right," Jestin said into her ear, not seeming to notice the others pouring into the room. "I've made my peace."

"Nay, Father, speak not of this." Tears filled her eyes, tears of regret and pain. "I've not made my peace with you, there is much to discuss." Her heart wrenched. Many times she'd cursed him, and just as many sung his praises. She couldn't lose him. Not yet. "I—I—"

"Shh." He patted her hands, then scowled. "You be bound," he murmured sluggishly, then his mind seemed to clear a bit as he touched her head. With a weak snap of his fingers, he glanced at a guard. "Cut these damned ropes upon my daughter's wrists and be quick about it." The man did as he was bid and Manning, who had entered the chamber, dared not argue with the Baron of Ogof. Glowering at Sheena, he stood to one side of Jestin's bed, the fingers of one gloved hand curled tightly over the hilt of his sword.

"What happened?" she asked her father as the guard cut her free. "Father, what happened to you?" She rubbed her wrists but watched Manning from the corner of her eye.

"'Tis only old age, daughter. I be sick for a while. Knew it, I did, but . . . I felt not too poorly. I could still run the castle, still hunt." He looked up toward a window, but she knew his vision was turned inward. "Then the babe was born and there was all that trouble. . . ." His voice faded, and he closed his eyes for a second. Then he cleared his throat, shoved himself up on the bed. As he did, some of his color returned.

"What babe? Fawn's child?"

"Aye. My son—" A catch stopped him from saying more.

"Where is he, this brother of mine?" Sheena asked through her tears and she saw the hint of a grin curve Manning's evil face.

"With the angels," Father Godfrey offered. "He—he was born wrong, never ate and fussed and just yesterday morn . . ." The priest crossed himself. "The babe, he drew his last breath."

"Nay," Manning whispered, his eyes thinning on Father Godfrey.

Jestin closed his eyes for a second, as if the conversation was much too painful.

"Oh, Father, 'tis sorry I be," Sheena said feeling the lack of warmth in this chamber with its roaring fire and torches glowing, where coming death and desperation could not be heated.

"You lie," Manning accused the priest. Rage flared in his eyes and color swept up his cheeks as he approached the man of God. His nostrils flared, his shoulders bunched in anger, and the lines around his mouth were etched deep with hatred. "The boy, Fawn's son, be fit and hale." He stalked toward the priest, the toes of his boots forced against the priest's shoes, his expression warning that he wanted to tear Father Godfrey limb from pious limb. "Say it!"

"Nay." Godfrey shook his head, cast down his eyes, the bald pate within his ring of fine hair dripping sweat and reflecting the firelight. "I cannot. 'Tis a pity, but God's will. I have prayed much for his little soul, a soul brought into the world in a sorceress's hut, where pagan arts are practiced."

"I believe you not, you worm of a priest." He glanced around, his lips flat over his teeth. "Where be Fawn?" Manning demanded.

"My wife. You're speaking of my wife." Jestin's spine stiffened. "Mayhap I should remind you she is a lady."

Why was he so upset? Sheena wondered. 'Twas a pity that the babe did not survive, a tragedy, but never had Sheena witnessed Manning care a whit about man or beast. Yet the child's unfortunate death seemed to make him forget Sheena and his mission of returning her to meet her doom.

"I needs speak to *the lady*. Now."

"You forget yourself, Manning," Jestin said, eyes narrowed now, hand scratching his chin thoughtfully.

"Where is she?" Manning's face had become mottled with disbelief and rage, his eyes mere slits, his hand tight over his sword as he glared down at the priest.

"I—I know not."

"Enough. The babe is dead. That be the end of it—there is nothing more to say!" Jestin pinned the dark knight with his old eyes and some of the fire in his soul. The old warrior he'd once been was visible in his gaze. With great effort he threw his legs over the side of his bed and sat up tall. Pushing himself upward, he managed to stand and straighten his spine. Even in a dressing gown, he was an imposing figure. "I still be baron here. You will not make demands of me, nor my wife."

"I returned your daughter."

"That you did and for that you will be paid and paid well."

"She killed Tardiff."

Jestin appraised the man he'd once trusted with his own life with new eyes. His graying eyebrows drew together and 'twas as if he were putting together the parts of an intricate, bedeviling puzzle. "I will determine her fate. You needs not remind me, Manning. Again, ye've forgotten yer station." He reached for a mazer of water and took a long swallow. "There has been much treachery here," he said as he set the cup down. His gaze swept the room that had filled with soldiers and servants. "Many of you think I already be dead, that I know not of your plots against me, but be warned, I will suffer no treason." His gaze flicked to Manning. "From anyone. Now, daughter," he turned back to Sheena, "tell me of Tardiff."

Keegan oared the rowboat toward the rotting dock in the cove. Much of the pier had disappeared in the past eleven years and 'twas dark as the devil's soul, but using a torch for illumination, Keegan eased the rowboat close to a decaying piling.

After disposing of Manning's men one by one, and seeing that they were locked in the hold, he had anchored the *Dark Sapphire* in the bay and, with Bo, rowed back to this cavern which smelled of decay and mold. The boy had a personal score to settle and though he was not as strong as some of the men, he was small and wiry and sneaky. He'd insisted upon accompanying Keegan to save Sheena and Keegan had decided that he would help rather than hinder him.

"Come," Keegan ordered the boy as they tied the boat to a sagging post and scrambled up the slick, uneven planks. They carried weapons, rope, axes, and the torch, for Keegan knew not if these old corridors would take him to Sheena. His heart pumped in fear and the memory of kissing her here so long ago was vivid in his mind. Dear God, he felt as if he'd loved her forever.

He would find her. Save her. He couldn't fail.

Then there was Manning. Keegan would personally hunt down the cur.

If only he was not too late.

The thought that Sheena might already be in her grave, the victim of her father's cruel justice caused his soul to shrivel. If it be so, he would kill Jestin and Manning with his bare hands, or be sent to hell himself.

He cared not which.

The water lapped with dark calm around the boat. Keegan forced his legs to run up the stairs, to the first cobweb-strewn doorway. He leaned a shoulder against the ancient oak and it held. A kick. Still the old timbers didn't budge.

"God's teeth," he growled, grabbing an ax.

Throwing his shoulders into the blow, he swung hard. Wood splintered. A rusted lock fell away. Keegan stepped into a corridor that was as dark as Satan's heart. His skin prickled as he forged onward, holding the torch aloft, following its flickering, smoky light up the narrow corridor that he prayed would lead to the center of Ogof toward Sheena.

He only hoped he wasn't too late.

Desperately, Sheena grabbed her father's hand. "Before I tell you of Tardiff, please, I beg you, order Manning to release the men that he captured when he caught up with me." She held fast to her father, willing life and fire into his ailing body. She couldn't lose him. Wouldn't. Theirs had been a stormy relationship, aye, but he was the man who had sired her. "Please, command him to give Keegan back his ship and that all the crew be free and—"

"Hush, child. Slow down." Jestin's face had pinched together. "Who is Keegan?"

"The bastard son of Rourke," Manning offered.

"Rourke?" Pain swept through the older man's eyes, but a newfound vigor as well. "His soul now rots in hell as well it should. What has his son to do with you?"

"She's been with your old enemy, m'lord," Manning spat out. "His son somehow escaped during the fire here at Ogof years ago when Rourke was killed. In the confusion the lad stole the ring, the one with the Dark Sapphire of Ogof. For days, nay, weeks now, your daughter has been with the bastard, plotting against Ogof and Tardiff."

"Is this true?" Jestin turned condemning eyes toward Sheena.

"Nay, Father, never have I plotted against Ogof, or you. Ogof is my home."

From his pocket, Manning withdrew the ring. The blue stone glittered in the firelight. "She lies." Manning held the ring aloft so that the gem's deep blue facets winked seductively. Jestin stiffened at the sight of the gem.

"For the love of God, 'tis the Dark Sapphire," Jestin whispered and the servants who had followed Manning inside stepped backward.

"The evil stone," Father Godfrey whispered.

"'Twas to be my ring," Lady Fawn proclaimed in a voice without much vigor as she hurried into the room. Her pale skin was whiter still, her expression haunted. She wore a wrinkled gown over her still bloated body and her hair, usually neat, was straggly and unkempt. She stared at the ring and couldn't muster a smile. Fawn saw Sir Manning and nearly stumbled. "I heard you had come finally," she said, as if no one else, not even Sheena was in the room. Her throat worked and she opened supplicating pale fingers toward the beast of a knight. Tears filled her eyes and ran down her milky skin. "Oh, Manning, 'tis sorry, I be. So sorry," she whispered thickly as Zelda followed after her, then, stood silent and grim near the fire.

"The babe?" Manning asked, his voice rough. Everyone within the chamber grew silent.

A strangled mewling noise escaped Fawn's throat. Her knees wobbled, and for a second Sheena thought she might collapse. "Llywelyn," she murmured. "Precious Llywelyn. Your son, Manning, mine, oh, for the love of God, he is gone. . . ." She crumpled onto a corner of the bed, and Sheena felt as if she'd been slapped awake. Did Fawn say that the babe was not her brother? That the dark knight had . . . ? Bile crawled up her throat, for Fawn and Manning had betrayed them all.

"What happened?" Manning's eyes held no compassion as he stared at the woman he'd lain with.

"What the bloody hell is this?" Jestin demanded, but his wife did not hear, looked only up at the father of her dead child.

"Llywelyn . . . Oh, merciful God, he . . . was not born right." She was shaking her head, sniffing, denying the truth, even as it passed her lips. "I tried, Manning, God knows I tried to keep him alive, but I could not. One morning he was gone." Fawn's voice broke and she sobbed, her callous heart broken.

"*His* son?" Jestin growled. "*His?*" He glared down upon the limp creature that was his wife and contempt contorted his features, rage snapped in his old eyes.

"Nay . . . nay . . ." Fawn said, shaking her head as if realizing her confession. "Your son, husband, of course . . . I am grieving . . . confused." Steadying herself on a bedpost, she swiped back the tears from her eyes, and finally the realization that Sheena was in the room pierced her brain. Her countenance shifted abruptly from grief to a slow-rising anger that swept up her pale cheeks in a hot flush.

"You," she spat. "Leave the lord be, can't you see . . . that . . . you are the cause of all the trouble. All that has gone wrong here in Ogof as well as Tardiff can be laid at your feet!"

Her voice faltered again and when she turned back to Manning, she again saw the ring in his hand, the Dark Sapphire that she'd glimpsed, then forgotten with her grief. "You . . . you found it?" she whispered in awe, her eyes rounding in disbelief, her sadness vanishing for the moment.

"What of you, Sheena? What have you to say?" Jestin focused on his daughter, his eyebrows lowered, his lips tight as if he were trying to piece together all of the information. "Manning said you were with Rourke's son." Accusation filled his old eyes. Disappointment slumped his shoulders.

"Nay, Father, let me explain."

"Saints preserve us," the priest whispered.

Fawn whirled upon her husband. "She's a murderess. That be all there is to explain," she insisted, her grief forgotten for the moment. "She killed my brother, robbed him of the gems you gave him, then ran away like the coward she is." Fawn's face had transformed from sadness to a mask of fury and hatred. "But 'tis all over, Sheena. All over. Your true colors have been shown and you have proved yourself to be a traitor to your father, Ogof, Tardiff and God Himself."

"Nay, wife." Jestin raised a suddenly strong hand. "Let us not be so hasty. There be much deception here, aye, and I think you be at the heart of it. 'Tis you who betrayed me, you who have lain with another man, you who got with child and lied to me of his conception." Blue eyes snapped in disgust. "Leave now before I wring your pathetic neck. I need time alone with my daughter."

"Nay, oh, husband, nay! You have many daughters," Fawn pointed out, stung. "I gave them to you. Think of Mary and—"

"Be off woman, before I kill you here and now."

"Nay, I can't believe that you would." She looked quickly around, a pathetic creature backing out of the room and then her gaze landed full force on the ring again. "'Tis not I who betrayed you. 'Twas your firstborn . . . Sheena is a killer. Do you not remember what she did to poor Ellwynn?" Fawn's voice had raised an octave and she lifted her arms to all in the chamber. "Killed him she did, stabbed him and left him to die on her wedding night."

"I will hear it from her own lips," Jestin insisted. His old eyes found Sheena's. "In all the years I have known her, she has never lied."

"Nay! Nay! Look at her! For the love of God, she be a traitor!" Fawn's thin patience snapped. She leapt up to snag the ring from Manning's hand, curling her fingers tightly around the cursed stone. As if drawing strength from the gem, she advanced with new determination upon her ailing husband. Sheena was poised to fling herself between husband and wife. Manning's hand was on his sword. The priest scrabbled for his rosary and one of the serving girls ran from the room.

Fawn's expression was hard and accusing as she glared at the man who was her husband. "You don't care, though, do you, Jestin? Because Sheena was born of Bertrice, you think she can do no harm," she accused, her lips turning downward as if the taste of Jestin's first wife's name was bitter. "Saint Bertrice, the woman who loved another man, yet married you. Oh, she did no wrong in your eyes and now her daughter, too, is above the law." She pointed a long, shaking finger at Sheena and her voice was tremulous. "But this one, this one, she be a murderer, a thief and a—"

"Nay, Father, listen not to her lies," Sheena said, unable to witness this outrage a moment longer. For months she had run and cowardly not faced the truth or her father. Now she could no longer listen to her accusers without defending herself. "'Tis true I stabbed my husband," she admitted, the painful night screaming behind her eyes. She remembered Tardiff as he was, a cold, cruel beast filled with lust and depravity. But no love. "I killed him because, upon our wedding night he placed a knife to my throat."

"She lies!" Fawn shrieked.

"'Twas not enough for me to take his bed, but he demanded that I share the bed with him and . . . and another woman." She stared at the floor for a second and the room was silent, only the hiss of the fire to be heard. "I could not. Would not. He laughed, then insisted he would bend my will to his with the knife. I struggled and fought, the dagger fell and . . . 'tis true, then I used his own blade against him, and ran. I grabbed the stones and escaped." She lifted her head, met her father's gaze with her own. "Aye, I be a murderer and aye, I be a thief. I make no excuse."

"Lies!" Fawn said, spinning and leveling a hideous, desperate glare at Sheena. "My brother would not do anything so vile."

"Father protect us," Father Godfrey intoned.

"Lady Sheena speaks the truth," Zelda said quietly from her corner. All eyes turned to the old maidservant. The lines around her mouth and eyes seemed deeper in the reflection of the fire. "Come inside, Fannie," she called across the chamber and Sheena's heart froze. Turning toward the doorway she spied the blond serving girl who had saved her life that night. Fannie, hands wringing her skirt, eyes downcast, cheeks flushed with embarrassment, edged slowly inside. "Tell the lord what happened."

Fannie cringed.

"Now, Fannie," Zelda ordered with sudden strength, then supplicated the baron. "Please, m'lord, listen. My daughter has something she must tell you."

Fawn's eyebrows drew together. "How dare you say anything, you simpleton!" she scolded, advancing upon the maidservant.

"I shall hear this," Jestin said softly.

Fawn raised a hand to slap the taller woman.

"Do not strike her!" Jestin warned. "Or I shall have you locked away. I would hear the girl speak."

The blond girl gulped. Her eyes were as large as goose eggs as everyone's attention turned toward her. "'Tis true . . . m'lord," she whispered, her worried gaze flicking from Fawn to Sir Manning. "I . . . I was there. Sheena wounded her husband on her wedding night because . . . because he wanted her to lie with him and another woman. 'Twas me. I was Lord Ellwynn's lover . . . and he forced me to join them in their chamber so that he could humiliate his new wife . . . break her spirit. But the lady . . . she would not yield, and the lord, he had a knife . . . 'tis as she says."

Tears of shame ran down Sheena's face, though she forced her spine to be stiff, her chin raised.

"Nay, nay, nay!" Fawn screeched, pointing an accusing finger at Fannie. "Lie no more! How much did you gain by warming my brother's bed only to turn on him now."

"As you turned on your own husband?" Zelda asked.

Fawn gasped, sputtering at her lady-in-waiting's damning accusation. "You're a ninny, a simpleton," Fawn spat at Zelda.

"But, m'lady 'tis true. We all heard it, that the babe you bore, the one who is now in his grave, was not the baron's. Did not Serena say so? Did not you yourself admit it just now when you first saw Sir Manning?"

Fawn scowled desperately. "Nay—"

Manning stepped forward, his fingers curling over his sword.

"Sir Manning fathered poor little Llywelyn. I saw him many a night go to the lady's chamber."

"Nay! You lie," Fawn snarled, her face turning the color of old ashes. "You all lie! And you will pay for it." She snapped her fingers at a guard, pointing at Sheena. "Take the traitor and this, this lying servant and her slutty daughter to the dungeons! Now!"

"Wait!" Jestin cried, his voice louder than it had been. He pinned the serving maid in his stare. "You swear this to be true?"

"Aye m'lord, I swear it on the Holy Mother's soul," Zelda vowed as Fawn raged. "And . . . and that is not all. Fannie," she prodded, her voice ringing through the chamber.

Smack! Fawn slapped the taller woman and Zelda's head snapped back. A huge red welt appeared on her cheek. Manning unsheathed his sword.

"Let there be no bloodshed," Father Godfrey insisted.

Fawn's lips pulled back into an ugly scowl. Motioning to Manning, she ordered, "Take them away! To the dungeon."

"Stop!" With more strength than Sheena thought he had, Jestin bent down, reached beneath his bed and slowly withdrew his sword. He held it high, its blade shining gold in the firelight, his bearing reminiscent of the leader he'd once been. Fire burned in his eyes and he swept a long, steady gaze through the chamber. "I still be lord here." His voice was fierce. It resounded against the coved ceilings and bounced from the rafters. "No one will take my daughter to the dungeon. Nor anyone else, unless it is my command."

Fawn stepped forward.

"That includes you, Wife. Did I not tell you that I would lock you away? Do not," he warned. "Do not defy me again. Ever." He pinned Manning in his hard glare and Sheena's heart froze for there was blood lust in his gaze. "Drop your weapon."

"You would stop me?" Manning sneered.

"If needs be."

"Father, please—" Sheena cried, fearful for his life. If only she had a weapon! She glanced quickly about, searching for a dagger, a sword, a bow, anything!

"Do not do anything stupid," Fawn said, closing the distance between her and Manning. "Not here. Not now."

"Get back, you lying whore. I've listened to you long enough," Manning ordered.

"Nay, Manning!"

Smack! He cuffed her hard across the cheek. She stumbled backward, her eyes round with horror, a huge welt forming on her ashen cheek. Manning wheeled on Jestin. "You *m'lord*," he said, sneering, "are on your way to hell."

Sheena moved, searching for a stone to throw, hot water to hurl, a stick, a weapon of any kind.

"You would kill me?" Jestin asked the man he'd once trusted.

"You are but a feeble old man."

"Be careful, my lord. Sir Manning, he has killed before," Fannie blurted. "'Twas not Sheena who took Lord Ellwynn's life. Nay. 'Twas Manning. I . . . I saw him thrust a dagger into Lord Ellwynn's chest when I returned to the chamber after I showed Sheena the corridor to the moat." Fanny swallowed hard. "Sheena did not kill the baron. Sir Manning did. At the lady's request."

"Lying bitch!" Manning cried, lifting his sword.

"What?" Sheena nearly lost her footing.

Manning didn't bother denying the deed and Sheena thought she might throw up. She hadn't killed Tardiff? It wasn't her wound that took his life? Tears filled her eyes and she felt an incredible relief, though she didn't have time to think of it. Not now. Not when her father's life was in peril of being taken from him by the very killer who had slain Tardiff, then let her take the blame. And Fawn had been behind it all? The scheming, the plotting, the sheer bloody horror of it!

"Bastard," Sheena muttered under her breath and Manning, curse him, smiled with pure evil.

"You ordered your own brother's death?" Sheena was ready to wring Fawn's pathetic neck. She advanced upon her stepmother.

Father Godfrey shook his head. "Nay, nay. Let there be no more blood spilled."

Fawn began to shake.

"Is this true?" Jestin asked his wife. "You would have your brother killed, then deceive me with a son who was not mine?"

"Nay, Husband. Never." Fawn, pale as goat's milk, shook her head. "I have been faithful to you. I love you, Jestin, and you know this to be true," she insisted far too quickly, her deception and lies propelling her into a last desperate attempt at denial. "If Sir Manning had anything to do with my brother's death, then he will be punished—"

Manning's eyes narrowed. "I'll hear no more of your lies, woman! I've done yer bidding, been yer damned slave and whipped cur far too long. Aye, the babe was mine, and she intended to pass it off as yours until you died. If I ever told the truth, she promised to accuse me of rape." With a snarl, he lunged at Fawn, as if determined to strike her dead.

Jestin sprang, his tired old body responding to the call of battle as he shielded his wife.

Sheena screamed.

Manning's blade swung downward. Hard. Jestin slid to one side, but not before the sword bit into his shoulder.

"Ahhhggghhh." Blood spurted.

"Stop! Do not do this!" Sheena yelled, frantic as she stripped a nearby guard of his weapon, the man paralyzed by the drama unfolding before him. Jestin rounded, his blade sharp and deadly. But Manning was quick, agilely ducking the blow only to face Sheena and her small dagger. "Stop," she commanded again.

Alarm bells clanged, ringing loudly throughout the castle. Footsteps pounded up the stairs. Men shouted and the walls of Ogof shook.

"What is it?" Fawn cried.

Soldiers burst into the room. One of the guards turned, Sheena grabbed his sword, and with a blade in each hand, faced the man who had so ruthlessly hunted her down. "Drop your sword, Sir Manning," she ordered.

From the corner of her eye she saw blood, thick and purple-red oozing from her father's wound. Jestin was unsteady on his feet, yet he held up a hand.

"Do not take him on, Daughter. This be my battle."

"And mine as well," Sheena replied, training her eyes upon Manning's sword hand.

Manning's smile was inhuman and cruel.

"Drop your weapon or die!"

"Sheena!" Keegan's voice rang through the castle. Her heart took flight and for a second she could not think, losing her concentration. Was it possible? Was Keegan here or was her mind playing tricks upon her again?

"Watch out!" Zelda warned as she turned and saw a flash in her peripheral vision.

Manning swung downward, but Sheena dodged to the right, caught a glimpse of Keegan, her beloved, his face a grim mask, his eyes filled with horror, his bow at his shoulder. "Don't!" he ordered the dark knight, but it was too late.

Manning struck hard. Sheena threw herself to the floor and rolled. The blade of the sword cleaved the air to crash against the floor.

Thwang!

An arrow sizzled past Sheena's head just as she covered it.

Thunk! Manning bellowed in rage as the deadly missile lodged deep in his chest. "You sea-loving bastard," he roared, dropping his sword, both hands surrounding the shaft of the arrow.

"Nay!" Fawn screamed as Manning, stunned, yanked at the horrid shaft and sank to his knees. "Murderer!" she cried, turning startled, tragic eyes toward the captain, before reaching Manning, falling to his side and cradling his great head in her arms. Blood trickled from the corner of his mouth and she leaned over to kiss his lips, her own becoming stained. She took the ring from his hand and put it into one of her pockets, all the while wailing, "Do not leave me, Manning, do not!" But the breath rasped and gurgled in his chest as he drew in his final gulps of air.

"You killed him!" As if catapulted, Fawn sprang at Keegan, clawing and scratching and he held her arms a second before the fight seemed to slip from her. Slowly, as she quit struggling, he released her and she collapsed near the slain soldier again.

Keegan went to Sheena and gathered her into his arms. "Sheena, oh, love, I feared that you . . ." He buried his face in her hair and beneath the strength of his arms, she felt him tremble.

"Nor did I believe that I would see you again."

"Oh, God, no," Fawn wailed, still clinging to the dead knight.

"Get up," Jestin commanded and when his wife sobbed and refused to stand, he motioned to one of the guards. "Take her away." To another, he pointed at Manning's carcass. "Clean up this mess."

Keegan's arm tightened around Sheena as Fawn was dragged off her lover. Blood smeared her dress, panic and disbelief in her eyes.

Jestin, weakened, fell back on the bed as his wife was dragged away. "You . . . you don't understand. . . ." Fawn was crying, sobbing, screaming, beseeching her husband with her outstretched bloodstained arms. "I had to do it. You wanted a son and . . . I . . ."

"You ordered your brother killed," Jestin charged, mopping his brow and refusing to look at the woman who'd sworn to love him for all their years.

"I did it only for you. To give you a son." Fawn shuddered and clutched herself.

Two heavy soldiers carried Manning's body away and no one, save Fawn, shed a tear for the Judas who had betrayed them all.

Keegan held tight to Sheena, his lips pressed into her hair, his arms as strong as the very walls of Ogof.

"The lord should rest," Zelda said and Keegan pulled on Sheena's arm, drew her past the crowd of servants, soldiers, and peasants and into a dark alcove of the hallway. Glances were sent their way and the whisper of gossip followed after them. Fannie could not help but grin and even Father Godfrey smothered a smile as he passed.

"Sheena!" Bo, carrying a thick coil of rope over his shoulder, threw himself at her. "I told him you would be fine," he said, throwing a glance over his shoulder to Hollis, who, with some of the other members of the *Dark Sapphire*'s crew, appeared. "But he worries always."

"Bah! The boy exaggerates." Hollis snorted and flicked Bo a warning glance.

"But you do not?" Sheena teased.

"Never."

Keegan grinned and Bo laughed out loud at Hollis's discomfiture.

"This be a grand castle," Bo said, his gaze roving through the corridor.

"The best. And I think if you go downstairs—Oh, wait! Fannie! See that these men are given food and drink and whatever else they desire."

The girl nodded and the cutthroats and pickpockets and thieves who had become close to Sheena followed her until at last, she and Keegan were alone in the hallway. He kissed the crown of her head gently.

"Thank God you be safe," Keegan whispered, his throat thick as the rush-lights burned low in their sconces. "I thought I'd lost you."

"And I you," she said sniffing and clinging tight to this man she loved with all her heart. Tears filled her eyes when she thought of how many times she'd nearly lost him, how she'd thought she'd never look upon him, never feel his strength or feel the beating of his heart.

"It won't happen again," he vowed and he cupped her chin with his fingers and tilted her face to his. His lips claimed hers and she sighed against him.

She closed her eyes and for a minute she was a young girl on a rotting dock experiencing her first kiss, then she was a woman held captive, half in love with a rogue captain and feeling the heat of his body, then she was a free woman, in love with the one man who had claimed her heart. Her blood heated, the castle seemed to disappear until she felt as if she and Keegan were the only man and woman in the universe.

Her skin tingled and deep inside she wanted more . . . oh, so much more.

When he lifted his head, his eyes shone with unshed tears. "I love you Sheena of Ogof," he vowed. "Whether you be a witch or an angel, a commoner or a lady, I swear on all that is holy that I love you with all my heart."

"And . . . and I love you."

His smile was a crooked slash of white. "You'll marry me, then?" he asked, a dark brow cocking as he looked down upon her.

She smiled through a sheen of tears and kissed him soundly on the lips. "What think you?"

"I think we'd best find that priest and have him do the honors now before you change your mind."

"Never will I," she vowed, laughing. "I shall see that you become Lord of Ogof."

"Mayhap we should wait until your father is no longer with us. He might disapprove."

"We shall see," she teased, shaking inside from relief and the ordeal. It was over. Now and evermore.

"Mayhap you, Lady, shall be the first and only mistress of the *Dark Sapphire*."

"A woman upon the sea? Is it not a curse?"

"Not when the captain loves the lady," he said.

"Your crew might not agree."

"My crew would rather see you at the helm than me," he said.

"So be it, then."

Again they kissed and again the corridor spun. He held her close, touched her lips with his tongue and she opened to him just as she always had, just as she always would.

"Ahem!"

Her father's voice startled her and she tried to pull away, but Keegan held her fast.

Jestin, with Zelda clucking her tongue and fussing at him to return to bed, glared at his daughter. He shook his head and rubbed his pate. "So this is how it is? You and the son of my enemy." Already his wound had been bound.

She stiffened, but held fast to Keegan. "Aye, Father, 'tis how it is."

"This will come to no good."

"It already has."

He sighed and rubbed his chin.

"Sheena and I will be married."

Jestin's jaw tightened. "'Tis a mistake."

"One I'm willing to make." Sheena notched up her chin. "This time, my husband will be my choice, Father. And you can banish me, never set eyes upon me or your grandchildren, but I hope not. You're ill and I . . . I want peace between you and the man I love."

Jestin hesitated. "'Twill take time and I may not have much."

"Then we will try."

He snorted, coughed and shook his head. "The folly of children," he muttered. "Do what ye will, Sheena. Ye always have. I must attend to my own wife and other children . . . but . . ." He cleared his throat. "Know that I'll never again doubt ye. As fer ye, Keegan, I hope ye're willing to roll the dice with me before I die."

"Mayhap." Keegan eyed the older man suspiciously. "But I will win."

"Will ye, now? That remains to be seen." With a grudging chuckle, Jestin waved them off, then ambled through the doorway and into his room. "I never could tell that girl what to do."

"Nor can I," Keegan admitted.

Sheena giggled, then slid from his embrace and tugged on his sleeve. With a twinkle in her eye, she pulled him down the stairs and through the series of tunnels that he had only recently run through. Dank and dark, wet and infested with rats and bats, they led ever downward past the chapel, under the curtain walls to the cover where the rowboat rocked on the swells coming in from the sea.

"Well?" she asked when they were standing on the very dock where they'd embraced so many years before.

"Well, what?"

"Take me with you."

He laughed and through the entrance to the cove he saw the silhouette of the *Dark Sapphire* riding high on the waves, sails full, spars cathedral-like as they reached for the heavens. The sun was setting behind the dark ship.

"Only if you agree to be my wife."

"Have I not?" She lifted a dark eyebrow.

"Then, aye, I shall. But first . . ." He held up her left hand and slipped the ring with the dark gem upon it over her finger.

"But how—?"

"I stripped it away from Fawn. She was so upset, she barely knew." He smiled slowly. "Remember, lady, I be my father's son. He taught me much, including his tricks and sleights of hand. Now, lady, let us start again."

"Aye, Captain," she teased, the stone shining bright upon her finger. "But how do I know this stone be not cursed?"

"Oh it is," he vowed. "For now you are mine."

"A blessed curse it be," she answered.

"Aye." Arms tightening around her, drawing her near, he kissed her.

Again.

The world seemed to melt around them. This kiss was as magical and breath stopping as the first time ever their lips had met. Sheena quivered inside, longed for more of his touch, wrapped her arms around his neck, and felt the breath of the sea against her skin. Here where it all began, they promised their love would last forever. And as the dark blue stone glimmered in the night, Sheena silently vowed to hold on to her rogue of a captain and never, ever, let go.

He was her destiny.

**The Dark Jewels trilogy
continues. . . .**

*Turn the page
for a thrilling peek
at Lisa Jackson's sexy
historical romance*

DARK EMERALD

Available from Signet

GAEAF FOREST, WALES
WINTER 1271

Lodema's skin prickled, though she warmed herself by the fire. Something was wrong. She felt it in her bones and sensed it in the frigid winter air.

Cold as a demon's breath, the wind whistled through the worn thatches of her small hut, and the premonition that there was death in the forest clung to her as hungrily as leeches to a naked man. 'Twas a feeling she couldn't ignore, a sensation that time and time again had proved to be a warning of worse times yet to come.

Using the charred wooden spoon, she stirred the mutton stew that bubbled in a blackened pot suspended over glowing coals. Her young cat, a mottled creature with glassy eyes, was perched on the shelf where she kept her herbs, candles, and lengths of cord. "Ye feel it, too, don't ye, Luna? There be trouble and it's comin' our way."

Luna lifted a paw and, using her long tongue, washed her face.

Somewhere not too distant a baby cried. Soft. Muffled.

Lodema stiffened.

The cat froze.

Nay. Couldn't be. No babe would be out on as dark and cold a night as this. Yet she heard it again. A pitiful, lonely wail.

"By the saints."

Lodema dropped the spoon. There was no babe. Couldn't be. Not this far into the forest in the dead of the coldest winter in years. 'Twas her tired mind playing tricks on her again. Had to be.

Again the muted cry, barely heard over the rush of wind that swept through the timbers. Ears straining, she heard the plop of horse's hooves and the creak of cart wheels.

For the love of Cerridwen, who would be out in the middle of the night?

Spine arched, fur ruffled, Luna hissed, as if whoever it was outside was pure evil. Like a blaze of lightning, she leaped to the floor and streaked to her hiding spot in the shadows of the firewood stacked near the grate. Footsteps crunched in the snow outside the door.

"Lord, be merciful," Lodema whispered under her breath, but she had more faith in the tiny knife tucked deep in her pocket than in the Christian God's protection. She braced herself. Only fools and devils walked about in the middle of the night.

Bam! Bam! Bam! A fist pounded her door. Fingering the knife with one hand, she cinched the neckline of her wool tunic more tightly around her throat.

"Lodema!" A male voice boomed, and memories, not quite formed, tugged at the edges of her brain. " 'Tis I. Simon."

"Simon?" she whispered, disbelieving. Could it be—after so many years? Her throat tightened and her scarred heart galumphed in her chest as she threw the bolt and tugged the heavy door open. A gust of icy wind raced through her and into the cabin, causing the fire to glow more brightly.

And there he was.

Tall as ever. Pride stiffening his spine.

A priest for too many years to count, Simon wore fine robes and a harsh expression on a face that, Lodema suspected, smiled rarely. In one arm he carried a fancy basket covered in blankets. "Simon—?" How long had it been? A decade? Two? The wind tore through the woods, rattling the dry, naked branches and snatching at Lodema's brown curls. "Mother of God, what brings ye out this night?" Memories of a much younger man and stolen minutes of passion the like of which she'd never since known flitted seductively through her mind.

" 'Tis best if you ask no questions." His gaze touched hers for the briefest of moments, and she noticed that guilt still lingered in his eyes.

"I—I never do."

"Aye, that is why I came to you."

"Is it now?" she taunted, and his lips clamped together. She studied the man she'd adored in her youth, a man who had professed to love God more than a lowly peasant girl, a man who had seduced her and lain with her time and time again, only to leave her for his work in the church. Even now, it made her ache for the naive child she'd been.

"None of your tongue, woman. 'Tis a blessing I bring to you." He held the basket a little higher, and again she heard the pitiful, soulful wail.

"A babe?" Her throat went dry.

"Aye."

"Come in, come in, 'tis freezing." She stepped out of the doorway and for the first time saw Simon's wagon, little more than a cart pulled by a fine brown mare and driven by a lad who could not have been more than eight. The boy huddled against the night, his fingers poking out from tattered gloves, his head covered by the hood of his cloak, his face averted. "Bring the boy in for—"

"Nay. There is no time." Simon breezed past her, and she noticed the spatters of blood on his wool mantle, the worry etching his brow, the sense of haunted desperation in his eyes. A thin man, taller than most, with graying hair that touched his shoulders, he went quickly about his business. He set his basket on the single scarred table and folded back the lamb's-wool blanket. From beneath the soft covers a newborn baby with dark hair and a red face blinked against the sudden rush of light. Tiny fists curled and flailed by her head.

"Whose child is this?" Lodema asked.

"She is yours now."

Lodema's heart nearly stopped. She sucked in a whistling breath and didn't for a second believe him. *A child? For her?* Oh, by the saints, how she would love to have a newborn. But she didn't dare. From the corner of her eye she saw Luna, huddled behind the woodpile, feline eyes staring unblinkingly at Simon as if he were the embodiment of hell. "Surely the babe has a mother . . . or a father."

"None that can care for her."

Somewhere intricately entwined within his words there was a lie.

"There are many who would want a child." Lodema was cautious, for she smelled a trap—but oh, such a lovely trap. "Those who are more deserving of a child."

"Mayhap, but I offer her to you, Lodema."

"In exchange for what?"

"Silence."

She looked down on the child blinking up at her. Dark black curls topped the infant's head, sooty eyelashes curved over rosy cheeks, and tiny lips moved gently, as if she wished to suckle. The ice around Lodema's barren heart cracked and began to melt. "Ye and I, Simon, have not always seen eye to eye."

He glanced at her, then looked away, as if he, too, remembered the lost innocence of their youth.

" 'Tis true, but I forgive you," he said, warming his hands by the fire.

" 'Tis too kind ye be," she said sarcastically, stiffening, unable to soften the bite to her words.

"That is why I came to you, Lodema. There are those who would have had you hanged for a witch long ago were it not for my words on your behalf. 'Tis well known that you practice the dark arts."

"Nay—"

"Hush, woman," he snapped, turning swiftly, his eyes suddenly harsh as the winter wind that raced through the brittle branches of the trees and moaned in the chimney. "I have stilled their voices by reminding them that you have helped with the birthing of many a child and seen to the sick when physicians, apothecaries, and prayers seemed to fail." He cleared his throat. "I have not agreed with your ways, but you have a true soul, Lodema. I know this, though ofttimes it seems you be misguided."

She didn't answer. Oh, how she wanted this child. But the baby came with trouble; she could feel it deep in the marrow of her bones.

"I am offering you a chance to be a mother, a true woman. All I ask is that you raise her as a Christian, that you show her not the dark arts—that she learns not to chant spells, call the wind, speak to the beasts, or see into the future. You must agree to tell no one that she is not of your womb. You are a recluse and still young enough to have borne a child. No one sees you for weeks or months at a time. 'Twould raise nary an eyebrow if you were to appear next spring with a child and no husband. Oh, a few tongues would wag, of course, but 'tis of no consequence. You have never concerned yourself with what others say."

The baby gave off a quiet whimper.

"She is hungry," Lodema said.

"Aye." The priest's gaze held hers. " 'Tis up to you now." Slowly he took off his glove, exposing long, soft fingers—fingers that had once, oh, so many years ago, caressed her, working a wanton magic that even now at the memories caused her blood to heat and stirred a long-forgotten yearning deep in her center.

"I know I can trust you, Lodema," he said quietly, and his voice was like a feather against her skin. Just as it had always been.

"Aye, Simon, that ye can."

With his gloved hand he removed a ring, a gold band with a dark jewel that winked forest green in the firelight. "This will be yours. As payment."

"I need not—"

"Of course you do." The hard edges of his face eased a bit, and he looked like the lad she'd known in her youth, the boy she'd loved with all of her foolish heart. He set the ring on the table near the basket, then delved deep into the pockets of his mantle. Retrieving a small leather pouch, he withdrew a few coins and placed them near the ring.

The baby began to cry and Father Simon sighed heavily. His haughty demeanor evaporated, and for a second Lodema thought he would put his arms around her and kiss her as he had when they were young. Instead he slowly replaced his glove, working his fingers into the soft doeskin.

"Simon," she said, addressing him as she had so many years before, "who does this girl belong to?"

"You will know in time, and then you will understand why you must keep her identity to yourself. 'Tis for your safety and hers." His eyes were suddenly weary. "Please, Lodema, give me your word."

"You have it," she said without thinking, and he smiled, the lines of worry vanishing from his brow.

"Who else knows of this?"

"No one."

"You brought a driver with you."

Simon stroked one eyebrow thoughtfully. "He is but a lad and is paid to keep what he has seen to himself."

"Then he knows?"

"Only that I am delivering an orphan to a woman who would be her mother." He thought for a moment. "Worry not of him, Lodema."

"What is his name?"

Simon sighed. " 'Tis Henry. He is but a stableboy. He works for me because he was caught stealing and I offered him a chance to redeem himself by working for me rather than see him cast into the dungeon and lose his soul." Simon pulled his cowl over his head. "He will not betray me, Lodema."

"Nor will I," she said.

"I know." Gently he touched the side of her face with one gloved finger, and she, whom so many called tough as dried meat, felt the urge to weep for a love that had died so long ago.

"I knew I could trust you," he whispered.

Oh, Morrigu, save me.

"Always." Her throat clogged.

His eyes grew sad.

"Simon—"

"Say not a word, sweet Lodema." Then, as if he'd revealed far too much, he turned so swiftly his mantle billowed. He strode to the door, made a quick sign of the cross over his chest at the threshold, and disappeared into the night. The door closed behind him with a bone-jarring thud.

Rooted to the spot where she'd stood when he touched her, Lodema heard the sharp crack of a whip and the creak of wheels as the wagon rolled away.

The baby gave out a lusty wail.

Lodema snapped back to the here and now. "Shh. All will be well, little one," she murmured, hurriedly picking up the warm bundle and wishing she could believe her words. The baby needed a mother, aye, and, oh, by the gods, how Lodema needed a little one, but somehow this seemed wrong. So wrong. Rocking softly, she held the child close and kissed her downy curls.

From the corner of her eye she caught sight of the emerald ring, its stone dark and cold as it lay on the table. Firelight played on the many facets, but the emerald's reflection held no spark.

Pocketing the jewel, she stared down at the infant's perfect little face. "This will be yours, child, and from now on, you shall be known as Tara, daughter of Lodema. I will raise you as my own." Aye, as a Christian, but one who will know of the old gods as well, a girl who would love air, water, and fire as well as Father, Son, and Holy Ghost.

She brushed her lips across the baby's soft forehead and only hoped she hadn't cursed them both.

Read on for more
Lisa Jackson!

Catch a special preview of
her newest medieval romance

TEMPTRESS

Available from Onyx

*M*orwenna moved upon the bed.

Her bed?

Or another's?

Lifting her head, she saw the glowing embers of the fire, red coals casting golden shadows upon the castle walls. But what castle? Where was she? There were no windows, and high above the walls, past creaking crossbeams, she spied the night sky, dozens of stars winking far in the distance.

Where was she?

In a prison? Held captive in an old, forsaken keep whose roof had blown away?

"Morwenna."

Her name echoed against the thick walls, reverberating and turning her blood to ice.

She twisted on the bed and stared into the shadows. "Who goes there?" she breathed, her heart thudding.

" 'Tis I." A deep male voice, one she should recognize, whispered from the dark corners of this seemingly endless chamber. Her skin crawled. With one hand she clamped the bedding to her breast and realized that she was naked. With the other hand she searched the bed, fingers scrabbling for her dagger, but it, like her clothes, was missing.

"Wh-who?" she demanded.

"Don't you know?"

Was he teasing her?

"Nay. Who are you?"

A deep chuckle from the gloom.

Oh, God!

"Carrick?" she whispered as he appeared, stepping into the light, a tall warrior with

broad shoulders, deep-set eyes and a chiseled chin. She couldn't trust him. Not again. And yet a thrill pulsed through her veins and erotic images stole through her mind.

He stepped closer to the bed, and her heart pounded, her mouth suddenly desert dry. She couldn't help but remember the feel of his sinewy muscles beneath her fingertips, the salty taste of his skin, the male smell of him that had always stirred her.

"What are you doing here . . . how did you get in?" she asked, but realized she didn't know where she was.

"I came for you," he said, and she trembled inside.

"I don't believe you."

"You never did." He was close to the bed now and leaned even nearer. Her heart thudded as he slowly pulled his tunic over his head, and the fire glow caught in his sinewy muscles as they moved. "Remember?"

Oh, yes . . . yes, she remembered.

And cursed herself for it.

"You should go."

"Where?"

"Anywhere but here." She forced the words out.

His smile flashed white. Knowing. Oh, he was a devil. Isa was right. Morwenna should never have allowed him close to her, let him into this room without a ceiling.

But you didn't. You don't even know where you are. Perhaps you're his captive and this is your prison cell. Could it not be that he is keeping you here as his slave, to minister to him, to lie with him, to do his bidding?

"If you won't leave, then I will," she said, her gaze sliding away from his face to search the floor and the pegs near the door for her clothes.

"Will you?" he taunted, settling onto the bed next to her and running a finger down the side of her jaw. Her skin prickled in delight. Her blood rippled with lust. "I think not."

"Bastard."

He laughed at her, ran his finger ever lower, pushing aside the bedclothes, baring her breast, watching the nipple pucker under his perusal, and though Morwenna knew she was making a devastating mistake, she turned her face up to his, felt the warmth of his breath against her skin, knew that she would never be able to resist him. A deep warmth invaded that most intimate of regions, and she sighed as he worked his way lower, callused fingers trickling down her willing flesh.

Lowering his head, he placed a kiss upon her bare abdomen.

She moaned, heat pulsing through her body. Then she sensed they were not alone; that unseen eyes were watching their every move. Someone or something with evil intent.

From where? The open ceiling where she saw stars shooting across the heavens . . . or closer? In the room with them?

"Morwenna!" Someone was calling her, but she could not be disturbed, not when this man she had loved with all of her heart had returned. "Morwenna!"

"Morwenna!"

Her eyes flew open.

The dream evaporated like a ghost chased by morning's light.

The dog at her feet gave out a disgruntled snort.

"God's teeth!" She sat straight up in bed, pushed her hair out of her eyes. It had been a dream. All just a cursed dream. Again. When would she ever learn?

There was no one in her chamber, no mysterious warrior about to seduce her, no old lover returning. She was alone. And yet she sensed something was amiss. . . . Something was very, very wrong.